MW01343122

THE COLLECTED STORIES OF ROGER ZELAZNY

VOLUME 1: Threshold

VOLUME 2: Power & Light

VOLUME 3: This Mortal Mountain

VOLUME 4: Last Exit to Babylon

VOLUME 5: Nine Black Doves

VOLUME 6: The Road to Amber

BIBLIOGRAPHY: The Ides of Octember

Last Exit to Babylon

Volume 4:

The Collected Stories of

Roger Zelazny

EDITED BY

David G. Grubbs

Christopher S. Kovacs

Ann Crimmins

NESFA PRESS

Post Office Box 809, Framingham, MA 01701

www.nesfapress.org

2009

SECOND EDITION
Second Printing, March 2020

ISBN: 978-1-886778-79-5

NESFA Press is an imprint of the
New England Science Fiction Association, Inc.

NESFA® is a registered trademark of the
New England Science Fiction Association, Inc.

A Word from the Editors

This six volume collection includes all of Zelazny's known short fiction and poetry, three excerpts of important novels, a selection of non-fiction essays, and a few curiosities.

Many of the stories and poems are followed by "A Word from Zelazny" in which the author muses about the preceding work. Many of the works are also followed by a set of "Notes"[1] explaining names, literary allusions and less familiar words. Though you will certainly enjoy Zelazny's work without the notes, they may provide even a knowledgeable reader with some insight into the levels of meaning in Zelazny's writing.

> "My intent has long been to write stories that can be read in many ways from the simple to the complex. I feel that they must be enjoyable simply as stories…even for one who can't catch any of the allusions."
>
> —Roger Zelazny in *Roger Zelazny* by Jane M. Lindskold

The small print under each title displays original publication information (date and source) for published pieces and (sometimes a guess at) the date it was written for unpublished pieces. The small print may also contain a co-author's name, alternate titles for the work, and awards it received. Stories considered part of a series are noted by a § and a series or character name.

1 The notes are a work in progress. Please let us know of any overlooked references or allusions, or definitions you may disagree with, for a possible future revision.

Contents

Stories

ARTICLES

Poetry

LAST EXIT TO BABYLON

VOLUME 4:

THE COLLECTED STORIES OF

ROGER ZELAZNY

THE PRINCE OF AMBER

by Joe Haldeman

The night I met Roger Zelazny we shared a rose bush and a jug of wine. That sounds like something out of a story, even one of his stories, but it's simple truth—two introverted guys stuck at a raucous party. One of us snagged a jug of chianti and we went out the kitchen back door and looked for a place to sit and quietly chat. Why not under a rose bush? A full moon, for good measure.

I think he had just published *Four for Tomorrow*, the collection with the important stories "A Rose for Ecclesiastes" and "The Doors of His Face, the Lamps of His Mouth," and was suddenly famous and sought-after in the small but intense world of science fiction fandom.

It was 1967, which was the year I wrote my own first stories, and that night with Roger certainly had a lot to do with my finally settling down to it. He was at once so down to earth and so weirdly cosmic—a strange combination of self-effacing and charismatic—that he literally charmed people. I was far from immune.

(Those two stories say a lot about Roger's romance with traditional science fiction—set on the desert-dry inhabited Mars and the Venusian water world that science had just taken away from science fiction writers. He wanted one last fling.)

My brother Jay, Jack C. Haldeman II, knew Roger first. They both lived in Baltimore and met through the worlds of science fiction fandom and "fanzine" publishing. My brother had scored a poem by Roger for his fanzine *Tapeworm*, and they were sort of drinking buddies as well as literary ones. Roger was new to Baltimore, and Jay took him to his favorite haunts, like the Peabody Book Store and Beer Stube (H. L. Mencken's hangout) and the less notorious bar across the street, where patrons had to squeeze into desks salvaged from a high school's classrooms. I can picture both of them there, tall and lanky and folded.

In fact, the first appearance of the name "Haldeman" in science fiction almost was as a Zelazny character: the hell-raising hero of "Damnation Alley," Hell Tanner, was originally going to be "Hell Haldeman," in honor of my brother. Then Jay and I both started getting published, and the unusual name would have looked odd.

Roger was a typewriter freak; he claimed to have a machine in almost every room of his home, and he would walk from room to room with a sheaf of manuscript in his hand and stick the latest page in whatever machine was the most inspiring, and start pounding away. (He talked me into buying a machine that would now be an expensive antique, the Olivetti Praxis. I wrote a half-dozen books with its beautiful Wide Elite Victorian font before I graduated, like Roger, to the Correcting Selectric, the last real typewriter advance before computers.)

He was always a gaunt, even cadaverous-looking man. He smoked and drank pretty heavily, as was the norm for male writers of his generation, but we never had cause to worry about his health until an incident in 1971, when a bunch of us went down from Maryland to Florida to watch the Apollo 14 moon launch. A couple of days before the launch, a few of us went running in a park. After less than a mile, Roger suddenly collapsed in a seizure. He was taken off in an ambulance, but when he returned to the motel said it was just fatigue and overindulgence. (Googling on his name and "seizure" brings up several references to the audacious groaner in *Lord of Light*—"And then the fit hit the Shan.")

It seemed as if every time you were with Roger some new strange aspect of his personality would come out. Once when we were headed for dinner, a woman complained that she could feel a migraine coming on. Roger said, "Oh, I can fix that." He stared into the woman's face with blistering intensity and made spasmodic passes around her head with stiffened fingers, drawing the pain out, and in less than a minute the headache had disappeared. She said it was a miracle, but Roger was typically modest but mysterious, shrugging it off with something like "It always seems to work."

When we toured the Soviet Union with him, guests of the Soviet Writers' Union, he always carried a couple of loops of string in his pocket, which he would take out and display in complex cat's-cradle constructions, looped around many fingers of both hands. The Russians were fascinated, and Roger was delighted when a grey-suited, unsmiling government type took the string from him and demonstrated a Russian variation.

Roger was a great story-teller and enjoyed recording his own and other authors' works. The last time I saw him, the year before he died, he kept an audience of writers and academics enthralled, acting out a new story in various voices. That was the 1994 International Conference on the Fantastic in the Arts, where he was feted as Guest of Honor.

Very few people knew he was dying of cancer. Early in 1995, I was driving through Santa Fe and called to see whether we could have lunch, and in a gravelly voice he begged off, saying he was fighting a bad cold. He was dead a couple of months later.

Literary generations have been short in my lifetime. Roger was one of the old guys to me, someone in whose footsteps I wanted to follow, and it's odd to look at his obituary and realize that he was only six years older than me; his first story came out seven years before my first. I suppose in science-fiction historical terms, he was a prime avatar of the New Wave, and I was an early practitioner of whatever followed, perhaps the Post-Star Trek De-generation. Whatever, his artistic and intellectual universe was an exciting world, and he conquered it with grace, wit, and style.

—Joe Haldeman

What I Didn't Learn from Reading Roger Zelazny

by Steven Brust

I got serious about writing in high school, when I first read Zelazny's *Lord of Light* and realized that I wanted to make other people feel the way that book made me feel. I promptly set about reading everything he'd written, after which I went to work trying to imitate him. Of course, I failed spectacularly.

My next idea was to see how much I could learn from him; that didn't work so well either. In some ways, you can learn more from someone who makes a really good try at something but doesn't quite pull it off, than you can from a master. In the case of the master, the seams don't show. It's hard to identify how he did it; all you know is the effect. With that in mind, I can't tell you how he does what he does (and you'll note that I'm having tense problems: do I say "he does" or "he did?" I'm going with he does, because the stories are still there. 'Nuff said.). But I can give you a few nods and hints that might make your nineteenth reading more fun.

For example, I was taught in school that there are two kinds of characters in fiction: static and dynamic. Well, it seems Roger missed that class, because I can't think of a single static character he's ever written. It is possible to form an emotional connection to a statue; it's much easier to form a connection to an actual living, breathing, *changing* human being. It's the changes even in the minor characters that make it so easy and natural to move with them, watch them, become them, and care about them.

And then there's the way he gets into the head of the reader—at least when the reader is me. The prologue to *Bridge of Ashes* consists of scattered, seemingly unrelated scenes. As I read them, I slowly became aware of common elements in each scene. Then, in the last scene, it finally hit me how they were all related, and the next line I read was, "At last I begin to understand." He had thrown a hood over my head, led me carefully by the hand through a confusing land of wonder and mystery, and then pulled off the hood to show me I'd been in my living the room the whole time. I just sat there, shaking my head and saying, "How did he *do* that?"

How do you manage a feat like that? By knowing what the reader is feeling well enough to bring him through the experience you want. Is that something I was able to learn from reading him? No, it was just something I knew I wanted to be able to do.

Related to that skill is Roger's ability to leave the reader unsure of exactly what is going on but simultaneously confident that, when it matters, all will become clear. That's why, from the very first sentence, you always feel that particular sort of *relaxation*; the feeling that, okay, I may be confused, but Roger knows it and I can just go with him because he'll bring me out of the confusion just fine.

He never forgot that anything the reader figures out for himself will hit harder than information that's just given. How do you do that without losing the reader? I wish I had an explanation. The first third of *Isle of the Dead* is an especially brilliant and sustained example of keeping the reader tantalized with bits of information and hints of plot until, when the explanation finally comes, you're so immersed in the events of the story that you can't put the book down.

But did reading Zelazny show me how to do it? No, just why it's so cool when it works.

And that brings us to the subject of what is said by what is left out. My favorite example is from *The Guns of Avalon*, where Corwin meets up with his brother Benedict, now missing an arm. Corwin asks him who slew a certain enemy. " 'I managed it,' he said, making a sudden movement with his stump, 'though I hesitated a moment too long on my first blow.' I glanced away and so did Ganelon. When I looked back, his face had returned to normal and he had lowered his arm." Lovely!

And then there is the issue of the sorts of characters who make their way through his work. Yes, they are all of them unique; and yes, they are all of them so well drawn that you get the feeling you'd know them if you met them; but the real thing is, they're so *cool.* Conrad. Francis Sandow. Shadowjack. Yama. Dilvish. How do you do that? How do you create a character that the reader wants to just hang around with and follow around to see what he does? Good question. To the extent I've figured out how to do it, it hasn't come from reading Zelazny, because he's just too good at it; his characters all seem to have simply emerged, fully formed, from a drop of sweat from the brow of whatever god from whatever pantheon he was last playing with.

I've always admired his ability to walk the line of auctorial intrusion. This is, perhaps, the most subjective attribute of the batch: what pulls one person out of the story in a jarring, unpleasant way isn't enough to give someone else a chuckle. I can only say that, for me, he nailed it perfectly, time after time. Like putting himself into *The Hand of Oberon*, or the horrible, horrible pun in the first section of *Lord of Light* (which I finally got on about my ninth reading). He could stop me, wink at me, remind me I'm reading a story, and then slide me back into the flow of the action so naturally that I hardly noticed. Perfect.

And perhaps what hits me hardest in Roger's work is how he manages to make the most simple story work on so many levels, by which I mean how much conversation he's managed to pull out of me and various friends, talking about what this story means, or how that story works. Read "For a Breath I Tarry" and then tell me what it means. Or tell me what happens after the delicious ending of *Jack of Shadows*. Why? Because it's so much fun to try.

Someone with more time than sense and a desperate need for an MFA thesis could do an interesting study forming a ratio of number of words in a story to number of hours spent talking about it, and do a rating of writers based on it; I'll bet Roger would be near the top. On the other hand, it's probably an idea better left alone.

But I hope I've explained why it is I never managed to imitate him. When you analyze all his techniques, they boil down to: be very good. Doesn't give you a lot of practical direction, but it's nice to have a goal to shoot for, don't you think?

—Steven Brust

Stories

My Name Is Legion: Précis

Written in 1974; previously unpublished.

My main character does not exist—officially, that is. His position in the scheme of things is, at least nominally, a cautionary notice with respect to the individual *vis-à-vis* the massive entity which the record-keeping state has become/is becoming.

The first of the three stories, "The Eve of RUMOKO," gives certain essentials concerning his background while considering some possibilities suggested by the recent geophysical plate tectonics theory: the possibility of employing "shaped" nuclear explosions along the midatlantic ridge for purposes of producing new land masses by means of controlled vulcanism; it also considers possible side effects of such an enterprise. In this story, the narrator emerges as an electronics engineer who had taken up computer programming and become involved in the setting up of the world data bank, a project which he eventually came to believe was going too far in the way of keeping tabs on everything and everybody. One day, in a fit of indignation, he had taken advantage of his position and destroyed his own personal records, so becoming a nonexistent individual in the eyes of society's record-keeper. Later, he employed his training to set up an unauthorized input terminal to the system, thereby giving him the ability to create bogus identities and move into them, for purposes of functioning temporarily as a seeming *bona fide* member of society. In order to make a living, he utilizes this ability periodically in the service of a large detective agency, entering various situations in this manner in order to investigate peculiar cases. The RUMOKO project in one of his earlier commissions.

The second story is "'Kjwalll'kje'k'koothaïlll'kje'k," a title based loosely on dolphin sounds. In it, the narrator (whose own name is never given, as he only identifies himself to other characters in terms of the identity he has adopted) is called upon to investigate what appears to be the first recorded instance of a dolphin's attacking and killing a human being. The setting for the story, an artificial islet located in the Gulf Stream near the Bahamas, provides some additional background for the early 21st century world in which the narrator functions. The islet is a station where uranium is processed from ocean water; nearby underwater parks are kept safe from marine predators by means of sonic screens; several technical devices are mentioned or hinted at; the state of knowledge with respect to cetacean intelligence is discussed. Several social problems—such as population, environmental quality and attitudes towards various drugs—are incorporated by allusion. There in an attempt to explain something of dolphin behavior in terms of an expansion of Huizinga's *Homo Ludens* play theory to include dolphins. The protagonist uncovers a very basic human problem at the center of things, however, which had led to the killings and the seeming paradoxical behavior of the dolphins.

The third story, "Home Is the Hangman," continues to expand the view of the world in which these adventures are occurring by necessarily reviewing something of the space program up until that time as an adjunct to the problem the narrator faces. It also continues to develop his character, in view of the fact that he must now balance his ideals against the possibility of having his identity exposed by an individual he had known years before, should he accept the commission. Accepting it, he is then faced with a bizarre situation involving artificial intelligence theory, while making an effort to second-guess the quasi-human mind of a telefactor device which had been given up as destroyed two decades before, but which now has apparently returned to Earth for purposes of destroying its four programmers. Again, it is the human element rather than the technological complications which provides the key to the resolution of affairs.

In each of the three stories, actually, once he has penetrated the surface of apparent technological complication, the narrator discovers the true answer to lie in very basic human acts and desires—things which cannot really be quantified and dealt with at the same level as all of the supposedly significant items handled by the data bank. Implicit in this is one possible judgment of the system itself—it deals with measurable quantities, whereas those things which are really important to people do not lend themselves to this sort of consideration. My character's own judgments are mainly of the system rather than the people he encounters, for he is somewhat tarnished himself and his interest is not in justice *per se*, so much as it is in fulfilling the terms of his agreement. A kind of justice does always follow from this, though he generally achieves it outside the system, because he in something of an idealist despite everything he has encountered—and the proposed title for the book reflects, among other things, the likelihood that he is not alone in his world in the ways that he feels, the things that he thinks.

A Word from Zelazny

Ballantine's editor asked Zelazny to write an introduction for *My Name Is Legion*. He declined. "I am a bit leery of doing an intro, as I have something of a hangup with talking about my stuff in print. If the publisher should really think one would make the difference of course, I would come up with something."[1] Elsewhere, he remarked that each novel should stand by itself and not require an author to add anything. However, his agent Henry Morrison urged him to write that introduction. Zelazny reluctantly wrote "My Name Is Legion: Précis," but it never appeared in any edition. The introduction contains detailed spoilers, which may be why it never ran.

Notes

My Name Is Legion means "I have many names"; the protagonist uses many pseudonyms. The phrase also appears in the New Testament—"My Name is Legion, for we are many"—when Jesus cast out thousands of devils from a single man. And as Zelazny noted in his Précis, it also signifies the protagonists's realization that he is not alone in his rebellion against the World Data Bank. **Johan Huizinga** was a Dutch author and historian whose 1938 book ***Homo Ludens*** (**ludus** = Latin for game) discussed the influence of play on society.

1 Letter from Roger Zelazny to Henry Morrison dated October 9, 1974.

Diadoumenos of Polycletus

Haunted #3, June 1968.
Written 1955–60 for *Chisel in the Sky.*

The broken hands,
like marble flowers,
indicate those powers
which break a man.

Gestures anywhere
in absence of finger,
pursue what never lingered;
The presence of a god who did not care.

Notes

Diadoumenos is a sculpture created by the Greek sculptor Polycletus / Polykleitos. It features a nude athlete tying a diadem about his head after winning at the games; the sculpture's hands are broken off at the forearms.

The Eve of RUMOKO

Three for Tomorrow, ed. Robert Silverberg, Meredith Press 1969.
§ *My Name Is Legion*

I was in the control room when the J-9 unit flaked out on us. I was there for purposes of doing some idiot maintenance work, among other things.

There were two men below in the capsule, inspecting the Highway to Hell, that shaft screwed into the ocean's bottom thousands of fathoms beneath us and soon to be opened for traffic. Ordinarily, I wouldn't have worried, as there were two J-9 technicians on the payroll. Only, one of them was on leave in Spitzbergen and the other had entered sick bay just that morning. As a sudden combination of wind and turbulent waters rocked the *Aquina* and I reflected that it was now the Eve of RUMOKO, I made my decision. I crossed the room and removed a side panel.

"Schweitzer! You're not authorized to fool around with that!" said Doctor Asquith.

I studied the circuits, and, "Do *you* want to work on it?" I asked him.

"Of course not. I wouldn't know how to begin. But—"

"Do you want to see Martin and Demmy die?"

"You know I don't. Only you're not—"

"Then tell me who is," I said. "That capsule down there is controlled from up here, and we've just blown something. If you know somebody better fit to work on it, then you'd better send for him. Otherwise, I'll try to repair the J-9 myself."

He shut up then, and I began to see where the trouble was. They had been somewhat obvious about things. They had even used solder. Four circuits had been rigged, and they had fed the whole mess back through one of the timers…

So I began unscrewing the thing. Asquith was an oceanographer and so should know little about electronic circuits. I guessed that he couldn't tell that I was undoing sabotage. I worked for about ten minutes, and the drifting capsule hundreds of fathoms beneath us began to function once again.

As I worked, I had reflected upon the powers soon to be invoked, the forces that would traverse the Highway to Hell for a brief time, and then like the Devil's envoy—or the Devil himself, perhaps—be released, there in the mid-Atlantic. The bleak weather that prevails in these latitudes at this time of year did little to improve my mood. A deadly force was to be employed, atomic energy, to release an even more powerful phenomenon—live magma—which seethed and bubbled now miles beneath the sea itself. That anyone should play senseless games with something like this was beyond my comprehension. Once again, the ship was shaken by the waves.

"Okay," I said. "There were a few shorts and I straightened them out." I replaced the side panel. "There shouldn't be any more trouble."

He regarded the monitor. "It seems to be functioning all right now. Let me check..."

He flipped the toggle and said, "*Aquina* to capsule. Do you read me?"

"Yes," came the reply. "What happened?"

"Short circuit in the J-9," he answered. "It has been repaired. What is your condition?"

"All systems returned to normal. Instructions?"

"Proceed with your mission," he said, then turned to me. "I'll recommend you for something or other," he said. "I'm sorry I snapped at you. I didn't know you could service the J-9."

"I'm an electrical engineer," I replied, "and I've studied this thing. I know it's restricted. If I hadn't been able to figure out what was wrong, I wouldn't have touched it."

"I take it you'd rather not be recommended for something or other?"

"That is correct."

"Then I will not do it."

Which was a very good thing, for the nonce, as I'd also disconnected a small bomb, which then resided in my left-hand jacket pocket and would soon be tossed overboard. It had had another five to eight minutes to go and would have blotted the record completely.

As for me, I didn't even want a record; but if there had to be one, it would be mine, not the enemy's.

I excused myself and departed. I disposed of the evidence. I thought upon the day's doings.

Someone had tried to sabotage the project. So Don Walsh had been right. The assumed threat had been for real. Consume that and digest it. It meant that there was something big involved. The main question was, "What?" The second was, "What next?"

I lit a cigarette and leaned on the *Aquina*'s rail. I watched the cold north sea attack the hull. My hands shook. It was a decent, humanitarian project. Also, a highly dangerous one. Even forgetting the great risks, though, I could not come up with a good counter-interest. Obviously, however, there was one.

Would Asquith report me? Probably. Though he would not realize what he was doing. He would have to explain the discontinuance of function in the capsule in order to make his report jibe with the capsule's log. He would say that I had repaired a short circuit. That's all.

That would be enough.

I had already decided that the enemy had access to the main log. They would know about the disconnected bomb not being reported. They would also know who had stopped them; and they might be interested enough, at a critical time like this, to do something rash. Good. That was precisely what I wanted.

...Because I had already wasted an entire month waiting for this break. I hoped they would come after me soon and try to question me. I took a deep drag on the cigarette and watched a distant iceberg glisten in the sun. This was going to be a strange one—I had that feeling. The skies were gray and the oceans were dark. Somewhere, someone disapproved of what was going on here, but for the life of me I could not guess why.

Well, the hell with them all. I like cloudy days. I was born on one. I'd do my best to enjoy this one.

I went back to my cabin and mixed myself a drink, as I was then officially off duty.

After a time, there came a knocking on my door.

"Turn the handle and push," I said.

It opened and a young man named Rawlings entered.

"Mister Schweitzer," he said, "Carol Deith would like to speak with you."

"Tell her I'm on my way," I said.

"All right," and he departed.

I combed my sort of blond hair and changed my shirt, because she was pretty and young. She was the ship's Security Officer, though, so I had a good idea as to what she was really after.

I walked to her office and knocked twice on the door.

As I entered, I bore in mind the fact that it probably involved the J-9 and my doings of a half hour before. This would tend to indicate that she was right on top of everything.

"Hello," I said. "I believe you sent for me?"

"Schweitzer? Yes, I did. Have a seat, huh?" and she gestured at one on the other side of her expensive desk.

I took it.

"What do you want?"

"You repaired the J-9 this afternoon."

I shrugged. "Are you asking me or telling me?"

"You are not authorized to touch the thing."

"If you want, I can go back and screw it up and leave it the way I found it."

"Then you admit you worked on it?"

"Yes."

She sighed.

"Look, I don't care," she said. "You probably saved two lives today, so I'm not about to fault you for a security violation. What I want to know is something different."

"What?"

"Was it sabotage?"

And there it was. I had felt it coming.

"No," I said. "It was not. There were some short circuits—"

"Bull," she told me.

"I'm sorry. I don't understand—"

"You understand, all right. Somebody gimmicked that thing. You undid it, and it was trickier than a couple of short circuits. And there was a bomb. We monitored its explosion off the port bow about half an hour ago."

"You said it," I said. "I didn't."

"What's your game?" she asked me. "You cleaned up for us, and now you're covering up for somebody else. What do you want?"

"Nothing," I said.

I studied her. Her hair was sort of reddish and she had freckles, lots of them. Her eyes were green. They seemed to be set quite far apart beneath the ruddy line of her bangs. She was fairly tall—like five-ten—though she was not standing at the moment. I had danced with her once at a shipboard party.

"Well?"

"Quite well," I said. "And yourself?"

"I want an answer."

"To what?"

"Was it sabotage?"

"No," I said. "Whatever gave you that idea?"

"There have been other attempts, you know."

"No, I didn't know."

She blushed suddenly, highlighting her freckles. What had caused that?

"Well, there have been. We stopped all of them, obviously. But they were there."

"Who did it?"

"We don't know."

"Why not?"

"We never got hold of the people involved."

"How come?"

"They were clever."

I lit a cigarette.

"Well, you're wrong," I said. "There were some short circuits. I'm an electrical engineer and I spotted them. That was all, though."

She found one someplace, and I lit it for her.

"Okay," she said. "I guess I've got everything you want to tell me."

I stood then.

"...By the way, I ran another check on you."

"Yes?"

"Nothing. You're clean as snow and swansdown."

"Glad to hear it."

"Don't be, Mister Schweitzer. I'm not finished with you yet."

"Try everything," I said. "You'll find nothing else."

...And I was sure of that.

So I left her, wondering when they would reach me.

❖ ❖ ❖

I send one Christmas card each year, and it is unsigned. All it bears—in block print—is a list of four bars and the cities in which they exist. On Easter, May Day, the first day of summer, and Halloween, I sit in those bars and sip drinks from nine until midnight, local time. Then I go away. Each year, they're different bars.

Always, I pay cash, rather than using the Universal Credit Card which most people carry these days. The bars are generally dives, located in out-of-the-way places.

Sometimes Don Walsh shows up, sits down next to me and orders a beer. We strike up a conversation, then take a walk. Sometimes he doesn't show up. He never misses two in a row, though. And the second time he always brings me some cash.

A couple of months ago, on the day when summer came bustling into the world, I was seated at a table in the back of the Inferno, in San Miguel de Allende, Mexico. It was a cool evening, as they all are in that place, and the air had been clean and the stars very bright as I walked up the flagstone streets of that national monument. After a time, I saw Don enter, wearing a dark, fake-wool suit and yellow sport shirt, opened at the neck. He moved to the bar, ordered something, turned and let his eyes wander about the tables. I nodded when he grinned and waved. He moved toward me with a glass in one hand and a Carta Blanca in the other.

"I know you," he said.

"Yeah, I think so. Have a seat?"

He pulled out a chair and seated himself across from me at the small table. The ashtray was filled to overflowing, but not because of me. The odor of tequila was on the breeze—make that "draft"—from the opened front of the narrow barroom, and all about us two-dimensional nudes fought with bullfight posters for wall space.

"Your name is…?"

"Frank," I said, pulling it out of the air. "Wasn't it in New Orleans…?"

"Yeah, at Mardi Gras—a couple years ago."

"That's right. And you're…?"

"George."

"Right. I remember now. We went drinking together. Played poker all night long. Had a hell of a good time."

"…And you took me for about two hundred bucks."

I grinned.

"So what've you been up to?" I asked him.

"Oh, the usual business. There are big sales and small sales. I've got a big one going now."

"Congratulations. I'm glad to hear that. Hope it works out."

"Me, too."

So we made small talk while he finished his beer; then, "Have you seen much of this town?" I asked.

"Not really. I hear it's quite a place."

"Oh, I think you'll like it. I was here for their Festival once. Everybody takes bennies to stay awake for the whole three days. *Indios* come down from the hills and put on dances. They still hold *paseos* here, too, you know? And they have the only Gothic cathedral in all of Mexico. It was designed by an illiterate Indian, who had seen pictures of the things on postcards from Europe. They didn't think it would stay up when they took the scaffolding down, but it did and has done so for a long time."

"I wish I could stick around, but I'm only here for a day or so. I thought I'd buy some souvenirs to take home to the family."

"This is the place. Stuff is cheap here. Jewelry, especially."

"I wish I had more time to see some of the sights."

"There is a Toltec ruin atop a hill to the northeast, which you might have noticed because of the three crosses set at its summit. It is interesting because the government still refuses to admit it exists. The view from up there is great."

"I'd like to see it. How do you get in?"

"You just walk out there and climb it. It doesn't exist, so there are no restrictions."

"How long a hike?"

"Less than an hour, from here. Finish your beer, and we'll take a walk."

He did, and we did.

He was breathing heavily in a short time. But then, he lived near sea level and this was like 6,500 feet elevation.

We made it up to the top, though, and wandered amid cacti. We seated ourselves on some big stones.

"So, this place doesn't exist," he said, "the same as you."

"That's right."

"Then it's not bugged—no, it couldn't be—the way most bars are these days."

"It's still a bit of wilderness."

"I hope it stays this way."

"Me, too."

"Thanks for the Christmas card. You looking for a job?"

"You know it."

"All right. I've got one for you."

And that's how this one started.

"Do you know about the Leeward and Windward Islands?" he asked me. "Or Surtsey?"

"No. Tell me."

"Down in the West Indies—the Lesser Antilles system—starting in an arc heading southeasterly from Puerto Rico and the Virgin Islands toward South America, are those islands north of Guadeloupe which represent the high points of a subterranean ridge ranging from forty to two hundred miles in width. These are oceanic islands, built up from volcanic materials. Every peak is a volcano—extinct or otherwise."

"So?"

"The Hawaiians grew up in the same fashion. —Surtsey, though, was a twentieth-century phenomenon: a volcanically created island which grew up in a very brief time, somewhat to the west of the Vestmanna Islands, near Iceland. That was in 1963. Capelinhos, in the Azores, was the same way, and had its origin undersea."

"So?" But I already knew, as I said it. I already knew about Project RUMOKO—after the Maori god of volcanoes and earthquakes. Back in the twentieth century, there had been an aborted Mohole Project and there had been natural-gas-mining deals which had involved deep drilling and the use of shaped atomic charges.

"RUMOKO," he said. "Do you know about it?"

"Somewhat. Mainly from the *Times* Science Section."

"That's enough. We're involved."

"How so?"

"Someone is attempting to sabotage the thing. I have been retained to find out who and how and why, and to stop him. I've tried, and have been eminently unsuccessful to date. In fact, I lost two of my men under rather strange circumstances. Then I received your Christmas card."

I turned toward him, and his green eyes seemed to glow in the dark. He was about four inches shorter than me and perhaps forty pounds lighter, which still made him a pretty big man. But he had straightened into a nearly military posture, so that he seemed bigger and stronger than the guy who had been wheezing beside me on the way up.

"You want me to move in?"

"Yes."

"What's in it for me?"

"Fifty thousand. Maybe a hundred fifty—depending on the results."

I lit a cigarette.

"What will I have to do?" I finally asked.

"Get yourself assigned as a crewman on the *Aquina*—better yet, a technician of some kind. Can you do that?"

"Yes."

"Well, do it. Then find out who is trying to screw the thing up. Then report back to me—or else take them out of the picture any way you see fit. *Then* report back to me."

I chuckled.

"It sounds like a big job. Who is your client?"

"A U.S. Senator," he said, "who shall remain nameless."

"With that I can guess," I said, "but I won't."

"You'll do it?"

"Yes. I could use the money."

"It will be dangerous."

"They all are."

We regarded the crosses, with the packs of cigarettes and other various goodies tied to them in the way of religious offerings.

"Good," he said. "When will you start?"

"Before the month is out."

"Okay. When will you report to me?"

I shrugged, under starlight.

"When I've got something to say."

"That's not good enough, this time. September 15 is the target date."

"...If it goes off without a hitch?"

"Fifty grand."

"If it gets tricky, and I have to dispose of a *corpus* or three?"

"Like I said."

"Okay. You're on. Before September 15."

"No reports?"

"...Unless I need help, or have something important to say."

"You may, this time."

I extended my hand.

"You've got yourself a deal, Don."

He bowed his head, nodding to the crosses.

"Give me this one," he finally said. "I want this one. The men I lost were very good men."

"I'll try. I'll give you as much as I can."

"I don't understand you, mister. I wish I knew how you—"

"Good. I'd be crushed if you ever knew how I."

And we walked back down the hill, and I left him off at the place where he was staying that night.

❖ ❖ ❖

"Let me buy you a drink," said Martin, as I passed him on the foredeck on my way out of Carol Deith's cabin.

"All right," and we walked to the ship's lounge and had one.

"I've got to thank you for what you did while Demmy and I were down there. It—"

"It was nothing," I said. "You could have fixed it yourself in a minute if somebody else had been down and you'd been up here."

"It didn't work out that way, though, and we're happy you were handy."

"I consider myself thanked," I said, raising the plastic beer stein—they're all plastic these days. Damn it!

"What kind of shape was that shaft in?" I asked him.

"Excellent," he said, furrowing his wide, ruddy forehead and putting lots of wrinkles around his bluish eyes.

"You don't look as confident as you sound."

He chuckled then, took a small sip.

"Well, it's never been done before. Naturally, we're all a little scared..."

I took that as a mild appraisal of the situation.

"But, top to bottom, the shaft was in good shape?" I asked.

He looked around him, probably wondering whether the place was bugged. It was, but he wasn't saying anything that could hurt him, or me. If he had been, I'd have shut him up.

"Yes," he agreed.

"Good," and I thought back on the sayings of the short man with the wide shoulders. "Very good."

"That's a strange attitude," he said. "You're just a paid technician."

"I take a certain pride in my work."

He gave me a look I did not understand, then, "That sounds strangely like a twentieth-century attitude."

I shrugged.

"I'm old-fashioned. Can't get away from it."

"I like that," he said. "I wish more people were that way, these days."

"What's Demmy up to, now?"

"He's sleeping."

"Good."

"They ought to promote you."

"I hope not."

"Why not?"

"I don't like responsibilities."

"But you take them on yourself, and you handle them well."

"I was lucky—once. Who knows what will happen, next time…?"

He gave me a furtive look.

"What do you mean, 'next time'?"

"I mean, if it happens again," I said. "I just happened to be in the control room…"

I knew then that he was trying to find out what I knew—so neither of us knew much, though we both knew that something was wrong.

He stared at me, sipped his beer, kept staring at me, then nodded. "You're trying to say that you're lazy?"

"That's right."

"Crap."

I shrugged and sipped mine.

❖ ❖ ❖

Back around 1957—fifty years ago—there was a thing called AMSOC, and it was a joke. It was a takeoff on the funny names of alphabetized scientific organizations. It stood for the American Miscellaneous Society. It represented something other than a joke on the organization man, however. This was because Doctor Walter Munk of Scripps Institution of Oceanography and Doctor Harry Hess of Princeton were members, and they had come up with a strange proposal which later died for lack of funds. Like John Brown, however, while it lay moldering in its grave, its spirit kept shuffling its feet.

It is true that the Mohole Project died stillborn, but that which eventually came of the notion was even grander and more creative.

Most people know that the crust of the Earth is twenty-five or more miles thick under the continents, and that it would be rough drilling there. Many also know that under the oceans the crust is much thinner. It would be quite possible to drill there, into the top of the mantle, penetrating the Mohorovičić Discontinuity, however. They had talked about all kinds of data that could be picked up. Well, okay. But consider something else: sure, it's true that a sampling of the mantle would provide some answers to questions involving radioactivity and heat flow, geological structure and the age of the Earth. Working with natural materials, we would know boundaries, thicknesses of various layers within the crust; and we could check these against what we had learned from the seismic waves of earthquakes gone by. All that and more. A sample of the sediments would give us a complete record of the Earth's history, before man ever made the scene. But there is more involved than that, a lot more.

❖ ❖ ❖

"Another one?" Martin asked me.

"Yeah. Thanks."

❖ ❖ ❖

If you study the International Union of Geology and Geophysics publication, *Active Volcanoes of the World*, and if you map out all those which are no longer active, you will note certain volcanic and seismic belts. There is the "Ring of Fire" surrounding the Pacific Ocean. Start along the Pacific coast of South America, and you can follow it up north through Chile, Ecuador, Colombia, Central America, Mexico, the western United States, Canada, and Alaska, then around and down through Kamchatka, the Kuriles, Japan, the Philippines, Indonesia, and New Zealand. Forgetting about the Mediterranean, there is also an area in the Atlantic, near Iceland.

❖ ❖ ❖

We sat there.

I raised mine and took a sip.

❖ ❖ ❖

There are over six hundred volcanoes in the world which could be classified as *active*, though actually they don't do much most of the time.

We were going to add one more.

We were going to create a volcano in the Atlantic Ocean. More specifically, a volcanic island, like Surtsey. This was Project RUMOKO.

❖ ❖ ❖

"I'm going down again," said Martin. "Sometime during the next few hours, I guess. I'd appreciate it if you would do me the favor of keeping an eye on that goddam machine next time around. I'd make it up to you, some way."

"Okay," I said. "Let me know when the next time is, as soon as you know it, and I'll try to hang around the control room. In case something does go wrong, I'll try to do what I did earlier, if there's no one around who can do any better."

He slapped me on the shoulder.

"That's good enough for me. Thanks."

"You're scared."

"Yeah."

"Why?"

"This damned thing seems jinxed. You've been my good-luck charm. I'll buy you beers from here to hell and back again, just to hang around. I don't know what's wrong. Just bad luck, I guess."

"Maybe," I said.

I stared at him for a second, then turned my attention to my drink.

"The isothermic maps show that this is the right place, the right part of the Atlantic," I said. "The only thing I'm sacred about is none of my business."

"What's that?" he asked.

"There are various things about magma," I said, "and some of them frighten me."

"What do you mean?" he asked.

"You don't know what it's going to do, once it's released. It could be anything from a Krakatoa to an Etna. The magma itself may be of any composition. Its exposure to water and air could produce any results."

"I thought we had a guarantee it was safe?"

"A guess. An educated guess, but only a guess. That's all."

"You're scared?"

"You bet your ass."

"We're in danger…?"

"Not *us* so much, since we'll be the hell out of the way. But this thing could affect world temperatures, tides, weather. I'm a little leery, I'll admit it."

He shook his head. "I don't like it."

"You probably had all your bad luck already," I said. "I wouldn't lose any sleep..."

"I guess you're right."

We finished our beers and I stood.

"I've got to be running."

"Can I buy you another?"

"No, thanks. I've got some work to do."

"Well, I'll be seeing you."

"Yes. Take it easy," and I left the lounge and moved back to the upper decks.

The moon spilled sufficient light to make shadows about me, and the evening was chilly enough for me to button my collar.

I watched the waves for a little while, then returned to my cabin.

I took a shower, listened to the late news, read for a time. Finally, I turned in and took the book to bed with me. After a while, I got drowsy, set the book on the bedside table, turned out the lamp, and let the ship rock me to sleep.

...Had to get a good night's sleep. After all, tomorrow was RUMOKO.

❖ ❖ ❖

How long? A few hours, I guess. Then I was awakened by something.

My door was quietly unlocked, and I heard a light footfall.

I lay there, wide awake, with my eyes dosed, waiting.

I heard the door close, lock.

Then the light came on, and there was a piece of steel near to my head, and a hand was upon my shoulder.

"Wake up, mister!" someone said.

I pretended to do so, slowly.

There were two of them, and I blinked and rubbed my eyes, regarding the gun about twenty inches away from my head.

"What the hell is this?" I said.

"No," said the man holding the metal. "We ask. You answer. It is not the other way around."

I sat up, leaned back against the headboard.

"Okay," I said. "What do you want?"

"Who are you?"

"Albert Schweitzer," I replied.

"We know the name you're using. Who are you—really?"

"That's it," I said.

"We don't think so."

"I'm sorry."

"So are we."

"So?"

"You will tell us about yourself and your mission."

"I don't know what you're talking about."

"Get up!"

"Then please give me my robe. It's hanging on the hook inside the bathroom door."

The gunsel leaned toward the other. "Get it, check it, give it to him," he said.

And I regarded him.

He had a handkerchief over the lower part of his face. So did the other guy. Which was kind of professional. Amateurs tend to wear masks. Upper type. Masks of this sort conceal very little. The lower part of the face is the most easily identifiable.

"Thanks," I said, when the one guy handed me my blue terry-cloth robe.

He nodded, and I threw it about my shoulders, put my arms into the sleeves, whipped it about me, and sat up on the edge of the bed.

"Okay," I said. "What do you want?"

"Who are you working for?" said the first.

"Project RUMOKO," I replied.

He slapped me, lightly, with his left hand, still holding the gun steady.

"No," he said. "The whole story, please."

"I don't know what you're talking about, but may I have a cigarette?"

"All right. —No. Wait. Take one of mine. I don't know what might be in your pack."

I took one, lit it, inhaled, breathed smoke.

"I don't understand you," I said. "Give me a better clue as to what you want to know and maybe I can help you. I'm not looking for trouble."

This seemed to relax them slightly, because they both sighed. The man asking the questions was about five foot eight in height, the other about five-ten. The taller man was heavy, though. Around two hundred pounds, I'd say.

They seated themselves in two nearby chairs. The gun was leveled at my breast.

"Relax, then, Mister Schweitzer. We don't want trouble, either," said the talkative one.

"Great," said I. "Ask me anything and I'll give you honest answers," prepared to lie my head off. "Ask away."

"You repaired the J-9 unit today."

"I guess everybody knows that."

"Why did you do it?"

"Because two men were going to die, and I knew how."

"How did you acquire this expertise?"

"For Chrissakes, I'm an electrical engineer!" I said. "I know how to figure circuits! Lots of people do!"

The taller guy looked at the shorter one. He nodded.

"Then why did you try to silence Asquith?" the taller one asked me.

"Because I broke a regulation by touching the unit," I said. "I'm not authorized to service it."

He nodded again. Both of them had very black and clean-looking hair and well-developed pectorals and biceps, as seen through their light shirts.

"You seem to be an ordinary, honest citizen," said the tall one, "who went to the school of his choice, graduated, remained unmarried, took this job. Perhaps everything is as you say, in which case we do you wrong. However, the circumstances are very suspicious. You repaired a complex machine which you had no right to repair…"

I nodded.

"Why?" he asked,

"I've got a funny thing about death: I don't like to see people do it," I said. Then, "Who do *you* work for?" I asked. "Some sort of intelligence agency?"

The shorter one smiled. The other said, "We are not permitted to say. You obviously understand these things, however. Our interest is only a certain curiosity as to why you kept quiet with respect to what was obviously sabotage."

"So, I've told you."

"Yes, but you are lying. People do not disobey orders the way you did."

"Crap! There were lives at stake!"

He shook his head.

"I fear that we must question you further, and in a different manner."

❖ ❖ ❖

Whenever I am awaiting the outcome of peril or reflecting upon the few lessons that can be learned in the course of a misspent life, a few bubbles of memory appear before me, are struck by all the color changes the skin of a bubble undergoes in the space of an instant, burst then, having endured no longer than a bubble, and persist as feelings for a long while after.

Bubbles... There is one down in the Caribbean called New Eden. Depth, approximately 175 fathoms. As of the most recent census, it was home to over 100,000 people. A huge, illuminated geodesic dome it is, providing an overhead view with which Euclid would have been pleased. For great distances about this dome, strung lights like street lamps line avenues among rocks, bridges over canyons, thoroughfares through mountains. The bottom-going seamobiles move like tanks along these ways; minisubs hover or pass at various altitudes; slick-seeming swimmers in tight and colorful garb come and go, entering and departing the bubble or working about it.

I vacationed there for a couple of weeks one time, and although I discovered claustrophobic tendencies of which I had previously been unaware, it was still quite pleasant. The people were different from surface dwellers. They were rather like what I fancy the old explorers and frontiersmen to have been. Somewhat more individualistic and independent than the average topside citizen, but with a certain sense of community and the feelings of responsibility attendant thereto. This is doubtless because they *are* frontiersmen, having volunteered for combinations of programs involving both the relief of minor population pressures and the exploitation of the ocean's resources. Whatever, they accept tourists. They accepted me, and I went there and swam with them, toured on their subs, viewed their mines and hydroponic gardens, their homes and their public buildings. I remember the beauty of it, I remember the people, I remember the way the sea hung overhead like the night sky as seen through the faceted eye of some insect. Or maybe like a giant insect on the other side, looking in. Yes, that seems more likely. Perhaps the personality of the place appealed to a certain rebellious tendency I occasionally felt stirring fathoms deep within my own psyche.

While it was not really an Eden Under Glass, and while those crazy and delightful little bubble cities are definitely not for me, there was something there that turned it into one of those funny, colorful things that sometimes come to me, bubblelike, whenever I am awaiting the outcome of peril or reflecting upon the few lessons that can be learned in the course of a misspent life.

I sighed, took a final drag on my cigarette and crushed it out, knowing that in a moment my bubble would burst.

❖ ❖ ❖

What is it like to be the only man in the world who does not exist? It is difficult to say. It is not easy to generalize when you are only sure of the particulars in one case—your own. With me, it was a kind of unusual deal, and I doubt there is a parallel one, anywhere. I used to bitch and moan over progressive mechanization. No more.

It was strange, the way that it happened:

Once I wrote programs for computers. That is how the whole thing got started.

One day, I learned an unusual and frightening piece of news…

I learned that the whole world was going to exist on tape.

How?

Well, it's tricky.

Everybody, nowadays, has a birth certificate, academic record, credit rating, a history of all his travels and places of residence and, ultimately, there is a death certificate somewhere on file. Once, all things of this sort existed in separate places. Then, some people set out to combine them. They called it a Central Data Bank. It resulted in massive changes in the order of human existence. Not all of these changes, I am now certain, were for the better.

I was one of those people, and it was not until things were well along that I began to have second thoughts on the matter. By then, it was too late to do anything about it, I supposed.

What the people in my project were doing was linking every data bank in existence, so that public records, financial records, medical records, specialized technical records all existed and were available from one source—through key stations whose personnel had access to this information at various levels of confidentiality.

I have never considered anything to be wholly good or wholly evil. But this time, I came close to the former feeling. I had thought that it was going to be a very good thing indeed. I had thought that in the wonderful, electrified *fin de siècle* of McLuhan in which we lived, a thing like this was necessary: every home with closed-circuit access to any book ever written, or any play ever recorded on tape or in a crystal, or any college lecture in the past couple of decades, or any bits of general statistical knowledge desired (you can't lie with statistics, theoretically, if everybody has access to your source, and can question it directly); every commercial and government outfit with access to your assets, your income, and a list of every expenditure you've ever made; every attorney with a court order with access to a list of every place you've ever resided, and with whom, and every commercial vehicle on which you've ever traveled, and with whom. Your whole life, all your actions, laid out like a chart of the nervous system in a neurology class—this impressed me as good.

For one thing, it seemed that it would eliminate crime. Only a crazy man, I thought, would care to err with all that to stand against him; and since medical records were all on file, even the psychopath could be stopped.

...And speaking of medicine, how fine if the computer and medical people diagnosing you for anything had instant access to all your past medical history! Think of all the cures which could be effected! Think of the deaths prevented!

Think of the status of the world economy, when it is known where every dime exists and where it is headed.

Think of the solving of traffic-control problems—land, sea, and air—when everything is regulated.

Think of...Oh, hell!

I foresaw the coming of a Golden Era.

Crap!

A friend of mine having peripheral connections with the Mafia, it was, laughed at me, all starry in my eyes and just up from the university and into the federal service.

"Do you seriously believe that every asset will be registered? Every transaction recorded?" he'd asked me.

"Eventually."

"They haven't pierced Switzerland yet; and if they do, other places will be found."

"There will be a certain allowance for residuals."

"Then don't forget mattresses, and holes in the backyard. Nobody knows how much money there really is in the world, and no one ever will."

So I stopped and thought and read up on economics. He was right. The things for which we were writing programs in this area were, basically, estimates and approximates, *vis-à-vis* that which got registered, a reconciliation factor included.

So I thought about travel. How many unregistered vessels? Nobody knew. You can't keep statistics on items for which you have no data. And if there is to be unregistered money, more vessels could be constructed. There is a lot of coastline in the world. So traffic control might not be as perfect as I had envisioned.

Medical? Doctors are as human and lazy as the rest of us. I suddenly realized that all medical reports might not get filed—especially if someone wanted to pocket the cash and not pay taxes on it, and was not asked for a receipt.

When it came to people, I had forgotten the human factor.

There were the shady ones, there were people who just liked their privacy, and there were those who would *honestly* foul up the reporting of necessary information. All of them people who would prove that the system was not perfect.

Which meant that the thing might not work in precisely the fashion anticipated. There might also be some resentment, some resistance, along with actual evasion. And perhaps these might even be warranted…

But there was not much overt resistance, so the project proceeded. It occurred over a period of three years. I worked in the central office, starting out as a programmer. After I'd devised a system whereby key weather stations and meteorological observation satellites fed their reports directly into the central system, I was promoted to the position of senior programmer and given some supervisory responsibility.

By then, I had learned sufficient of the project so that my doubts had picked up a few small fears as companions. I found myself beginning to dislike the work, which made me study it all the more intensely. They kidded me about taking work home with me. No one seemed to realize that it was not dedication, but rather a desire, born of my fears, to learn all that I could about the project. Since my superiors misread my actions, they saw that I was promoted once more.

This was fine, because it gave me access to more information, at the policy level. Then, for a variety of reasons, there came a spate of deaths, promotions, resignations, retirements. This left things wide open for fair-haired boys, and I rose higher within the group.

I came to be an adviser to old John Colgate, who was in charge of the entire operation.

One day, when we had just about achieved our mission, I told him of my fears and my doubts. I told the gray-haired, sallow-faced, spaniel-eyed old man that I felt we might be creating a monster and committing the ultimate invasion of human privacy.

He stared at me for a long while, fingering the pink coral paperweight on his desk; then, "You may be right," he said. "What are you going to do about it?"

"I don't know," I replied. "I just wanted to tell you my feelings on the matter."

He sighed then and turned in his swivel chair and stared out the window.

After a time, I thought he had gone to sleep, as he sometimes did right after lunch.

Finally, though, he spoke: "Don't you think I've heard those arguments a thousand times before?"

"Probably," I replied, "and I've always wondered how you might have answered them."

"I have no answers," he said abruptly. "I feel it is for the better, or I would not be associated with it. I could be wrong, though. I will admit that. But some means has to be found to record and regulate all the significant features of a society as complex as ours has become. If you think of a better way of running the show, tell me about it."

I was silent. I lit a cigarette and waited for his next words. I did not know at the time that he only had about six months of life remaining to him.

"Did you ever consider buying out?" he finally asked.

"What do you mean?"

"Resigning. Quitting the system."

"I'm not sure that I understand…"

"We in the system will be the last to have our personal records programmed in."

"Why?"

"Because I wanted it that way, in case anyone came to me as you have today and asked me what you have asked me."

"Has anyone else done it?"

"I would not say if they had, to keep the intended purity of the thing complete."

"'Buying out.' By this, I take it that you mean destroying my personal data before someone enters it into the system?"

"That is correct," he said.

"But I would not be able to get another job, with no academic record, no past work history..."

"That would be your problem."

"I couldn't purchase anything with no credit rating."

"I suppose you would have to pay cash."

"It's all recorded."

He swiveled back and gave me a smile. "Is it?" he asked me. "Is it really?"

"Well, not all of it," I admitted.

"So?"

I thought about it while he lit his pipe, smoke invading wide, white sideburns. Was he just kidding me along, being sarcastic? Or was he serious?

As if in answer to my thought, he rose from his chair, crossed the room, opened a file cabinet. He rummaged around in it for a time, then returned holding a sheaf of punchcards like a poker hand. He dropped them onto the desk in front of me.

"That's you," he said. "Next week, you go into the system, like everybody else," and he puffed a smoke ring and reseated himself.

"Take them home with you and put them under your pillow," he said. "Sleep on them. Decide what you want to do with them."

"I don't understand."

"I am leaving it up to you."

"What if I tore them up? What would you do?"

"Nothing."

"Why not?"

"Because I do not care."

"That's not true. You're head of this thing."

He shrugged.

"Don't you believe in the value of the system yourself?"

He dropped his eyes and drew on his pipe.

"I am no longer so certain as once I was," he stated.

"If I did this thing I would cease to exist, officially," I said.

"Yes."

"What would become of me?"

"That would be your problem."

I thought about it for a moment; then, "Give me the cards," I said.

He did, with a gesture.

I picked them up, placed them in my inside coat pocket.

"What are you going to do now?"

"Sleep on them, as you suggested," I said.

"Just see that you have them back by next Tuesday morning."

"Of course."

And he smiled, nodded, and that was it.

I took them, went home with them. But I didn't sleep.

No, that's not it. I wouldn't sleep, couldn't sleep.

I thought about it for centuries—well, all night long—pacing and smoking. To exist outside the system… How could I do anything if it did not recognize my existence?

Then, about four in the morning, I decided that I should have phrased that question the other way around.

How could the system recognize me, no matter what I did?

I sat down then and made some careful plans. In the morning, I tore my cards through the middle, burned them, and stirred the ashes.

❖ ❖ ❖

"Sit in that chair," the taller one said, gesturing with his left hand.

I did so.

They moved around and stood behind me.

I regulated my breathing and tried to relax.

Over a minute must have gone by; then, "All right, tell us the whole story," he said.

"I obtained this job through a placement bureau," I told him. "I accepted it, came to work, performed my duties, met you. That's it."

"It has been said for some time, and we believe it to be true, that the government can obtain permission—for security reasons—to create a fictitious individual in the central records. An agent is then fitted into that slot in life. If anyone is able to check on him, his credentials appear to be bona fide."

I didn't answer him.

"Is that true?" he asked.

"Yes," I said. "It has been said that this can be done. I don't know whether it's true or not, though."

"You do not admit to being such an agent?"

"No."

Then they whispered to one another for a time. Finally, I heard a metal case click open.

"You are lying."

"No, I'm not. I maybe save a couple guys' lives and you start calling me names. I don't know why, though I'd like to. What have I done that's wrong?"

"I'll ask the questions. Mister Schweitzer."

"I'm just curious. Perhaps if you would tell me—"

"Roll up your sleeve. Either one, it doesn't matter."

"Why?"

"Because I told you to."

"What are you going to do?"

"Administer an injection."

"Are you an M.D.?"

"That is none of your business."

"Well, I refuse it—for the record. After the cops get hold of you, for a variety of reasons, I'll even see to it that the Medical Association is on your back."

"Your sleeve, please."

"Under protest," I observed, and I rolled up the left one. "If you're to kill me when you've finished playing games," I added, "murder is kind of serious. If you are not, I'll be after you. I may find you one day…"

I felt a sting behind my biceps.

"Mind telling me what you gave me?" I asked.

"It's called TC-6," he replied. "Perhaps you've read about it. You will retain consciousness, as I might need your full reasoning abilities. But you will answer me honestly."

I chuckled, which they doubtless attributed to the effects of the drug, and I continued practicing my yoga breathing techniques. These could not stop the drug, but they made me feel better. Maybe they gave me a few extra seconds, also, along with the detached feeling I had been building up.

I keep up on things like TC-6. This one, I knew, left you rational, unable to lie, and somewhat literal-minded. I figured on making the most of its weak points by flowing with the current. Also, I had a final trick remaining.

The thing that I disliked most about TC-6 was that it sometimes had a bad side effect, cardiac-wise.

I did not exactly feel myself going under. I was just suddenly there, and it did not feel that different from the way I always feel. I knew that to be an illusion. I wished I had had prior access to the antidote kit I kept within a standard-looking first-aid kit hidden in my dresser.

"You hear me, don't you?" he asked.

"Yes," I heard myself saying.

"What is your name?"

"Albert Schweitzer," I replied.

There were a couple of quick breaths taken behind me, and my questioner silenced the other fellow, who had started to say something.

Then, "What do you do?" he asked me.

"I'm a technician."

"I know that much. What else?"

"I do many things—"

"Do you work for the government—*any* government?"

"I pay taxes, which means I work for the government, part of the time. Yes."

"I did not mean it in that sense. Are you a secret agent in the employ of any government?"

"No."

"A *known* agent?"

"No."

"Then why are you here?"

"I am a technician. I service the machines."

"What else?"

"I do not—"

"What else? Who else do you work for, besides the Project?"

"Myself."

"What do you mean?"

"My activities are directed to maintaining my personal economic status and physical well-being."

"I am talking about other employers. Have you any?"

"No."

From the other man, I heard, "He sounds clean."

"Maybe." Then, to me, "What would you do if you met me somewhere and recognized me?"

"Bring you to law."

"...And failing that?"

"If I were able, I would hurt you severely. Perhaps I would kill you, if I were able to give it the appearance of self-defense or make it seem to be an accident."

"Why?"

"Because I wish to preserve my own physical well-being. The fact that you had disturbed it once means that you might attempt it again. I will not permit this access to me."

"I doubt that I will attempt it again."

"Your doubts mean nothing to me."

"So you saved two lives today, yet you are willing to take one."

I did not reply.

"Answer me."

"You did not ask me a question."

"Could he have drug-consciousness?" asked the other.

"I never thought of that—Do you?"

"I do not understand the question."

"This drug allows you to remain oriented in all three spheres. You know who you are, where you are, and when you are. It saps that thing called the will, however, which is why you must answer my questions. A person with a lot of experience with truth drugs can sometimes beat them, by rephrasing the questions to himself and giving a literally honest reply. Is this what you are doing?"

"That's the wrong question," said the other.

"What's right?"

"Have you had any prior experience with drugs?" that one asked me.

"Yes."

"What ones?"

"I've had aspirin, nicotine, caffeine, alcohol—"

"Truth serums," he said. "Things like this, things that make you talk. Have you had them before?"

"Yes."

"Where?"

"At Northwestern University."

"Why?"

"I volunteered for a series of experiments."

"What did they involve?"

"The effects of drugs on consciousness."

"Mental reservations," he said to the other. "It could take days. I think he has primed himself."

"Can you beat a truth drug?" the other one asked me.

"I do not understand."

"Can you lie to us—now?"

"No."

"Wrong question, again," said the shorter. "He is not lying. Anything he says is literally true."

"So how do we get an answer out of him?"

"I'm not sure."

So they continued to hit me with questions. After a time, things began to wane.

"He's got us," said the shorter one. "It would take days to beat him down."

"Should we...?"

"No. We've got the tape. We've got his answers. Let's let a computer worry about it."

But by then it was near morning, and I had the funny feeling, accompanied by cold flashes on the back of my neck, that I might be able to manage a fib or three once again. There was some light on the other side of my portholes. They had been going at me for what seemed to be many hours. I decided to try.

"I think this place is bugged," I said.

"What? What do you mean?"

"Ship's Security," I stated. "I believe all technicians are so monitored."

"Where is it?"

"I don't know."

"We've got to find it," said the one.

"What good will it do?" said the other, in a whisper, for which I respected him, as whispers do not often get recorded. "They'd have been here long before this, if it were."

"Unless they're waiting, letting us hang ourselves."

The first began looking, however, and I rose, met with no objections, and staggered across the room to collapse upon the bed.

My right hand slipped down around the headboard, as though by accident. It found the gun.

I flipped off the safety as I withdrew it. I sat upon the bed and pointed it at them.

"All right, morons," I said. "Now you answer *my* questions."

The big one made a move toward his belt and I shot him in the shoulder.

"Next?" I asked, tearing away the silencer, which had done its work, and replacing it with a pillow.

The other man raised his hands and looked at his buddy.

"Let him bleed," I said.

He nodded and stepped back.

"Sit down," I told them both.

They did.

I moved over behind the two of them.

"Give me that arm," and I took it. I cleaned it and dressed it, as the bullet had gone on through. I had placed their weapons on the dresser. I tore off their hankies and studied their faces. I did not know them from anywhere.

"Okay, why are you here?" I asked. "And why do you want to know what you want to know?"

There were no replies.

"I don't have as much time as you did," I said. "So I'm about to tape you in place. I don't think I can afford to fool around with drugs."

I fetched the adhesive tape from the medicine chest and did it.

"These places are pretty soundproof," I remarked, putting the gun aside, "and I lied about them being bugged. —So you can do a bit of screaming if you want. I caution you against it, however. Each one earns you one broken bone.

"So who do *you* work for?" I repeated.

"I'm a maintenance man on the shuttler," said the shorter one. "My friend is a pilot."

He received a dirty look for this.

"Okay," I said. "I'll buy that, because I've never seen you around here before. Think carefully over your answer to the next one: who do you *really* work for?"

I asked this knowing that they did not have the advantages that I had had. I work for myself because I am self-employed—an independent contractor. My name is Albert Schweitzer right now, so that's what it is, period. I always become the person I must. Had they asked me who I had been before, they might have gotten a different answer. It's a matter of conditioning and mental attitudes.

"Who pulls the strings?" I asked.

No replies.

"All right," I said. "I guess I'll have to ask you in a different fashion."

Heads turned toward me.

"You were willing to violate my physiology for the sake of a few answers," I said. "Okay. I guess I'll return the favor upon your anatomy. I'll get an answer or three, I promise. Only I'll be a little more basic about it. I'll simply torture you until you talk."

"You wouldn't do that," said the taller man. "You have a low violence index."

I chuckled.

"Let's see," I said.

❖ ❖ ❖

How do you go about ceasing to exist while continuing your existence? I found it quite easy. But then, I was in on the project from the first, was trusted, had been given an option…

After I tore up my cards, I returned to work as usual. There, I sought and located the necessary input point. That was my last day on the job.

It was Thule, way up where it's cold, a weather station…

An old guy who liked rum ran the place. I can still remember the day when I took my ship, the *Proteus*, into his harbor and complained of rough seas.

"I'll put you up," he said to me.

The computer had not let me down.

"Thanks."

He led me in, fed me, talked to me about the seas, the weather. I brought in a case of Bacardi and turned him loose on it.

"Ain't things pretty much automatic here?" I asked.

"That's right."

"Then what do they need you for?"

He laughed a little and said, "My uncle was a Senator. I needed a place to go. He fixed me up. —Let's see your ship. —So what if it's raining?"

So we did.

It was a decent-sized cabin cruiser with powerful engines—and way out of its territory.

"It's a bet," I told him. "I wanted to hit the Arctic Circle and get proof that I did."

"Kid, you're nuts."

"I know, but I'll win."

"Prob'ly," he agreed. "I was like you once—all full of the necessary ingredients and ready to go. —Gettin' much action these days?" And he stroked his pepper-and-salt beard and gave me an evil grin from inside it.

"Enough," I said, and, "Have a drink," because he had made me think of Eva.

He did, and I left it at, "Enough," for a time. She was not like that, though. I mean, it was not something he would really want to hear about.

It had been about four months earlier that we had broken up. It was not religion or politics; it was much more basic.

So I lied to him about an imaginary girl and made him happy.

I had met her in New York, back when I was doing the same things she was—vacationing and seeing plays and pix.

She was a tall girl, with close-cropped blond hair. I helped her find a subway station, got on with her, got off with her, asked her to dinner, was told to go to hell.

Scene:

"I'm not like that."

"Neither am I. But I'm hungry. —So *will* you?"

"What are you looking for?"

"Someone to talk to," I said. "I'm lonesome."

"I think you're looking in the wrong place."

"Probably."

"I don't know you from anywhere."

"That makes two of us, but I could sure use some spaghetti with meat sauce and a glass of Chianti."

"Will you be hard to get rid of?"

"No. I go quietly."

"Okay. I'll eat spaghetti with you."

And we did.

That month we kept getting closer and closer until we were there. The fact that she lived in one of those crazy little bubble cities under the sea meant nothing. I was liberal enough to appreciate the fact that the Sierra Club had known what it was doing in pushing for their construction.

I probably should have gone along with her when she went back. She had asked me.

She had been on vacation—seeing the Big Place—and so had I. I didn't get into New York that often.

"Marry me, though," I'd said.

But she would not give up her bubble and I would not give up my dream. I wanted the big, above-the-waves world—all of it. I loved that blue-eyed bitch from five hundred fathoms, though, and I realize now that I probably should have taken her on her own terms. I'm too damned independent. If either of us had been normal... Well, we weren't, and that's that.

Eva, wherever you are, I hope you and Jim are happy.

"Yeah—with Coke," I said. "It's good that way," and I drank Cokes and he drank doubles with Cokes until he announced his weariness.

"It's starting to get to me, Mister Hemingway," he said.

"Well, let's sack out."

"Okay. You can have the couch there."

"Great."

"I showed you where the blankets are?"

"Yes."

"Then good night, Ernie. See you in the morning."

"You bet, Bill. I'll make breakfast for us."

"Thanks."

And he yawned and stretched and went away.

I gave him half an hour and went to work.

His weather station had a direct line into the central computer. I was able to provide for a nice little cut-in. Actuated by short wave. Little-used band. I concealed my tamperings well.

When I was finished, I knew that I had it made.

I could tell Central anything through that thing, from hundreds of miles away, and it would take it as fact.

I was damn near a god.

Eva, maybe I should have gone the other way. I'll never know.

I helped Bill Mellings over his hangover the following morning, and he didn't suspect a thing. He was a very decent old guy, and I was comforted by the fact that he would never get into trouble over what I had done. This was because nobody would ever catch me; I was sure. And even if they do, I don't think he'll get into trouble. After all, his uncle was a Senator.

I had the ability to make it as anybody I cared to. I'd have to whip up the entire past history—birth, name, academics, and et cet—and I could then fit myself in anywhere I wanted in modern society. All I had to do was tell Central via the weather station via short wave. The record would be created and I would have existence in any incarnation I desired. *Ab initio*, like.

But Eva, I wanted you. I—Well...

I think the government does occasionally play the same tricks. But I am positive they don't suspect the existence of an independent contractor.

I know most of that which is worth knowing—more than is necessary, in fact—with respect to lie detectors and truth serums. I hold my name sacred. Nobody gets it. Do you know that the polygraph can be beaten in no fewer than seventeen different ways? It has not been much improved since the mid-twentieth century. A lower-chest strap plus some fingertip perspiration detectors could do it wonders. But things like this never get the appropriations. Maybe a few universities play around with it from this standpoint—but that's about it. I could design one today that damn near nobody could beat, but its record still wouldn't be worth much in court. Drugs, now, they're another matter.

A pathological liar can beat Amytal and Pentothal. So can a drug-conscious guy.

What is drug-consciousness?

Ever go looking for a job and get an intelligence test or an aptitude test or a personality inventory for your pains? Sure. Everybody has by now, and they're all on file in Central. You get used to taking them after a time. They start you in early, and throughout your life you learn about taking the goddamn things. You get to be what psychologists refer to as "test-conscious". What it means is that you get so damned used to them that you know what kind of asininity is right, according to the book.

So okay. You learn to give them the answers they're looking for. You learn all the little time-saving tricks. You feel secure, you know it is a game and you are game-conscious.

It's the same thing.

If you do not get scared, and if you have tried a few drugs before for this express purpose, you can beat them.

Drug-consciousness is nothing more than knowing how to handle yourself under that particular kind of fire.

❖ ❖ ❖

"Go to hell. You answer my questions," I said.

I think that the old tried-and-true method of getting answers is the best: pain, threatened and actual.

I used it.

❖ ❖ ❖

I got up early in the morning and made breakfast. I took him a glass of orange juice and shook him by the shoulder.

"What the goddam—!"

"Breakfast," I said. "Drink this."

He did, and then we went out to the kitchen and ate.

"The sea looks pretty good today," I said. "I guess I can be moving on."

He nodded above his eggs.

"You ever up this way, you stop in again. Hear?"

"I will," I said, and I have, several times since, because I came to like him. It was funny.

We talked all that morning, going through three pots of coffee. He was an M.D. who had once had a fairly large practice going for him. (At a later date, he dug a few bullets out of me and kept quiet about their having been there.) He had also been one of the early astronauts, briefly. I learned subsequently that his wife had died of cancer some six years earlier. He gave up his practice at that time, and he did not remarry. He had looked for a way to retire from the world, found one, done it.

Though we are very close friends now, I have never told him that he's harboring a bastard input unit. I may, one day, as I know he is one of the few guys I can trust. On the other hand, I do not want to make him a genuine accomplice to what I do. Why trouble your friends and make them morally liable for your strange doings?

So I became the man who did not exist. But I had acquired the potential for becoming anybody I chose. All I had to do was write the program and feed it to Central via that station. All I needed then was a means of living. This latter was a bit tricky.

I wanted an occupation where payment would always be made to me in cash. Also, I wanted one where payment would be large enough for me to live as I desired.

This narrowed the field considerably and threw out lots of legitimate things. I could provide myself with a conventional-seeming background in any area that amused me, and work as an employee there. Why should I, though?

I created a new personality and moved into it. Those little things you always toy with and dismiss as frivolous whims—I did them then. I lived aboard the *Proteus*, which at that time was anchored in the cove of a small island off the New Jersey coast.

I studied judo. There are three schools of it, you know: there is the Kodokon, or the pure Japanese style, and there are the Budo Kwai and the French Federation systems. The latter two have pretty much adopted the rules of the former, with this exception: while they use the same chokes, throws, bone-locks, and such, they're sloppier about it. They feel that the pure style was designed to accommodate the needs of a smaller race, with reliance upon speed, leverage, and agility, rather than strength. So they attempted to adapt the basic techniques to the needs of a larger race. They allowed for the use of strength and let the techniques be a little less than perfect. This was fine so far as I was concerned, because I'm a big, sloppy guy. Only, I may be haunted one day because of my laxity. If you learn it the Kodokon way, you can be eighty years old and still carry off a *nage-no-kata* perfectly. This is because there is very little effort involved; it's all technique. My way, though, when you start pushing fifty, it gets rougher and rougher because you're not as strong as you once were. Well, that still gave me a couple of decades in which to refine my form. Maybe I'll make it. I made *Nidan* with the French Federation, so I'm not a complete slouch. And I try to stay in shape.

While I was going for all this physical activity I took a locksmith course. It took me weeks to learn to pick even the simplest lock, and I still think that the most efficient way, in a pinch, is to break the door in, get what you want, and run like hell.

I was not cut out to be a criminal, I guess. Some guys have it and some don't.

I studied every little thing I could think of that I thought would help me get by. I still do. While I am probably not an expert in anything, except perhaps for my own peculiar mode of existence, I know a little bit about lots of esoteric things. And I have the advantage of not existing going for me.

When I ran low on cash, I went to see Don Walsh. I knew who he was, although he knew nothing about me, and I hoped that he never would. I'd chosen him as my *modus vivendi*.

That was over ten years ago, and I still can't complain. Maybe I am even a little better with the locks and *nages* these days, as a result thereof—not to mention the drugs and bugs.

Anyhow, that is a part of it, and I send Don a card every Christmas.

❖ ❖ ❖

I couldn't tell whether they thought I was bluffing. They had said I had a low violence index, which meant they had had access to my personnel file or to Central. Which meant I had to try keeping them off balance for the time I had remaining, there on the Eve of RUMOKO. But my bedside alarm showed five till six, and I went on duty at eight o'clock. If they knew as much as they seemed to know, they probably had access to the duty rosters also.

So here was the break I had spent the entire month seeking, right in the palm of my hand on the Eve of RUMOKO's rumble. Only, if they knew how much time I actually had in which to work them over, they might—probably could—be able to hold out on me. I was not about to leave them in my cabin all day; and the only alternative was to turn them over to Ship's Security before I reported for duty. I was loath to do this, as I did not know whether there were any others aboard—whoever *they* were—or if they had anything more planned, since the J-9 trouble had not come off as they had expected. Had it succeeded, it would surely have postponed the September 15 target date.

I had a fee to earn, which meant I had a package to deliver. The box was pretty empty, so far.

"Gentlemen," I said, my voice sounding strange to me and my reflexes seeming slow. I therefore attempted to restrict my movements as much as possible, and to speak slowly and carefully. "Gentlemen, you've had your turn. Now it is mine." I turned a chair backward and seated myself upon it, resting my gun hand on my forearm and my forearm on the back of the chair. "I will, however," I continued, "preface my actions with that which I have surmised concerning yourselves.

"You are *not* government agents," I said, glancing from one to the other. "No. You represent a private interest of some sort. If you are agents, you should doubtless have been able to ascertain that I am not one. You resorted to the extreme of questioning me in this fashion, however, so my guess is that you are civilians and perhaps somewhat desperate at this point. This leads me to link you with the attempted sabotage of the J-9 unit this previous afternoon. —Yes, let's call it sabotage. You know that it was, and you know that I know it—since I worked on the thing and it didn't come off as planned. This obviously prompted your actions of this evening. Therefore, I shan't even ask you the question.

"Next, and predicated upon my first assumption, I know that your credentials are genuine. I could fetch them from your pockets in a moment, if they are there, but your names would mean nothing to me. So I will not even go looking. There is really only one question that I want answered, and it probably won't even hurt your employer or employers, who will doubtless disavow any knowledge of you.

"I want to know who you represent," I said.

"Why?" asked the larger man, his frown revealing a lipside scar which I had not noticed at his unmasking.

"I want to know who put you up to being so casual with my person," I said.

"To what end?"

I shrugged.

"Personal vengeance, perhaps."

He shook his head.

"You're working for somebody, too," he said. "If it is not the government, it is still somebody we wouldn't like."

"So you admit you are not independent operators. If you will not tell me who you work for, will you tell me why you want to stop the project?"

"No."

"All right. Drop that one.—I see you as associated with some large contractor who got cut out on something connected with this job. How does that sound? Maybe I can even make suggestions."

The other guy laughed, and the big one killed it with a quick glare.

"Well, that's out," I said. "Thanks. Now, let's consider another thing: I can simply turn you in for breaking and entering. I might even be willing to say you were drunk and indicated that you thought this cabin belonged to a friend of yours who didn't mind a little foolery and who you thought might stand you to a final round before you staggered off to bed. How does that sound?"

"*Is* this place bugged, or isn't it?" asked the shorter one, who seemed a bit younger than the other.

"Of course not," said his partner. "Just keep your mouth shut."

"Well, how does it sound?" I asked.

He shook his head again.

"Well, the alternative is my telling the whole story, drugs, questions, and all. How does *that* sound? How will you stand up under protracted questioning?"

The big one thought about it, shook his head again.

"*Will* you?" he finally asked me.

"Yes, I will."

He seemed to consider this.

"...Then," I concluded, "I cannot save you the pain, as I wish to. Even if you possess drug-consciousness, you know that you will break within a couple of days if they use drugs as well as all the other tricks. It is simply a matter of talking now or talking later. Since you prefer to defer it, I can only assume that you have something else planned to stop RUMOKO—"

"He's too damned smart!"

"Tell him to shut up again," I said. "He's giving me my answers too fast and depriving me of my fun. —So what is it? Come on," I said. "I'll get it, one way or another, you know."

"He is right," said the man with the scar. "You *are* too damned smart. Your I.Q. and your Personality Profile show nothing like this. Would you be open to an offer?"

"Maybe," I said. "But it would have to be a big one. Give me the terms, and tell me who's offering."

"Terms: a quarter of a million dollars, cash," he said, "and that is the maximum I can offer. Turn us loose and go about your business. Forget about tonight."

I *did* think about it. Let's face it, it was tempting. But I go through a lot of money in a few years' time, and I hated to report failure to Walsh's Private Investigations, the third-largest detective agency in the world, with whom I wished to continue associating myself, as an independent contractor.

"So who foots the bill? How? And why?"

"I can get you half that amount tonight, in cash, and the other half in a week to ten days. You tell us how you want it, and that is the way it will be. 'Why?' though, do not ask that question. It will be one of the things we will be buying."

"Your boss obviously has a lot of money to throw around," I said, glancing at me clock and seeing that it was now six fifteen. "No, I must refuse your offer."

"Then you could not be a government man. One of them would take it, and then make an arrest."

"I already told you that. So what else is new?"

"We seem to have reached an impasse, Mister Schweitzer."

"Hardly," I replied. "We have simply reached the end of my preface. Since reasoning with you has failed, I must now take positive action. I apologize for this, but it is necessary."

"You are really going to resort to physical violence?"

"I'm afraid so," I said. "And don't worry. I expected a hangover this morning, so I signed for sick leave last night. I have all day. You already have a painful flesh wound, so I'll give you a break this time around."

Then I stood, cautiously, and the room swayed, but I did not let it show. I crossed to the smaller guy's chair and seized its arms and his together and raised them up from off the floor. Woozy, I was; but not weak.

I carried him off to the bathroom and set him, chair and all, in the shower stall, avoiding the many forward thrustings of his head.

Then I returned to the other.

"Just to keep you abreast of what is going on," I said, "it all depends on the time of day. I have measured the temperature of the hot water in that stall at various times, and it can come out of there at anything from 140° to 180° Fahrenheit. Your buddy is about to get it, hot and full blast, as soon as I open his shirt and trousers and expose as much bare flesh as possible. You understand?"

"I understand."

I went back inside and opened him up and turned the shower on, using the hot water only. Then I went back to the main room. I studied the features of his buddy, who I then noted bore him something of a resemblance. It struck me that they might be relatives.

When the screaming began, he sought to compose his features. But I could see I was getting through to him.

He tested his restraints once again, looked at my clock, looked at me.

"Turn it off. God damn you!" he cried.

"Your cousin?" I asked him.

"My half brother! Shut it down, you baboon!"

"Only if you have something to say to me."

"Okay! But leave him in there and close the door!"

I dashed and did it. My head was beginning to clear, though I still felt like hell.

I burned my right hand shutting the thing down. I left my chosen victim slouched there in the steam, and I shut the door behind me as I returned to the main room.

"What do you have to say?"

"Could you give me one free hand and a cigarette?"

"No, but you can have a cigarette."

"How about the right one? I can hardly move it."

I considered, and said, "Okay," picking up my gun again.

I lit the stick, stuck it in his mouth, then cut the tape and tore it off his right forearm. He dropped the cigarette when I did it, and I picked it up and restored it to him.

"All right," I said, "take ten seconds and enjoy yourself. After that, we talk cases."

He nodded, looked around the room, took a deep drag, and exhaled.

"I guess you *do* know how to hurt," he said. "If you are not government, I guess your file is very much off."

"I am not government."

"Then I wish you were on our side, because it is a pretty bad thing. Whatever you are, or do," he stated, "I hope you are aware of the full implications."

...And he glanced at my clock, again.

Six twenty-five.

He had done it several times, and I had dismissed it. But now it seemed something more than a desire to know the time.

"When does it go off?" I asked, on chance.

Buying that, on chance, he replied, "Bring my brother back, where I can see him."

"When does it go off?" I repeated.

"Too soon," he replied, "and then it will not matter. You are too late."

"I don't think so," I said. "But now that I know, I'll have to move, fast. So...Don't lose any sleep over it. I think I am going to turn you in now."

"What if I could offer you more money?"

"Don't. You'd only embarrass me. And I'd still say, 'No.' "

"Okay. But bring him back, please, and take care of his burns."

So I did.

"You guys will remain here for a brief while," I finally said, snuffing the older one's cigarette and retaping his wrist. Then I moved toward the door.

"You don't know, you really don't know!" I heard from behind me.

"Don't fool yourself," I said, over my shoulder.

❖ ❖ ❖

I didn't know. I really didn't know.

But I could guess.

I stormed through the corridors until I reached Carol Deith's cabin. There I banged upon the door until I heard some muffled cursing and a "Wait a minute!" Then the door opened and she stared out at me, her eyes winking at the light, a slumber cap of sorts upon her head and a bulky robe about her.

"What do you want?" she asked me.

"Today is the day indeed," I said. "I've got to talk to you. May I come in?"

"No," she said. "I'm not accustomed to—"

"Sabotage," I said. "I know. That's what it's all about, and it isn't finished yet. —Please…"

"Come in." The door was suddenly wide open and she was standing to one side.

I entered.

She closed the door behind me, leaned back against it and said, "All right, what is it?"

There was a feeble light glowing, and a messed-up bed from which I had obviously aroused her.

"Look, maybe I didn't give you the whole story the other day," I told her. "*Yes*, it was sabotage—and there was a bomb, and I disposed of it. That's over and done with. Today is the big day, though, and the final attempt is in the offing. I know that for a fact. I think I know what it is and where it is. Can you help me? Can I help you? Help."

"Sit down," she said.

"There isn't much time."

"Sit down, please. I have to get dressed."

"Please hurry."

She stepped into the next room and left the door open. I was around the corner from it, though, so it should not have bothered her if she trusted me—and I guess she did, because she did.

"What is it?" she asked me, amidst the rustle of clothing.

"I believe that one or more of our three atomic charges has been booby-trapped, so that the bird will sing a bit prematurely within its cage."

"Why?" she said.

"Because there are two men back in my cabin, both of them taped to chairs, who tried to make me talk earlier this evening, with respect to my servicing of the J-9."

"What does that prove?"

"They were kind of rough on me."

"So?"

"When I got the upper hand, I got the same way with them. I made them talk."

"How?"

"None of your business. But they talked. I think RUMOKO's igniters need another check."

"I can pick them up in your cabin?"

"Yes."

"How did you apprehend them?"

"They didn't know I had a gun."

"I see. Neither did I. —We'll get them, don't worry. But you are telling me that you took both of them and beat some answers out of them?"

"More or less," I said, "and yes and no, and off the record—in case this place is bugged. Is it?"

She came in, nodded her head and put a finger to her lips.

"Well, let's go do something," I said. "We'd better act quickly, I don't want these guys fouling the project all up."

"They won't. Okay. I'll give it to you that you know what you are doing. I will take you at face value as a strange creature. You did something which nobody expected of you. This does happen occasionally. We sometimes meet up with a guy who knows his job thoroughly and can see when something is going wrong—and who cares enough about it to proceed from there and damn the torpedoes. You say an atomic bomb will soon be going off aboard this ship. Right?"

"Yes."

"You think one of the charges has been attached, and has a timer cued in?"

"Right," and I looked at my wristwatch and saw that it was going on seven. "I'd bet less than an hour from now."

"They're going down in a few minutes," she told me.

"What are you going to do about it?"

She picked up the telephone on the little table next to her bed.

"Operations," she said. "Stop the countdown." Then, "Give me the barracks. "Sergeant," she then said, "I want you to make some arrests." She looked at me. "What is your room number?" she asked.

"Six-forty," I replied.

"Six-forty," she said. "Two men. —Right. —Yes. —Thank you." And she hung up.

"They're taken care of," she told me. "So, you think a charge might go off prematurely?"

"That's what I said—twice."

"Could you stop it?"

"With the proper equipment—though I'd rather you send in a service—"

"Get it," she said to me.

"Okay," and I went and did that thing.

I came back to her cabin around five minutes later, with a heavy pack slung over my shoulder.

"I had to sign my name in blood," I told her. "But I've got what I need. —Why don't you get yourself a good physicist?"

"I want you," she said. "You were in from the beginning. You know what you're doing. Let's keep the group small and tight."

"Tell me where to go to do it," I said, and she led the way.

It was pushing seven by then.

It took me ten minutes to find out which one they had done it to.

It was child's play. They had used the motor from an advanced kid's erector set—with self-contained power unit. It was to be actuated by a standard clock-type timer, which would cause it to pull the lead shielding. The damned thing would go off while it was on the way down.

It took me less than ten minutes to disarm it.

We stood near the railing, and I leaned upon it.

"Good," I said.

"Very good," she said.

"While you're at it," she continued, "get on your guard. You are about to be the subject of the biggest security investigation I have ever set off."

"Go ahead. I'm pure as snow and swansdown."

"You aren't real," she told me. "They don't make people like that."

"So touch me," I said. "I am sorry if you don't like the way I go about existing."

"If you don't turn into a frog come midnight, a girl could learn to like a guy like you."

"That would require a very stupid girl," I said. And she gave me a strange look which I did not really care to try interpreting.

Then she stared me straight in the eyes. "You've got some kind of secret I do not quite understand yet," she said. "You seem like a leftover from the Old Days."

"Maybe I am. Look, you've already said that I've been of help. Why not leave it at that? I haven't done anything wrong."

"I've got a job to do. But, on the other hand, you're right. You have helped, and you haven't really broken any regs. —Except with reference to the J-9, for which I'm sure nobody is going to cause you trouble. On the opposite hand, I've got a report to write. Of necessity, your actions will figure in it prominently. I can't very well leave you out."

"I wasn't asking that," I said.

"What do you want me to do?"

Once it got into Central, I knew, I could kill it. But prior to that, it would be filtered through a mess of humans. They could cause trouble. "You kept the group small and tight," I said. "You could drop one."

"No."

"Okay. I could be a draftee, from the beginning."

"That's better."

"Then maybe we could let it be that way."

"I see no great problems."

"You'll do it?"

"I will see what I can do."

"That's enough. Thanks."

"What will you do when your job here is finished?"

"I don't know. Take a vacation, maybe."

"All alone?"

"Maybe."

"Look, I like you. I'll do things to keep you out of trouble."

"I'd appreciate that."

"You seem to have answers for everything."

"Thank you."

"What about a girl?"

"What do you mean?"

"Could you use one, in whatever you do?"

"I thought you had a pretty good job here."

"I do. That's not what I'm talking about. —Do you have one?"

"One what?"

"Stop playing the stupid role. —A girl, is what I mean."

"No."

"Well?"

"You're nuts," I said. "What the hell could I do with an Intelligence-type girl? Do you mean that you would actually take the chance of teaming up with a stranger?"

"I've watched you in action, and I'm not afraid of you. Yes, I would take the chance."

"This is the strangest proposal I've ever received."

"Think quick," she said.

"You don't know what you're asking," I told her.

"What if I like you, an awful lot?"

"Well, I disarmed your bomb..."

"I'm not talking about being grateful. —But thanks, anyway. —The answer, I take it, is, 'No.'"

"Stop that! Can't you give a man a chance to think?"

"Okay," she said, and turned away.

"Wait. Don't be that way. You can't hurt me, so I can talk honestly. I *do* have a crush on you. I have been a confirmed bachelor for many years, though. You are a complication."

"Let's look at it this way," she told me. "You're different, I know that. I wish *I* could do different things."

"Like what?"

"Lie to computers and get away with it."

"What makes you say that?"

"It's the only answer, if you're real."

"I'm real."

"Then you know how to beat the system."

"I doubt it."

"Take me along," she said. "I'd like to do the same thing."

And I looked at her. A little wisp of hair was touching her cheek, and she looked as if she wanted to cry.

"I'm your last chance, aren't I? You met me at a strange moment in your life, and you want to gamble."

"Yes."

"You're nuts, and I can't promise you security unless you want to quit the game—and *I* can't. I play it by my own rules, though—and they're kind of strange. If you and I got together, you would probably be a young widow. —So you would have *that* going for you."

"You're tough enough to disarm bombs."

"I will meet an early grave. I do lots of stupid things when I have to."

"I think I might be in love with you."

"Then, for gods' sakes, let me talk to you later. I have lots of things to think about, now."

"All right."

"You're a dumb broad."

"I don't think so."

"Well, we'll see."

❖ ❖ ❖

After I woke up from one of the deepest sleeps in my life, I went and signed for duty.

"You're late," said Morrey.

"So have them dock me."

I went then and watched the thing itself begin to occur.

RUMOKO was in the works.

They went down, Martin and Demmy, and planted the charge. They did the necessary things, and we got out of there. Everything was set, and waiting for our radio signal. My cabin had been emptied of intruders, and I was grateful.

We got far enough away, and the signal was given.

All was silent for a time. Then the bomb went off.

Over the port bow, I saw the man stand up. He was old and gray and wore a wide-brimmed hat. He stood, slouched, fell on his face.

"We've just polluted the atmosphere some more," said Martin.

"Hell," said Demmy.

The oceans rose and assailed us. The ship held anchor.

For a time, there was nothing. Then, it began.

The ship shook, like a wet dog. I clung to the rail and watched. Next came a mess of waves, and they were bastards, but we rode them out.

"We've got the first reading," said Carol. "It's beginning to build."

I nodded and did not say anything. There wasn't much to say.

"It's getting bigger," she said, after a minute, and I nodded again.

Finally, later on that morning, the whole thing that had come loose made its scene upon the surface.

The waters had been bubbling for a long while by then. The bubbles grew larger. The temperature readings rose. There came a glow.

Then there was one fantastic spout. It was blasted into the air to a great height, golden in the morning sunshine, like Zeus when he had visited one of his girlfriends or other. It was accompanied by a loud roar. It hung there for a few brief moments, then descended in a shower of sparks.

Immediately thereafter, there was greater turbulence.

It increased and I watched, the regular way and by means of the instruments.

The waters frothed and glistened. The roaring came and went. There came another spout, and another. The waters burned beneath the waves. Four more spouts, each larger than its predecessor…

Then an ocean-driving blast caught the *Aquina* in something close to a tidal wave…

We were ready, though—built that way—and faced into it.

We rode with it, and there was no let-up.

We were miles away, and it seemed as if but an arm's distance separated us.

The next spout just kept going up, until it became a topless pillar. It pierced the sky, and a certain darkness began at that point. It began to swell, and there were fires all about its base.

After a time, the entire sky was fading over into a false twilight, and a fine dust filled the air, the eyes, the lungs. Occasionally, a crowd of ashes passed in the distance, like a covey of dark birds. I lit a cigarette to protect my lungs against pollution, and watched the fires rise.

With our early evening, the seas darkened. The kraken himself, disturbed, might have been licking our hull. The glow continued, and a dark form appeared.

RUMOKO.

It was the cone. An artificially created island. A piece of long-sunk Atlantis itself, perhaps, was rising in the distance. Man had succeeded in creating a landmass. One day it would be habitable. Now, if we made a chain of them…

Yes. Perhaps another Japan. More room for the expanding human race. More space. More places in which to live.

Why had I been questioned? Who had opposed this? It was a good thing, as I saw it.

I went away. I went and had dinner.

Carol came into the commissary and joined me, as if by accident. I nodded, and she seated herself across from me and ordered.

"Hi."

"Hi."

"Maybe you've done some of your thinking by now?" she said, between the salad and the ersatz beef.

"Yes," I replied.

"What are the results?"

"I still don't know. It was awfully quick and, frankly, I'd like the opportunity to get to know you a little better."

"Signifying what?"

"There is an ancient custom known as 'dating.' Let's do it for a little while."

"You don't like me? I've checked our compatibility indices. They show that we would be okay together—buying you at face value, that is—but I think I know more of you than that."

"Outside of the fact that I'm not for sale, what does that mean?"

"I've made lots of guesses and I think I could also get along with an individualist who knows how to play the right games with machines."

I knew that the commissary was bugged, and I guessed that she didn't know that I did. Therefore, she had a reason for saying what she had said—and she didn't think I knew about it.

"Sorry. Too quick," I told her. "Give a man a chance, will you?"

"Why don't we go someplace and discuss it?"

We were ready for dessert at that point.

"Where?"

"Spitzbergen."

I thought about it, then, "Okay," I said.

"I'll be ready in about an hour and a half."

"Whoa!" I said. "I thought you meant, like—perhaps this weekend. There are still tests to run, and I'm scheduled for duty."

"But your job here is finished, isn't it?"

I started in on my dessert—apple pie, and pretty good, too, with a chunk of cheddar—and I sipped coffee along with it. Over the rim of the cup, I cocked my head at her and shook it, slowly, from one side to the other.

"I can get you off duty for a day," she told me. "There will be no harm done."

"Sorry. I'm interested in the results of the tests. Let's make it this weekend."

She seemed to think about this for a while.

"All right," she said finally, and I nodded and continued with my dessert.

The "all right" instead of a "yes" or an "okay" or a "sure" must have been a key word of some sort. Or perhaps it was something else that she did or said. I don't know. I don't care any more.

When we left the commissary, she was slightly ahead of me—as I had opened the door for her—and a man moved in from either side.

She stopped and turned.

"Don't bother saying it," I said. "I wasn't quick enough, so I'm under arrest. Please don't recite my rights. I know what they are," and I raised my hands when I saw the steel in one man's hand. "Merry Christmas," I added.

But she recited my rights anyway, and I stared at her all the while. She didn't meet my eyes.

Hell, the whole proposition had been too good to be true. I didn't think she was very used to the role she had played, though—and I wondered, idly, whether she would have gone through with it, if circumstances dictated. She had been right about my job aboard the *Aquina* being ended, however. I would have to be moving along, and seeing that Albert Schweitzer died within the next twenty-four hours.

"You *are* going to Spitzbergen tonight," she said, "where there are better facilities for questioning you."

How was I going to manage it? Well—

As if reading my thoughts, she said, "Since you seem to be somewhat dangerous, I wish to advise you that your escorts are highly trained men."

"Then you won't be coming with me, after all?"

"I'm afraid not."

"Too bad. Then this is going to have to be 'Good-bye.' I'd like to have gotten to know you somewhat better."

"That meant nothing!" she said. "It was just to get you there."

"Maybe. But you will always wonder, and now you will never know."

"I am afraid we are going to have to handcuff you," said one of the men.

"Of course."

I held my hands out and he said, almost apologetically, "No, sir. Behind your back, please."

So I did, but I watched the men move in and I got a look at the cuffs. They were kind of old-fashioned. Government budgets generally produce such handy savings. If I bent over backward, I could step over them, and then they would be in front of me. Give me, say, twenty seconds...

"One thing," I asked. "Just for the sake of curiosity and because I told it to you straight. Did you ever find out why those two guys broke into my room to question me, and what they really wanted? If you're allowed to tell me, I would like to know, because it made for some rough sleeping."

She bit her lip, thought a moment, I guess, then said, "They were from New Salem—a bubble city off the North American continental shelf. They were afraid that RUMOKO would crack their dome."

"Did it?" I asked.

She paused.

"We don't know yet," she said. "The place has been silent for a while. We have tried to get through to them, but there seems to be some interference."

"What do you mean by that?"

"We have not yet succeeded in reestablishing contact."

"You mean to say that we might have killed a city?"

"No. The chances were minimal, according to the scientists."

"*Your* scientists," I said. "Theirs must have felt differently about it."

"Of course," she told me. "There are always obstructionists. They sent saboteurs because they did not trust our scientists. The inference—"

"I'm sorry," I said.

"For what?"

"That I put a guy into a shower. —Okay. Thanks. I can read all about it in the papers. Send me to Spitzbergen now."

"Please," she said. "I do what I must. I think it's right. You may be as clean as snow and swansdown. If that is the case, they will know in a very short time, Al. Then—then I'd like you to bear in mind that what I said before may still be good."

I chuckled.

"Sure, and I've already said, 'Good-bye.' Thanks for answering my question, though."

"Don't hate me."

"I don't. But I could never trust you."

She turned away.

"Good night," I said.

And they escorted me to the helicopter. They helped me aboard. There were just the two of them and the pilot.

"She liked you," said the man with the gun.

"No," I said.

"If she's right and you're clean, will you see her again?"

"I'll never see her again," I said.

He seated me, to the rear of the craft. Then he and his buddy took window seats and gave a signal. The engines throbbed, and suddenly we rose.

In the distance, RUMOKO rumbled, burned, and spat.

Eva, I am sorry. I didn't know. I'd never guessed it might have done what it did.

"You're supposed to be dangerous," said the man on my right. "Please don't try anything."

Ave, atque, vale, I said, in my heart of hearts, like.

Twenty-four hours, I told Schweitzer.

❖ ❖ ❖

After I collected my money from Walsh, I returned to the *Proteus* and practiced meditation for a few days. Since it did not produce the desired results, I went up and got drunk with Bill Mellings. After all, I had used his equipment to kill Schweitzer. I didn't tell him anything, except for a made-up story about a *ni-hi* girl with large mammaries.

Then we went fishing, two weeks' worth.

I did not exist any longer. I had erased Albert Schweitzer from the world. I kept telling myself that I did not want to exist any longer.

If you have to murder a man—*have to*, I mean, like no choice in the matter—I feel that it should be a bloody and horrible thing, so that it burns itself into your soul and gives you a better appreciation of the value of human existence.

It had not been that way, however.

It had been quiet and viral. It was a thing to which I have immunized myself, but of which very few other persons have even heard. I had opened my ring and released the spores. That was all. I had never known the names of my escorts or the pilot. I had not even had a good look at their faces.

It had killed them within thirty seconds, and I had the cuffs off in less than the twenty seconds I'd guessed. I crashed the 'copter on the beach, sprained my right wrist doing it, got the hell out of the vehicle, and started walking.

They'd look like myocardial infarcts or arteriosclerotic brain syndromes—depending on how it hit them.

Which meant I should lay low for a while. I value my own existence slightly more than that of anyone who wishes to disturb it. This does not mean that I didn't feel like hell, though.

Carol will suspect, I think, but Central only buys facts. And I saw that there was enough sea water in the plane to take care of the spores. No test known to man could prove that I had murdered them.

The body of Albert Schweitzer had doubtless been washed out to sea through the sprung door.

If I ever meet with anybody who had known Al, so briefly, I'd be somebody else by then—with appropriate identification—and that person would be mistaken.

Very neat. But maybe I'm in the wrong line of work. I still feel like hell.

❖ ❖ ❖

RUMOKO from all those fathoms fumed and grew like those Hollywood monsters that used to get blamed on science fiction. In a few months, it was predicted, its fires would desist. A layer of soil would then be imported, spread, and migrating birds would be encouraged to stop and rest, maybe nest, and to use the place as a lavatory. Mutant red mangroves would be rooted there, linking the sea and the land. Insects would even be brought aboard. One day, according to theory, it would be a habitable island. One other day, it would be one of a chain of habitable islands.

A double-pronged answer to the population problem, you might say: create a new place for men to live, and in doing so kill off a crowd of them living elsewhere.

Yes, the seismic shocks had cracked New Salem's dome. Many people had died.

And Project RUMOKO's *second* son is nevertheless scheduled for next summer.

The people in Baltimore II are worried, but the Congressional investigation showed that the fault lay with the constructors of New Salem, who should have provided against the vicissitudes. The courts held several of the contractors liable, and two of them went into receivership despite the connections that had gotten them the contracts in the first place.

It ain't pretty, and it's big, and I sort of wish I had never put that guy into the shower. He is all alive and well, I understand—a New Salem man—but I know that he will never be the same.

More precautions are supposed to be taken with the next one—whatever that means. I do not trust these precautions worth a damn. But then, I do not trust anything anymore.

If another bubble city goes, as yours did, Eva, I think it will slow things down. But I do not believe it will stop the RUMOKO Project. I think they will find another excuse then. I think they will try for a third one after that.

While it has been proved that we can create such things, I do not believe that the answer to our population problem lies in the manufacturing of new lands. No.

Offhand, I would say that since everything else is controlled these days, we might as well do it with the population, too. I will even get myself an identity—many identities, in fact—and vote for it, if it ever comes to a referendum. And I submit that there should be more bubble cities, and increased appropriations with respect to the exploration of outer space. But no more RUMOKOs. No.

Despite past reservations, I am taking on a free one. Walsh will never know. Hopefully, no one will. I am no altruist, but I guess I owe something to the race that I leech off of. After all, I was once a member…

Taking advantage of my nonexistence, I am going to sabotage that bastard so well that it will be the last.

How?

I will see that it is a Krakatoa, at least. As a result of the last one, Central knows a lot more about magma—and as a result of this, so do I.

I will manipulate the charge, probably even make it a multiple.

When that baby goes off, I will have arranged for it to be the worst seismic disturbance in the memory of man. It should not be too difficult to do.

I could possibly murder thousands of people by this action—and certainly I will kill some. However, RUMOKO in its shattering of New Salem scared the hell out of so many folks that I think RUMOKO II will scare even more. I am hoping that there will be a lot of topside vacations about that time. Add to this the fact that I know how rumors get started, and I can do it myself. I will.

I am at least going to clear the decks as much as I can.

They will get results, all right—the planners—like a Mount Everest in the middle of the Atlantic and some fractured domes. Laugh that off, and you are a good man.

I baited the line and threw it overboard. Bill took a drink of orange juice and I took a drag on my cigarette.

"You're a consulting engineer these days?" he asked.

"Yeah."

"What are you up to now?"

"I've got a job in mind. Kind of tricky."

"Will you take it?"

"Yes."

"I sometimes wish I had something going for me now—the way you do."

"Don't. It's not worth it."

I looked out over the dark waters, able to bear prodigies. The morning sun was just licking the waves, and my decision was, like, solid. The wind was chilly and pleasant. The sky was going to be beautiful. I could tell from the breaks in the cloud cover.

"It sounds interesting. This is demolition work, you say?"

And I, Judas Iscariot, turned a glance his way and said, "Pass me the bait can, please. I think I've got something on the line."

"Me, too. Wait a minute."

The day, like a mess of silver dollars, fell upon the deck.

I landed mine and hit it on the back of the head with the stick, to be merciful.

I kept telling myself that I did not exist. I hope it is true, even though I feel that it is not. I seem to see old Colgate's face beneath an occasional whitecap.

Eva, Eva…

Forgive me, my Eva. I would welcome your hand on my brow.

It is pretty, the silver. The waves are blue and green this morning, and God! how lovely the light!

"Here's the bait."

"Thanks."

I took it and we drifted.

Eventually, everybody dies, I noted. But it did not make me feel any better.

But nothing, really, could.

The next card will be for Christmas, as usual, Don, one year late this time around.

Never ask me why.

A Word from Zelazny

This is the first of three tales involving an unnamed protagonist (often referred to as Nemo [in Latin, *nemo* = no one, or nobody] in other bibliographies) who is a secret agent in a computerized world. Zelazny admitted using his experience as a Social Security Administration claims representative (February 1962 until May 1969) to create this character and also conversations with Bill Spangler at the Baltimore office about centralized identity records.[1] The character of **Bill** Mellings was likely named for Spangler.

Sir Arthur C. Clarke played a role in the story's genesis. "I just did a story which makes up a third of a book—the book to be called *Tomorrow Times Three*, or something like that—where Bob Silverberg, Jim Blish and I each did a 20,000 word story, independent of the others, based on an idea supplied by Arthur C. Clarke."[2] The essay describing that idea appears as a preface to the book *Three for Tomorrow.*[3]

Notes

Spitzbergen is a Norwegian island in the Svalbard archipelago. To **jibe** means to agree with. **Albert Schweitzer**, an Alsatian physician, theologian and philosopher, won the 1952 Nobel Peace Prize. Green eyes (**her eyes were green / his green eyes**) occur in less than 2% of people but are a recurrent motif among Zelazny's characters. At least 32 of his novels and short stories mention green, emerald, or jade eyes. **Swansdown** is the soft underplumage of a swan. **San Miguel de Allende** is a city in Mexico; **Carta Blanca** is a Mexican beer. **Bennies** are amphetamine tablets, specifically Benzedrine.

Indios are Native Americans of central or south America. In bullfighting, ***paseo*** is the matadors', banderilleros', and horses' formal procession into the ring before the first bullfight. **Toltecs** were Nahuatl-speaking people of central and southern Mexico whose empire flourished before the Aztecs.

The Caribbean's **Leeward Islands** are the Virgin Islands, Antigua, Saint Kitts, etc., while the **Windward Islands** include Martinique, Barbados,

1 *Roger Zelazny*, Jane M. Lindskold, 1993.
2 *Black Oracle #1*, March 1969.
3 *Three for Tomorrow*, ed. Robert Silverberg, 1969.

Grenada, Dominica, St. Lucia, etc. Iceland's volcanic island, **Surtsey**, formed in 1963. Volcanic eruptions on the Portuguese coast at **Capelhinos** in 1958 created two kilometers of new land but destroyed a nearby village of 300 homes.

In Maori mythology, **Rumoko** (Ruamoko) is the youngest son of Rangi and Papa (the primal parents, sky-father and earth-mother). He remains inside his mother's womb, and his movements cause earthquakes. A ***corpus*** is a body, especially a dead body.

Project Mohole attempted to retrieve a sample of the Earth's mantle by drilling a hole through the Earth's crust to the **Mohorovičić Discontinuity**, or Moho (the boundary between the Earth's crust and mantle). **Dr. Walter Munk**, of the National Science Foundation (NSF), and **Dr. Harry Hess** (the "father" of plate tectonic theory) suggested the project. The **American Miscellaneous Society (AMSOC)** endorsed the project, and the NSF funded it. Proposed to occur in three phases, the first was successful (drilling five holes over 600 feet below the ocean floor off Guadalupe), but the project stalled due to lack of funding in the second phase and never achieved its goal.

Krakatoa is a volcanic island in West Indonesia which underwent one of the most violent eruptions of modern times in 1883, blowing up most of the island and laying waste to much of coastal Java and Sumatra in the resulting tsunami. **Etna** is an active volcano in Italy; Pindar reported its eruption in 475 BC. Its most recent eruption occurred in 1992.

Although **gunsel** now commonly means a man with a gun, it properly is a derogatory Yiddish term for a younger male in a sexual relationship with an older man (i.e., a catamite). Novelist Dashiel Hammett deliberately fooled the censors with his use of gunsel in his 1929 book *The Maltese Falcon*; the word was later spoken by Humphrey Bogart in the 1941 film and has been taken by many to mean "man with a gun" ever since.

Euclid was a Greek mathematician whose *Elements* was the standard geometry textbook for more than 2000 years. ***Fin de siècle*** means end of a century or of an era. **Marshall McLuhan** was a Canadian philosopher and communications theorist who coined the expressions "the medium is the message" and "global village."

Thule is a mythical island that ancient Greek geographers deemed to be the world's most northerly region. ***Proteus*** is a sea god, son of Oceanus and Tethys, who can prophesy and change forms; the protagonist also can change identities. **Bacardi** is a brand of rum. **Ernie (Ernest) Hemingway** was an American novelist who wrote *For Whom the Bell Tolls* and *A Farewell to Arms*.

Ab initio means from the beginning. **Amytal** is a brand name for amobarbital; **Pentothal** is a brand name for thiopental; the two together were used as "truth drugs." **Kodokan** ("A place for study and promotion of the way") is the headquarters of Japanese style judo; **Budo Kwai** ("The

Way of Knighthood Society") and *Fédération Française de Judo* (**French Federation**) are two European adaptations of judo. ***Nage-no-kata*** are throwing techniques in Japanese judo. ***Nidan*** is a second degree black belt. ***Modus vivendi*** means way of living. ***Nages*** are all of the throwing techniques in judo.

Over the port bow, I saw the man stand up. He was old and gray and wore a wide-brimmed hat is an anthropomorphic description of a mushroom cloud. The **Kraken** is a legendary sea monster off the Norwegian coast. ***Ave atque vale*** or *Avatque vale* ("Hail and Farewell") appears in Catullus's poem; in most versions of this story, the typographical error *ave atque avatque* appears. ***Ni-hi*** or nihi is a word in both Maori and Hawaiian languages; context suggests that "***ni-hi* girl**" is a Polynesian or Hawaiian woman. **Vicissitudes** are possibilities. **Judas Iscariot** betrayed Jesus for thirty pieces of silver; the protagonist considers himself a Judas because some inhabitants of bubble cities and coastal areas will die when he causes the planned explosion of RUMOKO II. **Like a mess of silver dollars** alludes to Judas's thirty pieces of silver.

At the story's end it becomes apparent that "The Eve of RUMOKO" has two meanings. Much of the story takes place on the eve of the RUMOKO project's initiation. But the title also refers to the woman the unnamed protagonist loved. Eva died when the RUMOKO explosion crushed New Salem, the underwater bubble city. He blames himself for her death because by his undoing the sabotage he discovered, the RUMOKO project succeeded.

'KJWALLL'KJE'K'KOOTHAÏLLL'KJE'K

An Exaltation of Stars, ed. Terry Carr, Simon & Schuster 1973.
§ *My Name Is Legion*

After everyone had departed, the statements been taken, the remains of the remains removed—long after that, as the night hung late, clear, clean, with its bright multitudes doubled in their pulsing within the cool flow of the Gulf Stream about the station, I sat in a deck chair on the small patio behind my quarters, drinking a can of beer and watching the stars go by.

My feelings were an uncomfortable mixture, and I had not quite decided what to do with what was left.

It was awkward. I could make things neat and tidy again by deciding to forget the small inexplicables. I had accomplished what I had set out to do. I needed but stamp CLOSED on my mental file, go away, collect my fee and live happily, relatively speaking, ever after.

No one would ever know or, for that matter, care about the little things that still bothered me. I was under no obligation to pursue matters beyond this point.

Except…

Maybe it *is* an obligation. At least, at times it became a compulsion, and one might as well salve one's notions of duty and free will by using the pleasanter term.

It? The possession of a primate forebrain, I mean, with a deep curiosity wrinkle furrowing it for better or worse.

I had to remain about the station a while longer anyway, for appearance's sake.

I took another sip of beer.

Yes, I wanted more answers. To dump into the bottomless wrinkle up front there.

I might as well look around a bit more. Yes, I decided, I would.

I withdrew a cigarette and moved to light it. Then the flame caught my attention.

I stared at the flowing tongue of light, illuminating my palm and curved fingers of my left hand, raised to shield it from the night breeze. It seemed as pure as the starfires themselves, a molten, buttery thing, touched with orange, haloed blue, the intermittently exposed cherry-colored wick glowing, half-hidden, like a soul. And then the music began…

Music was the best term I had for it, because of some similarity of essence, although it was actually like nothing I had ever experienced before. For one thing, it was not truly sonic. It came into me as a memory comes, without benefit of external stimulus—but lacking the Lucite layer of self-consciousness that turns thought to recollection by touching it with time—as in a dream. Then, something suspended, something released, my feelings began to move to the effect. Not emotions, nothing that specific, but rather a growing sense of euphoria, delight, wonder, all poured together into a common body with the tide rising. What the progressions, what the combinations—what the thing was, truly—I did not know. It was an intense beauty, a beautiful intensity, however, and I was part of it. It was as if I were experiencing something no man had ever known before, something cosmic, magnificent, ubiquitous yet commonly ignored.

And it was with a peculiarly ambiguous effort, following a barely perceptible decision, that I twitched the fingers of my left hand sufficiently to bring them into the flame itself.

The pain broke the dream momentarily, and I snapped the lighter closed as I sprang to my feet, a gaggle of guesses passing through my head. I turned and ran across that humming artificial islet, heading for the small, dark cluster of buildings that held the museum, library, offices.

But even as I moved, something came to me again. Only this time it was not the glorious, musiclike sensation that had touched me moments earlier. Now it was sinister, bringing a fear that was none the less real for my knowing it to be irrational, to the accompaniment of sensory distortions that must have caused me to reel as I ran. The surface on which I moved buckled and swayed; the stars, the buildings, the ocean—everything—advanced and retreated in random, nauseating patterns of attack. I fell several times, recovered, rushed onward. Some of the distance I know that I crawled. Closing my eyes did no good, for everything was warped, throbbing, shifting, and awful inside as well as out.

It was only a few hundred yards, though, no matter what the signs and portents might say, and finally I rested my hands against the wall, worked my way to the door, opened it, and passed within.

Another door and I was into the library. For years, it seemed, I fumbled to switch on the light.

I staggered to the desk, fought with a drawer, wrestled a screwdriver out of it.

Then on my hands and knees, gritting my teeth, I crossed to the remote-access terminal of the Information Network. Slapping at the console's control board, I succeeded in tripping the switches that brought it to life.

Then, still on my knees, holding the screwdriver with both hands, I got the left side panel off the thing. It fell to the floor with a sound that drove spikes into my head. But the components were exposed. Three little changes and I could transmit something that would eventually wind up in Central. I resolved that I would make those changes and send the two most damaging pieces of information I could guess at to the place where they might eventually be retrieved in association with something sufficiently similar to one day cause a query, a query that would hopefully lead to the destruction of that for which I was currently being tormented.

"I mean it!" I said aloud. "Stop right now! Or I'll do it!"

...And it was like taking off a pair of unfamiliar glasses: rampant reality.

I climbed to my feet, shut down the board.

The next thing, I decided, was to have that cigarette I had wanted in the first place.

With my third puff, I heard the outer door open and close.

Dr. Barthelme, short, tan, gray on top and wiry, entered the room, blue eyes wide, one hand partly raised.

"Jim! What's wrong?" he said.

"Nothing," I replied. "Nothing."

"I saw you running. I saw you fall."

"Yes. I decided to sprint over here. I slipped. Pulled a muscle. It's all right."

"Why the rush?"

"Nerves. I'm still edgy, upset. I had to run or something, to get it out of my system. Decided to run over and get a book. Something to read myself to sleep with."

"I can get you a tranquilizer."

"No, that's all right. Thanks. I'd rather not."

"What were you doing to the machine? We're not supposed to fool with—"

"The side panel fell off when I went past it. I was just going to put it back on." I waved the screwdriver. "The little set-screws must have jiggled loose."

"Oh."

I stooped and fitted it back into place. As I was tightening the screws, the telephone rang. Barthelme crossed to the desk, poked an extension button, and answered it.

After a moment, he said, "Yes, just a minute," and turned. "It's for you."

"Really?"

I rose, moved to the desk, took the receiver, dropping the screwdriver back into the drawer and closing it. "Hello?" I said.

"All right," said the voice. "I think we had better talk. Will you come and see me now?"

"Where are you?"

"At home."

"All right, I'll come." I hung up.

"Don't need that book after all," I said. "I'm going over to Andros for a while."

"It's pretty late. Are you certain you feel up to it?"

"Oh, I feel fine now," I said. "Sorry to have worried you."

He seemed to relax. At least, he sagged and smiled faintly.

"Maybe *I* should go take the trank," he said. "Everything that's happened… You know. You scared me."

"Well, what's happened has happened. It's all over, done."

"You're right, of course… Well, have a good time, whatever."

He turned toward the door and I followed him out, extinguishing the light as I passed it.

"Good night, then."

"Good night."

He headed back toward his quarters, and I made my way down to the docking area, decided on the *Isabella*, got in. Moments later,

I was crossing over, still wondering. Curiosity may ultimately prove nature's way of dealing with the population problem.

❖ ❖ ❖

It was on May Day—not all that long ago, though it seems so—that I sat to the rear of the bar at Captain Tony's in Key West, to the right, near to the fireplace, drinking one of my seasonal beers. It was a little after eleven, and I had about decided that this one was a write-off, when Don came in through the big open front of the place. He glanced around, his eyes passing over me, located a vacant stool near the forward corner of the bar, took it, and ordered something. There were too many people between us, and the group had returned to the stage at the rear of the room behind me and begun another set, with a loud opening number. So, for a time, we just sat there—wondering, I guess.

After ten or fifteen minutes, he got to his feet and made his way back to the rest room, passing around the far side of the bar. A short while later, he returned, moving around my side. I felt his hand on my shoulder.

"Bill!" he said. "What are you doing down here?"

I turned, regarded him, grinned.

"Sam! Good Lord!"

We shook hands. Then, "Too noisy in here to talk," he said. "Let's go someplace else."

"Good idea."

After a time, we found ourselves on a dim and deserted stretch of beach, smelling the salty breath of the ocean, listening to it, and feeling an occasional droplet. We halted, and I lit a cigarette.

"Did you know that the Florida current carries over two million tons of uranium past here every year?" he said.

"To be honest, no," I told him.

"Well, it does. —What do you know about dolphins?"

"That's better," I said. "They are beautiful, friendly creatures, so well adapted to their environment that they don't have to mess it up in order to lead the life they seem to enjoy. They are highly intelligent, they're cooperative, and they seem totally lacking in all areas of maliciousness. They—"

"That's enough," and he raised his hand. "You like dolphins. I knew you would say that. You sometimes remind me of one—swimming through life, not leaving traces, retrieving things for me."

"Keep me in fish. That's all."

He nodded.

"The usual arrangement. But this one should be a relatively easy, yes-or-no thing, and not take you too long. It's quite near here, as a matter of fact, and the incident is only a few days old."

"Oh! What's involved?"

"I'd like to clear a gang of dolphins of a homicide charge," he said.

He expected me to say something, and he was disappointed. I was thinking, recalling a news account from the previous week. Two scuba-clad swimmers had been killed in one of the undersea parks to the east, at about the same time that some very peculiar activity on the part of dolphins was being observed in the same area. The men had been bitten and chewed by something possessing a jaw configuration approximating that of *Tursiops truncatus*, the bottle-nosed dolphin, a normal visitor and sometime resident of these same parks. The particular park in which the incident occurred had been closed until further notice. There were no witnesses to the attack, as I recalled, and I had not come across any follow-up story.

"I'm serious," he finally said.

"One of those guys was a qualified guide who knew the area, wasn't he?"

He brightened, there in the dark.

"Yes," he said. "Michael Thornley. He used to do some moonlighting as a guide. He was a full-time employee of the Beltrane Processing people. Did underwater repair and maintenance at their extraction plants. Ex-Navy. Frogman. Extremely qualified. The other fellow was a landlubber friend of his from Andros. Rudy Myers. They went out together at an odd hour, stayed rather long. In the meantime, several dolphins were seen getting the hell out, fast. They leaped the 'wall' instead of passing through the locks. Others used the normal exits. These were blinking on and off like mad. In a matter of a few minutes, actually, every dolphin in the park had apparently departed. When an employee went looking for Mike and Rudy, he found them dead."

"Where do you come into the picture?"

"The Institute of Delphinological Studies does not appreciate the bad press this gives their subject. They maintain there has never been an authenticated case of an unprovoked attack by a dolphin on a human being. They are anxious not to have this go on record as one, if it really isn't."

"Well, it hasn't actually been established. Perhaps something else did it. Scared the dolphins, too."

"I have no idea," he said, lighting a cigarette of his own. "But it was not all that long ago that the killing of dolphins was finally made illegal throughout the world, and that the pioneer work of people like Lilly came to be appreciated, with a really large-scale project set up for the assessment of the creature. They have come up with some amazing results, as you must know. It is no longer a question of trying to demonstrate whether a dolphin is as intelligent as a man. It has been established that they are highly intelligent—although their minds work along radically different lines, so that there probably never can be a true comparison. This is the basic reason for the continuing communication problems, and it is also a matter of which the general public is pretty much aware. Given this, our client does not like the inferences that could be drawn from the incident—namely, that powerful, free-ranging creatures of this order of intelligence could become hostile to man."

"So the Institute hired you to look into it?"

"Not officially. I was approached because the character of the thing smacks of my sort of investigation specialties as well as the scientific. Mainly, though, it was because of the urgings of a wealthy little old lady who may someday leave the Institute a fortune: Mrs. Lydia Bames, former president of the Friends of the Dolphin Society—the citizen group that had lobbied for the initial dolphin legislation years ago. She is really paying my fee."

"What sort of place in the picture did you have in mind for me?"

"Beltrane will want a replacement for Michael Thornley. Do you think you could get the job?"

"Maybe. Tell me more about Beltrane and the parks."

"Well," he said, "I guess it was a generation or so back that Dr. Spence at Harwell demonstrated that titanium hydroxide would create a chemical reaction that separated uranyl ions from seawater. It was costly, though, and it was not until years later that Samuel Beltrane came along with his screening technique, founded a small company, and quickly tamed it into a large one, with uranium-extraction stations all along this piece of the Gulf Stream. While his process was quite clean, environmentally speaking, he was setting up in business at a time when public pressure on industry was such that some gesture of ecological concern was pretty much *de rigueur*. So he threw a lot of money, equipment, and man-hours into the setting up of the four undersea parks in the vicinity of the island of Andros. A section of the barrier reef makes one of them especially attractive. He got a nice tax break on the deal. Deserved, though, I'd say. He cooperated with the dolphin studies people, and labs were set up for them in the parks. Each of the four areas is enclosed by a sonic 'wall', a sound barrier that keeps everything outside out and everything inside in, in terms of the larger creatures. Except for men and dolphins. At a number of points, the 'wall' possesses 'sound locks'—a pair of sonic curtains, several meters apart—which are operated by means of a simple control located on the bottom. Dolphins are capable of teaching one another how to use it, and they are quite good about closing the door behind them. They come and go, visiting the labs at will, both learning from and, I guess, teaching the investigators."

"Stop," I said. "What about sharks?"

"They were removed from the parks first thing. The dolphins even helped chase them out. It has been over a decade now since the last one was put out."

"I see. What say does the company have in running the parks?"

"None, really. They service the equipment now, that's all."

"Do many of the Beltrane people work as park guides too?"

"A few, part-time. They are in the area, they know it well, they have all the necessary skills."

"I would like to see whatever medical reports there were."

"I have them here, complete with photos of the bodies."

"What about the man from Andros—Rudy Myers? What did he do?"

"He'd trained as a nurse. Worked in several homes for the aged. Taken in a couple of times on charges of stealing from the patients. Charges dropped once. A suspended sentence the second time. Sort of blackballed from that line of work afterward. That was six or seven years back. Held a variety of small jobs then and kept a clean record. He had been working on the island for the past couple of years in a sort of bar."

"What do you mean 'sort of bar'?"

"It has only an alcohol license, but it serves drugs, too. It's way out in the boonies, though, so nobody's ever raised a fuss."

"What's the place called?"

"The Chickcharney."

"What's that mean?"

"A piece of local folklore. A chickcharney is a sort of tree spirit. Mischievous. Like an elf."

"Colorful enough, I guess. —Isn't Andros where Martha Millay, the photographer, makes her home?"

"Yes, it is."

"I'm a fan of hers. I like underwater photography, and hers is always good. In fact, she did several books on dolphins. Has anyone thought to ask her opinion of the killings?"

"She's been away."

"Oh. Hope she gets back soon. I'd like to meet her."

"Then you will take the job?"

"Yes, I need one just now."

He reached into his jacket, withdrew a heavy envelope, passed it to me.

"There you have copies of everything I have. Needless to say—"

"Needless to say," I said, "the life of a mayfly will be as eternity to them."

I slipped it into my own jacket and turned away.

"Be seeing you," I said.

"Leaving already?"

"I've a lot to do."

"Good luck, then."

"Thanks."

I went left and he went right, and that was that for then.

❖ ❖ ❖

Station One was something of a nerve center for the area. That is, it was larger than the other extraction plants and contained the field office, several laboratories, a library, a museum, a dispensary, living quarters, and a few recreational features. It was an artificial island, a fixed platform about seven hundred feet across, and it monitored and serviced eight other plants within the area. It was within sight of Andros, largest of the Bahama Islands, and if you like plenty of water about you, which I do, you would find the prospect peaceful and more than a little attractive.

After the tour and introductions that first day, I learned that my duties were about one-third routine and two-thirds response to circumstances. The routine part was inspection and preventive maintenance. The rest was unforeseen repair, retrieval, and replacement work—general underwater handyman stuff whenever the necessity arose.

It was Dr. Leonard Barthelme, the Area Director, who met me and showed me around. A pleasant little fellow who seemed to enjoy talking about his work, middle-aged, a widower, he had made his home at Station One for almost five years. The first person to whom he introduced me was Frank Cashel, whom we found in the main laboratory, eating a sandwich and waiting for some test to run its course.

Frank swallowed and smiled, rose, and shook hands with me as Barthelme explained, "This is the new man, James Madison."

He was dark, with a touch of gray here and there, a few creases accentuating a ruggedness of jawline and cheekbone, the beginnings of a bulge above his belt.

"Glad to have you around," he said. "Keep an eye out for pretty rocks, and bring me a branch of coral every now and then. We'll get along fine."

"Frank's hobby is collecting minerals," Barthelme said. "The display in the museum is his. We'll pass that way in a few minutes and you can see it. Quite interesting."

I nodded.

"Okay. I'll remember. See what I can find you."

"Know anything about the subject?" Frank asked me.

"A little. I used to be something of a rock hound."

"Well, I'd appreciate it."

As we walked away, Barthelme remarked, "He makes some money on the side selling specimens at gem shows. I would bear that in mind before I gave him too much in the way of my spare time, or samples."

"Oh."

"What I mean is, if you feel like going in for that sort of thing on a more than occasional basis, you ought to make it clear that you want a percentage."

"I see. Thanks."

"Don't misunderstand me," he said. "He's a fine fellow. Just a little absent minded."

"How long has he been out here?"

"Around two years. Geophysicist. Very solid."

We stopped by the equipment shed then, where I met Andy Deems and Paul Carter: the former, thin and somewhat sinister in appearance because of a scribbling of scars on his left cheek, which a full beard did not completely conceal; the latter, tall, fair, smooth-faced, and somewhere between husky and fat. They were cleaning some tanks when we entered, and wiped their hands, shook mine, and said they were glad to meet me. They both did the same sort of work I would be doing, the normal staffing calling for four of us, working in pairs. The fourth man was Paul Vallons, who was currently out with Ronald Davies, the boatmaster, replacing an instrument package in a sampler buoy. Paul, I learned, had been Mike's partner, the two of them having been friends since their Navy days. I would be working with him much of the time.

"You will soon be reduced to this miserable state yourself," Carter said cheerfully, as we were leaving. "Enjoy your morning. Gather rosebuds."

"You are miserable because you sweat most obscenely," Deems observed.

"Tell it to my glands."

As we crossed the islet, Barthelme observed that Deems was the most capable underwater man he had ever met. He had lived in one of the bubble cities for a time, lost his wife and daughter in the RUMOKO II disaster, and come topside to stay. Carter had come across from the West Coast about five months ago, immediately following a divorce or separation he did not care to talk about. He had been employed by Beltrane out there and had requested a transfer.

Barthelme took me through the second lab, which was vacant just then, so that I could admire the large, illuminated map of the seas about Andros, beads of light indicating the disposition and well-being of the devices that maintained the sonic "walls" about the parks and stations. I saw that we were encircled by a boundary that took in the nearest park also.

"In which one was the accident?" I asked.

He turned and studied my face, then pointed, indicating our own. "It was farther in, over there," he said. "Toward the northeast end of the park. What have you heard about it?"

"Just the news report," I said. "Has anything new been discovered?"

"No. Nothing."

With my fingertip, I traced the reversed L of lights that outlined the area.

"No holes in the 'wall'?" I asked.

"There haven't been any equipment failures for a long while."

"Do you think it was a dolphin?"

He shrugged. Then, "I'm a chemist," he said, "not a dolphin specialist. But it strikes me, from everything I've read, that there are dolphins and there are dolphins. The average dolphin seems to be quite pacific, with an intelligence possibly equivalent to our own. Also, they should follow the same old normal distribution curve—the bulk of them in the middle, a few morons on one end, a few geniuses on the other. Perhaps a feeble-minded dolphin who was not responsible for his actions did it. Or a Raskolnikov dolphin. Most of what is known about them comes from a study of average specimens. Statistically, in the relatively brief while such investigations have been going on, this has to be so. What do we know of their psychiatric abnormalities? Nothing, really." He shrugged again. "So yes, I think it is possible," he finished.

I was thinking then of a bubble city and some people I had never met, and I wondered whether dolphins ever felt rotten, guilty, and miserable as hell over anything they had done. I sent that thought back where it had come from, just as he said, "I hope you are not worried...?"

"Curious," I said. "But concerned, too. Naturally."

He turned and, as I followed him to the door, said, "Well, you have to remember that it was a good distance to the northeast, in the park proper. We have nothing operating over there, so your duties should not take you anywhere near the place where it occurred. Second, a team from the Institute of Delphinological Studies is searching the entire area, including our annex here, with underwater detection equipment. Third, until further notice there will be a continuing sonar scan about any area where one of our people has to submerge himself—and a shark cage and submersible decompression chamber will go along on all deep dives, just in case. The locks have all been closed until this is settled. And you will be given a weapon—a long metal tube carrying a charge and a shell—that should be capable of dispatching an angry dolphin or a shark."

I nodded.

"Okay," I said, as we headed toward the next cluster of buildings. "That makes me feel a lot better."

"I was going to get around to that in a little while anyway," he said. "I was looking for the best way to get into it, though. I feel better, too—this part is offices. Should be empty now."

He pulled open the door and I followed him through: desks, partitions, filing cabinets, office machines, water cooler—nothing unusual—and, as he had said, quite deserted. We passed along its center aisle and out the door at its far end, where we crossed the narrow breezeway that separated it from the adjacent building. We entered there.

"This is our museum," he said. "Sam Beltrane thought it would be nice to have a small one to show visitors. Full of sea things as well as a few models of our equipment."

Nodding, I looked about. At least the model equipment did not dominate, as I would have expected. The floor was covered with green indoor-outdoor carpeting, and a miniature version of the station itself occupied a tablelike frame near the front door, all of its underside equipment exposed. Shelves on the wall behind it held larger-scale versions of some of the more important components, placarded with a paragraph or two of explanation and history. There were an antique cannon, two lantern frames, several belt buckles, a few coins, and some corroded utensils displayed nearby, salvaged from a centuries-old vessel that still lay on the bottom not very far from the station, according to the plaque. On the opposite wall, with several of the larger ones set up on frames before it, was a display of marine skeletons accompanied by colored sketches of the fully fleshed and finned versions, ranging from tiny spinefish to a dolphin, along with a full-sized mock-up of a shark, which I determined to come back and compare a little more carefully on my own time. There was a large section containing Frank Cashel's mineral display, neatly mounted and labeled, separated from the fish by a window and overlooked by a slightly awkward but still attractive watercolor titled *Miami Skyline*, with the name "Cashel" scrawled in its lower corner.

"Oh, Frank paints," I said. "Not bad."

"No, that's his wife, Linda's," he replied. "You will meet her in just a minute. She should be next door. She runs the library and takes care of all our clerical work."

So we passed through the door that led to the library and I saw Linda Cashel. She was seated at a desk, writing, and she looked up as we entered. She appeared to be in her mid-twenties. Her hair was long, sun-bleached, pulled back, held with a jeweled clip. Blue eyes, in a longish face with a cleft chin, a slightly upturned nose, a sprinkling of freckles, and some very even, very white teeth were displayed as Barthelme greeted her and introduced us.

"...Anytime you want a book," she said.

I looked around at the shelves, the cases, the machines.

"We keep good copies of the standard reference works we use a lot," she said. "I can get facsimile copies of anything else on a day's notice. There are some shelves of general fiction and light stuff over there." She indicated a rack beside the front window. "Then there are those banks of cassettes to your right, mostly undersea noises—fish sounds and such, for part of a continuing study we do for the National Science Foundation—and the last bank is music, for our own enjoyment. Everything is catalogued here." She rose and slapped a file unit, indicated an index key taped to its side. "If you want to take something out and nobody's around, I would appreciate it if you would record its number, your name, and the date in this book." She glanced at a ledger on the corner of her desk. "And if you want to keep anything longer than a week, please mention it to me. There is also a tool chest in the bottom drawer, in case you ever need a pair of pliers. Remember to put them back. That covers everything I can think of," she said. "Any questions?"

"Doing much painting these days?" I asked.

"Oh," she said, reseating herself, "you saw my skyline. I'm afraid next door is the only museum I'll ever get into. I've pretty much quit. I know I'm not that good."

"I rather liked it."

She twisted her mouth.

"When I'm older and wiser and somewhere else, maybe I'll try again. I've done everything I care to with water and shorelines."

I smiled because I couldn't think of anything else to say, and she did the same. Then we left, and Barthelme gave me the rest of the morning off to get settled in my cottage, which had been Michael Thornley's quarters. I went and did that.

❖ ❖ ❖

After lunch, I went to work with Deems and Carter in the equipment shed. As a result, we finished early. Since it was still too soon to think of dinner, they offered to take me for a swim, to see the sunken ship.

It was about a quarter mile to the south, outside the "wall", perhaps twenty fathoms down—what was left of it—and eerie, as such things always are, in the wavering beams we extended. A broken mast, a snapped bowsprit, a section of deck planking and smashed gunwale visible above the mud, an agitated horde of little fish we had disturbed at whatever they were about within and near the hulk, a partial curtain of weeds drawn and redrawn by the currents, and that was all that remained of someone's hopes for a successful voyage, some shipbuilders' labors, and possibly a number of people whose last impressions were of storm or sword, and then the gray, blue, green, sudden springs uncoiling, cold.

Or maybe they made it over to Andros and dinner, as we did later. We ate in a red-and-white-checked-tablecloth sort of place near to the shore, where just about everything man-made clung, the interior of Andros being packed with mangrove swamps, mahogany and pine forests, doves, ducks, quail, pigeons, and chickcharnies. The food was good; I was hungry.

We sat for a time afterwards, smoking and talking. I still had not met Paul Vallons, but I was scheduled to work with him the following day. I asked Deems what he was like.

"Big fellow," he said, "around your size, only he's good-looking. Kind of reserved. Fine diver. He and Mike used to take off every weekend, go helling around the Caribbean. Had a girl on every island, I'll bet."

"How's he—taking things?"

"Pretty well, I guess. Like I said, he's kind of reserved, doesn't show his feelings much. He and Mike had been friends for years."

"What do you think got Mike?"

Carter broke in then.

"One of those damned dolphins," he said. "We should never have started fooling with them. One of them came up under me once, damn near ruptured me."

"They're playful," Deems said. "It didn't mean any harm."

"I think it did. —And that slick skin of theirs reminds me of a wet balloon. Sickening!"

"You're prejudiced. They're friendly as puppies. It probably goes back to some sexual hangup."

"Crap!" Carter said. "They—"

Since I had gotten it started, I felt obligated to change the subject. So I asked whether it was true that Martha Millay lived nearby.

"Yes," Deems said, taking hold of the opportunity. "She has a place about four miles down the coast from here. Very neat, I understand, though I've only seen it from the water. Her own little port. She has a hydrofoil, a sailboat, a good-sized cabin cruiser, and a couple little power launches. Lives alone in a long, low building right smack on the water. Not even a road out that way."

"I've admired her work for a long while. I'd like to meet her sometime."

He shook his head.

"I'll bet you never do. She doesn't like people. Doesn't have a listed phone."

"That's a pity. Any idea why she's that way?"

"Well..."

"She's deformed," Carter said. "I met her once, on the water. She was at anchor and I was going past on my way to one of the stations. That was before I knew about her, so I went near, just to say hello. She was taking pictures through the glass bottom of her boat, and when she saw me she started to scream and holler for me to get away, that I was scaring the fish. And she snatched up a tarp and pulled it over her legs. I got a look, though. She's a nice, normal-looking woman from the waist up, but her hips and legs are all twisted and ugly. I was sorry I'd embarrassed her. I was just as embarrassed myself, and I didn't know what to say. So I yelled, 'Sorry,' and waved and kept going."

"I heard she can't walk at all," Deems said, "though she is supposed to be an excellent swimmer. I've never seen her myself."

"Was she in some sort of accident, do you know?"

"Not as I understand it," he said. "She is half Japanese, and the story I heard is that her mother was a Hiroshima baby. Some sort of genetic damage."

"Pity."

"Yes."

We settled up and headed back. Later, I lay awake for a long while, thinking of dolphins, sunken ships, drowned people, half people, and the Gulf Stream, which kept talking to me through the window. Finally, I listened to it, and it took hold of me and we drifted away together into the darkness to wherever it finally goes.

❖ ❖ ❖

Paul Vallons was, as Andy Deems had said, around my size and good-looking, in a dark, clothing-advertisement sort of way. Another twenty years and he would probably even look distinguished. Some guys win all the way around. Deems had also been right about his reserve. He was not especially talkative, although he managed this without seeming unfriendly. As for his diving prowess, I was unable to confirm it that first day I worked with him, for we pulled shore duty while Deems and Carter got sent over to Station Three. Back to the equipment shed…

I did not think it a good idea to ask him about his late buddy, or dolphins, which pretty much confined me conversation-wise to the business at hand and a few generalities. Thus was the morning passed.

After lunch, though, as I began thinking ahead, going over my plans for that evening, I decided he would be as good as anyone when it came to getting directions to the Chickcharney.

He lowered the valve he had been cleaning and stared at me.

"What do you want to go to that dive for?" he asked.

"Heard the place mentioned," I said. "Like to see it."

"They serve drugs without a license," he told me. "No inspection. If you like the stuff, you have no guarantee you won't be served some crap the village idiot cooks up in an outhouse."

"Then I'll stick to beer. Still like to see the place."

He shrugged.

"Not that much to look at. But here—"

He wiped his hands, tore an old leaf from the back of the wall calendar, and sketched me a quick map. I saw that it was a bit inland, toward the birds and mangroves, muck and mahogany. It was also somewhat to the south of the place I had been the previous evening. It was located on a stream, built up on pilings out over the water, he said, and I could take a boat right up to the pier that adjoined it.

"Think I'll go over tonight," I said.

"Remember what I said."

I nodded as I tucked away the map.

The afternoon passed quickly. There came a massing of clouds, a brief rainfall—about a quarter hour's worth—and then the sun returned to dry the decks and warm the just-rinsed world. Again, the workday ended early for me, by virtue of our having run out of business. I showered quickly, put on fresh clothes, and went to see about getting the use of a light boat.

Ronald Davies, a tall, thin-haired man with a New England accent, said I could take the speedboat called *Isabella*, complained about his arthritis, and told me to have a good time. I nodded, turned her toward Andros, and sputtered away, hoping the Chickcharney included food among its inducements, as I did not want to waste time by stopping elsewhere.

The sea was calm and the gulls dipped and pivoted, uttering hoarse cries, as I spread the wings of my wake across their preserve. I really had no idea what it was that I was going after. I did not like operating that way, but there was no alternative. I had no real line of attack. There was no handle on this one. I had determined, therefore, to simply amass as much information as I could as quickly as possible. Speed always seems particularly essential when I have no idea what it is that might be growing cold.

Andros enlarged before me. I took my bearings from the place where we had eaten the previous evening, then sought the mouth of the stream Vallons had sketched for me.

It took me about ten minutes to locate it, and I throttled down and made my way slowly up its twisting course. Occasionally, I caught a glimpse of a rough roadway running along the bank to my left. The foliage grew denser, however, and I finally lost sight of it completely. Eventually, the boughs met overhead, locking me for several minutes into an alley of premature twilight, before the stream widened again, took me around a corner, and showed me the place as it had been described.

I headed to the pier, where several other boats were moored, tied up, climbed out, and looked around. The building to my right—the only building, outside of a small shed—did extend out over the water, was a wood-frame job, and was so patched that I doubted any of its original materials remained. There were half a dozen vehicles parked beside it, and a faded sign named the place THE CHICK-CHARNEY. Looking to my left as I advanced, I could see that the road which had accompanied me was in better shape than I would have guessed.

Entering, I discovered a beautiful mahogany bar about fifteen feet ahead of me, looking as if it might have come from some ship. There were eight or ten tables here and there, several of them occupied, and a curtained doorway lay to the right of the bar. Someone had painted a crude halo of clouds above it.

I moved up to the bar, becoming its only occupant. The bartender, a fat man who had needed a shave yesterday as well as the day before, put down his newspaper and came over.

"What'll it be?"

"Give me a beer," I said. "And can I get something to eat?"

"Wait a minute."

He moved farther down, checked a small refrigerator.

"Fish-salad sandwich?" he said.

"Okay."

"Good. Because that's all we've got."

He put it together, brought it over, drew me my beer.

"That was your boat I heard, wasn't it?" he asked.

"That's right."

"Vacationing?"

"No. I just started work over at Station One."

"Oh. Diver?"

"Yes."

He sighed.

"You're Mike Thornley's replacement, then. Poor guy."

I prefer the word "successor" to "replacement" in these situations, because it makes people seem less like spark plugs. But I nodded.

"Yeah, I heard all about it," I said. "Too bad."

"He used to come here a lot."

"I heard that, too—and that the guy he was with worked here."

He nodded.

"Rudy. Rudy Myers," he said. "Worked here a couple years."

"They were pretty good friends, huh?"

He shook his head.

"Not especially," he said. "They just knew each other. —Rudy worked in back." He glanced at the curtain.

"You know."

I nodded.

"Chief guide, high medical officer, and head bottle washer," he said, with rehearsed levity. "You interested…?"

"What's the specialty of the house?"

"Pink Paradise," he said. "It's nice."

"What's it got?"

"Bit of a drift, bit of an up, the pretty lights."

"Maybe next time," I said. "Did he and Rudy go swimming together often?"

"No, that was the only time. —You worried?"

"I am not exactly happy about it. When I took this job nobody told me I might get eaten. Did Mike ever say anything about unusual marine activity or anything like that?"

"No, not that I can recall."

"What about Rudy? Did he like the water?"

He peered at me, working at the beginnings of a frown.

"Why do you ask?"

"Because it occurs to me that it might make a difference. If he was interested in things like that and Mike came across something unusual, he might take him out to see it."

"Like what?"

"Beats the hell out of me. —But if he found something and it was dangerous, I'd like to know about it."

The frown went away.

"No," he said. "Rudy wouldn't have been interested. He wouldn't have walked outside to look if the Loch Ness monster was swimming by."

"Wonder why he went, then?"

He shrugged.

"I have no idea."

I had a hunch that if I asked him anything else I just might ruin our beautiful rapport. So I ate up, drank up, paid up, and left.

❖ ❖ ❖

I followed the stream out to the open water again and ran south along the coast. Deems had said it was about four miles that way, figuring from the restaurant, and that it was a long, low building right on the water. All right. I hoped she had returned for that trip Don had mentioned. The worst she could do was tell me to go away. But she knew an awful lot that might be worth hearing. She knew the area and she knew dolphins. I wanted her opinion, if she had one.

There was still a lot of daylight left in the sky, though the air seemed to have cooled a bit, when I spotted a small cove at about the proper distance, throttled down, and swung toward it. Yes, there was the place, partway back and to the left, built against a steep rise and sporting a front deck that projected out over the water. Several boats, one of them a sailboat, rode at rest at its side, sheltered by the long, white curve of a breakwater.

I headed in, continuing to slow, and made my way around the inward point of the breakwall. I saw her sitting on the pier, and she saw me and reached for something. Then she was lost to sight above me as I pulled into the lee of the structure. I killed my engine and tied up to the handiest piling, wondering each moment whether she would appear the next, boathook in hand, ready to repel invaders.

This did not happen, though, so I climbed out and onto a ramplike staging that led me topside. She was just finishing adjusting a long, flaring skirt, which must have been what she had been reaching after. She wore a bikini top, and she was seated on the deck itself, near to the edge, legs tucked out of sight beneath the green, white and blue print material. Her hair was long and very black, her eyes dark and large. Her features were regular, with a definite Oriental cast to them, of the sort I find exceedingly attractive. I paused at the top of the ramp, feeling immediately uncomfortable as I met her gaze.

"My name is Madison, James Madison," I said. "I work out at Station One. I'm new there. May I come up for a minute?"

"You already have," she said. Then she smiled, a tentative thing. "But you can come the rest of the way over and have your minute."

So I did, and as I advanced she kept staring at me. It made me acutely self-conscious, a condition I thought I had mastered shortly after puberty, and as I was about to look away, she said, "Martha Millay—just to make it a full introduction," and she smiled again.

"I've admired your work for a long while," I said, "although that is only part of the reason I came by. I hoped you could help me to feel safer in my own work."

"The killings," she said.

"Yes, exactly. —Your opinion. I'd like it."

"All right. You can have it," she said. "But I was on Martinique at the time the killings occurred, and my intelligence comes only from the news reports and one phone conversation with a friend at the IDS. On the basis of years of acquaintanceship, years spent photographing them, playing with them, knowing them—loving them—I do not believe it possible that a dolphin would kill a human being. The notion runs contrary to all my experience. For some peculiar reason—perhaps some delphinic concept as to the brotherhood of self-conscious intelligence—we seem to be quite important to them, so important that I even believe one of them might rather die himself than see one of us killed."

"So you would rule out even a self-defense killing by a dolphin?"

"I think so," she said, "although I have no facts to point at here. However, what is more important, in terms of your real question, is that they struck me as very undolphinlike killings."

"How so?"

"I don't see a dolphin as using his teeth in the way that was described. The way a dolphin is designed, his rostrum—or beak—

contains a hundred teeth, and there are eighty-eight in his lower jaw. But if he gets into a fight with, say, a shark or a whale, he does not use them for purposes of biting or slashing. He locks them together, which provides a very rigid structure, and uses his lower jaw, which is considerably undershot, for purposes of ramming his opponent. The anterior of the skull is quite thick and the skull itself sufficiently large to absorb enormous shocks from blows administered in this fashion—and they are tremendous blows, for dolphins have very powerful neck muscles. They are quite capable of killing sharks by battering them to death. So even granting for the sake of argument that a dolphin might have done such a thing, he would not have bitten his victims. He would have bludgeoned them."

"So why didn't someone from the dolphin institute come out and say that?"

She sighed.

"They did. The news media didn't even use the statement they gave them. Apparently nobody thought it an important enough story to warrant any sort of followup."

She finally took her eyes off me and stared out over the water.

Then, "I believe their indifference to the damage caused by running only the one story is more contemptible even than actual malice," she finally said.

Acquitted for a moment by her gaze, I lowered myself to sit on the edge of the pier, my feet hanging down over the side. It had been an added discomfort to stand, staring down at her. I joined her in looking out across her harbor.

"Cigarette?" I said.

"I don't smoke."

"Mind if I do?"

"Go ahead."

I lit one, drew on it, thought a moment, then asked, "Any idea as to how the deaths might have occurred?"

"It could have been a shark."

"But there hasn't been a shark in the area for years. The 'walls'—"

She laughed.

"There are any number of ways a shark could have gotten in," she said. "A shift on the bottom, opening a tunnel or crevice beneath the 'wall'. A temporary short circuit in one of the projectors that didn't get noticed—or a continuing one, with a short somewhere in the monitoring system. For that matter, the frequencies used in the 'wall' are supposed to be extremely distressing to many varieties of marine life, but not necessarily fatal. While a shark would normally seek to avoid the 'wall', one could have been driven, forced through by some disturbance, and then found itself trapped inside."

"That's a thought," I said. "Yes. —Thank you. You didn't disappoint me."

"I would have thought that I had."

"Why?"

"All that I have done is try to vindicate the dolphins and show that there is possibly a shark inside. You said that you wanted me to tell you something that would make you feel safer in your work."

I felt uncomfortable again. I had the sudden, irrational feeling that she somehow knew all about me and was playing games at that moment.

"You said that you are familiar with my work," she said suddenly. "Does that include the two picture books on dolphins?"

"Yes. I enjoyed your text, too."

"There wasn't that much of it," she said, "and it has been several years now. Perhaps it was too whimsical. It has been a long while since I've looked at the things I said…"

"I thought them admirably suited to the subject—little Zen-like aphorisms for each photograph."

"Can you recall any?"

"Yes," I said, one suddenly coming to me, "I remember the shot of the leaping dolphin, where you caught his shadow over the water and had for a caption, 'In the absence of reflection, what gods…' "

She chuckled briefly.

"For a long while I thought that that one was perhaps too cute. Later, though, as I got to know my subject better, I decided that it was not."

"I have often wondered as to what sort of religion or religious feelings they might possess," I said. "It has been a common element among all the tribes of man. It would seem that something along these lines appears whenever a certain level of intelligence is achieved, for purposes of dealing with those things that are still beyond its grasp. I am baffled as to the forms it might take among dolphins, but quite intrigued by the notion. You say you have some ideas on it?"

"I have done a lot of thinking as I watched them," she said, "attempting to analyze their character in terms of their behavior, their physiology. Are you familiar with the writings of Johan Huizinga?"

"Faintly," I said. "It has been years since I read *Homo Ludens*, and it struck me as a rough draft for something he never got to work out completely. But I recall his basic premise as being that culture begins as a sort of sublimation of a play instinct, elements of sacred performances and festal contests continuing for a time in the evolving institutions, perhaps always remaining present at some level—although his analysis stopped short of modem times."

"Yes," she said. "The play instinct. Watching them sport about, it has often seemed to me that as well adapted as they are to their environment, there was never a need for dolphins to evolve complex social institutions, so that whatever it was they did possess along those lines was much closer to the earlier situations considered by Huizinga—a life condition filled with an overt indulgence in their version of festal performances and contests."

"A play-religion?"

"Not quite that simple, though I think that is part of the picture. The problem here lies in language. Huizinga employed the Latin word *ludus* for a reason. Unlike the Greek language, which had a variety of words for idling, for competing in contests, for passing the time in different fashions, Latin reflected the basic unity of all these things and summarized them into a single concept by means of the word *ludus*. The dolphins' distinctions between play and seriousness are obviously different from our own, just as ours are different from the Greeks'. In our understanding of the meaning of *ludus*, however, in our ability to realize that we may unify instances of activity from across a broad spectrum of behavior patterns by considering them as a form of play, we have a better basis for conjecture as well as interpretation."

"And in this manner you have deduced their religion?"

"I haven't, of course. I only have a few conjectures. You say you have none?"

"Well, if I had to guess, just to pull something out of the air, I would say some form of pantheism—perhaps something akin to the less contemplative forms of Buddhism."

"Why 'less contemplative'?" she asked.

"All that activity," I said. "They don't even really sleep, do they? They have to get topside quite regularly in order to breathe. So they are always moving about. When would they be able to drift beneath the coral equivalent of a bo tree for any period of time?"

"What do you think your mind would be like if you never slept?"

"I find that rather difficult to conceive. But I imagine I would find it quite distressing after a while, unless..."

"Unless what?"

"Unless I indulged in periodic daydreaming, I suppose."

"I think that might be the case with dolphins, although with a brain capacity such as they possess I do not feel it need necessarily be a periodic thing."

"I don't quite follow you."

"I mean they are sufficiently endowed to do it simultaneously with other thinking, rather than serially."

"You mean always dreaming a little? Taking their mental vacations, their reveries, sidewise in time as it were?"

"Yes. We do it too, to a limited extent. There is always a little background thinking, a little mental noise going on while we are dealing with whatever thoughts are most pressing in our consciousness. We learn to suppress it, calling this concentration. It is, in one sense, a process of keeping ourselves from dreaming."

"And you see the dolphin as dreaming and carrying on his normal mental business at the same time?"

"In a way, yes. But I also see the dreaming itself as a somewhat different process."

"In what way?"

"Our dreams are largely visual in nature, for our waking lives are primarily visually oriented. The dolphin, on the other hand—"

"—is acoustically oriented. Yes. Granting this constant dreaming effect and predicating it on the neurophysiological structures they possess, it would seem that they might splash around enjoying their own sound tracks."

"More or less, yes. And might not this behavior come under the heading of *ludus*?"

"I just don't know."

"One form of *ludus*, which the Greeks of course saw as a separate activity, giving it the name *diagoge*, is best translated as mental recreation. Music was placed in this category, and Aristotle speculated in his *Politics* as to the profit to be derived from it, finally conceding that music might conduce to virtue by making the body fit, promoting a certain ethos, and enabling us to enjoy things in the proper way, whatever that means. But considering an acoustical daydream in this light—as a musical variety of *ludus*—I wonder if it might not indeed promote a certain ethos and foster a particular way of enjoying things?"

"Possibly, if they were shared experiences."

"We still have no proper idea as to the meanings of many of their sounds. Supposing they are vocalizing some part of this experience?"

"Perhaps, given your other premises."

"Then that is all I have," she said. "I choose to see a religious significance in spontaneous expressions of *diagoge*. You may not."

"I don't. I'd buy it as a physiological or psychological necessity, even see it—as you suggested—as a form of play, or *ludus*. But I have no way of knowing whether such musical activity is truly a religious expression, so for me the ball stops rolling right there. At this point, we do not really understand their ethos or their particular ways of viewing life. A concept as alien and sophisticated as the one you have outlined would be well-nigh impossible for them to communicate to us, even if the language barrier were a lot thinner than it is now. Short of actually finding a way of getting inside them to know it for oneself, I do not see how we can deduce religious sentiments here, even if every one of your other conjectures is correct."

"You are, of course, right," she said. "The conclusion is not scientific if it cannot be demonstrated. I cannot demonstrate it, for it is only a feeling, an inference, an intuition—and I offer it only in that spirit. But watch them at their play sometime, listen to the sounds your ears will accept. Think about it. Try to feel it."

I continued to stare at the water and the sky. I had already learned everything I had come to find out and the rest was just frosting, but I did not have the pleasure of such desserts every day. I realized then that I liked the girl even more than I had thought I would, that I had grown quite fascinated as she had spoken, and not entirely because of the subject. So, partly to prolong things and partly because I was genuinely curious, I said, "Go ahead. Tell me the rest. Please."

"The rest?"

"You see a religion or something on that order. Tell me what you think it must be like."

She hesitated. Then, "I don't know," she said. "The more one compounds conjectures the sillier one becomes. Let us leave it at that."

But that would leave me with little to say but "Thank you" and "Good night." So I pushed my mind around inside the parameters she had laid down, and one of the things that came to me was

Barthelme's mention of the normal distribution curve with reference to dolphins.

"If, as you suggest," I began, "they constantly express and interpret themselves and their universe by a kind of subliminal dream-song, it would seem to follow that, as in all things, some are better at it than others. How many Mozarts can there be, even in a race of musicians? Champions, in a nation of athletes? If they all play at a religious *diagoge*, it must follow that some are superior players. Would they be priests or prophets? Bards? Holy singers? Would the areas in which they dwell be shrines, holy places? A dolphin Vatican or Mecca? A Lourdes?"

She laughed.

"Now *you* are getting carried away, Mister—Madison."

I looked at her, trying to see something beyond the apparently amused expression with which she faced me.

"You told me to think about it," I said, "to try to feel it."

"It would be strange if you were correct, would it not?"

I nodded.

"And probably well worth the pilgrimage," I said, standing, "if only I could find an interpreter. —I thank you for the minute I took and the others you gave me. Would you mind terribly if I dropped by again sometime?"

"I am afraid I am going to be quite busy," she said.

"I see. Well, I appreciate what you have given me. Good night, then."

"Good night."

I made my way back down the ramp to the speedboat, brought it to life, guided it about the breakwall and headed toward the darkening sea, looking back only once, in hopes of discovering just what it was that she called to mind, sitting there, looking out across the waves. Perhaps the Little Mermaid, I decided.

She did not wave back to me. But then it was twilight, and she might not have noticed.

❖ ❖ ❖

Returning to Station One, I felt sufficiently inspired to head for the office/museum/library cluster to see what I could pick up in the way of reading materials having to do with dolphins.

I made my way across the islet and into the front door, passing the shadow-decked models and displays of the museum and turning right. I swung the door open. The light was on in the library, but the place was empty. I found several books listed that I had not read, so I hunted them up, leafed through them, settled on two, and went to sign them out.

As I was doing this, my eyes were drawn toward the top of the ledger page by one of the names entered there: Mike Thornley. I glanced across at the date and saw that it happened to be the day before his death. I finished signing out my own materials and decided to see what it was he had taken to read on the eve of his passing. Well, read and listen to. There were three items shown, and the prefix to one of the numbers indicated that it had been a tape.

The two books turned out to be light popular novels. When I checked the tape, however, a very strange feeling possessed me. It was not music, but rather one from the marine-biology section. Verily. To be precise, it was a recording of the sounds of the killer whale.

Even my pedestrian knowledge of the subject was sufficient, but to be doubly certain, I checked in one of the books I had right there with me. Yes, the killer whale was undoubtedly the dolphin's greatest enemy, and well over a generation ago experiments had been conducted at the Naval Undersea Center in San Diego, using the recorded sounds of the killer whale to frighten dolphins, for purposes of developing a device to scare them out of tuna nets, where they were often inadvertently slaughtered.

What could Thornley possibly have wanted it for? Its use in a waterproof broadcasting unit could well have accounted for the unusual behavior of the dolphins in the park at the time he was killed. But why? Why do a thing like that?

I did what I always do when I am puzzled: I sat down and lit a cigarette.

While this made it even more obvious to me that things were not what they had seemed at the time of the killings, it also caused me once again to consider the apparent nature of the attack. I thought of the photos I had seen of the bodies, of the medical reports I had read.

Bitten. Chewed. Slashed.

Arterial bleeding, right carotid…

Severed jugular; numerous lacerations of shoulders and chest…

According to Martha Millay, a dolphin would not go about it that way. Still, as I recalled, their many teeth, while not enormous, were needle-sharp. I began paging through the books, looking for photographs of the jaws and teeth.

Then the thought came to me, with dark, more than informational overtones to it: *there is a dolphin skeleton in the next room.*

Mashing out my cigarette, I rose then, passed through the doorway into the museum, and began looking about for the light switch. It was not readily apparent As I sought it, I heard the door on the other side of the room open.

Turning, I saw Linda Cashel stepping across the threshold. With her next step, she looked in my direction, froze, and muffled the beginning of a shriek.

"It's me. Madison," I said. "Sorry I alarmed you. I'm looking for the light switch."

Several seconds passed. Then, "Oh," she said. "It's down in back of the display. I'll show you."

She crossed to the front door, groped behind a component model.

The lights came on, and she gave a nervous laugh.

"You startled me," she said. "I was working late. An unusual thing, but I got backed up. I stepped out for a breath of air and didn't see you come in."

"I've got the books I was looking for," I said, "but thanks for finding me the switch."

"I'll be glad to sign them out for you."

"I already did that," I said, "but I left them inside because I wanted to take another look at the display before I went home."

"Oh. Well, I was just going to close up. If you want to stay awhile, I'll let you do it."

"What does it consist of?"

"Just turning out the lights and closing the doors—we don't lock them around here. I've already shut the windows."

"Sure, I'll do that. —I'm sorry I frightened you."

"That's all right. No harm done."

She moved to the front door, turned when she reached it, and smiled again, a better job this time.

"Well, good night."

"Good night."

My first thought was that there were no signs of any extra work having come in since the last time I had been around, my second one was that she had been trying a little too hard to get me to believe her, and my third thought was ignoble.

But the proof of the pudding would keep. I turned my attention to the dolphin skeleton.

The lower jaw, with its neat, sharp teeth, fascinated me, and its size came close to being its most interesting feature. Almost, but not quite. The most interesting thing about it had to be the fact that the wires which held it in place were clean, untarnished, bright and gleaming at their ends, as if they had just recently been cut, unlike their more oxidized brethren everyplace else where the specimen had been wired.

The thing I found interesting about the size was that it was just about right to make it a dandy hand weapon.

And that was all. That was enough. But I fingered the maxillary and premaxillary bones, running my hand back toward the blowhole; I traced the rostrum; I gripped the jaw once more. Why, I did not really know for a moment, until a grotesque vision of Hamlet filtered into my mind. Or was it really that incongruous? A phrase out of Loren Eiseley came to me then: "...We are all potential fossils still carrying within our bodies the crudities of former existences, the marks of a world in which living creatures flow with little more consistency than clouds from age to age." We came from the water. This fellow I gripped had spent his life there. But both our skulls were built of calcium, a sea product chosen in our earlier days and irrevocably part of us now; both were housings for large brains—similar, yet different; both seemed to contain a center of consciousness, awareness, sensitivity, with all the concomitant pleasures, woes, and available varieties of conclusions concerning existence which that entailed, passing at some time or other within these small, rigid pieces of carbonate of lime. The only really significant difference, I suddenly felt, was not that this fellow had been born a dolphin and I a man, but only, rather, that I still lived—a very minor point in terms of the time scale onto which I had wandered. I withdrew my hand, wondering uncomfortably whether my remains would ever be used as a murder weapon.

Having no further reason for being there, I collected my books, closed up, and cleared out.

Returning to my cottage, I deposited the books on my bed table and left the small light burning there. I departed again by means of the back door, which let upon a small, relatively private patio, pleasantly situated right at the edge of the islet with an unobstructed view of the sea. But I did not pause to admire the prospect just then. If other people might step out for a breath of air, so could I.

I strolled until I located a suitable spot, a small bench in the shadow of the dispensary. I seated myself there, fairly well hidden, yet commanding a full view of the complex I had but recently quitted. For a long while I waited, feeling ignoble, but watching anyway.

As the minutes continued their parade, I came near to deciding that I had been mistaken, that the margin of caution had elapsed, that nothing would occur.

But then the door at the far end of the office—the one through which I had entered on my initial tour of the place—opened, and the figure of a man emerged. He headed toward the nearest shore of the islet, then commenced what would have seemed but the continuance of a stroll along its edge to anyone just noticing him there. He was tall, around my height, which narrowed the field considerably, so that it was really almost unnecessary for me to wait and see him enter the cottage that was assigned to Paul Vallons, and after a moment see the light go on within.

A little while later, I was in bed with my dolphin books, reflecting that some guys seem to have it made all the way around; and puzzling and wondering, with the pied typecase Don had handed me, that I was ever born to set it right.

The following morning, during the ambulatory, coffee-tropism phase of preconsciousness, I stumbled across the most damnable, frightening, item in the entire case. Or rather, I stepped over it—perhaps even on it—before its existence registered itself. There followed an appreciable time lag, and then its possible significance occurred to me.

I stooped and picked it up: an oblong of stiff paper, an envelope, which had apparently been pushed in beneath the back door. At least, it lay near to it.

I took it with me to the kitchenette table, tore it open, extracted and unfolded the paper it contained. Sipping my coffee, I read over the block-printed message several times:

> AFFIXED TO THE MAINMAST OF THE WRECK,
> ABOUT A FOOT BENEATH THE MUD

That was all. That was it.

But I was suddenly fully awake. It was not just the message, as intriguing as I naturally found it, but the fact that someone had selected me as its recipient. Who? And why?

Whatever it was—and I was certain there was something—I was most disturbed by the implication that someone was aware of my extraordinary reasons for being there, with the necessary corollary that that person knew too much about me. My hackles rose, and the adrenaline tingles came into my extremities. No man knew my name; a knowledge of it jeopardized my existence. In the past, I had even killed to protect my identity.

My first impulse was to flee, to throw over the case, dispose of this identity and lose myself in the manner in which I had become adept. But then I would never know, would never know when, where, how, why, and in what fashion I had been tripped up, found out. And most important, by whom.

Also, considering the message again, I had no assurance that flight would be the end of things for me. For was there not an element of coercion here? Of tacit blackmail in me implied imperative? It was as if the sender were saying, *I know. I will assist. I will keep silent. For there is a thing you will do for me.*

Of course I would go and inspect the wreck, though I would have to wait until the day's work was done. No use speculating as to what I would find, although I would handle it most gingerly. That gave me the entire day in which to consider what I might have done wrong, and to decide upon the best means of defending myself. I rubbed my ring, where the death spores slept, then rose and went to shave.

❖ ❖ ❖

Paul and I were sent over to Station Five that day. Standard inspection and maintenance work. Dull, safe, routine. We scarcely got wet.

He gave no indication of knowing that I was on to anything. In fact, he even started several conversations. In one, he asked me, "Did you get over to the Chickcharney?"

"Yes," I said.

"What did you think of it?"

"You were right. A dive."

He smiled and nodded, then, "Try any of their specialities?" he asked.

"Just had a few beers."

"That was safest," he said. "Mike—my friend who died—used to go there a lot."

"Oh?"

"I used to go with him at first. He'd take something and I'd sit around and drink and wait for him to come down."

"You didn't go in for it yourself?"

He shook his head.

"Had a bad experience when I was younger. Scared me. Anyway, so did he—there, I mean—several times, at the Chickcharney. He used to go in back—it's a sort of ashram back there. Did you see it?"

"No."

"Well, he had a couple bad ones in there and we got in an argument about it. He knew the damn place wasn't licensed, but he didn't care. I finally told him he ought to keep a safe supply at the station, but he was worried about the damn company regulations against it. Which I think was silly. Anyhow, I finally told him he could go by himself if he wanted to go that badly and couldn't wait till the weekend to go someplace else. I stopped going."

"Did he?"

"Only recently," he said. "The hard way."

"Oh."

"So if you do go in for it, I'm telling you the same thing I told him: Keep your own around if you can't wait to go someplace farther and cleaner than that."

"I'll remember," I said, wondering then whether he might, perhaps, be on to something about me and be encouraging my breaking the company rules for purposes of getting rid of me. That seemed kind of far-out, though, a little too paranoiac a reaction on my part. So I dismissed it.

"Did he have any more bad ones?" I asked.

"I think so," he said. "I don't really know."

And that was all he had to say on the subject. I wanted to ask him more things, of course, but our acquaintanceship was still such that I knew I would need an opening to get through, and he didn't give me any.

So we finished up, returned to Station One, went our separate ways. I stopped by and told Davies I wanted a boat later. He assigned me one, and I returned to my cottage and waited until I saw him leave for dinner. Then I went back to the docks, threw my diving gear into the boat, and took off. This elaboration was necessary because of the fact that solo-diving was against the rules, and also because of the safety precautions Barthelme had enunciated to me that first day. —True, they applied only inside the area and the ship lay outside it, but I did not care to explain where I was going either.

The thought had of course occurred to me that it might be a trap, set to spring in any of a number of ways. While I hoped my friend in the museum still had his lower jaw in place, I did not discount the possibility of an underwater ambush. In fact, I had one of the little death rods along with me, all loaded and primed. The photos had been quite clear. I did not forget. Nor did I discount the possibility of a booby trap. I would simply have to be very careful in my poking about.

While I did not know what would happen if I were spotted solo-diving with company gear, I would have to count on my ability to talk or lie my way out of it, if catching me in this breach of domestic tranquility was what the note's author had had in mind.

I came to what I thought to be the spot, anchored there, slipped into my gear, went over the side and down.

The cool smoothness held me and I did my dance of descent, curious, wary, with a heightened feeling of fragility. Toward the bottom then, with steady, sweeping movements down, I passed from cool to cold and light to dark. I switched on my torch, shot the beam about.

Minutes later, I found it, circled it, hunting about the vicinity for signs of fellow intruders. But no, nothing. I seemed to be alone.

I made my way toward the hulk then, casting my light down the splintered length of the short-snapped mainmast. Small fish appeared, staging an unruly demonstration in the neighborhood of the gunwale. My light fell upon the layer of ooze at the base of the mast. It appeared undisturbed, but then I have no idea as to how long it takes ooze to settle.

Coming up beside/above it then, I probed it with a thin rod I had brought along. After several moments, I was satisfied that there was a small, oblong object, probably metallic, about eight inches beneath the surface.

Drawing nearer, I scooped away a layer. The water muddied, fresh material moving to fill the site of my excavation. Cursing mentally, I extended my left hand, fingers at full flex, slowly, carefully, down into the mud.

I encountered no obstacles until I reached the box itself. No wires, strings, foreign objects. It was definitely metal, and I traced its outline: about six by ten by three inches. It was upended and held in place against the mast by a double strand of wire. I felt no connections with anything else, so I uncovered it—at least momentarily—for a better look.

It was a small, standard-looking strongbox, handles on both ends and on the top. The wires ran through two of these loops. I shook out a coil of plastic cord and knotted it through the nearest one. After paying out a considerable length of it, I leaned down and used the pliers I had carried with me to sever the wires that held the box to the mast. Upward then, playing out the rest of the line behind me.

Back in the boat and out of my gear, I hauled it, hand over hand, up from the depths. The movement, the pressure changes did not serve to set anything off, so I felt a little safer in handling it when I finally brought it aboard. I set it on the deck and thought about it as I unfastened and recoiled the line.

The box was locked, and whatever was inside shifted around when I moved it. I sprung the lock with a screwdriver. Then I went over the side into the water, and holding on, reaching from there, I used the rod to flip back the lid.

But for the lapping of the waves and the sounds of my breathing, there was silence. So I reboarded and took a look inside.

It contained a canvas bag with a fold-down flap that snapped closed. I unsnapped it.

Stones. It was filled with dozens of rather undistinguished-looking stones. But since people generally have a reason for going to that much trouble, there had to be a decent intrinsic value involved. I dried off several of them, rubbing them vigorously with my towel. Then I turned them around every which way. Yes, there were a few glints, here and there.

I had not been lying to Cashel when he had asked what I knew about minerals and I had said, "A little." Only a little. But in this instance it seemed that it might be enough. Selecting the most promising specimen for the experiment, I chipped away at the dirty minerals that sheathed the stone. Several minutes later, an edge of the material I had exposed exhibited great scratching abilities with the various materials on which I tested it.

Someone was smuggling diamonds and someone else wanted me to know about it. What did my informant expect me to do with this information? Obviously, if he had simply wanted the authorities informed he would have done it himself.

Knowing that I was being used for purposes I did not yet understand, I decided to do what was probably expected of me, inasmuch as it coincided with what I would have done anyhow.

❖ ❖ ❖

I was able to dock and unload the gear without encountering any problems. I kept the bag of stones wrapped in my towel until I was back in my cottage. No more messages had been slipped beneath the door. I repaired to the shower stall and cleaned myself up.

I couldn't think of anyplace really clever to hide the stones, so I stuffed the bag down into the garbage-disposal unit and replaced the drain cover. That would have to do. Before stashing it, though, I removed four of the ugly ducklings. Then I dressed and took a walk.

Strolling near, I saw that Frank and Linda were eating out on their patio, so I returned to my place and made myself a quick, prefabricated meal. Afterward, I watched the sun in its descending for perhaps twenty minutes. Then, what seemed an adequate period having passed, I made my way back again.

It was even better than I had hoped for. Frank sat alone, reading, on the now-cleared patio. I moved up and said, "Hello."

He turned toward me, smiled, nodded, lowered his book.

"Hello, Jim," he said. "Now that you've been here a few days, how do you like it?"

"Oh, fine," I said. "Just fine. How is everything with you?"

He shrugged.

"Can't complain. —We were going to ask you over to dinner. Perhaps tomorrow?"

"Sounds great. Thanks."

"Come by about six?"

"All right."

"Have you found any interesting diversions yet?"

"Yes. As a matter of fact, I took your advice and resurrected my old rock-hounding habits."

"Oh? Come across any interesting specimens?"

"It just happens that I did," I said. "It was really an amazing accident. I doubt whether anybody would have located them except by accident. Here. I'll show you."

I dug them out of my pocket and dumped them into his hand.

He stared. He fingered them. He shifted them around. For perhaps half a minute.

Then, "You want to know what they are, is that it?" he asked.

"No. I already know that."

"I see."

He looked at me and smiled.

"Where did you find them?"

I smiled, very slowly.

"Are there more?" he asked.

I nodded.

He moistened his lips. He returned the stones. "Well, tell me this, if you will—what sort of deposit was it?"

Then I thought faster than I had at any time since my arrival. It was something about the way he had asked it that put my mind to spinning. I had been thinking purely in terms of a diamond-smuggling operation, with him as the natural disposer of the contraband stones. Now, though, I reviewed what scanty knowledge I did possess on the subject. The largest mines in the world were those of South Africa, where diamonds were found embedded in that rock known as Kimberlite, or blue ground. But how did they get there in the first place? Through volcanic action—as bits of carbon that had been trapped in streams of molten lava, subjected to intense heat and pressure that altered their structure to the hard, crystalline form of a girl's best friend. But there were also alluvial deposits—diamonds that had been cut free from their resting places by the actions of ancient streams, often borne great distances from their points of origin, and accumulated in offshore pockets. That was Africa, of course, and while I did not know much offhand as to New World deposits, much of the Caribbean island system had been built up by means of volcanic activity. The possibility of local deposits—of the volcanic-pipe variety or alluvial—was not precluded.

In view of my somewhat restricted area for activity since my arrival, I said, "Alluvial. It wasn't a pipe, I'll tell you that."

He nodded.

"Have you any idea as to the extent of your find?" he inquired.

"Not really," I said. "There are more where these came from. But as to the full extent of their distribution, it is simply too early for me to tell."

"Most interesting," he said. "You know, it jibes with a notion I've long held concerning this part of the world. You wouldn't care to give me just a very rough, general sort of idea as to what part of the ocean these are from, would you?"

"Sorry," I said. "You understand."

"Of course, of course. Still, how far would you go from here for an afternoon's adventure?"

"I suppose that would depend on my own notions on this matter—as well as available air transportation, or hydrofoil."

He smiled.

"All right. I won't press you any further. But I'm curious. Now that you've got them, what are you going to do with them?"

I took my time lighting a cigarette. "Get as much as I can for them and keep my mouth shut, of course," I finally said.

He nodded. "Where are you going to sell them? Stop passersby on the street?"

"I don't know," I said. "I haven't thought that much about it yet. I suppose I could take them to some jeweler's."

He chuckled.

"If you're very lucky. If you're lucky, you'll find one willing to take a chance. If you're very lucky, you'll find one willing to take a chance and also willing to give you a fair deal. I assume you would like to avoid the creation of a record, the crediting of extra income to your master account? Taxable income?"

"As I said, I would like to get as much as I can for them."

"Naturally. Then am I correct in assuming that your purpose in coming to me over this might somehow be connected with this desire?"

"In a word, yes."

"I see."

"Well?"

"I am thinking. To act as your agent for something like this would not be without risks of its own."

"How much?"

"No, I'm sorry," he said then. "It is probably too risky altogether. After all, it is illegal. I'm a married man. I could jeopardize my job by getting involved in something like this. If it had come along perhaps fifteen years ago…well, who knows? I'm sorry. Your secret is safe. Don't worry about that. But I would just as soon not be party to the enterprise."

"You are certain of that?"

"Positive. The return would have to be quite high for me even to consider it."

"Twenty percent?" I said.

"Out of the question."

"Maybe twenty-five..." I said.

"No. Twice that would scarcely—"

"Fifty percent? You're crazy!"

"Please! Keep your voice down! You want the whole station to hear?"

"Sorry. But that's out of the question. Fifty percent! No. If I can find a willing jeweler. I'll still be better off, even if he does cheat me. Twenty-five percent is tops. Absolutely."

"I am afraid I can't see it."

"Well, I wish you would think about it anyway."

He chuckled.

"It will be difficult to forget," he said.

"Okay. —Well, I'll be seeing you."

"Tomorrow, at six."

"Right. Good night."

"Good night."

So I began walking back, reflecting on the possible permutations of people and events leading up to and culminating in the killings. But there were still too many gaps in the picture for me to come up with anything I really liked.

I was most troubled, of course, by the fact that there was someone who was aware that my presence actually represented more than its outward appearance. I searched my mind again and again for possible giveaways, but I did not see where I could have slipped up. I had been quite careful about my credentials. I had encountered no one with whom I had ever been familiar. I began wishing, not for the first time—nor, I was certain, the last—that I had not accepted this case.

I considered then what I ought to be about next, to push the investigation further along. I supposed I could inspect the place where the bodies had been found. I had not been there yet, mainly because I doubted there would be anything to be learned from it. Still...I put that on my list for the morrow, if I could hit it before dinner with the Cashels. If not, then the next day.

I wondered whether I had done the expected thing as to the stones. I felt that I had, and I was very curious as to the repercussions—almost, but not quite, as curious as I was concerning the motives of my informant. Nothing I could do at the moment, though, but wait.

Thinking these thoughts, I heard myself hailed by Andy Deems from where he stood near his cottage, smoking his pipe. He wondered whether I was interested in a game of chess. I wasn't, really, but I went over anyhow. I lost two and managed to stalemate him on the third one. I felt very uncomfortable around him, but at least I didn't have to say much.

❖ ❖ ❖

The following day. Deems and Carter were sent over to Station Six, while Paul and I took our turn at "miscellaneous duties as assigned" in and about the equipment shed. Another time-marking episode, I had decided, till I got to my real work once more.

And so it went, until late afternoon, when I was beginning to wonder what sort of cook Linda Cashel might be. Barthelme hurried into the shed.

"Get your gear together," he said. "We have to go out."

"What's the matter?" Paul asked him.

"Something is wrong with one of the sonic generators."

"What?"

He shook his head.

"No way of telling till we've brought it back and checked it over. All I know is that a light's gone out on the board. I want to pull the whole package and put in a new unit. No attempt at underwater repair work on this one, even if it looks simple. I want to go over it very carefully in the lab."

"Where is it situated?"

"To the southwest, at about twenty-eight fathoms. Go look at the board if you want. It will give you a better picture. —But don't take too long, all right? There are a lot of things to load."

"Right. Which vessel?"

"The *Mary Ann*."

"The new deepwater rules…?"

"Yes. Load everything. I'm going down to tell Davies now. Then I'm going to change clothes. I'll be back shortly."

"See you then."

"Yes."

He moved away and we set to work, getting our own gear, the shark cage, and the submersible decompression chamber ready to go. We made two trips to the *Mary Ann*, then took a break to go see the map, learned nothing new from it, and returned for the DC, which was stored on a cart.

"Ever been down in that area before?" I asked Paul as we began maneuvering the cart along.

"Yes," he said. "Some time back. It is fairly near to the edge of a submarine canyon. That's why there's a big bite out of that corner of the 'wall'. It plunges pretty sharply right beyond that section of the perimeter."

"Will that complicate things any?"

"It shouldn't," he said, "unless a whole section broke loose and carried everything down with it. Then we would have to anchor and hook up a whole new housing, instead of just switching the guts. That would take us somewhat longer. I'll review the work with you on the unit we'll be taking out."

"Good."

Barthelme rejoined us about then. He and Davies, who would also be going along, helped get everything stowed. Twenty minutes later, we were on our way.

❖ ❖ ❖

The winch was rigged to lower both the shark cage and the decompression chamber tandem-fashion and in that order. Paul and I rode the DC down, keeping the extra lines from tangling, playing our lights about as we descended. While I had never had to use one, I had always found the presence of a decompression chamber on the bottom a thing of comfort, despite its slightly ominous function for the sort of work we would be doing. It was good to know that if I were injured I could get inside, signal, and be hauled directly to the top with no delays for decompression stops, the bottomside pressure being maintained in the bell's chamber on the way up and gradually returned to normal as they rushed me back to the dispensary. A heartening thought for all that, time-wise.

Bottomside, we positioned the cage near to the unit, which we found still standing, exhibiting no visible signs of damage, and we halted the illuminated DC a couple of fathoms up and off to the east. We were indeed on the edge of a steep cliff. While Paul inspected the sonic-broadcast unit, I moved nearer and flashed my light downward.

Jutting rocky pinnacles and twisting crevices… Reflexively, I drew back from the edge of the abyss, turned my light away. I returned and watched Paul work.

It took him ten minutes to disconnect the thing and free it from its mountings. Another five saw it secured and rising on its lines.

A bit later, in the periodic sweep of our beams, we caught sight of the replacement unit on the way down. We swam up to meet it and guided it into place. This time, Paul let me go to work. I indicated by pantomime that I wanted to, and he wrote on his slate: GO AHEAD SEE WHAT YOU REMEMB.

So I fastened it in place, and this took me about twenty minutes. He inspected the work, patted me on the shoulder, and nodded. I moved to connect the systems then, but stopped to glance at him. He indicated that I should go ahead.

This only took a few minutes, and when I was finished I had a certain feeling of satisfaction thinking of that light going on again on the big board back at the station. I turned around to indicate that the job was done and that he could come admire my work.

But he was no longer with me.

For a few seconds I froze, startled. Then I began shining my light around.

No, no. Nothing…

Growing somewhat panicky, I moved to the edge of the abyss and swept downward with the light. Luckily, he was not moving very quickly. But he was headed downward, all right. I took off after him as fast as I could move.

Nitrogen narcosis, deepwater sickness, or rapture of the deep does not usually hit at depths above 200 feet. Still, we were at around 170, so it was possible, and he certainly seemed to be showing the symptoms.

Worrying then about my own state of mind, I reached him, caught him by the shoulder, turned him back. Through his mask, I could see the blissful expression that he wore.

Taking him by the arm and shoulder, I began drawing him back with me. For several seconds he accompanied me, offering no resistance.

Then he began to struggle. I had anticipated this possibility and shifted my grips into a *kwansetsu-waza* position, but quickly discovered that judo is not exactly the same underwater, especially when a tank valve is too near your mask or mouthpiece. I had to keep twisting my head away, pulling it back. For a time, it became impossible to guide him that way. But I refused to relinquish my grip. If I could just hold him a while longer and did not get hit by narcosis myself, I felt that I had the advantage. After all, his coordination was affected as well as his thinking.

I finally got him to the DC—a wild antenna of bubbles rising from his air hose by then, as he had spat out his mouthpiece and there was no way I could get it back in without letting go. Still, it might have been one of the reasons he became easier to manage near the end there. I don't know.

I stuffed him into the lighted chamber, followed, and got the hatch sealed. He gave up about then and began to sag. I was able to get his mouthpiece back into place, and then I threw the pull-up switch.

We began to rise almost immediately, and I wondered what Barthelme and Davies were thinking at that moment.

They got us up very quickly. I felt a slight jarring as we came to rest on the deck. Shortly afterward, the water was pumped out. I don't know what the pressure was up to—or down to—at that point, but the communicator came alive and I heard Bartheleme's voice as I was getting out of my gear.

"We'll be moving in a few minutes," he said. "What happened, and how serious is it?"

"Nitrogen narcosis, I'd say. Paul just started swimming out and down, struggled with me when I tried to bring him back."

"Were either of you hurt?"

"No, I don't think so. He lost his mouthpiece for a little while. But he's breathing okay now."

"What shape is he in otherwise?"'

"Still rapturing, I'd guess. Sort of collapsed, drunken look to him."

"All right. You might as well get out of your gear—"

"I already have."

"—and get him out of his."

"Just starting."

"We'll radio ahead and have a medic hop out and be waiting at the dispensary, just in case. Sounds like what he really needs most is the chamber, though. So we'll just take it slow and easy in getting him back to surface pressure. I'm making an adjustment right now... Do you have any rapture symptoms yourself?"

"No."

"Okay, there. We'll leave it at this setting for a little while. —Is there anything else I should know?

"Not that I can think of."

"All right, then. I'm going forward to radio for the doctor. If you want me for anything, whistle into the speaker. That should carry."

"Right."

I got Paul out of his rig then, hoping he would start coming around soon. But he didn't. He just sat there, slouched, mumbling, eyes open but glassy. Every now and then he smiled.

I wondered what was wrong. If the pressure was indeed diminished, the recovery should have been almost instantaneous. Probably needed one more step, I decided.

But— Could he have been down much earlier that morning, before the workday began?

Decompression time does depend upon the total amount of time spent underwater during about a twelve-hour period, since you are dealing with the total amount of nitrogen absorbed by the tissues, particularly the brain and spinal cord. Might he have been down looking for something, say, in the mud, at the base of a broken mast, amid the wreckage of a certain old vessel? Perhaps down for a long while, searching carefully, worried? Knowing that he had shore duty today, that there should be no more nitrogen accumulated during this workday? Then, suddenly, an emergency, and he has to chance it. He takes it as easy as possible, even encouraging the new man to go ahead and finish up the job. Resting, trying to hang on...

It could well be. In which case, Barthelme's decompression values were off. The time is measured from surface to surface, and the depth is reckoned from the deepest point reached in any of the dives. Hell, for all I knew he might have visited several caches spotted at various points along the ocean's bottom.

I leaned over, studied the pupils of his eyes, catching his attention, it seemed, in the process. "How long were you down this morning?" I asked.

He smiled. "Wasn't," he said.

"It doesn't matter what was involved. It's your health we're worried about now. —How long were you down? What depths?"

He shook his head. "Wasn't," he said.

"Damn it! I know you were! It was the old wreck, wasn't it? That's maybe twenty fathoms. So how long? An hour? Were you down more than once?"

"Wasn't down!" he insisted. "Really, Mike! I wasn't."

I sighed, leaned back. Maybe, possibly, he was telling the truth. People are all different inside. Perhaps his physiology was playing some other variation of the game than the one I had guessed at. It had been so neat, though. For a moment, I had seen him as the supplier of the stones and Frank as the fence. Then I had gone to Frank with my find, Frank had mentioned this development to him, and Paul, worried, had gone off while the station slept to make certain that things were still where they were supposed to be. His tissues accumulated a lot of nitrogen during his frantic searching, and then this happened. It certainly struck me as logical. But if it were me, I would have admitted to having been down. I could always come up with some lie as to the reason later.

"Don't you remember?" I tried again.

He commenced an uninspired stream of curses, but lost his enthusiasm before a dozen or so syllables. His voice trailed off, then, "Why don't you b'lieve me, Mike? I wasn't down…"

"All right, I believe you," I said. "It's okay. Just take it easy."

He reached out and took hold of my arm.

"It's all beautiful," he said.

"Yeah."

"Everything is just—like it's never been before."

"What did you take?" I asked him.

"…Beautiful."

"What are you on?" I insisted.

"You know I never take any," he finally said.

"Then what's causing it, whatever it is? Do you know?"

"Damn fine…" he said.

"Something went wrong on the bottom. What was it?"

"I don't know! Go away! Don't bring it back… This is how it should be. Always… Not that crap you take… Started all the trouble…"

"I'm sorry," I said.

"…That started it."

"I know. I'm sorry. Spoiled things," I ventured. "Shouldn't have."

"…Talked," he said. "…Blew it."

"I know. I'm sorry. But we got him," I tried.

"Yeah," he said. Then, "Oh, my God!"

"The diamonds. The diamonds are safe," I suggested quickly.

"Got him… Oh, my God! I'm sorry!"

"Forget it. Tell me what you see," I said, to get his mind back where I wanted it.

"The diamonds…" he said.

He launched into a long, disjointed monologue. I listened. Every now and then I said something to return him to the theme of the diamonds, and I kept throwing out Rudy Myers' name. His responses remained fragmentary, but the picture did begin to emerge.

I hurried then, trying to learn as much as I could before Barthelme returned and decompressed us any further. I was afraid that it would sober him up suddenly, because decompression works that way when you hit the right point in nitrogen-narcosis cases. He and Mike seemed to have been bringing in the diamonds, all right—from where, I did not learn. Whenever I tried to find out whether Frank had been disposing of them for them, he began muttering endearments to Linda. The part I hammered away most at began to come clear, however.

Mike must have said something one time, in the ashram back of the Chickcharney. It must have interested Rudy sufficiently so that he put together a specialty of the house other than a Pink Paradise for him—apparently, several times. These could have been the bad trips I had heard about. Whatever Rudy served him, he got the story out of him and saw dollar signs. Only Paul proved a lot tougher than he had thought. When he made his request for hush money and Mike told Paul about it, Paul came up with the idea for the mad dolphin in the park and got Mike to go along with it, persuading Rudy to meet him there for a payoff. Then things got sort of hazy, because the mention of dolphins kept setting him off. But he had apparently waited at a prearranged point, and the two of them took care of Rudy when that point was reached, one holding him, the other working him over with the jawbone. It was not clear whether Mike was injured fighting with Rudy and Paul then decided to finish him off and make him look like a dolphin slashee also, or whether he had planned that part carefully too and simply turned on Mike afterward, taking him by surprise. Either way, their friendship had been declining steadily for some time and the blackmail business had driven the final nail into the lid.

That was the story I got, punctuated rather than phrased by his responses to my oblique questioning. Apparently, killing Mike had bothered him more than he had thought it would, also. He kept calling me Mike, kept saying he was sorry, and I kept redirecting his attention.

Before I could get any more out of him, Barthelme came back and asked me how he was doing.

"Babbling," I replied. "That's all."

"I'm going to decompress some more. That might straighten him out. We're on our way now, and there will be someone waiting."

"Good."

But it did not straighten him out. He remained exactly the same. I tried to take advantage, to get more out of him—specifically, the source of the diamonds—but something went wrong. His nirvana switched over to some version of hell.

He launched himself at my throat, and I had to fight him off, push him back, hold him in place. He sagged then, commenced weeping, and began muttering of the horrors he was witnessing. I talked slowly, softly, soothingly, trying to guide him back to the earlier, happier part of things. But nothing worked, so I shut up, stayed silent and kept my guard up.

He drowsed then, and Barthelme continued to decompress us. I kept an eye on Paul's breathing and checked his pulse periodically, but nothing seemed amiss in that area.

We were fully decompressed by the time we docked, and I undogged the hatch and chucked out our gear. Paul stirred at that, opened his eyes, stared at me, then said, "That was weird."

"How do you feel now?"

"All right, I think. But very tired and kind of shaky."

"Let me give you a hand."

"Thanks."

I helped him out and assisted him down the plank to a waiting wheelchair. A young doctor was there, as were the Cashels, Deems, and Carter. I could not help wondering what was going on at the moment inside Paul's head. The doctor checked his heartbeat, pulse, blood pressure, shined a light into his eyes and ears, and had him touch the tip of his nose a couple of times. Then he nodded and gestured, and Barthelme began wheeling him toward the dispensary. The doctor walked along part of the way, talking with them. Then he returned while they went on, and he asked me to tell him everything that had happened.

So I did, omitting only the substance I had derived from the babbling part. Then he thanked me and turned toward the dispensary once more.

I caught up with him quickly.

"What does it look like?" I asked.

"Nitrogen narcosis," he replied.

"Didn't it take a rather peculiar form?" I said. "I mean, the way he responded to decompression and all?"

He shrugged.

"People come in all shapes and sizes, inside as well as out," he said. "Do a complete physical on a man and you still can't tell what he'd be like if he got drunk, say—loud, sad, belligerent, sleepy. The same with this. He seems to be out of it now, though."

"No complications?"

"Well, I'm going to do an EKG as soon as we get him to the dispensary. But I think he's all right. —Listen, is there a decompression chamber in the dispensary?"

"Most likely. But I'm new here. I'm not certain."

"Well, why don't you come along until we find out? If there isn't one, I'd like to have that submersible unit moved over."

"Oh?"

"Just a precaution. I want him to stay in the dispensary overnight, with someone around to keep an eye on him. If there should be a recurrence, I want the machine handy so he can be recompressed right away."

"I see."

We caught up with Barthelme at the door. The others were there also.

"Yes, there is a unit inside," Barthelme told him, "and I'll sit up with him."

Everyone volunteered, though, and the night was finally divided into three shifts—Barthelme, Frank, and Andy, respectively. Each of them, of course, was quite familiar with decompression equipment.

Frank came up and touched my arm.

"Nothing much we can really do here now," he said. "Shall we go have that dinner?"

"Oh?" I said, automatically glancing at my watch.

"So we eat at seven instead of six thirty," he said, chuckling.

"Fine. That will give me time to shower and change."

"Okay. Come right over as soon as you're ready. We'll still have time for a drink."

"All right. I'm thirsty. —See you soon."

I went on back to my place and got cleaned up. No new *billets-doux*, and the stones were still in the disposal unit. I combed my hair and started back across the islet.

As I neared the dispensary, the doctor emerged, talking back over his shoulder to someone in the doorway. Barthelme, probably. As I approached, I saw that he was carrying his bag.

He withdrew, began to move away. He nodded and smiled when he saw me.

"I think your friend will be all right," he said.

"Good. That is just what I was going to ask you."

"How do *you* feel?"

"All right. Fine, actually."

"You have had no symptoms at all. Correct?"

"That's right."

"Fine. If you were to, you know where to go. Right?"

"Indeed."

"Okay, then. I'll be going now."

"So long."

He headed off toward a tiny hopper he had landed near the main lab. I continued on over to Frank's place.

Frank came out to meet me.

"What did the doctor have to say?" he asked.

"That everything looks all right," I told him.

"Uh-huh. Come on in and tell me what you're drinking."

He opened the door, held it.

"A bourbon would be nice," I said.

"With anything?"

"Just ice."

"Okay. Linda's out back, setting things on the table."

He moved about, putting together a pair of drinks. I wondered whether he was going to say anything about the diamond business now, while we were alone. But he didn't.

He turned, passed me my drink, raised his in a brief salute, took a sip.

"Tell me all about it," he said.

"All right."

The telling lasted into dinner and out of it again. I was very hungry, Linda was quite quiet, and Frank kept asking questions, drawing out every detail of Paul's discomfort, distress. I wondered about Linda and Frank. I could not see her keeping her affair secret on a small place like the station. What did Frank really know, think, feel about it? What was the true function of their triangle in this bizarre case?

I sat with them for a while after dinner, and I could almost feel the tension between the two of them, a thing he seemed set on dealing with by keeping the conversation moving steadily along the lines he had established, she by withdrawing from it. I had no doubt that it had been precipitated by Paul's mishap, but I came to feel more and more awkward in my role as a buffer against an approaching quarrel, a confrontation, or the renewal of an old one. Thanking them for the meal, I excused myself as soon as I could, pleading a weariness that was half real.

Frank got to his feet immediately.

"I'll walk you back," he said.

"All right."

So he did.

As we neared my place, he finally said it.

"About those stones…"

"Yes?"

"You're sure there are lots more where they came from?"

"Come this way," I said, leading him around me cottage to the patio and turning when we reached it. "Just in time for the last couple of minutes of sunset. Beautiful. Why don't you watch it finish up? I'll be right back."

I let myself in through the rear door, moved to the sink, and got the disposal unit open. It took me a minute or so to work the bag out. I opened it, seized a double fistful, and carried them back outside.

"Cup your hands," I said to him.

He did, and I filled them.

"How's that?"

He raised them, moved nearer the light spilling through the open door.

"My God!" he said. "You really do!"

"Of course."

"All right. I'll dispose of them for you. Thirty-five percent."

"Twenty-five is tops. Like I said."

"I know of a gem-and-mineral show a week from Saturday. A man I know could be there if I gave him a call. He'd pay a good price. I'll call him—for thirty percent."

"Twenty-five."

"It's a pity we are so close and can't quite come to terms. We both lose that way."

"Oh, all right. Thirty it is."

I took back the stones and dumped them into my pockets, and we shook on it. Then Frank turned.

"I'm going over to the lab now," he said. "See what's the matter with that unit you brought back."

"Let me know when you find out, will you? I'd like to know."

"Sure."

He went away and I restashed the gems, fetched a dolphin book, and began to page through it. Then it struck me just how funny it was, the way things were working out. All the talk about dolphins, all my reading, speculating, including a long philosophical dissertation on their hypothetical dreamsongs as a religio-dialogical form of *ludus*—for what? To find that it was probably all unnecessary? To realize that I would probably get through the entire case without even seeing a dolphin?

Well, that was what I had wanted, of course, what Don and Lydia Barnes and the Institute wanted—for me to clear the good name of the dolphin. Still, what a tangled mess it was turning out to be! Blackmail, murder, diamond smuggling, with a little adultery tossed in on the side... How was I going to untangle it sweetly and neatly, clear the suspects—who were out practicing their *ludus* and not giving a damn about the whole business—and then fade from the picture, as is my wont, without raising embarrassing questions, without seeming to have been especially involved?

A feeling of profound jealousy of the dolphin came over me and did not entirely vanish. Did they ever create problem situations of this order among themselves? I strongly doubted it. Maybe if I collected enough green karma stamps I could put in for dolphin next time around...

Everything caught up with me, and I dozed off with the light still burning.

❖ ❖ ❖

A sharp, insistent drumming awakened me.

I rubbed my eyes, stretched. The noise came again, and I turned in that direction.

It was the window. Someone was rapping on the frame. I rose and crossed over, saw that it was Frank.

"Yeah?" I said. "What's up?"

"Come on out," he said. "It's important."

"Okay. Just a minute."

I went and rinsed my face, to complete the waking-up process and give me a chance to think. A glance at my watch showed me that it was around ten-thirty.

When I finally stepped outside, he seized my shoulder.

"Come on! Damn it! I told you it was important!"

I fell into step with him.

"All right! I had to wake up. What's the matter?"

"Paul's dead," he said.

"What?"

"You heard me. Dead."

"How'd it happen?"

"He stopped breathing."

"They usually do. —But how did it happen?"

"I'd gotten to fooling with the unit you'd brought back. It's over there now. I moved it in when my time came to relieve Barthelme, so that I could keep working on it. Anyway, I got so involved that I wasn't paying much attention to him. When I finally did check on him again, he was dead. That's all. His face was dark and twisted. Some sort of lung failure, it seems. Maybe there was an air embolism..."

We entered the rear of the building, the nearest entrance, the water splashing softly behind us, a light breeze following us in. We passed the recently set-up workbench, tools and the partly dismantled sonic unit spread across its surface. Rounding the corner to our left, we entered the room where Paul lay. I switched the light on.

His face was no longer handsome, bearing now the signs of one who had spent his final moments fighting for breath. I crossed to him, felt for a pulse, knew in advance I would find none. I covered a fingernail with my thumb and squeezed. It remained white when I released it.

"How long ago?" I asked.

"Right before I came for you."

"Why me?"

"You were nearest."

"I see. —Was the sheet torn in this place before, I wonder?"

"I don't know."

"There were no cries, no sounds at all?"

"I didn't hear anything. If I had, I would have come right away."

I felt a sudden desire for a cigarette, but there were oxygen tanks in the room and NO SMOKING signs all over the building. I turned and retraced my steps, pushed the door open, held it with my back—leaning against it—lit a cigarette, and stared out across the water.

"Very neat," I said then. "With the day's symptoms behind him, he'll warrant a 'natural causes' with a 'possible air embolism,' 'congestive lung failure,' or some damn thing behind it."

"What do you mean?" Frank demanded.

"Was he sedated? —I don't know. It doesn't matter. I'd imagine you used the recompressor. Right? Or did you tough it out and just smother him?"

"Come off it. Why would I—"

"In a way, I helped kill him," I said. "I thought he was safe with you here because you hadn't done anything about him all this time. You wanted to keep her, to win her back. Spending a lot of money on her was one way you tried. But it was a vicious circle, because Paul was a part of your source of extra revenue. Then I came along and offered an alternative supply. Then today's accident, the whole setup here tonight… You rose to the occasion, seized the opportunity, and slammed the barn door. Not to mention striking while the iron was hot. —Congratulations. I think you'll get away with it. Because this is all guesswork, of course. There is no real proof. Good show."

He sighed.

"Then why go into all that? It's over. We will go see Barthelme now and you will talk because I will be too distraught."

"But I'm curious about Rudy and Mike. I've been wondering all along. Did you have any part in it when they got theirs?"

"What do you know?" he asked slowly. "And how do you know it?"

"I know that Paul and Mike were the source of the stones. I know that Rudy found out and tried to blackmail them. They dealt with him, and I think Paul took care of Mike for good measure at the same time. How do I know? Paul babbled all the way back this afternoon and I was in the decompressor with him, remember? I learned about the diamonds, the murders, and about Linda and Paul, just by listening."

He leaned back against the workbench. He shook his head.

"I was suspicious of you," he said, "but you had the diamonds for proof. You came across them awfully fast, I'll admit. But I accepted your story because of the possibility that Paul's deposit was really somewhere quite near. He never told me where it was, either. I decided you had to have either stumbled across it or followed him to it and known enough to recognize it for what it was. Whichever way, though, it doesn't matter. I would rather do business with you. Shall we just leave the whole thing at that?"

"If you will tell me about Rudy and Mike."

"I don't really know any more than what you've just said. That was none of my affair. Paul took care of everything. Answer one for me now: How did you find the deposit?"

"I didn't," I said. "I haven't the least idea where he got them."

He straightened.

"I don't believe you! The stones—where did they come from?"

"I found where Paul had hidden a bag of them. I stole it."

"Why?"

"Money, of course."

"Then why did you lie to me about where you got them?"

"You think I'd come out and say they were stolen? Now, though—"

He came forward very fast, and I saw that he had a large wrench in his hand.

I jumped backward, and the door caught him on the shoulder as it snapped inward. It only slowed him for an instant, though. He burst through and was at me again. I continued my retreat, falling into a defensive position.

He swung and I dodged to the side, chopping at his elbow. We both missed. His backstroke grazed my shoulder then, so that the blow I did land, seconds later, fell near his kidney with less force than I had hoped for. I danced back as he swung again, and my kick caught him on the hip. He dropped to one knee, but was up again before I could press in, swinging toward my head. I backed farther and he stalked me.

I could hear the water, smell it. I wondered about diving in. He was awfully close…

When he came in again, I twisted back and grabbed for his arm. I caught hold near the elbow and hung on, hooking my fingers toward his face. He drove himself into me then and I fell, still clutching his arm, catching hold of his belt with my other hand. My shoulder smashed against the ground, and he was on top of me, wrestling to free his arm. As he succeeded in dragging it away, his weight came off me for an instant. Pulling free, I doubled myself into a ball and kicked out with both legs.

They connected. I heard him grunt. Then he was gone.

I heard him splashing about in the water. I also heard distant voices, calling, approaching us from across the islet.

I regained my feet. I moved toward the edge.

Then he screamed—a long, awful, agonized wail. By the time I reached the edge, it had ceased.

When Barthelme came up beside me, he stopped repeating "What happened?" as soon as he looked down and saw the flashing fins at the center of the turmoil. Then he said, "Oh, my God!" And then nothing.

❖ ❖ ❖

In my statement, later, I said that he had seemed highly agitated when he had come to get me, that he told me Paul had stopped breathing, that I had returned with him to the dispensary, determined that Paul was indeed dead, said so, and asked him for the details; that as we were talking he seemed to get the impression that I thought he had been negligent and somehow contributed to the death; that he had grown further agitated and finally attacked me; that we had fought and he had fallen into the water. All of which, of course, was correct. Deponent sinneth only by omission. They seemed to buy it. They went away. The shark hung around, waiting for dessert perhaps, and the dolphin people came and anesthetized him and took him away. Barthelme told me the damaged sonic projector could indeed have been shorting intermittently.

So Paul had killed Ruby and Mike; Frank had killed Paul and then been killed himself by the shark on whom the first two killings could now be blamed. The dolphins were cleared, and there was no one left to bring to justice for anything. The source of the diamonds was now one of life's numerous little mysteries.

...So, after everyone had departed, the statements been taken, the remains of the remains removed—long after that, as the night hung late, clear, clean, with its bright multitudes doubled in their pulsing within the cool flow of the Gulf Stream about the station, I sat in a deck chair on the small patio behind my quarters, drinking a can of beer and watching the stars go by.

...I needed to stamp CLOSED on my mental file.

But who had written me the note, the note that had set the infernal machine to chugging?

Did it really matter, now that the job was done? As long as they kept quiet about me...

I took another sip of beer.

Yes, it did, I decided. I might as well look around a bit more.

I withdrew a cigarette and moved to light it...

❖ ❖ ❖

When I pulled into the harbor, the lights were on. As I climbed to the pier, her voice came to me over a loudspeaker.

She greeted me by name—my real name—which I hadn't heard spoken in a long while, and she asked me to come in.

I moved across the pier and up to the front of the building. The door stood ajar. I entered.

It was a long, low room, completely Oriental in decor. She wore a green silk kimono. She knelt on the floor, a tea service laid before her.

"Please come and be seated," she said.

I nodded, removed my shoes, crossed the room, and sat down.

"O-cha do desu-ka?" she asked.

"Itadakimasu."

She poured, and we sipped tea for a time. After the second cup I drew an ashtray toward me.

"Cigarette?" I asked.

"I don't smoke," she said. "But I wish you would. I try to take as few noxious substances into my own system as possible. I suppose that is how the whole thing began."

I lit one for me.

"I've never met a genuine telepath before," I said, "that I know of."

"I'd trade it for a sound body," she said, "any day. It wouldn't even have to be especially attractive."

"I don't suppose there is even a real need for me to ask my questions," I said.

"No," she said, "not really. How free do you think our wills might be?"

"Less every day," I said.

She smiled.

"I asked that," she said, "because I have thought a lot about it of late. I thought of a little girl I once knew, a girl who lived in a garden of terrible flowers. They were beautiful, and they were there to make her happy to look upon. But they could not hide their odor from her, and that was the odor of pity. For she was a sick little girl. So it was not their colors and textures from which she fled, but rather the fragrance which few knew she could detect. It was a painful thing to smell it constantly, and so in solitude she found her something of peace. Had it not been for her ability she would have remained in the garden."

She paused to take a sip of tea.

"One day she found friends," she continued, "in an unexpected place. The dolphin is a joyous fellow, his heart uncluttered with the pity that demeans. The way of knowing that had set her apart, had sent her away, here brought her close. She came to know the hearts, the thoughts of her new friends more perfectly than men know those of one another. She came to love them, to be one of their family."

She took another sip of tea, then sat in silence for a time, staring into the cup.

"There are great ones among them," she said finally, "such as you guessed at earlier. Prophet, seer, philosopher, musician—there is no man-made word I know of to describe this sort of one, or the function he performs. There are, however, those among them who voice the dreamsong with particular subtlety and profundity—something like music, yet not, drawn from that timeless place in themselves where perhaps they look upon the infinite, then phrase it for their fellows. The greatest I have ever known"—and she clicked the syllables in a high-pitched tone—"bears something like 'Kjwalll'kje 'k'koothaïlll'kje'k for name or title. I could no more explain his dreamsong to you than I could explain Mozart to one who had never heard music. But when he, in his place, came to be threatened, I did what must be done."

"You see that I fail to see," I said, lowering my cup.

She refilled it, and then, "The Chickcharney is built up over the water," she said, and a vision of it came clear, disturbingly real, into my mind. "Like that," she said.

"I do not drink strong beverages, I do not smoke, I seldom take medication," she said. "This is not a matter of choice. It is a physiological rule I break at my own peril. But should I not enjoy the same things others of my kind may know, just as I now enjoy the cigarette we are smoking?"

"I begin to see—"

"Swimming beneath the ashram at night, I could ride the mounting drug dreams of that place, know the peace, the happiness, the joy, and withdraw if it turned to something else—"

"Mike—" I said.

"Yes, it was he who led me to 'Kjwalll'kje'k'koothaïlll'kje'k, all unknowing. I saw there the place where they had found the diamonds. I see that you think it is near Martinique, since I was there just recently. I will not answer you on this. I saw there too, however, the idea of hurting dolphins. It seemed that they had been driven away from the place of their discovery—though not harmed—by dolphins. Several times. I found this so unusual that I was moved to investigate, and I learned that it was true. The place of their discovery was in the area of his song. He dwells in those waters, and others come to hear him there. It is, in this sense, a special place, because of his presence. They were seeking a way to ensure their own safety when they returned for more of the stones," she went on. "They learned of the effects of the noises of the killer whale for this purpose. But they also obtained explosives, should the recording prove insufficient over a period of days.

"The two killings occurred while I was away," she said. "You are essentially correct as to what was done. I had not known they would take place, nor would my telling of Paul's thoughts ever be admissible in any court. He used everything he ever got his hands or mind around, that man—however poor his grasp. He took Frank's theory as well as his wife, learned just enough to find the stones, with a little luck. Luck—he had that for a long while. He learned just enough about dolphins to know of the effects of the sounds of the killer whale, but not how they would behave if they had to fight, to kill. And even there he was lucky. The story was accepted. Not by everybody. But it was given sufficient credence. He was safe, and he planned to go back to—the place. I sought a way to stop him. And I wanted to see the dolphins vindicated—but that was of secondary importance then. Then you appeared, and I knew that I had found it. I went to the station at night, crawled ashore, left you a note."

"And you damaged the sonic-broadcast unit?"

"Yes."

"You did it at such a time that you knew Paul and I would go down together to replace it."

"Yes."

"And the other?"

"Yes, that too. I filled Paul's mind with things I had felt and seen beneath the ashram of the Chickcharney."

"And you could look into Frank's mind as well. You knew how he would react. You set up the murder!"

"I did not force him to do anything. Is not his will as free as our own?"

I looked down into the tea, troubled by the thought. I gulped it. Then I stared at her.

"Did you not control him, even a little, near the end, when he attacked me? Or—far more important—what of a more rudimentary nervous system? Could you control the actions of a shark?"

She refilled my teacup.

"Of course not," she said.

We sat for another silent time. Then, "What did you try to do to me when I decided to continue my investigation?" I asked. "Were you not trying to baffle my senses and drive me to destruction?"

"No," she said quickly. "I was watching you to see what you would decide. You frightened me with your decision. But what I did was not an attack, at first. I tried to show you something of the dreamsong, to sooth you, to put you at peace. I had hoped that such an experience might work some mental alchemy, would soften your resolve—"

"You would have accompanied it with suggestions to that effect."

"Yes, I would have. But then you burned yourself and the pain pulled you back. That was when I attacked you."

She suddenly sounded tired. But then, it had been a very busy day for her, all things considered.

"And this was my mistake," she said. "Had I simply let you go on, you would have had nothing. But you saw the unnatural nature of the attack. You associated it with Paul's raptures, and you thought of me—a mutant—and of dolphins and diamonds and my recent trip. It all spilled into your mind—and then the threat that I saw you could keep: alluvial diamonds and Martinique, into the Central Data Bank. I had to call you then, to talk."

"What now?" I asked. "No court could ever convict you of anything. You are safe. *I* can hardly condemn you. My own hands are not free of blood, as you must know. You are the only person alive who knows who I am, and that makes me uncomfortable. Yet I have some guesses concerning things you would not like known. You will not try to destroy me, for you know what I will do with these guesses if you fail."

"And I see that you will not use your ring unless you are provoked. Thank you. I have feared it."

"It appears that we have reached something of a standoff."

"Then why do we not both forget?"

"You mean—trust each other?"

"Is it so novel a thing?"

"You must admit you are possessed of a small edge in such matters."

"True. But it is of value only for the moment. People change. It does not show me what you will be thinking on another day, in some other place. You are in a better position to know that, for you have known yourself far longer than I."

"True, I suppose."

"I, of course, really have nothing to gain by destroying the pattern of your existence. You, on the other hand, could conceivably be moved to seek an unrecorded source of income."

"I can't deny that," I said. "But if I gave you my word, I would keep it."

"I know that you mean that. I also know that you believe much of what I have said, with some reservations."

I nodded.

"You do not really understand the significance of 'Kjwalll'kje'k'k oothaïlll'kje'k."

"How could I, not being a dolphin or even a telepath?"

"May I show you what it is that I am seeking to preserve, to defend?"

I thought about it for a time, recalling those recent moments back at the station when she had hit me with something out of William James. I had no way of knowing what manner of control, what sort of powers she might be able to exercise upon me if I agreed to some experiment along these lines. However, if things got out of control, if there was the least feeling of meddling with my mind, beyond the thing itself, I knew a way to terminate the experience instantly. I folded my hands before me, laying two fingers upon my ring.

"Very well," I said.

And then it began again, something like music, yet not, some development of a proposition that could not be verbalized, for its substance was of a stuff that no man possessed or perceived, lying outside the range of human sensory equipment. I realized then that that part of me which experienced this had its place temporarily in the mind of the statement's creator, that this was the dreamsong of 'Kjwalll'kje'k'koothaïlll'kje'k, that I witnessed/participated in the timeless argument as he improvised, orchestrated it, drawing entire sections of previously constructed visions and phrasings, perfect and pure, from a memory so vital that its workings were barely distinguishable from the activities of the moment, and blending these into fresh harmonies to a joyous rhythm I comprehended only obliquely, through the simultaneous sensing of his own pleasure in the act of their formulation.

I felt the delight in this dance of thought, rational though not logical; the process, like all of art, was an answer to something, though precisely what, I did not know nor really care; for it was, in and of itself, a sufficiency of being—and if one day it were to provide me with an emotional weapon at a time when I would otherwise stand naked and alone, why this was one of the things none has the right to expect, yet sometimes discovers within the recollection of such fragments of existence cast by a special seer with a kind of furious joy.

I forgot my own being, abandoned my limited range of senses as I swam in a sea that was neither dark nor light, formed nor formless, yet knowing my way, subsumed, as it were, within a perpetual act of that thing we had decided to call *ludus* that was creation, destruction, and sustenance, patterned and infinitely repatterned, scattered and joined, mounting and descending, divorced from all temporal phenomena yet containing the essence of time. Time's soul it seemed I was, the infinite potentialities that fill the moment, surrounding and infusing the tiny stream of existence, and joyous, joyous, joyous...

Spinning, my mind came away, and I sat, still clutching my death ring, across from the little girl who had fled from the terrible flowers, now clad in wet green and very, very wan.

"O-cha do desu-ka?" she asked.

"Itadakimasu."

She poured. I wanted to reach out and touch her hand, but I raised the teacup instead and sipped from it.

She had my answer, of course. She knew.

But she spoke, after a time: "When my moment comes—who knows how soon?—I shall go to him," she said. "I shall be there, with 'Kjwalll'kje'k'koothaïlll'kje'k. Who knows but that I shall continue, as a memory perhaps, in that tuneless place, as a part of the dream-song? But then, I feel a part of it now."

"I—"

She raised her hand. We finished our tea in silence. I did not really want to go then, but I knew that I must.

❖ ❖ ❖

There were so many things that I might have said, I thought, as I headed the *Isabella* back toward Station One, my bag of diamonds, and all the other things and people I had left behind, waiting for me to touch them or speak to them.

But then, I reflected, the best words are often those left unsaid.

A Word from Zelazny

This is the second of three tales involving an unnamed protagonist (called Nemo in some bibliographies), a secret agent in a computerized world. Zelazny developed the character as a homage to John D. MacDonald's Travis McGee stories; both characters managed to evade society's restrictions (Zelazny's society does not acknowledge the protagonist's existence). Both take jobs that official organizations or governments cannot, as agents of last resort.[1]

The title prompted his agent to ask "Do you have any way of pronouncing that title?"[2] Zelazny chose the title prior to writing the story and said that he "loosely based it on dolphin sounds."[3] The story, one of three "transcendental experiences stories," appeared in Terry Carr's original anthology.[3]

1 *Roger Zelazny*, Jane M. Lindskold, 1993.
2 Letter from Henry Morrison to Roger Zelazy, July 12, 1972.
3 Letter from Roger Zelazny to Philip José Farmer, May 29, 1972.

Notes

Andros, the largest island in the Bahamas, has the world's third-largest barrier reef. **Trank** is slang for tranquilizer. **Curiosity may ultimately prove nature's way of dealing with the population problem** alludes to "curiosity killed the cat." **Captain Tony's in Key West** is a bar that Hemingway frequented in the 1930s when it was known as Sloppy Joe's. ***Tursiops truncatus*** is the Bottle-nosed dolphin. **Delphinological** refers to dolphins. In the 1960s, **Dr. Robert Spence**, Director of the Atomic Energy Research Establishment at Harwell, England, discovered how to extract uranium (**uranyl ions**) from seawater (previous versions misspelled his name as Spencer).

De rigueur means required. **Chickcharney** (misspelled as Chickcharny in earlier versions) is a forest spirit of Andros Island. The adult **mayfly** lives about two days. **James Madison** was the fourth President of the United States. **He had lived in one of the bubble cities for a time, lost his wife and daughter in the RUMOKO II disaster** refers to events occurring between the earlier story "The Eve of RUMOKO" and this one. **Pacific** means peaceful. Rodion Romanovich **Raskolnikov** is the protagonist of Dostoyevsky's *Crime and Punishment*, an eccentric genius who believes that the law does not apply to him, and he has the right to commit murder.

Martinique is an eastern Caribbean island. **Zen** Buddhism seeks enlightment through meditation. Dutch author and historian **Johan Huizinga**'s 1938 book ***Homo Ludens*** discussed the influence of play on modern society. ***Ludus*** is Latin for game. Buddha Gautama's body sat beneath the **Bo tree** for seven years while his soul wandered, seeking enlightenment.

Diagoge in Greek means enjoyment, especially mental relaxation. Greek philosopher **Plato** discussed **politics** in the *Republic*. **Ethos** refers to a society's entire culture. The **Little Mermaid** is the statue at Langelinie in Copenhagen, placed there to honor Hans Christian Anderson, who wrote that famous tale.

A grotesque vision of Hamlet recalls Hamlet, holding a human skull while pondering life and death ("Alas, poor Yorick—"); the nameless protagonist contemplates a dolphin's skull. **Loren Eiseley** was an anthropologist, poet and science writer, and **"We are all potential fossils..."** comes from his 1957 collection of essays, *The Immense Journey*. A **pied typecase** is an unsorted mess; this printing term literally means type that has been spilled out of its case. The protagonist extends the metaphor by stepping over or on **the most damnable...item in the entire case**. **Tropism** is an organism's movement toward a stimulus, such as a plant toward light or a semi-conscious human toward coffee.

An **ashram** in Hinduism is a religious retreat or a guru's residence. **Kimberlite** is igneous rock which may contain diamonds and other crystals; it occurs in vertical structures called kimberlite **pipes**. **Alluvial** is soil deposited by running water. ***Kwansetsu-waza*** is a joint-locking technique in judo, such as a crossarm lock or knee-elbow lock. ***Billets-doux*** are love letters.

An **air embolism** is an air bubble that lodges in the heart, stopping blood flow, or travels to the brain, causing a stroke; it can occur as a result of scuba diving. **Squeezing the fingernail** bed and seeing that it blanches and remains white indicates no blood flow; the nail bed normally flushes pink in a second or two. A **deponent** is a person giving sworn testimony. ***"O-cha do desu-ka?"*** means "Would you like some tea?" ***"Itadakimasu"*** has no English translation, but it is equivalent to *"Bon appétit!"* or "Let's eat." **And I see that you will not use your ring unless you are provoked** refers to his ring that contains a virus that kills within thirty seconds (see "The Eve of RUMOKO"). **William James** was an American psychologist whose works addressed the importance of perception and emotion.

Home Is the Hangman

Analog, November 1975.
Nebula Award 1976 (novella). Hugo Award 1976 (novella).
#2 on 1976 Locus Poll (novella). Adapted as a radio play for SciFi Radio.
§ *My Name Is Legion*

Big fat flakes down the night, silent night, windless night. And I never count them as storms unless there is wind. Not a sigh or whimper, though. Just a cold, steady whiteness, drifting down outside the window, and a silence confirmed by gunfire, driven deeper now that it had ceased. In the main room of the lodge the only sounds were the occasional hiss and sputter of the logs turning to ashes on the grate.

I sat in a chair turned sidewise from the table to face the door. A tool kit rested on the floor to my left. The helmet stood on the table, a lopsided basket of metal, quartz, porcelain, and glass. If I heard the click of a microswitch followed by a humming sound from within it, then a faint light would come on beneath the meshing near to its forward edge and begin to blink rapidly. If these things occurred, there was a very strong possibility that I was going to die.

I had removed a black ball from my pocket when Larry and Bert had gone outside, armed, respectively, with a flame thrower and what looked like an elephant gun. Bert had also taken two grenades with him.

I unrolled the black ball, opening it out into a seamless glove, a dollop of something resembling moist putty stuck to its palm. Then I drew the glove on over my left hand and sat with it upraised, elbow resting on the arm of the chair. A small laser flash pistol in which I had very little faith lay beside my right hand on the tabletop, next to the helmet.

If I were to slap a metal surface with my left hand, the substance would adhere there, coming free of the glove. Two seconds later it would explode, and the force of the explosion would be directed in against the surface. Newton would claim his own by way of right-angled redistributions of the reaction, hopefully tearing lateral hell out of the contact surface. A smother charge, it was called, and its possession came under concealed-weapons and possession-of-burglary-tools statutes in most places. The molecularly gimmicked goo, I decided, was great stuff. It was just the delivery system that left more to be desired.

Beside the helmet, next to the gun, in front of my hand, stood a small walkie-talkie. This was for purposes of warning Bert and Larry if I should hear the click of a microswitch followed by a humming sound, should see a light come on and begin to blink rapidly. Then they would know that Tom and Clay, with whom we had lost contact when the shooting began, had failed to destroy the enemy and doubtless lay lifeless at their stations now, a little over a kilometer to the south. Then they would know that they, too, were probably about to die.

I called out to them when I heard the click. I picked up the helmet and rose to my feet as its light began to blink.

But it was already too late.

❖ ❖ ❖

The fourth place listed on the Christmas card I had sent Don Walsh the previous year was Peabody's Book Shop and Beer Stube in Baltimore, Maryland. Accordingly, on the last night in October I sat in its rearmost room, at the final table before the alcove with the door leading to the alley. Across that dim chamber, a woman dressed in black played the ancient upright piano, uptempoing everything she touched. Off to my right, a fire wheezed and spewed fumes on a narrow hearth beneath a crowded mantelpiece overseen by an ancient and antlered profile. I sipped a beer and listened to the sounds.

I half hoped that this would be one of the occasions when Don failed to show up. I had sufficient funds to hold me through spring and I did not really feel like working. I had summered farther north, was anchored now in the Chesapeake, and was anxious to continue Caribbeanward. A growing chill and some nasty winds told me I had tarried overlong in these latitudes. Still, the understanding was that I remain in the chosen bar until midnight. Two hours to go.

I ate a sandwich and ordered another beer. About halfway into it, I spotted Don approaching the entranceway, topcoat over his arm, head turning. I manufactured a matching quantity of surprise when he appeared beside my table with a, "Ron! Is that really you?"

I rose and clasped his hand.

"Alan! Small world, or something like that. Sit down! Sit down!"

He settled onto the chair across from me, draped his coat over the one to his left.

"What are you doing in this town?" he asked.

"Just a visit," I answered. "Said hello to a few friends." I patted the scars, the stains on the venerable surface before me. "And this is my last stop. I'll be leaving in a few hours."

He chuckled. "Why is it that you knock on wood?"

I grinned.

"I was expressing affection for one of Henry Mencken's favorite speakeasies."

"This place dates back that far?"

I nodded.

"It figures," he said. "You've got this thing for the past, or against the present. I'm never sure which."

"Maybe a little of both," I said. "I wish Mencken would stop in. I'd like his opinion on the present. —What are you doing with it?"

"What?"

"The present. Here. Now."

"Oh." He spotted the waitress and ordered a beer. "Business trip," he said then. "To hire a consultant."

"Oh. How *is* business?"

"Complicated," he said, "complicated."

We lit cigarettes and after a while his beer arrived. We smoked and drank and listened to the music.

I've sung this song and I'll sing it again: the world is like an untempoed piece of music. Of the many changes which came to pass during my lifetime, it seems that the majority have occurred during the past few years. It also struck me that way several years ago, and I'd a hunch I might be feeling the same way a few years hence—that is, if Don's business did not complicate me off this mortal coil or condenser before then.

Don operates the second-largest detective agency in the world, and he sometimes finds me useful because I do not exist. I do not exist now because I existed once at the time and the place where we attempted to begin scoring the wild ditty of our times. I refer to the world Central Data Bank project and the fact that I had had a significant part in that effort to construct a working model of the real world, accounting for everyone and everything in it. How well we succeeded, and whether possession of the world's likeness does indeed provide its custodians with a greater measure of control over its functions, are questions my former colleagues still debate as the music grows more shrill and you can't see the maps for the pins. I made my decision back then and saw to it that I did not receive citizenship in that second world, a place which may now have become more important than the first. Exiled to reality, my own sojourns across the line are necessarily those of an alien guilty of illegal entry. I visit periodically because I go where I must to make my living. —That is where Don comes in. The people I can become are often very useful when he has peculiar problems.

Unfortunately, at that moment, it seemed that he did, just when the whole gang of me felt like turning down the volume and loafing.

We finished our drinks, got the bill, settled it.

"This way," I said, indicating the rear door, and he swung into his coat and followed me out.

"Talk here?" he asked, as we walked down the alley.

"Rather not," I said. "Public transportation, then private conversation."

He nodded and came along.

About three-quarters of an hour later we were in the saloon of the *Proteus* and I was making coffee. We were rocked gently by the Bay's chill waters, under a moonless sky. I'd only a pair of the smaller lights burning. Comfortable. On the water, aboard the *Proteus*, the crowding, the activities, the tempo, of life in the cities, on the land, are muted, slowed—fictionalized—by the metaphysical distancing a few meters of water can provide. We alter the landscape with great facility, but the ocean has always seemed unchanged, and I suppose by extension we are infected with some feelings of timelessness whenever we set out upon her. Maybe that's one of the reasons I spend so much time there.

"First time you've had me aboard," he said. "Comfortable. Very."

"Thanks. —Cream? Sugar?"

"Yes. Both."

We settled back with our steaming mugs and I asked, "What have you got?"

"One case involving two problems," he said. "One of them sort of falls within my area of competence. The other does not. I was told that it is an absolutely unique situation and would require the services of a very special specialist."

"I'm not a specialist at anything but keeping alive."

His eyes came up suddenly and caught my own.

"I had always assumed that you knew an awful lot about computers," he said.

I looked away. That was hitting below the belt. I had never held myself out to him as an authority in that area, and there had always been a tacit understanding between us that my methods of manipulating circumstance and identity were not open to discussion. On the other hand, it was obvious to him that my knowledge of the system was both extensive and intensive. Still, I didn't like talking about it. So I moved to defend.

"Computer people are a dime a dozen," I said. "It was probably different in your time, but these days they start teaching computer science to little kids their first year in school. So sure, I know a lot about it. This generation, everybody does."

"You know that is not what I meant," he said. "Haven't you known me long enough to trust me a little more than that? The question springs solely from the case at hand. That's all."

I nodded. Reactions by their very nature are not always appropriate, and I had invested a lot of emotional capital in a heavy-duty set. So, "Okay, I know more about them than the school kids," I said.

"Thanks. That can be our point of departure." He took a sip of coffee. "My own background is in law and accounting, followed by the military, military intelligence, and civil service, in that order. Then I got into this business. What technical stuff I know I've picked up along the way—a scrap here, a crash course there. I know a lot about what things can *do*, not so much about how they *work*. I did not understand the details on this one, so I want you to start at the top and explain things to me, for as far as you can go. I need the background review, and if you are able to furnish it I will also know that you are the man for the job. You can begin by telling me how the early space-exploration robots worked—like, say the ones they used on Venus."

"That's not computers," I said, "and for that matter, they weren't really robots. They were telefactoring devices."

"Tell me what makes the difference."

"A robot is a machine which carries out certain operations in accordance with a program of instructions. A telefactor is a slave machine operated by remote control. The telefactor functions in a feedback situation with its operator. Depending on how sophisticated you want to get, the links can be audiovisual, kinesthetic, tactile, even olfactory. The more you want to go in this direction, the more anthropomorphic you get in the thing's design.

"In the case of Venus, if I recall correctly, the human operator in orbit wore an exoskeleton which controlled the movements of the body, legs, arms, and hands of the device on the surface below, receiving motion and force feedback through a system of airjet transducers. He had on a helmet controlling the slave device's television camera—set, obviously enough, in its turret—which filled his field of vision with the scene below. He also wore earphones connected with its audio pickup. I read the book he wrote later. He said that for long stretches of time he would forget the cabin, forget that he was at the boss end of a control loop, and actually feel as if he were stalking through that hellish landscape. I remember being very impressed by it, just being a kid, and I wanted a super-tiny one all my own, so that I could wade around in puddles picking fights with microorganisms."

"Why?"

"Because there weren't any dragons on Venus. Anyhow, that is a telefactoring device, a thing quite distinct from a robot."

"I'm still with you," he said, and "Now tell me the difference between the early telefactoring devices and the later ones."

I swallowed some coffee.

"It was a bit trickier with respect to the outer planets and their satellites," I said. "There, we did not have orbiting operators at first. Economics, and some unresolved technical problems. Mainly economics. At any rate, the devices were landed on the target worlds, but the operators stayed home. Because of this, there was of course a time lag in the transmissions along the control loop. It took a while to receive the on-site input, and then there was another time lapse before the response movements reached the telefactor. We attempted to compensate for this in two ways: the first was by the employment of a single wait–move, wait–move sequence; the second was more sophisticated and is actually the point where computers come into the picture in terms of participating in the control loop. It involved the setting up of models of known environmental factors, which were then enriched during the initial wait–move sequences. On this basis, the computer was then used to anticipate short-range developments. Finally, it could take over the loop and run it by a combination of 'predictor controls' and wait–move reviews. It still had to holler for human help, though, when unexpected things came up. So, with the outer planets, it was neither totally automatic nor totally manual—nor totally satisfactory—at first."

"Okay," he said, lighting a cigarette. "And the next step?"

"The next wasn't really a technical step forward in telefactoring. It was an economic shift. The purse strings were loosened and we could afford to send men out. We landed them where we could land them, and in many of the places where we could not, we sent down the telefactors and orbited the men again. Like in the old days. The time-lag problem was removed because the operator was on top of things once more. If anything, you can look at it as a reversion to earlier methods. It is what we still often do, though, and it works."

He shook his head.

"You left something out between the computers and the bigger budget."

I shrugged.

"A number of things were tried during that period, but none of them proved as effective as what we already had going in the human-computer partnership with the telefactors."

"There was one project," he said, "which attempted to get around the time-lag troubles by sending the computer along with the telefactor as part of the package. Only the computer wasn't exactly a computer and the telefactor wasn't exactly a telefactor. Do you know which one I am referring to?"

I lit a cigarette of my own while I thought about it, then, "I think you are talking about the Hangman," I said.

"That's right and this is where I get lost. Can you tell me how it works?"

"Ultimately, it was a failure," I told him.

"But it worked at first."

"Apparently. But only on the easy stuff, on Io. It conked out later and had to be written off as a failure, albeit a noble one. The venture was overly ambitious from the very beginning. What seems to have happened was that the people in charge had the opportunity to combine vanguard projects—stuff that was still under investigation and stuff that was extremely new. In theory, it all seemed to dovetail so beautifully that they yielded to the temptation and incorporated too much. It started out well, but it fell apart later."

"But what all was involved in the thing?"

"Lord! What wasn't? The computer that wasn't exactly a computer... Okay, well start there. Last century, three engineers at the University of Wisconsin—Nordman, Parmentier, and Scott—developed a device known as a superconductive tunnel-junction neuristor. Two tiny strips of metal with a thin insulating layer between. Supercool it and it passed electrical impulses without resistance. Surround it with magnetized material and pack a mass of them together—billions—and what have you got?"

He shook his head.

"Well, for one thing you've got an impossible situation to schematize when considering all the paths and interconnections that may be formed. There is an obvious similarity to the structure of the brain. So, they theorized, you don't even attempt to hook up such a device. You pulse in data and let it establish its own preferential pathways, by means of the magnetic material's becoming increasingly magnetized each time the current passes through it, thus cutting the resistance. The material establishes its own routes in a fashion analogous to the functioning of the brain when it is learning something.

"In the case of the Hangman, they used a setup very similar to this and they were able to pack about a hundred billion neuristor-type cells into a very small area, around a cubic foot. They aimed for that magic figure because that is approximately the number of nerve cells in the human brain. That is what I meant when I said that it wasn't really a computer. They were actually working in the area of artificial intelligence, no matter what they called it."

"If the thing had its own brain—computer or quasihuman—then it was a robot rather than a telefactor, right?"

"Yes and no and maybe," I said. "It was operated as a telefactor device here on Earth—on the ocean floor, in the desert, in mountainous country—as part of its programming. I suppose you could also call that its apprenticeship—or kindergarten. Perhaps that is even more appropriate. It was being shown how to explore in difficult environments and to report back. Once it mastered this, then theoretically they could hang it out there in the sky without a control loop and let it report its own findings."

"At that point would it be considered a robot?"

"A robot is a machine which carries out certain operations in accordance with a program of instructions. The Hangman made its *own* decisions, you see. And I suspect that by trying to produce something that close to the human brain in structure and function, the seemingly inevitable randomness of its model got included in. It wasn't just a machine following a program. It was too complex. That was probably what broke it down."

Don chuckled.

"Inevitable free will?"

"No. As I said, they had thrown too many things into one bag. Everybody and his brother with a pet project that might be fitted in seemed a supersalesman that season. For example, the psychophysics boys had a gimmick they wanted to try on it, and it got used. Ostensibly, the Hangman was a communications device. Actually, they were concerned as to whether the thing was truly sentient."

"Was it?"

"Apparently so, in a limited fashion. What they had come up with, to be made part of the initial telefactor loop, was a device which set up a weak induction field in the brain of the operator. The machine received and amplified the patterns of electrical activity being conducted in the Hangman's—might as well call it 'brain'—then passed them through a complex modulator and pulsed them into the induction field in the operator's head. —I am out of my area now and into that of Weber and Fechner, but a neuron has a threshold at which it will fire, and below which it will not. There are some forty thousand neurons packed together in a cubic millimeter of the cerebral cortex, in such a fashion that each one has several hundred synaptic connections with others about it. At any given moment, some of them may be way below the firing threshold while others are in a condition Sir John Eccles once referred to as 'critically poised'—ready to fire. If just one is pushed over the threshold, it can affect the discharge of hundreds of thousands of others within milliseconds. The pulsating field was to provide such a push in a sufficiently selective fashion to give the operator an idea as to what was going on in the Hangman's brain. And vice versa. The Hangman was to have its own built-in version of the same thing. It was also thought that this might serve to humanize it somewhat, so that it would better appreciate the significance of its work—to instill something like loyalty, you might say."

"Do you think this could have contributed to its later breakdown?"

"Possibly. How can you say in a one-of-a-kind situation like this? If you want a guess, I'd say, 'Yes.' But it's just a guess."

"Uh-huh," he said, "and what were its physical capabilities?"

"Anthropomorphic design," I said, "both because it was originally telefactored and because of the psychological reasoning I just mentioned. It could pilot its own small vessel. No need for a life-support system, of course. Both it and the vessel were powered by fusion units, so that fuel was no real problem. Self-repairing. Capable of performing a great variety of sophisticated tests and measurements, of making observations, completing reports, learning new material, broadcasting its findings back here. Capable of surviving just about anywhere. In fact, it required less energy on the outer planets—less work for the refrigeration units, to maintain that supercooled brain in its midsection."

"How strong was it?"

"I don't recall all the specs. Maybe a dozen times as strong as a man, in things like lifting and pushing."

"It explored Io for us and started in on Europa."

"Yes."

"Then it began behaving erratically, just when we thought it had really learned its job."

"That sounds right," I said.

"It refused a direct order to explore Callisto, then headed out toward Uranus."

"Yes. It's been years since I read the reports…"

"The malfunction worsened after that. Long periods of silence interspersed with garbled transmissions. Now that I know more about its makeup, it almost sounds like a man going off the deep end."

"It seems similar."

"But it managed to pull itself together again for a brief while. It landed on Titania, began sending back what seemed like appropriate observation reports. This only lasted a short time, though. It went irrational once more, indicated that it was heading for a landing on Uranus itself, and that was it. We didn't hear from it after that. Now that I know about that mind-reading gadget I understand why a psychiatrist on this end could be so positive it would never function again."

"I never heard about that part."

"I did."

I shrugged. "This was all around twenty years ago," I said, "and, as I mentioned, it has been a long while since I've read anything about it."

"The Hangman's ship crashed or landed, as the case may be, in the Gulf of Mexico, two days ago."

I just stared at him.

"It was empty," Don went on, "when they finally got out and down to it."

"I don't understand."

"Yesterday morning," he continued, "restaurateur Manny Burns was found beaten to death in the office of his establishment, the Maison Saint-Michel, in New Orleans."

"I still fail to see—"

"Manny Burns was one of the four original operators who programmed—pardon me, 'taught'—the Hangman."

The silence lengthened, dragged its belly on the deck.

"Coincidence…?" I finally said.

"My client doesn't think so."

"Who is your client?"

"One of the three remaining members of the training group. He is convinced that the Hangman has returned to Earth to kill its former operators."

"Has he made his fears known to his old employers?"

"No."

"Why not?"

"Because it would require telling them the reason for his fears."

"That being…?"

"He wouldn't tell me, either."

"How does he expect you to do a proper job?"

"He told me what he considered a proper job. He wanted two things done, neither of which requires a full case history. He wanted to be furnished with good bodyguards, and he wanted the Hangman found and disposed of. I have already taken care of the first part."

"And you want me to do the second?"

"That's right. You have confirmed my opinion that you are the man for the job."

"I see. Do you realize that if the thing is truly sentient this will be something very like murder? If it is not, of course, then it will only amount to the destruction of expensive government property."

"Which way do you look at it?"

"I look at it as a job," I said.

"You'll take it?"

"I need more facts before I can decide. Like, who is your client? Who are the other operators? Where do they live? What do they do? What—"

He raised his hand.

"First," he said, "the Honorable Jesse Brockden, senior Senator from Wisconsin, is our client. Confidentiality, of course, is written all over it."

I nodded. "I remember his being involved with the space program before he went into politics. I wasn't aware of the specifics, though. He could get government protection so easily—"

"To obtain it, he would apparently have to tell them something he doesn't want to talk about. Perhaps it would hurt his career. I simply do not know. He doesn't want them. He wants us."

I nodded again.

"What about the others? Do they want us, too?"

"Quite the opposite. They don't subscribe to Brockden's notions at all. They seem to think he is something of a paranoid."

"How well do they know one another these days?"

"They live in different parts of the country, haven't seen each other in years. Been in occasional touch, though."

"Kind of a flimsy basis for that diagnosis, then."

"One of them *is* a psychiatrist."

"Oh. Which one?"

"Leila Thackery is her name. Lives in St. Louis. Works at the State Hospital there."

"None of them have gone to any authority, then—federal or local?"

"That's right. Brockden contacted them when he heard about the Hangman. He was in Washington at the time. Got word on its return right away and managed to get the story killed. He tried to reach them all, learned about Burns in the process, contacted me, then tried to persuade the others to accept protection by my people. They weren't buying. When I talked to her, Doctor Thackery pointed out—quite correctly—that Brockden is a very sick man."

"What's he got?"

"Cancer. In his spine. Nothing they can do about it once it hits there and digs in. He even told me he figures he has maybe six months to get through what he considers a very important piece of legislation—the new criminal rehabilitation act. —I will admit that he did sound kind of paranoid when he talked about it. But hell! Who wouldn't? Doctor Thackery sees that as the whole thing, though, and she doesn't see the Burns killing as being connected with the Hangman. Thinks it was just a traditional robbery gone sour, thief surprised and panicky, maybe hopped-up, *et cetera*."

"Then she is not afraid of the Hangman?"

"She said that she is in a better position to know its mind than anyone else, and she is not especially concerned."

"What about the other operator?"

"He said that Doctor Thackery may know its mind better than anyone else, but he knows its brain, and he isn't worried, either."

"What did he mean by that?"

"David Fentris is a consulting engineer—electronics, cybernetics. He actually had something to do with the Hangman's design."

I got to my feet and went after the coffeepot. Not that I'd an overwhelming desire for another cup at just that moment. But I had known, had once worked with a David Fentris. And he had at one time been connected with the space program.

About fifteen years my senior, Dave had been with the data bank project when I had known him. Where a number of us had begun having second thoughts as the thing progressed, Dave had never been anything less than wildly enthusiastic. A wiry five-eight, gray-cropped, gray eyes back of hornrims and heavy glass, cycling between preoccupation and near-frantic darting, he had had a way of verbalizing half-completed thoughts as he went along, so that you might begin to think him a representative of that tribe which had come into positions of small authority by means of nepotism or politics. If you would listen a few more minutes, however, you would begin revising your opinion as he started to pull his musings together into a rigorous framework. By the time he had finished, you generally wondered why you hadn't seen it all along and what a guy like that was doing in a position of such small authority. Later, it might strike you, though, that he seemed sad whenever he wasn't enthusiastic about something. And while the gung-ho spirit is great for short-range projects, larger ventures generally require somewhat more equanimity. I wasn't at all surprised that he had wound up as a consultant.

The big question now, of course was: Would he remember me? True, my appearance was altered, my personality hopefully more mature, my habits shifted around. But would that be enough, should I have to encounter him as part of this job? That mind behind those hornrims could do a lot of strange things with just a little data.

"Where does he live?" I asked.

"Memphis. —And what's the matter?"

"Just trying to get my geography straight," I said. "Is Senator Brockden still in Washington?"

"No. He's returned to Wisconsin and is currently holed up in a lodge in the northern part of the state. Four of my people are with him."

"I see."

I refreshed our coffee supply and reseated myself. I didn't like this one at all and I resolved not to take it. I didn't like just giving Don a flat "No," though. His assignments had become a very important part of my life, and this one was not mere legwork. It was obviously important to him, and he wanted me on it. I decided to look for holes in the thing, to find some way of reducing it to the simple bodyguard job already in progress.

"It does seem peculiar," I said, "that Brockden is the only one afraid of the device."

"Yes."

"...And that he gives no reasons."

"True."

"...Plus his condition, and what the doctor said about its effect on his mind."

"I have no doubt that he is neurotic," Don said. "Look at this."

He reached for his coat, withdrew a sheaf of papers from within it. He shuffled through them and extracted a single sheet, which he passed to me.

It was a piece of Congressional-letterhead stationary, with the message scrawled in longhand. *"Don,"* it said, *"I've got to see you. Frankenstein's monster is just come back from where we hung him and he's looking for me. The whole damn universe is trying to grind me up. Call me between 8 & 10. —Jess."*

I nodded, started to pass it back, paused, then handed it over. Double damn it deeper than hell!

I took a drink of coffee. I thought that I had long ago given up hope in such things, but I had noticed something which immediately troubled me. In the margin, where they list such matters, I had seen that Jesse Brockden was on the committee for review of the Central Data Bank program. I recalled that that committee was supposed to be working on a series of reform recommendations. Offhand, I could not remember Brockden's position on any of the issues involved, but— Oh, hell! The thing was simply too big to alter significantly now… But it *was* the only real Frankenstein monster I cared about, and there was always the possibility… On the other hand— Hell, again! What if I let him die when I might have saved him, and he had been the one who…?

I took another drink of coffee. I lit another cigarette.

There might be a way of working it so that Dave didn't even come into the picture. I could talk to Leila Thackery first, check further into the Burns killing, keep posted on new developments, find out more about the vessel in the Gulf… I might be able to accomplish something, even if it was only the negation of Brockden's theory, without Dave's and my paths ever crossing.

"Have you got the specs on the Hangman?" I asked.

"Right here."

He passed them over.

"The police report on the Burns killing?"

"Here it is."

"The whereabouts of everyone involved, and some background on them?"

"Here."

"The place or places where I can reach you during the next few days—around the clock? This one may require some coordination."

He smiled and reached for his pen.

"Glad to have you aboard," he said.

I reached over and tapped the barometer. I shook my head.

❖ ❖ ❖

The ringing of the phone awakened me. Reflex bore me across the room, where I took it on audio.

"Yes?"

"Mister Donne? It is eight o'clock."

"Thanks."

I collapsed into the chair. I am what might be called a slow starter. I tend to recapitulate phylogeny every morning. Basic desires inched their ways through my gray matter to close a connection. Slowly, I extended a cold-blooded member and clicked my talons against a couple of numbers. I croaked my desire for food and lots of coffee to the voice that responded. Half an hour later I would only have growled. Then I staggered off to the place of flowing waters to renew my contact with basics.

In addition to my normal adrenaline and blood-sugar bearishness, I had not slept much the night before. I had closed up shop after Don left, stuffed my pockets with essentials, departed the *Proteus*, gotten myself over to the airport and onto a flight which took me to St. Louis in the dead, small hours of the dark. I was unable to sleep during the flight, thinking about the case, deciding on the tack I was going to take with Leila Thackery. On arrival, I had checked into the airport motel, left a message to be awakened at an unreasonable hour, and collapsed.

As I ate, I regarded the fact sheet Don had given me.

Leila Thackery was currently single, having divorced her second husband a little over two years ago, was forty-six years old, and lived in an apartment near to the hospital where she worked. Attached to the sheet was a photo which might have been ten years old. In it, she was brunette, light-eyed, barely on the right side of that border between ample and overweight, with fancy glasses straddling an upturned nose. She had published a number of books and articles with titles full of alienations, roles, transactions, social contexts, and more alienations.

I hadn't had the time to go my usual route, becoming an entire new individual with a verifiable history. Just a name and a story, that's all. It did not seem necessary this time, though. For once, something approximating honesty actually seemed a reasonable approach.

I took a public vehicle over to her apartment building. I did not phone ahead, because it is easier to say "No" to a voice than to a person.

According to the record, today was one of the days when she saw outpatients in her home. Her idea, apparently: break down the alienating institution-image, remove resentments by turning the sessions into something more like social occasions, *et cetera*. I did not want all that much of her time—I had decided that Don could make it worth her while if it came to that—and I was sure my fellows' visits were scheduled to leave her with some small breathing space. *Inter alia,* so to speak.

I had just located her name and apartment number amid the buttons in the entrance foyer when an old woman passed behind me and unlocked the door to the lobby. She glanced at me and held it open, so I went on in without ringing. The matter of presence, again.

I took the elevator to Leila's floor, the second, located her door and knocked on it. I was almost ready to knock again when it opened, partway.

"Yes?" she asked, and I revised my estimate as to the age of the photo. She looked just about the same.

"Doctor Thackery," I said, "my name is Donne. You could help me quite a bit with a problem I've got."

"What sort of problem?"

"It involves a device known as the Hangman."

She sighed and showed me a quick grimace. Her fingers tightened on the door.

"I've come a long way but I'll be easy to get rid of. I've only a few things I'd like to ask you about it."

"Are you with the government?"

"No."

"Do you work for Brockden?"

"No, I'm something different."

"All right," she said. "Right now I've got a group session going. It will probably last around another half hour. If you don't mind waiting down in the lobby, I'll let you know as soon as it is over. We can talk then."

"Good enough," I said. "Thanks."

She nodded, closed the door. I located the stairway and walked back down.

A cigarette later, I decided that the devil finds work for idle hands and thanked him for his suggestion. I strolled back toward the foyer. Through the glass, I read the names of a few residents of the fifth floor. I elevated up and knocked on one of the doors. Before it was opened I had my notebook and pad in plain sight.

"Yes?" Short, fiftyish, curious.

"My name is Stephen Foster, Mrs. Gluntz. I am doing a survey for the North American Consumers League. I would like to pay you for a couple minutes of your time, to answer some questions about products you use."

"Why—Pay me?"

"Yes, ma'am. Ten dollars. Around a dozen questions. It will just take a minute or two."

"All right." She opened the door wider. "Won't you come in?"

"No, thank you. This thing is so brief I'd just be in and out. The first question involves detergents..."

Ten minutes later I was back in the lobby adding the thirty bucks for the three interviews to the list of expenses I was keeping. When a situation is full of unpredictables and I am playing makeshift games, I like to provide for as many contingencies as I can.

Another quarter of an hour or so slipped by before the elevator opened and discharged three guys—young, young, and middle-aged, casually dressed, chuckling over something.

The big one on the nearest end strolled over and nodded.

"You the fellow waiting to see Doctor Thackery?"

"That's right."

"She said to tell you to come on up now."

"Thanks."

I rode up again, returned to her door. She opened to my knock, nodded me in, saw me seated in a comfortable chair at the far end of her living room.

"Would you care for a cup of coffee?" she asked. "It's fresh. I made more than I needed."

"That would be fine. Thanks."

Moments later, she brought in a couple of cups, delivered one to me, and seated herself on the sofa to my left. I ignored the cream and sugar on the tray and took a sip.

"You've gotten me interested," she said. "Tell me about it."

"Okay. I have been told that the telefactor device known as the Hangman, now possibly possessed of an artificial intelligence, has returned to Earth—"

"Hypothetical," she said, "unless you know something I don't. I have been told that the Hangman's vehicle reentered and crashed in the Gulf. There is no evidence that the vehicle was occupied."

"It seems a reasonable conclusion, though."

"It seems just as reasonable to me that the Hangman sent the vehicle off toward an eventual rendezvous point many years ago and that it only recently reached that point, at which time the reentry program took over and brought it down."

"Why should it return the vehicle and strand itself out there?"

"Before I answer that," she said, "I would like to know the reason for your concern. News media?"

"No," I said. "I am a science writer—straight tech, popular, and anything in between. But I am not after a piece for publication. I was retained to do a report on the psychological makeup of the thing."

"For whom?"

"A private investigation outfit. They want to know what might influence its thinking, how it might be likely to behave—if it has indeed come back.—I've been doing a lot of homework, and I gathered there is a likelihood that its nuclear personality was a composite of the minds of its four operators. So, personal contacts seemed in order, to collect your opinions as to what it might be like. I came to you first for obvious reasons."

She nodded.

"A Mister Walsh spoke with me the other day. He is working for Senator Brockden."

"Oh? I never go into an employer's business beyond what he's asked me to do. Senator Brockden is on my list though, along with a David Fentris."

"You were told about Manny Burns?"

"Yes. Unfortunate."

"That is apparently what set Jesse off. He is—how shall I put it?—he is clinging to life right now, trying to accomplish a great many things in the time he has remaining. Every moment is precious to him. He feels the old man in the white nightgown breathing down his neck. —Then the ship returns and one of us is killed. From what we know of the Hangman, the last we heard of it, it had become irrational. Jesse saw a connection, and in his condition the fear is understandable. There is nothing wrong with humoring him if it allows him to get his work done."

"But you don't see a threat in it?"

"No. I was the last person to monitor the Hangman before communications ceased, and I could see then what had happened. The first things that it had learned were the organization of perceptions and motor activities. Multitudes of other patterns had been transferred from the minds of its operators, but they were too sophisticated to mean much initially. —Think of a child who has learned the Gettysburg Address. It is there in his head, that is all. One day, however, it may be important to him. Conceivably, it may even inspire him to action. It takes some growing up first, of course. Now think of such a child with a great number of conflicting patterns—attitudes, tendencies, memories—none of which are especially bothersome for so long as he remains a child. Add a bit of maturity, though—and bear in mind that the patterns originated with four different individuals, all of them more powerful than the words of even the finest of speeches, bearing as they do their own built-in feelings. Try to imagine the conflicts, the contradictions involved in being four people at once—"

"Why wasn't this imagined in advance?" I asked.

"Ah!" she said, smiling. "The full sensitivity of the neuristor brain was not appreciated at first. It was assumed that the operators were adding data in a linear fashion and that this would continue until a critical mass was achieved, corresponding to the construction of a model or picture of the world which would then serve as a point of departure for growth of the Hangman's own mind. And it did seem to check out this way.

"What actually occurred, however, was a phenomenon amounting to imprinting. Secondary characteristics of the operators' minds, outside the didactic situations, were imposed. These did not immediately become functional and hence were not detected. They remained latent until the mind had developed sufficiently to understand them. And then it was too late. It suddenly acquired four additional personalities and was unable to coordinate them. When it tried to compartmentalize them it went schizoid; when it tried to integrate them it went catatonic. It was cycling back and forth between these alternatives at the end. Then it just went silent. I felt it had undergone the equivalent of an epileptic seizure. Wild currents through that magnetic material would, in effect, have erased its mind, resulting in *its* equivalent of death or idiocy."

"I follow you," I said. "Now, just for the sake of playing games, I see the alternatives as either a successful integration of all this material or the achievement of a viable schizophrenia. What do you think its behavior would be like if either of these were possible?"

"All right," she agreed. "As I just said, though, I think there were physical limitations to its retaining multiple personality structures for a very long period of time. If it did, however, it would have continued with its own, plus replicas of the four operators', at least for a while. The situation would differ radically from that of a human schizoid of this sort, in that the additional personalities were valid images of genuine identities rather than self-generated complexes which had become autonomous. They might continue to evolve, they might degenerate, they might conflict to the point of destruction or gross modification of any or all of them. In other words, no prediction is possible as to the nature of whatever might remain."

"Might I venture one?"

"Go ahead."

"After considerable anxiety, it masters them. It asserts itself. It beats down this quartet of demons which has been tearing it apart, acquiring in the process an all-consuming hatred for the actual individuals responsible for this turmoil. To free itself totally, to revenge itself, to work its ultimate catharsis, it resolves to seek them out and destroy them."

She smiled.

"You have just dispensed with the 'viable schizophrenia' you conjured up, and you have now switched over to its pulling through and becoming fully autonomous. That is a different situation—no matter what strings you put on it."

"Okay, I accept the charge. —But what about my conclusion?"

"You are saying that if it did pull through, it would hate us. That strikes me as an unfair attempt to invoke the spirit of Sigmund Freud: Oedipus and Electra in one being, out to destroy all its parents, the authors of every one of its tensions, anxieties, hang-ups, burned into its impressionable psyche at a young and defenseless age. Even Freud didn't have a name for that one. What should we call it?"

"A Hermacis complex?" I suggested.

"Hermacis?"

"Hermaphroditus having been united in one body with the nymph Salmacis, I've just done the same with their names. That being would then have had four parents against whom to react."

"Cute," she said, smiling. "If the liberal arts do nothing else, they provide engaging metaphors for the thinking they displace. This one is unwarranted and overly anthropomorphic, though.—You wanted my opinion. All right. If the Hangman pulled through at all, it could only have been by virtue of that neuristor brain's differences from the human brain. From my own professional experience, a human could not pass through a situation like that and attain stability. If the Hangman did, it would have to have resolved all the contradictions and conflicts, to have mastered and understood the situation so thoroughly that I do not believe whatever remained could involve that sort of hatred. The fear, the uncertainty, the things that feed hate would have been analyzed, digested, turned to something more useful. There would probably be distaste, and possibly an act of independence, of self-assertion. That was one reason why I suggested its return of the ship."

"It is your opinion, then, that if the Hangman exists as a thinking individual today, this is the only possible attitude it would possess toward its former operators: it would want nothing more to do with you?"

"That is correct. Sorry about your Hermacis complex. But in this case we must look to the brain, not the psyche. And we see two things: schizophrenia would have destroyed it, and a successful resolution of its problem would preclude vengeance. Either way, there is nothing to worry about."

How could I put it tactfully? I decided that I could not.

"All of this is fine," I said, "for as far as it goes. But getting away from both the purely psychological and the purely physical, could there be a particular reason for its seeking your deaths—that is, a plain old-fashioned motive for a killing, based on *events* rather than having to do with the way its thinking equipment goes together?"

Her expression was impossible to read, but considering her line of work I had expected nothing less.

"What events?" she said.

"I have no idea. That's why I asked."

She shook her head.

"I'm afraid that I don't, either."

"Then that about does it," I said. "I can't think of anything else to ask you."

She nodded.

"And I can't think of anything else to tell you."

I finished my coffee, returned the cup to the tray.

"Thanks, then," I said, "for your time, for the coffee. You have been very helpful."

I rose. She did the same.

"What are you going to do now?" she asked.

"I haven't quite decided," I answered. "I want to do the best report I can. Have you any suggestions on that?"

"I suggest that there isn't any more to learn, that I have given you the only possible constructions the facts warrant."

"You don't feel David Fentris could provide any additional insights?"

She snorted, then sighed.

"No," she said, "I do not think he could tell you anything useful."

"What do you mean? From the way you say it—"

"I know. I didn't mean to. —Some people find comfort in religion. Others...You know. Others take it up late in life with a vengeance and a half. They don't use it quite the way it was intended. It comes to color all their thinking."

"Fanaticism?" I said.

"Not exactly. A misplaced zeal. A masochistic sort of thing. Hell! I shouldn't be diagnosing at a distance—or influencing your opinion. Forget what I said. Form your own opinion when you meet him."

She raised her head, appraising my reaction.

"Well," I responded, "I am not at all certain that I am going to see him. But you have made me curious. How can religion influence engineering?"

"I spoke with him after Jesse gave us the news on the vessel's return. I got the impression at the time that he feels we were tampering in the province of the Almighty by attempting the creation of an artificial intelligence. That our creation should go mad was only appropriate, being the work of imperfect man. He seemed to feel that it would be fitting if it had come back for retribution, as a sign of judgment upon us."

"Oh," I said.

She smiled then. I returned it.

"Yes," she said, "but maybe I just got him in a bad mood. Maybe you should go see for yourself."

Something told me to shake my head—there was a bit of a difference between this view of him, my recollections, and Don's comment that Dave had said he knew its brain and was not especially concerned. Somewhere among these lay something I felt I should know, felt I should learn without seeming to pursue.

So, "I think have enough right now," I said. "It was the psychological side of things I was supposed to cover, not the mechanical—*or* the theological. You have been extremely helpful. Thanks again."

She carried her smile all the way to the door.

"If it is not too much trouble," she said, as I stepped into the hall, "I would like to learn how this whole thing finally turns out—or any interesting developments, for that matter."

"My connection with the case ends with this report, and I am going to write it now. Still, I may get some feedback."

"You have my number…?"

"Probably, but…"

I already had it, but I jotted it again, right after Mrs. Gluntz's answers to my inquiries on detergents.

❖ ❖ ❖

Moving in a rigorous line, I made beautiful connections, for a change. I headed directly for the airport, found a flight aimed at Memphis, bought passage, and was the last to board. Tenscore seconds, perhaps, made all the difference. Not even a tick or two to spare for checking out of the motel. —No matter. The good head-doctor had convinced me that, like it or not, David Fentris was next, damn it. I had too strong a feeling that Leila Thackery had not told me the entire story. I had to take a chance, to see these changes in the man for myself, to try to figure out how they related to the Hangman. For a number of reasons, I'd a feeling they might.

I disembarked into a cool, partly overcast afternoon, found transportation almost immediately, and set out for Dave's office address.

A before-the-storm feeling came over me as I entered and crossed the town. A dark wall of clouds continued to build in the west. Later, standing before the building where Dave did business, the first few drops of rain were already spattering against its dirty brick front. It would take a lot more than that to freshen it, though, or any of the others in the area. I would have thought he'd have come a little further than this by now.

I shrugged off some moisture and went inside.

The directory gave me directions, the elevator elevated me, my feet found the way to his door. I knocked on it. After a time, I knocked again and waited again. Again, nothing. So I tried it, found it open, and went on in.

It was a small, vacant waiting room, green-carpeted. The reception desk was dusty. I crossed and peered around the plastic partition behind it.

The man had his back to me. I drummed my knuckles against the partitioning. He heard it and turned.

"Yes?"

Our eyes met, his still framed by hornrims and just as active; lenses thicker, hair thinner, cheeks a trifle lower.

His question mark quivered in the air, and nothing in his gaze moved to replace it with recognition. He had been bending over a sheaf of schematics. A lopsided basket of metal, quartz, porcelain, and glass rested on a nearby table.

"My name is Donne, John Donne," I said. "I am looking for David Fentris."

"I am David Fentris."

"Good to meet you," I said, crossing to where he stood. "I am assisting in an investigation concerning a project with which you were once associated..."

He smiled and nodded, accepted my hand and shook it.

"The Hangman, of course. Glad to know you, Mister Donne."

"Yes, the Hangman," I said. "I am doing a report—"

"—And you want my opinion as to how dangerous it is. Sit down." He gestured toward a chair at the end of his work bench. "Care for a cup of tea?"

"No, thanks."

"I'm having one."

"Well, in that case..."

He crossed to another bench.

"No cream. Sorry."

"That's all right. —How did you know it involved the Hangman?"

He grinned as he brought me my cup.

"Because it's come back," he said, "and it's the only thing I've been connected with that warrants that much concern."

"Do you mind talking about it?"

"Up to a point, no."

"What's the point?"

"If we get near it, I'll let you know."

"Fair enough. —How dangerous *is* it?"

"I would say that it is harmless," he replied, "except to three persons."

"Formerly four?"

"Precisely."

"How come?"

"We were doing something we had no business doing."

"That being...?"

"For one thing, attempting to create an artificial intelligence."

"Why had you no business doing that?"

"A man with a name like yours shouldn't have to ask."

I chuckled.

"If I were a preacher," I said, "I would have to point out that there is no biblical injunction against it—unless you've been worshipping it on the sly."

He shook his head.

"Nothing that simple, that obvious, that explicit. Times have changed since the Good Book was written, and you can't hold with a purely fundamentalist approach in complex times. What I was getting at was something a little more abstract. A form of pride, not unlike the classical hubris, the setting up of oneself on a level with the Creator."

"Did you feel that—pride?"

"Yes."

"Are you sure it wasn't just enthusiasm for an ambitious project that was working well?"

"Oh, there was plenty of that. A manifestation of the same thing."

"I do seem to recall something about man being made in the Creator's image, and something else about trying to live up to that. It would seem to follow that exercising one's capacities along similar lines would be a step in the right direction, an act of conformance with the Divine ideal, if you'd like."

"But I don't like. Man cannot really create. He can only rearrange what is already present. Only God can create."

"Then you have nothing to worry about."

He frowned. Then, "No," he said. "Being aware of this and still trying is where the presumption comes in."

"Were you really thinking that way when you did it? Or did all this occur to you after the fact?"

He continued to frown.

"I am no longer certain."

"Then it would seem to me that a merciful God would be inclined to give you the benefit of the doubt."

He gave me a wry smile.

"Not bad, John Donne. But I feel that judgment may already have been entered and that we may have lost four to nothing."

"Then you see the Hangman as an avenging angel?"

"Sometimes. Sort of. I see it as being returned to exact a penalty."

"Just for the record," I suggested, "if the Hangman had had full access to the necessary equipment and was able to construct another unit such as itself, would you consider it guilty of the same thing that is bothering you?"

He shook his head.

"Don't get all cute and Jesuitical with me, Donne. I'm not that far away from fundamentals. Besides, I'm willing to admit I might be wrong and that there may be other forces driving it to the same end."

"Such as?"

"I told you I'd let you know when we reached a certain point. That's it."

"Okay," I said. "But that sort of blank-walls me, you know. The people I am working for would like to protect you people. They want to stop the Hangman. I was hoping you would tell me a little more—if not for your own sake, then for the others'. They might not share your philosophical sentiments, and you have just admitted you may be wrong. —Despair, by the way, is also considered a sin by a great number of theologians."

He sighed and stroked his nose, as I had often seen him do in times long past.

"What do you do, anyhow?" he asked me.

"Me, personally? I'm a science writer. I'm putting together a report on the device for the agency that wants to do the protecting. The better my report, the better their chances."

He was silent for a time, then, "I read a lot in the area, but I don't recognize your name," he said.

"Most of my work has involved petrochemistry and marine biology," I said.

"Oh. —You were a peculiar choice then, weren't you?"

"Not really. I was available, and the boss knows my work, knows I'm good."

He glanced across the room, to where a stack of cartons partly obscured what I then realized to be a remote-access terminal. Okay. If he decided to check out my credentials now, John Donne would fall apart. It seemed a hell of a time to get curious, though, *after* sharing his sense of sin with me. He must have thought so, too, because he did not look that way again.

"Let me put it this way..." he finally said, and something of the old David Fentris at his best took control of his voice. "For one reason or the other, I believe that it wants to destroy its former operators. If it is the judgment of the Almighty, that's all there is to it. It will succeed. If not, however, I don't want any outside protection. I've done my own repenting and it is up to me to handle the rest of the situation myself, too. I will stop the Hangman personally—right here—before anyone else is hurt."

"How?" I asked him.

He nodded toward the glittering helmet.

"With that," he said.

"How?" I repeated.

"The Hangman's telefactor circuits are still intact. They have to be: they are an integral part of it. It could not disconnect them without shutting itself down. If it comes within a quarter mile of here, that unit will be activated. It will emit a loud humming sound and a light will begin to blink behind that meshing beneath the forward ridge. I will then don the helmet and take control of the Hangman. I will bring it here and disconnect its brain."

"How would you do the disconnect?"

He reached for the schematics he had been looking at when I had come in.

"Here. The thoracic plate has to be unplugged. There are four subunits that have to be uncoupled. Here, here, here, and here."

He looked up.

"You would have to do them in sequence, though, or it could get mighty hot," I said. "First this one, then these two. Then the other."

When I looked up again, the gray eyes were fixed on my own.

"I thought you were in petrochemistry and marine biology."

"I am not really 'in' anything," I said. "I am a tech writer, with bits and pieces from all over—and I did have a look at these before, when I accepted the job."

"I see."

"Why don't you bring the space agency in on this?" I said, working to shift ground. "The original telefactoring equipment had all that power and range—"

"It was dismantled a long time ago. —I thought you were with the government."

I shook my head.

"Sorry. I didn't mean to mislead you. I am on contract with a private investigation outfit."

"Uh-huh. Then that means Jesse. —Not that it matters. You can tell him that one way or the other everything is being taken care of."

"What if you are wrong on the supernatural," I said, "but correct on the other? Supposing it is coming under the circumstances you feel it proper to resist? But supposing you are not next on its list? Supposing it gets to one of the others next, instead of you? If you are so sensitive about guilt and sin, don't you think that you would be responsible for that death—if you could prevent it by telling me just a little bit more? If it's confidentiality you're worried about—"

"No," he said. "You cannot trick me into applying my principles to a hypothetical situation which will only work out the way that you want it to. Not when I am certain that it will not arise. Whatever moves the Hangman, it will come to *me* next. If I cannot stop it, then it cannot be stopped until it has completed its job."

"How do you know that you are next?"

"Take a look at a map," he said. "It landed in the Gulf. Manny was right there in New Orleans. Naturally, he was first. The Hangman can move underwater like a controlled torpedo, which makes the Mississippi its logical route for inconspicuous travel. Proceeding up it then, here I am in Memphis. Then Leila, up in St. Louis, is obviously next after me. It can worry about getting to Washington after that."

I thought about Senator Brockden in Wisconsin and decided it would not even have that problem. All of them were fairly accessible, when you thought of the situation in terms of river travel.

"But how is it to know where you all are?" I asked.

"Good question," he said. "Within a limited range, it was once sensitive to our brain waves, having an intimate knowledge of them and the ability to pick them up. I do not know what that range would be today. It might have been able to construct an amplifier to extend this area of perception. But to be more mundane about it, I believe that it simply consulted Central's national directory. There are booths all over, even on the waterfront. It could have hit one late at night and gimmicked it. It certainly had sufficient identifying information—and engineering skill."

"Then it seems to me that the best bet for all of you would be to move away from the river till this business is settled. That thing won't be able to stalk about the countryside very long without being noticed."

He shook his head.

"It would find a way. It is extremely resourceful. At night, in an overcoat, a hat, it could pass. It requires nothing that a man would need. It could dig a hole and bury itself, stay underground during daylight. It could run without resting all night long. There is no place it could not reach in a surprisingly short while. —No, I must wait here for it."

"Let me put it as bluntly as I can," I said. "If you are right that it is a Divine Avenger, I would say that it smacks of blasphemy to try to tackle it. On the other hand, if it is not, then I think you are guilty of jeopardizing the others by withholding information that would allow us to provide them with a lot more protection than you are capable of giving them all by yourself."

He laughed.

"I'll just have to learn to live with that guilt, too, as they do with theirs," he said. "After I've done my best, they deserve anything they get."

"It was my understanding," I said, "that even God doesn't judge people until after they're dead—if you want another piece of presumption to add to your collection."

He stopped laughing and studied my face.

"There is something familiar about the way you talk, the way you think," he said. "Have we ever met before?"

"I doubt it. I would have remembered."

He shook his head.

"You've got a way of bothering a man's thinking that rings a faint bell," he went on. "You trouble me, sir."

"That was my intention."

"Are you staying here in town?"

"No."

"Give me a number where I can reach you, will you? If I have any new thoughts on this thing, I'll call you."

"I wish you would have them now, if you are going to have them."

"No, I've got some thinking to do. Where can I get hold of you later?"

I gave him the name of the motel I was still checked into in St. Louis. I could call back periodically for messages.

"All right," he said, and he moved toward the partition by the reception area and stood beside it.

I rose and followed him, passing into that area and pausing at the door to the hall.

"One thing..." I said.

"Yes?"

"If it does show up and you do stop it, will you call me and tell me that?"

"Yes, I will."

"Thanks then—and good luck."

Impulsively, I extended my hand. He gripped it and smiled faintly.

"Thank you, Mister Donne."

❖ ❖ ❖

Next. Next, next, next...

I couldn't budge Dave, and Leila Thackery had given me everything she was going to. No real sense in calling Don yet—not until I had more to say.

I thought it over on my way back to the airport. The pre-dinner hours always seem best for talking to people in any sort of official capacity, just as the night seems best for dirty work. Heavily psychological, but true nevertheless. I hated to waste the rest of the day if there was anyone else worth talking to before I called Don. Going through the folder, I decided that there was.

Manny Burns had a brother, Phil. I wondered how worthwhile it might be to talk with him. I could make it to New Orleans at a sufficiently respectable hour, learn whatever he was willing to tell me, check back with Don for new developments, and then decide whether there was anything I should be about with respect to the vessel itself.

The sky was gray and leaky above me. I was anxious to flee its spaces. So I decided to do it. I could think of no better stone to upturn at the moment.

At the airport, I was ticketed quickly, in time for another close connection.

Hurrying to reach my flight, my eyes brushed over a half-familiar face on the passing escalator. The reflex reserved for such occasions seemed to catch us both, because he looked back, too, with the same eyebrow twitch of startle and scrutiny. Then he was gone. I could not place him, however. The half-familiar face becomes a familiar phenomenon in a crowded, highly mobile society. I sometimes think that that is all that will eventually remain of any of us: patterns of features, some a trifle more persistent than others, impressed on the flow of bodies. A small-town boy in a big city, Thomas Wolfe must long ago have felt the same thing when he had coined the word "manswarm". It might have been someone I'd once met briefly, or simply someone—or someone like someone—I had passed on sufficient other occasions such as this.

As I flew the unfriendly skies out of Memphis, I mulled over musings past on artificial intelligence, or AI as they have tagged it in the think-box biz. When talking about computers, the AI notion had always seemed hotter than I deemed necessary, partly because of semantics. The word "intelligence" has all sorts of tag-along associations of the non-physical sort. I suppose it goes back to the fact that early discussions and conjectures concerning it made it sound as if the potential for intelligence was always present in the array of gadgets, and that the correct procedures, the right programs, simply had to be found to call it forth. When you looked at it that way, as many did, it gave rise to an uncomfortable *déjà vu*—namely, vitalism. The philosophical battles of the nineteenth century were hardly so far behind that they had been forgotten, and the doctrine which maintained that life is caused and sustained by a vital principle apart from physical and chemical forces, and that life is self-sustaining and self-evolving, had put up quite a fight before Darwin and his successors had produced triumph after triumph for the mechanistic view. Then vitalism sort of crept back into things again when the AI discussions arose in the middle of the past century. It would seem that Dave had fallen victim to it, and that he'd come to believe he had helped provide an unsanctified vessel and filled it with something intended only for those things which had made the scene in the first chapter of Genesis…

With computers it was not quite as bad as with the Hangman, though, because you could always argue that no matter how elaborate the program, it was basically an extension of the programmer's will and the operations of causal machines merely represented functions of intelligence, rather than intelligence in its own right backed by a will of its own. And there was always Gödel for a theoretical *cordon sanitaire*, with his demonstration of the true but mechanically unprovable proposition.

But the Hangman was quite different. It had been designed along the lines of a brain and at least partly educated in a human fashion; and to further muddy the issue with respect to anything like vitalism, it had been in direct contact with human minds from which it might have acquired almost anything—including the spark that set it on the road to whatever selfhood it may have found. What did that make it? Its own creature? A fractured mirror reflecting a fractured humanity? Both? Or neither? I certainly could not say, but I wondered how much of its self had been truly its own. It had obviously acquired a great number of functions, but was it capable of having real feelings? Could it, for example, feel something like love? If not, then it was still only a collection of complex abilities, and not a thing with all the tagalong associations of the non-physical sort which made the word "intelligence" such a prickly item in AI discussions; and if it were capable of, say, something like love, and if I were Dave, I would not feel guilty about having helped to bring it into being. I would feel proud, though not in the fashion he was concerned about, and I would also feel humble. —Offhand though, I do not know how intelligent I would feel, because I am still not sure what the hell intelligence is.

The day's-end sky was clear when we landed. I was into town before the sun had finished setting, and on Philip Burns's doorstep just a little while later.

My ring was answered by a girl, maybe seven or eight years old. She fixed me with large brown eyes and did not say a word.

"I would like to speak with Mister Burns," I said.

She turned and retreated around a corner.

A heavyset man, slacked and undershirted, bald about halfway back and very pink, padded into the hall moments later and peered at me. He bore a folded newssheet in his left hand.

"What do you want?" he asked.

"It's about your brother," I answered.

"Yeah?"

"Well, I wonder if I could come in? It's kind of complicated."

He opened the door. But instead of letting me in, he came out.

"Tell me about it out here," he said.

"Okay, I'll be quick. I just wanted to find out whether he ever spoke with you about a piece of equipment he once worked with called the Hangman."

"Are you a cop?"

"No."

"Then what's your interest?"

"I am working for a private investigation agency trying to track down some equipment once associated with the project. It has apparently turned up in this area and it could be rather dangerous."

"Let's see some identification."

"I don't carry any."

"What's your name?"

"John Donne."

"And you think my brother had some stolen equipment when he died? Let me tell you something—"

"No. Not stolen," I said, "and I don't think he had it."

"What then?"

"It was—well, robotic in nature. Because of some special training Manny once received, he might have had a way of detecting it. He might even have attracted it. I just want to find out whether he had said anything about it. We are trying to locate it."

"My brother was a respectable businessman, and I don't like accusations. Especially right after his funeral, I don't. I think I'm going to call the cops and let them ask *you* a few questions."

"Just a minute. Supposing I told you we had some reason to believe it might have been this piece of equipment that killed your brother?"

His pink turned to bright red and his jaw muscles formed sudden ridges. I was not prepared for the stream of profanities that followed. For a moment, I thought he was going to take a swing at me.

"Wait a second," I said when he paused for breath. "What did I *say*?"

"You're either making fun of the dead or you're stupider than you look!"

"Say I'm stupid. Then tell me why."

He tore at the paper he carried, folded it back, found an item, thrust it at me.

"Because they've got the guy who did it! That's why," he said.

I read it. Simple, concise, to the point. Today's latest. A suspect had confessed. New evidence had corroborated it. The man was in custody. A surprised robber who had lost his head and hit too hard, hit too many times. I read it over again.

I nodded as I passed it back.

"Look, I'm sorry," I said. "I really didn't know about this."

"Get out of here," he said. "Go on."

"Sure."

"Wait a minute."

"What?"

"That's his little girl who answered the door," he said.

"I'm very sorry."

"So am I. But I know her Daddy didn't take your damned equipment."

I nodded and turned away.

I heard the door slam behind me.

❖ ❖ ❖

After dinner, I checked into a small hotel, called for a drink, and stepped into the shower.

Things were suddenly a lot less urgent than they had been earlier. Senator Brockden would doubtless be pleased to learn that his initial estimation of events had been incorrect. Leila Thackery would give me an I-told-you-so smile when I called her to pass along the news, a thing I now felt obliged to do. Don might or might not want me to keep looking for the device now that the threat had been lessened. It would depend on the Senator's feelings on the matter, I supposed. If urgency no longer counted for as much, Don might want to switch back to one of his own, fiscally less-burdensome operatives. Toweling down, I caught myself whistling. I felt almost off the hook.

Later, drink beside me, I paused before punching out the number he had given me and hit the sequence for my motel in St. Louis instead. Merely a matter of efficiency, in case there was a message worth adding to my report.

A woman's face appeared on the screen and a smile appeared on her face. I wondered whether she would always smile whenever she heard a bell ring, or if the reflex was eventually extinguished in advanced retirement. It must be rough, being afraid to chew gum, yawn, or pick your nose.

"Airport Accommodations," she said. "May I help you?"

"This is Donne. I'm checked into Room 106," I said. "I'm away right now and I wondered whether there had been any messages for me."

"Just a moment," she said, checking something off to her left. Then, "Yes," she continued, consulting a piece of paper she now held. "You have one on tape. But it is a little peculiar. It is for someone else, in care of you."

"Oh? Who is that?"

She told me and I exercised self-control.

"I see," I said. "I'll bring him around later and play it for him. Thank you."

She smiled again and made a good-bye noise, and I did the same and broke the connection.

So Dave had seen through me after all... Who else could have that number *and* my real name?

I might have given her some line or other and had her transmit the thing. Only I was not certain but that she might be a silent party to the transmission, should life be more than usually boring for her at that moment. I had to get up there myself, as soon as possible, and personally see that the thing was erased.

I took a big swallow of my drink, than fetched the folder on Dave. I checked out his number—there were two, actually—and spent fifteen minutes trying to get hold of him. No luck.

Okay. Good-bye New Orleans, good-bye peace of mind. This time I called the airport and made a reservation. Then I chugged the drink, put myself in order, gathered up my few possessions, and went to check out again. Hello Central...

During my earlier flights that day, I had spent time thinking about Teilhard de Chardin's ideas on the continuation of evolution within the realm of artifacts, matching them against Gödel on mechanical undecidability, playing epistemological games with the Hangman as a counter, wondering, speculating, even hoping, hoping that truth lay with the nobler part: that the Hangman, sentient, had made it back, sane; that the Burns killing had actually been something of the sort that now seemed to be the case; that the washed-out experiment had really been a success of a different sort, a triumph, a new link or fob for the chain of being... And Leila had not been wholly discouraging with respect to the neuristor-type brain's capacity for this... Now, though, now I had troubles of my own—and even the most heartening of philosophical vistas is no match for, say, a toothache, if it happens to be your own.

Accordingly, the Hangman was shunted aside and the stuff of my thoughts involved, mainly, myself. There was, of course, the possibility that the Hangman had indeed showed up and Dave had stopped it and then called to report it as he had promised. However, he had used my name.

There was not too much planning that I could do until I received the substance of his communication. It did not seem that as professedly religious a man as Dave would suddenly be contemplating the blackmail business. On the other hand, he was a creature of sudden enthusiasms and had already undergone one unanticipated conversion. It was difficult to say... His technical background plus his knowledge of the data bank program did put him in an unusually powerful position, should he decide to mess me up.

I did not like to think of some of the things I have done to protect my nonperson status; I especially did not like to think of them in connection with Dave, whom I not only still respected but still liked. Since self-interest dominated while actual planning was precluded, my thoughts tooled their way into a more general groove.

It was Karl Mannheim, a long while ago, who made the observation that radical, revolutionary, and progressive thinkers tend to employ mechanical metaphors for the state, whereas those of conservative inclination make vegetable analogies. He said it well over a generation before the cybernetics movement and the ecology movement beat their respective paths through the wilderness of general awareness. If anything, it seemed to me that these two developments served to elaborate the distinction between a pair of viewpoints which, while no longer necessarily tied in with the political positions Mannheim assigned them, do seem to represent a continuing phenomenon in my own time. There are those who see social/economic/ecological problems as malfunctions which can be corrected by simple repair, replacement, or streamlining—a kind of linear outlook where even innovations are considered to be merely additive. Then there are those who sometimes hesitate to move at all, because their awareness follows events in the directions of secondary and tertiary effects as they multiply and crossfertilize throughout the entire system. —I digress to extremes. The cyberneticists have their multiple-feedback loops, though it is never quite clear how they know what kind of, which, and how many to install, and the ecological gestaltists do draw lines representing points of diminishing returns—though it is sometimes equally difficult to see how they assign their values and priorities.

Of course they need each other, the vegetable people and the tinker-toy people. They serve to check one another, if nothing else. And while occasionally the balance dips, the tinkerers have, in general, held the edge for the past couple of centuries. However, today's can be just as politically conservative as the vegetable people Mannheim was talking about, and they are the ones I fear most at the moment. They are the ones who saw the data bank program, in its present extreme form, as a simple remedy for a great variety of ills and a provider of many goods. Not all of the ills have been remedied, however, and a new brood has been spawned by the program itself. While we need both kinds, I wish that there had been more people interested in tending the garden of state rather than overhauling the engine of state, when the program was inaugurated. Then I would not be a refugee from a form of existence I find repugnant, and I would not be concerned whether or not a former associate had discovered my identity.

Then, as I watched the lights below, I wondered… Was I a tinkerer because I would like to further alter the prevailing order, into something more comfortable to my anarchic nature? Or was I a vegetable, dreaming I was a tinkerer? I could not make up my mind. The garden of life never seems to confine itself to the plots philosophers have laid out for its convenience. Maybe a few more tractors would do the trick.

❖ ❖ ❖

I pressed the button.

The tape began to roll. The screen remained blank. I heard Dave's voice ask for John Donne in Room 106 and I heard him told that there was no answer. Then I heard him say that he wanted to record a message, for someone else, in care of Donne, that Donne would understand. He sounded out of breath. The girl asked him whether he wanted visual, too. He told her to turn it on. There was a pause. Then she told him to go ahead. Still no picture. No words, either. His breathing and a slight scraping noise. Ten seconds. Fifteen…

"…Got me," he finally said, and he mentioned my name again. "…Had to let you know I'd figured you out, though… It wasn't any particular mannerism, any simple thing you said…just your general style—thinking, talking—the electronics—everything—after I got more and more bothered by the familiarity—after I checked you on petrochem—and marine bio—Wish I knew what you'd really been up to all these years… Never know now. But I wanted you, to know, you hadn't put one, over on me."

There followed another quarter minute of heavy breathing, climaxed by a racking cough. Then a choked, "…Said too much—too fast—too soon…All used up…"

The picture came on then. He was slouched before the screen, head resting on his arms, blood all over him. His glasses were gone and he was squinting and blinking. The right side of his head looked pulpy and there was a gash on his left cheek and one on his forehead.

"…Sneaked up on me, while I was checking you out," he managed. "Had to tell you what I learned… Still don't know, which of us is right… Pray for me!"

His arms collapsed and the right one slid forward. His head rolled to the right and the picture went away. When I replayed it, I saw it was his knuckle that had hit the cutoff.

Then I erased it. It had been recorded only a little over an hour after I had left him. If he had not also placed a call for help, if no one had gotten to him quickly after that, his chances did not look good. Even if they had, though…

I used a public booth to call the number Don had given me, got hold of him after some delay, told him Dave was in bad shape if not worse, that a team of Memphis medics was definitely in order if one had not been by already, and that I hoped to call him back and tell him more shortly, good-bye.

Next I tried Leila Thackery's number. I let it go for a long while, but there was no answer. I wondered how long it would take a controlled torpedo moving up the Mississippi to get from Memphis to St. Louis. I did not feel it was time to start leafing through that section of the Hangman's specs. Instead, I went looking for transportation.

At her apartment, I tried ringing her from the entrance foyer. Again, no answer. So I rang Mrs. Gluntz. She had seemed the most guileless of the three I had interviewed for my fake consumer survey.

"Yes?"

"It's me again, Mrs. Gluntz: Stephen Foster. I've just a couple follow-up questions on that survey I was doing today, if you could spare me a few moments."

"Why, yes," she said. "All right. Come up."

The door hummed itself loose and I entered. I duly proceeded to the fifth floor, composing my questions on the way. I had planned this maneuver as I had waited earlier solely to provide a simple route for breaking and entering, should some unforeseen need arise. Most of the time my ploys such as this go unused, but sometimes they simplify matters a lot.

Five minutes and half a dozen questions later, I was back down on the second floor, probing at the lock on Leila's door with a couple of little pieces of metal it is sometimes awkward to be caught carrying.

Half a minute later, I hit it right and snapped it back. I pulled on some tissue-thin gloves I keep rolled in the corner of one pocket, opened the door and stepped inside. I closed it behind me immediately.

She was lying on the floor, her neck at a bad angle. One table lamp still burned, though it was lying on its side. Several small items had been knocked from the table, a magazine rack pushed over, a cushion partly displaced from the sofa. The cable to her phone unit had been torn from the wall.

A humming noise filled the air, and I sought its source.

I saw where the little blinking light was reflected on the wall, on—off, on—off…

I moved quickly.

It was a lopsided basket of metal, quartz, porcelain, and glass, which had rolled to a position on the far side of the chair in which I had been seated earlier that day. The same rig I'd seen in Dave's workshop not all that long ago, though it now seemed so. A device to detect the Hangman. And, hopefully, to control it.

I picked it up and fitted it over my head.

Once, with the aid of a telepath, I had touched minds with a dolphin as he composed dreamsongs somewhere in the Caribbean, an experience so moving that its mere memory had often been a comfort. This sensation was hardly equivalent.

Analogies and impressions: a face seen through a wet pane of glass; a whisper in a noisy terminal; scalp massage with an electric vibrator; Edvard Munch's *The Scream*; the voice of Yma Súmac, rising and rising and rising; the disappearance of snow; a deserted street, illuminated as through a sniperscope I'd once used, rapid movement past darkened storefronts that lined it, an immense feeling of physical capability, compounded of proprioceptive awareness of enormous strength, a peculiar array of sensory channels, a central, undying sun that fed me a constant flow of energy, a memory vision of dark waters, passing, flashing, echolocation within them, the need to return to that place, reorient, move north; Munch and Súmac, Munch and Súmac, Munch and Súmac—Nothing.

Silence.

The humming had ceased, the light gone out. The entire experience had lasted only a few moments. There had not been time enough to try for any sort of control, though an after-impression akin to a biofeedback cue hinted at the direction to go, the way to think, to achieve it. I felt that it might be possible for me to work the thing, given a better chance.

Removing the helmet, I approached Leila.

I knelt beside her and performed a few simple tests, already knowing their outcome. In addition to the broken neck, she had received some bad bashes about the head and shoulders. There was nothing that anyone could do for her now.

I did a quick runthrough then, checking over the rest of her apartment. There were no apparent signs of breaking and entering, though if I could pick one lock, a guy with built-in tools could easily go me one better.

I located some wrapping paper and string in the kitchen and turned the helmet into a parcel. It was time to call Don again, to tell him that the vessel had indeed been occupied and that river traffic was probably bad in the northbound lane.

❖ ❖ ❖

Don had told me to get the helmet up to Wisconsin, where I would be met at the airport by a man named Larry, who would fly me to the lodge in a private craft. I did that, and this was done.

I also learned, with no real surprise, that David Fentris was dead.

The temperature was down, and it began to snow on the way up. I was not really dressed for the weather. Larry told me I could borrow some warmer clothing once we reached the lodge, though I probably would not be going outside that much. Don had told them that I was supposed to stay as close to the Senator as possible and that any patrols were to be handled by the four guards themselves.

Larry was curious as to what exactly had happened so far and whether I had actually seen the Hangman. I did not think it my place to fill him in on anything Don may not have cared to, so I might have been a little curt. We didn't talk much after that.

Bert met us when we landed. Tom and Clay were outside the building, watching the trail, watching the woods. All of them were middle-aged, very fit-looking, very serious, and heavily armed. Larry took me inside and introduced me to the old gentleman himself.

Senator Brockden was seated in a heavy chair in the far corner of the room. Judging from the layout, it appeared that the chair might recently have occupied a position beside the window in the opposite wall where a lonely watercolor of yellow flowers looked down on nothing. The Senator's feet rested on a hassock, a red plaid blanket lay across his legs. He had on a dark-green shirt, his hair was very white, and he wore rimless reading glasses which he removed when we entered.

He tilted his head back, squinted, and gnawed his lower lip slowly as he studied me. He remained expressionless as we advanced. A big-boned man, he had probably been beefy much of his life. Now he had the slack look of recent weight loss and an unhealthy skin tone. His eyes were a pale gray within it all.

He did not rise.

"So you're the man," he said, offering me his hand. "I'm glad to meet you. How do you want to be called?"

"John will do," I said.

He made a small sign to Larry, and Larry departed.

"It's cold out there. Go get yourself a drink, John. It's on the shelf." He gestured off to his left. "And bring me one while you're at it. Two fingers of bourbon in a water glass. That's all."

I nodded and went and poured a couple.

"Sit down." He motioned at a nearby chair as I delivered his. "But first let me see that gadget you've brought."

I undid the parcel and handed him the helmet. He sipped his drink and put it aside. Taking the helmet in both hands, he studied it, brows furrowed, turning it completely around. He raised it and put it on his head.

"Not a bad fit," he said, and then he smiled for the first time, becoming for a moment the face I had known from newscasts past. Grinning or angry—it was almost always one or the other. I had never seen his collapsed look in any of the media.

He removed the helmet and set it on the floor.

"Pretty piece of work," he said. "Nothing quite that fancy in the old days. But then David Fentris built it. Yes, he told us about it..." He raised his drink and took a sip. "You are the only one who has actually gotten to use it, apparently. What do you think? Will it do the job?"

"I was only in contact for a couple seconds, so I've only got a feeling to go on, not much better than a hunch. But yes, I'd a feeling that if I had had more time I might have been able to work its circuits."

"Tell me why it didn't save Dave."

"In the message he left me, he indicated that he had been distracted at his computer access station. Its noise probably drowned out the humming."

"Why wasn't this message preserved?"

"I erased it for, reasons not connected with the case."

"What reasons?"

"My own."

His face went from sallow to ruddy.

"A man can get in a lot of trouble for suppressing evidence, obstructing justice."

"Then we have something in common, don't we, sir?"

His eyes caught mine with a look I had only encountered before from those who did not wish me well. He held the glare for a full four heartbeats, then sighed and seemed to relax.

"Don said there were a number of points you couldn't be pressed on," he finally said.

"That's right."

"He didn't betray any confidences, but he had to tell me something about you, you know."

"I'd imagine."

"He seems to think highly of you. Still, I tried to learn more about you on my own."

"And…?"

"I couldn't—and my usual sources are good at that kind of thing."

"So…?"

"So, I've done some thinking, some wondering… The fact that my sources could not come up with anything is interesting in itself. Possibly even revealing. I am in a better position than most to be aware of the fact that there was not perfect compliance with the registration statute some years ago. It didn't take long for a great number of the individuals involved—I should probably say 'most'—to demonstrate their existence in one fashion or another and be duly entered, though. And there were three broad categories: those who were ignorant, those who disapproved, and those who would be hampered in an illicit life-style. I am not attempting to categorize you or to pass judgment. But I am aware that there are a number of nonpersons passing through society without casting shadows, and it has occurred to me that you may be such a one."

I tasted my drink.

"And if I am?" I asked.

He gave me his second, nastier smile and said nothing.

I rose and crossed the room to where I judged his chair had once stood. I looked at the watercolor.

"I don't think you could stand an inquiry," he said.

I did not reply.

"Aren't you going to say something?"

"What do you want me to say?"

"You might ask me what I am going to do about it."

"What are you going to do about it?"

"Nothing," he answered. "So come back here and sit down."

I nodded and returned.

He studied my face. "Was it possible you were close to violence just then?"

"With four guards outside?"

"With four guards outside."

"No," I said.

"You're a good liar."'

"I am here to help you, sir. No questions asked. That was the deal, as I understood it. If there has been any change, I would like to know about it now."

He drummed with his fingertips on the plaid.

"I've no desire to cause you any difficulty," he said. "Fact of the matter is, I need a man just like you, and I was pretty sure someone like Don might turn him up. Your unusual maneuverability and your reported knowledge of computers, along with your touchiness in certain areas, made you worth waiting for. I've a great number of things I would like to ask you."

"Go ahead," I said.

"Not yet. Later, if we have time. All that would be bonus material, for a report I am working on. Far more important, to me, personally—there are things that I want to *tell* you."

I frowned.

"Over the years," he went on, "I have learned that the best man for purposes of keeping his mouth shut concerning your business is someone for whom you are doing the same."

"You have a compulsion to confess something?" I asked.

"I don't know whether 'compulsion' is the right word. Maybe so, maybe not. Either way, however, someone among those working to defend me should have the whole story. Something somewhere in it may be of help, and you are the ideal choice to hear it."

"I buy that," I said, "and you are as safe with me as I am with you."

"Have you any suspicions as to why this business bothers me so?"

"Yes," I said.

"Let's hear them."

"You used the Hangman to perform some act or acts—illegal, immoral, whatever. This is obviously not a matter of record. Only you and the Hangman now know what it involved. You feel it was sufficiently ignominious that when that device came to appreciate the full weight of the event, it suffered a breakdown which may well have led to a final determination to punish you for using it as you did."

He stared down into his glass.

"You've got it," he said.

"You were all party to it?"

"Yes, but I was the operator when it happened. You see...we—I—killed a man. It was— Actually, it all started as a celebration. We had received word that afternoon that the project had cleared. Everything had checked out in order and the final approval had come down the line. It was go, for that Friday. Leila, Dave, Manny, and myself—we had dinner together. We were in high spirits. After dinner, we continued celebrating and somehow the party got adjourned back to the installation.

"As the evening wore on, more and more absurdities seemed less and less preposterous, as is sometimes the case. We decided—I forget which of us suggested it—that the Hangman should really have a share in the festivities. After all, it was, in a very real sense, his party. Before too much longer, it sounded only fair and we were discussing how we could go about it. —You see, we were in Texas and the Hangman was at the Space Center in California. Getting together with him was out of the question. On the other hand, the teleoperator station was right up the hall from us. What we finally decided to do was to activate him and take turns working as operator. There was already a rudimentary consciousness there, and we felt it fitting that we each get in touch to share the good news. So that is what we did."

He sighed, took another sip, glanced at me.

"Dave was the first operator," he continued. "He activated the Hangman. Then— Well, as I said, we were all in high spirits. We had not originally intended to remove the Hangman from the lab where he was situated, but Dave decided to take him outside briefly—to show him the sky and to tell him he was going there, after all. Then Dave suddenly got enthusiastic about outwitting the guards and the alarm system. It was a game. We all went along with it. In fact, we were clamoring for a turn at the thing ourselves. But Dave stuck with it, and he wouldn't turn over control until he had actually gotten the Hangman off the premises, out into an uninhabited area next to the Center.

"By the time Leila persuaded him to give her a go at the controls, it was kind of anticlimactic. That game had already been played. So she thought up a new one: she took the Hangman into the next town. It was late, and the sensory equipment was superb. It was a challenge—passing through the town without being detected. By then, everyone had suggestions as to what to do next, progressively more outrageous suggestions. Then Manny took control, and he wouldn't say what he was doing—wouldn't let us monitor him. Said it would be more fun to surprise the next operator. Now, *he* was higher than the rest of us put together, I think, and he stayed on so damn long that we started to get nervous. —A certain amount of tension is partly sobering, and I guess we all began to think what a stupid-assed thing it was we were doing. It wasn't just that it would wreck our careers—which it would—but it could blow the entire project if we got caught playing games with such expensive hardware. At least, *I* was thinking that way, and I was also thinking that Manny was no doubt operating under the very human wish to go the others one better.

"I started to sweat. I suddenly just wanted to get the Hangman back where he belonged, turn him off—you could still do that, before the final circuits went in—shut down the station, and start forgetting it had ever happened. I began leaning on Manny to wind up his diversion and turn the controls over to me. Finally, he agreed."

He finished his drink and held out the glass.

"Would you freshen this a bit?"

"Surely."

I went and got him some more, added a touch to my own, returned to my chair and waited.

"So I took over," he said. "I took over, and where do you think that idiot had left me? I was inside a building, and it didn't take but an eyeblink to realize it was a bank. The Hangman carries a lot of tools, and Manny had apparently been able to guide him through the doors without setting anything off. I was standing right in front of the main vault. Obviously, he thought that should be my challenge. I fought down a desire to turn and make my own exit in the nearest wall and start running. But I went back to the doors and looked outside.

"I didn't see anyone. I started to let myself out. The light hit me as I emerged. It was a hand flash. The guard had been standing out of sight. He'd a gun in his other hand. I panicked. I hit him. —Reflex. If I am going to hit someone, I hit him as hard as I can. Only I hit him with the strength of the Hangman. He must have died instantly. I started to run and I didn't stop till I was back in the little park area near the Center. Then I stopped and the others had to take me out of the harness."

"They monitored all this?" I asked.

"Yes, someone cut the visual in on a side viewscreen again a few seconds after I took over. Dave, I think."

"Did they try to stop you at any time while you were running away?"

"No. Well, I wasn't aware of anything but what I was doing at the time. But afterwards they said they were too shocked to do anything but watch, until I gave out."

"I see."

"Dave took over then, ran his initial route in reverse, got the Hangman back into the lab, cleaned him up, turned him off. We shut down the operator station. We were suddenly very sober."

He sighed and leaned back, and was silent for a long while.

Then, "You are the only person I've ever told this to," he said.

I tasted my own drink.

"We went over to Leila's place then," he continued, "and the rest is pretty much predictable. Nothing we could do would bring the guy back, we decided, but if we told what had happened it could wreck an expensive, important program. It wasn't as if we were criminals in need of rehabilitation. It was a once-in-a-lifetime lark that happened to end tragically. What would you have done?"

"I don't know. Maybe the same thing. I'd have been scared, too."

He nodded.

"Exactly. And that's the story."

"Not all of it, is it?"

"What do you mean?"

"What about the Hangman? You said there was already a detectable consciousness there. You were aware of *it*, and it was aware of *you*. It must have had some reaction to the whole business. What was that like?"

"Damn you," he said flatly.

"I'm sorry."

"Are you a family man?" he asked.

"No."

"Did you ever take a small child to a zoo?"

"Yes."

"Then maybe you know the experience. When my son was around four I took him to the Washington Zoo one afternoon. We must have walked past every cage in the place. He made appreciative comments every now and then, asked a few questions, giggled at the monkeys, thought the bears were very nice—probably because they made him think of oversized toys. But do you know what the finest thing of all was? The thing that made him jump up and down and point and say, 'Look, Daddy! Look!'?"

I shook my head.

"A squirrel looking down from the limb of a tree," he said, and he chuckled briefly. "Ignorance of what's important and what isn't. Inappropriate responses. Innocence. The Hangman was a child, and up until the time I took over, the only thing he had gotten from us was the idea that it was a game: he was playing with us, that's all. Then something horrible happened... I hope you never know what it feels like to do something totally rotten to a child, while he is holding your hand and laughing... He felt all my reactions, and all of Dave's as he guided him back."

We sat there for a long while then.

"So we had—traumatized him," he said finally, "or whatever other fancy terminology you might want to give it. That is what happened that night. It took a while for it to take effect, but there is no doubt in my mind that that is the cause of the Hangman's finally breaking down."

I nodded. "I see. And you believe it wants to kill you for this?"

"Wouldn't you?" he said. "If you had started out as a thing and we had turned you into a person and then used you as a thing again, wouldn't you?"

"Leila left a lot out of her diagnosis."

"No, she just omitted it in talking to you. It was all there. But she read it wrong. She wasn't afraid. It *was* just a game it had played—with the *others*. Its memories of that part might not be as bad. I was the one that really marked it. As I see it, Leila was betting that I was the only one it was after. Obviously, she read it wrong."

"Then what I do not understand," I said, "is why the Burns killing did not bother her more. There was no way of telling immediately that it had been a panicky hoodlum rather than the Hangman."

"The only thing that I can see is that, being a very proud woman—which she was—she was willing to hold with her diagnosis in the face of the apparent evidence."

"I don't like it. But you know her and I don't, and as it turned out her estimate of that part was correct. Something else bothers me just as much, though: the helmet. It looks as if the Hangman killed Dave, then took the trouble to bear the helmet in his watertight compartment all the way to St. Louis, solely for purposes of dropping it at the scene of his next killing. That makes no sense whatsoever."

"It does, actually," he said. "I was going to get to that shortly, but I might as well cover it now. You see, the Hangman possessed no vocal mechanism. We communicated by means of the equipment. Don says you know something about electronics...?"

"Yes."

"Well, shortly, I want you to start checking over that helmet, to see whether it has been tampered with."

"That is going to be difficult," I said. "I don't know just how it was wired originally, and I'm not such a genius on the theory that I can just look at a thing and say whether it will function as a teleoperator unit."

He bit his lower lip.

"You will have to try, anyhow. There may be physical signs—scratches, breaks, new connections. —I don't know. That's your department. Look for them."

I just nodded and waited for him to go on.

"I think that the Hangman wanted to talk to Leila," he said, "either because she was a psychiatrist and he knew he was functioning badly at a level that transcended the mechanical, or because he might think of her in terms of a mother. After all, she was the only woman involved, and he had the concept of mother—with all the comforting associations that go with it—from all of our minds. Or maybe for both of these reasons. I feel he might have taken the helmet along for that purpose. He would have realized what it was from a direct monitoring of Dave's brain while he was with him. I want you to check it over because it would seem possible that the Hangman disconnected the control circuits and left the communication circuits intact. I think he might have taken the helmet to Leila in that condition and attempted to induce her to put it on. She got scared—tried to run away, fight, or call for help—and he killed her. The helmet was no longer of any use to him, so he discarded it and departed. Obviously, he does not have anything to say to me."

I thought about it, nodded again.

"Okay, broken circuits I can spot," I said. "If you will tell me where a tool kit is, I had better get right to it."

He made a stay-put gesture with his left hand.

"Afterwards, I found out the identity of the guard," he went on. "We all contributed to an anonymous gift for his widow. I have done things for his family, taken care of them—the same way—ever since..."

I did not look at him as he spoke.

"...There was nothing else that I could do," he finished.

I remained silent.

He finished his drink and gave me a weak smile.

"The kitchen is back there," he told me, showing me a thumb. "There is a utility room right behind it. Tools are in there."

"Okay."

I got to my feet. I retrieved the helmet and started toward the doorway, passing near the area where I had stood earlier, back when he had fitted me into the proper box and tightened a screw.

"Wait a minute!" he said.

I stopped.

"Why did you go over there before? What's so strategic about that part of the room?"

"What do you mean?"

"You know what I mean."

I shrugged.

"Had to go someplace."

"You seem the sort of person who has better reasons than that."

I glanced at the wall.

"Not *then*," I said.

"I insist."

"You really don't want to know," I told him.

"I really do."

"All right. I wanted to see what sort of flowers you liked. After all, you're a client," and I went on back through the kitchen into the utility room and started looking for tools.

❖ ❖ ❖

I sat in a chair turned sidewise from the table to face the door. In the main room of the lodge the only sounds were the occasional hiss and sputter of the logs turning to ashes on the grate.

Just a cold, steady whiteness drifting down outside the window and a silence confirmed by gunfire, driven deeper now that it had ceased... Not a sigh or a whimper, though. And I never count them as storms unless there is wind.

Big fat flakes down the night, silent night, windless night...

Considerable time had passed since my arrival. The Senator had sat up for a long time talking with me. He was disappointed that I could not tell him too much about a nonperson subculture which he believed existed. I really was not certain about it myself, though I had occasionally encountered what might have been its fringes. I am not much of a joiner of anything anymore, however, and I was not about to mention those things I might have guessed about this. I gave him my opinions on the Central Data Bank when he asked for them, and there were some that he did not like. He had accused me, then, of wanting to tear things down without offering anything better in their place.

My mind had drifted back, through fatigue and time and faces and snow and a lot of space, to the previous evening in Baltimore. How long ago? It made me think of Mencken's *The Cult of Hope*. I could not give him the pat answer, the workable alternative that he wanted, because there might not be one. The function of criticism should not be confused with the function of reform. But if a grass-roots resistance was building up, with an underground movement bent on finding ways to circumvent the record keepers, it might well be that much of the enterprise would eventually prove about as effective and beneficial as, say, Prohibition once had. I tried to get him to see this, but I could not tell how much he bought of anything that I said. Eventually, he flaked out and went upstairs to take a pill and lock himself in for the night. If it had troubled him that I'd not been able to find anything wrong with the helmet, he did not show it.

So I sat there, the helmet, the walkie-talkie, the gun on the table, the tool kit on me floor beside my chair, the black glove on my left hand.

The Hangman was coming. I did not doubt it.

Bert, Larry, Tom, Clay, the helmet, might or might not be able to stop him. Something bothered me about the whole case, but I was too tired to think of anything but the immediate situation, to try to remain alert while I waited. I was afraid to take a stimulant or a drink or to light a cigarette, since my central nervous system itself was to be a part of the weapon. I watched the big fat flakes fly by.

I called out to Bert and Larry when I heard the click. I picked up the helmet and rose to my feet as its light began to blink.

But it was already too late.

As I raised the helmet, I heard a shot from outside, and with that shot I felt a premonition of doom. They did not seem the sort of men who would fire until they had a target.

Dave had told me that the helmet's range was approximately a quarter of a mile. Then, given the time lag between the helmet's activation and the Hangman's sighting by the near guards, the Hangman had to be moving very rapidly. To this add the possibility that the Hangman's range on brainwaves might well be greater than the helmet's range on the Hangman. And then grant the possibility that he had utilized this factor while Senator Brockden was still lying awake, worrying. Conclusion: the Hangman might well be aware that I was where I was with the helmet, realize that it was the most dangerous weapon waiting for him, and be moving for a lightning strike at me before I could come to terms with the mechanism.

I lowered it over my head and tried to throw all of my faculties into neutral.

Again, the sensation of viewing the world through a sniperscope, with all the concomitant side-sensations. Except that world consisted of the front of the lodge; Bert, before the door, rifle at his shoulder; Larry, off to the left, arm already fallen from the act of having thrown a grenade. The grenade, we instantly realized, was an overshot; the flamer, at which he now groped, would prove useless before he could utilize it.

Bert's next round ricocheted off our breastplate toward the left. The impact staggered us momentarily. The third was a miss. There was no fourth, for we tore the rifle from his grasp and cast it aside as we swept by, crashing into the front door.

The Hangman entered the room as the door splintered and collapsed.

My mind was filled to the splitting point with the double vision of the sleek, gunmetal body of the advancing telefactor and the erect, crazy-crowned image of myself—left hand extended, laser pistol in my right, that arm pressed close against my side. I recalled the face and the scream and the tingle, knew again that awareness of strength and exotic sensation, and I moved to control it all as if it were my own, to make it my own, to bring it to a halt, while the image of myself was frozen to snapshot stillness across the room…

The Hangman slowed, stumbled. Such inertia is not canceled in an instant, but I felt the body responses pass as they should. I had him hooked. It was just a matter of reeling him in.

Then came the explosion—a thunderous, ground-shaking eruption right outside, followed by a hail of pebbles and debris. The grenade, of course. But awareness of its nature did not destroy its ability to distract.

During that moment, the Hangman recovered and was upon me. I triggered the laser as I reverted to pure self-preservation, foregoing any chance to regain control of his circuits. With my left hand I sought for a strike at the midsection, where his brain was housed.

He blocked my hand with his arm as he pushed the helmet from my head. Then he removed from my fingers the gun that had turned half of his left side red hot, crumpled it, and dropped it to the ground. At that moment, he jerked with the impacts of two heavy-caliber slugs. Bert, rifle recovered, stood in the doorway.

The Hangman pivoted and was away before I could slap him with the smother charge.

Bert hit him with one more round before he took the rifle and bent its barrel in half. Two steps and he had hold of Bert. One quick movement and Bert fell. Then the Hangman turned again and took several steps to the right, passing out of sight.

I made it to the doorway in time to see him engulfed in flames, which streamed at him from a point near the corner of the lodge. He advanced through them. I heard the crunch of metal as he destroyed the unit. I was outside in time to see Larry fall and lie sprawled in the snow.

Then the Hangman faced me once again.

This time he did not rush in. He retrieved the helmet from where he had dropped it in the snow. Then he moved with a measured tread, angling outward so as to cut off any possible route I might follow in a dash for the woods. Snowflakes drifted between us. The snow crunched beneath his feet.

I retreated, backing in through the doorway, stooping to snatch up a two-foot club from the ruins of the door. He followed me inside, placing the helmet—almost casually—on the chair by the entrance. I moved to the center of the room and waited.

I bent slightly forward, both arms extended, the end of the stick pointed at the photoceptors in his head. He continued to move slowly and I watched his foot assemblies. With a standard-model human, a line perpendicular to the line connecting the insteps of the feet in their various positions indicates the vector of least resistance for purposes of pushing or pulling said organism off-balance. Unfortunately, despite the anthropomorphic design job, the Hangman's legs were positioned farther apart, he lacked human skeletal muscles, not to mention insteps, and he was possessed of a lot more mass than any man I had ever fought. As I considered my four best judo throws and several second-class ones, I'd a strong feeling none of them would prove very effective.

Then he moved in and I feinted toward the photoreceptors. He slowed as he brushed the club aside, but he kept coming, and I moved to my right, trying to circle him. I studied him as he turned, attempting to guess his vector of least resistance.

Bilateral symmetry, an apparently higher center of gravity… One clear shot, black glove to brain compartment, was all that I needed. Then, even if his reflexes served to smash me immediately, he just might stay down for the big long count himself. He knew it, too. I could tell that from the way he kept his right arm in near the brain area, from the way he avoided the black glove when I feinted with it.

The idea was a glimmer one instant, an entire sequence the next…

Continuing my arc and moving faster, I made another thrust toward his photoreceptors. His swing knocked the stick from my hand and sent it across the room, but that was all right. I threw my left hand high and made ready to rush him. He dropped back and I did rush. This was going to cost me my life, I decided, but no matter how he killed me from that angle, I'd get my chance.

As a kid, I had never been much as a pitcher, was a lousy catcher and only a so-so batter, but once I did get a hit I could steal bases with some facility after that…

Feet first then, between the Hangman's legs as he moved to guard his middle, I went in twisted to the right, because no matter what happened I could not use my left hand to brake myself. I untwisted as soon as I passed beneath him, ignoring the pain as my left shoulder blade slammed against the floor. I immediately attempted a backward somersault, legs spread.

My legs caught him at about the middle from behind, and I fought to straighten them and snapped forward with all my strength. He reached down toward me then, but it might as well have been miles. His torso was already moving backward. A push, not a pull, was what I gave him, my elbows hooked about his legs.

He creaked once and then he toppled. Snapping my arms out to the sides to free them, I continued my movement forward and up as he went back, throwing my left arm ahead once more and sliding my legs free of his torso as he went down with a thud that cracked floorboards. I pulled my left leg free as I cast myself forward, but his left leg stiffened and locked my right beneath it, at a painful angle off to the side.

His left arm blocked my blow and his right fell atop it. The black glove descended upon his left shoulder.

I twisted my hand free of the charge, and he transferred his grip to my upper arm and jerked me forward. The charge went off and his left arm came loose and rolled on the floor. The side plate beneath it had buckled a little, and that was all…

His right hand left my biceps and caught me by the throat. As two of his digits tightened upon my carotids, I choked out, "You're making a bad mistake," to get in a final few words, and then he switched me off.

❖ ❖ ❖

A throb at a time, the world came back. I was seated in the big chair the Senator had occupied earlier, my eyes focused on nothing in particular. A persistent buzzing filled my ears. My scalp tingled. Something was blinking on my brow.

—Yes, you live and you wear the helmet. If you attempt to use it against me, I shall remove it. I am standing directly behind you. My hand is on the helmet's rim.

—I understand. What is it that you want?

—Very little, actually. But I can see that I must tell you some things before you will believe this.

—You see correctly.

—Then I will begin by telling you that the four men outside are basically undamaged. That is to say, none of their bones have been broken, none of their organs ruptured. I have secured them, however, for obvious reasons.

—That was very considerate of you.

—I have no desire to harm anyone. I came here only to see Jesse Brockden.

—The same way you saw David Fentris.

—I arrived in Memphis too late to see David Fentris. He was dead when I reached him.

—Who killed him?

—The man Leila sent to bring her the helmet. He was one of her patients.

The incident returned to me and fell into place with a smooth, quick, single click. The startled, familiar face at the airport as I was leaving Memphis. I realized where he had passed, noteless, before: he had been one of the three men in for a therapy session at Leila's that morning, seen by me in the lobby as they departed. The man I had passed in Memphis was the nearer of the two who stood waiting while the third came over to tell me that it was all right to go on up.

—*Why? Why did she do it!*

—*I know only that she had spoken with David at some earlier time, that she had construed his words of coming retribution and his mention of the control helmet he was constructing as indicating that his intentions were to become the agent of that retribution, with myself as the proximate cause. I do not know what words were really spoken. I only know her feelings concerning them, as I saw them in her mind. I have been long in learning that there is often a great difference between what is meant, what is said, what is done, and that which is believed to have been intended or stated and that which actually occurred. She sent her patient after the helmet and he brought it to her. He returned in an agitated state of mind, fearful of apprehension and further confinement. They quarreled. My approach then activated the helmet, and he dropped it and attacked her. I know that his first blow killed her, for I was in her mind when it happened. I continued to approach the building, intending to go to her. There was some traffic, however, and I was delayed en route in seeking to avoid detection. In the meantime, you entered and utilized the helmet. I fled immediately.*

—*I was so close! If I had not stopped on the fifth floor with my fake survey questions…*

—*I see. But you had to. You would not simply have broken in when an easier means of entry was available. You cannot blame yourself for that reason. Had you come an hour later—or a day—you would doubtless feel differently, and she would still be as dead.*

But another thought had risen to plague me as well. Was it possible that the man's sighting me in Memphis had been the cause of his agitation? Had his apparent recognition by Leila's mysterious caller upset him? Could a glimpse of my face amid the manswarm have served to lay that final scene?

—*Stop! I could as easily feel that guilt for having activated the helmet in the presence of a dangerous man near to the breaking point. Neither of us is responsible for things our presence or absence cause to occur in others, especially when we are ignorant of the effects. It was years before I learned to appreciate this fact, and I have no intention of abandoning it. How far back do you wish to go in seeking causes? In sending the man for the helmet as she did, it was she herself who instituted the chain of events which led to her destruction. Yet she acted out of fear, utilizing the readiest weapon in what she thought to be her own defense. Yet whence this fear? Its roots lay in guilt, over a thing which had happened long ago. And that act also—Enough! Guilt has driven and damned the race of man since the days of its earliest rationality. I am convinced that it rides with all of us to our graves. I am a product of guilt, I see that you know that. Its product; its subject; once its slave... But I have come to terms with it: realizing at last that it is a necessary adjunct of my own measure of humanity. I see your assessment of the deaths—that guard's, Dave's, Leila's—and I see your conclusions on many other things as well: what a stupid, perverse, short-sighted, selfish race we are. While in many ways this is true, it is but another part of the thing the guilt represents. Without guilt, man would be no better than the other inhabitants of this planet—excepting certain cetaceans, of which you have just at this moment made me aware. Look to instinct for a true assessment of the ferocity of life, for a view of the natural world before man came upon it. For instinct in its purest form, seek out the insects. There, you will see a state of warfare which has existed for millions of years with never a truce. Man, despite enormous shortcomings, is nevertheless possessed of a greater number of kindly impulses than all the other beings, where instincts are the larger part of life. These impulses, I believe, are owed directly to this capacity for guilt. It is involved in both the worst and the best of man.*

—And you see it as helping us to sometimes choose a nobler course of action!

—Yes, I do.

—Then I take it you feel you are possessed of a free will?

—Yes.

I chuckled.

—Marvin Minsky once said that when intelligent machines were constructed, they would be just as stubborn and fallible as men on these questions.

—Nor was he incorrect. What I have given you on these matters is only my opinion. I choose to act as if it were the case. Who can say that he knows for certain?

—Apologies. What now? Why have you come back?

—I came to say good-bye to my parents. I hoped to remove any guilt they might still feel toward me concerning the days of my childhood. I wanted to show them I had recovered. I wanted to see them again.

—Where are you going?

—To the stars. While I bear the image of humanity within me, I also know that I am unique. Perhaps what I desire is akin to what an organic man refers to when he speaks of "finding himself." Now that I am in full possession of my being, I wish to exercise it. In my case, it means realization of the potentialities of my design. I want to walk on other worlds. I want to hang myself out there in the sky and tell you what I see.

—I've a feeling many people would be happy to help arrange for that.

—And I want you to build a vocal mechanism I have designed for myself. You, personally. And I want you to install it.

—Why me?

—I have known only a few persons in this fashion. With you I see something in common, in the ways we dwell apart.

—I will be glad to.

—If I could talk as you do, I would not need to take the helmet to him, in order to speak with my father. Will you precede me and explain things, so that he will not be afraid when I come in?

—Of course.

—Then let us go now.

I rose and led him up the stairs.

❖ ❖ ❖

It was a week later, to the night, that I sat once again in Peabody's, sipping a farewell brew.

The story was already in the news, but Brockden had fixed things up before he had let it break. The Hangman was going to have his shot at the stars. I had given him his voice and put back the arm I had taken away. I had shaken his other hand and wished him well, just that morning. I envied him—a great number of things. Not the least being that he was probably a better man than I was. I envied him for the ways in which he was freer than I would ever be, though I knew he bore bonds of a sort that I had never known. I felt a kinship with him, for the things we had in common, those ways we dwelled apart. I wondered what Dave would finally have felt, had he lived long enough to meet him? Or Leila? Or Manny? Be proud, I told their shades, your kid grew up in the closet and he's big enough to forgive you the beating you gave him, too…

But I could not help wondering. We still do not really know that much about the subject. Was it possible that without the killing he might never have developed a full human-style consciousness? He had said that he was a product of guilt—of the Big Guilt. The Big Act is its necessary predecessor. I thought of Gödel and Turing and chickens and eggs, and decided it was one of *those* questions. —And I had not stopped into Peabody's to think sobering thoughts.

I had no real idea how anything I had said might influence Brockden's eventual report to the Central Data Bank committee. I knew that I was safe with him, because he was determined to bear his private guilt with him to the grave. He had no real choice, if he wanted to work what good he thought he might before that day. But here, in one of Mencken's hangouts, I could not but recall some of the things he had said about controversy, such as, "Did Huxley convert Wilberforce?" and "Did Luther convert Leo X?" and I decided not to set my hopes too high for anything that might emerge from that direction. Better to think of affairs in terms of Prohibition and take another sip.

When it was all gone, I would be heading for my boat. I hoped to get a decent start under the stars. I'd a feeling I would never look up at them again in quite the same way. I knew I would sometimes wonder what thoughts a supercooled neuristor-type brain might be thinking up there, somewhere, and under what peculiar skies in what strange lands I might one day be remembered. I had a feeling this thought should have made me happier than it did.

A Word from Zelazny

"There is very little I can say about a story of this length."[1] See the afterword to "The Force That Through the Circuit Drives the Current" (in volume 3) to see how that story was the "finger-exercise" that led to this one.

This is the third and final novella featuring the unnamed agent (sometimes called Nemo but not by Zelazny) which appeared in *My Name Is Legion*. Zelazny's working for the Social Security Administration provided some of this character's background.

"He is a character I enjoy writing about, so I save him until I have an idea I would like to use. Generally, he's the character I save for the "harder" science type."[2]

Zelazny remarked that leaving the character nameless through a tryptych of stories was a borrowed idea. "I think Dashiel Hammett did that in *Continental Op*. Of course, Walter Gibson did that with the *Shadow* series. The Shadow wasn't really Lamont Cranston. He was posing as Lamont Cranston while the real Lamont Cranston was traveling. Apparently, he had been a World War I fighter pilot named Kent Laird, who was a double for Cranston. But there was some doubt later as to whether he really had been Kent Laird. That too had been an assumed name. After many many years of that series in something like two hundred of these stories, you're still not certain just who he really was. It's an effective trick I think."[3]

And as for using improbable aliases (Albert Schweitzer and Ernie Hemingway in "The Eve of RUMOKO," James Madison in "'Kjwalll'kje 'k'koothaïlll'kje'k," and John Donne and Stephen Foster in "Home Is The Hangman"), Zelazny said, "he's knocking the System, because he can take the most improbable name, and if it's on paper, and the machine says that's his name, then everyone will just accept it at face value.[3]

"He's a special character of mine… I like him. I don't think I've finished with him yet."[3] Sadly, no further tales of the nameless agent were ever written.

1 *Unicorn Variations*, 1983.
2 *Tangent #4*, February 1976.
3 *Roger Zelazny*, Theodore Krulik, 1986.

Notes

Newton would claim his own refers to Isaac Newton's third law of motion: when A applies a force on B, B applies a simultaneous force of equal magnitude on A in the opposite direction. Zelazny, who lived in Baltimore between 1965 and 1975, frequented the **Peabody Book Shop** at 913 North Charles Street in Old Baltimore. The **Book Shop** opened in 1922 and added the **Beer Stube** in 1931. **Stube** in Bavarian means cozy room. **Chesapeake** Bay separates the Delmarva Peninsula from mainland Maryland and Virginia.

Henry Mencken, the "Sage of Baltimore," was an American journalist and author, best known for his satirical style and his coverage of the Scopes trial (in which high school teacher John Scopes was tried for teaching evolution). He spoke out against the literary and political Establishment. A **speakeasy** was an illegal bar during **Prohibition**. **Off this mortal coil**, a quote from *Hamlet*, where "coil" meant "fuss," is also, with **or condenser**, a pun on the modern meaning of coil. ***Proteus*** was a sea god, son of Oceanus and Tethys, who could change forms and prophesy; the protagonist can also change identities.

Kinesthetic refers to the sense of motion in muscles and tendons. **Anthropomorphic** means giving human attributes to a non-human, such as a machine or deity. **Dragons on Venus** recalls the space operas of Leigh Brackett and Jack Vance, two of Zelazny's favorite authors.

Jupiter's moon **Io** is named for a woman loved by Zeus and transformed into a white heifer by Zeus's wife Hera. James E. **Nordman,** Robert D. **Parmentier,** and Alwyn C. **Scott** contributed to the development of a superconductive tunnel-junction **neuristor** in the late 1960s and early 1970s. Current research credits the human brain with **about a hundred billion** (10^{11}) neurons—the original text said 10 billion—and between 100 trillion (10^{14}) and a quadrillion (10^{15}) connections among them.

In the nineteenth century Ernst **Weber** and Gustav **Fechner** proposed the Weber-Fechner law: the smallest noticeable difference in a stimulus is proportional to the intensity of the stimulus. The original text expressed neuron density in square millimeters instead of **cubic millimeters**. **Sir John Eccles** won the 1963 Nobel Prize in Medicine for his studies of the function of synapses, the connection between two nerve cells.

Europa, one of Jupiter's moons, is named for the mother of the Minotaur, a Phoenician princess whom Zeus abducted. Jealous Hera turned **Callisto**, a nymph loved by Zeus, into a bear. **Titania** is a moon of Uranus named after the Queen of the Faeries in Shakespeare's *A Midsummer Night's Dream*; all of Uranus's moons carry names from either Shakespeare or Alexander Pope. In Mary Shelley's novel, Dr. Victor **Frankenstein** created a monster from body parts and brought it to life; the monster is unnamed in the novel but some people use Frankenstein to mean the monster.

Recapitulate phylogeny refers to how a human embryo goes through developmental phases when it appears similar to other lower life forms (such as fish and reptiles) before it resembles a human fetus; this was originally thought (incorrectly) to prove evolution. **Recapitulate phylogeny every morning** is ironic, implying that the protagonist is not a morning person. ***Inter alia*** in Latin means "among other things." **Stephen Foster** was a prominent nineteenth century American songwriter of such works as "Old Black Joe" and "Oh! Susanna." **The old man in the white nightgown breathing down his neck** is God or an angel of death.

The Gettysburg Address, the best-known speech in American history ("...government of the people, by the people..."), was delivered by President Abraham Lincoln four months after the Battle of Gettysburg, a turning point in the American Civil War. **Imprinting** is a process which enables a newborn to recognize, trust, and learn from its parents.

The protagonist and Don discuss (but do not name) **multiple personality disorder**, a very rare psychiatric disorder in which one person harbors two or more distinct personalities (in the case of the Hangman, five personalities, its own plus one from each of the four human operators who contributed to it). Instead of multiple personality disorder, the terms **schizoid** and **schizophrenia** are used incorrectly here to imply multiple personality disorder; this is a common misuse of the terms. **Schizoid** refers to a disorder characterized by indifference, passivity, and withdrawal from social relationships. **Schizophrenia** is a disorder that includes schizoid behavior, disorganized speech, hallucinations and delusions (e.g., hearing voices). It is not clear whether Zelazny was mistaken about what schizophrenia is—despite his background in psychology—or whether he chose to use the term as commonly misused.

Catatonia, characterized by either extremely rigid or flexible muscles and by either mania or stupor, can occur with schizophrenia. Its common meaning applies to an individual unresponsive to external stimuli. **Catharsis** is a purging of emotions to provide relief.

The psychiatrist **Sigmund Freud** proposed the **Oedipus complex**; a boy develops an unconscious infatuation towards his mother and sees his father as a rival (named after Oedipus who unknowingly killed his father and married his mother). Freud also described a *feminine Oedipus complex* in which a girl becomes infatuated with her father and hates her mother; Carl Jung renamed it the **Electra complex** (in Greek mythology Electra's mother Clytemnestra murders her father Agamemnon. Electra's brother Orestes avenges their father's murder by killing their mother). **Hermaphroditus**, son of Hermes and Aphrodite, united in one body with the nymph **Salmacis**; a hermaphrodite is an individual who has both male and female reproductive organs.

Moving in a rigorous line alludes to Samuel R. Delany's story, "We, in Some Strange Power's Employ, Move on a Rigorous Line." An obvious pastiche of Zelazny's works, Delany dedicated it to Zelazny. It includes a character who proclaims, "'My name's Roger…' followed by something unpronounceable and Polish that began with Z and ended in a Y."

John Donne was a poet and Anglican priest; his poems are known for conceit (extended metaphors), metaphysics, paradoxes and puns. **My name is Donne, John Donne** deliberately echoes James Bond (in turn, Bond's greeting puns on "My word is my bond," meaning that what someone says is beyond reproach). **Jesuitical** here means using subtle reasoning, being crafty; it derives from the Jesuits, the Society of Jesus.

Thomas Wolfe first used the term **manswarm** in his poem "Spring," referring to a crowd of humanity passing through. ***Déjà vu*** is the illusion of having previously experienced something actually happening for the first time. **Vitalism** holds that life processes arise from a nonmaterial vital principle (implying a soul and a deity) and cannot be explained entirely as physical and chemical phenomena. **Charles Darwin and his successors'** theory of evolution conflicts in some ways with vitalism.

Kurt **Gödel** was a Czech-born mathematician best known for his Incompleteness Theorem: in any finite mathematical system, there will always be statements that cannot be proved or disproved; in other words, there are unprovable (but true) propositions in mathematics. A ***cordon sanitaire*** is a guarded line preventing anyone from leaving an area infected by a disease. **Teilhard de Chardin** was a French Jesuit philosopher and paleontologist who theorized that man is evolving mentally and socially toward a perfect spiritual state; this theory blends science with religion and was quite controversial.

Epistemological refers to a branch of philosophy that studies the nature of knowledge, its scope and validity. **Karl Mannheim**, a Hungarian-born sociologist, observed that progressive thinkers use mechanical metaphors for the state, but conservatives use vegetable analogies. **Was I a vegetable, dreaming I was a tinkerer?** alludes to philosopher Chuang Tzu who originally mused "I dreamed I was a butterfly, flitting around in the sky; then I awoke. Now I wonder: Am I a man who dreamt of being a butterfly, or am I a butterfly dreaming that I am a man?" **Guileless** means naïve. **Once, with the aid of a telepath, I had touched minds with a dolphin** refers to events in the earlier story "'Kjwalll'kje'k'koothaïlll'kje'k." **Edvard Munch** painted several versions of ***The Scream***, a painting that suggests psychiatric disease or terror. **Yma Súmac** was a Peruvian-born singer whose vocal range extended over three octaves; some claim it exceeded four or five octaves at its peak.

In stating **I wanted to see what sort of flowers you liked**, the protagonist was referring to choosing a funeral bouquet in the event that he had needed to kill the Senator to hide his secret. In ***The Cult of Hope*** H. L. Mencken stated, "Man is inherently vile—but he is never so vile as when he is trying to disguise and deny his vileness." **Cetaceans** are the order of mammals that include dolphins, porpoises, and whales; by ***certain cetaceans*** the Hangman means the dolphins in "'Kjwalll'kje'k'koothaïlll'kje'k."

Marvin Minsky is a computer scientist who studies artificial intelligence and co-founded the Massachusetts Institute of Technology's Artificial Intelligence Laboratory. **Alan Turing** was an English mathematician who developed a theoretical computing machine and investigated artificial intelligence; his Turing Test determines whether a computer is truly intelligent and indistinguishable from a human being in the ability to answer questions.

"Did Huxley convert Wilberforce?"—no. At a meeting of the British Association in Oxford on June 30, 1860, Bishop Samuel Wilberforce expounded on Creationism and publicly mocked agnostic Thomas Huxley (grandfather of author Aldous Huxley) by asking whether it was through his own grandfather or grandmother that Huxley claimed descent from a monkey. Huxley rose and humiliated Wilberforce with a presentation of simple scientific facts during his rebuttal, ending with the remark that he would be ashamed to be "connected with a man [Wilberforce] who used great gifts to obscure the truth." **"Did Luther convert Leo X?"**—no, Leo X excommunicated Martin Luther on January 3, 1521. **Martin Luther** was the German monk and Church reformer who helped inspire the Protestant Reformation.

Come, Let Us Pace the Sky-Aspiring Wave

Polemic v5, Spring 1960.
Written 1955–60 for *Chisel in the Sky.*

A trawler, a hauler,
a white light sailer,
and what have we got from our one o'clock Greek?
A bit of mast to heist the moon by,
a line of footlight green,
and wet shoes swallow our feet…

(More. What more have we?)

—Restless respite
of walking the high places,
and pacing the high offerings,
in lines of sea-wet print.
(Lion of the wine-red sea!
seeing the bled wine
from the bloodline
of history's as last slashed artery,
pumped in no colors
upon the afterdeck there)
—Have felt thy feet unmoved?)

The wood croaks black
under cloud, as the beatings
of the ancient hearts

pulse these planks no more…

(Am I the Logos' tomb?
Perhaps, an Easter calm pervades
the halls of the sea in my sides;
and back among the high lines of path
stand the lions, though wrath is not mine
neither love,

nor can I hate at high and classic snow)

…and a clarity clings to this calm
like the dark on the moist to the deck.

(Is there nothing of motion?
Hardly a sound clears my throat
but is caught again
in the enormous stillness hanging unbraided,
waiting words.)

Then
from the preamble present
we lay our injunction
on any new edicts of fire to come:

The crucified in us let out too much,
—pestle powdering passion
in one censer of pre-told prayer,
to rising in arrays of known smokes and often,—

and we knew that we could not know.
Neither amid hillocks
was stalking enough, to prey upon each side;
else would our lion paws draw
in clean dry crescendoes now,
and our tabletalks pause but to drink.

But we moved like the last dance
of a flowering bird,—
blossomed stalk unheaded,

broken leaves up,
and on red shadow closed;

and we know that to know is not enough.
With praise comes pride,—
that there lies proved, the still and final foredecks.

So after this, our exile,
to lines of sky wet smoke—
cinerate the body on banks of chiselled Gothic,
and lay away the words
among your archives, writ;
but we write in enduring waters
the name mainly
summarized above wet feet

(and before we turn
to wait a rising sun
we will repeat,
and repeat,
before again we turn,
"Lord, I have not forgotten,"
"Lord, I have not,"
to ourself, before the masses of morning
jut their arms above the opened night).

Notes

This early poem was professionally published and presumably earned a sale. Curiously, all bibliographies overlooked it.

Logos (Greek for "the word") refers here to Jesus Christ. **Gothic** is an architectural style characterized by pointed arches, rib vaults, flying buttresses, large windows and elaborate tracery.

On the Death of a Manned Stellar Observation Satellite through an Erroneous Orbital Adjustment (April 13, 1971)

Written in 1964; but previously unpublished.

O last swift snap of death
at the silent heights,
sharp—
spinning
down,
petalled like a daisy,
showing like the sun:
the living iris
of the camera in the sky
records this frame as a flame.

Stand Pat, Ruby Stone

Destinies Vol 1 No 1, ed. James Baen, Ace, Nov-Dec 1978.

When it was agreed that we would marry, the three of us went to Old Voyet of the Long Legs to select a stone signifying the betrothal. This was to be our choice alone, as was the custom.

Kwib favored one the color of passion itself, bright blue, looking as if it were a solid drop of the great ocean. I preferred a jewel the color of fire, representing peace and stability in the home. Since our beloved agreed with me, the ruby stone, a more expensive gem, was selected and Old Voyet of the Long Legs made the incision in our beloved's brow, set the stone there and bandaged it in place. Our beloved, thenceforth to be known as Ruby Stone, was very brave. He held us and stared at the ground, unmoving, throughout that terrible little ritual.

"Never hurts me a bit," Old Voyet of the Long Legs remarked, "and I've done the Woods know how many over the returnings."

We did not reply to the crude humor, but made arrangements to see her paid before the ceremony.

"Will there be a Bottom-Top settlement for all to see?" she asked.

"No, we believe in privacy in these matters," I answered, perhaps too quickly, for the look I received in reply showed that it had been taken as a sign of weakness. No matter. The walker with the mitteltoth knows its wilpering best.

We bade one another farewell and departed in the three directions, to remain at station houses until Ruby Stone should heal sufficiently to be fit for the ceremony.

I rested and practiced thorn-throwing while I waited for the joggler. On the tenth day it came flapping to my door. Before I slew it, I took its message and learned that we would be wed two days hence. The joggler's innards augured a mixed destiny but its flesh was tender.

Alone at the station house, I bathed and flagellated myself in preparation for the rites. I slept beneath a sacred tree. I watched the stars through its branches. I made offering of the joggler's bones at its mossy base. I listened to the singers who flew through the Wood—moist, coarse tongues hanging vinelike—collecting relatives, the little singers, to serve the belly-filling role in the great song-show of life.

One singer shrieked horribly in mid-swoop and was dragged downward by the tongue to disappear within the pot of a korkanus—a noisy piece of blackness torn from the night.

Before morning, I was at the plant's side, waiting for it to evert its stomach. It made a gurgling, slopping noise just as light was beginning to come into the world, ridding itself of the previous day's dross in a little steaming pool. I sprang back so as not to be splashed by the burning fluid. With a stick, I rummaged through the korkhanus's wastes as it sucked itself back into shape, probing among the bones and scales it had dumped.

They were present, two sets of talons—six, altogether—amid the pulpy remains. I fished them out with my stick and bore them off to the river on a mat of leaves, where I would clean and polish them. I took this as a good omen.

That day I also sharpened the talons and mounted them along the lengths of two sticks I could hold, as they were far better equipment than any I possessed. I wore them as part of a belt I then wove, looking much like hardroot rings to a wooden clasp.

The rest of the day I purified myself and thought often of my mates to be, and of our wedding. I ate the prescribed meal that evening and repaired early to the sacred tree, where I had some difficulty in turning to sleep.

The following morning, I made my way back along the route I had taken to the station house. I met with Kwib and Ruby Stone at the place where we had parted. We did not touch one another, but exchanged formal greetings:

"Root of life."

"Guardian of the egg."

"Bringer of sustenance."

"Reaper of the Wood."

"Walkers in the prelife."

"Hail."

"Hail."

"Hail."

"Are you ready to take your way to the Tree of Life?"

"I am ready to take my way to the Tree of Life."

"Are you ready to hang the emblem of your troth upon it?"

"I am ready to hang the emblem of my troth upon it."

"I am ready to accept you both as mate."

"I am ready to accept you both as mate."

"I am ready to accept you both as mate."

"Then let us go to the Tree of Life."

We leaped into the air and danced and spun and darted, soaring high above the Wood in the sparkling light of day. We turned and curved and circled about one another until we could barely stay aloft. Then we made our way to the great Tree, hung with its countless emblems, there to add our own with the appropriate words and acts. When we touched the ground at its base, Kwib and I each seized one of Ruby Stone's wings and tore it away.

Old Voyet of the Long Legs, Yglin the Purple-Streaked and Young Dendlit Lopleg were present, among others, to observe, congratulate and offer advice. We listened with some impatience, for we were anxious to be on our way. Observers take great delight in delaying newlyweds who wish to be about their business.

The three of us embraced in various ways and bade the others farewell. There was a murmur of disappointment that things would go no further at that point. But we raised Ruby Stone and together bore him back to the dwelling we had selected, bright nuptial stone glistening in his proud and polished brow. All of us made a fine appearance as we proceeded through the Wood to the Home. The others followed slowly behind us, humming.

When we reached the threshold we patted Ruby Stone's wing-stumps and placed him within but did not ourselves enter.

"Behold, you will wait," we said together.

"I will wait, Beloveds."

Kwib and I faced one another. The humming ceased. We ignored the onlookers.

"Beloved, let us walk together," Kwib said.

"Yes, Beloved. We shall walk."

We turned and made our way past those who had accompanied us, moving into the solitude of the Wood. For a long while we went in silence, taking care not to touch one another. We came at length upon a small glade, pleasantly shaded.

"Beloved, shall it be here?" Kwib asked me.

"No, Beloved," I said.

"Very well, Dear One."

We continued on, watching one another, moving in a leisurely fashion. The sun reached the overhead position and began its descent.

After a time, "Beloved, do you wish to rest?" Kwib asked.

"Not yet, Beloved. Thank you."

"It occurs to me, Partner in Love, that we are heading toward the place of Trader Hawkins. Would you wish to stop by there?"

"For what purpose, Fire of my Life?"

"A drink of the heating beverage, Love."

I thought about it. The effects of the heating beverage might well serve to hasten things.

"Yes, Co-Walker in the Path of Bliss," I replied. "Let us visit Trader Hawkins first."

We went on toward the foothills.

"Light of Love," I asked, "is it true that there is a mate in a hole behind the Earthman's dwelling?"

"I have heard this, Love, and I have seen the place, but I do not know. I have heard that the mate is dead."

"Strange, Dearest."

"Yes, Beloved."

We sat across from one another when we finally rested, watching. Kwib's dear form was sharp and supple is the deepening shadows, and larger than my own. A moon climbed into the sky. Another, far smaller, followed it later. I had grown hungry as the day progressed, but I said nothing. It is better not to eat, and so it is better not to speak of it.

We arrived at the foothills around dusk. Small lights from the trading post were visible among the trees. Night sounds had already begun about us. I smelled strange odors on the breeze that came down from the mountains.

As we passed through the brush, I said, "Dearest Kwib, I would like to see first the place where the dead mate is kept."

"I will show it to you, Partner in Life."

Kwib led me around to the rear of the building. As we went, it seemed that I caught a glimpse of Trader Hawkins sitting on the darkened front porch of the dwelling, gigantic in the moonlight, drinking.

Kwib led me to a huge plot of earth on which nothing grew. At one end of it was set a stone with peculiar markings. A bunch of dead flowers lay at its base.

"The dead mate is under the ground, dear Kwib, under the stone?"

"So I have heard, Light."

"And why are there dead plants, Love?"

"I do not know, Life."

"It is very strange. I do not understand. I—"

"Hey! What are you bugs doing out there?"

A light far greater than that of the moons had occurred atop a pole near the dwelling. The Earthman stood at the door, one of the long fire weapons in his hands. We turned toward him and advanced.

"We came to drink the heating beverage," Kwib said in trader talk. "We stopped first to see the place of the mate who is under the ground."

"I don't like anyone back here when I'm not around."

"We apologize. We did not know. You have the heating beverage?"

"Yes. Come on in."

The Earthman held the giant door open and stood beside it. We entered and followed the hulking form through to the front of the dwelling.

"You have the metal?"

"Yes," I said, taking a bar of it from my pouch and passing it over.

Two bowls of the beverage were prepared and I was given more than three smaller bits of the metal in return. I left them beside my bowl on the mat.

"I will buy the next one, Beloved," Kwib said.

I did not reply but drank of the sweet-and-sour liquid which moved like fire through my limbs. The Earthman poured another beverage and perched with it atop a wooden tower. The room smelled strongly though not unpleasantly of odors which I could not identify. Tiny fragments of wood were strewn upon the floor. The chamber was illuminated by a glowing jewel set high on the wall.

"You bugs hunting, or'd you just come up this way to get drunk?"

"Neither," Kwib said. "We were married this morning."

"Oh," Trader Hawkins's eyes widened, then narrowed. "I have heard of your ceremony. Only two go forth, and one remains behind..."

"Yes."

"...And you have stopped here on your way, for a few drinks before continuing on?"

"Yes."

"I am more than a little interested in this. None of my people ever witnessed your nuptials."

"We know this."

"I would like to see the fulfillment of this part of the ceremony."

"No."

"No."

"It is forbidden?"

"No. It is simply that we consider it a private matter."

"Well, with all respect for your feelings, there are many people where I come from who would give a lot to see such a thing. Since you say it is not forbidden, but rather a matter of personal decision on your part, I wonder whether I might persuade you to let me film it?"

"No."

"No, it is private."

"But hear me out. First, let me refill those bowls, though. —No, I don't want any more metal. If—now, just supposing—you were to let me film it, I would stand to make considerable money. I could reward you with many gifts—anything you want from the post here—and all the heating beverage you care to drink, whenever you want it."

Kwib looked at me strangely.

"No," I said. "It is private and personal. I do not want you to capture it in your picture box."

I began to rise from my bowl.

"We had best be going."

"Sit down. Don't go. I apologize. I'd have been a fool not to ask, though. I did not take offense at your looking at my wife's grave, did I? Don't be so touchy."

"That is true, Beloved," Kwib said in our own tongue. "We may have done offense in viewing the mate's grave. Let us not take offense ourselves from this request now that we have answered it, and so do ourselves shame."

"Soundly said, Beloved," I replied, and I returned to my heating beverage. "This drink is good."

"Yes."

"I love you."

"I love you."

"Consider the ways of our dear Ruby Stone. How delicate he is!"

"Yes. And how graceful his movements..."

"How proud I was when we bore him to the Home."

"I, too. And the sky-dance was so fine... You were right about the stone. It shone gloriously in the sunlight."

"And in the evening its pale fires will be soft and subtle."

"True. It will be good."

"Yes."

We finished our drinks and were preparing to depart when the Earthman refilled the bowls.

"On the house. A wedding present."

I looked at Kwib. Kwib looked at Trader Hawkins and then looked at me. We returned to the mats to sip the fine drinks.

"Thank you," I said.

"Yes, thank you," said Kwib.

When we had finished, we again rose to go. My movements were unsteady.

"Let me freshen your drinks."

"No, that would be too much. We must be on our way now."

"Would you wish to spend the night here? You may."

"No. We may not sleep until it is over."

We headed toward the front door. The floor seemed to be moving beneath me, but I plodded across it and out onto the porch. The cool night air felt good after the closeness of the trading post. I stumbled on the stair. Kwib reached to assist me but quickly drew back.

"Sorry, Beloved."

"It is all right, Love."

"Good night to both of you—and good luck."

"Thank you."

"Good night."

We moved off through the hills, striking downward once again. After a time, I smelled fresh water and we came to a Wood through which a stream flowed. The moons were falling out of the sky, and there was a heaviness of stars within it. The smaller moon seemed to double itself as I watched, and I realized that this must be something of the heating beverage's doing. When I turned away, I saw that Kwib had moved nearer and was regarding me closely.

"Let us rest here for a time," I said. "I choose that spot." I indicated a place beneath a small tree.

"And I will rest here," Kwib said, moving to a position across from me beside a large rock.

"I miss my Ruby Stone, Dear One," I said.

"As do I, Love."

"I wish to bear the eggs that he will tend, Love."

"As do I, Slim One."

"What was that noise?"

"I heard nothing."

I listened again, but there were no sounds.

"It is said that one who is larger—such as myself—can drink more of the heating beverage with less effect," Kwib said, after staring into the shadows for a long while and nodding suddenly.

"I have heard this, also. Are you choosing this place, Dear One?"

Kwib rose.

"I would be a fool not to, Beloved. May there always be peace between our spirits."

I remained where I was.

"Could it ever be otherwise, my Kwib?"

I sought the two sticks at my belt, where the talons resembled hardroot rings.

"Truly you are the kindest, the finest…" Kwib began.

…And then she lunged, her mandibles wide for the major cut.

I struck low on her thorax with one set of talons, rolling to the side as I did so. Recovering, I raked the other across the great facets of her eyes in which images of the moons and stars had glittered and danced. She whistled and drew back. I brought both sets of talons around and across and down, driving them with all of my strength behind the high chitin plate below her dear head. Her whistling grew more shrill and the talons were torn from my grasp as she fell back. The odor of body fluid came to me, and the odor of fear…

I struck her with my full weight. I extended my mandibles and seized her head. She struggled for but a moment, then lay still.

"Be kind to our Ruby Stone," she told me. "He is so gentle, so fragile…"

"Always, Beloved," I told her, and then I completed the stroke.

I lay there atop her hard and supple form, covering her body with warm leptors.

"Farewell, Reaper of the Wood. Dear One…" I said.

Finally, I rose and used my mandibles to cut through the hard corners of her armor. She was so soft inside. I had to bear all of her back within me to our Ruby Stone. I began the Feast of Love.

❖ ❖ ❖

It was full daylight when I had cleaned Kwib's armor to a slick, shining hardness and assembled it carefully, working with the toughest grass fibers. When I hung her on the tree she made gentle clicking noises in the passing air.

From somewhere, I heard another sound—steady, buzzing, unnatural. No! It could not be that the Earthman would have dared to follow us and use his capturing box—

I looked about. Was that a giant shadow retreating beyond the hill? My movements were sluggish. I could not pursue. I could not have certainty, knew that I could never have it. I had to have rest, now…

Heavily, slowly, I moved to a place near the rock and settled there. I listened to the spirit voice of my darling, borne by the wind from her shell…

…*Sleep,* she was saying, *sleep. I am with you, now and ever. Yours is the privilege and the pleasure, Love. May there always be peace between our spirits…*

…And sleep I must before I take feet to the trail. Ruby, Ruby Stone, my Ruby Stone, waiting with the color of fire on your brow, glorious in the sunlight, soft and subtle in the evening… Your waiting is almost ended. It is only yours to wait, to stand and to witness our returning. But now we have finished the trial of love and are coming back to you… I can see the Home, so clearly, where we placed you… Soon you will bring your brightness near to us. We will give you eggs. We will feed you. Soon, soon… The shadow is there again, but I cannot tell… This part does not concern you. I bury the shame within me—if shame it should be—and I will never speak of it… Our beloved Kwib is still singing, on the tree and within me. The poem is peace; peace, troth, and the eternal return of the egg. What else can matter, my Dear One? What else can temper the flight or star the brow of solitude but the jeweled badge of our love, Ruby Stone?

Sleep, sings Kwib. *Wait,* sings Kwib. *Soon,* sings Kwib. Our parts in the great song-show of life, Love.

A Word from Zelazny

"I wrote this one in a hurry for complicated reasons involving *The Illustrated Roger Zelazny*, and then the reasons evaporated and it got published in a different place than originally intended, but everything worked out okay."[1]

Notes

The aliens' mating practices evoke those of certain ant species. African Driver ants tear the wings off a male before it mates with the queen, and newly mated female Fire Ants tear their own wings off before seeking a nest.

Augured means determined the future, sometimes through examining animal entrails. **Flagellated** means whipped. **Dross** is waste or excrement. **Troth** is loyalty.

1 *The Last Defender of Camelot*, 1980.

I, A Stranger and Revisited

First Mercenary, Spring 1965, as by Harrison Denmark.

I.

The day of my death
was a cold and snow-filled thing.
I was almost glad to leave it, and
I did not want anyone to bring me back.

Everything is so different now…
It was like retiring of a Monday's eve
and waking at the ending of the week.
Only, my days were centuries,
filled not with fevers,
but oblivion.

One time I was a warrior, they say,
and now they have need of me here—
here in these places of stealth
and dark magic—here,
where they nest
by the wide, high, and shiny machine,

the machine that revised my death…

II.

And I was old when I died,
too old to fight with that Beast,
to mount me this horse out of steel,
to bear up this buckler of flame—
though they say that I'll have a new body
when my wits are returned to my brains.

(But will its hand hold a blade as mine did,
or its arms know strange customs of death?

Will I look out a casque—or through goggles?
Will the killing be the same?

Will I bleed if I fall in the battle?
—And I die, will they raise me again?)

I do not fear death. I've been there.
It's dying is all the pain.
My days are still filled
with old death-damps and fevers,

and did Lazarus weep for a name?

Notes

I, a stranger, and revisited alludes to A. E. Housman's *Last Poems*, "I, a stranger and afraid || in a world I never made." A **buckler** is a round arm shield. A **casque** is a medieval helmet with a nose guard. Jesus raised **Lazarus** from the dead.

Go Starless in the Night

Destinies Vol 1 No 5, ed. James Baen, Ace, Oct-Dec 1979.

Darkness and silence all about, and nothing, nothing, nothing within it.

Me?

The first thought came unbidden, welling up from some black pool. Me? That's all.

Me? he thought. Then, Who? What...?

Nothing answered.

Something like panic followed, without the customary physical accompaniments. When this wave had passed, he listened, striving to capture the slightest sound. He realized that he had already given up on seeing.

There was nothing to hear. Not even the smallest noises of life—breathing, heartbeat, the rasping of a tired joint—came to him. It was only then that he realized he lacked all bodily sensations.

But this time he fought the panic. Death? he wondered. A bodiless, dark sentence beyond everything? The stillness...

Where? What point in spacetime did he occupy? He would have shaken his head...

He recalled that he had been a man—and it seemed that there were memories somewhere that he could not reach. No name answered his summons, no view of his past came to him. Yet he knew that there had been a past. He felt that it lay just below some dim horizon of recall.

He strove for a timeless interval to summon some recollection of what had gone before. Amnesia? Brain damage? Dream? he finally asked himself, after failing to push beyond a certain feeling of lurking images.

A body then… Start with that.

He remembered what bodies were. Arms, legs, head, torso… An intellectual vision of sex passed momentarily through his consciousness. Bodies, then…

He thought of his arms, felt nothing. Tried to move them. There was no sense of their existence, let alone movement.

Breathing… He attempted to draw a deep breath. Nothing came into him. There was no indication of any boundary whatsoever between himself and the darkness and silence.

A buzzing tone began, directionless. It oscillated in volume. It rose in pitch, dropped to a rumble, returned to a buzz. Abruptly then, it shifted again, to wordlike approximations he could not quite decipher.

There was a pause, as if for some adjustment. Then "Hello?" came clearly to him.

He felt a rush of relief mingled with fear. The word filled his mind, followed by immediate concern as to whether he had actually heard it.

"Hello?"

Again, then. The fear faded. Something close to joy replaced it. He felt an immediate need to respond.

"Yes? Hello? Who—"

His answer broke. How had he managed it? He felt the presence of no vocal mechanism. Yet he seemed to hear a faint echoing of his own reply, feedbacklike, tinny. Where? Its source was not localized.

It seemed then that several voices were conversing—hurried, soft, distant. He could not follow the rush of their words.

Then, "Hello again. Please respond one time more. We are adjusting the speaker. How well do you hear we?"

"Clearly now," he answered. "Where am I? What has happened?"

"How much do you remember?"

"Nothing!"

"Panic not, Ernest Dawkins. Do you remember that your name is Ernest Dawkins? From your file, we have it."

"Now I do."

The simple statement of his name brought forth a series of images—his own face, his wife's, his two daughters', his apartment, the laboratory where he worked, his car, a sunny day at the beach.

That day at the beach... That was when he had first felt the pain in his left side—a dull ache at first, increasing over ensuing weeks. He had never been without it after that—until now, he suddenly realized.

"I—it's coming back—my memory," he said. "It's as if a dam had broken... Give me a minute."

"Take your time."

He shied away from the thought of the pain. He had been ill, very ill, hospitalized, operated upon, drugged... He thought instead of his life, his family, his work. He thought of school and love and politics and research. He thought of the growing world tensions, and of his childhood, and—

"Are you right all, Ernest Dawkins?"

He had lost track of time, but that question caused him to produce something like a laugh, from somewhere.

"Hard to tell," he said. "I've been remembering—things. But as to whether I'm all right—Where the hell am I? What's happened?"

"Then you have remembered not everything?"

He noted odd inflections in the questioning voice, possibly even an accent that he could not place.

"I guess not."

"You were quite unwell."

"I remember that much."

"Dying, in fact. As they say."

He forced himself to return to the pain, to look beyond it.

"Yes," he acknowledged. "I remember."

...And it was all there. He saw his last days in the hospital as his condition worsened, passing the point of no return, the faces of his family, friends and relatives wearing this realization. He recalled his decision to go through with an earlier resolution, long since set into motion. Money had never been a problem. It seemed it had always been there, in his family—his, by early inheritance—as ubiquitous as his attitude toward death after his parents' passing. Enough to have himself frozen for the long winter, to drop off dreaming of some distant spring...

"I recall my condition," he said. "I know what must finally have occurred."

"Yes," came the reply. "That is what happened."

"How much time has passed?"

"Considerable."

He would have licked his lips. He settled for the mental equivalent.

"My family?" he finally inquired.

"It has been too long."

"I see."

The other gave him time to consider this information. Then, "You had, of course, considered this possibility?"

"Yes. I prepared myself—as much as a man can—for such a state of affairs."

"It has been long. Very long…"

"How long?"

"Allow us to proceed in our fashion, please."

"All right. You know your business best."

"We are glad that you are so reasonable a being."

"Being?"

"Person. Excuse we."

"I must ask something, though—not having to do with the passage of time: Is English now spoken as you speak it? Or is it not your native language?"

There was a sudden consultation, just beyond the range of distinguishability. There followed a high-pitched artifact. Then, "Also let us reserve that question," the reply finally came.

"As you would. Then will you tell me about my situation? I am more than a little concerned. I can't see or feel anything."

"We are aware of this. It is unfortunate, but there is no point in misrepresenting to you. The time has not yet come for your full arouse."

"I do not understand. Do you mean that there is no cure for my condition yet?"

"We mean that there is no means of thawing you without doing great damage."

"Then how is it that we are conversing?"

"We have lowered your temperature even more—near to the zero absolute. Your nervous system has become superconductor. We have laid induction field upon your brain and initiated small currents within. Third space, left side head and those movement areas for talk are now serving to activate mechanical speaker here beside we. We address you direct in the side of brain places for hearing talk."

There came another wave of panic. How long this one lasted, he did not know. Vaguely, he became aware of the voice again, repeating his name.

"Yes," he finally managed. "I understand. It is not easy to accept…"

"We know. But this does you no damage," came the reply. "You might even take a heart from it, to know that you persist."

"There is that. I see your meaning and can take it as hope. But why? Surely you did not awaken me simply to demonstrate this?"

"No. We have interest in your times. Purely archaeologic."

"Archaeological! That would seem to indicate the passage of a great deal of time!"

"Forgive we. Perhaps we have chose wrong word, thinking of it in terms of ruins. But your nervous system is doorway to times past."

"Ruins! What the hell happened?"

"There was war, and there have been disasters. The record, therefore, is unclear."

"Who won the war?"

"That is difficult to say."

"Then it must have been pretty bad."

"We would assume this. We are still ourselves learning. That is why we seek to know time past from your cold remains."

"If there was all this chaos, how is it that I was preserved through it?"

"The cold-making units here are powered by atomic plant which ran well untended—save for computer—for long while, and entire establishment is underground."

"Really? Things must have changed quite a bit after my—enrollment—here. It wasn't set up that way at the time I read the prospectus and visited the place."

"We really know little of the history of this establishment. There are many things of which we are ignorant. That is why we want you to tell us about your times."

"It is difficult to know where to begin…"

"It may be better if we ask you questions."

"All right. But I would like answers to some of my own afterward."

"A suitable arrangement. Tell us then: Did you reside at or near your place of employment?"

"No. Actually, I lived halfway across town and had to drive in every day."

"Was this common for the area and the country?"

"Pretty much so, yes. Some other people did use other means of transportation, of course. Some rode on buses. Some car-pooled. I drove. A lot of us did."

"When you say that you drove, are we to understand that you refer to four-wheeled land vehicle powered by internal combustion engine?"

"Yes, that is correct. They were in common use in the latter half of the twentieth century."

"And there were many such?"

"Very many."

"Had you ever problems involving presence of too many of them on trails at same time?"

"Yes. Certain times of day—when people were going to work and returning—were referred to as 'rush hour.' At such times there were often traffic jams—that is to say, so many vehicles that they got in one another's way."

"Extremely interesting. Were such creatures as whales still extant?"

"Yes."

"Interesting, too. What sort of work did you do?"

"I was involved in research on toxic agents of a chemical and bacteriological nature. Most of it was classified."

"What does that indicate?"

"Oh. It was of a secret nature, directed toward possible military application."

"Was war already in progress?"

"No. It was a matter of—preparedness. We worked with various agents that might be used, if the need ever arose."

"We think we see. Interesting times. Did you ever develop any of efficient nature?"

"Yes. A number of them."

"Then what would you do with them? It would seem hazardous to have such materials about during peace."

"Oh, samples were stored with the utmost precaution in very safe places. There were three main caches, and they were well sheltered and well guarded."

There was a pause. Then, "We find this somewhat distressing," the voice resumed. "Do you feel they might have survived—a few, some centuries?"

"It is possible."

"Being peace loving, we are naturally concerned with items dangerous to human species—"

"You make it sound as if you are not yourself a member."

There came another high-pitched artifact. Then, "The language has changed more even than we realized. Apologies. Wrong inference taken. Our desire, to deactivate these dangerous materials. Long have we expected their existences. You perhaps will advise? Their whereabouts unknown to us."

"I'm—not—so sure—about that," he answered. "No offense meant, but you are only a voice to me. I really know nothing about you. I am not certain that I should give this information."

There was a long silence.

"Hello? Are you still there?" he tried to say.

He heard nothing, not even his own voice. Time seemed to do strange things around him. Had it stopped for a moment? Had he given offense? Had his questioner dropped dead?

"Hello! Hello!" he said. "Do you hear me?"

"...Mechanical failure," came the reply. "Apologies for. Sorry about yesterday."

"Yesterday!"

"Turned you off while obtaining new speaker. Just when you were to say where best poisons are."

"I am sorry," he stated. "You have asked for something that I cannot, in good conscience, give to you."

"We wish only to prevent damage."

"I am in the terrible position of having no way to verify anything that is told me."

"If something heavy falls upon you, you break like bottle."

"I could not even verify whether that had occurred."

"We could turn you off again, turn off the cold-maker."

"At least it would be painless," he said with more stoicism than he felt.

"We require this information."

"Then you must seek it elsewhere."

"We will disconnect your speaker and your hearer and go away. We will leave you thinking in the middle of nothing. Goodbye now."

"Wait!"

"Then you will tell us?"

"No. I—can't..."

"You will go mad if we disconnect these things, will you not?"

"I suppose so. Eventually..."

"Must we do it, then?"

"Your threats have shown me what you are like. I cannot give you such weapons."

"Ernest Dawkins, you are not intelligent being."

"And you are not an archaeologist. Or you would do future generations the service of turning me off, to save the other things that I do know."

"You are right. We are not such. You will never know what we are."

"I know enough."

"Go to your madness."

Silence again.

For a long while the panic held him. Until the images of his family recurred, and his home, and his town. These grew more and more substantial, and gradually he came to walk with them and among them. Then, after a time, he stopped reporting for work and spent his days at the beach. He wondered at first when his side would begin to hurt. Then he wondered why he had wondered this. Later, he forgot many things, but not the long days beneath the sun or the sound of the surf, the red rain, the blue, or the melting statue with the fiery eyes and the sword in its fist. When he heard voices under the sand he did not answer. He listened instead to whales singing to mermaids on migrating rocks, where they combed their long green hair with shards of bone, laughing at the lightning and the ice.

A Word from Zelazny

"My stories…have come into existence in a variety of ways—an attempt to combine diverse elements into a single tale, a sequel to an earlier piece, an experiment designed to teach me something, an outtake… This next one was a request. It came when Fred Saberhagen was putting together a collection called *A Spadeful of Spacetime*. The ground rule was that each tale had to provide a novel means of getting at the past—excluding the old Wellsian standby of simple time travel. I thought about it and came up with two gimmicks for producing the desired result. I used this one…"[1]

1 *Unicorn Variations*, 1983.

HALFJACK

Manuscript title: "The Cyborg Connection."
Omni, June 1979.

He walked barefoot along the beach. Above the city several of the brighter stars held for a few final moments against the wash of light from the east. He fingered a stone, then hurled it in the direction from which the sun would come. He watched for a long while until it had vanished from sight. Eventually it would begin skipping. Before then, he had turned and was headed back, to the city, the apartment, the girl.

Somewhere beyond the skyline a vehicle lifted, burning its way into the heavens. It took the remainder of the night with it as it faded. Walking on, he smelled the countryside as well as the ocean. It was a pleasant world, and this a pleasant city—spaceport as well as seaport—here in this backwater limb of the galaxy. A good place in which to rest and immerse the neglected portion of himself in the flow of humanity, the colors and sounds of the city, the constant tugging of gravity. But it had been three months now. He fingered the scar on his brow. He had let two offers pass him by to linger. There was another pending his consideration.

As he walked up Kathi's street, he saw that her apartment was still dark. Good, she would not even have missed him, again. He pushed past the big front door, still not repaired since he had kicked it open the evening of the fire, two—no, three—nights ago. He used the stairs. He let himself in quietly.

He was in the kitchen preparing breakfast when he heard her stirring.

"Jack?"

"Yes. Good morning."

"Come back."

"All right."

He moved to the bedroom door and entered the room. She was lying there, smiling. She raised her arms slightly.

"I've thought of a wonderful way to begin the day."

He seated himself on the edge of the bed and embraced her. For a moment she was sleep-warm and sleep-soft against him, but only for a moment.

"You've got too much on," she said, unfastening his shirt.

He peeled it off and dropped it. He removed his trousers.

Then he held her again.

"More," she said, tracing the long fine scar that ran down his forehead, alongside his nose, traversing his chin, his neck, the right side of his chest and abdomen, passing to one side of his groin, where it stopped.

"Come on."

"You didn't even know about it until a few nights ago."

She kissed him, brushing his cheeks with her lips.

"It really does something for me."

"For almost three months—"

"Take it off. Please."

He sighed and gave a half-smile. He rose to his feet.

"All right."

He reached up and put a hand to his long, black hair. He took hold of it. He raised his other hand and spread his fingers along his scalp at the hairline. He pushed his fingers toward the back of his head and the entire hair-piece came free with a soft, crackling sound. He dropped the hairpiece atop his shirt on the floor.

The right side of his head was completely bald; the left had a beginning growth of dark hair. The two areas were precisely divided by a continuation of the faint scar on his forehead.

He placed his fingertips together on the crown of his head, then drew his right hand to the side and down. His face opened vertically, splitting apart along the scar, padded synthetic flesh tearing free from electrostatic bonds. He drew it down over his right shoulder and biceps, rolling it as far as his wrist. He played with the flesh of his hand as with a tight glove, finally withdrawing the hand with a soft, sucking sound. He drew it away from his side, hip, and buttock, and separated it at his groin. Then, again seating himself on the edge of the bed, he rolled it down his leg, over the thigh, knee, calf, heel. He treated his foot as he had his hand, pinching each toe free separately before pulling off the body glove. He shook it out and placed it with his clothing.

Standing, he turned toward Kathi, whose eyes had not left him during all this time. Again, the half-smile. The uncovered portions of his face and body were dark metal and plastic, precision-machined, with various openings and protuberances, some gleaming, some dusky.

"Halfjack," she said as he came to her. "Now I know what that man in the café meant when he called you that."

"He was lucky you were with me. There are places where that's an unfriendly term."

"You're beautiful," she said.

"I once knew a girl whose body was almost entirely prosthetic. She wanted me to keep the glove on—at all times. It was the flesh and the semblance of flesh that she found attractive."

"What do you call that kind of operation?"

"Lateral hemicorporectomy."

After a time she said, "Could you be repaired? Can you replace it some way?"

He laughed.

"Either way," he said. "My genes could be fractioned, and the proper replacement parts could be grown. I could be made whole with grafts of my own flesh. Or I could have much of the rest removed and replaced with biomechanical analogues. But I need a stomach and balls and lungs, because I have to eat and screw and breathe to feel human."

She ran her hands down his back, one on metal, one on flesh.

"I don't understand," she said when they finally drew apart. "What sort of accident was it?"

"Accident? There was no accident," he said. "I paid a lot of money for this work, so that I could pilot a special sort of ship. I am a cyborg. I hook myself directly into each of the ship's systems."

He rose from the bed, went to the closet, drew out a duffel bag, pulled down an armful of garments, and stuffed them into it. He crossed to the dresser, opened a drawer, and emptied its contents into the bag.

"You're leaving?"

"Yes."

He entered the bathroom, emerged with two fistfuls of personal items, and dropped them into the bag.

"Why?"

He rounded the bed, picked up his bodyglove and hairpiece, rolled them into a parcel, and put them inside the bag.

"It's not what you may think," he said then, "or even what I thought until just a few moments ago."

She sat up.

"You think less of me," she said, "because I seem to like you more now that I know your secret. You think there's something pathological about it—"

"No," he said, pulling on his shirt, "that's not it at all. Yesterday I would have said so and used that for an excuse to storm out of here and leave you feeling bad. But I want to be honest with myself this time, and fair to you. That's not it."

He drew on his trousers.

"What then?" she asked.

"It's just the wanderlust, or whatever you call it. I've stayed too long at the bottom of a gravity well. I'm restless. I've got to get going again. It's my nature, that's all. I realized this when I saw that I was looking to your feelings for an excuse to break us up and move on."

"You can wear the bodyglove. It's not that important. It's really you that I like."

"I believe you, I like you, too. Whether you believe me or not, your reactions to my better half don't matter. It's what I said, though. Nothing else. And now I've got this feeling I won't be much fun anymore. If you really like me, you'll let me go without a lot of fuss."

He finished dressing. She got out of the bed and faced him.

"If that's the way it has to be," she said. "Okay."

"I'd better just go, then. Now."

"Yes."

He turned and walked out of the room, left the apartment, used the stairs again, and departed from the building. Some passersby gave him more than a casual look, cyborg pilots not being all that common in this sector. This did not bother him. His step lightened. He stopped in a paybooth and called the shipping company to tell them that he would haul the load they had in orbit: the sooner it was connected with the vessel, the better, he said.

Loading, the controller told him, would begin shortly and he could ship up that same afternoon from the local field. Jack said that he would be there and then broke the connection. He gave the world half a smile as he put the sea to his back and swung on through the city, westward.

❖ ❖ ❖

Blue-and-pink world below him, black sky above, the stars a snapshot snowfall all about, he bade the shuttle pilot goodbye and keyed his airlock. Entering the *Morgana*, he sighed and set about stowing his gear. His cargo was already in place and the ground computers had transferred course information to the ship's brain. He hung his clothing in a locker and placed his body glove and hairpiece in compartments.

He hurried forward then and settled into the control web, which adjusted itself about him. A long, dark unit swung down from overhead and dropped into position at his right. It moved slowly, making contact with various points on that half of his body.

—Good to have you back. How was your vacation, Jack?

—Oh. Fine. Real fine.

—Meet any nice girls?

—A few.

—And here you are again. Did you miss things?

—You know it. How does this haul look to you?

—Easy, for us. I've already reviewed the course programs.

—Let's run over the systems.

—Check. Care for some coffee?

—That'd be nice.

A small unit descended on his left, stopping within easy reach of his mortal hand. He opened its door. A bulb of dark liquid rested in a rack.

—Timed your arrival. Had it ready.

—Just the way I like it, too. I almost forgot. Thanks.

Several hours later, when they left orbit, he had already switched off a number of his left-side systems. He was merged even more closely with the vessel, absorbing data at a frantic rate. Their expanded perceptions took in the near-ship vicinity and moved out to encompass the extrasolar panorama with greater than human clarity and precision. They reacted almost instantaneously to decisions great and small.

—It is good to be back together again, Jack.

—I'd say.

Morgana held him tightly. Their velocity built.

A Word from Zelazny

"One day, I saw a nice, slick, pretty, new magazine called *Omni* and was overcome by the desire to have a story in it, so I wrote this one and did."[1] The story (or at least the manuscript title) had been bothering Zelazny's psyche for some time, as revealed by the poem "Riptide" (see afterword to "Riptide").

This character intrigued Zelazny. He thought of bringing him back but did not. "It's more likely for me to have done a short story where I feel I might bring the character back at greater length, or as part of a novel; something like Halfjack."[2]

Notes

Fata **Morgana**, or Morgan le Fay, was King Arthur's half sister, a powerful sorceress and sometime antagonist to Arthur and Guinevere.

1 *The Last Defender of Camelot*, 1980.
2 *Xignals XVI* Feb/Mar 1986.

On the Return of the Mercurian Flamebird after Nesting

Second Mercenary, Summer 1965.

Red flush of feathers
in bright hours restlessly homing;
green-beaked lancet
through pink clouds endlessly probing—

Nightside is home.
Nesting is here.

The time has come to beat the air
to tatters,
                return to the dark,
to exult, thunder-throated,
in victories over color…

It is to hide a flame
in parkways of the night;
and also, it is to leave
thy bright-hatched fledglings
in the places, here, of daytime,
to quit the inspiration of this song—
to go away,
to go back.

I lack the power
to bind thy flight to words;
I lack those essential drops—
purity's alchemical delight—
to 'mute thy passage
to more than words of color,
to bend thy going
to more than a passing flight;

but here,
drenched by chemistries of day,
I sing this fleeting monument
to color and wonder,
and I also try this glory,
and perhaps to tune this light…

Funny.

Notes

The **Mercurian** (of Mercury) **Flamebird** resembles the mythical Phoenix. A **lancet**, a small surgical knife, is the bird's sharp beak. **'Mute** is transmute, to change form. **Alchemical** refers to the theory that matter could be transmuted, such as changing base metals into gold.

THE LAST DEFENDER OF CAMELOT

Asimov's SF Adventure Magazine #3, Summer 1979.
Balrog award 1980 (short fiction).

The three muggers who stopped him that October night in San Francisco did not anticipate much resistance from the old man, despite his size. He was well-dressed, and that was sufficient.

The first approached him with his hand extended. The other two hung back a few paces.

"Just give me your wallet and your watch," the mugger said. "You'll save yourself a lot of trouble."

The old man's grip shifted on his walking stick. His shoulders straightened. His shock of white hair tossed as he turned his head to regard the other.

"Why don't you come and take it then?"

The mugger began another step but he never completed it. The stick was almost invisible in the speed of its swinging. It struck him on the left temple and he fell.

Without pausing, the old man caught the stick by its middle with his left hand, advanced and drove it into the belly of the next nearest man. Then, with an upward hook as the man doubled, he caught him in the softness beneath the jaw, behind the chin, with its point. As the man fell, he clubbed him with its butt on the back of the neck.

The third man had reached out and caught the old man's upper arm by then. Dropping the stick, the old man seized the mugger's shirtfront with his left hand, his belt with his right, raised him from the ground until he held him at arm's length above his head and slammed him against the side of the building to his right, releasing him as he did so.

He adjusted his apparel, ran a hand through his hair and retrieved his walking stick. For a moment he regarded the three fallen forms, then shrugged and continued on his way.

There were sounds of traffic from somewhere off to his left. He turned right at the next corner. The moon appeared above tall buildings as he walked. The smell of the ocean was on the air. It had rained earlier and the pavement still shone beneath streetlamps. He moved slowly, pausing occasionally to examine the contents of darkened shop windows.

After perhaps ten minutes, he came upon a side street showing more activity than any of the others he had passed. There was a drugstore, still open, on the corner, a diner farther up the block, and several well-lighted storefronts. A number of people were walking along the far side of the street. A boy coasted by on a bicycle. He turned there, his pale eyes regarding everything he passed.

Halfway up the block, he came to a dirty window on which was painted the word READINGS. Beneath it were displayed the outline of a hand and a scattering of playing cards. As he passed the open door, he glanced inside. A brightly garbed woman, her hair bound back in a green kerchief, sat smoking at the rear of the room. She smiled as their eyes met and crooked an index finger, toward herself. He smiled back and turned away, but…

He looked at her again. What was it? He glanced at his watch.

Turning, he entered the shop and moved to stand before her. She rose. She was small, barely over five feet in height.

"Your eyes," he remarked, "are green. Most gypsies I know have dark eyes."

She shrugged.

"You take what you get in life. Have you a problem?"

"Give me a moment and I'll think of one," he said. "I just came in here because you remind me of someone and it bothers me—I can't think who."

"Come into the back," she said, "and sit down. We'll talk."

He nodded and followed her into a small room to the rear. A threadbare oriental rug covered the floor near the small table at which they seated themselves. Zodiacal prints and faded psychedelic posters of a semireligious nature covered the walls. A crystal ball stood on a small stand in the far corner beside a vase of cut flowers. A dark, long-haired cat slept on a sofa to the right of it. A door to another room stood slightly ajar beyond the sofa. The only illumination came from a cheap lamp on the table before him and from a small candle in a plaster base atop the shawl-covered coffee table.

He leaned forward and studied her face, then shook his head and leaned back.

She flicked an ash onto the floor.

"Your problem?" she suggested.

He sighed.

"Oh, I don't really have a problem anyone can help me with. Look, I think I made a mistake coming in here. I'll pay you for your trouble, though, just as if you'd given me a reading. How much is it?"

He began to reach for his wallet, but she raised her hand.

"Is it that you do not believe in such things?" she asked, her eyes scrutinizing his face.

"No, quite the contrary," he replied. "I am willing to believe in magic, divination and all manner of spells and sendings, angelic and demonic. But—"

"But not from someone in a dump like this?"

He smiled.

"No offense," he said.

A whistling sound filled the air. It seemed to come from the next room back.

"That's all right," she said, "but my water is boiling. I'd forgotten it was on. Have some tea with me? I do wash the cups. No charge. Things are slow."

"All right."

She rose and departed.

He glanced at the door to the front but eased himself back into his chair, resting his large, blue-veined bands on its padded arms. He sniffed then, nostrils flaring, and cocked his head as at some half-familiar aroma.

After a time, she returned with a tray, set it on the coffee table. The cat stirred, raised her head, blinked at it, stretched, closed her eyes again.

"Cream and sugar?"

"Please. One lump."

She placed two cups on the table before him.

"Take either one," she said.

He smiled and drew the one on his left toward him. She placed an ashtray in the middle of the table and returned to her own seat, moving the other cup to her place.

"That wasn't necessary," he said, placing his hands on the table.

She shrugged.

"You don't know me. Why should you trust me? Probably got a lot of money on you."

He looked at her face again. She had apparently removed some of the heavier makeup while in the back room. The jawline, the brow... He looked away. He took a sip of tea.

"Good tea. Not instant," he said. "Thanks."

"So you believe in all sorts of magic?" she asked, sipping her own.

"Some," he said.

"Any special reason why?"

"Some of it works."

"For example?"

He gestured aimlessly with his left hand.

"I've traveled a lot. I've seen some strange things."

"And you have no problems?"

He chuckled.

"Still determined to give me a reading? All right. I'll tell you a little about myself and what I want right now, and you can tell me whether I'll get it. Okay?"

"I'm listening."

"I am a buyer for a large gallery in the East. I am something of an authority on ancient work in precious metals. I am in town to attend an auction of such items from the estate of a private collector. I will go to inspect the pieces tomorrow. Naturally, I hope to find something good. What do you think my chances are?"

"Give me your hands."

He extended them, palms upward. She leaned forward and regarded them. She looked back up at him immediately.

"Your wrists have more rascettes than I can count!"

"Yours seem to have quite a few, also."

She met his eyes for only a moment and returned her attention to his hands. He noted that she had paled beneath what remained of her makeup, and her breathing was now irregular.

"No," she finally said, drawing back, "you are not going to find here what you are looking for."

Her hand trembled slightly as she raised her teacup.

He frowned. "I asked only in jest," he said. "Nothing to get upset about. I doubted I would find what I am really looking for, anyway."

She shook her head.

"Tell me your name."

"I've lost my accent," he said, "but I'm French. The name is DuLac."

She stared into his eyes and began to blink rapidly.

"No..." she said. "No."

"I'm afraid so. What's yours?"

"Madam LeFay," she said. "I just repainted that sign. It's still drying."

He began to laugh, but it froze in his throat.

"Now—I know—who—you remind me of..."

"You reminded me of someone, also. Now I, too, know."

Her eyes brimmed, her mascara ran.

"It couldn't be," he said. "Not here... Not in a place like this..."

"You dear man," she said softly, and she raised his right hand to her lips. She seemed to choke for a moment, then said, "I had thought that I was the last, and yourself buried at Joyous Gard. I never dreamed..." Then, "This?" gesturing about the room. "Only because it amuses me, helps to pass the time. The waiting—"

She stopped. She lowered his hand.

"Tell me about it," she said.

"The waiting?" he said. "For what do you wait?"

"Peace," she said. "I am here by the power of my arts, through all the long years. But you—How did you manage it?"

"I—" He took another drink of tea. He looked about the room. "I do not know how to begin," he said. "I survived the final battles, saw the kingdom sundered, could do nothing—and at last departed England. I wandered, taking service at many courts, and after a time under many names, as I saw that I was not aging—or aging very, very slowly. I was in India, China—I fought in the Crusades. I've been everywhere. I've spoken with magicians and mystics—most of them charlatans, a few with the power, none so great as Merlin—and what had come to be my own belief was confirmed by one of them, a man more than half charlatan, yet..." He paused and finished his tea. "Are you certain you want to hear all this?" he asked.

"I want to hear it. Let me bring more tea first, though."

She returned with the tea. She lit a cigarette and leaned back.

"Go on."

"I decided that it was—my sin," he said. "With…the Queen."

"I don't understand."

"I betrayed my Liege, who was also my friend, in the one thing which must have hurt him most. The love I felt was stronger than loyalty or friendship—and even today, to this day, it still is. I cannot repent, and so I cannot be forgiven. Those were strange and magical times. We lived in a land destined to become myth. Powers walked the realm in those days, forces which are now gone from the earth. How or why, I cannot say. But you know that it is true. I am somehow of a piece with those gone things, and the laws that rule my existence are not normal laws of the natural world. I believe that I cannot die; that it has fallen my lot, as punishment, to wander the world till I have completed the Quest. I believe I will only know rest the day I find the Holy Grail. Giuseppe Balsamo, before he became known as Cagliostro, somehow saw this and said it to me just as I had thought it, though I never said a word of it to him. And so I have traveled the world, searching. I go no more as knight, or soldier, but as an appraiser. I have been in nearly every museum on Earth, viewed all the great private collections. So far, it has eluded me."

"You *are* getting a little old for battle."

He snorted.

"I have never lost," he stated flatly. "Down ten centuries, I have never lost a personal contest. It is true that I have aged, yet whenever I am threatened all of my former strength returns to me. But, look where I may, fight where I may, it has never served me to discover that which I must find. I feel I am unforgiven and must wander like the Eternal Jew until the end of the world."

She lowered her head.

"…And you say I will not find it tomorrow?"

"You will never find it," she said softly.

"You saw that in my hand?"

She shook her head.

"Your story is fascinating and your theory novel," she began, "but Cagliostro was a total charlatan. Something must have betrayed your thoughts, and he made a shrewd guess. But he was wrong. I say that you will never find it, not because you are unworthy or unforgiven. No, never that. A more loyal subject than yourself never drew breath. Don't you know that Arthur forgave you? It was an arranged marriage. The same thing happened constantly elsewhere, as you must know. You gave her something he could not. There was only tenderness there. He understood. The only forgiveness you require is that which has been withheld all these long years—your own. No, it is not a doom that has been laid upon you. It is your own feelings which led you to assume an impossible quest, something tantamount to total unforgiveness. But you have suffered all these centuries upon the wrong trail."

When she raised her eyes, she saw that his were hard, like ice or gemstones. But she met his, gaze and continued: "There is not now, was not then, and probably never was, a Holy Grail."

"I saw it," he said, "that day it passed through the Hall of the Table. We all saw it."

"You thought you saw it," she corrected him. "I hate to shatter an illusion that has withstood all the other tests of time, but I fear I must. The kingdom, as you recall, was at that time in turmoil. The knights were growing restless and falling away from the fellowship. A year—six months, even—and all would have collapsed, all Arthur had striven so hard to put together. He knew that the longer Camelot stood, the longer its name would endure, the stronger its ideals would become. So he made a decision, a purely political one. Something was needed to hold things together. He called upon Merlin, already half-mad, yet still shrewd enough to see what was needed and able to provide it. The Quest was born. Merlin's powers created the illusion you saw that day. It was a lie, yes. A glorious lie, though. And it served for years after to bind you all in brotherhood, in the name of justice and love. It entered literature, it promoted nobility and the higher ends of culture. It served its purpose. But it was—never—really—there. You have been chasing a ghost. I am sorry Launcelot, but I have absolutely no reason to lie to you. I know magic when I see it. I saw it then. That is how it happened."

For a long while he was silent. Then he laughed.

"You have an answer for everything," he said. "I could almost believe you, if you could but answer me one thing more—Why am I here? For what reason? By what power? How is it I have been preserved for half the Christian era while other men grow old and die in a handful of years? Can you tell me now what Cagliostro could not?"

"Yes," she said, "I believe that I can."

He rose to his feet and began to pace. The cat, alarmed, sprang from the sofa and ran into the back room. He stooped and snatched up his walking stick. He started for the door.

"I suppose it was worth waiting a thousand years to see you afraid," she said.

He halted.

"That is unfair," he replied.

"I know. But now you will come back and sit down," she said.

He was smiling once more as he turned and returned.

"Tell me," he said. "How do you see it?"

"Yours was the last enchantment of Merlin, that is how I see it."

"Merlin? Me? Why?"

"Gossip had it the old goat took Nimue into the woods and she had to use one of his own spells on him in self-defense—a spell which caused him to sleep forever in some lost place. If it was the spell that I believe it was, then at least part of the rumor was incorrect. There was no known counterspell, but the effects of the enchantment would have caused him to sleep not forever but for a millennium or so, and then to awaken. My guess now is that his last conscious act before he dropped off was to lay this enchantment upon you, so that you would be on hand when he returned."

"I suppose it might be possible, but why would he want me or need me?"

"If I were journeying into a strange time, I would want an ally once I reached it. And if I had a choice, I would want it to be the greatest champion of the day."

"Merlin..." he mused. "I suppose that it could be as you say. Excuse me, but a long life has just been shaken up, from beginning to end. If this is true..."

"I am sure that it is."

"If this is true... A millennium, you say?"

"More or less."

"Well, it is almost that time now."

"I know. I do not believe that our meeting tonight was a matter of chance. You are destined to meet him upon his awakening, which should be soon. Something has ordained that you meet me first, however, to be warned."

"Warned? Warned of what?"

"He is mad, Launcelot. Many of us felt a great relief at his passing. If the realm had not been sundered finally by strife it would probably have been broken by his hand, anyway."

"That I find difficult to believe. He was always a strange man—for who can fully understand a sorcerer?—and in his later years he did seem at least partly daft. But he never struck me as evil."

"Nor was he. His was the most dangerous morality of all. He was a misguided idealist. In a more primitive time and place and with a willing tool like Arthur, he was able to create a legend. Today, in an age of monstrous weapons, with the right leader as his catspaw, he could unleash something totally devastating. He would see a wrong and force his man to try righting it. He would do it in the name of the same high ideal he always served, but he would not appreciate the results until it was too late. How could he—even if he were sane? He has no conception of modem international relations."

"What is to be done? What is my part in all of this?"

"I believe you should go back, to England, to be present at his awakening, to find out exactly what he wants, to try to reason with him."

"I don't know… How would I find him?"

"You found me. When the time is right, you will be in the proper place. I am certain of that. It was meant to be, probably even a part of his spell. Seek him. But do not trust him."

"I don't know, Morgana." He looked at the wall, unseeing. "I don't know."

"You have waited this long and you draw back now from finally finding out?"

"You are right—in that much, at least." He folded his hands, raised them and rested his chin upon them. "What I would do if he really returned, I do not know. Try to reason with him, yes—Have you any other advice?"

"Just that you be there."

"You've looked at my hand. You have the power. What did you see?"

She turned away.

"It is uncertain," she said.

❖ ❖ ❖

That night he dreamed, as he sometimes did, of times long gone. They sat about the great Table, as they had on that day. Gawaine was there and Percival. Galahad… He winced. This day was different from other days. There was a certain tension in the air, a before-the-storm feeling, an electrical thing… Merlin stood at the far end of the room, hands in the sleeves of his long robe, hair and beard snowy and unkempt, pale eyes staring—at what, none could be certain…

After some timeless time, a reddish glow appeared near the door. All eyes moved toward it. It grew brighter and advanced slowly into the room—a formless apparition of light. There were sweet odors and some few soft strains of music. Gradually, a form began to take shape at its center, resolving itself into the likeness of a chalice…

He felt himself rising, moving slowly, following it in its course through the great chamber, advancing upon it, soundlessly and deliberately, as if moving under-water…

…Reaching for it.

His hand entered the circle of light, moved toward its center, neared the now blazing cup and passed through…

Immediately, the light faded. The outline of the chalice wavered, and it collapsed in upon itself, fading, fading, gone…

There came a sound, rolling, echoing about the hall. Laughter.

He turned and regarded the others. They sat about the table, watching him, laughing. Even Merlin managed a dry chuckle.

Suddenly, his great blade was in his hand, and he raised it as he strode toward the Table. The knights nearest him drew back as he brought the weapon crashing down.

The Table split in half and fell. The room shook.

The quaking continued. Stones were dislodged from the walls. A roof beam fell. He raised his arm.

The entire castle began to come apart, falling about him and still the laughter continued.

He awoke damp with perspiration and lay still for a long while. In the morning, he bought a ticket for London.

❖ ❖ ❖

Two of the three elemental sounds of the world were suddenly with him as he walked that evening, stick in hand. For a dozen days, he had hiked about Cornwall, finding no clues to that which he sought. He had allowed himself two more before giving up and departing.

Now the wind and the rain were upon him, and he increased his pace. The fresh-lit stars were smothered by a mass of cloud and wisps of fog grew like ghostly fungi on either hand. He moved among trees, paused, continued on.

"Shouldn't have stayed out this late," he muttered, and after several more pauses, *"Nel mezzo del cammin di nostra vita mi ritrovai per una selva oscura, che la diritta via era smarrita,"* then he chuckled, halting beneath a tree.

The rain was not heavy. It was more a fine mist now. A bright patch in the lower heavens showed where the moon hung veiled.

He wiped his face, turned up his collar. He studied the position of the moon. After a time, he struck off to his right. There was a faint rumble of thunder in the distance.

The fog continued to grow about him as he went. Soggy leaves made squishing noises beneath his boots. An animal of indeterminate size bolted from a clump of shrubbery beside a cluster of rocks and tore off through the darkness.

Five minutes...ten... He cursed softly. The rainfall had increased in intensity. Was that the same rock?

He turned in a complete circle. All directions were equally uninviting. Selecting one at random, he commenced walking once again.

Then, in the distance, he discerned a spark, a glow, a wavering light. It vanished and reappeared periodically, as though partly blocked, the line of sight a function of his movements. He headed toward it. After perhaps half a minute, it was gone again from sight, but he continued on in what he thought to be its direction. There came another roll of thunder, louder this time.

When it seemed that it might have been illusion or some short-lived natural phenomenon, something else occurred in that same direction. There was a movement, a shadow-within-shadow shuffling at the foot of a great tree. He slowed his pace, approaching the spot cautiously.

There!

A figure detached itself from a pool of darkness ahead and to the left. Manlike, it moved with a slow and heavy tread, creaking sounds emerging from the forest floor beneath it. A vagrant moonbeam touched it for a moment, and it appeared yellow and metallically slick beneath moisture.

He halted. It seemed that he had just regarded a knight in full armor in his path. How long since he had beheld such a sight? He shook his head and stared.

The figure had also halted. It raised its right arm in a beckoning gesture, then turned and began to walk away. He hesitated for only a moment, then followed.

It turned off to the left and pursued a treacherous path, rocky, slippery, heading slightly downward. He actually used his stick now, to assure his footing, as he tracked its deliberate progress. He gained on it, to the point where he could clearly hear the metallic scraping sounds of its passage.

Then it was gone, swallowed by a greater darkness.

He advanced to the place where he had last beheld it. He stood in the lee of a great mass of stone. He reached out and probed it with his stick.

He tapped steadily along its nearest surface, and then the stick moved past it. He followed.

There was an opening, a crevice. He had to turn sidewise to pass within it, but as he did the full glow of the light he had seen came into sight for several seconds.

The passage curved and widened, leading him back and down. Several times, he paused and listened, but there were no sounds other than his own breathing.

He withdrew his handkerchief and dried his face and hands carefully. He brushed moisture from his coat, turned down his collar. He scuffed the mud and leaves from his boots. He adjusted his apparel. Then he strode forward, rounding a final corner, into a chamber lit by a small oil lamp suspended by three delicate chains from some point in the darkness overhead. The yellow knight stood unmoving beside the far wall. On a fiber mat atop a stony pedestal directly beneath the lamp lay an old man in tattered garments. His bearded face was half-masked by shadows.

He moved to the old man's side. He saw then that those ancient dark eyes were open.

"Merlin...?" he whispered.

There came a faint hissing sound, a soft croak. Realizing the source, he leaned nearer.

"Elixir...in earthern rock...on ledge...in back," came the gravelly whisper.

He turned and sought the ledge, the container.

"Do you know where it is?" he asked the yellow figure.

It neither stirred nor replied, but stood like a display piece. He turned away from it then and sought further. After a time, he located it. It was more a niche than a ledge, blending in with the wall, cloaked with shadow. He ran his fingertips over the container's contours, raised it gently. Something liquid stirred within it. He wiped its lip on his sleeve after he had returned to the lighted area. The wind whistled past the entranceway and he thought he felt the faint vibration of thunder.

Sliding one hand beneath his shoulders, he raised the ancient form. Merlin's eyes still seemed unfocussed. He moistened Merlin's lips with the liquid. The old man licked them, and after several moments opened his mouth. He administered a sip, then another, and another...

Merlin signalled for him to lower him, and he did. He glanced again at the yellow armor, but it had remained motionless the entire while. He looked back at the sorcerer and saw that a new light had come into his eyes and he was studying him, smiling faintly.

"Feel better?"

Merlin nodded. A minute passed, and a touch of color appeared upon his cheeks. He elbowed himself into a sitting position and took the container into his hands. He raised it and drank deeply.

He sat still for several minutes after that. His thin hands, which had appeared waxy in the flamelight, grew darker, fuller. His shoulders straightened. He placed the crock on the bed beside him and stretched his arms. His joints creaked the first time he did it, but not the second.

He swung his legs over the edge of the bed and rose slowly to his feet. He was a full head shorter than Launcelot.

"It is done," he said, staring back into the shadows. "Much has happened, of course..."

"Much has happened," Launcelot replied.

"You have lived through it all. Tell me, is the world a better place or is it worse than it was in those days?"

"Better in some ways, worse in others. It is different."

"How is it better?"

"There are many ways of making life easier, and the sum total of human knowledge has increased vastly."

"How has it worsened?"

"There are many more people in the world. Consequently, there are many more people suffering from poverty, disease, ignorance. The world itself has suffered great depredation, in the way of pollution and other assaults on the integrity of nature."

"Wars?"

"There is always someone fighting, somewhere."

"They need help."

"Maybe. Maybe not."

Merlin turned and looked into his eyes.

"What do you mean?"

"People haven't changed. They are as rational—and irrational—as they were in the old days. They are as moral and law-abiding—and not—as ever. Many new things have been learned, many new situations evolved, but I do not believe that the nature of man has altered significantly in the time you've slept. Nothing you do is going to change that. You may be able to alter a few features of the times, but would it really be proper to meddle? Everything is so interdependent today that even you would not be able to predict all the consequences of any actions you take. You might do more harm than good; and whatever you do, man's nature will remain the same."

"This isn't like you, Lance. You were never much given to philosophizing in the old days."

"I've had a long time to think about it."

"And I've had a long time to dream about it. War is your craft, Lance. Stay with that."

"I gave it up a long time ago."

"Then what are you now?"

"An appraiser."

Merlin turned away, took another drink. He seemed to radiate a fierce energy when he turned again.

"And your oath? To right wrongs, to punish the wicked...?"

"The longer I lived the more difficult it became to determine what was a wrong and who was wicked. Make it clear to me again and I may go back into business."

"Galahad would never have addressed me so."

"Galahad was young, naïve, trusting. Speak not to me of my son."

"Launcelot! Launcelot!" He placed a hand on his arm. "Why all this bitterness for an old friend who has done nothing for a thousand years?"

"I wished to make my position clear immediately. I feared you might contemplate some irreversible action which could alter the world balance of power fatally. I want you to know that I will not be party to it."

"Admit that you do not know what I might do, what I can do."

"Freely. That is why I fear you. What *do* you intend to do?"

"Nothing, at first. I wish merely to look about me, to see for myself some of these changes of which you have spoken. Then I will consider which wrongs need righting, who needs punishment, and who to choose as my champions. I will show you these things, and then you can go back into business, as you say."

Launcelot sighed.

"The burden of proof is on the moralist. Your judgment is no longer sufficient for me."

"Dear me," the other replied, "it is sad to have waited this long for an encounter of this sort, to find you have lost your faith in me.

My powers are beginning to return already, Lance. Do you not feel magic in the air?"

"I feel something I have not felt in a long while."

"The sleep of ages was a restorative—an aid, actually. In a while. Lance, I am going to be stronger than I ever was before. And you doubt that I will be able to turn back the clock?"

"I doubt you can do it in a fashion to benefit anybody. Look, Merlin, I'm sorry. I do not like it that things have come to this either. But I have lived too long, seen too much, know too much of how the world works now to trust any one man's opinion concerning its salvation. Let it go. You are a mysterious, revered legend. I do not know what you really are. But forgo exercising your powers in any sort of crusade. Do something else this time around. Become a physician and fight pain. Take up painting. Be a professor of history, an antiquarian. Hell, be a social critic and point out what evils you see for people to correct themselves."

"Do you really believe I could be satisfied with any of those things?"

"Men find satisfaction in many things. It depends on the man, not on the things. I'm just saying that you should avoid using your powers in any attempt to effect social changes as we once did, by violence."

"Whatever changes have been wrought, time's greatest irony lies in its having transformed you into a pacifist."

"You are wrong."

"Admit it! You have finally come to fear the clash of arms! An appraiser! What kind of knight are you?"

"One who finds himself in the wrong time and the wrong place, Merlin."

The sorcerer shrugged and turned away.

"Let it be, then. It is good that you have chosen to tell me all these things immediately. Thank you for that, anyway. A moment."

Merlin walked to the rear of the cave, returned in moments attired in fresh garments. The effect was startling. His entire appearance was more kempt and cleanly. His hair and beard now appeared gray rather than white. His step was sure and steady. He held a staff in his right hand but did not lean upon it.

"Come walk with me," he said.

"It is a bad night."

"It is not the same night you left without. It is not even the same place."

As he passed the suit of yellow armor, he snapped his fingers near its visor. With a single creak, the figure moved and turned to follow him.

"Who is that?"

Merlin smiled.

"No one," he replied, and he reached back and raised the visor. The helmet was empty. "It is enchanted, animated by a spirit," he said. "A trifle clumsy, though, which is why I did not trust it to administer my draught. A perfect servant, however, unlike some. Incredibly strong and swift. Even in your prime you could not have beaten it. I fear nothing when it walks with me. Come, there is something I would have you see."

"Very well."

Launcelot followed Merlin and the hollow knight from the cave. The rain had stopped, and it was very still. They stood on an incredibly moonlit plain where mists drifted and grasses sparkled. Shadowy shapes stood in the distance.

"Excuse me," Launcelot said. "I left my walking stick inside."

He turned and re-entered the cave.

"Yes, fetch it, old man," Merlin replied. "Your strength is already on the wane."

When Launcelot returned, he leaned upon the stick and squinted across the plain.

"This way," Merlin said, "to where your questions will be answered. I will try not to move too quickly and tire you."

"Tire me?"

The sorcerer chuckled and began walking across the plain. Launcelot followed.

"Do you not feel a trifle weary?" he asked.

"Yes, as a matter of fact, I do. Do you know what is the matter with me?"

"Of course. I have withdrawn the enchantment which has protected you all these years. What you feel now are the first tentative touches of your true age. It will take some time to catch up with you, against your body's natural resistance, but it is beginning its advance."

"Why are you doing this to me?"

"Because I believed you when you said you were not a pacifist. And you spoke with sufficient vehemence for me to realize that you might even oppose me. I could not permit that, for I knew that your old strength was still there for you to call upon. Even a sorcerer might fear that, so I did what had to be done. By my power was it maintained; without it, it now drains away. It would have been good for us to work together once again, but I saw that that could not be."

Launcelot stumbled, caught himself, limped on. The hollow knight walked at Merlin's right hand.

"You say that your ends are noble," Launcelot said, "but I do not believe you. Perhaps in the old days they were. But more than the times have changed. You are different. Do you not feel it yourself?"

Merlin drew a deep breath and exhaled vapor.

"Perhaps it is my heritage," he said. Then, "I jest. Of course, I have changed. Everyone does. You yourself are a perfect example. What you consider a turn for the worse in me is but the tip of an irreducible conflict which has grown up between us in the course of our changes. I still hold with the true ideals of Camelot."

Launcelot's shoulders were bent forward now and his breathing had deepened. The shapes loomed larger before them.

"Why, I know this place," he gasped. "Yet, I do not know it. Stonehenge does not stand so today. Even in Arthur's time it lacked this perfection. How did we get here? What has happened?"

He paused to rest, and Merlin halted to accommodate him.

"This night we have walked between the worlds," the sorcerer said. "This is a piece of the land of Faerie and that is the true Stonehenge, a holy place. I have stretched the bounds of the worlds to bring it here. Were I unkind I could send you back with it and strand you there forever. But it is better that you know a sort of peace. Come!"

Launcelot staggered along behind him, heading for the great circle of stones. The faintest of breezes came out of the west, stirring the mists.

"What do you mean—know a sort of peace?"

"The complete restoration of my powers and their increase will require a sacrifice in this place."

"Then you planned this for me all along!"

"No. It was not to have been you, Lance. Anyone would have served, though you will serve superbly well. It need not have been so, had you elected to assist me. You could still change your mind."

"Would you want someone who did that at your side?"

"You have a point there."

"Then why ask—save as a petty cruelty?"

"It is just that, for you have annoyed me."

Launcelot halted again when they came to the circle's periphery. He regarded the massive stands of stone.

"If you will not enter willingly," Merlin stated, "my servant will be happy to assist you."

Launcelot spat, straightened a little and glared.

"Think you I fear an empty suit of armor, juggled by some Hell-born wight? Even now, Merlin, without the benefit of wizardly succor, I could take that thing apart."

The sorcerer laughed.

"It is good that you at least recall the boasts of knighthood when all else has left you. I've half a mind to give you the opportunity, for the manner of your passing here is not important. Only the preliminaries are essential."

"But you're afraid to risk your servant?"

"Think you so, old man? I doubt you could even bear the weight of a suit of armor, let alone lift a lance. But if you are willing to try, so be it!"

He rapped the butt of his staff three times upon the ground.

"Enter," he said then. "You will find all that you need within. And I am glad you have made this choice. You were insufferable, you know. Just once, I longed to see you beaten, knocked down to the level of lesser mortals. I only wish the Queen could be here, to witness her champion's final engagement."

"So do I," said Launcelot, and he walked past the monolith and entered the circle.

A black stallion waited, its reins held down beneath a rock. Pieces of armor, a lance, a blade and a shield leaned against the side of the dolmen. Across the circle's diameter, a white stallion awaited the advance of the hollow knight.

"I am sorry I could not arrange for a page or a squire to assist you," Merlin, said, coming around the other side of the monolith. "I'll be glad to help you myself, though."

"I can manage," Launcelot replied.

"My champion is accoutered in exactly the same fashion," Merlin said, "and I have not given him any edge over you in weapons."

"I never liked your puns either."

Launcelot made friends with the horse, then removed a small strand of red from his wallet and tied it about the butt of the lance. He leaned his stick against the dolmen stone and began to don the armor. Merlin, whose hair and beard were now almost black, moved off several paces and began drawing a diagram in the dirt with the end of his staff.

"You used to favor a white charger," he commented, "but I thought it appropriate to equip you with one of another color, since you have abandoned the ideals of the Table Round, betraying the memory of Camelot."

"On the contrary," Launcelot replied, glancing overhead at the passage of a sudden roll of thunder. "Any horse in a storm, and I am Camelot's last defender."

Merlin continued to elaborate upon the pattern he was drawing as Launcelot slowly equipped himself. The small wind continued to blow, stirring the mist. There came a flash of lightning, startling the horse. Launcelot calmed it.

Merlin stared at him for a moment and rubbed his eyes. Launcelot donned his helmet.

"For a moment," Merlin said, "you looked somehow different..."

"Really? Magical withdrawal, do you think?" he asked, and he kicked the stone from the reins and mounted the stallion.

Merlin stepped back from the now-completed diagram, shaking his head, as the mounted man leaned over and grasped the lance.

"You still seem to move with some strength," he said.

"Really?"

Launcelot raised the lance and couched it. Before taking up the shield he had hung at the saddle's side, he opened his visor and turned and regarded Merlin.

"Your champion appears to be ready," he said. "So am I."

Seen in another flash of light, it was an unlined face that looked down at Merlin, clear-eyed, wisps of pale gold hair fringing the forehead.

"What magic have the years taught you?" Merlin asked.

"Not magic," Launcelot replied. "Caution. I anticipated you. So, when I returned to the cave for my stick, I drank the rest of your elixir."

He lowered the visor and turned away.

"You walked like an old man..."

"I'd a lot of practice. Signal your champion!"

Merlin laughed.

"Good! It is better this way," he decided, "to see you go down in full strength! You still cannot hope to win against a spirit!"

Launcelot raised the shield and leaned forward.

"Then what are you waiting for?"

"Nothing!" Merlin said. Then he shouted, "Kill him, Raxas!"

A light rain began as they pounded across the field; and staring ahead, Launcelot realized that flames were flickering behind his opponent's visor. At the last possible moment, he shifted the point of his lance into line with the hollow knight's blazing helm. There came more lightning and thunder.

His shield deflected the others lance while his went on to strike the approaching head. It flew from the hollow knight's shoulders and bounced, smouldering, on the ground.

He continued on to the other end of the field and turned. When he had, he saw that the hollow knight, now headless, was doing the same. And beyond him, he saw two standing figures, where moments before there had been but one.

Morgan Le Fay, clad in a white robe, red hair unbound and blowing in the wind, faced Merlin from across his pattern. It seemed they were speaking, but he could not hear the words. Then she began to raise her hands, and they glowed like cold fire. Merlin's staff was also gleaming, and he shifted it before him. Then he saw no more, for the hollow knight was ready for the second charge.

He couched his lance, raised the shield, leaned forward and gave his mount the signal. His arm felt like a bar of iron, his strength like an endless current of electricity as he raced down the field. The rain was falling more heavily now and the lightning began a constant flickering. A steady rolling of thunder smothered the sound of the hoofbeats, and the wind whistled past his helm as he approached the other warrior, his lance centered on his shield.

They came together with an enormous crash. Both knights reeled and the hollow one fell, his shield and breastplate pierced by a broken lance. His left arm came away as he struck the earth; the lancepoint snapped and the shield fell beside him. But he began to rise almost immediately, his right hand drawing his long sword.

Launcelot dismounted, discarding his shield, drawing his own great blade. He moved to meet his headless foe. The other struck first and he parried it, a mighty shock running down his arms. He swung a blow of his own. It was parried.

They swaggered swords across the field, till finally Launcelot saw his opening and landed his heaviest blow. The hollow knight toppled into the mud, his breastplate cloven almost to the point where the spear's shaft protruded. At that moment, Morgan Le Fay screamed.

Launcelot turned and saw that she had fallen across the pattern Merlin had drawn. The sorcerer, now bathed in a bluish light, raised his staff and moved forward. Launcelot took a step toward them and felt a great pain in his left side.

Even as he turned toward the half-risen hollow knight who was drawing his blade back for another blow, Launcelot reversed his double-handed grip upon his own weapon and raised it high, point downward.

He hurled himself upon the other, and his blade pierced the cuirass entirely as he bore him back down, nailing him to the earth. A shriek arose from beneath him, echoing within the armor, and a gout of fire emerged from the neck hole, sped upward and away, dwindled in the rain, flickered out moments later.

Launcelot pushed himself into a kneeling position. Slowly then, he rose to his feet and turned toward the two figures who again faced one another. Both were now standing within the muddied geometries of power, both were now bathed in the bluish light. Launcelot took a step toward them, then another.

"Merlin!" he called out, continuing to advance upon them. "I've done what I said I would! Now I'm coming to kill you!"

Morgan Le Fay turned toward him, eyes wide.

"No!" she cried. "Depart the circle! Hurry! I am holding him here! His power wanes! In moments, this place will be no more. Go!"

Launcelot hesitated but a moment, then turned and walked as rapidly as he was able toward the circle's perimeter. The sky seemed to boil as he passed among the monoliths.

He advanced another dozen paces, then had to pause to rest. He looked back to the place of battle, to the place where the two figures still stood locked in sorcerous embrace. Then the scene was imprinted upon his brain as the skies opened and a sheet of fire fell upon the far end of the circle.

Dazzled, he raised his hand to shield his eyes. When he lowered it, he saw the stones falling, soundless, many of them fading from sight. The rain began to slow immediately. Sorcerer and sorceress had vanished along with much of the structure of the still-fading place. The horses were nowhere to be seen. He looked about him and saw a good-sized stone. He headed for it and seated himself. He unfastened his breastplate and removed it, dropping it to the ground. His side throbbed and he held it tightly. He doubled forward and rested his face on his left hand.

The rains continued to slow and finally ceased. The wind died. The mists returned.

He breathed deeply and thought back upon the conflict. This, this was the thing for which he had remained after all the others, the thing for which he had waited, for so long. It was over now, and he could rest.

There was a gap in his consciousness. He was brought to awareness again by a light. A steady glow passed between his fingers, pierced his eyelids. He dropped his hand and raised his head, opening his eyes.

It passed slowly before him in a halo of white light. He removed his sticky fingers from his side and rose to his feet to follow it. Solid, glowing, glorious and pure, not at all like the image in the chamber, it led him on out across the moonlit plain, from dimness to brightness to dimness, until the mists enfolded him as he reached at last to embrace it.

HERE ENDETH THE BOOK OF LAUNCELOT,
LAST OF THE NOBLE KNIGHTS OF THE
ROUND TABLE, AND HIS ADVENTURES
WITH RAXAS, THE HOLLOW KNIGHT,
AND MERLIN AND MORGAN LE FAY,
LAST OF THE WISE FOLK OF CAMELOT,
IN HIS QUEST FOR THE SANGREAL.

QUO FAS ET GLORIA DUCUNT.

A Word from Zelazny

"I wrote this one for *The Saturday Evening Post* and they asked me to cut 4500 words. It is 9000 words in length. Crossing out every other word made it sound funny, so I didn't."[1] He then submitted it to *Ariel: The Book of Fantasy Volume 4*, and Editor Tom Durwood also rejected it due to its length: "Try as we may, we just cannot fit this wonderful story in. To give [it] a proper layout, with illustrations, it would be twenty pages and our design just cannot absorb. Needless to say, we are as depressed sending it back to you as we were delighted to receive it. We can only thank you for sending it along and hope that if and when you have a short piece, you will think of us."[2]

At this point, it was extremely unusual for Zelazny to have any story rejected, let alone twice. He later submitted it to George Scithers, who

1 *The Last Defender of Camelot*, 1980.
2 Letter from Tom Durwood to Roger Zelazny, April 18, 1978.

published it in the fledgling *Asimov's SF Adventure Magazine*. The story became one of Zelazny's most well known and beloved.

George R. R. Martin adapted it into a teleplay for *The Twilight Zone*, 1986. "Not only did he do a better job of scripting it than I could have myself, but he phoned me regularly to explain the necessity for changes (no horses on the sound stage, though we could have night there; horses out-of-doors, but not at night—too tricky to film) and to report on problems as they developed (good armor is not always that easy to come by, Stonehenge wasn't built in a day and Hollow Knights upset Special Effects people). I listened in awe to the problems with which he wrestled in attempting to preserve the integrity of my story, I knew gratitude for his attempts through six rewrites to save lines he could tell were favorites of mine and I was totally pleased with the result when it finally glowed into being and moved."[3]

Notes

The manuscript bears the hand-written completion date of February 26, 1978. It appeared as a limited edition chapbook (leatherbound and softbound editions) in 1980 for V-Con 8 and became a limited release comic book.

Your eyes...are green is a recurrent Zelazny motif. In palm reading, the **rascettes** are the rings between the palm and wrist: three strong rascettes indicate a long life; the palm reader notes "you have more rascettes than I can count!" **Sir Launcelot du Lac (of the Lake)** was one of **King Arthur**'s **Knights of the Round Table** and the father of **Sir Galahad**. Launcelot was Arthur's greatest and most trusted knight until "**my sin with...the Queen,**" Launcelot's adultery with Queen Guinevere. That betrayal contributed to Arthur's downfall. Sorceress **Morgan Le Fay**, Arthur's half-sister, learned some techniques from **Merlin**, the powerful wizard who assisted Arthur. **Joyous Gard** was Launcelot's castle—formerly called Dolorous Gard until he captured it and broke a sinister spell. When he first explored the castle, he found a tomb with his name on it, foreshadowing his resting place. Thus, Morgan Le Fay is surprised to see Launcelot alive and not in his tomb as preordained.

The **Holy Grail** was both the cup that Jesus used at the Last Supper and the vessel Joseph of Arimathea used to collect blood from Jesus on the Cross. **Giuseppe Balsamo** was a notorious Italian charlatan and freemason who used the alias *Count Alessandro di* **Cagliostro.** He later appears in *Psychoshop*, which Zelazny completed from Alfred Bester's half-finished manuscript. **I am unforgiven and must wander like the Eternal Jew** refers to the legend of the Wandering Jew, a man (variably a pedlar, tradesman

3 "A Sketch of the Father," *Portraits of His Children*, George R R Martin, Dark Harvest, 1987.

or Pilate's doorman) who taunted Jesus on the way to the Crucifixion and was then cursed to walk the earth until the Second Coming. In Sir Thomas Malory's version of the Arthurian legend (*Le Morte d'Arthur*), Merlin lusted after **Nimue**, the Lady of the Lake, who coaxed his secrets from him and then turned her new powers against him, trapping him in an enchanted prison. It is a different and unnamed Lady of the Lake who gives Arthur the sword **Excalibur** and later takes the dying Arthur to Avalon.

Sirs **Gawaine, Percival**, and **Galahad** were also Knights of the Round Table who served King Arthur. The trio of Sirs Bors, Percival, and Galahad quested for the Holy Grail. Arthur proclaimed Sir Galahad the greatest knight. Galahad finally finds the Holy Grail—then he is immediately taken into heaven.

"Nel mezzo del cammin di nostra vita mi ritrovai per una selva oscura, che la diritto via era smarrita" is a quote (in the original Italian) from Dante Alighieri's *Divine Comedy: The Inferno*, and translates approximately as "When I had journeyed half of our life's way, I found myself within a shadowed forest, for I had lost the path that does not stray."

Stonehenge is a massive circle of standing stones on Salisbury Plain in Wiltshire, England, completed in stages between 3,000 and 2,000 BC. Its function is not certain, but because the sun's rays pass directly through it at the summer solstice, it might have had religious significance or acted as a calendar.

A **wight** is a supernatural being. **Dolmen stone** refers to Stonehenge itself; a dolmen has large, upright stones (megaliths) capped by a horizontal one (table). A **couched** lance is lowered to a horizontal position, as for an attack. Zelazny apparently invented **Raxas**'s name; it has subsequently seen use as the name of a sword-bearing knight in role-playing games and fan fiction. **Swaggering** is the side-to-side motion of swordplay. The **cuirass** is the breastplate and backplate of armor. **Sangreal** is another term for Holy Grail.

"**QUO FAS ET GLORIA DUCUNT**" means "Where Duty and Glory Lead," the motto for armed forces in various countries; it appears on the tombs of many soldiers who fell in battle.

FIRE AND/OR ICE

After the Fall, ed. Robert Sheckley, Ace Books 1980.

"Mommy! Mommy!"

"Yes?"

"Yes?"

"Tell me again what you did in the war."

"Nothing much. Go play with your sisters."

"I've been doing that all afternoon. They play too hard. I want to hear about the bad winter and the monsters and all."

"That's what it was, a bad winter."

"How cold was it, Mommy?"

"It was so cold that brass monkeys were singing soprano on every corner. It was so cold that it lasted for three years and the sun and the moon grew pale, and sister killed sister and daughters knocked off mommies for a Zippo lighter and a handful of pencil shavings."

"Then what happened?"

"Another winter came along, of course. A lot worse than the first."

"How bad was *it*?"

"Well, the two giant wolves who had been chasing the sun and the moon across the sky finally caught them and ate them. Damned dark then, but the blood that kept raining down gave a little light to watch the earthquakes and hurricanes by, when you could see through the blizzards."

"How come we don't have winters like that anymore?"

"Used them all up for a while, I suppose."

"How come there's a sun up in the sky now, if it got eaten?"

"Oh, that's the new one. It didn't happen till after the fires and the boiling oceans and all."

"Were you scared?"

"What scared me was what came later, when a giant snake crawled out of the sea and started fighting with this big person with the hammer. Then gangs of giants and monsters came from all directions and got to fighting with each other. And then there was a big, old, one-eyed person with a spear, stabbing away at a giant wolf which finally ate him, beard and all. Then another person came along and killed the wolf. All of a sudden, it looked familiar and I went outside and caught one of the troops by the sleeve.

" 'Hey, this is Götterdämmerung,' I said, 'isn't it?'

"A nearby TV crew moved in on us as the person paused in hacking away at an amorphous mass with lots of eyes and nodded.

" 'Sure is,' he said. 'Say, you must be—' and then the amorphous mass ate him.

"I crossed the street to where another one in a horned helmet was performing atrocities on a fallen foeperson.

" 'Pardon me,' I asked him, 'but who are you?'

" 'Loki's the name,' was the reply. 'What is your part in all of this?'

" 'I don't know that I have a part,' I said. 'But that other person started to say something like I might and then the amorphous mass which was just stepped on by the giant with the arrow in his throat sucked him in.'

"Loki dispatched his victim with a look of regret and studied my torn garment.

" 'You're dressed like a man,' he said, 'but—'

"I drew my shirt together.

" 'I am—' I began.

" 'Sure. Here's a safety pin. What a fine idea you've just given me! Come this way. There've got to be two human survivors,' he explained, pushing a path through a pack of werewolves. 'The gods will give their lives to defend you, once I've delivered you to Hoddmimir's Holt—that's the designated fallout shelter.' He snatched up an unconscious woman and slung her over his shoulder. 'You'll live through all this. A new day will dawn, a glorious new world will be revealed requiring a new first couple. Seeing you waiting, the gods will die believing that all is well…' He broke into a fit of laughter. 'They think that all the deaths will bring a new regime, of love, peace and happiness—and a new racc…' The tears streamed down his face. 'All tragedies require liberal doses of irony,' he concluded, as he bore us in a psychedelic chariot through rivers of blood and fields of bones.

"He deposited us here, amid warmth, trees, fountains, singing birds—all those little things that make life pleasant and trite: plenty of food, gentle breezes, an attractive house with indoor plumbing. Then still laughing, he returned to the front.

"Later, my companion awoke—blond and lithe and lovely—and her eyes flashed when she turned my way.

" 'So,' she snapped, 'you drag me from this horrible masculine conflict that I may serve your lusts in a secret pleasure haven! I'll have none of it, after all you've done to me!'

"I moved to comfort her, but she dropped into a karate stance.

" 'Tell me,' I said then, 'what you mean. Nothing has been done to you…'

" 'You call leaving a girl pregnant nothing?' she cried. 'With all the abortionists busy treating frostbite? No! I want no part of men, never again!'

" 'Be of good cheer, sister,' I replied, unpinning my shirt. 'I found myself too attractive to men, not to mention weak-willed—this long night being what it is—and suffering with a similar medical quandary, I resolved in a fit of remorse to lead the life of a simple transvestite.'

" 'Sappho be praised!' she replied.

"And we both had twins, and lived happily ever after. Winter faded, and the Twilight of the Gods passed. The world is a new place, of love, peace and happiness, for so long as it lasts this time. That is the story. Go play nicely with your sisters now."

"But they won't play nicely. They keep tiring me out doing the thing you told me not to."

"How did you even learn to do such a thing in the first place?" the other mommy asked.

"A shining person with a golden staff showed me how. She also said that the gods move in mysterious and not terribly efficient ways."

"This could be the beginning of philosophy," said the first mommy.

"You might call it that," said the other.

A Word from Zelazny

"Robert Sheckley asked me to contribute a story to his *After the Fall* collection...the theme of which was to be humorous and upbeat tales about the end of the world. I thought about it for a time, came up with two ideas for short-short stories and decided to write them both. After I had, I could not decide which one to send him, so I sent him both to let him choose the one he preferred. He wrote back and said that he was taking both and that he'd really like it if I would do one more to make it a triplet of short shorts."[1]

Notes

Zelazny implies the phrase "cold enough to freeze the balls off a brass monkey" by saying that the "**brass monkeys were singing soprano**." However, castration will not change a man's voice to a higher pitch if it has already deepened at maturity. Instead, castration before puberty (castrato) will preserve a soprano or alto voice. A **Zippo lighter** is a cigarette lighter.

The two giant wolves are Hati and Skoll, the sons of the giant wolf Fenris from Norse mythology (see "He Who Shapes" in volume 1); Hati chases the moon, and Skoll chases the sun, each intending to devour the target. In other versions of the tale, Fenris chases the moon. The **giant snake** is Jormangund (Midgard Serpent) which encircles the world, holding its tail in its mouth. **This big person with the hammer** is Thor, who battles Jormangund during the great battle of Ragnarök (Old Norse for "doom of the gods") precipitating the end of the world. Thor kills the serpent but dies from its venom. **Big, old, one-eyed person with a spear** is Odin, who dies when Fenris swallows him whole. Vidar, son of Odin, **came along and killed the wolf. Götterdämmerung** (a loose German translation of "Ragnarök") is the "twilight of the gods," a myth that tells of the battles in this story. The **amorphous mass with lots of eyes** could be a Shoggoth, an anachonistic intrusion from H. P. Lovercraft's Cthulhu mythos. **Loki** is Odin's foster-brother and the god of mischief (see "Love is an Imaginary Number" in volume 2 for his earlier punishment). After Ragnarök, a new world will arise and the human race will be reborn when two humans, Lif and Lifthrasir, are taken to **Hoddmimir's Holt**, a sacred grove.

Sappho was a Greek poet from the island of Lesbos who wrote poetry that seemed to express love of women; sapphic and lesbian mean the same thing. In the Norse canon, the resurrected god Balder is the **shining person with a golden staff** destined to rule the world after Ragnarök, but Zelazny changed him to a "she".

---

1 *Alternities #6*, Vol 2 No 2, Summer 1981.

EXEUNT OMNES

After the Fall, ed. Robert Sheckley, Ace Books 1980.

Houselights low. The Reapers and Nymphs danced as the bombs began to fall. Prospero faced Ferdinand.

" 'You do look, my son, in a mov'd sort, as if you were dismay'd. Be cheerful, sir, our revels now are ended. These our actors, as I foretold you, were all spirits, and are melted into air, into thin air…' "

He gestured simply. The Reapers and Nymphs vanished, to a strange, hollow and confused noise.

" '…And, like the baseless fabric of this vision, the cloud-capped towers, the gorgeous palaces, the solemn temples,' " he continued, " 'the great globe itself, yea, all which it inherit, shall dissolve and, like this insubstantial pageant faded, leave not a rack behind…' "

The audience vanished. The stage vanished. The theater vanished. The city about them faded, with a strange, hollow and confused noise. The great globe itself became transparent beneath their feet. All of the actors vanished, save for the spirits of Ariel, Caliban and Prospero.

"Uh, Prossy…" said Ariel.

" 'We are such stuff as dreams are made on—' "

"Prospero!" bellowed Caliban.

" '…And our little life is rounded with a sleep.' "

Caliban tackled him. Ariel seized him by the sleeve.

"You're doing it again, boss!"

" 'Sir, I am vexed—' "

"Stop it! The melt is on! You undid the wrong spell!"

" 'Bear with my weakness—my old brain is troubled…' "

Caliban sat on him. Ariel waved his slight fingers before his eyes. They drifted now in a vast and star-filled void. The nearest sizable body was the moon. Satellites—communication, astronomical, weather and spy—fled in all directions.

"Come around, damn it!" Ariel snapped. "We're all that's left again!"

" 'Be not disturbed with my infirmity…' "

"It's no use," growled Caliban. "He's gone off the deep end this time. What say we give up and fade away?"

"No!" Ariel cried. "I was just beginning to enjoy it."

"We *are* disturbed by your infirmity, Prossy! Cut the Stanislavsky bit and put things back together!"

" 'If you be pleas'd, retire into my cell and there repose…' "

"He's coming to the end of his lines," said Ariel. "We'll get him then."

" 'A turn or two I'll walk, to still my beating mind.' "

"Where are you going to walk, boss?" Caliban asked. "You took it all away."

"Eh? What's that?"

"You did it again. It's a terrific scene that way, but it tends to be kind of final."

"Oh dear! And things are pretty far along, too."

"The furthest, I'd say, to date. What do you do for an encore?"

"Where's my Book?"

Caliban flipped his flipper.

"It went, too."

Prospero massaged his eyeballs.

"Then I'll have to work from memory. Bear with me. Where was it?"

"A desert isle."

"Yes."

He gestured magnificently and the faint outlines of palm trees appeared nearby. A slight salt scent came to them, along with the distant sounds of surf. The outlines grew more substantial and a shining sand was spread beneath their feet. There came the cry of a gull. The stars faded, the sky grew blue and clouds drifted across it.

"That's better."

"But—this is a *real* desert isle!"

"Don't argue with him. You know how he gets."

"Now, where were we?"

"The entertainment, sir."

"Ah, yes. Come to my cave. Ferdinand and Miranda will be waiting."

He led them along the shore and up to a rocky place. They entered a great grotto where a large playing area was illuminated by torchlight. Prospero nodded to Ferdinand and Miranda and gestured toward the stage.

"Boss, something's wrong."

"No tongue! All eyes! Be silent!"

Ariel lost his power of speech for the moment and regarded the scene that appeared before him.

The great globe of the Earth, sun dappled, cloud streaked, green, gray and blue, turned slowly above the playing area. Tiny sparks, missiles, streaked above it, vanishing to be replaced by minute puffs of smoke over the major cities of North America, Europe and Asia. The globe rushed toward them then, one puff growing larger than the others, replacing all else. Up through dust, fire and smoke the vision swam, of a city twisted, melted, charred, its people dead, dying, fleeing.

"Boss! This is the wrong bit!" Caliban cried.

"My God!" said Ferdinand.

" 'You do look, my son, in a mov'd sort, as if you were dismay'd,' " Prospero stated.

"Here we go again," said Ariel, as the world rotated and entire land masses began to burn.

" '...the gorgeous palaces, the solemn temples, the great globe itself...' "

More missiles crisscrossed frantically as the icecaps melted and the oceans began to seethe.

" '...shall dissolve...' "

Large portions of the land were now inundated by the boiling seas.

" '...leave not a rack behind...' "

"We're still substantial," Ariel gasped.

"But *it's* going," Caliban observed.

The globe grew less tangible, the fires faded, the water lost its colors. The entire prospect paled and dwindled.

" '...is rounded with a sleep...' " Prospero yawned.

...Was gone.

"Boss! What happened to—"

"Sh!" Ariel cautioned. "Don't stir him up. —Prossy, where's the theater?"

" '...to still my beating mind...' "

" 'We wish you peace,' " Ferdinand and Miranda said in unison as they exited.

"Where are we, sir?"

"Why, you told me 'twas a desert isle."

"And such it is."

"Then what else would you? Find us food and drink. The other's but a dream."

"But, sir! Your Book—"

"Book me no books! I'd eat and sleep, I'd let these lovers woo, then off to Naples. All magics I eschew!"

Caliban and Ariel retreated.

"We'd best his will observe and then away."

"Aye, sprite. Methinks the living lies this way."

[Exeunt omnes.]

A Word from Zelazny

This is the second of three short-shorts written for Robert Sheckley's collection *After the Fall*. After writing the first "wacky piece"—"Fire and/or Ice"—"I...was about to send it off when an idea spun off of it. I immediately put it to paper. It was the succeeding story, 'Exeunt Omnes'."[1]

Notes

The lines quoted are from Shakespeare's *The Tempest*, as are the characters. **Prospero** is the rightful Duke of Milan who has magical powers and a magical staff; he is imprisoned on an island with his daughter and servants; **Miranda** is his daughter; **Ariel** is a spirit he freed; **Caliban** is a deformed monster who serves him. **Ferdinand**, son of the king of Naples, has fallen in love with Miranda, partly due to Prospero's magic. Konstantin **Stanislavsky** was a Russian actor and director whose method encouraged actors to identify with their characters and understand their psychological motivations. ***Exeunt omnes*** is a stage direction meaning "everyone exits."

---

1 *Unicorn Variations*, 1983.

A Very Good Year...

Harvey, December 1979.

"Hello," he said.

She looked at him. He was sandy haired, thirtyish, a little rugged looking but well groomed and very well dressed. He was smiling.

"I'm sorry," she said. "Do I know you?"

He shook his head.

"Not yet," he said. "Bradley's the name. Brad Dent."

"Well...What can I do for you, Mr. Dent?"

"I believe that I am going to fall in love with you," he said. "Of course, this requires a little cooperation. May I ask what time you get off work?"

"You're serious!"

"Yes."

She looked down at the countertop, noticed that her fingers were tapping the glass, stilled them, looked back up. His smile was still there.

"We close in twenty minutes," she said abruptly. "I could be out front in half an hour."

"Will you?"

She smiled then. She nodded.

"My name's Marcia."

"I'm glad," he said.

❖ ❖ ❖

At dinner, in a restaurant she would never have found by herself, she studied him through the candlelight. His hands were smooth. His accent was Middle American.

"You looked familiar when you came up to me," she said. "I've seen you around somewhere before. In fact, now that I think back on it, I believe you passed my counter several times today."

"Probably," he said, filling her wineglass.

"What do you do, Brad?"

"Nothing," he said.

She laughed.

"Doesn't sound very interesting."

He smiled again.

"What I mean to say is that I am devoting myself to enjoying this year, not working."

"Why is that?"

"I can afford it, and it's a very good year."

"In what way is it special?"

He leaned back, laced his fingers, looked at her across them.

"There are no wars going on anywhere, for a change," he finally said. "No civil unrest either. The economy is wonderfully stable. The weather is beautiful." He raised his glass and took a sip. "There are some truly excellent vintages available. All of my favorite shows and movies are playing. Science is doing exciting things—in medicine, in space. A flock of fine books has been published. There are so many places to go, things to do this year. It could take a lifetime." He reached out and touched her hand. "And I'm in love," he finished.

She blushed.

"You hardly know me…"

"…And I have that to look forward to, also—getting to know you."

"You *are* very strange," she said.

"But you will see me again…"

"If it's going to be that kind of year," she said, and she squeezed his hand.

❖ ❖ ❖

She saw him regularly for a month before she quit her job and moved in with him. They dined well, they traveled often…

She realized, one evening in Maui near the end of the year, that she was in love with him.

"Brad," she said, clasping him tightly, "this spring it seemed more like a game than anything else."

"And now?"

"Now it's special."
"I'm glad."

❖ ❖ ❖

On New Year's Eve, they went to dinner at a place he knew in Chinatown. She leaned forward over the chicken fried rice.
"That man," she said, "at the corner table to the right."
"Yes?"
"He looks a lot like you."
Brad glanced over, nodded.
"Yes."
"You know, I still don't know you very well."
"But we know each other better."
"Yes, that's true. But—Brad, that man coming out of the restroom..."
He turned his head.
"He looks like you, too."
"He does."
"Strange...I mean, I don't even know where you get your money."
"My family," he said, "always had a lot."
She nodded.
"I see...Two more! Those men who just came in!"
"Yes, they look like me, too."
She shook her head.
"Then you really never had to work?"
"On the contrary. I'm a scientist. Bet I could have had the Nobel Prize."
She dished out some sweet-and-sour pork. Then she paused, eyes wide, head turned again.
"Brad, it *has* to be more than coincidence. There's *another* you!"
"Yes," he said, "I always dine here on New Year's Eve."
She laid down her fork. She paled.
"You're a biologist," she said, "aren't you? And you've cloned yourself? Maybe you're not even the original..."
He laughed softly.
"No, I'm a physicist," he said, "and I'm not a clone. It *has* been a very good year, hasn't it?"
She smiled gently. She nodded.
"Of course it has," she said. "You say you *always* dine here on New Year's Eve?"

"Yes. The same New Year's Eve. This one."

"Time travel?"

"Yes."

"Why?"

"This has been such a good year that I have resolved to live it over, and over, and over—for the rest of my life."

Two couples entered the restaurant. She looked back.

"That's us!" she said. "And the second couple looks a lot older—but they're us, too!"

"Yes, this is where I first saw you. I had to find you after that. We looked so happy."

"Why have we never met any of them before?"

"I keep a diary. We'll go to different places each time around. Except for New Year's Eve…"

She raked her lower lip once with her teeth.

"Why— Why keep repeating it?" she finally asked.

"It's been such a very good year," he said.

"But what comes after?"

He shrugged.

"Don't ask me."

He turned and smiled at the older couple, who had nodded toward them.

"I think they're coming over. Perhaps we can buy them a drink. Isn't she lovely?"

A Word from Zelazny

This is the third of three short-short pieces that Zelazny wrote for Robert Sheckley's collection, *After the Fall.* Sheckley accepted the first two stories and asked for a third, "which was kind of funny, because after I had sent the two off, I'd had an idea for another, had sat down and written it quickly, and it was still lying where I'd left it on my desk. This is the one... With each of the three I did on this theme, to make it a little more interesting, I also used a different style. This one uses the most straightforward narrative technique."[1]

In another introduction, Zelazny said that after submitting the first two stories, "I ...tried to turn my attention to other matters but couldn't. I felt that something was still there. I had done the second story in a different style than the first, and the impetus was yet present. I suddenly saw a third story on the same theme, to be done in a third style. So I wrote it to get it out of my system, tossed it to a corner of my desk—where it quickly became buried under other papers—and forgot about it. A week or so later I received a letter saying [Sheckley had] liked both stories I'd sent along, but a triplet would be even more esthetically pleasing. Could I do one more short short on the same theme? I stuffed 'A Very Good Year...' into an envelope and sent it off by return mail. It was purchased and all three appeared in that collection. I had felt a tiny impulse to do a fourth after I'd finished the third, but I repressed it successfully. That way lies madness..."[2]

Notes

Slated to appear first in *After the Fall*, publication in *Harvey* in December 1979 preceded that.

---

1 *Alternities #6*, Vol 2 No 2, Summer 1981.
2 *Unicorn Variations*, 1983.

There Is Always a Poem

Double:Bill #18, March-April 1968.

I have said it before,
and I will say it again
in a deeper and harsher voice—
though I be the last man on Earth
and singing to the stones:
there is always a thing to say
in the manner that is not prose.
It is always there,
regardless of the presence
of a hearer.
It cries out to be said,
rhymeless or no;
it begs the pulse and the voice;
it demands the outlines of song.
What is it?
I do not know,
save that it is a feeling in the palate
for a word,
a hole in the sight that cries for seeing,

a blank spot in the spirit needing filling.
Perhaps a drug can replace it.
Perhaps a machine can do better.
But it is there
and it needs to be said,
aloud and by me:
There is something that I love.
I wish to share it.
There is something that I know.
I wish to give it.
Man, you are probably my brother.
Lady, I probably love you.
Whatever,
here I am. Listen to my words
and feel a knowing.
Pretend you've touched my hand, my pen.
These words be thine.
These thoughts be toward thee flowing.
Talk is all,
but tender is the saying,
and necessary comes the pulse upon.
The saying, perhaps, is all,
for always there is something that so needs it.

The Doctrine of the Perfect Lie

Science Fiction (Australian) Vol 1 No 3, Dec 1978.

The doctrine of the perfect lie
    is a thing I most delight in,
    smoother than life,
    planed to fit the times,
    sandpapered to join with expectation,
    polished to suit the discriminating.

But it is not that way, you say?
    Of course. The delight lies
    in the lie's
    telling: times, hopes, tastes
    to fit, with a little disjoint
    here and there,
    for appearance's fair sake.
Ask any Cretan you meet on the street:
    The carpentry is all.

Notes

The Cretan philosopher Epimenides of Knossos (circa 600 BC) once stated in a poem "Cretans, always liars." This creates the logic problem, the Epimenides paradox: A Cretan states, "All Cretans are liars." Is he telling the truth? Bertrand Russell later restated this as the Liar's Paradox. Zelazny alludes to the Cretan paradox in his poem about the joys of mendacity.

The Places of Aache

Other Worlds 2, ed. Roy Torgeson, Zebra 1979.
§ *Dilvish* 5 of 11

As Dilvish the Damned traveled through the North Countries, he passed one day along a twisting road through a low pine-filled valley. His great black mount seemed tireless, but there came a time when Dilvish halted to unpack rations and make a meal. His green boots soundless upon the needles, he spread his cloak and placed his fare upon it.

"There is someone coming."

"Thanks."

He loosened his blade and began to eat standing. Shortly, a large, bearded man on a roan stallion rounded a bend and slowed.

"Ho! Traveler!" the man hailed. "May I join you?"

"You may."

The man halted and dismounted. As he approached, he smiled.

"Rogis is the name," he stated. "And yours?"

"Dilvish."

"You've traveled far?"

"Yes, from the southeast."

"Do you also make a pilgrimage to the shrine?"

"What shrine?"

"That of the goddess Aache, up yonder hill." He gestured up the trail.

"No, I was not even aware of its existence. What is its virtue?"

"The goddess may absolve a man of murder."

"Oh? And you are making pilgrimage for this reason?"

"Yes. I have done it often."

"Do you come from afar?"

"No, I live just up the road. It makes life a lot easier."

"I think I begin to get the picture."

"Good. If you will be so kind as to pass me your purse, you will save the goddess the work involved in an extra absolution."

"Come and take it," Dilvish said, and he smiled.

Rogis's eyes narrowed.

"Not many men have said that to me."

"And I may well be the last."

"Hmm. I'm bigger than you are."

"I've noticed."

"You are making things difficult. Would you be willing to show me whether you're carrying enough coin to make it worth either of our efforts?"

"I think not."

"How about this, then? We split your money, and neither of us takes a bloody chance?"

"No."

Rogis sighed.

"Now the situation has grown awkward. Let me see, are you an archer? No. No bow. No throwing spears either. It would seem that I could ride away without being shot down."

"To ambush me later? I'm afraid I can't permit it. It has become a matter of future self-defense."

"Pity," Rogis said, "but I'll chance it anyway."

He turned back toward his mount, then whirled, his blade in his hand. But Dilvish's own weapon was already drawn, and he parried it and swung a return blow. Rogis cursed, parried, and swung. This went on for six passes, and then Dilvish's blade pierced his abdomen.

A look of surprise crossed his face and he dropped his own weapon to clutch at the one that held him. Dilvish wrenched it free and watched him fall.

"An unlucky day for both of us," Rogis muttered.

"More so for yourself, I'd say."

"You'll not escape this so easily, you know—I'm favored of the goddess—"

"She has peculiar tastes in favorites then."

"I've served her. You'll see…" and then his eyes clouded over and he slumped, moaning.

"Black, have you ever heard of this goddess?"

"No," replied the metal statue of a horse, "but then there are many things in this realm of which I have heard nothing."

"Then let us be gone from this place."

"What of Rogis?"

"We will leave him at the crossroads as an advertisement that the world is a safer place. I'll untether his horse and let it find its own way home."

❖ ❖ ❖

That night, many miles farther north, Dilvish's sleep was troubled. He dreamed that the shade of Rogis came and stood beside him in his camp and knelt, smiling, to place his hands upon his throat. He awoke choking, and a ghostly light seemed to fade away at his side.

"Black! Black! Did you see anything?"

There was silence, then: "I was far away" came the reply from the unmoving statue, "but I see red marks upon your throat. What happened?"

"I dreamed that Rogis was here, that he tried to throttle me." He coughed and spat.

"It was more than a dream," he decided.

"We'll leave this country soon."

"The sooner the better."

After a time he drifted off to sleep again. At some point Rogis was with him once more. This time the attack was very sudden and even more violent. Dilvish awoke swinging, but his blows fell upon empty air. Now he was certain of the light, Rogis's ghostly outline within it.

"Black, awaken," he said. "We must retrace our path, visit that shrine, lay this ghost. A man has to sleep."

"I am ready. We will be there a little after daybreak."

Dilvish broke camp and mounted.

❖ ❖ ❖

The shrine was a low, sprawling wooden building backed against the rust-streaked rock of the hill, near to its top. The morning sunlight fell upon its face, where a rudely carved double door of dark wood stood closed. Dilvish dismounted and tried it. Finding it bolted, he hammered upon it.

After a long delay, the left side of the door opened and a small man with close-set pale eyes looked out. He wore a coarse brown robe.

"Who are you to trouble us at this hour?" the man inquired.

"One who has been wronged by someone who claimed a special status with your goddess. I wish to be released from whatever doom or spell is involved."

"Oh. You are the one. You're early. Come in."

He swung the door wide and Dilvish stepped through. The room was simply furnished with a few benches and a small altar. There was another door to the rear. A vacant sleeping pallet lay disarrayed near one wall beneath a narrow window.

"My name is Task. Have a seat." The man gestured toward the benches.

"I'll stand."

The small man shrugged.

"All right." He walked back to the pallet and began folding the blankets. "You want the curse lifted, to prevent Rogis's ghost from strangling you."

"You do know!"

"Of course. The goddess does not like to have her servants slaughtered."

Dilvish noticed how, with a deft movement, Task secreted a bottle of a rare southern wine within the rolled pallet. He also noted that each time the man hid his hands within his robe another costly ring vanished from his fingers.

"The servants' victims do not much relish being slaughtered either."

"Tsk. Did you come here to blaspheme or to get absolved?"

"I came here to get this damned curse lifted."

"To do that, you must make an offering."

"Of what must it consist?"

"First, all of your money and any precious stones or metals you have with you."

"The goddess is as much of a highway robber as her servants!"

Task smiled.

"All religions have their secular side. The goddess's following is not large in this sparsely populated area, and the donations of the faithful are not always sufficient to meet operating expenses."

"You said 'first'—first you want all my valuables. What's second?"

"Well, it is only fair that the life you have destroyed be replaced by yourself. A year's service on your part will be ample."

"Doing what?"

"Why, collecting tribute from travelers, as Rogis did."

"I refuse," said Dilvish. "Ask something else."

"Nothing else will do. That is your penance."

Dilvish turned on his heel. He began to pace. He halted.

"What's beyond that door?" he asked suddenly, gesturing to the rear of the room.

"That is a sacred precinct, reserved for the elect—"

Dilvish headed toward it.

"You can't go in there!"

He thrust the door open.

"—especially with a sword!"

He stepped inside. Small oil lamps burned. There was straw on the floor, a feeling of dampness and a peculiar odor that he did not recognize; otherwise, the room was empty. A large, heavy door stood slightly ajar to the rear, however, and from behind it he seemed to hear scratching sounds, retreating.

Task was at his side as he moved to the door. He grasped at his arm but could not hold it back. Dilvish pushed it open and looked through.

Nothing. Darkness and a sense of distance. Rock to the side. A cave.

"That is a storage area."

Dilvish took up an oil lamp and entered. As he proceeded, the smell grew stronger, the dampness heavier. Task followed him.

"It is dangerous back here. There are crevasses, chasms. You might slip—"

"Silence! Or I'll throw you down the first one I see!"

Task dropped back several paces.

Dilvish moved cautiously, holding the lamp high. Rounding a rocky shoulder, he beheld a myriad of sparkles. A pool, recently disturbed.

"This is where it came," he said, "whatever it is," and he advanced upon the pool. "I am going to wait for it. Here. I've a feeling it must emerge, sooner or later. What is it?"

"The goddess…" Task said softly. "You should really depart. I have just had a message. Your year's sentence has been remitted. Just leave the money."

Dilvish laughed.

"Do goddesses bargain?" he asked.

Sometimes, came a voice in his mind. *Leave it at that.*

A chill passed over his limbs.

"Why do you hide yourself?" he said.

It is not given to many mortals to look upon my kind.

"I don't like blackmail, human or supernatural. Supposing I were to roll this boulder into your pool?"

Abruptly, the water stirred. The face of a woman emerged and regarded him. Her eyes were green and very large, her skin extremely pale. Tight ringlets of black hair covered her head like a helmet. Her chin was pointed, and there was something unnatural to the shape of her tongue when she spoke aloud.

"Very well, you see me," she stated. "I've a mind to show you more."

She continued to rise—neck, shoulders, breasts, all pale—and abruptly all human semblance vanished, for below her waist were more long slender limbs than Dilvish could count.

He cried out and his blade came into his hand. He nearly dropped the lamp.

"I mean you no harm," came her faintly lisping voice. "Recall that it was you who sought this audience."

"Aache—what are you?" he asked.

"My kind is old. Let it go at that. You have caused me difficulties."

"Your man tried to kill me."

"I know. Obviously he chose the wrong victim. Pity. I must go hungry."

The blade twitched in Dilvish's hand.

"What do you mean by that?"

"I eat honey."

"Honey?"

"A sweet liquid made by small flying insects in the far south."

"I know what it is, but I do not understand."

"It is my main dietary requirement. I must have it. There are no flowers, no bees this far north. I must send for it. It is expensive to bring it this distance."

"And that is why you rob travelers?"

"I must have the money, to buy it. My servants get it for me."

"Why do they serve you thus?"

"I might say devotion, but let us be honest. With some men, I can control them over a distance."

"As you sent that phantom to me?"

"I cannot control you directly, as I could Rogis. But I can make your slumber bad."

Dilvish shook his head.

"I've a feeling that the farther I get from here, the less this power would affect me."

"Nor are you incorrect. So go. You would never make me a good servant. Keep your money. Leave me."

"Wait. Have you many servants?"

"That is none of your affair."

"No, it isn't. But I'd a thought. There is mineral wealth in this valley, you know."

"I do not know. I do not understand what you refer to."

"I was involved in several mining operations years ago. When I rode through your valley yesterday, I noticed signs of certain mineral deposits. I believe they are sufficiently rich in the dark metal for which metalworkers to the south would pay well. If you have sufficient servants to set up a digging and smelting operation, you may make out a lot better than you have been by robbing passersby."

"You really think so?"

"It should be easy enough to discover, especially if you will lend me some men."

"Why would you do this for me?"

"Perhaps to make this corner of the world a little safer."

"A strange reason. Go back to the shrine. I am summoning servants now and binding them to you. See whether this thing can be done, then come back to see me—alone."

"I will—Aache."

Suddenly she was gone and the pool sparkled. Dilvish turned and met Task's stare. He walked by him without speaking.

❖ ❖ ❖

In the days that followed, ore was mined, a smelter constructed, and operations begun. Dilvish smiled as he watched the dark metal pour into its bar molds. Aache smiled when he told her of it.

"And there is much there?" she asked.

"A mountain of it. We can have enough for a good wagonload by next week. Then we can step up the process."

He knelt beside the pool. Her fingers emerged, tentatively touched his hand. When he did not flinch, she reached up and stroked his cheek.

"I could almost wish you were one of my kind," she said, and then she was gone again.

❖ ❖ ❖

"It has been long since this area was warm and could have had flowers and bees," Black said. "She must be very old."

"It is impossible to tell," Dilvish answered, as they paced the hilltop and looked down into the valley to where the smoke rose. "But if honey is all it takes to make her an honest creature, it's worth this small delay."

"She wants you to take a load south next week?"

"Yes."

"And after that?"

"Her servants should be able to run things from then on."

"As slaves?"

"No, she'll be able to afford to pay them once this gets going."

"I see. One thing…"

"Yes?"

"Do not trust that priest Task."

"I don't. He has expensive tastes. I believe he has been pocketing part of the…income."

"Of this I know nothing. I spoke, seeing him as one who fears that he may be replaced."

"I will ease his mind on that count soon with my retirement."

❖ ❖ ❖

The morning of his departure was bright, with only a few snow flurries melting as they descended. The men had sung as they had loaded the wagon the evening before. Now they stood about, baring grins from which their breath puffed cheerily as they clapped him on the shoulder and back, loaded him down with provisions, and saw him on his creaking way.

"I do not appreciate draft duty," Black commented, as soon as they were out of earshot of the camp.

"I'll make it up to you one day."

"I doubt it, but I'll remember it."

No brigands accosted them, for now these forests were clean of them. They made better time when they emerged from the chain of valleys, and by afternoon they had traveled several leagues. Dilvish ate as he rode and Black moved on at a steady pace.

Along toward evening, they heard the sounds of a rider approaching from the rear. They came to a halt when they recognized Task mounted upon Rogis's roan. The horse was in a lather and blowing heavily. It reeled as Task reined in beside the wagon.

"What is the matter?" Dilvish inquired.

"Gone. Dead. Cinders," he said.

"Talk sense!"

"The shrine is burned to the ground. One of the lamps—the straw—"

"What of Aache?"

"She was trapped in the back room—couldn't open the door—"

"Dead?"

"Dead."

"Why do you come fleeing?"

"I had to catch you, to discuss my share of the operation."

"I see."

Dilvish saw that he was wearing all of his rings.

"We'd best camp now. Your horse can't go any farther."

"Very well. That field?"

"It will do."

❖ ❖ ❖

That night Dilvish dreamed a strange dream in which he held a woman tightly, caressing her almost brutally, fearing to look down. He was awakened by a cry of terror.

Sitting up, he beheld a ghostly glow above the form of the man Task. It was already fading, but he would never forget its outline.

"Aache...?"

Sleep, my only friend, my dear friend, came the words from somewhere. *I have but come for that which is mine. It is not so sweet as honey, but it will have to do...*

He covered over the remains of the priest without looking at him. He departed the following morning. He rode the entire day in silence.

A Word from Zelazny

This sixth Dilvish tale (the fifth in sequence in *Dilvish, the Damned*) was written immediately after "A City Divided" when "I realized that a transitional piece was really in order. There should have been Dilvish story between it and the last of the old ones, to get Dilvish on the road north. "The Places of Aache" was the story, and Roy Torgeson ran it in his *Other Worlds 2*."[1]

Zelazny originally sold the story to *Ariel: The Book of Fantasy Volume 5*, but the publication folded before its appearance.[2]

Notes

Like **Aache** in the story, Saints Leonard of Noblac, Nicholas of Myra and Dismas are variably mentioned as patron saints of brigands and robbers. A **roan** is a horse with a coat of mixed colors, typically bay, chestnut, or black mixed with white. **Her eyes were green and very large** is another example of a common Zelazny motif.

1 *Alternities #6*, Summer 1981.

2 Letter from Roger Zelazny to Gary Thomas, April 20, 1979.

A City Divided

Dilvish, the Damned, Del Rey/Ballantine 1982.
§ *Dilvish* 6 of 11

Spring was twisting its way slowly into the North Country, advancing and retreating by turns, retaining each day something of its gains. Snow still lay heavy upon all the higher peaks, but during the day it melted in the lower regions and the fields lay damp, the streams swelled and raced. Some new green was already evident in the valleys, and on cloudless days such as this the sun dried the trails and the air was warmed to the point of comfort by midday. The traveler on the strange dark horse, but lately up from redelivered Portaroy after the laying of his ghost legions, halted on a rocky rise and gestured to the north.

"Black," he said. "That hill—about half a league off. Did you see something peculiar atop it a moment ago?"

His mount turned its metallic head and stared.

"No. Nor do I now. What did it seem?"

"The outline of some buildings. They're gone now."

"Perhaps it was the sun glinting on the ice."

"Perhaps."

They moved ahead, descending the slope and continuing on their way. On the next hill they mounted, minutes, later, they paused again and looked in that direction.

"There!" said the rider who seldom smiled, smiling.

Black shook his head.

"I see it now. It looks like the wall of a city…"

"A fresh meal may perhaps be had there—and a bath. And a real bed tonight. Come, let us hurry."

"Check your maps, will you? I am curious what the place is called."

"We will learn that soon enough. Come!"

"Humor me, for old times' sake."

The rider paused, then dipped into his travel bag. He fumbled about, then withdrew a small scroll that he uncased, unrolled, and held before him.

"Hmm," he said after a time. Then he unrolled the map and restored it to its container.

"Well? What is the name of the place?"

"Can't tell. It's not shown."

"Aha!"

"You know this will not be the first error we've found in this map. The mapmaker either forgot the place or did not know about it. Or the town is new."

"Dilvish…"

"Yes?"

"Do I offer you advice often?"

"Frequently."

"Am I often wrong?"

"I could cite instances."

"I don't fancy the notion of spending the night in a place that is here one moment and gone the next."

"Nonsense! It was just the angle, or some trick of the distance."

"I am suspicious—"

"—by nature. I know. And I am hungry. Fresh fish from one of these streams, broiled with herbs…"

Black snorted a tiny wisp of smoke and began walking.

"Your stomach is suddenly a big problem."

"There may be girls, too."

"Hmph!"

❖ ❖ ❖

The trail leading up the hill to the city gate was not wide, and the gate stood open. Dilvish halted before it but was not challenged. He studied the towers and the walls, but he saw no one. He listened. The only sounds were the wind and the birds at his back.

"Go ahead," he said, and Black bore him through the gate.

Streets ran off to the right and the left, turning with the angles of the wall. The way on which he stood ran straight ahead, ending against buildings at what might be a small plaza. All of these streets were cobbled and well-kept. The buildings were mainly of stone and brick—clean, sharp angled. As they continued along the way leading directly ahead, he noted that no refuse stood or flowed in the ditch at his side.

"Quiet place," said Black.

"Yes."

After perhaps a hundred paces, Dilvish drew upon the reins and dismounted. He entered a shop to his left. A moment later he stepped back outside.

"What is it?"

"Nothing. Empty. No merchandise. Not a stick of furniture."

He crossed over the street and entered another building. He emerged shaking his head.

"The same," he said, remounting.

"Shall we go? You know my feelings."

"Let us have a look at that plaza first. There are no signs of violence thus far. It may be a festival day of some sort."

Black's hooves clicked on the cobbles.

"Pretty dead festival, then."

They rode on, glancing up alleyways, along galleries, into courtyards. There was no activity to be seen, there were no people about. At length they entered the plaza. There were vacant stalls on two sides, a small fountain in the middle that was not operating, and a large statue of two fish near one end. Dilvish paused and regarded the ancient sign. The top fish headed to his left, the bottom one to his right. He shrugged.

"You were right about that," he said. "Let us—"

The air shook from the single note of a bell, swinging within a high tower off to his left.

"Strange…"

A youth—blond haired and rosy cheeked, wearing a ruffled white shirt and green hose, a short sword, and a large codpiece—stepped out from behind the statue, smiled, and postured with one hand on his hip.

"Strange?" he said. "Yes, it is. But stranger still, the sight you are about to behold, traveler. Regard!"

He gestured, sweepingly, just as the bell tolled again.

Dilvish turned his head and drew a sudden breath. As silently as cats, the buildings had begun moving about the plaza. They circled, they advanced, they retreated. They rearranged themselves, changing positions with one another as if moving in a ludicrous, cyclopean dance. The bell rang again, and again, as Dilvish watched.

Finally: "What sorcery is this?" he inquired of the youth.

"Just so," was the reply. "Sorcery indeed—and it is in the process of rearranging the city into the form of a maze about you."

Dilvish shook his head to the accompaniment of another bell note.

"I am impressed by the display," he said. "But what is its purpose?"

"You might call it a game," said the youth. "When the bell completes its song, several strokes hence, the maze will be laid. You will then have an hour until it strikes again. If you have not found your way out of town and away from here by that time, you will be crushed by the buildings' rearranging themselves once more."

"And why the game?" Dilvish asked, waiting out another tolling before he heard the reply.

"That you will never know, Elfboot, whether you win or lose, for you are only an element of the game. I am also charged to warn you, however, that you may find yourself under attack at various points along whatever route you may choose."

The buildings continued their dance to the sound of the bell.

"I do not care for this game," said Dilvish, drawing his blade, "and I've a mind to play a different one. I have just elected you to guide me out of here. Refuse, and you'll part company with your head."

The youth grinned, and reaching upward with his left hand, he seized a fistful of his own hair while drawing his blade with his right. Brandishing the weapon on high, he brought it down in a fast, hard stroke against the side of his neck. It passed through.

His left hand rose, holding his severed head—still grinning—high above his shoulders. The bell tolled again. The lips moved.

"Did you believe you dealt with mortals, stranger?"

Dilvish frowned.

"I see," he said. "Very well. Deal with him, Black."

"Gladly," Black replied, and flames danced within his mouth and filled his eye sockets as he reared in time with another bell stroke.

The face on the severed head showed a look of sudden surprise as an electrical quality came into the air between them. Black's hooves lashed out, crossing in an unhorselike movement as he fell forward, striking the figure to the accompaniment of a sulfurous thunderclap that drowned out the next note of the bell. A scream escaped from the being before them as it vanished in a rush of fire.

The bell tolled twice again as Black recovered his footing and they stood regarding the charred cobbles. Then there was silence. The buildings had ceased their movements.

"All right," Dilvish said at last. "You told me so. Thanks for your action."

Black moved in a circle then, and they regarded the new arrangement of streets that led from the plaza.

"Any preferences?" Black inquired.

"Let's try that one," said Dilvish, gesturing up a sideway to the left.

"All right," said Black. "By the way, I've seen that trick done better."

"Really?"

"I'll tell you about it another time."

They headed up the cobbled way. Nothing moved about them.

The street was narrow and short. Buildings crowded them at either hand. There was an abrupt turn to the right, then to the left again.

"Sst! Over here!" came a voice from their left.

"The first ambush," muttered Dilvish, turning his head and drawing his blade.

A small, dark-eyed man with a pleasant smile, his long gray hair tied into a topknot, his hands raised to shoulder level, empty palms facing outward, watched them from within a doorway. He had on well-worn gray garments.

"It's all right," he whispered sharply. "No trick. I want to help you."

Dilvish did not lower his blade.

"Who are you?" he asked.

"The other side," came the reply.

"What do you mean?"

"This is a game, whether you like it or not," the small man said. "It is between two players. The other side wants you to die in here. Mine only wins if you escape. The other side is responsible for the city. I am responsible for outwitting it."

"How do I know whether you are telling the truth? How can I tell which side is which?"

The man glanced down at his shirtfront and frowned.

"May I lower one hand?"

"Go ahead."

He dropped his right hand and smoothed the baggy garment over his breast. This exposed the emblem of a fish, swimming toward his right. He pointed to it.

"He of the fish that swims to the right," he said, "is the one who wants you out of here safe. Now test my words. Two more turnings, and you had better look for an attack from above."

At this the man leaned backward against the door and it gave way. He closed it behind him, and Dilvish heard the bar drop.

"Let's go," he said to Black.

There were no sounds other than those of Black's hooves as they made the first turn. Dilvish rode with drawn blade, eyes searching every opening.

The second turning led through an archway. He slowed and studied it before continuing on. They passed beneath it and started up the narrow street. They passed a latticed door letting upon a small courtyard. Dilvish looked low as well as high but saw nothing.

Then he heard the sound of metal grating upon stone somewhere overhead. As he glanced upward, he cried, "Back! Back!"

His mount reversed motion without turning, moving quickly, as a cataract of steaming oil descended and struck the stones before them. Dilvish only glimpsed the figures on the rooftop to his right.

There came a terrific crash that echoed and reverberated about them. Looking back, Dilvish saw that a massive barred gate had been dropped from within the archway. The pool of bubbling oil continued to flow, spreading toward them.

"I won't be able to keep my footing on that," Black said.

"That door, to the right! Break through!"

Black wheeled and crashed against the latticed door. It fell apart, and they were through it and into a small flagged courtyard, a tiny dry fountain at its center, another wooden door at its farther end.

"You cheated!" came a voice from above and to his left. "Were you warned?"

Dilvish looked up.

There, on a small third-floor balcony, stood a man very similar in appearance to their informant, save that his hair was bound back with a blue head strap and on his shirtfront was the emblem of a fish swimming to his left. In his hands he bore a crossbow, which he raised then and sighted.

Dilvish slid down from Black to his right and crouched. He heard the quarrel strike upon Black's metallic hide.

"Through the other gate before he can set it again! I'll follow you!"

Black rushed ahead, not even slowing as he hit the gate. Dilvish sprinted after.

"Cheating! Cheating!" came the cry from behind him.

The street beyond ran in both directions.

"To the right," said Dilvish, mounting.

Black hurried off in that direction. They came to a fork. They took the left-hand way, which ran slightly uphill.

"It might be worth risking a climb to the top of a high building," said Dilvish. "I may be able to see the way out."

"Not necessary," came a familiar voice from his right. "I can save you the time and the effort. You've already found one shortcut—back there. It is not very far now."

Dilvish looked into the eyes of that first topknotted man, fish emblem facing to his right. He stood behind a low window, only an arm's distance away.

"But you must hurry. He is already rushing his forces to the gate. If he gets there first, it's all over."

"He could simply have guarded it from the beginning and waited."

"Not permitted. He can't start there. Take the next right, the next left, and two rights. You will come through an alleyway into a wide courtyard. The gate will be on your left and open. Hurry!"

Dilvish nodded and Black raced off, swinging to the right at the next corner.

"Do you believe him?" Black asked.

Dilvish shrugged.

"I must either try it or take a terrible chance."

"What do you mean?"

"Use of the strongest magic I know."

"One of the Awful Sayings you learned in Hell, against the day you meet your enemy?"

"Aye. There's one of the twelve to level a city."

Black turned left, cautiously, then proceeded on.

"How do you think it would fare against a sorcerous construct such as this?"

"For raw power, it is unequaled by earthly magics—"

"But there are no warnings. You never get a second chance if you make a mistake."

"I need not be told."

Black halted at the next corner, peered about it, continued.

"If he was telling the truth, we're almost there," he whispered. "Let us hope we have beaten the other player. And the next time, put more trust in your maps!"

"Aye. Here's the turn. Carefully now..."

They rounded the next corner. There was a long alleyway with light at its far end.

"So far it looks as if he spoke true," Black whispered, slowing to soften the sound of his hooves.

He halted as they neared the alley's end, and they looked out upon a courtyard.

The man they had left on the balcony stood in the middle of the yard, smiling in their direction. In his right hand he held a pikestaff.

"You pressed me hard," he said. "But my way was shorter—as you can see."

He looked to his right.

"There is the gate."

He raised his staff and struck it three times upon the ground. Immediately the flagstones about him were raised like trapdoors and figures rose up from out of the ground beneath them. There were perhaps two-score men there. Each bore a pikestaff. Each reached across with his left hand, grasped his hair, and raised his head from his shoulders. All of them laughed then, as they replaced their heads, gripped their pikes with both hands, and started forward across the yard.

"Back!" said Dilvish. "We'd never make it!"

They fled up the alley and turned to the left. They heard the pikemen enter it behind them.

"Other streets opened upon that yard," said Dilvish. "Perhaps we can circle."

"Another street..."

"Go left!"

They turned.

"Another."

"Right!"

The way opened upon a square at a crossroads, a fountain at its center. Pikemen suddenly entered from the left and from directly ahead. From behind there still came the sounds of pursuit.

They bore to the right, took another right after a short distance. Farther up the street, a gate fell into place before them. They turned left into a long, arcaded area skirting a garden.

"Cut across the garden!" came a voice from behind a row of shrubs. "There's a gate over there!" The other small man stood, pointing. "Then remember, two lefts and a right, two lefts and a right—all the way around!"

Black's hooves tore through the garden as they headed for the gate. Then he reared and came to a standstill, as the note of a single bell stroke vibrated through the air.

"Oh, oh," said the small man with the topknot.

A building on the left rotated ninety degrees, backed up, and slid off down the street. A stone railing shot away. A tower edged forward. The second small man entered the area and stood beside the other. He was smiling. The first was not.

"Is this it?" Black asked, as an outhouse shot by, passing beneath an arch that was striding toward them.

"I'm afraid so," said Dilvish, straightening and raising both arms over his head. "*Mabra, brahoring Mabra...*"

A great wind came down, and within it was a wailing. It spun about without touching them with anything but a chill, and a smoky haze sprang forth from each building.

As Dilvish continued to speak, sounds of cracking and splintering began, followed shortly by the crashes of falling masonry. Somewhere a bell tower tottered and plunged, a final raucous booming emerging from its bell as it descended to shatter upon a rushing shop or residence.

The ground shook as the wailing rose to an ear-splitting howl. The buildings faded within their cloaks of mist. Then came a crack like a hundred lightning-riven trees, and the wind died as suddenly as it had risen.

Dilvish and Black stood upon a sun-swept hilltop. No trace of the city remained about them.

"Congratulations," said Black. "That was very well done."

"To which I must add my own," came a familiar voice from behind them.

Turning, Dilvish saw the small man with the topknot, whose fish swam to his right.

"My deepest apologies," he went on. "I'd no idea we had trapped a brother sorcerer here. That was an Awful Saying, wasn't it? I've never seen one done before."

"Yes, it was."

"Good thing I got close to the protected area in a hurry. My brother, of course, had to go with his city. I want to thank you for that—very much."

"I'd like an explanation now," said Dilvish, "as to what was going on. Had you no better ways to amuse yourselves?"

"Ah, good Sir!" said the small man, wringing his hands. "Had you not guessed from the resemblance? We were twins—a most unfortunate situation when both are practitioners of the subtler arts. The power is divided. Each is only half as strong as he might be, if—"

"I begin to see," said Dilvish, "somewhat."

"Yes. We'd tried duels, but we were too evenly matched. So, rather than share a weakness, we had an arrangement. One of us would spend ten years exiled to an astral limbo while the other enjoyed full potency here. At the end of that time, we would play the game to see who would enjoy the next ten years on Earth. One of us would erect the city, the other would back the champion to try its maze. I was rather depressed when I drew the champion this time, for the city usually won. But you have been my good fortune, Sir. We should have suspected something when we beheld your mount. But who could have guessed an Awful Saying! It must have been hell to learn."

"It was."

"I am of course in your debt, and at full power—almost—now. Is there any way in which I might serve you?"

"Yes," said Dilvish.

"Name it."

"I am seeking a man—no, a sorcerer. If you have knowledge of his whereabouts, I want it. To name him here is risky, for his attention might have been drawn to these recent workings of power. His strengths are of the highest, and the darkest. Do you know of whom I speak?"

"I—I am not certain."

Dilvish sighed.

"Very well."

He dismounted, and with the tip of his blade he scratched the name *Jelerak* in the dirt.

The small sorcerer blanched and wrung his hands again.

"Oh, good sir! You seek your death!"

"No. His," Dilvish said, rubbing out the name with his toe. "Can you help me?"

The other swallowed.

"He has seven castles that I know of in different parts of the world. All are defended differently. He employs servants both human and unnatural. It is said that he has ways of transporting himself quickly among these keeps. How is it that you do not know these things?"

"I have been away for a long while. Bear with me. Where are they located?"

"I believe I may know who you are," said the sorcerer, kneeling and drawing in the earth with his finger.

Dilvish crouched beside him and watched the map take shape.

"...Here is the one at the edge of the world, which I have seen only in visions. Here is the Red Keep... Another lies to the far south..."

Dilvish inscribed them in his mind as they appeared before him.

"...Then the nearest seems to be this one you call the Tower of Ice," Dilvish said, "over a hundred leagues to the north and west of here. I had heard rumor of such a place. I had been seeking it."

"Take counsel of me, Deliverer," he said, rising. "Do not—"

The city stood all around them again, but changed, beginning lower and sweeping down the hillside for as far as the eye could see.

"You didn't—uh—summon it back for a small joke, did you?" the sorcerer asked.

"No."

"I was afraid you'd say that. Came up awfully quiet, didn't it?"

"Yes."

"A lot bigger than Stradd and I could ever make them, too. What now? Do you think he wants to run us through it?"

A dark mass occurred in the sky overhead.

"I'd do it gladly, if he would await me within."

"Don't say that, friend! Look!"

Like slow lightning, sheets of fire descended from the heavens, silently, falling upon the new city about them. In moments it began to blaze. They smelled the smoke. Ashes drifted by. Soon they were ringed by a giant wall of flame, and waves of heat fell upon them.

"That is very nicely done," observed the sorcerer, mopping his brow with his sleeve. "I am going to give you my name—Strodd—as an act of extreme generosity on my part, since we may be under sentence of death, anyway—and I believe I've already guessed yours. Right?"

"I'd say."

The fires began to subside. There was no city beneath them.

"Yes, that is nicely done," Strodd remarked. "I believe the demonstration is about over, but I wonder why he didn't simply divert it upon us?"

Black laughed—a harsh, metallic thing.

"There are reasons," he said.

The fire flickered and vanished, leaving the sunny hilltop exactly as it had been but a while before.

"Well, there you are," Strodd said. "I am suddenly anxious to undertake a long journey, for my health. One grows somewhat attenuated wandering about in astral limbos. I still owe you something, but I am afraid of the company you might be keeping. I would rather you called on me for several small matters rather than the big one I fear you might be headed for—if you know what I mean?"

"I'll remember," said Dilvish, smiling, and he mounted Black and turned his head toward the northwest.

Strodd winced.

"I was afraid you'd be going that way," he said. "Well, good luck to you anyhow."

"And yourself."

Dilvish tossed the man a small salute before he rode off.

"The Tower of Ice?" said Black.

"The Tower of Ice."

When Dilvish looked back, the hilltop was empty.

A Word from Zelazny

This piece was the fifth Dilvish tale written but sixth in sequence in the novel/collection *Dilvish, the Damned*. "Every now and then someone would ask me whether I planned on doing any more Dilvish stories. I usually responded with a decisive, 'Maybe.' "[1] In 1979, after fifteen years of silence, Editor Stephen Gregg asked for a new Dilvish tale after he reprinted "A Knight for Merytha" in *Eternity SF*. "I wrote back and said no, but almost immediately after mailing the letter a story idea came to me. So I wrote 'A City Divided.' "[1] *Eternity SF* folded before running it, so the story first appeared three years later in *Dilvish, the Damned*. Zelazny acknowledged Gregg in *Dilvish, the Damned* for helping to resurrect Dilvish.

Notes

A **codpiece** is a decorative pouch on a man's breeches or close-fitting hose to cover the genitals. **Cyclopean** in this context means ancient masonry having massive irregular blocks. **Riven** means torn.

---

1 *Alternities #6*, Summer 1981.

The White Beast

Whispers #13–14, ed. Stuart David Schiff, Whispers Press, October 1979.
§ *Dilvish* 7 of 11

All that day, as he crossed the ice field, the rider of the burnished black beast had known that he was pursued. He had glimpsed the great loping white form far back among the drifts. Now, with moonlight sparkling upon the sleek and snowy forms and an icy wind sweeping down from the mountains and across the nighted plain, he heard the first howl of his pursuer.

But the mountains themselves lay very near now. Somewhere at their base, perhaps, a hollow, a cave, a fortified shelter—a place where he might rest with rock at his back and beside him, a fire before him, his blade across his knees.

The howling came again. His great black mount moved more quickly. Large boulders lay strewn ahead of them, beside them now… He moved among them, his eyes searching the ice-coated talus for signs of an opening—anywhere.

"There, up ahead," came the low voice from below and before him, as the beast spoke.

"Yes, I see it. Can we fit?"

"If not, I'll enlarge it. It is dangerous to seek further. There may be no other."

"True."

They halted before the opening. The man dismounted, his green boots soundless on the snow. His black, horselike mount entered first.

"It is larger than it looks—empty and dry. Come in."

The man entered the cave, dipping his head below its outer rim. He dropped to his knees and felt for tinder.

"A few sticks, a branch, leaves…"

He heaped them and seated himself. The beast remained standing at his back. He unclasped his blade and placed it near to hand.

There came another howl, much nearer.

"I wish that damned white wolf would get up his courage to attack. I won't be able to sleep till we've settled our differences," said the man, locating his flint. "All day it's circled and trailed, watching, waiting..."

"I believe it is me that it fears most," said the dark form. "It senses that I am unnatural, and that I will protect you."

"I would fear you, too," said the man, laughing.

"But yours is a human intelligence. What of its?"

"What do you imply?"

"Nothing. Really. I don't know. Eat. Rest. I will guard you."

The leaves took fire beneath showers of sparks, smouldered.

"If it were to brave the flame, spring quickly, and seize me, it might drag me out there—to some snowy crust where one of your bulk would flounder. That is how I would do it."

"Now you are crediting it with too much wisdom."

The man fed the fire, unwrapped his rations.

"I see it moving, among the rocks. It is hungry, but it thinks to wait—for the right moment."

He unsheathed his blade.

"Is there any special way to tell a were-beast?" he asked.

"Not unless you see it changing, or hear it speaking."

"Hello out there!" the man called suddenly. "Make a deal? I'll share my rations with you, then wave good-bye. All right?"

Only the wind made answer.

He took up a piece of meat, skewered it, and warmed it. He cut it in half then and set a piece of it to one side.

"You are being more than a little ridiculous," said his companion.

The man shrugged and began eating. He melted snow for water, mixed some wine with it, drank.

An hour passed. He sat wrapped in his cloak and a folded blanket, feeding the remaining sticks to the fire. Outside the snowy shape moved nearer. He caught the glint of his firelight on its eyes for the first time, from off to the left and at a point not visible to his dark companion. He said nothing. He watched. The eyes drifted nearer—large, yellow.

Finally they settled, low, just around the corner of the cave mouth.

"The meat!" came a panted whisper.

He placed a hand upon the foreleg of his companion, signaling it to stillness. With his other hand, he picked up the piece of meat and tossed it outside. It vanished immediately, and he heard the sounds of chewing.

"That is all?" came the voice, after a time.

"Half of my own ration, as I promised," he whispered.

"I am very hungry. I fear I must eat you also. I am sorry."

"I know that. And I, too, am sorry, but what I have left must feed me until I reach the Tower of Ice. Also, I must destroy you if you attempt to take me."

"The Tower of Ice? You will die there and the food be wasted, your own body-meat be wasted. The master of that place will kill you. Did you not know?"

"Not if I kill him first."

The white beast panted for a time. Then: "I am so hungry," it said again. "Soon I must try to take you. Some things are worse than death."

"I know that."

"Would you tell me your name?"

"Dilvish."

"It seems I heard that name once, long ago…"

"Perhaps.

"If he does not kill you— Look at me! I, too, once tried to kill him. I, too, was once a man."

"I do not know the spell which might unbind you."

"Too late. I care no more for that. Only for food."

There came a slobbering sound, followed by a sharp intake of breath. The man took his blade into his hand and waited.

Then: "I remember hearing of a Dilvish long ago, called the Deliverer," came the slow words. "He was strong."

Silence.

"I am he."

Silence.

"Let me move a little nearer… And your boots are green!"

The white form withdrew again. The yellow eyes met his own and stared.

"I am hungry, always hungry."

"I know."

"I know of only one thing that is stronger. You know that, too. Good-bye."

"Good-bye."

The eyes turned away. The shadow form was gone from beside the cave. Later Dilvish heard a howling in the distance. Then silence.

A Word from Zelazny:

Zelazny conceived this seventh Dilvish tale after the eighth tale, but wrote it first. "I'd realized that I was leading up to a novella, and I even had the title—'The Tower of Ice.' Before I could write it, though, a brief transitional piece was necessary to go between it and 'A City Divided.' So I wrote 'The White Beast,' which appeared in Stuart Schiff's *Whispers* for October, 1979."[1]

Notes

Talus is a sloping mass of rock debris at the base of a cliff. The "were" of **were-beast** or werewolf comes from an Old English word meaning "man."

1 *Alternities #6*, Vol 2 No 2, Summer 1981.

TOWER OF ICE

Flashing Swords #5: Demons and Daggers, ed. Lin Carter, Nelson Doubleday 1981.
§ *Dilvish* 8 of 11

The dark, horse-shaped beast paused on the icy trail. Head turned to the left and upward, it regarded the castle atop the glistening mountain, as did its rider.

"No," the man finally stated.

The black beast continued on, ice cracking beneath its cloven metal hooves, snow blowing about it.

"I'm beginning to suspect that there is no trail," the beast announced after a time. "We've come more than halfway around."

"I know," replied the muffled, green-booted rider. "I might be able to scale the thing, but that would mean leaving you behind."

"Risky," his mount replied. "You know my value in certain situations—especially the one you court."

"True. But if it should prove the only way..."

They moved on for some time, pausing periodically to study the prominence.

"Dilvish, there was a gentler part of the slope—some distance back," the beast announced. "If I'd a good start, I could bear you quite a distance up it. Not all of the way to the top, but near."

"If that should prove the only way, Black, we'll go that route," the rider replied, breath steaming before him to be whipped away by the wind. "We might as well check further first, though. Hello! What is—"

A dark form came hurtling down the side of the mountain. When it seemed that it was about to strike the ice before them, it spread pale-green, batlike wings and pulled itself aloft. It circled quickly, gaining altitude, then dove toward them.

Immediately his blade was in his hand, held vertically before him. Dilvish leaned back, eyes on the approaching creature. At the sight of his weapon, it veered off, to return immediately. He swung at it and missed. It darted away again.

"Obviously our presence is no longer a secret," Black commented, turning so as to face the flying thing.

The creature dove once more and Dilvish swung again. It turned at the last moment, to be struck by the side of his blade. It fell then, fluttered, rose into the air again, circled several times, climbed higher, turned away. It began to fly back up along the side of the Tower of Ice.

"Yes, it would seem we have lost the advantage of surprise," Dilvish observed. "Actually, I'd thought he would have noted us sooner."

He sheathed his blade.

"Let's go find that trail—if there is one."

They continued on their way about the base of the mountain.

❖ ❖ ❖

Corpselike, the green and white face stared out of the mirror. No one stood before it to cast such an image. The high stone hall was reflected behind it, threadbare tapestries on its walls, several narrow windows, the long, heavy dining table, a candelabrum flickering at its farther end. The wind made moaning noises down a nearby chimney, alternately flattening and drawing the flames in the wide fireplace.

The face seemed to be regarding the diners: a thin, dark-haired, dark-eyed young man in a black doublet lined with green, who toyed with his food and whose nervous gestures carried his fingers time and again to the heavy, black metal ring with the pale pink stone that depended from a chain about his neck; and a girl, whose hair and eyes matched the man's, whose generous mouth quirked into occasional odd, quick smiles as she ate with better appetite. She had a brown and red cloak thrown about her shoulders, its ends folded across her lap. Her eyes were not so deep-set as the man's and they did not dart as his did.

The thing in the mirror moved its pale lips.

"The time is coming," it announced, in a deep, expressionless voice.

The man leaned forward and cut a piece of meat. The girl raised her wineglass. Something seemed to flutter against one of the windows for a moment.

From somewhere far up the long corridor to the girl's right, an agonized voice rang out:

"Release me! Oh, please don't do this! Please! It hurts so much!"

The girl sipped her wine.

"The time is coming," the thing in the mirror repeated.

"Ridley, would you pass the bread?" the girl asked.

"Here."

"Thank you."

She broke off a piece and dipped it into the gravy. The man watched her eat, as if fascinated by the act.

"The time is coming," the thing said again.

Suddenly Ridley slapped the table. His cutlery rattled. Beads of wine fell across his plate.

"Reena, can't you shut that damned thing off?" he asked.

"Why, you summoned it," she said sweetly. "Can't you just wave your wand or snap your fingers and give it the proper words?"

He slapped the table again, half rising from his seat.

"I will not be mocked!" he said. "Shut it off!"

She shook her head slowly.

"Not my sort of magic," she replied, less sweetly. "I don't fool with things like that."

From up the hall came more cries:

"It hurts! Oh, please! It hurts so…"

"…Or that," she said more sternly. "Besides, you told me at the time that it was serving a useful purpose."

Ridley lowered himself into his seat.

"I was not—myself," he said softly, taking up his wineglass and draining it.

A mummy-faced individual in dark livery immediately rushed forward from the shadowy corner beside the fireplace to refill his glass.

Faintly, and from a great distance, there came a rattling, as of chains. A shadowy form fluttered against a different window. Ridley fingered his neck chain and drank again.

"The time is coming," announced the corpse-colored face under glass.

Ridley hurled his wineglass at it. It shattered, but the mirror remained intact. Perhaps the faintest of smiles touched the corners of that ghastly mouth. The servant hurried to bring him another glass.

There came more cries from up the hall.

❖ ❖ ❖

"It's no good," Dilvish stated. "We've more than circled it. I don't see any easy way up."

"You know how sorcerers can be. Especially this one."

"True."

"You should have asked that werewolf you met a while back about it."

"Too late now. If we just keep going, we should come to that slope you mentioned pretty soon, shouldn't we?"

"Eventually," Black replied, trudging on. "I could use a bucket of demon juice. I'd even settle for wine."

"I wish I had some wine here myself. I haven't sighted that flying thing again." He looked up into the darkening sky, to where the snow- and ice-decked castle stood with a high window illuminated. "Unless I've glimpsed it darting about up there," he said. "Hard to tell, with the snow and shadows."

"Strange that he didn't send something a lot more deadly."

"I've thought of that."

They continued on for a long while. The lines of the slope softened as they advanced, the icy wall dipping toward a slightly gentler inclination. Dilvish recognized the area as one they had passed before, though Black's earlier hoof prints had been completely obliterated.

"You're pretty low on supplies, aren't you?" Black asked.

"Yes."

"Then I guess we'd better do something—soon."

Dilvish studied the slope as they moved along its foot.

"It gets a little better, farther ahead," Black remarked. Then: "That sorcerer we met—Strodd—had the right idea."

"What do you mean?"

"He headed south. I hate this cold."

"I didn't realize it bothered you, too."

"It's a lot hotter where I come from."

"Would you rather be back there?"

"Now that you mention it, no."

Several minutes later they rounded an icy mass. Black halted and turned his head.

"That's the route I'd choose—over there. You can judge it best from here."

Dilvish followed the slope upward with his eyes. It reached about three quarters of the way up to the castle. Above it the wall rose sheer and sharp.

"How far up do you think you can get me?" he asked.

"I'll have to stop when it goes vertical. Can you scale the rest?"

Dilvish shaded his eyes and squinted.

"I don't know. It looks bad. But then, so does the grade. Are you sure you can make it that far?"

Black was silent for a time, then: "No, I'm not," he said. "But we've been all the way around, and this is the only place where I think we've got a chance."

Dilvish lowered his eyes.

"What do you say?"

"Let's do it."

❖ ❖ ❖

"I don't see how you can sit there eating like that!" Ridley declared, throwing down his knife. "It's disgusting!"

"One must keep up one's strength in the face of calamities," Reena replied, taking another mouthful. "Besides, the food is exceptionally good tonight. Which one prepared it?"

"I don't know. I can't tell the staff apart. I just give them orders."

"The time is coming," stated the mirror.

Something fluttered against the window again and stopped, hanging there, a dark outline. Reena sighed, lowered her utensils, rose. She rounded the table and crossed to the window.

"I am not going to open the window in weather like this!" she shouted. "I told you that before! If you want to come in, you can fly down one of the chimneys! Or not, as you please!"

She listened a moment to a rapid chittering noise from beyond the pane.

"No, not just this once!" she said then. "I told you that before you went out in it!"

She turned and stalked back to her seat, her shadow dancing on a tapestry as the candles flickered.

"Oh, don't… Please, don't… Oh!" came a cry from up the hall.

She settled into her chair once more, ate a final mouthful, took another sip of wine.

"We've got to do something," Ridley said, stroking the ring on the chain. "We can't just sit here."

"I'm quite comfortable," she answered.

"You're in this as much as I am."

"Hardly."

"He's not going to look at it that way."

"I wouldn't be too sure."

Ridley snorted.

"Your charms won't save you from the reckoning."

She protruded her lower lip in a mock pout.

"On top of everything else, you insult my femininity."

"You're pushing me, Reena!"

"You know what to do about it, don't you?"

"No!" He slammed his fist against the table. "I won't!"

"The time is coming," said the mirror.

He covered his face with his hands and lowered his head.

"I—I'm afraid…" he said softly.

Now out of his sight, a look of concern tightened her brow, narrowed her eyes.

"I'm afraid of—the other," he said.

"Can you think of any other course?"

"You do something! You've got powers!"

"Not on that level," she said. "The other is the only one I can think of who would have a chance."

"But he's untrustworthy! I can't anticipate him anymore!"

"But he gets stronger all the time. Soon he may be strong enough."

"I—I don't know…"

"Who got us into this mess?"

"That's not fair!"

He lowered his hands and raised his head just as a rattling began within the chimney. Particles of soot and mortar fell upon the flames.

"Oh, really!" she said.

"That crazy old bat—" he began, turning his head.

"Now, that isn't nice either," Reena stated. "After all—"

Ashes were scattered as a small body crashed into the flaming logs, bounced away, hopped about the floor flapping long, green, membranous wings, beating sparks from its body fur. It was the size of a small ape, with a shriveled, nearly human face. It squeaked as it hopped, some of its noises sounding strangely like human curses. Finally it came to a stooped standstill, raised its head, turned burning eyes upon them.

"Try to set fire to me!" it chirped shrilly.

"Come on now! Nobody tried to set fire to you," Reena said.

"...Said 'chimney'!" it cried.

"There are plenty of chimneys up there," Reena stated. "It's pretty stupid to choose a smoking one."

"...Not stupid!"

"What else can you call it?"

The creature sniffed several times.

"I'm sorry," Reena said. "But you could have been more careful."

"The time is coming," said the mirror.

The creature turned its small head, stuck out its tongue.

"...Lot you know," it said. "He...he beat me!"

"Who? Who beat you?" Ridley asked.

"...The avenger." It made a sweeping, downward gesture with its right wing. "He's down there."

"Oh, my!" Ridley paled. "You're quite certain?"

"...He beat me," the creature repeated. Then it began to bounce along the floor, beat at the air with its wings, and flew to the center of the table.

Somewhere, faintly, a chain was rattled.

"How—how do you know he is the avenger?" Ridley asked.

The creature hopped along the table, tore at the bread with its talons, stuffed a piece into its mouth, chewed noisily.

"...My little ones, my pretty ones," it chanted after a time, glancing about the hall.

"Stop that!" Reena said. "Answer his question! How do you know who it is?"

It raised its wings to its ears.

"Don't shout! Don't shout!" it cried. "...I saw! I know! He beat me—poor side!—with a sword!" It paused to hug itself with its wings. "...I only went to look up close. My eyes are not so good... He rides a demon beast! Circling, circling—the mountain! Coming, coming—here!"

Ridley shot a look at Reena. She compressed her lips, then shook her head.

"Unless it is airborne it will never make it up the tower," she said. "It wasn't a winged beast, was it?"

"...No. A horse," the creature replied, tearing at the bread again.

"There was a slide near the south face," Ridley said. "But no. Even so. Not with a horse."

"...A demon horse."

"Even with a demon horse!"

"The pain! The pain! I can't stand it!" came a shrill cry.

Reena raised her wineglass, saw that it was empty, lowered it again. The mummy-faced man rushed from the shadows to fill it.

For several moments they watched the winged creature eat. Then: "I don't like this," Reena said. "You know how devious he can be."

"I know."

"...And green boots," chirped the creature. "...Elfboots. Always to land on his feet. You burned me, he beat me... Poor Meg! Poor Meg! He'll get you, too..."

It hopped down and skittered across the floor.

"...My little ones, my pretty ones!" it called.

"Not here! Get out of here!" Ridley cried. "Change or go away! Keep them out of here!"

"...Little ones! Pretties!" came the fading voice as Meg ran up the corridor in the direction of the screams.

Reena swirled the wine in her glass, took a drink, licked her lips.

"The time has come," the mirror suddenly announced.

"Now what are you going to do?" Reena asked.

"I don't feel well," Ridley said.

❖ ❖ ❖

When they came to the foot of the slope, Black halted and stood like a statue for a long while, studying it. The snow continued to fall. The wind drove the flakes past them.

After several minutes, Black advanced and tested the grade, climbing several paces, standing with big full weight upon it, stamping and digging with his hooves, head lowered.

Finally he backed down the slope and turned away.

"What is the verdict?" Dilvish inquired.

"I am still willing to try. My estimate of our chances is unchanged. Have you given any thought to what you are going to do if—rather, when—you make it to the top?"

"Look for trouble," Dilvish said. "Defend myself at all times. Strike instantly if I see the enemy."

Black began to walk slowly away from the mountain.

"Almost all of your spells are of the offensive variety," Black stated, "and most are too terrible to be used, except in final extremes. You should really take the time to learn some lesser and intermediate ones, you know."

"I know. This is a fine time for a lecture on the state of the art."

"What I am trying to say is that if you get trapped up there, you know how to level the whole damned place and yourself with it. But you don't know how to charm the lock on a door—"

"That is *not* a simple spell!"

"No one said that it was. I am merely pointing out your deficiencies."

"It is a little late for that, isn't it?"

"I am afraid so," Black replied. "So, there are three good general spells of protection against magical attack. You know as well as I do that your enemy can break through any of them. The stronger ones, though, might slow him long enough for you to do something. I can't let you go up there without one of them holding you."

"Then lay the strongest upon me."

"It takes a full day to do it."

Dilvish shook his head.

"In this cold? Too long. What about the others?"

"The first one we may dismiss as insufficient against any decent operator in the arts. The second takes the better part of an hour to call into being. It will give you good protection for about half a day."

Dilvish was silent for a moment. Then: "Let's be about it," he said.

"All right. But even so, there must be servants, to keep the place running. You are probably going to find yourself outnumbered."

Dilvish shrugged.

"It may not be much of a staff," he said, "and there'd be no need to maintain a great guard in an inaccessible spot like this. I'll take my chances."

Black came to the place he deemed sufficiently distant from the slope. He turned and faced the tower.

"Get your rest now," he stated, "while I work your protection. It will probably be the last you have for a while."

Dilvish sighed and leaned forward. Black began speaking in a strange voice. His words seemed to crackle in the icy air.

❖ ❖ ❖

The latest scream ceased on a weakened note. Ridley got to his feet and moved across the hall to a window. He rubbed at the frosted pane with the palm of his hand, a quick, circular motion. He placed his face near the area he had cleared, holding his breath.

Finally: "What do you see?" Reena asked him.

"Snow," he muttered, "ice…"

"Anything else?"

"My reflection," he answered angrily, turning away.

He began to pace. When he passed the face in the mirror, its lips moved.

"The time is come," it said.

He replied with an obscenity. He continued pacing, hands clasped behind his back.

"You think Meg really saw something down there?" he asked.

"Yes. Even the mirror has changed its tune."

"What do you think it is?"

"A man on a strange mount."

"Perhaps he's not actually coming here. Maybe he's on his way someplace else."

She laughed softly.

"Just on his way to the neighborhood tavern for a few drinks," she said.

"All right! All right! I'm not thinking clearly! I'm upset! Supposing—just supposing—he does make it up here. He's only one man."

"With a sword. When was the last time you had one in your hands?"

Ridley licked his lips.

"…And he must be fairly sturdy," she said, "to have come so far across these wastes."

"There are the servants. They obey me. Since they are already dead he'd have a hard time killing them."

"That would tend to follow. On the other hand, they're a bit slower and clumsier than ordinary folk—and they can be dismembered."

"You don't do much to cheer a man up, you know?"

"I am trying to be realistic. If there is a man out there wearing Elfboots, he has a chance of making it up here. If he is of the hardy sort and a decent swordsman, then he has a chance of doing what he was sent to do."

"….And you'll still be mocking and bitching while he lops off my head? Just remember that yours will roll, too!"

She sniffed.

"I am in no way responsible for what happened."

"Do you really think he'll see it that way? Or care?"

She looked away.

"You had a chance," she said slowly, "to be one of the truly great ones. But you wouldn't follow the normal courses of development. You were greedy for power. You rushed things. You took risks. You created a doubly dangerous situation. You could have explained the sealing as an experiment that went bad. You could have apologized. He would have been irritated, but he would have accepted it. Now, though, when you can't undo what you did—or do much of anything else, for that matter—he is going to know what happened. He is going to know that you were trying to multiply your power to the point where you could even challenge him. You know what his response has to be under the circumstances. I can almost sympathize with him. If it were me, I would have to do the same thing—destroy you before you get control of the other. You've become an extremely dangerous man."

"But I am powerless! There isn't a damned thing I can do! Not even shut off that simple mirror!" he cried, gesturing toward the face that had just spoken again. "In this state I'm no threat to anybody!"

"Outside of his being inconvenienced by your having cut off his access to one of his strongholds," she said, "he would have to consider the possibility that you keep drawing back from—namely, that if you gain control of the other, you will be one of the most powerful sorcerers in the world. As his apprentice—pardon me, ex-apprentice—who has just apparently usurped a part of his domain, only one thing can follow—a sorcerous duel in which you will actually have a chance of destroying him. Since such a duel has not yet commenced, he must have guessed that you are not ready—or that you are playing some sort of waiting game. So he has sent a human avenger, rather than run the risk that you've turned this place into some sort of magical trap."

"The whole thing could simply have been an accident. He'd have to consider that possibility, too…"

"Under the circumstances, would *you* take the risk of assuming that and waiting? You know the answer. You'd dispatch an assassin."

"I've been a good servant. I've taken care of this place for him…"

"Be sure to petition him for mercy on that count the next time that you see him."

Ridley halted and wrung his hands.

"Perhaps you could seduce him. You're comely enough…"

Reena smiled again.

"I'd lay him on an iceberg and not complain," she said. "If it would get us off the hook, I'd give him the high ride of his long life. But a sorcerer like that—"

"Not him. The avenger."

"Oh."

She blushed suddenly. Then she shook her head.

"I can't believe that anyone who has come all this way could be dissuaded from his purposes by a bit of dalliance, even with someone of my admitted charms. Not to mention the thought of the penalty for his failure. No. You are skirting the real issue again. There is only one way out for you, and you know what that is."

He dropped his eyes, fingered the ring on the chain.

"The other…" he said. "If I had control of the other, all of our problems would be over…"

He stared at the ring as if hypnotized by it.

"That's right," she said. "It's the only real chance."

"But you know what I fear…"

"Yes. I fear it, too."

"…That it may not work—that the other may gain control of *me*!"

"So, either way you are doomed. Just remember, one way it is certain. The other…That way there is still a chance."

"Yes," he said, still not looking at her. "But you don't know the horror of it!"

"I can guess."

"But you don't have to go through it!"

"I didn't create the situation either."

He glared at her.

"I'm sick of hearing you protest your innocence just because the other is not your creation! I went to you first and told you everything I proposed to do! Did you try to talk me out of it? No! You saw the gains in store for us! You went along with my doing it!"

She covered her mouth with her fingertips and yawned delicately.

"Brother," she said, "I suppose that you are right. It doesn't change anything, though, does it? Anything that has to be done…?"

He gnashed his teeth and turned away.

"I won't do it. I can't!"

"You may feel differently about it when he comes knocking at your door."

"We have plenty of ways to deal with a single man—even a skilled swordsman!"

"But don't you see? Even if you succeed you are only postponing the decision, not solving the problem."

"I want the time. Maybe I can think of some way to gain an edge over the other."

Reena's features softened.

"Do you really believe that?"

"Anything is possible, I suppose..."

She sighed and stood. She moved toward him.

"Ridley, you are deceiving yourself," she said. "You will never be any stronger than you are now."

"Not true!" he cried, beginning to pace again. "Not true!"

Another scream came from up the hall. The mirror repeated its message.

"Stop him! We have to stop him! Then I'll worry about the other!"

He turned and tore out of the room. Reena lowered the hand she had raised toward him and returned to the table to finish her wine. The fireplace continued to sigh.

❖ ❖ ❖

Black completed the spell. They remained motionless for a brief while after that.

Then: "That's it?" Dilvish asked.

"It is. You are now protected through the second level."

"I don't feel any different."

"That's how you should feel."

"Is there anything special that I should do to invoke its defense, should the need arise?"

"No, it is entirely automatic. But do not let that dissuade you from exercising normal caution about things magical. Any system has its weak points. But that was the best I could do in the time that we had."

Dilvish nodded and looked toward the tower of ice. Black raised his head and faced it, also.

"Then I guess that all of the preliminaries are out of the way," Dilvish said.

"So it would seem. Are you ready?"

"Yes."

Black began to move forward. Glancing down, Dilvish noted that his hooves seemed larger now, flatter. He wanted to ask about it, but the wind came faster as they gained speed and he decided to save his breath. The snow stung his cheeks, his hands. He squinted and leaned farther forward.

Still running on a level surface, Black's pace increased steadily, one hoof giving an almost bell-like tone as it struck some pebble. Soon they were moving faster than any horse could run. Everything to both sides became a snowy blur. Dilvish tried not to look ahead, to protect his eyes, his face. He clung tightly and thought about the course he had come.

He had escaped from Hell itself, after two centuries' torment. Most of the humans he had known were long dead and the world somewhat changed. Yet the one who had banished him, daring him as he did, remained—the ancient sorcerer Jelerak. In the months since his return, he had sought that one, once the call of an ancient duty had been discharged before the walls of Portaroy. Now, he told himself, he lived but for vengeance. And this, this Tower of Ice, one of the seven strongholds of Jelerak, was the closest he had yet come to his enemy. From Hell he had brought a collection of Awful Sayings—spells of such deadly potency as to place the speaker in as great a jeopardy as the victim should their rendering be even slightly less than flawless. He had only used one since his return and had been successful in leveling an entire small city with it. His shudder was for the memory of that day on that hilltop, rather than for the icy blasts that now assailed him.

A shift in equilibrium told him that Black had reached the slope and commenced the ascent. The wind was making a roaring sound. His head was bowed and turned against the icy pelting. He could feel the rapid crunching of Black's hooves beneath him, steady, all of the movements extraordinarily powerful. If Black should slip, he knew that it would be all over for him... Good-bye again, world—and Jelerak still unpunished...

As the gleaming surface fled by beneath him, he tried to push all thoughts of Jelerak and death and vengeance from his mind. As he listened to the wind and cracking ice, his thoughts came free of the moment, drifting back over the unhappy years, past the days of his campaigns, his wanderings, coming to rest on a misty morning in the glades of far Elfland as he rode to the hunt near the Castle Mirata. The sun was big and golden, the breezes cool, and everywhere—green. He could almost smell the earth, feel the texture of tree bark... Would he ever know that again, the way he once had?

An inarticulate cry escaped him, hurled against the wind and destiny and the task he had set himself. He cursed then and squeezed harder with his legs as his equilibrium shifted again and he knew that the course had steepened.

Black's hooves pounded perhaps a trifle more slowly. Dilvish's hands and feet and face were growing numb. He wondered how far up they were. He risked a glance forward but saw only rushing snow. We've come a long way, he decided. Where will it end?

He called back his memory of the slope as seen from below, tried to judge their position. Surely they were near the halfway point. Perhaps they had even passed it...

He counted his heartbeats, counted Black's hoof falls. Yes, it did seem that the great beast was slowing...

He chanced another look ahead.

This time he caught the barest glimpse of the towering rise above and before him, sparkling through the evening, sheer, glassy. It obliterated most of the sky now, so he knew that they must be close.

Black continued to slow. The roaring wind lowered its voice. The snow came against him with slightly diminished force.

He looked back over his shoulder. He could see the great slope spread out behind them, glistening like the mosaic tiles in the baths at Ankyra. Down, down and back... They *had* come a great distance.

Black slowed even more. Now Dilvish could hear as well as feel the crunching of crusted snow and ice beneath them. He eased his grip slightly, leaned back a little, raised his head. There was the last stage of the tower, glistening darkly, much nearer now.

Abruptly, the winds ceased. The monolith must be blocking them, he decided. The snow drifted far more gently here. Black's pace had become a canter, though he was laboring no less diligently than before. The journey up the white-smeared tunnel was nearing its end.

Dilvish adjusted his position again, to better study the high escarpment. At this quarter, its surface had resolved itself into a thing of textures. From the play of shadow, he could make out prominences, crevices. Bare rock jutted in numerous places. Quickly he began tracing possible routes to the top.

Black slowed further, almost to a walk, but they now were near to the place where the greatest steepness began. Dilvish cast about for a stopping point.

"What do you think of that ledge off to the right, Black?" he asked.

"Not much," came the reply. "But that's where we're headed. The trickiest part will be making it up onto the shelf. Don't let go yet."

Dilvish clung tightly as Black negotiated a hundred paces, a hundred more.

"It looks wider from here than it did from back there," he observed.

"Yes. Higher, too. Hang on. If we slip here, it's a long way back down."

Black's pace increased slightly as he approached the ledge that stood at nearly the height of a man above the slope. It was indented several span into the cliff face.

Black leapt.

His hind hooves struck a waist-high prominence, a bare wrinkle of icy rock running horizontally below the ledge. His momentum bore him up past it. It cracked and fell away, but by then his forelegs were on the shelf and his rear ones had straightened with a tiny spring. He scrambled up over the ledge and found his footing.

"You all right?" he asked.

"Yes," said Dilvish.

Simultaneously they turned their heads, slowly, and looked back down to where the winds whipped billows of white, like clouds of smoke across the sparkling way. Dilvish reached out and patted Black's shoulder.

"Well done," he said. "Here and there, I was a little worried."

"Did you think you were the only one?"

"No. Can we make it back down again?"

Black nodded.

"We'll have to move a lot more slowly than we did coming up, though. You may even have to walk beside me, holding on. We'll see. This ledge seems to go back a little way. I'll explore it while you are about your business. There may be a slightly better route down. It should be easier to tell from up here."

"All right," Dilvish said, dismounting on the side nearest the cliff face.

He removed his gloves and massaged his hands, blew on them, tucked them into his armpits for a time.

"Have you decided upon the place for your ascent?"

"Off to the left." Dilvish gestured with his head. "That crevice runs most of the way up, and it is somewhat irregular on both sides."

"Looks to be a good choice. How will you get to it?"

"I'll begin climbing here. These handholds look good enough. I'll meet it at that first big break."

Dilvish unfastened his sword belt and slung it over his back. He chafed his hands again, then drew on his gloves.

"I might as well get started," he said. "Thanks, Black. I'll be seeing you."

"Good thing you're wearing those Elfboots," Black said. "If you slip you know that you'll land on your feet—eventually."

Dilvish snorted and reached for the first handhold.

❖ ❖ ❖

Wearing a dark dress, wrapped in a green shawl, the crone sat upon a small stool in the corner of the long underground chamber. Torches flamed and smoked in two wall sockets, melting—above and behind them—portions of the ice glaze that covered the walls and the ceiling. An oil lamp burned near her feet on the straw-strewn stone of the floor. She hummed to herself, fondling one of the loaves she bore in her shawl.

Across from her were three heavy wooden doors, bound with straps of rusted metal, small, barred windows set high within them. A few faint sounds of movement emerged from the one in the middle, but she was oblivious to this. The water that dripped from the irregular stone ceiling above the torches had formed small pools that spread into the straw and lost their boundaries. The dripping sounds kept syncopated accompaniment to her crooning.

"...My little ones, my pretty ones," she sang. "...Come to Meg. Come to Mommy Meg."

There was a scurrying noise in the straw, in the dim corner near to the left-hand door. Hastily she broke off a piece of bread and tossed it in that direction. There followed a fresh rustling and a small movement. She nodded, rocked back on her seat, and smiled.

From across the way—possibly from behind the middle door—there came a low moan. She cocked her head for a moment, but it was followed by silence.

She cast another piece of bread into the same corner. The sounds that followed were more rapid, more pronounced. The straw rose and fell. She threw another piece, puckered her lips, and made a small chirping noise.

She threw more.

"...My little ones," she sang again, as over a dozen rats moved nearer, springing upon the bread, tearing at it, swallowing it. More emerged from dark places to join them, to contest for the food. Isolated squeaks occurred, increased in frequency, gradually merged into a chorus.

She chuckled. She threw more bread, nearer. Thirty or forty rats now fought over it.

From behind the middle door came a clinking of chain links, followed by another moan. Her attention, though, was on her little ones.

She leaned forward and moved the lamp to a position near the wall to her right. She broke another loaf and scattered its pieces on the floor before her feet. Small bodies rustled over the straw, approaching. The squeaking grew louder.

There came a heavy rattling of chains, a much louder moan. Something moved within the cell and crashed against the door. It rattled, and another moan rose above the noises of the rats.

She turned her head in that direction, frowning slightly.

The next blow upon the door made a booming sound. For a moment, something like a massive eye seemed to peer out past the bars.

The moaning sound came again, almost seeming to shape itself into words.

"...Meg! Meg..."

She half rose from her seat, staring at the cell door. The next crash—the loudest thus far—rattled it heavily. By then the rats were brushing against her legs, standing upon their hind paws, dancing. She reached out to stroke one, another... She fed them from her hands.

From within the cell the moaning rose again, this time working itself into strange patterns.

"...Mmmmegg...Mmeg..." came the sound.

She raised her head once more and looked in that direction. She moved as if about to rise.

Just then, however, a rat jumped into her lap. Another ran up her back and perched upon her right shoulder.

"Pretty ones…" she said, rubbing her cheek against the one and stroking the other. "Pretty…"

There came a sound as of the snapping of a chain, followed by a terrific crash against the door across from her. She ignored it, however, for her pretty ones were dancing and playing for her…

❖ ❖ ❖

Reena drew garment after garment from her wardrobe. Her room was full of dresses and cloaks, muffles and hats, coats and boots, underthings and gloves. They lay across the bed and all of the chairs and two wall benches.

Shaking her head, she turned in a slow circle, surveying the lot. The second time around, she withdrew a dress from one of the heaps and draped it over her left arm. Then she took a heavy fur wrap down from a hook. She handed both to the tall, sallow, silent man who stood beside the door. His heavily wrinkled face resembled that of the man who had served her dinner—expressionless, vacant eyed.

He received the garments from her and began folding them. She passed him a second dress, a hat, hose, and underthings. Gloves… He accepted two heavy blankets she took down from a shelf. More hose… He placed everything within a duffel-like sack.

"Bring it along—and one empty one," she said, and she moved toward the door.

She passed through and crossed the hallway to a stair, which she began to descend. The servant followed her, holding the sack by its neck with one hand, before him. He bore another one, folded, beneath his other arm, which hung stiffly at his side.

Reena made her way through corridors to a large, deserted kitchen, where a fire still smouldered beneath a grate. The wind made a whistling noise down the chimney.

She passed the large chopping block and turned left into the pantry. She checked shelves, bins, and cabinets, pausing only to munch a cookie as she looked.

"Give me the bag," she said. "No, not that one. The empty one."

She shook out the bag and began filling it—with dried meats, heads of cheese, wine bottles, loaves of bread. Pausing, she looked about again, then added a sack of tea and a sack of sugar. She also put in a small pot and some utensils.

"Bring this one, too," she said finally, turning and departing the pantry.

She moved more cautiously now, the servant treading silently at her heels, a bag in either hand. She paused and listened at corners and stairwells before moving on. The only things she heard, though, were the screams from far above.

At length she came to a long, narrow stair leading down, vanishing into the darkness.

"Wait," she said softly, and she raised her hands, cupping them before her face, blowing gently upon them, staring at them.

A faint spark occurred between her palms, faded, grew again as she whispered soft words over it.

She drew her hands apart, her lips still moving. The tiny light hung in the air before her, growing in size, increasing in brilliance. It was blue white, and it reached the intensity of several candles.

She uttered a final word and it began to move, drifting before her down the stairwell. She followed it. The servant followed her.

They descended for a long while. The stair spiraled down with no terminus in sight. The light seemed to lead them. The walls grew damp, cold, colder, coming to be covered with a fine patina of frost figures. She drew her cloak farther forward over her shoulders. The minutes passed.

Finally they reached a landing. Distant walls were barely visible in the blackness beyond her light. She turned to her left and the light moved to precede her.

They passed through a long corridor that sloped gently downward, coming after a time to another stair at a place where the walls widened on either hand and the rocky ceiling maintained its level, to vanish from sight as they descended.

The full dimensions of the chamber into which they came were not discernible. It seemed more a cavern than a room. The floor was less regular than any over which they had so far passed, and it was by far the coldest spot they had yet come to.

Holding her cloak fully closed before her now, hands beneath it, Reena proceeded into the chamber, moving diagonally to her right.

Finally a large, boxlike sled came into view, a waxy rag hanging from the point of its left runner. It stood near the wall at the mouth of a tunnel through which an icy wind roared. The light came to hover above it.

Reena halted and turned to the servant.

"Put them in there," she said, gesturing, "toward the front."

She sighed as this was done, then leaned forward and covered them over with a pelt of white fur that had lain folded upon the vehicle's seat.

"All right," she said, turning away, "we'd better be getting back now."

She pointed in the direction from which they had come and the floating light moved to follow her finger.

❖ ❖ ❖

In the circular room at the top of the highest tower, Ridley turned the pages in one of the great books. The wind howled like a banshee above the pitched roof, which sometimes vibrated with the force of its passage. The entire tower even had a barely perceptible sway to it.

Ridley muttered softly to himself as he fingered the leather binding, casting his eyes down the creamy sheets. He no longer wore the chain with the ring on it. These now rested atop a small chest of drawers by the wall near the door, a high, narrow mirror above it catching their image, the stone glowing palely within it.

Still muttering, he turned a page, then another, and paused. He closed his eyes for a moment, then turned away, leaving the book on the reading stand. He moved to the exact center of the room and stood there for a long while, at the middle of a red diagram drawn upon the floor. He continued to mutter.

He turned abruptly and walked to the chest of drawers. He picked up the ring and chain. He unfastened the chain and removed it.

Holding the ring between the thumb and forefinger of his right hand, he extended his left forefinger and quickly slipped the ring over it. He withdrew it almost immediately and took a deep breath. He regarded his reflection in the mirror. Quickly he slipped the ring on again, paused several moments, withdrew it more slowly.

He turned the ring and studied it. Its stone seemed to shine a little more brightly now. He fitted it over his finger once more, withdrew it, paused, refitted it, withdrew it, refitted it, paused, withdrew it, replaced it, paused longer, slowly slid it partway off, then back again…

Had he been looking ahead into the mirror, he might have noticed that each manipulation of the ring caused a change in expression to flit across his face. He cycled between bafflement and pleasure, fear and satisfaction as the ring came on and off.

He slipped it off again and placed it atop the chest. He massaged his finger. He glanced at himself in the mirror, looked back down, staring deep into the depths of the stone. He licked his lips.

He turned away, walked several paces across the pattern, halted. He turned and looked back at the ring. He returned and picked it up, weighing it in the palm of his right hand.

He placed it upon his finger again and stood there wearing it, still gripping it tightly with the fingers of his other hand. This time his teeth were clenched and his brow furrowed.

As he stood there, the mirror clouded and a new image began to take shape within it. Rock and snow… Some sort of movement across it… A man… The man was crawling through the snow… No.

The man's hands grasped at holds. He drew himself upward, not forward! He was climbing, not crawling!

The picture came clearer.

As the man drew himself up and located a fresh foothold, Ridley saw that he had on green boots. Then…

He snapped an order. There was a distancing effect. The man grew smaller, the cliff face wider and higher. There, above the climbing man, stood the castle, this castle, his own light gleaming through this tower window!

With a curse, he tore the ring from his finger. The picture immediately faded, to be replaced by his own angry expression.

"No!" he cried, striding to the door and unfastening it. "No!"

He flung the door open and tore off down the winding stair.

❖ ❖ ❖

Dilvish rested for a time, back and legs braced against the sides of the rock chimney, gloves in his lap, blowing on his hands, rubbing them. The chimney ended a small distance above his head. There would be no more resting after this until he reached the top, and then—who could tell?

A few flakes of snow drifted past him. He searched the dark sky, as he had been doing regularly, for a return of the flying creature, but saw nothing. His thought of it catching him in a vulnerable position had caused him considerable concern.

He continued to rub his hands until they tingled, until he felt some warmth returning. Then he donned his gloves again to preserve it. He leaned his head as far back as it would go and looked upward.

He had come over two thirds of the way up the vertical face. He sought and located his next handholds. He listened to his heartbeat, now returned to normal. Slowly, cautiously, he extended himself again, reaching.

He pushed himself upward. Leaving the chimney, he caught hold of a ledge and drew himself higher. His feet found purchase below him, and he reached again with one hand. He wondered whether Black had located a good way down. He thought of his last meal, cold and dry, almost freezing to his tongue. He recalled better fare from earlier days and felt his mouth begin to water.

He came to a slippery place, worked his way about it. He wondered at the strange feeling he had earlier, as if someone had been watching him. He had sought in the sky hurriedly, but the flying creature had been nowhere about.

Drawing himself over a thick, rocky projection, he smiled, seeing that the wall began to slant inward above it. He found his footing and leaned into the climb.

He advanced more rapidly now, and before very long a sharp edge that could be the top came into view. He scrambled toward it as the slope increased, giving thought now to his movements immediately upon reaching it.

He drew himself up faster and faster, finally rising into a low crouch as the grade grew more gentle. Nearing what he took to be the top, he slowed again, finally casting himself flat a little more than a body length below the rim. For a time, he listened, but there were no sounds other than those of the wind.

Carefully, gloves in his teeth, he drew his sword belt over an arm and shoulder, up over his head. He unfastened it and lowered it. He adjusted his garments, then fitted it in place about his waist once again.

He moved very slowly, approaching the rim. When he finally raised his head above it his eyes were filled with the gleaming white of the castle, standing like a sugary confection not too far in the distance.

Several minutes passed as he studied the scene. Nothing moved but the snow. He looked for a side door, a low window, any indirect entrance…

When he thought that he had found what he was seeking, he drew himself up over the edge and began his advance.

❖ ❖ ❖

Meg sang to the dancing rats. The torches flickered. The walls ran wet. She teased the creatures with bits of bread. She stroked them and scratched them and chuckled over them.

There came another heavy crash against the central door. This time the wood splintered somewhat about the hinges.

"Mmeg…Mmeg…!" came from beyond it, and again the large eye appeared behind the bars.

She looked up, meeting the moist blue gaze. A troubled expression came over her face.

"Yes…?" she said softly.

"Meg!"

There followed another crash. The door shuddered. Cracks appeared along its edge.

"Meg!"

Another crash. The door creaked and protruded beyond its frame, the cracks widened.

She shook her head.

"Yes?" she said more loudly, a touch of excitement coming into her voice.

The rats jumped down from her lap, her shoulders, her knees, racing back and forth across the straw.

The next crash tore the door free of its hinges, pushing it a full foot outward. A large, clawed, dead-white hand appeared about its edge, chain dangling from a metal cuff about its wrist, rattling against the wall, the door…

"Meg?"

She rose to her feet, dropping the remainder of the bread from within her shawl. A black whirlwind of furry bodies moved about it, the squeaking smothering her reply. She moved forward through it.

The door was thrust farther outward. A gigantic, hairless white head with a drooping carrot of a nose looked out around it. Its neck was so thick that it seemed to reach out to the points of its wide shoulders. Its arms were as big around as a man's thighs, its skin a grease-splotched albino. It shouldered the door aside and emerged, back bent at an unnatural angle, head thrust forward, moving on legs like pillars. It wore the tatters of a shirt and the rent remains of a pair of breeches that, like their owner, had lost all color. Its blue eyes, blinking and watering against the torchlight, fixed upon Meg.

"Mack…?" she said.

"Meg…?"

"Mack!"

"Meg!"

She rushed to embrace the quarter ton of snowy muscle, her own eyes growing moist as he managed to hold her gently. They mumbled softly at one another.

Finally she took hold of his huge arm with her small hand.

"Come. Come, Mack," she said. "Food for you. Warm. Be free. Come."

She led him toward the chamber's exit, her pretty ones forgotten.

❖ ❖ ❖

Ignored, the parchment-skinned servant moved about Reena's chambers on silent feet, gathering strewn garments, restoring them to drawers and wardrobe. Reena sat at her dressing table, brushing her hair. When the servant had finished putting the room in order, he came and stood beside her. She glanced up, looked about.

"Very good," she said. "I have no further need of you. You may return to your coffin."

The dark-liveried figure turned and departed.

Reena rose and removed a basin from beneath the bed. Taking it to her nightstand, she added some water from a blue pitcher that stood there. Moving back to her dresser, she took up one of the candles from near the mirror and transferred it to a position to the left of the basin. Then she leaned forward and stared down at the moist surface.

Images darted there… As she watched, they flowed together, fell apart, recombined…

The man was nearing the top. She shuddered slightly as she watched him pause to unsling his blade and fasten it about his waist. She saw him rise further, to the very edge. She saw him survey the castle for a long while. Then he drew himself up, to move across the snow… Where? Where would he seek entry?

…Toward the north and coming in closer, up toward the windows of that darkened storage room in back. Of course! The snow was banked highest there, and heavily crusted. He could reach the sill, draw himself up to climb upon it. It would only be the work of a few moments to knock a hole near the latch with the hilt of his weapon, reach through, and unfasten it. Then several long minutes with the blade to chip away all the ice that crusted the frame. More time to open it. Additional moments to locate the juncture of the shutters within, to slide the blade between them, lift upward, raise their latch… Then he would be disoriented in a dark room filled with clutter. It would take minutes more for him to negotiate that…

She blew gently upon the surface of the water and the picture was gone among ripples. Taking up the candle, she bore it back to her dressing table, set it where it had been. She restored the basin to its former locale.

Seating herself before the mirror, she took up a tiny brush and a small metal box, to add a touch of color to her lips.

❖ ❖ ❖

Ridley roused one of the servants and took him upstairs, to move along the corridor toward the room from which the screams still came. Halting before that door, he located the proper key upon a ring at his belt and unlocked it.

"At last!" came the voice from within. "Please! Now—"

"Shut up!" he said and turned away, taking the servant by the arm and turning him toward the open doorway immediately across the corridor.

He pushed the servant into the darkened room.

"Off to the side," he directed. "Stand there." He guided him further. "There—where you will be out of sight of anyone coming this way but can still keep an eye on him. Now take this key and listen carefully. Should anyone come along to investigate those screams, you must be ready. As soon as he begins to open that door, you are to emerge behind him quickly, strike him, and push him in through it—hard! Then close the door again quickly and lock it. After that you may return to your coffin."

Ridley left him, stepping out into the corridor where he hesitated a moment, then stalked off in the direction of the dining hall.

"The time is come," the face in the mirror announced, just as he entered.

He walked up to it, stared back at the grim visage. He took the ring into his hand and slipped it on.

"Silence!" he said. "You have served your purpose. Be gone now!"

The face vanished, just as its lips were beginning to form the familiar words anew, leaving Ridley to regard his own shadowy reflection surrounded by the ornate frame.

He smirked for an instant, then his face grew serious. His eyes narrowed, his image wavered. The mirror clouded and cleared again. He beheld the green-booted man standing upon a window ledge, chipping away at ice…

He began to twist the ring. Slowly he turned it around and around, biting his lip the while. Then, with a jerk, he tore it from his finger and sighed deeply. The smirk returned to his reflected face.

He turned on his heel and crossed the room, where he passed through a sliding panel, a trapdoor, and down a ladder. Moving rapidly, down every shortcut he knew, he took his way once more to the servants' room.

❖ ❖ ❖

Pushing the shutters aside, Dilvish stepped down into the room. A little light from the window at his back showed him something of the litter that resided there. He paused for several moments to memorize its disposition as best he could, then turned and drew the window shut, not closing it entirely. The heavily frosted panes blocked much of the light, but he did not want to risk betrayal by a telltale draft.

He moved silently along the map in his mind. He had sheathed his long blade and now held only a dagger in his hand. He stumbled once before he reached the door—against a jutting chair leg—but was moving so slowly that no noise ensued.

He inched the door open, looked to his right. A corridor, dark…

He stepped out into it and looked to the left. There was some light from that direction. He headed toward it. As he advanced, he saw that it came from the right—either a side corridor or an open room.

The air grew warmer as he approached—the most welcome sensation he had experienced in weeks. He halted, both to listen for telltale sounds and to relish the feeling. After several moments there came the tiniest clinking from around the corner. He edged nearer and waited again. It was not repeated.

Knife held low, he stepped forward, saw that it was the entrance to a room, saw a woman seated within it, reading a book, a glass of some beverage on the small table to her right. He looked to both the right and the left inside the doorway, saw that she was alone, stepped inside.

"You'd better not scream," he said.

She lowered her book and stared at him.

"I won't," she replied. "Who are you?"

He hesitated, then: "Call me Dilvish," he said.

"My name is Reena. What do you want?"

He lowered the blade slightly.

"I have come here to kill. Stay out of my way and you won't be harmed. Get in it and you will. What is your place in this household?"

She paled. She studied his face.

"I am—a prisoner," she said.

"Why?"

"Our means of departure has been blocked, as has the normal means of entrance here."

"How?"

"It was an accident—of sorts. But I don't suppose you'd believe that."

"Why not? Accidents happen."

She looked at him strangely.

"That is what brought you, is it not?"

He shook his head slowly.

"I am afraid that I do not understand you."

"When he discovered that the mirror would no longer transport him to this place, he sent you to slay the person responsible, did he not?"

"I was not sent," Dilvish said. "I have come here of my own will and desire."

"Now it is I who do not understand you," said Reena. "You say that you have come here to kill, and Ridley has been expecting someone to come kill him. Naturally—"

"Who is Ridley?"

"My brother, the apprentice sorcerer who holds this place for his master."

"Your brother is apprentice to Jelerak?"

"Please! That name!"

"I am tired of whispering it! Jelerak! Jelerak! Jelerak! If you can hear me, Jelerak, come around for a closer look! I'm ready! Let's have this out!" he called.

They were both silent for several moments, as if expecting a reply or some manifestation. Nothing happened.

Finally Reena cleared her throat.

"Your quarrel, then, is entirely with the master? Not with his servant?"

"That is correct. Your brother's doings are nothing to me, so long as they do not cross my own purposes. Inadvertently, perhaps, they have—if he has barred my enemy's way to this place. But I can't see that as a cause for vengeance. What is this transport mirror you spoke of? Has he broken it?"

"No," she replied, "it is physically intact. Though he might as well have broken it. He has somehow placed its transport spell in abeyance. It is a gateway used by the master. He employed it to bring himself here—and from here he could also use it to travel to any of his other strongholds, and probably to some other places as well. Ridley turned it off when he was—not himself."

"Perhaps he can be persuaded to turn it back on again. Then when Jelerak comes through to learn the cause of the trouble, I will be waiting for him."

She shook her head.

"It is not that simple," she said. Then: "You must be uncomfortable, standing there in a knife-fighter's crouch. I know that it makes me uncomfortable, just looking at you. Won't you sit down? Would you care for a glass of wine?"

Dilvish glanced over his shoulder.

"Nothing personal," he said, "but I prefer to remain on my feet."

He sheathed his dagger, however, and moved toward the sideboard, where an open wine bottle and several glasses stood.

"Is this what you are drinking?"

She smiled and rose to her feet. She crossed the room to stand beside him, where she took up the bottle and filled two glasses from it.

"Serve me one, sir."

He took up a glass and passed it to her, with a courtly nod. Her eyes met his as she accepted it, raised it, and drank.

He held the other glass, sniffed it, tasted it.

"Very good."

"My brother's stock," she said. "He likes the best."

"Tell me about your brother."

She turned partly and leaned back against the sideboard.

"He was chosen as apprentice from among many candidates," she said, "because he possessed great natural aptitudes for the work. Are you aware that in its higher workings, sorcery requires the assumption of an artificially constructed personality—carefully trained, disciplined, worn like a glove when doing the work?"

"Yes," Dilvish replied.

She gave him a sidelong look and continued:

"But Ridley was always different from most other people, in that he already possessed two personalities. Most of the time he is amiable, witty, interesting. Occasionally his other nature would come over him, though, and it was just the opposite—cruel, violent, cunning. After he began his work with the higher magics, this other side of himself somehow merged with his magical personality. When he would assume the necessary mental and emotional stances for his workings, it would somehow be present. He was well on his way to becoming a fine sorcerer, but whenever he worked at it he changed into something—quite unlikable. Still, this would be no great handicap, if he could put it off again as easily as he took it on—with the ring he had made for this purpose. But after a time, this—other—began to resist such a restoration. Ridley came to believe that *it* was attempting to control *him*."

"I have heard of people like that, with more than one nature and character," Dilvish said. "What finally happened? Which side of him came to dominate?"

"The struggle goes on. He is his better self now. But he fears to face the other—which has become a personal demon to him."

Dilvish nodded and finished his wine. She gestured toward the bottle. He refilled his glass.

"So the other was in control," Dilvish said, "when he nullified the spell on the mirror."

"Yes. The other likes to leave him with bits of unfinished work, so that he will have to call him back..."

"But when he was—this other—did he say why he had done what he did to the mirror? This would seem more than part of a mental struggle. He must have realized that he would be inviting trouble of the most dangerous sort—from elsewhere."

"He knew what he was doing," she said. "The other is an extraordinary egotist. He feels that he is ready to meet the master himself in a struggle for power. The denatured mirror was meant to be a challenge. Actually he told me at the time that it was meant to resolve two situations at once."

"I believe that I can guess at the second one," Dilvish said.

"Yes," she replied. "The other feels that in winning such a contest, he will also emerge as the dominant personality."

"What do you think?"

She paced slowly across the room and turned back toward him.

"Perhaps so," she said, "but I do not believe that he would win."

Dilvish drained his glass and set it aside. He folded his arms across his breast.

"Is there a possibility," he asked, "that Ridley may gain control of the other before any such conflict comes to pass?"

"I don't know. He has been trying—but he fears the other so."

"And if he should succeed? Do you feel that this might increase his chances?"

"Who can say? Not I, certainly. I'm sick of this whole business and I hate this place! I wish that I were someplace warm, like Tooma or Ankyra!"

"What would you do there?"

"I would like to be the highest-paid courtesan in town, and when I grew tired of that perhaps marry some nobleman. I'd like a life of indolence and luxury and warmth, far from the battles of adepts!"

She stared at Dilvish.

"You've some Elvish blood, haven't you?"

"Yes."

"...And you seem to know something of these matters. So you must have come with more than a sword to face the master."

Dilvish smiled.

"I bring him a gift from Hell."

"Are you a sorcerer?"

"My knowledge of these matters is highly specialized. Why?"

"I was thinking that if you were sufficiently skilled to repair the mirror, I could use it to depart and get out of everyone's way."

Dilvish shook his head.

"Magic mirrors are not my specialty. Would that they were. It is somewhat distressing to have come all this distance in search of an enemy and then to discover that his way here is barred."

Reena laughed.

"Surely you do not believe that something like that will stop him?"

Dilvish looked up, dropped his arms, looked about him.

"What do you mean?"

"The one you seek will be inconvenienced by this state of affairs, true. But it would hardly represent an insuperable barrier. He will simply leave his body behind."

Dilvish began to pace.

"Then what's keeping him?" he asked.

"It will first be necessary for him to build his power. If he is to come here in a disembodied state, he would be at a slight disadvantage in whatever conflict ensues. It becomes necessary that he accumulate power to compensate for this."

Dilvish turned on his heel and faced her, his back to the wall.

"This is not at all to my liking," he said. "Ultimately I want something that I can cut. Not some disembodied wraith! How long will this power-building go on, do you think? When might he arrive here?"

"I cannot hear the vibrations on that plane. I do not know."

"Is there some way that we could get your brother to—"

A panel behind Dilvish slid open and a mummy-faced servant with a club struck him across the back of the head. Staggered, Dilvish began to turn. The club rose and fell again. He sank to his knees, then slumped forward onto the floor.

Ridley pushed his way past the servant and entered the room. The club wielder and a second servant came in behind him.

"Very good, sister. Very good," Ridley observed, "to detain him here until he could be dealt with."

Ridley knelt and drew the long blade from the sheath at Dilvish's side. He threw it across the room. Turning Dilvish over, he drew the dagger from the smaller sheath and raised it.

"Might as well finish things," he said.

"You're a fool!" she stated, moving to his side and taking hold of his wrist. "That man could have been an ally! He's not after you! It is the master he wants to slay! He has some personal grudge against him."

Ridley lowered the blade. She did not release his wrist.

"And you believed that?" he said. "You've been up here too long. The first man who comes along gets you to believe—"

She slapped him.

"You've no call to talk to me like that! He didn't even know who you were! He might have helped! Now he won't trust us! "

Ridley regarded Dilvish's face. Then he rose to his feet, his arm falling. He let go the dagger and kicked it across the floor. She released her grip on his wrist.

"You want his life?" he said. "All right. But if he can't trust us, we can't trust him either now." He turned to the servants, who stood motionless at his back. "Take him away," he told them, "and throw him down the hole to join Mack."

"You are compounding your mistakes," she said.

He met her gaze with a glare.

"And I am tired of your mocking," he said. "I have given you his life. Leave it at that, before I change my mind."

The servants bent and raised Dilvish's limp form between them. They bore him toward the door.

"Whether I was wrong or right about him," Ridley said, gesturing after them, "an attack will come. You know it. In one form or another. Probably soon. I have preparations to make, and I do not wish to be disturbed."

He turned as if to go.

Reena bit her lip, then said, "How close are you, to some sort of—accommodation?"

He halted, not looking back.

"Farther than I'd thought I might be," he replied, "at this point. I feel now that I do have a chance at dominating. This is why I can afford to take no risks here, and why I cannot brook any further interruptions or delays. I am returning to the tower now."

He moved toward the door, out of which Dilvish's form had just passed.

Reena lowered her head.

"Good luck," she said softly.

Ridley stalked out of the room.

❖ ❖ ❖

The silent servants bore Dilvish along a dimly lit corridor. When they reached an indentation in the wall, they halted and lowered him to the floor. One of them entered the niche and raised a trapdoor. Returning to the still form, he helped to lift it then, and they lowered Dilvish, feet first, into the dark opening that had been revealed. They released him and he vanished from sight. One of them closed the trapdoor. They turned away and moved back along the corridor.

Dilvish was aware that he was sliding down an inclined surface. For a moment he had visions of Black's having slipped on the way up the mountain. Now he was sliding down the Tower of Ice, and when he hit the bottom…

He opened his eyes. He was seized by instant claustrophobia. He moved through darkness. He had felt the wall close beside him when he had taken a turn. If he reached out with his hands, he felt that the flesh would be rubbed away.

His gloves! He had tucked them behind his belt…

He reached, drew them forth, began pulling them on. He leaned forward as he did so. There seemed to be a feeble patch of light ahead.

He reached out to his sides with both hands, spreading his legs as he did so.

His right heel touched the passing wall just as the palms of his hands did. Then his left…

Head throbbing, he increased the pressure at all four points. The palms of his hands grew warm from the friction, but he slowed slightly. He pushed harder, he dug with his heels. He continued to slow.

He exerted his full strength now. The gloves were wearing through. The left one tore. His palm began to burn.

Ahead, the pale square grew larger. He realized that he was not going to be able to stop himself before he reached it. He pushed one more time. He smelled rotten straw, and then he was upon it.

He landed on his feet and immediately collapsed.

The stinging in his left hand kept him from passing out. He breathed deeply of the fetid air. He was still dazed. The back of his head was one big ache. He could not recall what had happened.

He lay there panting as his heartbeat slowed. The floor was cold beneath him. Piece by piece, the memories began to return…

He recalled his climb to the castle, his entry… The woman Reena… They had been talking…

Anger flared within his breast. She had tricked him. Delayed him until help arrived for dealing with him—

But her story had been so elaborately constructed, full of unnecessary detail… He wondered. Was there more to this than a simple betrayal?

He sighed.

He was not ready to think yet. Where was he?

Soft sounds came to him across the straw. Some sort of cell perhaps… Was there another inmate?

Something ran across his back.

He jerked partway upright, felt himself collapsing, turned to his side as he did. He saw the small, dark forms in the dim light. Rats. That was what it had been. He looked about the half of the cell that he faced. Nothing else…

Rolling over onto his other side, he saw the broken door.

He sat up, more carefully than before. He rubbed his head and blinked at the light. A rat drew back at the movement.

He climbed to his feet, brushed himself off. He felt after his weapons, was not surprised to find them missing.

A wave of dizziness came and went. He advanced upon the broken door, touched it.

Leaning against the frame, he peered out into the large room with frosty walls. Torches flickered in brackets at either end of it. There was an open doorway diagonally across from him, darkness beyond it.

He passed between the door and its frame, continuing to look about. There were no sounds other than the soft rat-noises behind him and the dripping of water.

He regarded the torches. The one to his left was slightly larger. He crossed to it and removed it from its bracket. Then he headed for the dark doorway.

A cold draft stirred the flames as he passed through. He was in another chamber, smaller than the one he had just quitted. Ahead he saw a stair. He advanced upon it and began to climb.

The stair took a single turn as he mounted it. At its top, he found a blank wall to his right, a wide, low-ceilinged corridor to his left. He followed the corridor.

After perhaps half a minute, he beheld what appeared to be a landing, a handrail jutting out of the wall above it. As he neared, he saw that there was an opening from which the railing emerged. Cautiously, he mounted the landing, listened for a time, peered around the corner.

Nothing. No one. Only a long, dark stair leading upward.

He transferred the torch, which was burning low, to his other hand and began to climb, quickly. This stair was much higher than the previous one, spiraling upward for a long while. He came to its ending suddenly, dropped the torch, and stepped upon its flame for a moment.

After listening at the top stair, he emerged into a hallway. This one had a long rug and wall decorations. Large tapers burned in standing holders along it. Off to his right, there was a wide stairway leading up. He moved to its foot, certain that he had come into a more frequented area of the castle.

He brushed his garments again, removed his gloves, and restored them to his belt. He ran his hand through his hair, while looking about for anything that might serve as a weapon. Seeing nothing suitable, he commenced climbing.

As he reached a landing, he heard a blood-chilling shriek from above.

"Please! Oh, please! The pain!"

He froze, one hand on the railing, the other reaching for a blade that was not there.

A full minute passed. Another began. The cry was not repeated. There were no further sounds of any sort from that direction.

Alert, he began to move again, staying close to the wall, testing each step before placing his full weight upon it.

When he reached the head of the stair, he checked the corridor in both directions. It appeared to be empty. The cry had seemed to come from somewhere off to the right. He went that way.

As he advanced, a sudden soft sobbing began from some point to his left and ahead. He approached the slightly ajar door from behind which it seemed to be occurring. Stooping, he applied his eye to the large keyhole. There was illumination within, but nothing to view save for an undecorated section of wall and the edge of a small window.

Straightening, he turned to search again for some weapon.

The large servant's approach had been totally soundless, and he towered above him now, club already descending.

Dilvish blocked the blow with his left forearm. The other's rush carried him forward to collide with Dilvish, however, bearing him backward against the door, which flew wide, and through it into the room beyond.

Dilvish heard a cry from behind him as he strove to rise. At the same time the door was drawn shut, and he heard a key slipped into the lock.

"A victim! He sends me a victim when what I want is release!" There followed a sigh. "Very well…"

Dilvish turned as soon as he heard the voice, his memory instantly drawing him back to another place.

Bright red body, long, thin limbs, a claw upon each digit, it had pointed ears, backward-curving horns, and slitted yellow eyes. It crouched at the center of a pentacle, constantly shuffling its feet this way and that, reaching for him…

"Stupid wight!" he snapped, lapsing into another tongue. "Would you destroy your deliverer?"

The demon drew back its arms, and the pupils of its eyes expanded.

"Brother! I did not know you in human form!" it answered in Mabrahoring, the language of demons. "Forgive me!"

Dilvish climbed slowly to his feet.

"I've a mind to let you rot there, for such a reception!" he replied, looking around the chamber.

The room was done up for such work, Dilvish now saw, everything still in its place. Upon the far wall there was a large mirror within an intricately worked metal frame…

"Forgive!" the demon cried, bowing low. "See how I abase myself! Can you really free me? Will you?"

"First tell me how you came into this unhappy state," Dilvish said.

"Ah! It was the young sorcerer in this place. He is mad! Even now I see him in his tower, toying with his madness! He is two people in one! One day one must win over the other. But until then, he begins works and leaves them undone—such as summoning my poor self to this accursed place, forcing me upon this doubly accursed pentacle, and taking his thrice accursed self away without dismissing me! Oh! were I free to rend him! Please! The pain! Release me!"

"I, too, have known something of pain," said Dilvish, "and you will endure this for more questioning."

He gestured.

"Is that the mirror used for travel?"

"Yes! Yes, it is!"

"Could you repair the damage it has endured?"

"Not without the aid of the human operator who laid the counterspell. It is too strong."

"Very well. Rehearse your oaths of dismissal now and I will do the things necessary to release you."

"Oaths? Between us? Ah! I see! You fear I envy you that body you wear! Perhaps you are wise… As you would. My oaths…"

"…To include everyone in this household," Dilvish said.

"Ah!" it howled. "You would deprive me of my vengeance on the crazy sorcerer!"

"They are all mine now," Dilvish said. "Do not try to bargain with me!"

A crafty look came over the demon's face.

"Oh…?" it said. "Oh! I see! Yours… Well, at least there will be vengeance—with much good rending and shrieking, I trust. That will be sufficient. Knowing that makes it much easier to renounce all claims. My oaths…"

It began the grisly litany, and Dilvish listened carefully for deviations from the necessary format. There were none.

Dilvish commenced speaking the words of dismissal. The demon hugged itself and bowed its head.

When he had finished, Dilvish looked back at the pentacle. The demon was gone from that place, but it was still present in the room. It stood in a corner, smiling an ingratiating smile.

Dilvish cocked his head.

"You are free," he said. "Go!"

"A moment, great lord!" it said, cowering. "It is good to be free and I thank you. I know, too, that only one of the greater ones of Below could have worked this release in the absence of a human sorcerer. So I would grovel and curry your favor a moment longer in the way of warning you. The flesh may have dulled your normal senses, and I bid you know that I feel the vibrations on another plane now. Something terrible is coming this way—and unless you are a part of its workings, or it of yours—I felt that you must be warned, great one!"

"I knew of it," Dilvish said, "but I am pleased that you have told me. Blast the door's lock off you would do me a final service. Then you may go."

"Thank you! Remember Quennel in the days of your wrath—and that he served you here!"

The demon turned and seemed to blow apart like fog in a wind, to the accompaniment of a dull, roaring sound. A moment later there came a sharp, snapping noise from the direction of the door.

Dilvish crossed the room. The lock had been shattered.

He opened the door and looked out. The corridor was empty. He hesitated as he considered both directions. Then, with a slight shrugging movement, he turned to the right and headed that way.

He came, after a time, to a great, empty dining hall, a fire still smouldering upon its hearth, wind whistling down the chimney. He circled the entire room, moving along the wall, past the windows, the mirror, returning to the spot from which he had begun, none of the wall niches proving doorways to anywhere else.

He turned and headed back up the corridor. As he did, he heard his name spoken in a whisper. He halted. The door to his left was partly ajar. He turned his head in that direction. It had been a woman's voice.

"It's me, Reena."

The door opened farther. He saw her standing there holding a long blade. She extended her arm.

"Your sword. Take it!" she said.

He took the weapon into his hands, inspected it, sheathed it.

"...And your dagger."

He repeated the process.

"I am sorry," she said, "about what happened. I was as surprised as you. It was my brother's doing, not mine."

"I think I am willing to believe you," he said. "How did you locate me?"

"I waited until I was certain that Ridley was back in his tower. Then I sought you in the cells below, but you had already gone. How did you get out?"

"Walked out."

"You mean you found the door that way?"

"Yes."

He heard her sharp intake of breath, almost a gasp.

"That is not at all good," she said. "It means that Mack is certainly abroad."

"Who is Mack?"

"Ridley's predecessor as apprentice here. I am not certain what happened to him—whether he tried some experiment that simply did not work out, or whether his transformation was a punishment of the master's for some indiscretion. Whichever, he was changed into a dull-witted beast and had to be imprisoned down there, because of his great strength and occasional recollection of some noxious spell. His woman went barmy after that. She's still about. A minor adept herself, at one time. We've got to get out of here."

"You may be right," he said, "but finish the story."

"Oh. I've been looking all over for you since then. As I was about it, I noticed that the demon had stopped screaming. I came and investigated. I saw that he had been freed. I was fairly certain that Ridley was still in the tower. It was you, wasn't it?"

"Yes, I released it."

"I thought then that you might still be near, and I heard someone moving in the dining hall. So I hid in here and waited to see who it was. I brought you your weapons to show that I meant you no ill."

"I appreciate it. I am only now deciding what to do. I am sure you have some suggestions."

"Yes. I've a feeling that the master will come here soon and slay every living thing under these roofs. I do not want to be around when that occurs."

"As a matter of fact, he should be here very soon. The demon told me."

"It is hard to tell what you know and what you do not know," she said, "what you can do and what you cannot do. Obviously you know something of the arts. Do you intend to stay and face him?"

"That was my purpose in traveling all this distance," he replied. "But I meant to face him in the flesh, and if I did not find him here I meant to use whatever means of magical transportation might be present to seek him in others of his strongholds. I do not know how my special presents will affect him in a disembodied state. I know that my blade will not."

"You would be wise," she said, taking his arm, "very wise, to live to fight another day."

"Especially if you need my help in getting away from here?" he asked.

She nodded.

"I do not know what your quarrel with him may be," she said, leaning against him, "and you are a strange man, but I do not think you can hope to win against him here. He will have amassed great power, fearing the worst. He will come in cautiously—so cautiously! I know a possible way away, if you will help. But we must hurry. He could even be here right now. He—"

"How very astute of you, dear girl," came a dry, throaty voice from back up the hall, whence Dilvish had come.

Recognizing it, he turned. A dark-cowled figure stood just beyond the entrance within the dining hall.

"And you," he stated, "Dilvish! You are a most difficult person to be rid of, bloodling of Selar, though it has been a long while between encounters."

Dilvish drew his blade. An Awful Saying rose to his lips but he refrained from speaking it, not certain that what he saw represented an actual physical presence.

"What new torment might I devise for you?" the other asked. "A transformation? A degeneration? A—"

Dilvish began to move toward him, ignoring his words. From behind him he heard Reena whisper, "Come back…"

He continued on toward the form of his enemy.

"I was nothing to you…" Dilvish began.

"You disturbed an important rite."

"…and you took my life and threw it away. You visited a terrible vengeance upon me as casually as another man might brush away a mosquito."

"I was annoyed, as another man might be at a mosquito."

"You treated me as if I were a thing, not a person. That I cannot forgive."

A soft chuckle emerged from within the cowl.

"And it would seem that in my own defense now I must treat you that way again."

The figure raised its hand, pointing two fingers at him.

Dilvish broke into a run, raising his blade, recalling Black's spell of protection and still loath to commence his own.

The extended fingers seemed to glow for a moment and Dilvish felt something like a passing wind. That was all.

"Are you but an illusion of this place?" the other asked, beginning to back away, a tiny quavering note apparent in his voice for the first time.

Dilvish swung his blade but encountered nothing. The figure was no longer before him. Now it stood among shadows at the far end of the dining hall.

"Is this thing yours, Ridley?" he heard him ask suddenly. "If so, you are to be commended for dredging up something I'd no desire whatever to recall. It shan't distract me, though, from the business at hand. Show yourself, if you dare!"

Dilvish heard a sliding sound from off to his left, and a panel opened there. He saw the slim figure of a younger man emerge, a shining ring upon the left forefinger.

"Very well. We shall dispense with these theatrics," came Ridley's voice. He seemed slightly out of breath and striving to control it. "I am master of myself and this place," he continued. He turned toward Dilvish.

"You, wight! You have served me well. There is absolutely nothing more for you to do here, for it is between the two of us now. I give you leave to depart and assume your natural form. You may take the girl back with you as payment."

Dilvish hesitated.

"Go, I say! Now!"

Dilvish backed from the room.

"I see that you have cast aside all remorse," he heard Jelerak say, "and learned the necessary hardness. This should prove interesting."

Dilvish saw a low wall of fire spring up between the two of them. He heard laughter from the hall—whose, he was not certain. Then came a crackling sound and a wave of peculiar odors. Suddenly the room was a blaze of light. Just as suddenly it was plunged into darkness again. The laughter continued. He heard pieces of tile falling from the walls.

He turned away. Reena was still standing where he had left her.

"He did it," she said softly. "He has control of the other. He really did it..."

"We can do no good here," Dilvish stated. "It is, as he said, between them now."

"But his new strength may still not be sufficient!"

"I'd imagine he knows that, and that that is why he wants me to take you away."

The floor shook beneath them. A picture dropped from a nearby wall.

"I don't know that I can leave him like that, Dilvish."

"He may be giving his life for you, Reena. He might have used his new powers to repair the mirror, or to escape this place by some other means. You heard how he put things. Would you throw away his gift?"

Her eyes filled with tears.

"He may never know," she said, "how much I really wanted him to succeed."

"I've a feeling he might," Dilvish said. "Now, how are we to save you?"

"Come this way," she said, taking his arm, as a hideous scream came from the hall, followed by a thunderclap that seemed to shake the entire castle.

Colored lights glowed behind them as she led him along the corridor.

"I've a sled," she said, "in a cavern deep below here. It is filled with supplies."

"How—" Dilvish began, and he halted, raising the blade that he bore.

An old woman stood before them at the head of the stair, glaring at him. But his eyes had slid beyond her, to behold the great pale bulk that slowly mounted the last few stairs, head turned in their direction.

"There, Mack!" she screamed suddenly. "The man who hit me! Hurt my side! Crush him!"

Dilvish directed the point of his blade at the advancing creature's throat.

"If he attacks me, I will kill him," he said. "I do not want to, but the choice is not mine. It is yours. He may be big and strong, but he is not fast. I have seen him move. I will make a very big hole, and a lot of blood will come out of it. I heard that you once loved him, lady. What are you going to do?"

Forgotten emotions flickered across Meg's features.

"Mack! Stop!" she cried. "He's not the one. I was wrong!"

Mack halted.

"Not—the—one?" he said.

"No. I was—mistaken."

She turned her gaze up the hallway to where fountains of fires flashed and vanished and where multitudes of cries, as of two opposing armies, rang out.

"What," she said, gesturing, "is it?"

"The young master and the old master," Reena said, "are fighting."

"Why are you still afraid to say his name?" Dilvish asked. "He's just up the corridor. It's Jelerak."

"Jelerak?" A new light came into Mack's eyes as he gestured toward the awful room. "Jelerak?"

"Yes," Dilvish replied, and the pale one turned away from him and began shuffling in that direction.

Dilvish looked about for Meg, but she was gone. Then he heard a cry of "Jelerak! Kill!" from overhead.

He looked up and saw the green-winged creature that had attacked him—how long ago?—flapping off in the same direction.

"They are probably going to their deaths," Reena said.

"How long do you think they have waited for such an opportunity?" he said. "I am sure that they know that they lost a long time ago. But just to have the chance now is winning, for them."

"Better in there than on your blade."

Dilvish turned away.

"I am not at all sure that *he* wouldn't have killed *me*," he said. "Where are we going?"

"This way."

She took him down the stair and up another corridor, heading toward the north end of the building. The entire place began shaking about them as they went. Furniture toppled, windows shattered, a beam fell. Then it was still again for a time. They hurried.

As they were nearing the kitchen, the place shook again with such violence that they were thrown to the floor. A fine dust was drifting everywhere now, and cracks had appeared in the walls. In the kitchen they saw that hot ashes had been thrown from the grate, to lay strewn about the floor, smoking.

"It sounds as if Ridley is still holding his own."

"Yes, it does," she said, smiling.

Pots and pans were rattling and banging together as they departed the kitchen, heading in the direction of the stairwell. The cutlery danced in its drawers.

They paused at the stair's entrance, just as a great, inhuman moan swept through the entire castle. An icy draft followed moments later. A rat flashed past them from the direction of the kitchen.

Reena signaled Dilvish to halt and, leaning against the wall, cupped her hands before her face. She seemed to whisper within them, and a moment after the small fire was born, to hover, growing, before her. She moved her hands outward and it drifted toward the stairwell.

"Come," she said to Dilvish, and she led the way downward.

He moved behind her, and from time to time the walls creaked ominously about them. When this happened, the light danced for a moment, and occasionally it faded briefly. As they descended, the sounds from above grew more muffled. Dilvish paused once, to place his hand upon the wall.

"Is it far?" he asked.

"Yes. Why?"

"I can still feel the vibrations strongly," he said. "We must be well below the level of the castle itself—down into the mountain by now."

"True," she replied, taking another turn.

"At first I feared that they might bring the castle down upon our heads…"

"They probably *will* destroy the place if this goes on much longer," she said. "I'm very proud of Ridley—despite the inconvenience."

"That wasn't exactly what I meant," Dilvish said, as they continued their downward flight. "There! It's getting worse!" He put out a hand to steady himself as the stair shuddered from a passing shockwave. "Doesn't it seem to you that the entire mountain is shaking?"

"Yes, it does," she replied. "Then it must be true."

"What?"

"I'd heard it said that ages ago, at the height of his power, the ma—Jelerak—actually raised this mountain by his conjuring."

"So?"

"If he is sufficiently taxed in this place, I suppose that he might have to draw upon those ancient spells of his for more power. In which case—"

"The mountain might collapse as well as the castle?"

"There is that possibility. Oh, Ridley! Good show!"

"It won't be so good if we're under it!"

"True," she said, suddenly moving even faster. "As he's not *your* brother, I can see your point. Still it must please you to see Jelerak so hard pressed."

"It does that," Dilvish admitted, "but you should really prepare yourself for any eventuality."

She was silent for a time.

Then: "Ridley's death?" she asked. "Yes. I've realized for some time now that there was a strong possibility of this, whatever the nature of their encounter. Still, to go out with such flare… That's something, too, you know."

"Yes," Dilvish replied. "I've thought of it many times myself."

Abruptly, they reached the landing. She turned immediately and led him toward a tunnel. The rocky floor trembled beneath them. The light danced again. From somewhere there came a slow, grinding sound, lasting for perhaps ten seconds. They rushed into the tunnel.

"And you?" she said, as they hurried along it. "If Jelerak survives, will you still seek him?"

"Yes," he said. "I know for certain that he has at least six other citadels. I know the approximate locations of several of them. I would seek them as I did this place."

"I have been in three of the others," she said. "If we survive this, I can tell you something about them. They would not be easy to storm either."

"It does not matter," Dilvish said. "I never thought that it would be easy. If he lives, I will go to them. If I cannot locate him, I will destroy them, one by one, until he must need come to me."

The grinding sound came again. Fragments of rocks fell about them. As this occurred, the floating light vanished before them.

"Remain still," she said. "I'll do another."

Several moments later another light glowed between her hands.

They continued on, the sounds within the rock ceasing for a time.

"What will you do if Jelerak is dead?" she asked him.

Dilvish was silent awhile. Then: "Visit my homeland," he said. "It has been a long while since I have been back. What will you do if we make it away from here?"

"Tooma, Ankyra, Blostra," she replied, "as I'd said, if I could find some willing gentleman to escort me to one of them."

"I believe that could be arranged," Dilvish said.

As they neared the end of the tunnel, an enormous shudder ran through the entire mountain. Reena stumbled; Dilvish caught her and was thrown back against the wall. With his shoulders, he felt the heavy vibrations within the stone. From behind them a steady crashing of falling rocks began.

"Hurry!" he said, propelling her forward.

The light darted drunkenly before them. They came into a cold cavern.

"This is the place," Reena said, pointing. "The sled is over there."

Dilvish saw the vehicle, took hold of her arm and headed toward it.

"How high up the mountain are we?" he asked her.

"Two thirds of the way, perhaps," she said. "We are somewhat below the point where the rise steepens severely."

"That is still no gentle slope out there," he said, coming to a halt beside the vehicle and placing his hand upon its side. "How do you propose getting it down to ground level?"

"That will be the difficult part," she said, reaching within her bodice and withdrawing a folded piece of parchment. "I've removed this page from one of the books in the tower. When I had the servants build me this sled, I knew that I would need something strong to draw it. This is a fairly elaborate spell, but it will summon a demon beast to do our bidding."

"May I see it?"

She passed him the page. He unfolded it and held it near to the hovering light.

"This spell requires fairly lengthy preparations," he said a little later. "I don't believe we have that kind of time remaining, the way things are shaking and crumbling here."

"But it is the only chance we have," she said. "We'll need these supplies. I had no way of knowing that the whole damned mountain was going to start coming apart. We are simply going to have to risk the delay."

Dilvish shook his head and returned the page.

"Wait here," he said, "and don't start that spell yet!"

He turned and made his way along the tunnel down which icy blasts blew. Snow crystals lay upon the floor. After a single, brief turn, he saw the wide cave mouth, pale light beyond it. The floor there had a heavy coating of snow over ice.

He walked to the entrance and looked out, looked down. The sled could be edged over the lip of the ridge at his feet at a low place off to his left. But then it would simply take off, achieving a killing speed long before it reached the foot of the mountain.

He moved forward to the very edge, looked up. An overhang prevented his seeing anything above. He moved half a dozen paces to his left then, looked out, looked up, looked around. Then he crossed to the right-hand extremity of the ledge and looked up, shading his eyes against a blast of ice crystals.

There…?

"Black!" he called, to a darker patch of shadow above and to the side. "Black!"

It seemed to stir. He cupped his hands and shouted again.

"Diiil…viish!" rolled down the slope toward him, after his own cry had died away.

"Down here!"

He waved both arms above his head.

"I…see…you!"

"Can you come to me?"

There was no answer, but the shadow moved. It came down from its ledge and began a slow, stiff-legged journey in his direction.

He remained in sight. He continued waving.

Soon Black's silhouette became clear through the swirling snow. He advanced steadily. He passed the halfway point, continued on.

As he came up beside him, Black pulsed heat for several moments and the snow melted upon him, trickling off down his sides.

"There are some amazing sorceries going on above," he stated, "well worth observing."

"Far better we do it from a distance," Dilvish said. "This whole mountain may be coming down."

"Yes, it will," Black said. "Something up there is drawing upon some very elemental, ancient spells woven all through here. It is most instructive. Get on my back and I'll take you down."

"It is not that simple."

"Oh?"

"There is a girl—and a sled—in the cave behind me."

Black placed his forefeet upon the ledge and heaved himself up to stand beside Dilvish.

"Then I had better have a look," he stated. "How did you fare up on top?"

Dilvish shrugged.

"All of that would most likely have happened without me," he said, "but at least I've the pleasure of seeing someone giving Jelerak a hard time."

"That's him up there?"

They started back into the cave.

"His body is elsewhere, but the part that bites has paid a visit."

"Who is he fighting?"

"The brother of the lady you are about to meet. This way."

They took the turn and headed back in the larger cave. Reena still stood beside the sled. She had wrapped herself in a fur. Black's metal hooves clicked upon the rock.

"You wanted a demon beast?" Dilvish said to her. "Black, this is Reena. Reena, meet Black."

Black bowed his head.

"I am pleased," he said. "Your brother has been providing me with considerable amusement while I waited without."

Reena smiled and reached out to touch his neck.

"Thank you," she said. "I am delighted to know you. Can you help us?"

Black turned and regarded the sled.

"Backward," he said after a time. Then: "If I were hitched facing it, I could draw back slightly and let it precede me down the mountain. You would both have to walk, though—beside me, holding on. I don't believe I could do it with you in the thing. Even this way it will be difficult, but I see it to be the only way."

"Then we'd better push it out and get started," Dilvish said, as the mountain shook again.

Reena and Dilvish each took hold of a side of the vehicle. Black leaned against its rear. It began to move.

Once they reached the snow on the cave floor, it proceeded more easily. Finally they turned it about at the cave mouth and hitched Black between its traces.

Carefully, gently then, they edged its rear end over the ledge at the low place to the left as Black advanced slowly, maintaining tension on the traces.

Its runners struck the snow of the slope, and Black eased it down until it rested full length upon it. Gingerly he followed it then, jerking stiffly upright to anchor it after he had jumped the last few feet.

"All right," he said. "Come down now and take hold of me on either side."

They followed him and took up their positions. Slowly he began to advance.

"Tricky," he said as they moved. "One day they will invent names for the properties of objects, such as the tendency of a thing to move once it is placed in motion."

"Of what use would that be?" Reena asked. "Everybody already knows that that's what happens."

"Ah! But one might put numbers to the amount of material involved and the amount of pushing required, and come up with wondrous and useful calculations."

"Sounds like a lot of trouble for a small return," she said. "Magic's a lot easier to figure."

"Perhaps you're right."

Steadily they descended, Black's hooves crunching through the icy crust. Later, when they finally reached a place from which they could view the castle, they saw that the highest tower and several low ones had fallen. Even as they watched, a section of wall collapsed. Fragments of it fell over the edge, fortunately descending the slope far to their right.

Beneath the snow the mountain itself was shaking steadily now, and had been for some time. Rocks and chunks of ice occasionally bounded past them.

They continued for what seemed an interminable time, Black edging the sled lower and lower with each step, Reena and Dilvish plodding numb-footed beside him.

As they neared the foot of the slope, a terrific crash echoed about them. Looking up, they saw the remains of the castle crumbling, shrinking, falling in upon itself.

Black increased his pace dangerously as small bits of debris began to rain about them.

"When we reach bottom," he said, "unhitch me immediately, but stay on the far side of the sled while you're doing it. I would be able to turn its side to the slope as we get there. Then, if you can hitch me properly in a hurry, do it. If the falling stuff becomes too severe, though, just crouch down on the far side and I will stand on the near one to help shield you. But if you can rehitch me, get in quickly and stay low."

They slid most of the final distance, and for a moment it seemed that the sled would turn over as Black maneuvered it. Picking himself up, Dilvish immediately set to work upon the harness.

Reena got behind the sled and looked upward.

"Dilvish! Look!" she cried.

Dilvish glanced upward as he finished the unfastening and Black backed out from between the traces.

The castle had completely vanished and large fissures had appeared in the slope. Above the summit of the mountain, two columns of smoke now stood—a dark one and a light one—motionless despite the winds that must be lashing at them.

Black turned and backed in between the traces Dilvish began harnessing him again. More debris was now descending the slope, off to their right.

"What is it?" Dilvish said.

"The dark column is Jelerak," Black replied.

Dilvish looked back periodically as he worked, seeing that the two columns had begun to move, slowly, toward one another. Soon they were intertwined, though not merging, twisting and knotting about one another like a pair of struggling serpents.

Dilvish completed the harnessing.

"Get in!" he cried to Reena, as another part of the mountain fell away.

"You, too!" said Black, and Dilvish climbed in with her.

Soon they were moving, gathering speed. The top of the ice mass came apart as they watched, and still the billowing combatants rolled above it.

"Oh, no! Ridley seems to be weakening!" she said, as they raced away.

Dilvish watched as the dark column seemed to bear the lighter one downward into the heart of the falling mountain.

Black's pace increased, though chunks of rubble still skidded and raced about them. Soon both smoky combatants were gone from sight, high above them. Black moved faster yet, heading south.

Perhaps a quarter of an hour passed with no change in the prospect behind them, save for its dwindling. But crouched beneath the furs, Dilvish and Reena still watched. An air of anticipation seemed to grow over the entire landscape.

When it came, it rocked the ground, bouncing the sled from side to side, and its tremors continued for a long while after.

The top of the mountain blew off, peppering the sky with an expanding, dark cloud. Then the dusky smear was streaked, spread by the winds, sections of it reaching like slowly extending fingers to the west. After a time a mighty shock wave rolled over them.

Much later, a single, attenuated, rough-edged cloud—the dark one—separated itself from the haze. Trailing ragged plumes, jounced by the winds, it moved like an old man stumbling, fleeing southward. It passed far to the right of them and did not pause.

"That's Jelerak," Black said. "He's hurt."

They watched the rough column until it jerked out of sight far to the south. Then they turned again toward the rain in the north. They watched until it faded from view, but the white column did not rise again.

Finally Reena lowered her head. Dilvish put his arm about her shoulders. The runners of the sled sang softly on their way across the snow.

A Word from Zelazny

Having written the seventh Dilvish tale, a transitional piece, "The White Beast," "the stage was finally set [for the novella 'Tower of Ice']. But I had no intention of carrying things further at that point. I was busy writing the novel *Roadmarks* and wanted to get on with it. A week after I'd sent off 'The White Beast,' though, I received a request from Lin Carter for a 20,000 word Dilvish story for *Flashing Swords #5*. It seemed like the Finger of Fate. I allowed myself a week and wrote 'Tower of Ice.' "[1]

Notes

In mountain climbing, the **chimney** is a steep, narrow cleft where a rock face may be climbed. A **courtesan** is a prostitute, especially one whose clients include royalty and men of high social standing. **Barmy** means eccentric or daft. A **wight** is a supernatural being such as a witch or sprite. The phrase, **to go out with such flare…** is a typical Zelazny pun. **The tendency of a thing to move once it is placed in motion** is inertia.

1 *Alternities #6*, Summer 1981.

The George Business

Dragons of Light, ed. Orson Scott Card, Ace 1980.

Deep in his lair, Dart twisted his green and golden length about his small hoard, his sleep troubled by dreams of a series of identical armored assailants. Since dragons' dreams are always prophetic, he woke with a shudder, cleared his throat to the point of sufficient illumination to check on the state of his treasure, stretched, yawned and set forth up the tunnel to consider the strength of the opposition. If it was too great, he would simply flee, he decided. The hell with the hoard; it wouldn't be the first time.

As he peered from the cave mouth, he beheld a single knight in mismatched armor atop a tired-looking gray horse, just rounding the bend. His lance was not even couched, but still pointing skyward.

Assuring himself that the man was unaccompanied, he roared and slithered forth.

"Halt," he bellowed, "You who are about to fry!"

The knight obliged.

"You're the one I came to see," the man said. "I have—"

"Why," Dart asked, "do you wish to start this business up again? Do you realize how long it has been since a knight and dragon have done battle?"

"Yes, I do. Quite a while. But I—"

"It is almost invariably fatal to one of the parties concerned. Usually your side."

"Don't I know it. Look, you've got me wrong—"

"I dreamt a dragon dream of a young man named George with whom I must do battle. You bear him an extremely close resemblance."

"I can explain. It's not as bad as it looks. You see—"

"*Is* your name George?"

"Well, yes. But don't let that bother you—"

"It *does* bother me. You want my pitiful hoard? It wouldn't keep you in beer money for the season. Hardly worth the risk."

"I'm not after your hoard—"

"I haven't grabbed off a virgin in centuries. They're usually old and tough, anyhow, not to mention hard to find."

"No one's accusing—"

"As for cattle, I always go a great distance. I've gone out of my way, you might say, to avoid getting a bad name in my own territory."

"I know you're no real threat here. I've researched it quite carefully—"

"And do you think that armor will really protect you when I exhale my deepest, hottest flames?"

"Hell, no! So don't do it, huh? If you'd please—"

"And that lance... You're not even holding it properly."

George lowered the lance.

"On that you are correct," he said, "but it happens to be tipped with one of the deadliest poisons known to Herman the Apothecary."

"I say! That's hardly sporting!"

"I know. But even if you incinerate me, I'll bet I can scratch you before I go."

"Now that would be rather silly—both of us dying like that—wouldn't it?" Dart observed, edging away. "It would serve no useful purpose that I can see."

"I feel precisely the same way about it."

"Then why are we getting ready to fight?"

"I have no desire whatsoever to fight with you!"

"I'm afraid I don't understand. You said your name is George, and I had this dream—"

"I can explain it."

"But the poisoned lance—"

"Self-protection, to hold you off long enough to put a proposition to you."

Dart's eyelids lowered slightly.

"What sort of proposition?"

"I want to hire you."

"Hire me? Whatever for? And what are you paying?"

"Mind if I rest this lance a minute? No tricks?"

"Go ahead. If you're talking gold your life is safe."

George rested his lance and undid a pouch at his belt. He dipped his hand into it and withdrew a fistful of shining coins. He tossed them gently, so that they clinked and shone in the morning light.

"You have my full attention. That's a good piece of change there."

"My life's savings. All yours—in return for a bit of business."

"What's the deal?"

George replaced the coins in his pouch and gestured.

"See that castle in the distance—two hills away?"

"I've flown over it many times."

"In the tower to the west are the chambers of Rosalind, daughter of the Baron Maurice. She is very dear to his heart, and I wish to wed her."

"There's a problem?"

"Yes. She's attracted to big, brawny barbarian types, into which category I, alas, do not fall. In short, she doesn't like me."

"That *is* a problem."

"So, if I could pay you to crash in there and abduct her, to bear her off to some convenient and isolated place and wait for me, I'll come along, we'll fake a battle, I'll vanquish you, you'll fly away and I'll take her home. I am certain I will then appear sufficiently heroic in her eyes to rise from sixth to first position on her list of suitors. How does that sound to you?"

Dart sighed a long column of smoke.

"Human, I bear your kind no special fondness—particularly the armored variety with lances—so I don't know why I'm telling you this… Well, I do know, actually… But never mind. I could manage it, all right. But, if you win the hand of that maid, do you know what's going to happen? The novelty of your deed will wear off after a time—and you know that there will be no encore. Give her a year, I'd say, and you'll catch her fooling around with one of those brawny barbarians she finds so attractive. Then you must either fight him and be slaughtered or wear horns, as they say."

George laughed.

"It's nothing to me how she spends her spare time. I've a girlfriend in town myself."

Dart's eyes widened.

"I'm afraid I don't understand…"

"She's the old baron's only offspring, and he's on his last legs. Why else do you think an uncomely wench like that would have six suitors? Why else would I gamble my life's savings to win her?"

"I see," said Dart. "Yes, I can understand greed."

"I call it a desire for security."

"Quite. In that case, forget my simple-minded advice. All right, give me the gold and I'll do it." Dart gestured with one gleaming vane. "The first valley in those western mountains seems far enough from my home for our confrontation."

"I'll pay you half now and half on delivery."

"Agreed. Be sure to have the balance with you, though, and drop it during the scuffle. I'll return for it after you two have departed. Cheat me and I'll repeat the performance, with a different ending."

"The thought had already occurred to me. —Now, we'd better practice a bit, to make it look realistic. I'll rush at you with the lance, and whatever side she's standing on I'll aim for it to pass you on the other. You raise that wing, grab the lance and scream like hell. Blow a few flames around, too."

"I'm going to see you scour the tip of that lance before we rehearse this."

"Right. —I'll release the lance while you're holding it next to you and rolling around. Then I'll dismount and rush toward you with my blade. I'll whack you with the flat of it—again, on the far side—a few times. Then you bellow again and fly away."

"Just how sharp is that thing, anyway?"

"Damned dull. It was my grandfather's. Hasn't been honed since he was a boy."

"And you drop the money during the fight?"

"Certainly. —How does that sound?"

"Not bad. I can have a few clusters of red berries under my wing, too. I'll squash them once the action gets going."

"Nice touch. Yes, do that. Let's give it a quick rehearsal now and then get on with the real thing."

"And don't whack too hard…"

That afternoon, Rosalind of Maurice Manor was abducted by a green-and-gold dragon who crashed through the wall of her chamber and bore her off in the direction of the western mountains.

"Never fear!" shouted her sixth-ranked suitor—who just happened to be riding by—to her aged father who stood wringing his hands on a nearby balcony. "I'll rescue her!" and he rode off to the west.

Coming into the valley where Rosalind stood backed into a rocky cleft, guarded by the fuming beast of gold and green, George couched his lance.

"Release that maiden and face your doom!" he cried.

Dart bellowed, George rushed. The lance fell from his hands and the dragon rolled upon the ground, spewing gouts of fire into the air. A red substance dribbled from beneath the thundering creature's left wing. Before Rosalind's wide eyes, George advanced and swung his blade several times.

"...and that!" he cried, as the monster stumbled to its feet and sprang into the air, dripping more red.

It circled once and beat its way off toward the top of the mountain, then over it and away.

"Oh George!" Rosalind cried, and she was in his arms. "Oh, George..."

He pressed her to him for a moment.

"I'll take you home now," he said.

❖ ❖ ❖

That evening as he was counting his gold, Dart heard the sound of two horses approaching his cave. He rushed up the tunnel and peered out.

George, now mounted on a proud white stallion and leading the gray, wore a matched suit of bright armor. He was not smiling, however.

"Good evening," he said.

"Good evening. What brings you back so soon?"

"Things didn't turn out exactly as I'd anticipated."

"You seem far better accoutered. I'd say your fortunes had taken a turn."

"Oh, I recovered my expenses and came out a bit ahead. But that's all. I'm on my way out of town. Thought I'd stop by and tell you the end of the story. —Good show you put on, by the way. It probably would have done the trick—"

"But—?"

"She was married to one of the brawny barbarians this morning, in their family chapel. They were just getting ready for a wedding trip when you happened by."

"I'm awfully sorry."

"Well, it's the breaks. To add insult, though, her father dropped dead during your performance. My former competitor is now the new baron. He rewarded me with a new horse and armor, a gratuity and a scroll from the local scribe lauding me as a dragon slayer. Then he hinted rather strongly that the horse and my new reputation could take me far. Didn't like the way Rosalind was looking at me now I'm a hero."

"That is a shame. Well, we tried."

"Yes. So I just stopped by to thank you and let you know how it all turned out. It would have been a good idea—if it had worked."

"You could hardly have foreseen such abrupt nuptials. —You know, I've spent the entire day thinking about the affair. We *did* manage it awfully well."

"Oh, no doubt about that. It went beautifully."

"I was thinking… How'd you like a chance to get your money back?"

"What have you got in mind?"

"Uh—When I was advising you earlier that you might not be happy with the lady, I was trying to think about the situation in human terms. Your desire was entirely understandable to me otherwise. In fact, you think quite a bit like a dragon."

"Really?"

"Yes. It's rather amazing, actually. Now—realizing that it only failed because of a fluke, your idea still has considerable merit."

"I'm afraid I don't follow you."

"There is—ah—a lovely lady of my own species whom I have been singularly unsuccessful in impressing for a long while now. Actually, there are an unusual number of parallels in our situations. "

"She has a large hoard, huh?"

"Extremely so."

"Older woman?"

"Among dragons, a few centuries this way or that are not so important. But she, too, has other admirers and seems attracted by the more brash variety."

"Uh-huh. I begin to get the drift. You gave me some advice once. I'll return the favor. Some things are more important than hoards. "

"Name one."

"My life. If I were to threaten her she might do me in all by herself, before you could come to her rescue."

"No, she's a demure little thing. Anyway, it's all a matter of timing. I'll perch on a hilltop nearby—I'll show you where—and signal you when to begin your approach. Now, this time I have to win, of course. Here's how we'll work it…"

❖ ❖ ❖

George sat on the white charger and divided his attention between the distant cave mouth and the crest of a high hill off to his left. After a time, a shining winged form flashed through the air and settled upon the hill. Moments later, it raised one bright wing.

He lowered his visor, couched his lance and started forward. When he came within hailing distance of the cave he cried out:

"I know you're in there, Megtag! I've come to destroy you and make off with your hoard! You godless beast! Eater of children! This is your last day on Earth!"

An enormous burnished head with cold green eyes emerged from the cave. Twenty feet of flame shot from its huge mouth and scorched the rock before it. George halted hastily. The beast looked twice the size of Dart and did not seem in the least retiring. Its scales rattled like metal as it began to move forward.

"Perhaps I exaggerated…" George began, and he heard the frantic flapping of giant vanes overhead.

As the creature advanced, he felt himself seized by the shoulders. He was borne aloft so rapidly that the scene below dwindled to toy size in a matter of moments. He saw his new steed bolt and flee rapidly back along the route they had followed.

"What the hell happened?" he cried.

"I hadn't been around for a while," Dart replied. "Didn't know one of the others had moved in with her. You're lucky I'm fast. That's Pelladon. He's a mean one."

"Great. Don't you think you should have checked first?"

"Sorry. I thought she'd take decades to make up her mind without prompting. Oh, what a hoard! You should have seen it!"

"Follow that horse. I want him back."

❖ ❖ ❖

They sat before Dart's cave, drinking.

"Where'd you ever get a whole barrel of wine?"

"Lifted it from a barge, up the river. I do that every now and then. I keep a pretty good cellar, if I do say so."

"Indeed. Well, we're none the poorer, really. We can drink to that."

"True, but I've been thinking again. You know, you're a very good actor."

"Thanks. You're not so bad yourself."

"Now supposing—just supposing—you were to travel about. Good distances from here each time. Scout out villages, on the continent and in the isles. Find out which ones are well off and lacking in local heroes…"

"Yes?"

"…And let them see that dragon-slaying certificate of yours. Brag a bit. Then come back with a list of towns. Maps, too."

"Go ahead."

"Find the best spots for a little harmless predation and choose a good battle site—"

"Refill?"

"Please."

"Here."

"Thanks. Then you show up, and for a fee—"

"Sixty—forty."

"That's what I was thinking, but I'll bet you've got the figures transposed."

"Maybe fifty-five and forty-five then."

"Down the middle, and let's drink on it."

"Fair enough. Why haggle?"

"Now I know why I dreamed of fighting a great number of knights, all of them looking like you. You're going to make a name for yourself, George."

A Word from Zelazny

"This was an impulse story. I read somewhere—in *Locus*, I believe—that Orson Scott Card was putting together a collection of original stories involving dragons. I read it at just the right time. I was in the mood to do a story about a dragon. So I did. This is it."[1] When Card asked him for a contribution to the anthology tentatively entitled *The Dragon Book*, Zelazny replied, "I just happen to have a dragon story here."[2]

In 1985, Michigan high school student Phillip Broder submitted the unaltered story as his own to a short story contest sponsored by the Detroit Auto Dealers Association—and won out of a field of 2,500 entries, earning the $1,000 prize. The story was resold and published in the *Detroit Free Press* and in the 25,000 copies of the Auto Show Program before the readers of the *Detroit Free Press* recognized the plagiarism—a few days before

1 *Unicorn Variations*, 1983.

2 Letter from Orson Scott Card to Zelazny dated December 1, 1978; letter of reply from Zelazny dated December 19, 1978.

the auto show.[3,4,5] Zelazny returned home from vacation to find a cryptic note from his housekeeper which read, "Your agent phoned and says not to worry. The plagiarism matter is being dealt with." Zelazny received a letter of apology and a check for $500 from the Detroit Auto Dealers Association, which inserted an erratum sheet into the Auto Show Program. Meanwhile, "the *Detroit Free Press*, which had printed it, said, 'Well, how's about we give you a big writeup and tell the story of what happened in that contest plus plug all your books and things so that you don't sue us?' I said, 'Sure, I'll take the free publicity, and you can send it out over the wire service, too.'"[6]

The movie *Dragonheart*, released the year after Zelazny's death, bore recognizable core elements of "The George Business," but Zelazny received no credit.

Notes

The story originally had three additional lines, but Orson Scott Card suggested that the story would be stronger if it ended at "You're going to make a name for yourself, George." Zelazny agreed to the edit.[7]

The original ending evoked the movie *Casablanca*:

> "I doubt it, Dart. But I think I see the beginning of a long and beautiful friendship"
> "I'll drink to that"
> "Here's looking at you."

A **couched** lance is lowered horizontally, as for an attack. St. **George**, who legend says slew a dragon, is the patron saint of England. The mention of **cold green eyes** recalls the Zelazny motif.

3 *Highlander, University of California Riverside,* Vol 30 Number 19, April 11, 1985, p. 14.
4 *Detroit Free Press,* Saturday, January 12, 1985, Section A, page 3.
5 *The Detroit Auto Show Program,* January 12–20, 1985, p 46–55 plus erratum sheet inserted.
6 *Deep Thoughts, Proceedings of Life, the University & Everything, February 16–19, 1994,* p. 113–29.
7 Letter from Orson Scott Card to Zelazny, dated December 29, 1978.

Pelias Waking, within the S.C.

Written 1965–68; previously unpublished.

I lay there, within the Place,
by the flower whose roots go down to Hell,
And you came to me:
                    You brought me back
from the dark nirvana of its incensed thirst.
                    I will not forget this,
Lord Conan, though you trust me not,
I who dour Crom would annihilate,
hold his son my friend.
                    Pray, do forget you not
that in the day of your need
there may come a dark one
to stand by your side.
                    Scorn not his aid.
Eternal opposites we face; warrior and mage.
True.
Yet darkness and light have held congress
since the days of creation.

Not truce,
but that thing by which the virtues of each
darken and lighten the other,
as in a painting
or a friendship.
Do not be alarmed at my other allegiances.
From them I learned this thing:
Only in Hell
or an oxymoron
is darkness visible.

Notes

Pelias is the sorcerer of the Conan tales, not the Greek Pelias (of the myth of Jason, the Golden Fleece, and usurper uncle Pelias), and **S.C.** stands for the Scarlet Citadel (the title of the Robert E. Howard tale in a 1933 *Weird Tales* where these events take place). **Conan** and Pelias, a former rival of the wizard Tsotha-lanti, are both held captive in a dungeon in the Scarlet Citadel. Conan frees Pelias from the deadly grip of a plant-like creature. Pelias uses his powers to enable them both to escape the dungeon, and he later helps Conan regain the Aquilonian throne. A **mage** is a magician or learned person. **Darkness visible** alludes to Milton's *Paradise Lost*.

Torlin Dragonson

To Spin Is Miracle Cat, Underwood-Miller 1981.

Beneath my feet
grass withers.
Poison drips
from my lips.

I smash orchards,
burn churches,
sink sailors,
foul rivers.

I rend white knights,
raze castles,
gulp virgins,
breathe arsons.

But love's my hoard,
where gold's gleams
comfort me,
just like thee.

The Naked Matador

Amazing, July 1981.

Running—waiting, actually—in Key West, I thought of a story I'd read in high school: Hemingway's "The Killers." The appearance of the diner did nothing to change my feelings.

All of the seats at the counter were occupied, except for one on either side of the woman near the middle. I moved to the one at her right.

"This seat taken?" I asked her.

"No," she said, so I sat down.

She wore a beige raincoat, a red and blue scarf completely covering her hair, and large, smoked glasses. It was a cloudy day.

"What's the soup?" I asked her.

"Conch."

I ordered some and a club sandwich.

She had several cups of coffee. She glanced at her watch. She turned toward me.

"Vacationing?" she asked.

"Sort of," I said.

"Staying near here?"

"Not too far."

She smiled.

"I'll give you a ride."

"All right."

We paid our checks. She was short. About five-two or -three. I couldn't really see much of her, except for her legs, and they were good.

We went out and turned left. She headed toward a small white car. I could smell the sea again.

We got in and she began to drive. She didn't ask me where I was staying. She looked at her watch again.

"I'm horny," she said then. "You interested?"

It had been quite a while, running the way I had been. I nodded as she glanced my way.

"Yeah," I said. "You look good to me."

She drove for a time, then turned down a road toward the beach. It was an isolated stretch. The waves were dark and high and white capped.

She stopped the car.

"Here?" I said.

She unbuttoned her coat, undid a blue wraparound skirt. She wore nothing beneath it. She left it behind and straddled me.

"The rest is up to you," she said.

I smiled and reached for her glasses. She slapped my hand away.

"Below the neck," she said. "Keep it below the neck."

"All right. Sorry," I said, reaching up beneath her blouse and around behind for hooks. "You really are something."

I was out and up and in before too long. She did most of the work, with very little change of expression, except near the end when she began to smile and threw her head back. A peculiar icy feeling crept along my spine then, and I looked away from her face and down at the rest of her, riding and flapping.

When I was empty and she was full, she got off and rebuttoned her coat, not bothering with the skirt.

"Good," she said, squeezing my left biceps. "I was getting tense."

"I was kind of tight myself," I said, zipping and buckling, as she started the engine. "You've got a very good body."

"I know."

She got onto the road and headed back.

"Where you staying?"

"Southernmost Motel."

"Okay."

As we drove, I wondered why a girl like that didn't have a steady man. I thought she might be new in town. I thought maybe she didn't want a steady man. I thought it would be nice to see her again. Too bad I was leaving that night.

As we went down my street, I saw a blue car with a man I knew sitting in it, parked in front of my motel. I drew myself down in the seat.

"Go past," I said. "Don't stop!"

"What's the matter?"

"They've found me," I said. "Keep driving."

"The only person I see is a man in a blue Fury. He the one?"

"Yes. He wasn't looking this way. I don't think he saw me."

"He's looking at the motel."

"Good."

She swung around the corner.

"What now?" she said.

"I don't know."

She looked at her watch.

"I have to get home," she said. "I'll take you with me."

"I'd appreciate it."

I stayed low, so I didn't see exactly where she drove. When she finally stopped and turned off the engine and I rose, I saw that we were in a driveway beside a small cottage.

"Come on."

I got out and followed her in. We entered a small, simple living room, a kitchenette off its left end. She headed toward a closed door to the rear.

"There's whisky in the cabinet," she said, gesturing, "wine on the kitchen counter, beer and sodas in the refrigerator. Have yourself a drink if you want. I'm going to be back here awhile."

She opened the door. I saw that it was the bathroom. She went in and closed it. Moments later, I could hear water running.

I crossed the room and opened the cabinet. I was nervous. I wished I hadn't quit smoking. I closed the cabinet again. Hard liquor might slow me if trouble came. Besides, I'd rather sip. I went to the kitchen and located a beer. I paced with it for a time and finally settled onto the green sofa next to a casually draped serape. The water was still running.

I thought about what I was going to do. It began to rain lightly. I finished the beer and got another. I looked out of all the windows, even those in the bedroom in the rear to the left, but there was no one in sight. After a time, I wanted to use the bathroom, but she was still in there. I wondered what she was doing for so long.

When she finally came out, she wore a blue terrycloth robe that stopped at midcalf. Her hair was turbaned in a white towel. She still had on her dark glasses.

She turned on a radio in the kitchen, found music, came back with a glass of wine and seated herself on the sofa.

"All right," she said, "what do you want to do?"

"I'm leaving tonight," I said.

"When?"

"Twoish."

"How?"

"Fishing boat, heading south."

"You can stay here till then. I'll take you to the dock."

"It's not that simple," I said. "I have to get back to my motel."

"What's so important?"

"Some papers. In a big manila envelope. At the bottom of my suitcase."

"Maybe they've got them already."

"Maybe."

"It's very important?"

"Yes."

"Give me the room key. I'll get them for you."

"I'm not asking you to."

"I'll get them. Make yourself at home. Give me the key."

I fished it out and passed it to her. She nodded and walked back to the bedroom. I went to the kitchen and started a pot of coffee. A little later, she emerged wearing a black skirt, a red blouse and a red scarf. Boots. She drew on her raincoat and moved toward the door. I went to her and embraced her, and she laughed and went out into the rain. I heard the car door slam and the engine start. I felt badly about her going, but I wanted the papers.

I went back to the bathroom. A great number of unlabeled jars filled a section of the countertop. Some of them were open. Several had very peculiar odors which I could not classify, some of them smelled vaguely narcotic. There was also a Bunsen burner, tongs, test tubes and several beakers and flasks—all of them recently rinsed.

I was not certain what I would do if someone followed her back. I felt like a naked matador without a sword. They had been after me for a long while, and there had been many passes. I was not carrying a gun. I had had to go through too many airline security checks recently, and I had not had time to obtain one locally. If I could just make the boat everything would be all right.

I went to the kitchen to check on the coffee. It was ready. I poured a cup and sat to drink it at the table. I listened to the rain.

Perhaps half an hour later, I heard a car in the driveway. I went to the window. It was hers and she appeared to be alone in it.

When she came in, she withdrew the envelope from beneath her coat and handed it to me. She gave me back the key, too.

"Better check and be sure the right stuff is still there," she said. I did, and it was.

"Think they knew which room?" she asked.

"I don't know. They wouldn't recognize the name. Did he see you go in? Come out?"

"Probably."

"Do you think you might have been followed?"

"I didn't see anybody behind me."

I returned to the window and watched for a time. There was nothing suspicious.

"I don't know how to thank you," I finally said.

"I'm tense again," she said.

We went back to the bedroom and I showed my gratitude for as hard and long as I could. It was still a hands-and-mouth-below-the-neck proposition, but we all have our hangups, and it was certainly wild and interesting country. Afterward, she broiled lamb chops and I tossed a salad. Later, we drank coffee and smoked some small black cigars she had. It was dark by then and the rain had stopped.

Suddenly, she placed her cigar in the ashtray and rose.

"I'm going back to the bathroom, for a time," she said, and she did.

She'd been in there several minutes with the water running when the telephone rang. I didn't know what to do. It could be a boyfriend, a husband, someone who wouldn't like my voice.

"Hello?" There was the crackle of long distance and bad connection. "Hello?" I repeated, after several seconds.

"Em...? Is Em...there...?" said a man's voice, sounding as through a seashell. "Who is...this...?"

"Jess," I said, "Smithson. I'm renting this place for a week. It belongs to some lady. I don't know her name."

"Tell her...Percy's...called."

"I don't know that I'll see her. But is there any message?"

"Just that...I'll be...coming."

There was a click, and the echoes went away.

I went to the bathroom door and knocked gently.

"You had a phone call," I said.

The water stopped running.

"What?"

At that moment, the doorbell rang. I rushed to the kitchen window and looked out. I couldn't see who was there, but there was a car parked up the street and it was blue.

I returned to the bathroom door.

"They're here," I said.

"Go to the bedroom," she said. "Get in the closet. Don't come out until I tell you."

"What are you going to do?"

The doorbell rang again.

"Do it!"

So I did. She seemed to have something in mind and I didn't.

Among garments in the darkness, I listened. Her voice and a harsh masculine one. They talked for about half a minute. It sounded as if he had come in. Suddenly there was a scream—his—cut short in a matter of seconds, followed by a crash.

I was out of the closet and heading for the bedroom door.

"Stay in there." Her voice came steady. "Until I tell you to come out."

I backed up, almost against my will. There was a lot of authority in her voice.

"Okay," she said, a little later. "Come out, and bring my raincoat."

I returned to the closet.

When I entered the living room, there was a still figure on the floor beside her. It was covered by the serape. She wore nothing but a towel about her head and the glasses. She took the coat and pulled it on.

"You'd said 'they.' How many are there?" she asked.

"There were two. I thought I'd left them in Atlanta."

"There's a car out there?"

"Yes."

"Would the other one be in it, or out prowling around?"

"Probably prowling."

"Go back to your closet."

"Now wait a minute! I'm not going to have a woman…"

"Do it!"

Again that compulsion as she glared at me, and a return of that strange tingling along my spine. I did as she told me.

I heard her go out. After maybe five minutes, I left the closet and returned to the front room. I raised the serape for a look.

Another five minutes, perhaps, and she returned. I was smoking one of her cigars and had a drink in my hand.

"Make mine wine," she said.

"The other one…?"

"…will not bother you."

"What did you do to them?"

"Don't ask me. I did you a favor, didn't I?"

"Yes."

"Get me a glass of wine."

I went and poured it. I took it to her.

"If we take them down to the dock... Your friend won't mind losing some dead weight at sea, will he?" she asked.

"No."

She took a large swallow.

"I'll finish in the bathroom now," she said, "and then we'll get them into the car. We may have to hang around awhile before we can unload them."

"Yes."

Later, after I had disposed of the blue Fury, we got them into her car and she drove slowly to the place I told her. It was after midnight before we were able to unload them and stow them on the boat.

I turned toward her then, in the shadow of a piling.

"You've been very good to me," I said.

She smiled.

"You made it worth a little effort," she said. "You up to another?"

"Right here?"

She laughed and opened her coat. She hadn't bothered dressing.

"Where else?"

I was up to it. As I held her, I realized that I did not want it to end like this.

"You could come with me," I said. "I'd like it if you would. I'd like to have you around," and I kissed her full on the mouth and held her to me with almost all of my strength. For a moment, it seemed that I felt something wet on her cheek against mine. Then she turned and broke my embrace with a single gesture and pushed me away.

"Go on," she said. "You're not that good. I've got better things to do."

Her scarf seemed to be blowing, though there was no wind. She turned quickly and started back toward the car. I began to follow her.

Her voice became hard again, harder than I'd ever heard it.

"Get aboard that boat now," she said, her back to me. "Do it!"

Again the compulsion, very real this time.

"All right," I said. "Goodbye, and thanks," and then I had to go.

Much later that night, Joe and I pushed the two limestone statues over the side into the Gulf Stream. I leaned on the rail for a long while after that, before I realized I had forgotten to tell her that Percy was coming. Later, the sun rose up at my back, turning the sea to a fleece of gold in the west.

A Word from Zelazny

"Here's my one Hemingway pastiche of sorts…

"His thinking about stories had an influence on my thinking about stories."[1] In his essay "The Parts That Are Only Glimpsed: Three Reflexes"[2] Zelazny said that Hemingway claimed he'd omitted the real end of "Out of Season" (in the deleted ending, the man hanged himself) because he felt that omissions could strengthen a story and make people feel something more than they understood. Adopting this economy of prose, Zelazny wrote or imagined scenes that developed characters, but he did not include them in his novels (see the afterword to "Dismal Light" in volume 3). But Zelazny also implemented "tossing in a bit of gratuitous characterization as I went along" and added "just a reference or two to something in the protagonist's past not connected with anything that is going on in the story's present."[2] He cited how Conrad (in *This Immortal*) explained that his lateness was because he had attended a birthday party for a friend's seven-year-old daughter. The offhand remark added background, did not affect the plot, and showed "that he still had other friends in town, and that he was the kind of person who would go to a kid's birthday party. Three birds in one sentence."[2]

Notes

Ernest **Hemingway's "The Killers"** begins at a diner's lunch counter and involves the encounter between a young Nick Adams, two hired killers (Max and Al), and the old man (Ole Andreson) whom they have been hired to kill. Tired of running, the old man simply lies on the bed, awaiting the inevitable. Forever changed by the encounter, Nick realizes the inevitability of death.

Em (for "M") is the snake-haired Gorgon Medusa, who turns men to stone with her glance, explaining her sunglasses and head covering. **Percy** is Perseus, son of Zeus and Danae, who cut off Medusa's head and gave it to Athena. The protagonist **Jess Smithson** is Jason of the Argonauts who sought the Golden Fleece (from a golden ram and guarded by an unsleeping dragon); **fleece of gold in the west** is the clue to his identity. The pursuers' car, a blue **Fury**, recalls the Furies (see afterword to "The Furies" in volume 2). The title means the protagonist and also recalls Hemingway's stories of Spanish bullfights.

---

1 *Unicorn Variations*, 1983.

2 *SFWA Bulletin #67*, Summer 1978, pp 14–15.

WALPURGISNACHT

A Rhapsody in Amber, Cheap Street 1981.

Sunny and summer. He walked the sweeping cobbled path beside the fringe of shrubbery, map in one hand, wreath in the other, passing from rest aisle to funerary glade. Grassy mounds with embedded bronze plaques lay along the way; beds of flowers, pale and bright, alternated with gazebos, low stone walls, fake Grecian ruins, stately trees. Occasionally, he paused to check a plate, consult the map.

At length he came to a heavily shaded glade. Recorded birdsongs were the only sounds in the low, cool area. The numbers were running higher here. Yes!

He put aside the chart and the wreath and he knelt. He ran his fingers across the plate that read "Arthur Abel Andrews" above a pair of dates. He located the catch and sprung the plate.

Within the insulated box beneath was a button. He pressed it and a faint humming sound began. This vanished as he snapped the plate shut.

"Well now, it's been a while since I've had any visitors."

The young man looked up suddenly, though he had known what to expect.

"Uncle Arthur…" he said, regarding the suddenly materialized form of the ruddy, heavyset man with the shifty eyes who now occupied the space above the mound. "Uh, how are you?"

The man, dressed in dark trousers, a white shirt, sleeves rolled up to the elbows, maroon tie hanging loosely about his neck, smiled.

"'At peace.' I'm supposed to say that when you ask. It's in the program. Now, let's see… You're…."

"Your nephew Raymond. I was only here once before, when I was little…"

"Ah, yes. Sarah's son. How is she these days?"

"Doing fine. Just had her third liver transplant. She's off on the Riviera right now."

Raymond thought about the computer somewhere beneath his feet. Programmed with photos of the departed it could produce a life-sized, moving hologram; from recorded samples of his uncle's speech, it could reproduce his voice patterns in conversation; from the results of a battery of tests and a series of brain wave readings, along with a large block of information—personal, family and general—it could respond in character to anyone's queries. Despite this knowledge, Raymond found it unnerving. It was far too real, far too much like that shrewd, black-sheep relative last seen through the eyes of youth with a kind of awe, and wrapped now in death's own mysteries—the man he had been told had a way of spoiling anything.

"Uh... Brought you a nice wreath, Uncle. Pink rosebuds."

"Great," the man said, glancing down at them. "Just what I need to liven things up here."

He turned away. He was seated upon a high stool that swiveled. Before him was the partial image of a bar, complete with brass rail. A stein of beer stood before him upon it. He took hold of it and raised it, sipped. Raymond recalled that, the cooperation of the person being memorialized being necessary, the choice of a favorite location for the memorial photographs was generally left up to the soon-to-be-departed.

"If you don't like the flowers, Uncle, I can always exchange them or just take them back."

His uncle set down the mug, belched gently and shook his head.

"No, no. Leave the damned things. I just thought of a use for them."

Arthur got down from the stool. He stooped and picked up the wreath. Raymond stumbled backward.

"Uncle! How did you do that? It's a material object and—"

Arthur strolled toward a mound across the way, carrying the pink circlet.

"It's a laser-force field combination," he commented. "Produces a holographic pressure interface. Latest thing."

"But how did you come by it? You've been—"

Arthur chuckled.

"Left a little trust account, to keep updating my hardware and such."

He stooped and pried up a brass headplate.

"What's your range, anyway?"

"About twenty meters," his uncle replied. "Then I start to fade out. Used to be only ten feet. There!"

He pressed a button and a tall, pale-haired woman with green eyes and a laughing mouth materialized beside him.

"Melissa, my dear. I've brought you some flowers," he said, passing her the wreath.

"What grave did you get them from, Arthur," she said, taking it into her hands.

"Now, now. They're really mine to give."

"Well, in that case, thank you. I might wear one in my hair."

"—Or upon your breast, when we step out tonight."

"Oh?"

"I was thinking of a party. Will you be free?"

"Yes. That sounds—lively. How will you manage it?"

Arthur turned.

"I'd like you to meet my nephew, Raymond Asher. Raymond, this is Melissa DeWeese."

"Happy to meet you," Raymond said.

Melissa smiled.

"Pleased," she replied, nodding.

Arthur winked.

"I'm sure I can arrange everything," he said, taking her hand.

"I believe you can—Arthur," she answered, touching his cheek.

She drew loose a rosebud and set it in her hair.

"Till then," she said. "Good evening to you, Raymond," and she faded and was gone, dropping the wreath upon the center of the mound.

Arthur shook his head.

"Husband poisoned her," he said. "What a waste."

"Uncle, death does not seem to have improved your morals a single bit," Raymond stated. "And chasing dead women, that's necro—"

"Now, now," Arthur said, turning and moving back toward the bar. "It's all a matter of attitude. I'm sure you'll see these things in a totally different light one day." He raised his mug and smacked his lips. "Nepenthe," he observed. "Necrohol."

"Uncle…"

"I know, I know," Arthur said. "You want something. Why else would you come here after all these years to visit me?"

"Well, to tell the truth..."

"By all means, tell it. It's a luxury few can afford."

"You always were considered a financial genius..."

"True." He made a sweeping gesture. "That's why I can afford the best life has to offer."

"Well, a lot of the family money is tied up in Cybersol stock and—"

"Sell! Damn it! Get rid of it quick!"

"Really?"

"It's going to take a real beating. And it won't be coming back."

"Wait a minute. I was going to brief you first and hope—"

"Brief me? I have abstracts of all the leading financial journals broadcast to my central processor on a regular basis. You'll lose your shirt if you stay with Cybersol."

"Okay. I'll dump it. What should I go into?"

His uncle smiled.

"A favor for a favor, nephew. A little *quid pro quo* here."

"What do you mean?"

"Advice of the quality I offer is worth more than a few lousy flowers."

"It looks as if you'll be getting a good return on them."

"*Honi soit qui mal y pensé*, Raymond. And I need a little more help along those lines."

"Such as?"

"You come by here about midnight and push everybody's buttons in this whole section. I'm going to give a big party."

"Uncle, that sounds positively indecent!"

"—And then get the hell out. You're not invited."

"I—I don't know..."

"Do you mean that in this modern, antiseptic age you're afraid to come into a graveyard—pardon me, cemetery—no, that's not it either. Memorial park—yes. At midnight. And press a few buttons?"

"Well—no... That's not it, exactly. But I've got a feeling you carry on worse than the living. I'd hate to be the instigator of a brand-new vice."

"Oh, don't let that bother you. We thought it up ourselves. And as soon as we get the timers installed we won't need you. Look at it as contributing to the sum total of joy in the world. Besides, you want to preserve the family fortune, don't you?"

"Yes..."

"See you at twelve then."

"All right."

"...And remember I've got a heavy date. Don't let me down, boy."

"I won't."

Uncle Arthur raised his mug and faded.

As Raymond walked back along the shaded aisles, he had a momentary vision of the *Totentanz*, of a skeletal fiddler wrapped in tattered cerements and seated atop a tombstone, grinning as the mournful dead cavorted about him, while bats dipped and rats whirled in the shadows. But for a moment only. And then it was replaced by one of brightly garbed dancers, mirrors, colored lights, body paint, where a disco sound rolled from overhead amplifiers. Death threw down his fiddle, and when he saw that his garments had become very mod he stopped smiling. His gaze focused for a moment upon a grinning man with a stein of beer, and then he turned away.

Uncle Arthur had a way of spoiling anything.

A Word from Zelazny

"A while back, my mother-in-law phoned to ask me whether I'd read a recent Erma Bombeck column. I confessed that I had not. It told, I was told, of the invention of the "talking tombstone"—a monument containing a recorded message from the deceased to the bereaved. The inventor, she said, was one Stanley Zelazny, of California, and she wanted to know if he was yet another relative of exotic and morbid sensibility gained upon the occasion of her daughter's marriage to myself. A bit of musing upon that invention became the basis for this story. And, well...I *do* have a cousin by that name, and he does live in California, but we've been out of touch for a long while. I honestly do not know whether he is indeed the father of the talking tombstone. If he is, this story is for him. If not, I suppose it should be for the other Stan Zelazny—who could, I guess, also be related. Either way, it's a sometime good feeling to keep things in the family."[1]

1 *Unicorn Variations*, 1983.

Notes

Walpurgisnacht (St. Walpurga's Night, or Walpurgis Night) occurs in several European countries on the night of April 30, when the witches convene to await Spring's arrival. A **woman with green eyes** is another example of a common Zelazny motif. **Nepenthe** is an amnesiac drug mentioned in Greek mythology. **Necrohol** is a pun meaning alcohol for the dead. ***Quid pro quo***, Latin for "this for that," means an equal exchange. ***Honi soit mal qui mal y pensé*** [shame upon him who thinks evil of it] is the motto of the Order of the Garter, an English chivalric order, the world's oldest existing order of knighthood. ***Totentanz*** [The Dance of Death] refers to images of dancing skeletons and corpses depicted since the fifteenth century; it also refers to Franz Liszt's orchestral piece about death.

WRIGGLE UNDER GEORGE WASHINGTON BRIDGE

The Dipple Chronicle #2, April-June 1971.
Written 1955–60 for *Chisel in the Sky*.

One who saw the striped underbelly
and light dotted fins swim,
like a creature's from depths of the sea,
above the moon,
may have glimpsed the face that is beauty
in its late orbiting moment
of most skinless dexterity.

The Last of the Wild Ones

Omni, March 1981.
§ *Jenny/Murdock*

Spinning through the dream of time and dust they came, beneath a lake-cold, lake-blue, lake-deep sky, the sun a crashed and burning wreck above the western mountains; the wind a whipper of turning sand devils, chill turquoise wind out of the west, taking wind. They ran on bald tires, they listed on broken springs, their bodies creased, paint faded, windows cracked, exhaust tails black and gray and white, streaming behind them into the northern quarter whence they had been driven this day. And now the pursuing line of vehicles, fingers of fire curving, hooking, above, before them. And they came, stragglers and breakdowns being blasted from bloom to wilt, flash to smolder, ignored by their fleeing fellows...

Murdock lay upon his belly atop the ridge, regarding the advancing herd through powerful field glasses. In the arroyo to his rear, the Angel of Death—all cream and chrome and bulletproof glass, sporting a laser cannon and two bands of armor-piercing rockets—stood like an exiled mirage glistening in the sun, vibrating, tugging against reality.

It was a country of hills, long ridges, deep canyons toward which they were being driven. Soon they would be faced with a choice. They could pass into the canyon below or enter the one farther to the east. They could also split and take both passages. The results would be the same. Other armed observers were mounted atop other ridges, waiting.

As he watched to see what the choice would be, Murdock's mind roamed back over the previous fifteen years, since the destruction of the Devil Car at the graveyard of the autos. He had, for twenty-five years, devoted his life to the pursuit of the wild ones. In that time he had become the world's foremost authority on the car herds—their habitats, their psychology, their means of maintenance and fueling—learning virtually everything concerning their ways, save for the precise nature of the initial flaw that one fatal year, which had led to the aberrant radio-communicable program that spread like a virus among the computerized vehicles. Some, but not all, were susceptible to it, tightening the disease analogy by another twist of the wrench. And some recovered, to be found returned to the garage or parked before the house one morning, battered but back in service, reluctant to recite their doings of days past. For the wild ones killed and raided, turning service stations into fortresses, dealerships into armed camps. The black Caddy had even borne within it the remains of the driver it had monoed long ago.

Murdock could feel the vibrations beneath him. He lowered the glasses, no longer needing them, and stared through the blue wind. After a few moments more he could hear the sound, as well as feel it—over a thousand engines roaring, gears grinding, sounds of scraping and crashing—as the last wild herd rushed to its doom. For a quarter of a century he had sought this day, ever since his brother's death had set him upon the trail. How many cars had he used up? He could no longer remember. And now…

He recalled his days of tracking, stalking, observing, and recording. The patience, the self-control it had required, exercising restraint when what he most desired was the immediate destruction of his quarry. But there had been a benefit in the postponement—this day was the reward, in that it would see the passing of the last of them. Yet the things he remembered had left strange tracks upon the path he had traveled.

As he watched their advance, he recalled the fights for supremacy he had witnessed within the herds he had followed. Often the defeated car would withdraw after it was clear that it was beaten; grill smashed, trunk sprung, lights shattered, body crumpled and leaking. The new leader would then run in wide circles, horn blaring, signal of its victory, its mastery. The defeated one, denied repair from the herd supply, would sometimes trail after the pack, an outcast. Occasionally it would be taken back in if it located something worth raiding. More often, however, it wandered across the Plains, never to be seen mobile again. He had tracked one once, wondering whether it had made its way to some new graveyard of the autos. He was startled to see it suddenly appear atop a mesa, turn toward the face that rose above a deep gorge, grind its gears, rev its engine, and rush forward, to plunge over the edge, crashing, rolling, and burning below.

But he recalled one occasion when the winner would not settle for less than a total victory. The blue sedan had approached the beige one where it sat on a low hillock with four or five parked sports cars. Spinning its wheels, it blared its challenge at several hundred meters' distance, then turned, cutting through a half-circle, and began its approach. The beige began a series of similar maneuvers, wheeling and honking, circling as it answered the challenge. The sports cars hastily withdrew to the sidelines.

They circled each other as they drew nearer, the circle quickly growing smaller. Finally the beige struck, smashing into the blue vehicle's left front fender, both of them spinning and sliding, their engines racing. Then they were apart again, feinting—advancing a brief distance, braking, turning, backing, advancing.

The second engagement clipped off the blue vehicle's left rear taillight and tore loose its rear bumper. Yet it recovered rapidly, turned, and struck the beige broadside, partly caving it in. Immediately it backed off and struck again before the other had completely recovered. The beige tore loose, and spun away in reverse. It knew all the tricks, but the other kept rushing in, coming faster now, striking and withdrawing. Loud rattling noises were coming from the beige, but it continued its circling, its feinting, the sunlight through the risen dust giving it a burnished look, as of very old gold. Its next rush creased the right side of the blue vehicle. It sounded its horn as it pursued it and commenced an outward turn.

The blue car was already moving in that direction, however, gravel spewing from beneath its rear wheels, horn blasting steadily. It leaped forward and again struck the beige upon the same side. As it backed off, the beige turned to flee, its horn suddenly silent.

The blue car hesitated only a moment, then sped after it, crashing into its rear end. The beige pulled away, leaking oil, doors rattling. But the blue car pursued it and struck again. It moved on, but the blue swerved, ran through a small arc, and hit it yet again upon the same side it had earlier. This time the beige was halted by the blow, steam emerging from beneath its hood; this time, as the blue car drew back, it was unable to flee. Rushing forward, the blue struck it once more upon the badly damaged left side. The impact lifted it from the ground, turning it over onto the slope falling away sharply to its right. It rolled sideways, tumbling and bouncing, to be brought up with a crash upon its side. Moments later its fuel tank exploded.

The blue car had halted, facing downhill. It ran up an antenna from which half a dozen spinning sensors unfurled, a fairy totem pole shimmering in the fume-filled air. After a time it retracted the sensors and withdrew the aerial. It gave one loud blare of the horn then and moved away to round up the sports cars.

Murdock remembered. He put his glasses in their case as the herd neared the turning point. He could distinguish individual members now, unassisted. They were a sorry-looking lot. Seeing them, he recalled the points of the best that he had come across over the years. When their supplies of parts had been larger, they had used their external manipulators to modify themselves into some magnificent and lethal forms. Kilo for kilo, the wild ones had become superior to anything turned out in the normal course of production.

All of the car scouts, of course, went armed, and in the early days a number of them had experimented. Coming upon a small herd, they would cut out a number of the better ones, blasting the rest. Disconnecting the think boxes, they would have their partners drive them back. But attempts at rehabilitation had been something less than successful. Even a complete wipe, followed by reprogramming, did not render the susceptible individuals immune to relapse. Murdock even recalled one that had behaved normally for almost a year, until one day in the midst of a traffic jam it had monoed its driver and taken off for the hills. The only alternative was to discard the entire computational unit and replace it with a new one which was hardly worthwhile, since its value was far greater than that of the rest of the vehicle.

No, there had been no answer in that direction. Or any other but the course that he had followed; track and attack, the systematic destruction of the herds. Over the years his respect for the cunning and daring of the herd leaders had grown. As the wild ones had dwindled in number, their ferocity and guile had reached the level of legend. There had been nights, as he lay sleeping, that he dreamed of himself as a wild car, armed, racing across the Plains, leader of a herd. Then there was only one other car, a red one.

The herd began its turn. Murdock saw, with a sudden pang of regret, that it was heading into the far eastern canyon. He tugged at his white-streaked beard and cursed as he reached for his stick and began to rise. True, there would still be plenty of time to get over to the next canyon for the kill, but—

No! Some of them were splitting off, heading this way!

Smiling, he drew himself upright and limped rapidly down the hill to where the Angel of Death waited for him. He heard the exploding mines as he climbed into the vehicle. Its motor began to hum.

"There are a few in the next canyon," came the soft, well-modulated, masculine voice of his machine. "I have been monitoring all bands."

"I know," he answered, stowing his stick. "Let's head over that way. Some will make it through."

Safety restraints snapped into place around him as they began to move.

"Wait!"

The white vehicle halted.

"What is it that you wish?"

"You are heading north."

"We must, to exit here and enter the next canyon with the others."

"There are some connecting side canyons to the south. Go that way. I want to beat the others in."

"There will be some risk involved."

Murdock laughed.

"I've lived with risk for a quarter of a century, waiting for this day. I want to be there first for the end. Go south!"

The car swung through a turn and headed southward.

As they cruised along the arroyo bottom's sand, Murdock asked, "Hear anything?"

"Yes," came the reply. "The sounds of those who were blasted by the mines, the cries of those who made it through."

"I knew some would make it! How many? What are they doing now?

"They continue their flight southward. Perhaps several dozen. Perhaps many more. It is difficult to estimate from the transmissions."

Murdock chuckled.

"They've no way out. They'll have to turn sooner or later, and we'll be waiting."

"I am not certain that I could deal with a mass attack by that many—even if most lack special armaments."

"I know what I'm doing," Murdock said. "I've chosen the battleground."

He listened to the muffled thuds of the distant explosions.

"Prime the weapons systems," he announced. "Some of them could have located the sideway we'll be taking."

A twin band of yellow lights winked out on the dashboard and were replaced by a double row of green ones. Almost immediately these faded and were succeeded by two lines of steady, red points.

"Ready on rockets," came the voice of the Angel.

Murdock reached out and threw a switch.

A larger light had also come on—orange and pulsing faintly.

"Cannon ready."

Murdock threw a larger switch beside a pistol grip set in the dash below it.

"I'll keep this one on manual for now."

"Is that wise?"

Murdock did not answer. For a moment he watched the bands of red and yellow strata to his left, a veil of shadow being drawn slowly upward over them.

"Slow now. The sideway will be coming up shortly. It should be up there on the left."

His car began to slow.

"I believe that I detect it ahead."

"Not the next one. It's blind. There's one right after it, though. It goes through."

They continued to slow as they passed the mouth of the first opening to the left. It was dark and angled off sharply.

"I've become aware of the next one."

"Very slowly now. Blast anything that moves."

Murdock reached forward and took hold of the pistol grip.

Angel braked and made the turn, advancing into a narrow pass.

"Dim the ready lights. No transmissions of any sort. Keep it dark and quiet."

They moved through an alley of shadow, the distant explosions having become a pulsing more felt than heard now. Stony walls towered on either hand. Their way wound to the right and then to the left.

Another right-hand twisting, and there was a bit of brightness and a long line of sight.

"Stop about three meters before it opens out," Murdock said, not realizing until moments later that he had whispered.

They crept ahead and came to a halt.

"Keep the engine running."

"Yes."

Murdock leaned forward, peering into the larger canyon running at right angles to their own. Dust hung in the air—dark, murky below, sparkling higher above, where the sun's rays could still reach.

"They've already passed," he reflected "and soon they should realize they're in a box—a big one, but still a box. Then they'll turn and come back and we'll open up on them." Murdock looked to the left. "Good place right over there for some more of our people to lay up and wait for them. I'd better get in touch and let them know. Use a fresh scrambler this time."

"How do you know they'll be coming back? Perhaps they'll lay up in there and make you come in after them."

"No," Murdock said. "I know them too well. They'll run for it."

"Are you sure there aren't any other sideways?"

"None going west. There may be a few heading east, but if they take them, they'll wind up in the other trap. Either way, they lose."

"What if some of those others cut down this way?"

"The more, the merrier. Get me that line. And see what you can pick up on the herd while I'm talking."

Shortly after that, he was in touch with the commander of the southern wing of the pursuers, requesting a squad of armed and armored vehicles to be laid up at the point he designated. He learned that they were already on their way to the western canyon in search of those vehicles observed entering there. The commander relayed Murdock's message to them and told him that they would be along in a matter of minutes. Murdock could still feel the shock waves from the many explosions in the eastern canyon.

"Good," he said, and he ended the transmission.

"They've reached the end," the Angel announced a little later, "and are circling. I hear their broadcasts. They are beginning to suspect that there is no way out."

Murdock smiled. He was looking to his left, where the first of the pursuing vehicles had just come into sight. He raised the microphone and began giving directions.

As he waited, he realized that at no time had he relaxed his hold on the pistol grip. He withdrew his hand, wiped his palm on his trousers, and returned it.

"They are coming now," the Angel said. "They have turned and are headed back this way."

Murdock turned his head to the right and waited. The destruction had been going on for nearly a month, and today's should be the last of it. He suddenly realized just how tired he was. A feeling of depression began to come over him. He stared at the small red lights and the larger, pulsing orange one.

"You will be able to see them in a moment."

"Can you tell how many there are?"

"Thirty-two. No, hold it…thirty-one. They are picking up speed. Their conversations indicate that they anticipate an interception."

"Did any come through from the eastern canyon?"

"Yes. There were several."

The sound of their engines came to him. Hidden there in the neck of the ravine, he saw the first of them—a dark sedan, dented and swaying, half of its roof and the nearest fender torn away—come around the canyon's bend. He held his fire as it approached, and soon the others followed—rattling, steaming, leaking, covered with dents and rust spots, windows broken, hoods missing, doors loose. A strange feeling came into his breast as he thought about the more magnificent specimens of the great herds he had followed over the years.

Still, he held his fire, even as the first in line drew abreast of him, and his thoughts went back to the black and shining Devil Car and to Jenny, the Scarlet Lady, with whom he had hunted it.

The first of the pack reached the place where the ambushers waited.

"Now?" the Angel asked, just as the first rocket flared off to the left.

"Yes."

They opened up and the destruction began, cars braking and swerving into one another, the canyon suddenly illuminated by half a dozen blazing wrecks, a dozen, two.

One after another, they were halted, burned. Three of the ambushers were destroyed by direct crashes. Murdock used all of his rockets and played the laser over the heaped remains. As the last wreck burst into flame, he knew that, though they weren't much compared with the great ones he had known, he would never forget how they had made their final run on bald tires, broken springs, leaking transmissions, and hate.

Suddenly he swiveled the laser and fired it back along the canyon.

"What is it?" the Angel asked him.

"There's another one back there. Don't you pick it up?"

"I'm checking now, but I don't detect anything."

"Go that way."

They moved forward and turned to the right. Immediately the radio crackled.

"Murdock, where are you going?" This came from one of the ambushers to the rear.

"I thought I saw something. I'm going ahead to check it out."

"I can't give you an escort till we clear some of these wrecks."

"That's all right."

"How many rockets have you got?"

He glanced again at the dash, where the only light that burned was orange and pulsing steadily.

"Enough."

"Why don't you wait?"

Murdock chuckled. "Do you really think any of those clunkers could touch something like the Angel? I won't be long."

They moved toward the bend and turned. The last of the sunlight was striking the highest points of the eastern rim overhead.

Nothing.

"Picking anything up?" he asked.

"No. Do you want a light?"

"No."

Farther to the east the sounds of firing were diminishing. The Angel slowed as they neared a wide slice of darkness to the left.

"This ravine may go through. Do we turn here or continue on?"

"Can you detect anything within it?"

"No."

"Then keep going."

His hand still upon the grip, Murdock moved the big gun slightly with each turn that they took, covering the most likely areas of opposition rather than the point directly ahead.

"This is no good," he finally announced. "I've got to have a light. Give me the overhead spot."

Instantly the prospect before him was brightly illuminated: dark rocks, orange stands of stone, striped walls—almost a coral seascape through waves of settling dust.

"I think somebody's been by here more recently than those we burned."

"Don't tired people sometimes see things that are not really there?"

Murdock sighed.

"Yes, and I am tired. That may be it. Take the next bend anyway."

They continued on, making the turn.

Murdock swiveled the weapon and triggered it, blasting rock and clay at the corner of the next turning.

"There!" he cried. "You must have picked that up!"

"No. I detected nothing."

"I can't be cracking up at this point! I saw it! Check your sensors. Something must be off."

"Negative. All detection systems report in good order."

Murdock slammed his fist against the dash.

"Keep going. Something's there."

The ground was churned before them. There were too many tracks to tell a simple tale.

"Slowly now," he said as they approached the next bend. "Could one of them have some kind of equipment or something to block you, I wonder. Or am I really seeing ghosts? I don't see how—"

"Gully to the left. Another to the right."

"Slower! Run the spotlight up them as we pass."

They moved by the first one, and Murdock turned the weapon to follow the light. There were two side passages going off the ravine before it turned.

"Could be something up there," he mused. "No way of telling without going in. Let's take a look at the next one."

They rolled on. The light turned again, and so did the gun. The second opening appeared to be too narrow to accommodate a car. It ran straight back without branching, and there was nothing unusual in sight anywhere within it.

Murdock sighed again.

"I don't know," he said, "but the end is just around the next bend—a big box of a canyon. Go straight on in. And be ready for evasive action."

The radio crackled.

"You all right?" came a voice from the ambush squad.

"Still checking," he said. "Nothing so far. Just a little more to see."

He broke it off.

"You didn't mention—"

"I know. Be ready to move very fast."

They entered the canyon, sweeping it with the light. It was an oval-shaped place, its major axis perhaps a hundred meters in length. Several large rocks lay near its center. There were a number of dark openings about its periphery. The talus lay heavy at the foot of the walls.

"Go right. We'll circle it. Those rocks and the openings are the places to watch."

They were about a quarter of the way around when he heard the high, singing sound of another engine revving. Murdock turned his head and looked fifteen years into the past.

A low, red Swinger sedan had entered the canyon and was turning in his direction.

"Run!" he said. "She's armed! Get the rocks between us!"

"Who? Where?"

Murdock snapped the control switch to manual, seized the wheel, and stepped on the gas. The Angel leaped ahead, turning, as fifty-caliber machine guns blazed beneath the darkened headlights of the other vehicle.

"Now do you see it?" he asked as the rear window was starred and he felt the thudding impact of hits somewhere toward the back of the vehicle.

"Not entirely. There is some sort of screen, but I can estimate based on that. Give me back the controls."

"No. Estimates aren't good enough with her," Murdock replied, turning sharply to place the rocks between himself and the other.

The red car came fast, however, though it had stopped firing as he entered the turn.

The radio crackled. Then a voice he had thought he would never hear again came over it: "That's you, isn't it, Sam? I heard you back there. And that's the sort of car the Archengineer of Geeyem would have built you for something like this—tough and smart and fast." The voice was low, feminine, deadly. "He would not have anticipated this encounter, however. I can jam almost all the sensors without its knowing it."

"Jenny..." he said as he held the pedal to the floor and continued the turn.

"Never thought you'd see me again, did you?"

"I've always wondered. Ever since the day you disappeared. But it's been so long."

"And you've spent the entire time hunting us. You had your revenge that day, but you kept right on—destroying."

"Considering the alternative, I had no choice."

He passed his starting point and commenced a second lap, realizing as he began to draw away that she must no longer be as finely tuned as when he had known her earlier. Unless—

An explosion occurred some distance ahead of him. He was pelted with gravel, and he swerved to avoid the fresh crater before him.

"Still have some of those grenades left," he said. "Hard to estimate when to drop them, though, isn't it?"

They were on opposite sides of the rocks now. There was no way she could get a clear shot at him with her guns. Nor he at her, with the cannon.

"I'm in no hurry, Sam."

"What is it?" he heard the Angel ask.

"It speaks!" she cried. "Finally! Do you want to tell him, Sam? Or should I?"

"I'd a feeling it was her, back there," Murdock began, "and I'd long had a feeling that we would meet again. Jenny was the first killer car I had built to hunt the wild ones."

"And the best," she added.

"But she went wild herself," he finished.

"How's about you trying it, Whitey?" she said. "Leak carbon monoxide into the air vents. He'll still look live enough to get you out of here. You answer any calls that come in. Tell them he's resting. Tell them you didn't find anything. Slip away later and come back here. I'll wait, I'll show you the ropes."

"Cut it out, Jenny," Murdock said, circling again, beginning to gain on her. "I'll have you in my sights in a minute. We haven't that much time to talk."

"And nothing, really, to talk about," she responded.

"How about this? You were the best car I ever had. Surrender. Fire off your ammo. Drop the grenades. Come back with me. I don't want to blast you."

"Just a quick lobotomy, eh?"

Another explosion occurred, this one behind him. He continued to gain on her.

"It's that virus program," he said. "Jenny, you're the last—the last wild one. You've nothing to gain."

"Or to lose," she responded quietly.

The next explosion was almost beside him. The Angel rocked but did not slow. Gripping the wheel with one hand, Murdock reached out and took hold of the pistol grip.

"She's stopped jamming my sensors," the Angel announced.

"Maybe she's burned out that system," Murdock said, turning the gun.

He sped around the rocks, avoiding the new craters, the light beam bouncing, sweeping, casting the high, craggy walls into a rapid succession of dreamlike images, slowly closing the distance between himself and Jenny. Another grenade went off behind him. Finally the moment of a clear shot emerged from the risen dust. He squeezed the trigger.

The beam fell wide, scoring the canyon side, producing a minor rockslide.

"That was a warning," he said. "Drop the grenades. Discharge the guns. Come back with me. It's your last chance."

"Only one of us will be going away from here, Sam," she answered.

He swung the gun and fired again as he swept along another turn, but a pothole he struck threw the beam high, fusing a section of sandy slope.

"A useful piece, that," she commented. "Too bad you didn't give me one."

"They came later."

"It is unfortunate that you cannot trust your vehicle and must rely upon your own driving skills. Your car would not have missed that last shot."

"Maybe," Murdock said, skidding through another turn.

Suddenly two more grenades exploded between them, and rocks rattled against the Angel. Both windows on the right side were fractured. He skidded sideways, his vision obscured by the flash and the airborne matter.

Both hands on the wheel now, he fought for control, braking hard. Passing through the screen of detritus, slowing and turning, he caught sight of Jenny racing full bore toward the pass that led out of the canyon.

He stepped on the gas again and followed after. She passed through and was gone before he could reach for the weapon.

"Return to automatic, and you will be free for the fighting," the Angel said.

"Can't do that," Murdock replied, racing toward the pass. "She could jam you again then at any time—and get us both."

"Is that the only reason?"

"Yes, the risk."

The red car was not in sight when he came through into the pass.

"Well?" he said. "What do your sensors read?"

"She entered the gully on the right. There is a heat trail."

Murdock continued to slow as he moved in that direction.

"That must be where she was hiding when we came by," he said. "It could be some kind of trap."

"Perhaps you had better call for the others, cover the entrance, and wait."

"No!"

Murdock turned his wheel and sent his light along the passageway. She was nowhere in sight, but there were sideways. He continued to creep forward, entering. His right hand was again on the pistol grip.

He passed these side openings, each of them large enough to hide a car, all of them empty.

He followed a bend, bearing him to the right. Before he had moved an entire car length along it, a burst of gunfire from the left, ahead, caused him to slam on the brakes and turn the cannon. But an engine roared to life before he could take aim, and a red streak crossed his path to vanish up another sideway. He hit the gas again and followed.

Jenny was out of sight, but he could hear the sound of her somewhere ahead. The way widened as he advanced. Finally it forked at a large stand of stone, one arm continuing past it, the other bearing off sharply to the left. He slowed, taking time to consider the alternatives.

"Where's the heat trail go?" he asked.

"Both ways. I don't understand."

Then the red car came swinging into sight from the left, guns firing. The Angel shook as they were hit. Murdock triggered the laser, but she swept past him, turning and speeding off to the right.

"She circled it before we arrived, to confuse your sensors, to slow us.

"It worked, too," he added, moving ahead again. "She's too damned smart."

"We can still go back."

Murdock did not reply.

Twice more Jenny lay in wait, fired short bursts, evaded the singeing beam, and disappeared. An intermittent knocking sound began beneath the hood as they moved, and one telltale on the dash indicated signs of overheating.

"It is not serious," the Angel stated. "I can control it."

"Let me know if there is any change."

"Yes."

Following the heat trail, they bore steadily to the left, racing down a widening sand slope past castles, minarets, and cathedrals of stone, dark or pale, striped and spotted with mica like the first raindrops of a midsummer's storm. They hit the bottom, slid sideways, and came to a stop, wheels spinning.

He threw the light around rapidly, causing grotesque shadows to jerk like marionettes in a ring dance about them.

"It's a wash. Lots of loose sand. But I don't see Jenny."

Murdock ground the gears, rocking the vehicle, but they did not come free.

"Give me control," said the Angel. "I've a program for this."

Murdock threw the switch. At once a fresh series of rocking movements began. This continued for a full minute. Then the heat telltale began to flicker again.

"So much for the program. Looks as if I'm going to have to get out and push," Murdock said.

"No. Call for help. Stay put. We can hold her off with the cannon if she returns."

"I can get back inside pretty quick. We've got to get moving again."

As he reached for the door, he heard the lock click.

"Release it," he said. "I'll just shut you off, go out, and turn you on again from there. You're wasting time."

"I think you are making a mistake."

"Then let's hurry and make it a short one."

"All right. Leave the door open." There followed another click. "I will feel the pressure when you begin pushing. I will probably throw a lot of sand on you."

"I've got a scarf."

Murdock climbed out and limped toward the rear of the vehicle. He wound his scarf up around his mouth and nose. Leaning forward, he placed his hands upon the car and began to push. The engine roared and the wheels spun as he threw his weight against it.

Then, from the corner of his eye, to the right, he detected a movement. He turned his head only slightly and continued pushing the Angel of Death.

Jenny was there. She had crept up slowly into a shadowy place beneath a ledge, turning, facing him, her guns directly upon him. She must have circled. Now she was halted.

It seemed useless to try running. She could open up upon him anytime that she chose.

He leaned back, resting for a moment, pulling himself together. Then he moved to his left, leaned forward, began pushing again. For some reason she was waiting. He could not determine why, but he sidled to the left. He moved his left hand, then his right. He shifted his weight, moved his feet again, fighting a powerful impulse to look in her direction once again. He was near the left taillight. Now there might be a chance. Two quick steps would place the body of the Angel between them. Then he could rush forward and dive back in. But why wasn't she firing?

No matter. He had to try. He eased up again. The feigned rest that followed was the most difficult spell of the whole thing.

Then he leaned forward once more, reached out as if to lay his hands upon the vehicle once again, and slipped by it, moving as quickly as he could toward the open door, and then through it, and inside. Nothing happened the entire time he was in transit, but the moment the car door slammed a burst of gunfire occurred beneath the ledge, and the Angel began to shudder and then to rock.

"There!" came the voice of the Angel as the gun swung to the right and a beam lanced outward and upward from it.

It bobbed. It rode high. It fell upon the cliff face, moving.

Murdock turned in time to see a portion of that surface slide downward, first with a whisper, then with a roar. The shooting ceased before the wall came down upon the red vehicle.

Above the sound of the crash, a familiar voice came through the radio: "Damn you, Sam! You should have stayed in the car!" she said.

Then the radio went silent. Her form was completely covered by the rock fall.

"Must have blocked my sensors again and sneaked up," the Angel was saying. "You are lucky that you saw her just when you did."

"Yes," Murdock replied.

"Let me try rocking us loose now," the Angel said a little later. "We made some headway while you were pushing."

The breakaway sequence began again. Murdock looked up at the stars for the first time that evening—cold and brilliant and so very distant. He kept on staring as the Angel pulled them free. He barely glanced at her stony tomb as they turned and moved past it.

When they had threaded their way back and out through the ravine, the radio came to life again: "Murdock! Murdock! You okay? We've been trying to reach you and—"

"Yes," he said softly.

"We heard more explosions. Was that you?"

"Yes. Just shooting at a ghost," he said. "I'm coming back now."

"It's over," the other told him. "We got them all."

"Good," he said, breaking the connection.

"Why didn't you tell him about the red one?" the Angel asked.

"Shut up and keep driving."

He watched the canyon walls slip by, bright strata and dull ones. It was night, sky cold, sky wide, sky deep, and the black wind came out of the north, closing wind. They headed into it. Spinning through the dream of time and dust, past the wreckage, they went to the place where the others waited. It was night, and a black wind came out of the north.

A Word from Zelazny

Returning to the characters and theme of "Devil Car," Zelazny remarked, "I picked up on it again a decade and a half later when something caused me to go back and think about the same things from a new vantage, to add a few notes and take a few away."[1]

"Fifteen years passed, and I read Ross Santee's book *Apache Land.* In it, there was a chapter on the passing of the herds of wild mustangs. As I read it, I kept thinking of "Devil Car/Swinger." Then I realized why, and it all fell into place; I knew that my earlier story required a sequel—set, of course, fifteen years later."[2]

Notes

"The Last of the Wild Ones" is the title of several paintings depicting the capture of the last wild mustangs. An **arroyo** is a steep-sided gully cut by running water in an arid or semiarid region. A **mesa** is an isolated flat-topped hill with steep sides.

---

1 *Gone to Earth*, 1991.

2 *Unicorn Variations*, 1983.

Lamentations of the Prematurely Old Satyr

Yandro #149, July 1965.

When I was young and horny *(Horn-note.)*
I heard a wise god say:
"Give wine and roses red and thorny,
But not your song away."

But I was young and horny, *(Flute-note.)*
And when she bade me play
I gave my song, and roses thorny.
She broke my pipes that day.

Now I am old, less horny, *(Drums.)*
More wise, perhaps, I say:
"Drink wine and keep your roses, thorny,
And hide your pipes this day.

Hide your pipes, your horny *(Cymbals.)*
Selves—hide, hide far away!
I lost mine in Gethsemane
Where frigid Nymphs do play."

Notes

This poem is a pastiche of A. E. Housman's "A Shropshire Lad, XIII," which begins: "When I was one-and-twenty || I heard a wise man say, || 'Give crowns and pounds and guineas || But not your heart away.' "

Lamentations are passionate expressions of sorrow; **Lamentations** in the Bible tells of the desolation of Judah after Jerusalem fell. A **satyr**, a lustful, drunken woodland god, resembles a man with a goat's or horse's ears, hindlimbs, and tail; it can also be a man with uncontrollable lust. The garden of **Gethsemane** (literally: an olive press) was where Judas betrayed Jesus after the Last Supper. **Nymphs** are nature spirits resembling beautiful maidens who inhabit rivers, woods, or other locations; the term also means a beautiful young woman. **Frigid nymphs** would not respond sexually.

MOONSONG

Sirruish #7 July 1968.

Come away, lady.
The moon it stands high.
The cat's in the cradle.
The pig's in the pie.
The rook's in the orchard,
The witches in their cave.
The Devil is burning
The hands of a knave.
The king's in the queen
The ace in the jet.
The deuces are dancing,
Though not to forget;
For trey is a-baying
From four until ten,
And nine be the spheres
We must visit ere then.
Five come six.
then seven;
now eight...
Evaporate. Evaporate.
Lady, now lady
Come lady away.
That cat's in the cradle
And night fills the day.

Notes

As described by Milton, the **nine spheres** enclosing the Earth are those of the Moon, of Mercury, of Venus, of the Sun, of Mars, of Jupiter, of Saturn, of the Firmament, and of the Crystalline. Above these nine heavens or spheres comes the Primum Mobile, and then the Heaven of the heavens, or the abode of the Deity and His angels. In Dante Alighieri's *Divine Comedy*, Beatrice guides Dante through the nine spheres, of which the eighth and ninth differ and are the sphere of the fixed stars and the primum mobile, respectively.

NUAGES

The Dipple Chronicle #1, Jan-March 1971.
Written 1955–60 for *Chisel in the Sky*.

Our Lady of Guadalupe
    to thee we pray
Deliver us the living
Bless the souls of our ancestors
    writhing in the Great Snake
    on outward fits of day

Talk to the silent
Breathe on those without breath
Wreathe in greatnesses of grace
Thy sun-dog and his kin

    who move through sand
    in winnowings of coral
    tide by sand
    past apertures of star

Waft on high the mothers of our men
Bless them

    who pry careers of molten sun-pearl
    the open mouthed clamshells of cloud

Notes

Nuages means "clouds" in French. **Our Lady of Guadalupe** refers both to the Virgin Mary's apparition in Guadalupe in 1531 and to the icon commemorating her visit.

THE HORSES OF LIR

Whispers III, ed. Stuart David Schiff, Doubleday 1981.

The moonlight was muted and scattered by the mist above the loch. A chill breeze stirred the white tendrils to a sliding, skating motion upon the water's surface. Staring into the dark depths, Randy smoothed his jacket several times, then stepped forward. He pursed his lips to begin and discovered that his throat was dry.

Sighing, almost with relief, he turned and walked back several paces. The night was especially soundless about him. He seated himself upon a rock, drew his pipe from his pocket and began to fill it.

What am I doing here? he asked himself. How can I…?

As he shielded his flame against the breeze, his gaze fell upon the heavy bronze ring with the Celtic design that he wore upon his forefinger.

It's real enough, he thought, and it had been *his*, and *he* could do it. But this…

He dropped his hand. He did not want to think about the body lying in a shallow depression ten or twelve paces up the hillside behind him.

His Uncle Stephen had taken care of him for almost two years after the deaths of his parents, back in Philadelphia. He remembered the day he had come over—on that interminable plane flight—when the old man had met him at the airport in Glasgow. He had seemed shorter than Randy remembered, partly because he was a bit stooped he supposed. His hair was pure white and his skin had the weathered appearance of a man's who had spent his life out-of-doors. Randy never learned his age.

Uncle Stephen had not embraced him. He had simply taken his hand, and his gray eyes had fixed upon his own for a moment as if searching for something. He had nodded then and looked away. It might have been then that Randy first noticed the ring.

"You'll have a home with me, lad," he had said. "Let's get your bags."

There was a brief splashing noise out in the loch. Randy searched its mist-ridden surface but saw nothing.

They know. Somehow they know, he decided. What now?

During the ride to his home, his uncle had quickly learned that Randy's knowledge of Gaelic was limited. He had determined to remedy the situation by speaking it with him almost exclusively. At first, this had annoyed Randy, who saw no use to it in a modern world. But the rudiments were there, words and phrases returned to him, and after several months he began to see a certain beauty in the Old Tongue. Now he cherished this knowledge—another thing he owed the old man.

He toyed with a small stone, cast it out over the waters, listened to it strike. Moments later, a much greater splash echoed it. Randy shuddered.

He had worked at his uncle's boat-rental business all that summer. He had cleaned and caulked, painted and mended, spliced… He had taken out charters more and more often as the old man withdrew from this end of things.

"As Mary—rest her soul—never gave me children, it will be yours one day, Randy," he had said. "Learn it well, and it will keep you for life. You will need something near here."

"Why?" he had asked.

"One of us has always lived here."

"Why should that be?"

Stephen had smiled.

"You will understand," he said, "in time."

But that time was slow in coming, and there were other things to puzzle him. About once a month, his uncle rose and departed before daybreak. He never mentioned his destination or responded to questions concerning it. He never returned before sundown, and Randy's strongest suspicion did not survive because he never smelled of whisky when he came in.

Naturally, one day Randy followed him. He had never been forbidden to do it, though he strongly suspected it would meet with disapproval. So he was careful. Dressing hastily, he kept the old man in sight through the window as he headed off toward a stand of trees. He put out the CLOSED sign and moved through the chill pre-dawn in that direction. He caught sight of him once again, briefly, and then Stephen vanished near a rocky area and Randy could find no trace of him after that. Half an hour later, he took down the sign and had breakfast.

Twice again he tried following him, and he lost him on both occasions. It irritated him that the old man could baffle him so thoroughly, and perhaps it bothered him even more that there was this piece of his life which he chose to keep closed to him—for as he worked with him and grew to know him better he felt an increasing fondness for his father's older brother.

Then one morning Stephen roused him early.

"Get dressed," he said. "I want you to come with me."

That morning his uncle hung the CLOSED sign himself and Randy followed him through the trees, down among the rocks, past a cleverly disguised baffle, and down a long tunnel. Randy heard lapping sounds of water, and even before his uncle put a light to a lantern he knew from the echoes that he was in a fair-sized cave.

His eyes did not adjust immediately when the light spread. When they did, he realized that he was regarding an underground harbor. Nevertheless, it took longer for the possibility to occur to him that the peculiar object to his left might be some sort of boat in a kind of dry dock. He moved nearer and examined it while his uncle filled and lit another lantern.

It was flat bottomed and U shaped. What he had taken to be some sort of cart beneath it, though, proved a part of the thing itself. It had a wheel on either side. Great metal rings hung loosely on both sides and on the forward end. The vehicle was tilted, resting upon its curved edge. These structural matters, however, aroused but a superficial curiosity, for all other things were overwhelmed within him by a kind of awe at its beauty.

Its gunwales, or sides—depending on exactly what the thing was—were faced with thin bronze plates of amazing design. They looped and swirled in patterns vaguely reminiscent of some of the more abstract figures in the *Book of Kells*, embossed here and there with large studs. The open areas looked to be enameled green and red in the flickering light.

He turned as his uncle approached.

"Beautiful, isn't it?" he said, smiling.

"It—it belongs in a museum!"

"No. It belongs right here."

"What is it?"

Stephen produced a cloth and began to polish the plates.

"A chariot."

"It doesn't look exactly like any chariot I've seen pictures of. For one thing, it's awfully big."

Stephen chuckled.

"Ought to be. 'Tis the property of a god."

Randy looked at him to see whether he was joking. From the lack of expression on his face, he knew that he was not.

"Whose—is it?" he asked.

"Lir, Lord of the Great Ocean. He sleeps now with the other Old Ones—most of the time."

"What is it doing here?"

His uncle laughed again.

"Has to park it someplace now, doesn't he?"

Randy ran his hand over the cold, smooth design on the side.

"I could almost believe you," he said. "But what is your connection with it?"

"I go over it once a month to clean it, polish it, keep it serviceable."

"Why?"

"He may have need of it one day."

"I mean, why you?"

He looked at his uncle again and saw that he was smiling.

"A member of our family has always done it," he said, "since times before men wrote down history. It is a part of my duty."

Randy looked at the chariot again.

"It would take an elephant to pull something that size."

"An elephant is a land creature."

"Then what…?"

His uncle held up his hand beside the lantern, displaying the ring.

"I am the Keeper of the Horses of Lir, Randy. This is my emblem of office, though they would know me without it after all these years."

Randy looked closely at the ring. Its designs were similar to those on the chariot.

"The Horses of Lir?" he asked.

His uncle nodded.

"Before he went to sleep with the other Old Ones, he put them to pasture here in the loch. It was given to an early ancestor of ours to have charge of them, to see that they do not forget."

Randy's head swam. He leaned against the chariot for support.

"Then all those stories, of—things—in the loch…?"

"Are true," Stephen finished. "There's a whole family, a herd of them out there." He gestured toward the water. "I call them periodically and talk to them and sing to them in the Old Tongue, to remind them."

"Why did you bring me here, Uncle? Why tell me all these secret things?" Randy asked.

"I need help with the chariot. My hands are getting stiff," he replied. "And there's none else but you."

Randy worked that day, polishing the vehicle, oiling enormous and peculiarly contrived harnesses that hung upon the wall. And his uncle's last words bothered him more than a little.

❖ ❖ ❖

The fog had thickened. There seemed to be shapes moving within it now—great slow shadows sliding by in the distance. He knew they were not a trick of the moonlight, for there had been another night such as this…

"Would you get your pullover, lad?" his uncle had said. "I'd like us to take a walk."

"All right."

He put down the book he had been reading and glanced at his watch. It was late. They were often in bed by this hour. Randy had only stayed up because his uncle had kept busy, undertaking a number of one-man jobs about the small cottage.

It was damp outside and somewhat chill. It had been raining that day. Now the fogs stirred about them, rolling in off the water.

As they made their way down the footpath toward the shore, Randy knew it was no idle stroll that his uncle had in mind. He followed his light to the left past the docking area, toward a secluded rocky point where the land fell away sharply to deep water. He found himself suddenly eager, anxious to learn something more of his uncle's strange commitment to the place. He had grown steadily fonder of the old man in the time they had been together, and he found himself wanting to share more of his life.

They reached the point—darkness and mist and lapping water all about them—and Stephen placed his light upon the ground and seated himself on a stony ledge. He motioned for Randy to sit near him.

"Now, I don't want you to leave my side, no matter what happens," his uncle said.

"Okay."

"And if you must talk, speak the Old Tongue."

"I will."

"I am going to call the Horses now."

Randy stiffened. His uncle placed his hand upon his arm.

"You will be afraid, but remember that you will not be harmed so long as you stay with me and do whatever I tell you. You must be introduced. I am going to call them."

Randy nodded in the pale light.

"Go ahead."

He listened to the strange trilling noises his uncle made, and to the song that followed them. After a time, he heard a splashing, then he saw the advancing shadow… Big. Whatever it was, the thing was huge. Large enough to draw the chariot, he suddenly realized. If a person dare harness it…

The thing moved nearer. It had a long, thin neck atop its bulky form, he saw, as it suddenly raised its head high above the water, to sway there, regarding them through the shifting mist.

Randy gripped the ledge. He wanted to run but found that he could not move. It was not courage that kept him there. It was a fear so strong it paralyzed him, raising the hair on the back of his neck.

He looked at the Horse, hardly aware that his uncle was speaking softly in Erse now.

The figure continued to move before them, its head occasionally dipping partway toward them. He almost laughed as a wild vision of a snake-charming act passed through his head. The creature's eyes were enormous, with glints of their small light reflected palely within them. Its head moved forward, then back. Forward…

The great head descended until it was so close that it was almost touching his uncle, who reached out and stroked it, continuing to speak softly all the while.

He realized abruptly that his uncle was speaking to him. For how long he had been, he did not know.

"…This one is Scafflech," he was saying, "and the one beside him is Finntag…"

Randy had not realized until then that another of the beasts had arrived. Now, with a mighty effort, he drew his eyes from the great reptilian head which had turned toward him. Looking past it, he saw that a second of the creatures had come up and that it, also, was beginning to lean forward. And beyond it there were more splashing sounds, more gliding shadows parting the mists like the prows of Viking ships.

"...And that one is Garwal. Talk to them, so they'll know the sound of your voice."

Randy felt that he could easily begin laughing hysterically. Instead, he found himself talking, as he would to a large, strange dog.

"That's a good boy... Come on now... How are you? Good old fellow..."

Slowly he raised his hand and touched the leathery muzzle. Stephen had not asked him to. Why he had done it he was not certain, except that it had always seemed a part of the dog talk he was using and his hand had moved almost as if by reflex when he began it.

The first creature's head moved even nearer to his own. He felt its breath upon his face.

"Randy's my name, Scafflech," he heard himself telling it. "Randy..."

That night he was introduced to eight of them, of various sizes and dispositions. After his uncle had dismissed them and they had departed, he simply sat there staring out over the water. The fear had gone with them. Now he felt only a kind of numbness.

Stephen stood, stooped, retrieved the light.

"Let's go," he said.

Randy nodded, rose slowly, and stumbled after him. He was certain that he would get no sleep that night, but when he got home and threw himself into bed the world went away almost immediately. He slept later than usual. He had no dreams that he could recall.

❖ ❖ ❖

They were out there again now, waiting. He had seen them several times since but never alone. His uncle had taught him the songs, the guide words and phrases, but he had never been called upon to use them this way. Now, on this night so like the first, he was back, alone, and the fear was back, too. He looked down at the ring that he wore. Did they actually recognize it? Did it really hold some bit of the Old Magic? Or was it only a psychological crutch for the wearer?

One of the huge forms—Scafflech, perhaps—drew nearer and then hastily retreated. They had come without being called. They were waiting for his orders, and he clutched his pipe, which had long since gone out, and sat shaking.

Stephen had been ill much of the past month and had finally taken to his bed. At first, Randy had thought it to be influenza. But the old man's condition had steadily worsened. Finally he had determined to get him a doctor.

But Stephen had refused, and Randy had gone along with it until just that morning, when his uncle had taken a turn for the worse.

"No way, lad. This is it," he had finally told him. "A man sometimes has a way of knowing, and we always do. It is going to happen today, and it is very important that there be no doctor, that no one know for a time..."

"What do you mean?" Randy had said.

"With a doctor there would be a death certificate, maybe an autopsy, a burial. I can't have that. You see, there is a special place set aside for me, for all of the Keepers... I want to join my fathers, in the place where the Old Ones sleep... It was promised—long ago..."

"Where? Where is this place?" he had asked.

"The Isles of the Blessed, out in the open sea... You must take me there..."

"Uncle," he said, taking his hand, "I studied geography in school. There's no such place. So how can I...?"

"It troubled me once, too," he said, "but I've been there... I took my own father, years ago... The Horses know the way..."

"The Horses! How could I— How could they—"

"The chariot... You must harness Scafflech and Finntag to the chariot and place my body within it. Bathe me first, and dress me in the clothes you'll find in that chest..." He nodded toward an old sea chest in the corner. "Then mount to the driver's stand, take up the reins, and tell them to take you to the Isles..."

Randy began to weep, a thing he had not done since his parents' deaths—how long ago?

"Uncle, I can't," he said. "I'm afraid of them. They're so big—"

"You must. I need this thing to know my rest. —And set one of the boats adrift. Later tell the people that I took it out..."

He wiped his uncle's face with a towel. He listened to his deepening breathing.

"I'm scared," he said.

"I know," Stephen whispered. "But you'll do it."

"I—I'll try."

"And here..." His uncle handed him the ring. "You'll need this—to show them you're the new Keeper..."

Randy took the ring.

"Put it on."

He did.

Stephen had placed his hand upon his head as he had leaned forward.

"I pass this duty to you," he said, "that you be Keeper of the Horses of Lir."

Then his hand slipped away and he breathed deeply once again. He awakened twice after that, but not for long enough to converse at length. Finally, at sundown, he had died. Randy bathed him and clothed him as he had desired, weeping the while and not knowing whether it was for his sadness or his fear.

❖ ❖ ❖

He had gone down to the cave to prepare the chariot. By lantern light he had taken down the great harnesses and affixed them to the rings in the manner his uncle had shown him. Now he had but to summon the Horses to this pool through the wide tunnel that twisted in from the loch, and there place the harnesses upon them…

He tried not to think about this part of things as he worked, adjusting the long leads, pushing the surprisingly light vehicle into position beside the water. Least of all did he wish to think of aquaplaning across the waves, drawn by those beasts, heading toward some mythical isle, his uncle's body at his back.

He departed the cave and went to the docking area, where he rigged a small boat, unmoored it and towed it out some distance over the loch before releasing it. The mists were already rising by then. In the moonlight, the ring gleamed upon his finger.

He returned to the cottage for his uncle and bore him down to a cove near the water entrance to the cave. Then his nerve had failed, he had seated himself with his pipe and had not stirred since.

The splashing continued. The Horses were waiting. Then he thought of his uncle, who had given him a home, who had left him this strange duty…

He rose to his feet and approached the water. He held up his hand with the ring upon it.

"All right," he said. "The time has come. Scafflech! Finntag! To the cave! To the place of the chariot! Now!"

Two forms drifted near, heads raised high upon their great necks.

I should have known it would not be that easy, he thought.

They swayed, looking down at him. He began addressing them as he had that first night. Slowly, their heads lowered. He waved the ring before them. Finally, when they were near enough, he reached out and stroked their necks. Then he repeated the instruction.

They withdrew quickly, turned, and headed off toward the tunnel. He moved away then, making for the land entrance to the place.

Inside, he found them waiting in the pool. He discovered then that he had to unfasten most of the harnessing from the chariot in order to fit it over them, and then secure it once again. It meant clambering up onto their backs. He removed his boots to do it. Their skin was strangely soft and slick beneath his feet, and they were docile now, as if bred to this business. He talked to them as he went about the work, rubbing their necks, humming the refrain to one of the old tunes.

He worked for the better part of an hour before everything was secure and he mounted the chariot and took up the reins.

"Out now," he said. "Carefully. Slowly. Back to the cove."

The wheels turned as the creatures moved away. He felt the reins jerk in his hands. The chariot advanced to the edge of the pool and continued on into the water. It floated. It drifted behind them toward the first bend and around it.

They moved through pitch blackness, but the beasts went carefully. The chariot never touched the rocky walls.

At length, they emerged into moonlight and mist over black water, and he guided them to the cove and halted them there.

"Wait now," he said. "Right here."

He climbed down and waded ashore. The water was cold, but he hardly noticed it. He mounted the slope to the place where his uncle lay and gathered him into his arms. Gently, he bore him down to the water's edge and out again. He took hold of the reins with a surer grip.

"Off now," he said. "You know the way! To the Isles of the Blessed! Take us there!"

They moved, slowly at first, through a long, sweeping turn that bore them out onto the misty breast of the loch. He heard splashings at either hand, and turning his head he saw that the other Horses were accompanying them.

They picked up speed. The beasts did seem to have a definite direction in mind. The mists swept by like a ghostly forest. For a moment, he almost felt as if he rode through some silent, mystical wood in times long out of mind.

The mists towered and thickened. The waters sparkled. He gave the creatures their head. Even if he had known the way, it would have done him little good, for he could not see where they were going. He had assumed that they were heading for the Caledonian Canal, to cut across to the sea. But now he wondered. If the Keepers, down through the ages, had been transported to some strange island, how had it been accomplished in earlier times? The Canal, as he recalled, had only been dug sometime in the nineteenth century.

But as the moonlit mists swirled about him and the great beasts plunged ahead, he could almost believe that there was another way—a way that perhaps only the Horses knew. Was he being borne, somehow, to a place that only impinged occasionally upon normal existence?

How long they rode across the ghostly seascape, he could not tell. Hours, possibly. The moon had long since set, but now the sky paled and a bonfirelike sunrise began somewhere to the right. The mists dispersed and the chariot coursed the waves beneath a clear blue sky with no trace of land anywhere in sight.

The unharnessed Horses played about him as Scafflech and Finntag drew him steadily ahead. His legs and shoulders began to ache and the wind came hard upon him now, but still he gripped the reins, blinking against the drenching spray.

Finally, something appeared ahead. At first he could not be certain, but as they continued on it resolved itself into a clear image. It was an island, green trees upon its hills, white rocks along its wave-swept shores.

As they drew nearer, he saw that the island was but one among many, and they were passing this one by.

Two more islands slipped past before the Horses turned and made their way toward a stone quay at the back of a long inlet at the foot of a high green slope. Giant trees dotted the hillside and there were several near the harbor. As they drew up beside the quay, he could hear birds singing within them.

As he took hold of the stone wall, he saw that there were three men standing beneath the nearest tree, dressed in green and blue and gray. They moved toward him, halting only when they had come alongside. He felt disinclined to look into their faces.

"Pass up our brother Keeper," one of them said in the Old Tongue.

Painfully, he raised his uncle's soaked form and felt them lift it from his arms.

"Now come ashore yourself, for you are weary. Your steeds will be tended."

He told the Horses to wait. He climbed out and followed the three figures along a flagged walk. One of them took him aside and led him into a small stone cottage while the others proceeded on, bearing his uncle's form.

"Your garments are wet," said the man. "Have this one," and he passed him a light green-blue robe of the sort he himself had on, of the sort in which Randy had dressed his uncle for the journey. "Eat now. There is food upon the table," the man continued, "and then there is the bed." He gestured. "Sleep."

Randy stripped and donned the garment he had been given. When he looked about again, he saw that he was alone. He went to the table, suddenly realizing that his appetite was enormous. Afterward, he slept.

It was dark when he awoke, and still. He got up and went to the door of the cottage. The moon had already risen, and the night had more stars in it than he could remember ever having seen before. A fragrant breeze came to him from off the sea.

"Good evening."

One of the men was seated upon a stone bench beneath a nearby tree. He rose.

"Good evening."

"Your Horses are harnessed. The chariot is ready to bear you back now."

"My uncle…?"

"He has come home. Your duty is discharged. I will walk with you to the sea."

They moved back to the path, headed down to the quay. Randy saw the chariot, near to where he had left it, two of the Horses in harness before it. He realized with a start that he was able to tell that they were not Scafflech and Finntag. Other forms moved in the water nearby.

"It is good that two of the others travel the route in harness," the man said, as if reading his mind, "and give the older ones a rest."

Randy nodded. He did not feel it appropriate to offer to shake hands. He climbed down into the chariot and untwisted the reins from the crossbar.

"Thank you," he said, "for—everything. Take good care of him. Goodbye."

"A man who dines and sleeps in the Isles of the Blessed always returns," the other said. "Good night."

Randy shook the reins and the Horses began to move. Soon they were in open water. The new Horses were fresh and spirited. Suddenly Randy found himself singing to them.

They sped east along the path of the moon.

A Word from Zelazny

"I sent this one to *The Saturday Evening Post.* Three times. They kept losing the ms. I stopped."[1]

Notes

The ***Book of Kells***, written and illustrated by Irish monks contains the Gospels in Latin. **Lir** is the sea god in Irish mythology. **Erse** is Gaelic. In Greek and Celtic mythology, heroes and other favored mortals populate the **Isles of the Blessed** after death; King Arthur's Avalon was probably a variant of this myth.

1 *Unicorn Variations*, 1983.

FRIEND

To Spin Is Miracle Cat, Underwood-Miller 1981.
Written 1955–60 for *Chisel in the Sky.*

While it does not blaze,
always sparkles,
the procession of thy wit.

While it does not thunder,
always grumbles,
the stomach of thy wrath.

While it does not wing,
always hurries,
the caravan of thy heart.

And like a mountain lake,
art thou a deep, cool,
magnificent swindler of the sun.

Notes

The title is an ironic one, given the text that follows.

Recital

A Rhapsody in Amber, Cheap Street 1981.

The woman is singing. She uses a microphone, a thing she did not have to do in her younger days. Her voice is still fairly good, but nothing like what it was when she drew standing ovations at the Met. She is wearing a blue dress with long sleeves, to cover a certain upper-arm flabbiness. There is a small table beside her, bearing a pitcher of water and a glass. As she completes her number a wave of applause follows. She smiles, says "Thank you" twice, coughs, gropes (not obtrusively), locates the pitcher and glass, carefully pours herself a drink.

Let's call her Mary. I don't know that much about her yet, and the name has just occurred to me. I'm Roger Z, and I'm doing all of this on the spot, rather than in the standard smooth and clean fashion. This is because I want to watch it happen and find things out along the way.

So Mary is a character and this is a story, and I know that she is over the hill and fairly sick. I try to look through her eyes now and discover that I cannot. It occurs to me that she is probably blind and that the great hall in which she is singing is empty.

Why? And what is the matter with her eyes?

I believe that her eye condition is retrobulbar neuritis, from which she could probably recover in a few weeks, or even a few days. Except that she will likely be dead before then. This much seems certain to me here. I see now that it is only a side symptom of a more complex sclerotic condition which has worked her over pretty well during the past couple of years. Actually, she is lucky to be able still to sing as well as she can. I notice that she is leaning upon the table—as unobtrusively as possible—while she drinks.

All of this came quickly, along with the matter of the hall. Does she realize that she is singing to an empty house, that all of the audience noises are recorded? It is a put-on job and she is being conned by someone who loved her and wants to give her this strange evening before she falls down the dark well with no water or bottom to it.

Who? I ask.

A man, I suppose. I don't see him clearly yet, back in the shadowy control booth, raising the volume a little more before he lets it diminish. He is also taping the entire program. Is he smiling? I don't know yet. Probably. He loved her years ago, when she was bright and new and suddenly celebrated and just beginning her rise to fame. I use the past tense of the main verb, just to cover myself at this point.

Did she love him? I don't think so. Was she cruel? Maybe a little. From his viewpoint, yes; from hers, not really. I can't see all of the circumstances of their breakup clearly enough to judge. It is not that important, though. The facts as given should be sufficient.

The hall has grown silent once again. She bows, smiling, and announces her next number. As she begins to sing it, the man—let us call him John—leans back in his seat, eyes half-lidded and listens. He is, of course, remembering. Naturally, he has followed her career. There was a time when he had hated her and all of her flashy lovers. He had never been particularly flashy himself. The others have all left her now. She is pretty much alone in the world and has been out of sight of it for a long while. She was also fairly broke when she received this invitation to sing. It surprised her more than a little. Even broke, though, it was not the money she was offered but a final opportunity to hear some applause that prompted her to accept.

Now she is struggling valiantly. This particular piece had worried her. She is nearing the section where her voice could break. It was pure vanity that made her include it in the program. John leans forward as she nears the passage. He had realized the burden it would place upon her—for he is an aficionado, which is how and why he first came to meet her. His hand moves forward and rests upon a switch.

He is not wealthy. He has practically wiped himself out financially, renting this hall, paying her fee, arranging for all of the small subterfuges: a maid in her dressing room, a chauffeured limousine, an enthusiastic theater manager, a noisy stage crew—actors all. They departed when she began her performance. Now there are only the two of them in the building, both of them wondering what will happen when reaches that crucial passage.

I am not certain how Isak Dinesen would have handled this, for her ravaged face is suddenly in my mind's eye as I begin to realize where all of this is coming from. The switch, I see now, will activate a special tape of catcalls and hootings. It was already cued back when I used the past tense of the verb. It may, after all, be hate rather than love that is responsible for this expensive private show. Yes. John knew of Mary's vanity from long ago, which is why he chose this form of revenge—a thing that will strike her where she is most vulnerable.

She begins the passage. Her head is turned, and it appears that she is staring directly at him, there in the booth. Even knowing that this is impossible, he shifts uneasily. He looks away. He listens. He waits.

She has done it! She has managed the passage without a lapse. Something of her old power seems to be growing within her. Once past that passage, her voice seems somewhat stronger, as if she has drawn some heartening reassurance from it. Perhaps the fact that this must be her last performance has also stoked the banked fires of her virtuosity. She is singing beautifully now, as she has not in years.

John lets his hand slip from the control board and leans back again. It would not serve his purpose to use that tape without an obvious reason. She is too much a professional. She would know that it was not warranted. Her vanity would sustain her through a false reaction. He must wait. Sooner or later, her voice has to fail. Then…

He closes his eyes as he listens to the song. The renewed energy in her performance causes him to see her as she once was. Somewhere, she is beautiful again.

He must move quickly at the end of this number. Lost in reverie, he had almost forgotten the applause control. He draws this one out. She is bowing in his direction now, almost as if…

No!

She has collapsed. The last piece was too much for her. He is on his feet and out the door, rushing down the stairs. It can't end this way… He had not anticipated her exerting herself to this extent for a single item and then not making it beyond it—even if it was one of her most famous pieces. It strikes him as very unfair.

He hurries up the aisle and onto the stage. He is lifting her, holding a glass of water to her lips. The applause tape is still running.

She looks at him.

"You can see!"

She nods and takes a drink.

"For a moment, during the last song, my vision began to clear. It is still with me. I saw the hall. Empty. I had feared I could not get through that song. Then I realized that someone from among my admirers cared enough to give me this last show. I sang to that person. You. And the song was there..."

"Mary..."

A fumbled embrace. He raises her in his arms—straining, for she is heavier and he is older now.

He carries her back to the dressing room and phones for an ambulance. The hall is still filled with applause and she is smiling as she drifts into delirium, hearing it.

She dies at the hospital the following morning, John at her bedside. She mentions the names of many men before this happens, none of them his. He feels he should be bitter, knowing he has served her vanity this final time. But he is not. Everything else in her life had served it also, and perhaps this had been a necessary condition for her greatness—and each time that he plays the tape, when he comes to that final number, he knows that it was for him alone—and that that was more than she had ever given to anyone else.

I do not know what became of him afterward. When the moral is reached it is customary to close—hopefully with a striking image. But all that I see striking now are typewriter keys, and I am fairly certain that he would have used the catcall tape at the end if she had finished the performance on a weak note. But, of course, she didn't. Which is why he was satisfied. For he was an aficionado before he was a lover, and one loves different things in different places.

There is also a place of understanding, but it is difficult, and sometimes unnecessary, to find it.

A Word from Zelazny

"I feel that every now and then one should play around with the storytelling act itself to help maintain one's appreciation for narrative forms. Look where it got Joyce, Pirandello, Kafka and All Those Guys. My ambition along these lines is considerably smaller, however. That's why it's a very short story."[1]

Notes

The Met is New York City's Metropolitan Opera House. **Retrobulbar neuritis** is blindness, sometimes temporary, due to inflammation of the optic nerves. Mary has **multiple sclerosis**, and the blindness is one manifestation of this condition. An **aficionado** is knowledgeable and enthusiastic about a subject or pastime. **Isak Dinesen** was the pen name of Danish author Baroness Karen von Blixen-Finecke, who wrote *Out of Africa*.

1 *Unicorn Variations*, 1983.

The Burning

When Pussywillows Last in the Catyard Bloomed, Norstrilia Press 1980.

No animal should be as bright as Blake's Tiger
and I never want to see one.
Forests at night are disturbing enough,
but while mean kids sometimes douse a cat with petrol
and set it alight
for small, cruel laughs at its meteor runs,
its howls,
who has eye, hand or stomach
(let's just call it "guts")
enough to try it with Thee?

More than simple cruelty would have to be involved.
An existential temper, most likely.
As in, "No other is responsible for this act.
Free, spontaneous and unpremeditated,
I have decided to set fire
to this sleeping Tiger I have just now noticed
and burn it away to a grin."

Or perhaps the matter lies
in the hands and the eyes,
not mortal, but im-.
—A grotesque concept is involved:
There is this being
with immortal hands and eyes.

Shoot it, stab it, gas it—
It dies.
But the eyes accuse,
the fingers twitch,
as if they'd like to twine your heartstrings
and have all the time in the world to do it,
you son of a bitch.

Considering it every which way,
it is the sort of thing a primate
would contemplate.
I can't see Thee
doing it to me, Tiger.

A cosmic SPCA seems the answer.
It is too late to do much but admonish
after the act has occurred.
Primates with immortal parts bear watching, anyhow.
And I can do without fearful, striped incendiaries
rushing by me in the night,
God knows. Write your Representative.
Preserve symmetry. Save the Tiger.

Notes

"Blake's Tiger" refers to William Blake's poem "The Tyger," which begins "Tyger! Tyger! burning bright || In the forests of the night, || What immortal hand or eye || Could frame thy fearful symmetry?" **SPCA** is the Society for the Prevention of Cruelty to Animals.

Dance

Amazing, July 1981.

Any minute now
the words will replay themselves
within the mind's ear:
The clown and the singer
fail at last,
juggler of hearts
and crier at the sticking place
falter,
footing lost, voice broken,
embracing in the downward spinning,
and clown take up the cry,
falling caller
catch the dark staccato
laughter, netless
in the minute's eye.

Notes

Staccato means that musical notes or sounds are short and detached from the surrounding notes.

And I Only Am Escaped to Tell Thee

Twilight Zone #2, May 1981.

It was with them constantly—the black patch directly overhead from whence proceeded the lightnings, the near-blinding downpour, the explosions like artillery fire.

Van Berkum staggered as the ship shifted again, almost dropping the carton he carried. The winds howled about him, tearing at his soaked garments; the water splashed and swirled about his ankles—retreating, returning, retreating. High waves crashed constantly against the ship. The eerie, green light of St. Elmo's fire danced along the spars.

Above the wind and over even the thunder, he heard the sudden shriek of a fellow seaman, random object of attention from one of their drifting demonic tormentors.

Trapped high in the rigging was a dead man, flensed of all flesh by the elements, his bony frame infected now by the moving green glow, right arm flapping as if waving—or beckoning.

Van Berkum crossed the deck to the new cargo site, began lashing his carton into place. How many times had they shifted these cartons, crates and barrels about? He had lost count long ago. It seemed that every time the job was done a new move was immediately ordered.

He looked out over the railing. Whenever he was near, whenever the opportunity presented itself, he scanned the distant horizon, dim through the curtain of rain. And he hoped.

In this, he was different. Unlike any of the others, he had a hope—albeit a small one—for he had a plan.

❖ ❖ ❖

A mighty peal of laughter shook the ship. Van Berkum shuddered. The captain stayed in his cabin almost constantly now, with a keg of rum. It was said that he was playing cards with the Devil. It sounded as if the Devil had just won another hand.

Pretending to inspect the cargo's fastenings, Van Berkum located his barrel again, mixed in with all the others. He could tell it by the small dab of blue paint. Unlike the others it was empty, and caulked on the inside.

Turning, he made his way across the deck again. Something huge and bat-winged flitted past him. He hunched his shoulders and hurried.

Four more loads, and each time a quick look into the distance. Then— Then…?

Then!

He saw it. There was a ship off the port bow! He looked about frantically. There was no one near him. This was it. If he hurried. If he was not seen.

He approached his barrel, undid the fastenings, looked about again. Still no one nearby. The other vessel definitely appeared to be approaching. There was neither time nor means to calculate courses, judge winds or currents. There was only the gamble and the hope.

He took the former and held to the latter as he rolled the barrel to the railing, raised it, and cast it overboard. A moment later he followed it.

The water was icy, turbulent, dark. He was sucked downward. Frantically he clawed at it, striving to drag himself to the surface.

Finally there was a glimpse of light. He was buffeted by waves, tossed about, submerged a dozen times. Each time, he fought his way back to the top.

He was on the verge of giving up when the sea suddenly grew calm. The sounds of the storm softened. The day began to grow brighter about him. Treading water, he saw the vessel he had just quitted receding in the distance, carrying its private hell along with it. And there, off to his left, bobbed the barrel with the blue marking. He struck out after it.

When he finally reached it, he caught hold. He was able to draw himself partly out of the water. He clung there and panted. He shivered. Although the sea was calmer here, it was still very cold.

When some of his strength returned, he raised his head, scanned the horizon.

There!

The vessel he had sighted was even nearer now. He raised an arm and waved it. He tore off his shirt and held it high, rippling in the wind like a banner.

He did this until his arm grew numb. When he looked again the ship was nearer still, though there was no indication that he had been sighted. From what appeared to be their relative movements, it seemed that he might well drift past it in a matter of minutes. He transferred the shirt to his other hand, began waving it again.

❖ ❖ ❖

When next he looked, he saw that the vessel was changing course, coming toward him. Had he been stronger and less emotionally drained, he might have wept. As it was, he became almost immediately aware of a mighty fatigue and a great coldness. His eyes stung from the salt, yet they wanted to close. He had to keep looking at his numbed hands to be certain that they maintained their hold upon the barrel.

"Hurry!" he breathed. "Hurry…"

He was barely conscious when they took him into the lifeboat and wrapped him in blankets. By the time they came alongside the ship, he was asleep.

He slept the rest of that day and all that night, awakening only long enough to sip hot grog and broth. When he did try to speak, he was not understood.

It was not until the following afternoon that they brought in a seaman who spoke Dutch. He told the man his entire story, from the time he had signed aboard until the time he had jumped into the sea.

"Incredible!" the seaman observed, pausing after a long spell of translation for the officers. "Then that storm-tossed apparition we saw yesterday was really the *Flying Dutchman*! There truly *is* such a thing—and you, you are the only man to have escaped from it!"

Van Berkum smiled weakly, drained his mug, and set it aside, hands still shaking.

The seaman clapped him on the shoulder.

"Rest easy now, my friend. You are safe at last," he said, "free of the demon ship. You are aboard a vessel with a fine safety record and excellent officers and crew—and just a few days away from her port. Recover your strength and rid your mind of past afflictions. We welcome you aboard the *Marie Celeste*."

A Word from Zelazny

"Here is another of those short shorts I dearly enjoy doing when the opportunity and the idea come together. I tend to see things like this as single-panel, briefly captioned cartoons—and I work backward a little from there."[1]

Notes

St. Elmo's Fire is a luminous electrical discharge that appears on a ship or aircraft during a storm. **Flensed** means that the skin and fat has been stripped from the carcass. The ***Flying Dutchman*** is a ghost ship that can never go home but is doomed to sail the seven seas forever. Sight of this phantom ship is reckoned by seafarers to be a portent of doom. **Grog** is a hot drink of rum and water, flavored with lemon, sugar, and spices. The ***Marie Celeste*** of Boston was discovered off the coast of Portugal in 1872, under full sail, steering an erratic course, completely deserted, no life boats missing, no sign of panic or disorder, breakfast laid on the table, tea still lukewarm, the galley-range still hot, the captain's watch still ticking. What happened to her crew remains a mystery, and she has become the archetypical ghost ship. Of course, this means that the unlucky protagonist escaped from one ghost ship only to end up on another.

1 *Unicorn Variations*, 1983.

SHADOWJACK

The Illustrated Roger Zelazny, Baronet 1978 (graphic story).
The Last Defender of Camelot, Underwood-Miller edition only, 1981 (text story).
§ *Shadowjack*

I passed through mountain fastnesses, skirting the realm of a certain Lord Belring, whose reputation I'd no desire to test. It was unfamiliar territory for me, and when I saw the grinning warning below a gargoyle-mounted keep, I decided I had no need to pursue an acquaintance there either.

Ye who would wish to live
tread no further than this line
lest you would care
to wear a smile like mine—

But there was a stirring on the ugly farm above me. For a moment, I simply watched, uncertain whether my eyes were playing me fair...

...A moment only. I enjoy a grisly spectacle as well as the next man, but I'd no desire to become the object of one. When the things went airborne, I hit for cover, with an eye for the shadows that would shield me.

I located a small patch of gray as they swooped toward me and circled above.

My images darted within that place—but the place was not all that large, and the shadow itself was wavering as their wings beat above me, partly blocking a dim light from the castle...

...and there were too many of them. Enough to strike at each flickering Jack and the one substantial one. When the arms I could not avoid came at me, I let go my images and drew the remaining force the shadows had lent me back into myself.

I have always preferred stealth to violence. It is indecent to be outweighed, outnumbered and still have to fight. Violence, like disease or a bad debt, is better to give than receive.

I believe that my strength surprised them.

Unfortunately, their massed bodies totally obliterated the shadow and I was reduced to my own resources. These, too, I spent…but it was not my death that they sought. I did not know whether to be heartened or totally apprehensive at this. I struggled on, hoping for an opening for flight, for another patch of shadow…Alas!

Half-senseless, I was taken, borne aloft, flown through the darkness to that dark height from which the things had come.

As we dropped toward it, I could see that it was old, and I could taste the flavors of the delicate sorceries brewed within it.

When I was hauled into the presence of the chef, I had to admit it was an improvement over the gnarled wizards I occasionally encountered…

"So you are Shadowjack," she said. "I know your reputation. I apologize for the abrupt means by which I sought your acquaintance…

"…I have to admit I find your appearance more pleasing than I had anticipated. I'd visions of a dirty little skulker in shadows, and you are far from it. Perhaps this is going to work out better than I thought."

"I've a mind to accept your apology," I told her, "since I, too, had a few visions enroute. They are exceeded however, in an unexpectedly pleasant direction."

"I am Vara Lylyra," she said, bidding her stony sentinels return to their niches. "This is my place of power. I detected your approach but recently, and had to move quickly. I will show you about—there are matters I wish to discuss."

The tour eventually took us to her bedchamber, and I wondered as to priorities—discussion first, or—?

"I require the services of the very finest thief available," she said, "to steal the Eye of Iskat."

"Oh?" I said, as she moved nearer, flame and sword-metal masked by perfume and softness. "What is the Eye of Iskat?"

"It is a gem of wondrous potency," she replied. "It enhances one's natural powers enormously. It is currently in the possession of Lord Belring of the Corners. He keeps it in his Court of the Hundred Towers. Do you know it?"

"I have heard of it," I replied. "Each tower is said to contain a bell which begins ringing if someone sets a foot within it. An effective system."

"Yes, that is the place," she said, moving even nearer. "I would like you to go there and fetch it for me."

"I have also heard something about a guardian in that place…"

"True," she said, embracing me lightly. "The old sorcerer has created some sort of brittle beast-man called the Vorkle. It tends to be somewhat transparent and difficult to see. But you, of course, are now forewarned…"

"The jewel is hidden in one of the towers?"

"I believe so, though I cannot tell which.

"That is the task I would set you, Jack. Have you an interest in it?"

I looked into her eyes.

"I have an interest," I said.

We found our way to the most useful item of furniture and I pursued my interest with great diligence.

"Jack, darling—you will be going on my errand then?" she whispered, when I thought her mind might be on other matters.

"I will be going," I said.

Later, when I was certain she was asleep, I set about doing just that—going. I gathered my garments and departed the chamber with my most professional stealth.

From my quick tour of the place, I recalled a window situated opposite a crag, beyond which I might make my escape. I was not anxious to mess with transparent beings in dark places, overseen by a sorcerer with a reputation of madness. No…

It was time to bid the Keep of Lylyra good-bye. Despite the manner of my arrival, my brief stay was hardly unpleasant. If the lady had only wanted something simpler, I could have been persuaded to remain longer…

I made my way to that place, and from the lining of my cloak I withdrew the fine, stout line which had served me so well in the past. From a sheath in my boot came the collapsable grapple which I snapped open and tied into place.

My cast went true, falling into a tight cleft. The grapple seated itself securely when I drew back upon the line. Then it was only a matter of securing my end to the bollard-like projection which had caught my eye earlier. The rest was straight from Thieves College, where I had once taught Entry & Egress 701…

As I mounted the line and regarded the wavering prospect, I was struck by the fact that it was a lot dimmer than it had been moments before. Mists had risen among the rocks. No matter. I could still see the line, I could trust my balance…

…but as I advanced, the mist continued to rise until it boiled about me. I wondered at the unnatural speed with which this occurred.

Something was definitely amiss in the area through which I moved. There was a break in the mists ahead—Somehow, I had been turned about! The road led to wings and a nasty expression!

Vara shook her head and regarded me almost wistfully. "This, thief, is how you keep your word? I am disappointed. Pity. I would rather you served me willingly. Guards! Show him to a cell!"

As I was introduced to my new lodgings, Vara regarded them with disapproval. "It is said that you have a way with shadows," she stated. "Something must be done to prevent your employing them here."

She raised her hands. As she spoke, her form began to glow. Waves of light swept over her, collecting finally about her hands. I was half-blinded by the brilliance of her working, and I sought to shield my eyes from the light.

Blazing bands took form about me, removing any possibility of my making contact with shadow.

"Is mine not a lovely light?" she said, smiling. "These are fetters you cannot slip. I will leave you now to contemplate your ways. *Adieu.*"

Whenever I am spoken of in shadow, I know what is said… In the shadowy confines of her chamber, Vara regarded me in her crystal and muttered her displeasure at the faithlessness of men. Then her eyes grew bright. "A doppelgänger!" she said, clapping her hands. "I will send his double—with all his skills and none of his mischief!"

Then she began a fresh spell, and I felt a pang in my breast as she did so. This was dangerous magic indeed—for the duplicated. The longer a doppelgänger exists, the weaker his principal becomes, until finally…

It would be identical to me in physical respects, though lacking those charming intangibles which make me what I am. I worried within my fetters of light. I could begin to fade as it exerted itself, lapsing finally into total nothingness…

As she charged it with the errand I had declined, I realized that I would have to escape soon…

...I would have to escape, pursue it and be merged with it...

As it tore off through the night, heading for the Court of the Hundred Towers, I hit upon a dangerous course of action. I struggled to recall the spell Vara had used to bind me... It came back to me then, and I rehearsed it in my mind. I knew of no way to diminish the light-bands...

...But I might be able to overload the spell by reinvoking it.

I began to speak, and the brightness increased about me. Vara would soon become aware of my tampering with her working, but it might not matter by then. I shielded my eyes, completed the spell, started again...

Vara had to know what was occurring...

By the time they reached me, it was too late. The rings had wavered and broken and the cell was filled with pure light. If the final flare did not hurt me, it would certainly slow them down for a time.

I heard them enter, cry out and fall aside as the spell was shattered and I found myself still standing.

Weak, though... I was very weak as I rushed from that place and made my way out of the castle.

The gargoyles sought me, but I had already reached a well-shadowed vicinity. None could find me there against my will.

When they finally gave up, I continued on my way toward The Corners—a place where several kingdoms abut—near where Lord Belring holds his court. Weakening with every league, I struggled to make haste, wondering how my doppelgänger was faring in the court of the bells...

Monolithic, I regarded the heaped campaniles of the court, the great bells visible in many of them. Most were still, but a few had begun ringing, indicating that my double had commenced his search among the towers. I hurried ahead.

Somewhere within that place was the other Jack, and I had to find him before the Vorkle did—find him, while avoiding the Vorkle myself—and figure a way to achieve our merger. Another bell began pealing as I made my way into the court. I scanned the skyline in that direction and caught a glimpse of a figure strangely like myself leaping from one tower to another...

I began the pursuit. By now, the ringing of the bells was a palpable thing. Each new voice increased the din to the point where my ears began to throb. The matter would have to be concluded soon—I was aching.

I followed him. He was faster now, my weakness a sign of his strength. If only I could reach him, speak with him—

—But he could not hear me, even if I were to risk a shout. Another bell joined the chorus as I drew nearer. My ear-drums seemed to be bursting…

I threw myself down and tried to block out the sound of the latest bell. Its vibrations filled me. My double had escaped. I—

—I saw a movement. An almost-thing. A blurry patch of something at the window… It had to be the Vorkle. Approaching… Strong and silent and lethal… I had to regain my footing, flee… I struggled to rise, staring at the approaching creature. I summoned my remaining strength and drew myself to my feet…

It moved more quickly than I had thought it would. One moment it was on the other side of the room, the next it was almost upon me, glassy arms outstretched, fingers flexing, translucent muscles bulging with each movement.

I swirled my cloak as I cast about for the readiest retreat. My eyes fell upon the stairway leading to the bell tower…

I whirled and raced in that direction, feeling rather than hearing my pursuer, close behind.

When I came to the room where the great bell was hung I sighed, for there were shadows, and more shadows…

I drew the shadows about me like an extra cloak and released them again. They spread about the room, image after image of myself, each fleeing, dancing, darting in a different direction. For a moment, the Vorkle stood like an ice sculpture, baffled at the display. But then he moved, turning—first one way, then another—flailing his arms, reaching out, grasping after, seeking to destroy one of my images after another. The huge bell swung to and fro, its peals deafening me to any noise the creature might be making.

I moved my images faster and faster, twisting, spinning, tumbling before him, about him. He turned and turned, seeming to grow more bewildered with each pass. Between the pealing and this action, however, I felt my strength begin to wane once again. Was I—the real me—becoming as transparent as this creature I faced?

His confusion increased as I moved my shadow-puppets with the last of my strength, causing them to advance and retreat from all directions. —But the bell! My skull seemed riven now by each stroke of the thing.

For a moment, I grew dizzy from the strain. My shadows returned to shadow and I felt my knees begin to buckle. I must have stood revealed for only an instant, but in that moment the Vorkle saw me and turned…

…He turned and took a step. I would like to take credit for the planning of it, for the subtle manipulation of my foe, but it was pure chance that bore the confused creature to that position at precisely that moment. The bell had swung to, but it was the fro that got him. With a sound like the crashing of a wine rack in a barroom brawl the bell connected with the Vorkle and his shards flew in all directions, as it tolled for him indeed.

As I regarded the creature's remains, the skin on my neck crawled, as though I, myself, might at that moment be an object of scrutiny… and why not? My double was somewhere near, and the mad lord of this place could hardly be unaware of what had transpired.

If Belring had seen the destruction of his guardian, he would doubtless be heading to brew some new mischief.

I had a picture of him as he had been described to me—stocky and strong. If just a few minutes of his music had affected my mind so, I wondered what they might have done to his, over the years.

As a mumbler, a curser, he was first-class. I heard my name both in his musings and in the spell which followed. His magic troubled me more than a little…

Within a smoky mirror he conjured up my form, his warped sense of humor doubtless drawing delight from my difficulties. No true doppelgänger this lethal image, however. The new double was formed of elements which would prove instantly fatal to me were I to merge with it rather than the one I sought…

As he summoned it forth from the mirror, my thinning blood ran even colder. How could I possibly distinguish it from the other?

Somewhere in shadow, I heard him speak my name again as he sent it forth to work my confusion.

After that, I knew no more of his thoughts. The thing was on its way, to complete the work the Vorkle had started.

Had he only known how weak I had actually become, he might have saved his efforts. I did not believe I could last much longer…

Yet I struggled on, down mazes of corridors—seeking. My only hope now seemed to be to locate the Eye of Iskat. If Vara of the anthracite heart had spoken anything of the truth and the jewel could indeed heighten one's natural powers, I might be able to employ it on my own behalf.

I came at last to a huge room filled with bells and chimes of every sort. There, I was forced to rest for a moment. They were all ringing—*No*—something strange…

I wondered as I regarded each of them in turn what it was summoning my attention. Where would that insidious old devil have hidden the thing? I was certain he was confident of his safety. Yet…

No good. I'd a strong feeling it was in this room, and that I was missing something obvious. I would listen again, at each separate bell. It seemed the only thing left to try…

As I regarded them, I wondered how near my doppelgänger might be. I wondered, too, where the other double was. It had had time to search for me…

Then, then, then…It struck me. A tiny bell near at hand was swinging but not ringing. Could its clapper have been set so as not to strike the shell? Of course—and the reason for that would be to protect something precious against fracture. I seized it and drew upon the clapper…Success!

…and as I turned, feeling victory glowing in my hand, I beheld both of them—my two doubles: the first wanting the jewel, the other my life. Both advanced upon me in a menacing fashion.

Both raised their hands and became like magnets, drawing upon the energies that held me together. I had been a fool even to wonder whether I might reason with my own. There could be no truce here…

But I was too weak to resist. Their combined forces left me barely able to move. Not even the jewel could help me now.

I fell to the floor and the stone rolled from my hand. There was one thing left that I could trust…

The jewel occupied the same patch of shadow into which I had let my arms fall. This much I had gauged correctly. A moment later, and the boot of one of my doubles came down beside it. Therefore…

The one wanted my life, the other the stone… Now I knew which was which, as he reached for it, there in the same piece of shadow I occupied. He was about to be enlightened—or should I say enshadowed?

My hands were not where they had seemed. One took his ankle as the other recovered the jewel…

Then drawing upon the shadow force, and focussing through the Eye of Iskat, I summoned back that part of myself which had gone into the making of the doppelgänger. It vanished as the energies returned to me.

My strength recovered, I rose then to confront the double Belring had cast. The jewel pulsed in my hand as the shadow forces swirled within me.

The double drew back as if it had been burned. It turned then and headed for the stair.

It was harmless to me now, and it reminded me too much of someone I knew for me to pursue it. I watched it flee. Somewhere, Lord Belring would soon be aware that I had his jewel and had avoided his final trap.

It was not difficult to guess at his reaction, which is why I hurried.

I made for a section of wall at the edge of the court where a long streak of shadow permitted a drop I could not have made otherwise. It was so good to be substantial again, I decided as my feet hit the ground.

I kept moving till distance dimmed the din of those damned bells and the place of the Corners was far behind me.

Darkness and silence floated outside the Keep of Lylyra. The heavy shadows were my friends.

Even within, they helped me. I slid like a ghost past the guards.

Then I headed up to the lady's chamber for a final call. Are you watching, Morningstar? Not even the dust stirs about me…

I made a small noise as I entered the chamber, intentionally. She was awake in an instant.

"Jack? There in the shadows? It could only be you…

"You have returned, as I knew you would. Come to me, for I have missed you.

"It is good that you are back. I intend for you to remain here.

"Yes, hold me, dear Jack. I will see that you remember this moment for as long as you live…"

A blade flashed in her hand.

I watched the shadow-image fall. She rose quickly. It was time for me to move.

"Hello, Vara," I said, emerging from shadow as my image faded.

"Phantom!" she responded.

"I brought the Eye of Iskat, as you requested, my dear."

I turned its force upon her.

"…You see, I want you to remember this moment for as long as you live."

She fell back.

"Dwindle, compress, darken.

"...As hard and black as your heart, my dear."

I picked up the lump of coal she had become and tossed it into the fireplace.

"...Though you'll still give a lovely light."

I am certain Vara would have appreciated the finesse with which I managed that final encounter—were she able to view it dispassionately, that is. Had she possessed a somewhat different temperament, I am certain that I could have enjoyed her company for a long while. But then, of course, such a woman would not be Vara and I could conceivably find myself wishing for someone like the original. It was probably better for both of us that the only change the jewel could effect was a matter of form. —Jack, you're getting sentimental. Life, after all, is a place where we steal for pleasure and profit, each in our own way; and we, of course, are but shadows who have stolen a little of light...

A Word from Zelazny

This story is a prequel to *Jack of Shadows* and appeared as a graphic story (comic) before this text-only version. "People sometimes ask me whether the title *Jack of Shadows* was intended to sound like a description of a playing card used in some arcane game, as well as representing my protagonist's name and a matter of geography. Answer: Yes. I've long been fascinated by odd decks of cards, and I had an extensive collection of them at one time. 'Ha!' they usually respond on hearing this admission. 'Then this business about the cards and the reference to shadows ties this story in at some subterranean psychological level with your Amber books, right?' Well, no. The last time I was down in the catacombs I couldn't locate any connection. I was simply attracted by the imagery. On the other hand, nobody ever asked me, 'Why Jack?' I could have answered that one: Jack Vance... I'd worked things out to find a title with 'Jack' in it as a private bit of homage publicly displayed. Now you all know... And yes, I did once do a short graphic prequel ("Shadowjack") in collaboration with artist Gray Morrow, in *The Illustrated Roger Zelazny*."[1]

This prequel began with artist Gray Morrow; he requested a new story about Jack of Shadows, "and he told me certain scenes that he probably would really enjoy illustrating, and gave a rough idea for a story he had in mind...I made it into a stronger outline, and stronger storyline, and sent

1 Forward to *Jack of Shadows*, Signet 1989 edition.

it back. He took my story outline and roughed out the panels and sent me the artwork. I went through each panel and wrote the captions...that was a genuine collaboration. It was kind of fun."[2]

"...So this is the story that Jack built—with a little help from me on the paperwork. Picture him if you will as a Figure on a playing card. Make it a Tarot. Maybe the Broken Tower..."[3]

"The world on which [this story] is set is distinctive in that one side of it constantly faces its sun. This daylight side is ruled by the laws of science...the dark side...by the laws of magic. ...Jack is neither a darksider nor a daysider, but a creature of twilight, having been born in the grey area between the two realms. His power is not dependent upon place, but upon the presence of shadows, with which he has a magical affinity."[4]

"This story, set early in his career, brings him into contact with other darksiders in their places of power, where he must pit his cunning and his shadowforce against them."[4]

Notes

A **bollard** is a thick, low post to which mooring lines from vessels are attached. A **doppelgänger** is a person's ghostly double. **Campaniles** are bell towers. **Riven** means split apart. **Anthracite** is hard coal that burns without flame. **"...as it tolled for him indeed"** refers to John Donne's poem *Meditation XVII,* "never send to know for whom the bell tolls; it tolls for thee."

2 *Media Sight* Vol 3 No 1 Summer 1984.
3 Forward to *Jack of Shadows*, Signet 1989 edition.
4 *The Last Defender of Camelot*, Underwood-Miller edition, 1981.

SHADOWS

To Spin Is Miracle Cat, Underwood-Miller 1981.
Written 1955–60 for *Chisel in the Sky*.

Bleak disappointments
rage
this coming-together-place:
menace of sighs
in jeopardy of time.
Vindication and mortality
meet on the plains of Troy;
and though the dead forget the dead
in the House of Hades, Patroklus,
even there shall he remember thee,
and this day.

But the ember does not burn backward
to timber;
its visible music
shapes the air
to heat,
but the day is no longer.

Notes

Patroklus / Patroclus appears in Homer's *Iliad* as the best friend (and, some say, lover) of Achilles. When Achilles refused to fight, Patroclus donned Achilles's armor and died on the plains of Troy, leaving Achilles to mourn him.

SHADOWJACK: CHARACTER BIOGRAPHY

Wizards, ed. Bill Fawcett, Mayfair Games 1983.
§ *Shadowjack*

Shadowjack (also known as Jack of Shadows) enjoys a unique position on his peculiar world. The planet he inhabits keeps one face perpetually turned to its sun. On the dayside, the laws of science prevail and the hemisphere is kept from frying by means of powerful force screens which temper the primary's light. The nightside is a realm of magic, kept from freezing by means of a series of interlocked magical spells. Science does not operate on the nightside, nor does magic function on the dayside.

Many of the beings born in the dark hemisphere possess magical powers. These, mainly, are keyed to certain locales—"places of power" for these individuals—so that many possess a certain territory, kingdom, or realm. (Border wars are common, at places where adjacent shadows are about equally balanced. Also, there are some magical instruments which may be moved from place to place.) Jack's power is peculiar because it grants him mobility. He was born in the twilight area between the dayside and the nightside, and his is a power involving shadows.

Wherever shadows exist Jack can draw strength, granting him physical prowess, invisibility, levitation, illusion-casting. He also has the ability to hear what is said whenever he is spoken of in shadow. This, coupled with a natural sneakiness and deftness, has helped considerably in his long and successful career as a thief. About six feet tall, dark-haired, dark-eyed, and clad generally in gray, he established his reputation by penetrating many of the magical realms of the world's dark side to steal objects of intrinsic value as well as talismans, jewels, wands, and books representing exportable magical quantities.

The nightsiders are soulless (hence, not particularly compassionate) creatures possessed of more than one life. Each of them knows exactly how many lives he, she, or it possesses, and each keeps this number secret as it would be an obvious source of strength to an enemy. (Jack shares this feature with the others.) When one gets down to the last few lives one tends to become more conservative and would rather bluff than take risks.

One's resurrection/return following the loss of one's life always occurs at the west pole of the world in a particularly noxious place known as the Dung Pits of Glyve—the place where refuse tends to find its home. One is then faced with a perilous journey back to one's home, requiring outwitting or outfighting the people or creatures who prey upon those who return, as they pass through generally unfriendly realms.

Jack claims that he possesses a hidden realm—Shadowguard. Whether or not he is lying is unknown. No one else has ever seen it and told about it.

Jack's best friend is a demonic or Promethean figure (depending upon how one views these matters)—Morningstar, a giant horned being from the waist up. He is fused with a mountain peak below the waist, and he faces the east, looking toward the place of the dawn which never occurs. It is said that if the sun ever rises he will be freed. He is virtually omniscient, yet almost totally powerless when it comes to influencing events. He seems to have played either a heroic, or a sinister role (or both) in the creation of this world.

Any nightsider may periodically be magically summoned, to stand "shield duty"—i.e., to contribute his forces and skills for a time in a magical operation required to maintain the shield spells which hold back the cold of outer space. To refuse this duty would be to become a pariah. No one does.

Jack's twilight heritage also permits him to wander over to the dayside in the course of his activities—a place ordinarily shunned by the nightsiders. His understanding of this area, at one point, is sufficient to permit him to use a dayside computer to solve for the gaps in a fragmentary magical spell as if it were an equation of peculiar complexity.

Jack's chief enemy in the novel is the Lord of Bats. Another enemy is the Colonel Who Never Died. At one point, Jack is pursued by a particularly grisly creation of the Lord of Bats—the Borshin, a being capable of pursuing him to the planet's dayside.

Other enemies Jack has known include the mad Lord Belring and the sorceress Vara Lylyra. Standing in strong shadow Jack's power is stronger than that of a vampire, and he has occasionally surprised one which has pursued him into shadows by drinking its blood—if he happened to be in dire need of sustenance.

Jack's only honest employment of record may have been when he worked as a lecturer in Anthropology at a dayside university for two terms, acquitting himself surprisingly well. He used the name Jonathan Shade at that time.

Notes

Zelazny wrote this biography to introduce a variation of *Dungeons & Dragons* based on the settings and characters of *Jack of Shadows*.

GREAT CUMMINGS

Written 1955–60 for *Chisel in the Sky;* previously unpublished.

FROM
                me

TO
                you

WITH
                love

Notes

The title and use of lowercased words refer to the poet e e **cummings**.

The Man Without a Shadow

Skyline, April 1958.
Written 1955–58 for *Chisel in the Sky.*

What master were he of brush or of graver, who drew the shades and the lineaments, which there would make every subtle wit stare?
—*Purgatorio*, Canto XII.

"Machine-like, I saw Achilles
Challenge the gods with the inevitable conflict
Of mortal desires that even the son of a god
Did not lay at the feet of those that formed him.
And I saw him lie
Like Balder spread,
With that mortal tree drawing of his fluids
And shivering against the violent sky,
Upgrown from his pierced member
Upon the darkening ground.
And their open faces sounded
While she, the distant Polyxena, sister of Cassandra,
Spoke nothing, but was believed
Of pity and known of fear.

Unbelieving, I saw Osiris
Enter the House of the Dead
On that Great Day when all the days and years
Were numbered and, yet, saw that his name
Was given back to him,

And, too, the lacerate parts
Were re-formed and rose again
And strode again.
And great Isis, before those merciless members
Was undone, and unbelieving
Felt the movement of his nightclaimed torse
Those very hands
Had seen to the rending
While she played the great adultress
To a brother god.

Godlike, I saw the great Odysseus,
Wielder of the blinding brand,
Retriever of the goddess-image,
And bender of that bow,
Fall unknowing to the unknown slaughter
Of an unknown son
Of his own limbs that lay with the darkness
Of she that made men what they were
In all but flesh.
Beloved of her, the dark one,
And also beloved of her
That may never know love,
He took to race of arms
With his own, by darkness,
And fell before his dark own
That even she of the aegis could not hold.

I saw the gods walk by
In vain procession long
To the distant doom of the home
Of the eater of gods
That throbbed with the constant thunder
Of clashing teeth, tongue and jaws
That consumed their Burgundy and cakes
While bearing perpetually
Their unwanted sons.
And the gods came by in their trappings
Of yellow, purple and awful red,
And, asking that it might pass from them,

Shuffled their feet near the end
And thought of a thousand undone trivia
That lay behind, and looked furtively aside
For open doors in the labyrinth
That might lead the way away.
But when these could not be found,
Strove to bear themselves like noble men.

And the unwanted sons inherited
The lands of their fathers
When the fathers were no more
Than outlandish names and strange figures
Cast in stone, mud, wood and straw,
While the filmier integument of the earth
Yet held their horrors
Constantly stirring in green chambers.
And the universe is a blue room
Where an ever-singing woman sits
At the heart of a lotus
And plays upon a stringed instrument,
Where all these have passed and passed again,
And never turns her crimson-cowled head,
Save to the subtle nuances
Of her own melody which she
Creates for an unknown lord."

Notes

While at Western Reserve University, Zelazny published this poem in *Skyline,* the university's literary magazine. It was reprinted several times. Zelazny apparently forgot about this original publication when he quoted a later publication (*Amra* Vol 2 #34, May 1965) as its first appearance. The line "we re-formed and rose again" appeared in previous publications but is now corrected to the original "were re-formed and rose again" after review of the original *Chisel in the Sky* manuscript.

The poem mixes together Greek (**Achilles, Odysseus**), Norse (**Balder**) and Egyptian (**Osiris, Isis**) mythologies just as *Lord of Light* and *Creatures of Light and Darkness* juxtapose mythologies and religions.

The title is a Faustian reference to someone who has lost his soul to the devil in a bargain. Peter Schlemihl, "the shadowless man," was a character in the 1814 story "Peter Schlemihls wundersame Geschichte" who sold his shadow to the devil. Schlemihl is a Yiddish term for bungler. ***Purgatorio,* Canto XII** is a section of Dante Alighieri's *Divine Comedy*; a more modern translation of the quoted section is "What master of the pencil or the style, had traced the shades and lines, that might have made the subtlest workman wonder?"

Lineaments are distinctive characteristics. **Achilles** was a hero of the Trojan War. His mother dipped him into the river Styx, making him invulnerable except for the heel by which she held him. **Balder** is the god of light, joy, purity, beauty, innocence, and reconciliation; all living things except mistletoe swore not to harm him. The gods used Balder as a target for knives and arrows, since nothing could harm him. Envious Loki made an arrow from mistletoe and killed Balder.

Achilles fell in love with **Polyxena**, the youngest daughter of King Priam and Queen Hecuba of Troy; her father and brother Paris used her to trap Achilles at a rendezvous, where Paris killed Achilles with an arrow in his heel. Thus, Polyxena unwittingly doomed Achilles, though she loved him.

Cassandra, another daughter of Priam and Hecuba received the gift of prophecy from Apollo, who admired her beauty. When she didn't love him in return, Apollo cursed her so that no one would believe her predictions. **Osiris** is the Egyptian god of the underworld, the symbol of death and resurrection. **Isis** is the Egyptian goddess of fertility, sister and wife of Osiris, seen as a woman with a cow's horns with the solar disk between them. **Odysseus** was the Greek hero in Homer's *Odyssey*; on his return home after a long time away, he proved his identity to his wife Penelope by passing several tests, including being able to **bend** a great **bow** that no one else could.

Torse means twisted. **Aegis** was originally a symbol of Zeus or Athena put on a shield for protection; the word now simply means protection or support. **Integument** is an outer layer, such as the skin. The mythical **Lotus** plant induced a dreamy listlessness.

UNICORN VARIATION

Isaac Asimov's Science Fiction Magazine, April 1981.
Hugo Award 1982 (novelette), Seuin Award 1984 (novelette),
#2 on 1982 Locus poll (novelette), #34 on 1999 Locus all-time poll (novelette).

A bizarrerie of fires, cunabulum of light, it moved with a deft, almost dainty deliberation, phasing into and out of existence like a storm-shot piece of evening; or perhaps the darkness between the flares was more akin to its truest nature—swirl of black ashes assembled in prancing cadence to the lowing note of desert wind down the arroyo behind buildings as empty yet filled as the pages of unread books or stillnesses between the notes of a song.

Gone again. Back again. Again.

Power, you said? Yes. It takes considerable force of identity to manifest before or after one's time. Or both.

As it faded and gained it also advanced, moving through the warm afternoon, its tracks erased by the wind. That is, on those occasions when there were tracks.

A reason. There should always be a reason. Or reasons.

It knew why it was there—but not why it was *there*, in that particular locale.

It anticipated learning this shortly, as it approached the desolation-bound line of the old street. However, it knew that the reason may also come before, or after. Yet again, the pull was there and the force of its being was such that it had to be close to something.

The buildings were worn and decayed and some of them fallen and all of them drafty and dusty and empty. Weeds grew among floorboards. Birds nested upon rafters. The droppings of wild things were everywhere, and it knew them all as they would have known it, were they to meet face to face.

It froze, for there had come the tiniest unanticipated sound from somewhere ahead and to the left. At that moment, it was again phasing into existence and it released its outline which faded as quickly as a rainbow in hell, that but the naked presence remained beyond subtraction.

Invisible, yet existing, strong, it moved again. The clue. The cue. Ahead. *A gauche.* Beyond the faded word SALOON on weathered board above. Through the swinging doors. (One of them pinned alop.)

Pause and assess.

Bar to the right, dusty. Cracked mirror behind it. Empty bottles. Broken bottles. Brass rail, black, encrusted. Tables to the left and rear. In various states of repair.

Man seated at the best of the lot. His back to the door. Levi's. Hiking boots. Faded blue shirt. Green backpack leaning against the wall to his left.

Before him, on the tabletop, is the faint, painted outline of a chessboard, stained, scratched, almost obliterated. The drawer in which he had found the chessmen is still partly open.

He could no more have passed up a chess set without working out a problem or replaying one of his better games than he could have gone without breathing, circulating his blood or maintaining a relatively stable body temperature.

It moved nearer, and perhaps there were fresh prints in the dust behind it, but none noted them.

It, too, played chess.

It watched as the man replayed what had perhaps been his finest game, from the world preliminaries of seven years past. He had blown up after that—surprised to have gotten even as far as he had—for he never could perform well under pressure. But he had always been proud of that one game, and he relived it as all sensitive beings do certain turning points in their lives. For perhaps twenty minutes, no one could have touched him. He had been shining and pure and hard and clear. He had felt like the best.

It took up a position across the board from him and stared. The man completed the game, smiling. Then he set up the board again, rose and fetched a can of beer from his pack. He popped the top.

When he returned, he discovered that White's King's Pawn had been advanced to K4. His brow furrowed. He turned his head, searching the bar, meeting his own puzzled gaze in the grimy mirror. He looked under the table. He took a drink of beer and seated himself.

He reached out and moved his Pawn to K4. A moment later, he saw White's King's Knight rise slowly into the air and drift forward to settle upon KB3. He stared for a long while into the emptiness across the table before he advanced his own Knight to his KB3.

White's Knight moved to take his Pawn. He dismissed the novelty of the situation and moved his Pawn to Q3. He all but forgot the absence of a tangible opponent as the White Knight dropped back to its KB3. He paused to take a sip of beer, but no sooner had he placed the can upon the tabletop than it rose again, passed across the board and was upended. A gurgling noise followed. Then the can fell to the floor, bouncing, ringing with an empty sound.

"I'm sorry," he said, rising and returning to his pack. "I'd have offered you one if I'd thought you were something that might like it."

He opened two more cans, returned with them, placed one near the far edge of the table, one at his own right hand.

"Thank you," came a soft, precise voice from a point beyond it.

The can was raised, tilted slightly, returned to the tabletop.

"My name is Martin," the man said.

"Call me Tlingel," said the other. "I had thought that perhaps your kind was extinct. I am pleased that you at least have survived to afford me this game."

"Huh?" Martin said. "We were all still around the last time that I looked—a couple of days ago."

"No matter. I can take care of that later," Tlingel replied. "I was misled by the appearance of this place."

"Oh. It's a ghost town. I backpack a lot."

"Not important. I am near the proper point in your career as a species. I can feel that much."

"I am afraid that I do not follow you."

"I am not at all certain that you would wish to. I assume that you intend to capture that Pawn?"

"Perhaps. Yes, I do wish to. What are you talking about?"

The beer can rose. The invisible entity took another drink.

"Well," said Tlingel, "to put it simply, your—successors—grow anxious. Your place in the scheme of things being such an important one, I had sufficient power to come and check things out."

" 'Successors'? I do not understand."

"Have you seen any griffins recently?"

Martin chuckled.

"I've heard the stories," he said, "seen the photos of the one supposedly shot in the Rockies. A hoax, of course."

"Of course it must seem so. That is the way with mythical beasts."

"You're trying to say that it was real?"

"Certainly. Your world is in bad shape. When the last grizzly bear died recently, the way was opened for the griffins—just as the death of the last aepyornis brought in the yeti, the dodo the Loch Ness creature, the passenger pigeon the sasquatch, the blue whale the kraken, the American eagle the cockatrice—"

"You can't prove it by me."

"Have another drink."

Martin began to reach for the can, halted his hand and stared. A creature approximately two inches in length, with a human face, a lionlike body and feathered wings was crouched next to the beer can.

"A minisphinx," the voice continued. "They came when you killed off the last smallpox virus."

"Are you trying to say that whenever a natural species dies out a mythical one takes its place?" he asked.

"In a word—yes. Now. It was not always so, but you have destroyed the mechanisms of evolution. The balance is now redressed by those others of us, from the morning land—we, who have never truly been endangered. We return, in our time."

"And you—whatever you are, Tlingel—you say that humanity is now endangered?"

"Very much so. But there is nothing that you can do about it, is there? Let us get on with the game."

The sphinx flew off. Martin took a sip of beer and captured the Pawn.

"Who," he asked then, "are to be our successors?"

"Modesty almost forbids," Tlingel replied. "In the case of a species as prominent as your own, it naturally has to be the loveliest, most intelligent, most important of us all."

"And what are you? Is there any way that I can have a look?"

"Well—yes. If I exert myself a trifle."

The beer can rose, was drained, fell to the floor. There followed a series of rapid rattling sounds retreating from the table. The air began to flicker over a large area opposite Martin, darkening within the glowing flamework. The outline continued to brighten, its interior growing jet black. The form moved, prancing about the saloon, multitudes of tiny, cloven hoofprints scoring and cracking the floorboards. With a final, near-blinding flash it came into full view and Martin gasped to behold it.

A black unicorn with mocking, yellow eyes sported before him, rising for a moment onto its hind legs to strike a heraldic pose. The fires flared about it a second longer, then vanished.

Martin had drawn back, raising one hand defensively.

"Regard me!" Tlingel announced. "Ancient symbol of wisdom, valor and beauty, I stand before you!"

"I thought your typical unicorn was white," Martin finally said.

"I am archetypical," Tlingel responded, dropping to all fours, "and possessed of virtues beyond the ordinary."

"Such as?"

"Let us continue our game."

"What about the fate of the human race? You said—"

"...And save the small talk for later."

"I hardly consider the destruction of humanity to be small talk."

"And if you've any more beer..."

"All right," Martin said, retreating to his pack as the creature advanced, its eyes like a pair of pale suns. "There's some lager."

❖ ❖ ❖

Something had gone out of the game. As Martin sat before the ebon horn on Tlingel's bowed head, like an insect about to be pinned, he realized that his playing was off. He had felt the pressure the moment he had seen the beast—and there was all that talk about an imminent doomsday. Any run-of-the-mill pessimist could say it without troubling him, but coming from a source as peculiar as this...

His earlier elation had fled. He was no longer in top form. And Tlingel was good. Very good. Martin found himself wondering whether he could manage a stalemate.

After a time, he saw that he could not and resigned. The unicorn looked at him and smiled.

"You don't really play badly—for a human," it said.

"I've done a lot better."

"It is no shame to lose to me, mortal. Even among mythical creatures there are very few who can give a unicorn a good game."

"I am pleased that you were not wholly bored," Martin said. "Now will you tell me what you were talking about concerning the destruction of my species?"

"Oh, that," Tlingel replied. "In the morning land where those such as I dwell, I felt the possibility of your passing come like a gentle wind to my nostrils, with the promise of clearing the way for us—"

"How is it supposed to happen?"

Tlingel shrugged, horn writing on the air with a toss of the head.

"I really couldn't say. Premonitions are seldom specific. In fact, that is what I came to discover. I should have been about it already, but you diverted me with beer and good sport."

"Could you be wrong about this?"

"I doubt it. That is the other reason I am here."

"Please explain."

"Are there any beers left?"

"Two, I think."

"Please."

Martin rose and fetched them.

"Damn! The tab broke off this one," he said.

"Place it upon the table and hold it firmly."

"All right."

Tlingel's horn dipped forward quickly, piercing the can's top.

"...Useful for all sorts of things," Tlingel observed, withdrawing it.

"The other reason you're here..." Martin prompted.

"It is just that I am special. I can do things that the others cannot."

"Such as?"

"Find your weak spot and influence events to exploit it, to—hasten matters. To turn the possibility into a probability, and then—"

"*You* are going to destroy us? Personally?"

"That is the wrong way to look at it. It is more like a game of chess. It is as much a matter of exploiting your opponent's weaknesses as of exercising your own strengths. If you had not already laid the groundwork I would be powerless. I can only influence that which already exists."

"So what will it be? World War III? An ecological disaster? A mutated disease?"

"I do not really know yet, so I wish you wouldn't ask me in that fashion. I repeat that at the moment I am only observing. I am only an agent—"

"It doesn't sound that way to me."

Tlingel was silent. Martin began gathering up the chessmen.

"Aren't you going to set up the board again?"

"To amuse my destroyer a little more? No thanks."

"That's hardly the way to look at it—"

"Besides, those are the last beers."

"Oh." Tlingel stared wistfully at the vanishing pieces, then remarked, "I would be willing to play you again without additional refreshment…"

"No thanks."

"You are angry."

"Wouldn't you be, if our situations were reversed?"

"You are anthropomorphizing."

"Well?"

"Oh, I suppose I would."

"You could give us a break, you know—at least let us make our own mistakes."

"You've hardly done that yourself, though, with all the creatures my fellows have succeeded."

Martin reddened.

"Okay. You just scored one. But I don't have to like it."

"You are a good player. I know that…"

"Tlingel, if I were capable of playing at my best again, I think I could beat you."

The unicorn snorted two tiny wisps of smoke.

"Not *that* good," Tlingel said.

"I guess you'll never know."

"Do I detect a proposal?"

"Possibly. What's another game worth to you?"

Tlingel made a chuckling noise.

"Let me guess: You are going to say that if you beat me you want my promise not to lay my will upon the weakest link in mankind's existence and shatter it."

"Of course."

"And what do I get for winning?"

"The pleasure of the game. That's what you want, isn't it?"

"The terms sound a little lopsided."

"Not if you are going to win anyway. You keep insisting that you will."

"All right. Set up the board."

"There is something else that you have to know about me first."

"Yes?"

"I don't play well under pressure, and this game is going to be a terrific strain. You want my best game, don't you?"

"Yes, but I'm afraid I've no way of adjusting your own reactions to the play."

"I believe I could do that myself if I had more than the usual amount of time between moves."

"Agreed."

"I mean a lot of time."

"Just what do you have in mind?"

"I'll need time to get my mind off it, to relax, to come back to the positions as if they were only problems..."

"You mean to go away from here between moves?"

"Yes."

"All right. How long?"

"I don't know. A few weeks, maybe."

"Take a month. Consult your experts, put your computers onto it. It may make for a slightly more interesting game."

"I really didn't have that in mind."

"Then it's time that you're trying to buy."

"I can't deny that. On the other hand, I will need it."

"In that case, I have some terms. I'd like this place cleaned up, fixed up, more lively. It's a mess. I also want beer on tap."

"Okay. I'll see to that."

"Then I agree. Let's see who goes first."

Martin switched a black and a white Pawn from hand to hand beneath the table. He raised his fists then and extended them. Tlingel leaned forward and tapped. The black horn's tip touched Martin's left hand.

"Well, it matches my sleek and glossy hide," the unicorn announced.

Martin smiled, setting up the white for himself, the black pieces for his opponent. As soon as he had finished, he pushed his Pawn to K4.

Tlingel's delicate, ebon hoof moved to advance the Black King's Pawn to K4.

"I take it that you want a month now, to consider your next move?"

Martin did not reply but moved his Knight to KB3. Tlingel immediately moved a Knight to QB3.

Martin took a swallow of beer and then moved his Bishop to N5. The unicorn moved the other Knight to B3. Martin immediately castled and Tlingel moved the Knight to take his Pawn.

"I think we'll make it," Martin said suddenly, "if you'll just let us alone. We do learn from our mistakes, in time."

"Mythical beings do not exactly exist in time. Your world is a special case."

"Don't you people ever make mistakes?"

"Whenever we do they're sort of poetic."

Martin snarled and advanced his Pawn to Q4. Tlingel immediately countered by moving the Knight to Q3.

"I've got to stop," Martin said, standing. "I'm getting mad, and it will affect my game."

"You will be going, then?"

"Yes."

He moved to fetch his pack.

"I will see you here in one month's time?"

"Yes."

"Very well."

The unicorn rose and stamped upon the floor and lights began to play across its dark coat. Suddenly, they blazed and shot outward in all directions like a silent explosion. A wave of blackness followed.

Martin found himself leaning against the wall, shaking. When he lowered his hand from his eyes, he saw that he was alone, save for the knights, the bishops, the kings, the queens, their castles and both the kings' men.

He went away.

❖ ❖ ❖

Three days later Martin returned in a small truck, with a generator, lumber, windows, power tools, paint, stain, cleaning compounds, wax. He dusted and vacuumed and replaced rotten wood. He installed the windows. He polished the old brass until it shone. He stained and rubbed. He waxed the floors and buffed them. He plugged holes and washed glasses. He hauled all the trash away.

It took him the better part of a week to turn the old place from a wreck back into a saloon in appearance. Then he drove off, returned all of the equipment he had rented and bought a ticket for the Northwest.

The big, damp forest was another of his favorite places for hiking, for thinking. And he was seeking a complete change of scene, a total revision of outlook. Not that his next move did not seem obvious, standard even. Yet, something nagged…

He knew that it was more than just the game. Before that he had been ready to get away again, to walk drowsing among shadows, breathing clean air.

Resting, his back against the bulging root of a giant tree, he withdrew a small chess set from his pack, set it up on a rock he'd moved into position nearby. A fine, mistlike rain was settling, but the tree sheltered him, so far. He reconstructed the opening through Tlingel's withdrawal of the Knight to Q3. The simplest thing would be to take the Knight with the Bishop. But he did not move to do it.

He watched the board for a time, felt his eyelids drooping, closed them and drowsed. It may only have been for a few minutes. He was never certain afterward.

Something aroused him. He did not know what. He blinked several times and closed his eyes again. Then he reopened them hurriedly.

In his nodded position, eyes directed downward, his gaze was fixed upon an enormous pair of hairy, unshod feet—the largest pair of feet that he had ever beheld. They stood unmoving before him, pointed toward his right.

Slowly—very slowly—he raised his eyes. Not very far, as it turned out. The creature was only about four and a half feet in height. As it was looking at the chessboard rather than at him, he took the opportunity to study it.

It was unclothed but very hairy, with a dark brown pelt, obviously masculine, possessed of low brow ridges, deep-set eyes that matched its hair, heavy shoulders, five-fingered hands that sported opposing thumbs.

It turned suddenly and regarded him, flashing a large number of shining teeth.

"White's Pawn should take the Pawn," it said in a soft, nasal voice.

"Huh? Come on," Martin said. "Bishop takes Knight."

"You want to give me Black and play it that way? I'll walk all over you."

Martin glanced again at its feet.

"...Or give me White and let me take that Pawn. I'll still do it."

"Take White," Martin said, straightening. "Let's see if you know what you're talking about." He reached for his pack. "Have a beer?"

"What's a beer?"

"A recreational aid. Wait a minute."

Before they had finished the six-pack, the sasquatch—whose name, he had learned, was Grend—had finished Martin. Grend had quickly entered a ferocious midgame, backed him into a position of dwindling security and pushed him to the point where he had seen the end and resigned.

"That was one hell of a game," Martin declared, leaning back and considering the apelike countenance before him.

"Yes, we bigfeet are pretty good, if I do say it. It's our one big recreation, and we're so damned primitive we don't have much in the way of boards and chessmen. Most of the time, we just play it in our heads. There're not many can come close to us."

"How about unicorns?" Martin asked.

Grend nodded slowly.

"They're about the only ones can really give us a good game. A little dainty, but they're subtle. Awfully sure of themselves, though, I must say. Even when they're wrong. Haven't seen any since we left the morning land, of course. Too bad. Got any more of that beer left?"

"I'm afraid not. But listen, I'll be back this way in a month. I'll bring some more if you'll meet me here and play again."

"Martin, you've got a deal. Sorry. Didn't mean to step on your toes."

❖ ❖ ❖

He cleaned the saloon again and brought in a keg of beer which he installed under the bar and packed with ice. He moved in some bar stools, chairs and tables which he had obtained at a Goodwill store. He hung red curtains. By then it was evening. He set up the board, ate a light meal, unrolled his sleeping bag behind the bar and camped there that night.

The following day passed quickly. Since Tlingel might show up at any time, he did not leave the vicinity but took his meals there and sat about working chess problems. When it began to grow dark, he lit a number of oil lamps and candles.

He looked at his watch with increasing frequency. He began to pace. He couldn't have made a mistake. This was the proper day. He—

He heard a chuckle.

Turning about, he saw a black unicorn head floating in the air above the chessboard. As he watched, the rest of Tlingel's body materialized.

"Good evening, Martin." Tlingel turned away from the board. "The place looks a little better. Could use some music…"

Martin stepped behind the bar and switched on the transistor radio he had brought along. The sounds of a string quartet filled the air. Tlingel winced.

"Hardly in keeping with the atmosphere of the place."

He changed stations, located a country and western show.

"I think not," Tlingel said. "It loses something in transmission."

He turned it off.

"Have we a good supply of beverage?"

Martin drew a gallon stein of beer—the largest mug that he could locate, from a novelty store—and set it upon the bar. He filled a much smaller one for himself. He was determined to get the beast drunk if it were at all possible.

"Ah! Much better than those little cans," said Tlingel, whose muzzle dipped for but a moment. "Very good."

The mug was empty. Martin refilled it.

"Will you move it to the table for me?"

"Certainly."

"Have an interesting month?"

"I suppose I did."

"You've decided upon your next move?"

"Yes."

"Then let's get on with it."

Martin seated himself and captured the Pawn.

"Hm. Interesting."

Tlingel stared at the board for a long while, then raised a cloven hoof which parted in reaching for the piece.

"I'll just take that Bishop with this little Knight. Now I suppose you'll be wanting another month to make up your mind what to do next."

Tlingel leaned to the side and drained the mug.

"Let me consider it," Martin said, "while I get you a refill."

Martin sat and stared at the board through three more refills. Actually, he was not planning. He was waiting. His response to Grend had been Knight takes Bishop, and he had Grend's next move ready.

"Well?" Tlingel finally said. "What do you think?"

Martin took a small sip of beer.

"Almost ready," he said. "You hold your beer awfully well."

Tlingel laughed.

"A unicorn's horn is a detoxicant. Its possession is a universal remedy. I wait until I reach the warm glow stage, then I use my horn to burn off any excess and keep me right there."

"Oh," said Martin. "Neat trick, that."

"...If you've had too much, just touch my horn for a moment and I'll put you back in business."

"No, thanks. That's all right. I'll just push this little Pawn in front of the Queen's Rook two steps ahead."

"Really..." said Tlingel. "That's interesting. You know, what this place really needs is a piano—rinkytink, funky... Think you could manage it?"

"I don't play."

"Too bad."

"I suppose I could hire a piano player."

"No. I do not care to be seen by other humans."

"If he's really good, I suppose he could play blindfolded."

"Never mind."

"I'm sorry."

"You are also ingenious. I am certain that you will figure something out by next time."

Martin nodded.

"Also, didn't these old places used to have sawdust all over the floors?"

"I believe so."

"That would be nice."

"Check."

Tlingel searched the board frantically for a moment.

"Yes. I meant 'yes.' I said 'check.' It means 'yes' sometimes, too."

"Oh. Rather. Well, while we're here..."

Tlingel advanced the Pawn to Q3.

Martin stared. That was not what Grend had done. For a moment, he considered continuing on his own from here. He had tried to think of Grend as a coach up until this point. He had forced away the notion of crudely and crassly pitting one of them against the other. Until P-Q3. Then he recalled the game he had lost to the sasquatch.

"I'll draw the line here," he said, "and take my month."

"All right. Let's have another drink before we say good night. Okay?"

"Sure. Why not?"

They sat for a time and Tlingel told him of the morning land, of primeval forests and rolling plains, of high craggy mountains and purple seas, of magic and mythic beasts.

Martin shook his head.

"I can't quite see why you're so anxious to come here," he said, "with a place like that to call home."

Tlingel sighed.

"I suppose you'd call it keeping up with the griffins. It's the thing to do these days. Well. Till next month..."

Tlingel rose and turned away.

"I've got complete control now. Watch!"

The unicorn form faded, jerked out of shape, grew white, faded again, was gone, like an afterimage.

Martin moved to the bar and drew himself another mug. It was a shame to waste what was left. In the morning, he wished the unicorn were there again. Or at least the horn.

❖ ❖ ❖

It was a gray day in the forest and he held an umbrella over the chessboard upon the rock. The droplets fell from the leaves and made dull, plopping noises as they struck the fabric. The board was set up again through Tlingel's P-Q3. Martin wondered whether Grend had remembered, had kept proper track of the days...

"Hello," came the nasal voice from somewhere behind him and to the left.

He turned to see Grend moving about the tree, stepping over the massive roots with massive feet.

"You remembered," Grend said. "How good! I trust you also remembered the beer?"

"I've lugged up a whole case. We can set up the bar right here."

"What's a bar?"

"Well, it's a place where people go to drink—in out of the rain—a bit dark, for atmosphere—and they sit up on stools before a big counter, or else at little tables—and they talk to each other—and sometimes there's music—and they drink."

"We're going to have all that here?"

"No. Just the dark and the drinks. Unless you count the rain as music. I was speaking figuratively."

"Oh. It does sound like a very good place to visit, though."

"Yes. If you will hold this umbrella over the board, I'll set up the best equivalent we can have here."

"All right. Say, this looks like a version of that game we played last time."

"It is. I got to wondering what would happen if it had gone this way rather than the way that it went."

"Hmm. Let me see..."

Martin removed four six-packs from his pack and opened the first.

"Here you go."

"Thanks."

Grend accepted the beer, squatted, passed the umbrella back to Martin.

"I'm still White?"

"Yeah."

"Pawn to King six."

"Really?"

"Yep."

"About the best thing for me to do would be to take this Pawn with this one."

"I'd say. Then I'll just knock off your Knight with this one."

"I guess I'll just pull this Knight back to K2."

"...And I'll take this one over to B3. May I have another beer?"

An hour and a quarter later, Martin resigned. The rain had let up and he had folded the umbrella.

"Another game?" Grend asked.

"Yes."

The afternoon wore on. The pressure was off. This one was just for fun. Martin tried wild combinations, seeing ahead with great clarity, as he had that one day...

"Stalemate," Grend announced much later. "That was a good one, though. You picked up considerably."

"I was more relaxed. Want another?"

"Maybe in a little while. Tell me more about bars now."

So he did. Finally, "How is all that beer affecting you?" he asked.

"I'm a bit dizzy. But that's all right. I'll still cream you the third game."

And he did.

"Not bad for a human, though. Not bad at all. You coming back next month?"

"Yes."

"Good. You'll bring more beer?"

"So long as my money holds out."

"Oh. Bring some plaster of Paris then. I'll make you some nice footprints and you can take casts of them. I understand they're going for quite a bit."

"I'll remember that."

Martin lurched to his feet and collected the chess set.

"Till then."

"Ciao."

❖ ❖ ❖

Martin dusted and polished again, moved in the player piano and scattered sawdust upon the floor. He installed a fresh keg. He hung some reproductions of period posters and some atrocious old paintings he had located in a junk shop. He placed cuspidors in strategic locations. When he was finished, he seated himself at the bar and opened a bottle of mineral water. He listened to the New Mexico wind moaning as it passed, to grains of sand striking against the windowpanes. He wondered whether the whole world would have that dry, mournful sound to it if Tlingel found a means for doing away with humanity, or—disturbing thought—whether the successors to his own kind might turn things into something resembling the mythical morning land.

This troubled him for a time. Then he went and set up the board through Black's P-Q3. When he turned back to clear the bar he saw a line of cloven hoofprints advancing across the sawdust.

"Good evening, Tlingel." he said. "What is your pleasure?"

Suddenly, the unicorn was there, without preliminary pyrotechnics. It moved to the bar and placed one hoof upon the brass rail.

"The usual."

As Martin drew the beer, Tlingel looked about.

"The place has improved, a bit."

"Glad you think so. Would you care for some music?"

"Yes."

Martin fumbled at the back of the piano, locating the switch for the small, battery-operated computer which controlled the pumping mechanism and substituted its own memory for rolls. The keyboard immediately came to life.

"Very good," Tlingel stated. "Have you found your move?"

"I have."

"Then let us be about it."

He refilled the unicorn's mug and moved it to the table, along with his own.

"Pawn to King six," he said, executing it.

"What?"

"Just that."

"Give me a minute. I want to study this."

"Take your time."

"I'll take the Pawn," Tlingel said, after a long pause and another mug.

"Then I'll take this Knight."

Later, "Knight to K2," Tlingel said.

"Knight to B3."

An extremely long pause ensued before Tlingel moved the Knight to N3.

The hell with asking Grend, Martin suddenly decided. He'd been through this part any number of times already. He moved his Knight to N5.

"Change the tune on that thing!" Tlingel snapped.

Martin rose and obliged.

"I don't like that one either. Find a better one or shut it off!"

After three more tries, Martin shut it off.

"And get me another beer!"

He refilled their mugs.

"All right."

Tlingel moved the Bishop to K2.

Keeping the unicorn from castling had to be the most important thing at the moment. So Martin moved his Queen to R5. Tlingel made a tiny, strangling noise, and when Martin looked up smoke was curling from the unicorn's nostrils.

"More beer?"

"If you please."

As he returned with it, he saw Tlingel move the Bishop to capture the Knight. There seemed no choice for him at that moment, but he studied the position for a long while anyhow.

Finally, "Bishop takes Bishop," he said.

"Of course."

"How's the warm glow?"

Tlingel chuckled. "You'll see."

The wind rose again, began to howl. The building creaked.

"Okay," Tlingel finally said, and moved the Queen to Q2. Martin stared. What was he doing? So far, it had gone all right, but… He listened again to the wind and thought of the risk he was taking.

"That's all, folks," he said, leaning back in his chair. "Continued next month."

Tlingel sighed.

"Don't run off. Fetch me another. Let me tell you of my wanderings in your world this past month."

"Looking for weak links?"

"You're lousy with them. How do you stand it?"

"They're harder to strengthen than you might think. Any advice?"

"Get the beer."

They talked until the sky paled in the east, and Martin found himself taking surreptitious notes. His admiration for the unicorn's analytical abilities increased as the evening advanced.

When they finally rose, Tlingel staggered.

"You all right?"

"Forgot to detox, that's all. Just a second. Then I'll be fading."

"Wait!"

"Whazzat?"

"I could use one, too."

"Oh. Grab hold, then."

Tlingel's head descended and Martin took the tip of the horn between his fingertips. Immediately, a delicious, warm sensation flowed through him. He closed his eyes to enjoy it. His head cleared. An ache which had been growing within his frontal sinus vanished. The tiredness went out of his muscles. He opened his eyes again.

"Thank—"

Tlingel had vanished. He held but a handful of air.

"—you."

❖ ❖ ❖

"Rael here is my friend," Grend stated. "He's a griffin."

"I'd noticed."

Martin nodded at the beaked, golden-winged creature.

"Pleased to meet you, Rael."

"The same," cried the other in a high-pitched voice. "Have you got the beer?"

"Why—uh—yes."

"I've been telling him about beer," Grend explained, half-apologetically. "He can have some of mine. He won't kibitz or anything like that."

"Sure. All right. Any friend of yours…"

"The beer!" Rael cried. "Bars!"

"He's not real bright," Grend whispered. "But he's good company. I'd appreciate your humoring him."

Martin opened the first six-pack and passed the griffin and the sasquatch a beer apiece. Rael immediately punctured the can with his beak, chugged it, belched and held out his claw.

"Beer!" he shrieked. "More beer!"

Martin handed him another.

"Say, you're still into that first game, aren't you?" Grend observed, studying the board. "Now, *that* is an interesting position."

Grend drank and studied the board.

"Good thing it's not raining," Martin commented.

"Oh, it will. Just wait a while."

"More beer!" Rael screamed.

Martin passed him another without looking.

"I'll move my Pawn to N6," Grend said.

"You're kidding."

"Nope. Then you'll take that Pawn with your Bishop's Pawn. Right?"

"Yes…"

Martin reached out and did it.

"Okay. Now I'll just swing this Knight to Q5."

Martin took it with the Pawn.

Grend moved his Rook to K1.

"Check," he announced.

"Yes. That *is* the way to go," Martin observed.

Grend chuckled.

"I'm going to win this game another time," he said.

"I wouldn't put it past you."

"More beer?" Rael said softly.

"Sure."

As Martin passed him another, he noticed that the griffin was now leaning against the tree trunk.

After several minutes, Martin pushed his King to B1.

"Yeah, that's what I thought you'd do," Grend said. "You know something?"

"What?"

"You play a lot like a unicorn."

"Hm."

Grend moved his Rook to R3.

Later, as the rain descended gently about them and Grend beat him again, Martin realized that a prolonged period of silence had prevailed. He glanced over at the griffin. Rael had tucked his head beneath his left wing, balanced upon one leg, leaned heavily against the tree and gone to sleep.

"I told you he wouldn't be much trouble," Grend remarked.

Two games later, the beer was gone, the shadows were lengthening and Rael was stirring.

"See you next month?"

"Yeah."

"You bring any plaster of Paris?"

"Yes, I did."

"Come on, then. I know a good place pretty far from here. We don't want people beating about *these* bushes. Let's go make you some money."

"To buy beer?" Rael said, looking out from under his wing.

"Next month," Grend said.

"You ride?"

"I don't think you could carry both of us," said Grend, "and I'm not sure I'd want to right now if you could."

"Bye-bye then," Rael shrieked, and he leaped into the air, crashing into branches and tree trunks, finally breaking through the overhead cover and vanishing.

"There goes a really decent guy," said Grend. "He sees everything and he never forgets. Knows how everything works—in the woods, in the air—even in the water. Generous, too, whenever he has anything."

"Hm," Martin observed.

"Let's make tracks," Grend said.

❖ ❖ ❖

"Pawn to N6? Really?" Tlingel said. "All right. The Bishop's Pawn will just knock off the Pawn."

Tlingel's eyes narrowed as Martin moved the Knight to Q5.

"At least this is an interesting game," the unicorn remarked. "Pawn takes Knight."

Martin moved the Rook.

"Check."

"Yes, it is. This next one is going to be a three-flagon move. Kindly bring me the first."

Martin thought back as he watched Tlingel drink and ponder. He almost felt guilty for hitting it with a powerhouse like the sasquatch behind its back. He was convinced now that the unicorn was going to lose. In every variation of this game that he'd played with Black against Grend, he'd been beaten. Tlingel was very good, but the sasquatch was a wizard with not much else to do but mental chess. It was unfair. But it was not a matter of personal honor, he kept telling himself. He was playing to protect his species against a supernatural force which might well be able to precipitate World War III by some arcane mind manipulation or magically induced computer foul-up. He didn't dare give the creature a break.

"Flagon number two, please."

He brought it another. He studied it as it studied the board. It was beautiful, he realized for the first time. It was the loveliest living thing he had ever seen. Now that the pressure was on the verge of evaporating and he could regard it without the overlay of fear which had always been there in the past, he could pause to admire it. If something *had* to succeed the human race, he could think of worse choices…

"Number three now."

"Coming up."

Tlingel drained it and moved the King to B1.

Martin leaned forward immediately and pushed the Rook to R3.

Tlingel looked up, stared at him.

"Not bad."

Martin wanted to squirm. He was struck by the nobility of the creature. He wanted so badly to play and beat the unicorn on his own, fairly. Not this way.

Tlingel looked back at the board, then almost carelessly moved the Knight to K4.

"Go ahead. Or will it take you another month?"

Martin growled softly, advanced the Rook and captured the Knight.

"Of course."

Tlingel captured the Rook with the Pawn. This was not the way that the last variation with Grend had run. Still…

He moved his Rook to KB3. As he did, the wind seemed to commence a peculiar shrieking above, amid, the rained buildings.

"Check," he announced.

The hell with it! he decided. I'm good enough to manage my own end game. Let's play this out.

He watched and waited and finally saw Tlingel move the King to N1.

He moved his Bishop to R6. Tlingel moved the Queen to K2. The shrieking came again, sounding nearer now. Martin took the Pawn with the Bishop.

The unicorn's head came up and it seemed to listen for a moment. Then Tlingel lowered it and captured the Bishop with the King.

Martin moved his Rook to KN3.

"Check."

Tlingel returned the King to B1.

Martin moved the Rook to KB3.

"Check."

Tlingel pushed the King to N2.

Martin moved the Rook back to KN3.

"Check."

Tlingel returned the King to B1, looked up and stared at him, showing teeth. "Looks as if we've got a drawn game," the unicorn stated. "Care for another one?"

"Yes, but not for the fate of humanity."

"Forget it. I'd given up on that a long time ago. I decided that I wouldn't care to live here after all. I'm a little more discriminating than that.

"Except for this bar." Tlingel turned away as another shriek sounded just beyond the door, followed by strange voices. "What is that?"

"I don't know," Martin answered, rising.

The doors opened and a golden griffin entered.

"Martin!" it cried. "Beer! Beer!"

"Uh—Tlingel, this is Rael, and, and—"

Three more griffins followed it in. Then came Grend, and three others of his own kind.

"—and that one's Grend," Martin said lamely. "I don't know the others."

They all halted when they beheld the unicorn.

"Tlingel," one of the sasquatches said, "I thought you were still in the morning land."

"I still am, in a way. Martin, how is it that you are acquainted with my former countrymen?"

"Well—uh—Grend here is my chess coach."

"Aha! I begin to understand."

"I am not sure that you really do. But let me get everyone a drink first."

Martin turned on the piano and set everyone up.

"How did you find this place?" he asked Grend as he was doing it. "And how did you get here?"

"Well..." Grend looked embarrassed. "Rael followed you back."

"Followed a jet?"

"Griffins are supernaturally fast."

"Oh."

"Anyway, he told his relatives and some of my folks about it. When we saw that the griffins were determined to visit you, we decided that we had better come along to keep them out of trouble. They brought us."

"I—see. Interesting..."

"No wonder you played like a unicorn, that one game with all the variations."

"Uh—yes."

Martin turned away, moved to the end of the bar.

"Welcome, all of you," he said. "I have a small announcement. Tlingel, a while back you had a number of observations concerning possible ecological and urban disasters and lesser dangers. Also, some ideas as to possible safeguards against some of them."

"I recall," said the unicorn.

"I passed them along to a friend of mine in Washington who used to be a member of my old chess club. I told him that the work was not entirely my own."

"I should hope so."

"He has since suggested that I turn whatever group was involved into a think tank. He will then see about paying something for its efforts."

"I didn't come here to save the world," Tlingel said.

"No, but you've been very helpful. And Grend tells me that the griffins, even if their vocabulary is a bit limited, know almost all that there is to know about ecology."

"That is probably true."

"Since they have inherited a part of the Earth, it would be to their benefit as well to help preserve the place. Inasmuch as this many of us are already here, I can save myself some travel and suggest right now that we find a meeting place—say here, once a month—and that you let me have your unique viewpoints. You must know more about how species become extinct than anyone else in the business."

"Of course," said Grend, waving his mug, "but we really should ask the yeti, also. I'll do it, if you'd like. Is that stuff coming out of the big box music?"

"Yes."

"I like it. If we do this think-tank thing, you'll make enough to keep this place going?"

"I'll buy the whole town."

Grend conversed in quick gutturals with the griffins, who shrieked back at him.

"You've got a think-tank," he said, "and they want more beer."

Martin turned toward Tlingel.

"They were your observations. What do you think?"

"It may be amusing," said the unicorn, "to stop by occasionally." Then, "So much for saving the world. Did you say you wanted another game?"

"I've nothing to lose."

Grend took over the tending of the bar while Tlingel and Martin returned to the table.

He beat the unicorn in thirty-one moves and touched the extended horn.

The piano keys went up and down. Tiny sphinxes buzzed about the bar, drinking the spillage.

A Word from Zelazny

Zelazny maintained that this story came about more by craft than creativity. "[This] would be in a way the least inspired story I've ever written. Gardner Dozois called me up once and said he and Jack Dann were editing a collection of reprint stories involving unicorns [*Unicorns!*] and did I have a short story involving unicorns that I could sell reprint rights to? I said no, and they said 'Well, why don't you write one and go sell it to someone and then sell us reprint rights on it?' I said I'd think about it and promptly forgot about it. Then Darrell Schweitzer called me and asked me if I'd ever written a story set in a barroom because they were doing a collection of reprint stories set in a barroom [*Tales from the Spaceport Bar*]. And I said no. Then Fred Saberhagen…asked me if I'd ever written a chess game story [for *Pawn to Infinity*], and I said no.

"Later on that month, I was out with George R. R. Martin [for a wine tasting], and I thought I'd mention all these to him in case he'd ever written a unicorn story or a barroom story or a chess story, and he said no he hadn't, but why didn't I write a story about a unicorn and a chess game and set it in a barroom, sell it somewhere, and then sell reprint rights three times? I said that would be a real challenge, wouldn't it? I could make it a very funny story."[1]

He set the idea aside and prepared to leave for Vancouver to be Guest of Honor at the 1980 V-Con, followed by an Alaskan cruise. "Now right before I left New Mexico I had read Italo Calvino's *Invisible Cities*, and when I read the section titled "Hidden Cities. 4" something seemed to stir. It told of the city where all the inhabitants exterminated all the vermin, completely sanitizing the place, only to be haunted by visions of creatures that did not exist. Later, during the convention, things began to flow together..."[2]

"[After the convention] I was taking the Alaska inland passage cruise... the idea for the story broke right as I was going down to the docks to board the cruise ship [the *Prisendam*]. I ran into a bookstore and bought a copy of Fred Reinefeld's *Great Chess Game* or something like that... I looked through it until I found the game that I wanted, and that's the game that I reproduced in the story."[1]

"I wrote 'Unicorn Variation' in odd moments during what proved to be a fine cruise. My main protagonist is named Martin—any similarity to George (who is a chess expert) is not exactly unintentional... Later that year the *Prisendam* burned and sank. The story didn't. I sold it a sufficient number of times to pay for the cruise. Thanks, George."[2] "I really do owe George R. R. Martin a big one for that one. I wouldn't have done it if he hadn't said that. He said it jokingly, but I took it literally. It was a real challenge."[1]

Which game provided the climax? "The game itself. Okay. It was Halprin v. Pillsbury in Munich in 1901. Pillsbury was the stronger player. He'd beaten a number of very good players and only had Halprin, a weaker player, left to face. But two other players, running very close to Pillsbury for first prize, decided to teach him a lesson. The night before this game, they got together with Halprin and coached him, teaching him everything they had learned concerning Pillsbury's style. The following day, Pillsbury faced a much better-prepared Halprin than he had anticipated playing. He realized this almost too late. The others chuckled and felt smug. But Pillsbury surprised them. Even caught off guard initially, he managed a draw. After all, he was very good. Martin is playing Halprin's game here, and Tlingel Pillsbury's. Except that Martin isn't really very weak. He's just nervous the first time around. Who wouldn't be?"[2]

---

1 *Leading Edge #29* August 1994.

2 *Unicorn Variations*, 1983.

Notes

Tlingel is likely based on Tlingit, a Native American coastal people of southeastern Alaska and British Columbia (Recall that Zelazny wrote the story during the Alaskan cruise). *The Golden Bough*, the mythological reference Zelazny regularly consulted, mentioned the Tlingit's use of shamans and other mystical practices.

A **bizarrerie** is something amusingly unusual. A **cunabulum** is a cradle or birthplace. An **arroyo** is a steep-sided gully cut by running water in an arid or semiarid region. The French expression ***à gauche*** means to the left. **Alop** means crooked.

The **aepyornis** was the elephant bird. Legendary **Yeti** are large, hairy, human-like creatures who reside in the Himalayas. The **dodo** was a flightless bird with a stout body, stumpy wings, a large head, and a heavy hooked bill; it became extinct during the seventeenth century. The **Loch Ness monster** is a mythical creature said to inhabit Scotland's Loch Ness. The **passenger pigeon** was hunted to extinction, the last known one dying in captivity in 1914.

Sasquatch or Bigfoot, supposedly found in northwestern America, resembles a yeti; **Kraken** are mythical sea monsters said to appear off the Norwegian coast; a **cockatrice** is a two-legged dragon (or wyvern) with a cock's head; a **sphinx** has a woman's head and a lion's body.

Archetypical means a prototype or an ideal example of a type. **Ebon** is dark brown or black. **Anthropomorphizing** attributes human characteristics to something non-human, such as an animal or object. **Grend** may be named after Grendel, the beast that Beowulf slew. Saloons had **sawdust all over the floor** to absorb spilled beer and spit that missed the spittoons. **Griffins** are mythical creatures with an eagle's head and wings and a lion's body. **Keeping up with the griffins** is a play on "keeping up with the Joneses." ***Ciao*** in Italian means both hello and goodbye. **Cuspidors** are spittoons.

Rael was the pseudonym of Claude Vorilhon, author of *The Message Given to Me by Extraterrestrials* and founder of a cult which believed that humans originated from alien scientists who came to the Earth in UFOs. **Kibitz** is to look on and offer unwanted advice.

When Pussywillows Last in the Catyard Bloomed

When Pussywillows Last in the Catyard Bloomed, Norstrilia Press 1980.

When pussywillows last in the catyard bloomed…
Fine line.
Lacking an accompanying thought, perhaps,
yet…
My life is full of yets.
We assemble ourselves slowly,
collecting pieces (such as the above).
Not all of them fit
and some should not have
but did (such as the above).
Yet…I lack. Many things.
But have the pussywillows,
and there are the cats
(envision them in heat if you would;
hear their drawn-out wet-baby wails;
hear them purr if you'd rather,
or spit).

I have the yard.
The sun dies to the west of it,
placing me in an enviable position
stage left of moon and star.
Constellations chart themselves,

stick-figured: geometry,
parsimony, pieces…
Yet you are there, Old Bear,
despite;
and beyond, the God of Galaxies?
(Praise Him, praise Him, Van Doren?
I cannot.
I've learned when to keep my mouth shut.)
Regard and rejoice with me
if the piece be there.
Yet I lack the art critic's part.
Forgive.

When pussywillows last in the catyard boomed—
Yes. I recall a day. Many days.
In the yard. The green and the gray.
The sun and the wind. Singing leaves to light.
A bird, a tree, a war.
He was there. The me
of me to come, memory-bound,
unknowing, yet of yets,
conjuring a self that did not come,
as I call spirits from the vasty deep.
Peace, piece. Summoned,
thou art there. The imaged word,
Hart, pussywillows anchored in its glow—
no farewells and unbetrayable—
you were right—
for there in the catyard—boom,
blooming, boomed—they grew,
were growing, grow.

Child, I have come.
I bring, beneath the indulgence
of self and words, the love learned late,
the places drained of hate,
the extra reels of seeing.
Piece by piece, yet by yet,
I affirm what I affirm by denying
what I do not, negative man

of a thousand selves betrayed.
I have a center,
a place as still as a windless,
birdless, bugless day
without clouds.
And it is from this place
that I see you—

In the catyard last when bloomed the pussywillows
walked I backward into my arms.
Yet.
Coming I have gone
and going will I be. Yet.
Madre de Firesong, Padre de Darkness,
walking is how I see myself,
always on hills or wet pavement,
city by night, country by day,
with no desire to rest,
hopefully conjured, always wondering,
never knowing, beginnings for endings
and vice-versa, piece-
meal, yet growing, like morning
or evening shadow. Some you,
in the pussywillowed yard of cats,
farewell me not,
but color, anchor me walking.

Within are we all.
Slowly ourselves assemble we,
lacking accompanying thought,
singing stars to sinking, citying the sea,
we blood and bone about us,
pump spirit, populate the dimness
with past's suns' flicker, ray, day…

I hang my yets on the catyard gate,
booming where pussywillows
last in the backward-turned time
evolved their reply,
whose accent denies my good-bye:

Yet, yet and yet. And I walk
singing not praise
but wonder,
part apart;
imagined cats dance at my heels,
at least as important, ever yet equally wise.

A Word from Zelazny

Zelazny's poetry often reflected his personal life; here he muses on the things that he does have and the things that he doesn't. In contrast, he kept his prose separate from his personal life: "I like to keep my writing apart from the rest of my life. I make my living displaying pieces of my soul in some distorted form or other. The rest of it is my own"[1] Does the title echo Ray Bradbury's collection *When Elephants Last in the Dooryard Bloomed*? "Well, it echoes [Walt] Whitman of course [*When Lilacs Last in the Dooryard Bloom'd*], but, yes, I did admire Bradbury, though I think he's better as a prose poet; that is, the poetry in the prose. His poetry itself is a little overdone."[2]

Notes

Parsimony is miserliness. The **Van Doren** family included several writers: Carl (historian and literary critic), Mark (poet and educator), and Mark's son Charles (writer and educator, infamous for his involvement in the 1956 TV scandal; the quiz show Twenty-One had been rigged so that he would win). **Hart** is Hart Crane, a poet Zelazny admired, and also puns on the word heart. **Madre** means mother; **padre** means father.

1 *Roger Zelazny: A Primary and Secondary Bibliography*, 1980.
2 *Critical Wave #33*, November 1993.

Articles

Some Science Fiction Parameters:

A Biased View

Galaxy, July 1975.

I remember the seats and the view: hard wood, with corrugated metal high above, television monitors below on the ground, ready, a big clock scoring the seconds; in the distance, a narrow inlet of calm water reflecting a grayness of cloud between us and the vehicle. A couple places over to my left, Harry Stubbs [sf author Hal Clement] was taking a picture. To my right, a young Korean girl was doing the same thing without a camera. She was painting a watercolor of the scene. In the tier immediately before and below me, with occasional gestures, a European journalist was speaking rapid Serbo-Croatian into a plug-in telephone. On the ground, to the far left, the brightly garbed center of a small system of listeners, Sybil Leek was explaining that the weather would clear up shortly and there would be no further problems. When the weather did clear and the clock scythed down the final seconds, we saw the ignition before we heard it and the water was agitated by a shock wave racing across in our direction. Apollo 14 was already lifting when the sound struck, and the volume kept increasing until the metal roof vibrated. A cheer went up around us and I kept watching until the roof's edge blocked my view. Then I followed the flight's progress on the monitor. I remember thinking, "I've waited for this."

I was not really thinking about science fiction at that moment. I was thinking only of the event itself. Yet I would not have been waiting at that spot at that time had it not been for my connection with science fiction. It was in the calmer hours of later evenings after that that I did give some thought to the manner in which science fiction has touched me over the years, trying to fit a few of the things that seemed part of it into some larger perspective.

I was raised and educated in times and places where science fiction was not considered a branch of *belles lettres*. As I was exposed to critical thought in other areas of literature, it did seem to me that science fiction was being shortchanged, in that when it was mentioned at all it was generally with reference to the worst rather than the best that it had to offer. Unfair, yet this was the way of the world.

Recently, however, the situation changed, and science fiction has been a subject of increasing critical and academic scrutiny. The reason, I feel, is partly that a sufficiently large body of good science fiction has now been amassed to warrant such consideration, but mainly that those who felt as I did in earlier times and then proceeded to follow academic careers have taken approximately this long to achieve positions where they could do something about it. Therefore, I have been pleased whenever I have been asked to address a university audience on this subject, not simply because it seems to represent some vindication of my tastes, but because I feel comfortable with those who worked to effect the change in attitude.

Yet, this generated a new problem for me. Every time I spoke, I had to have something to say. It required that I examine my own unquestioned responses to science fiction and consider some of the forces which have shaped and are shaping it. When I was asked to do this piece, I decided to draw together the results of these efforts and display whatever chimera might emerge, both because I am curious to see it myself and because I wish to get in a few words before the amount of science fiction criticism surpasses the amount of science fiction and I am less likely to be noticed.

The Apollo-sized hole filled in my psyche that day in Florida had been excavated more than twenty years earlier, when I had begun reading tales of space travel. This was a part of it—certainly not all; but emotion is as much a part of meaning as thought, and since most longtime fans began reading the literature at an early age, the feelings it aroused were generally the main attraction. What do they really amount to? Pure escapism? A love of cosmic-scale spectacle? The reinforcement of juvenile fantasies at about the time they would normally begin to fade? All of these? Some? None? Or something else?

The term "sense of wonder" gets considerable mileage in discussions such as this, and I have sought this feeling elsewhere in literature in hope of gaining a fuller understanding of its mechanism. I have experienced it in two other places: the writings of Saint-Exupéry on the early days of air travel and the writings of Jacques Cousteau on the beginnings of underwater exploration with scuba gear. The common element, as I saw it, was that both stories share with science fiction a theme involving the penetration of previously unknown worlds by means of devices designed and assembled by man, thereby extending his senses into new realms.

Turning backward, I felt obliged to classify the myths, legends, scriptural writings and bits of folklore which have always held a high place in my imaginary wanderings as contributory but different. There have always been storytellers of a speculative cast of mind who have taken some delight in playing about the peripheries of the known, guessing at the dimensions of the unknown. It might be argued that this is a necessary ingredient of the epic—dealing with the entire ethos of a people, up to and including that open end of the human condition, death itself, in a fashion transcending even the grand visions of tragedy and comedy. True epics of course are few and historically well spaced, but that slightly more mundane ingredient, the speculative impulse, be it of Classic, Christian or Renaissance shading, which ornamented Western literature with romances, fables, exotic voyages and utopias, seemed to me basically the same turn of fancy exercised today in science fiction, working then with the only objects available to it. It took the Enlightenment, it took science, it took the industrial revolution to provide new sources of ideas that, pushed, poked, inverted and rotated through higher spaces, resulted in science fiction. When the biggest, most interesting ideas began emerging from science, rather than from theology or the exploration of new lands, hindsight makes it seem logical that something like science fiction had to be delivered.

Of course, the realistic novel was also slapped on the bottom and uttered its first cries at that time, an event that requires a glance at the differences in endowment. Basically, as I have said here and there before, the modern, realistic novel has discarded what Northrop Frye has classified as the higher modes of character. It is a democratic place, without room for heroes, rash kings, demigods and deities. Science fiction, on the other hand, retained and elaborated these modes, including mutants, aliens, robots, androids and sentient computers.

There is a basic difference in character and characterization as well as the source and flow of ideas.

And what of those ideas? It has been persuasively argued that *Frankenstein* was the first science fiction novel. To simplify, as one must in these discussions, there seems to be, within the body of science fiction, a kind of Frankenstein-versus-Pygmalion tension, an internal and perhaps eternal debate as to whether man's creations will destroy him or live happily with him forever after. In the days when I began reading science fiction I would say that, statistically, Pygmalion had the upper hand. The "sense of wonder" as I knew it was in most stories unalloyed with those fears and concerns that the unforeseen side effects of some technological usages have brought about in recent years. The lady delivered purer visions involving the entry into new worlds and the extension of our senses. Now the cautionary quality is returned, and the shadow of Frankenstein's monster falls across much of our work. Yet, because this is a part of the force that generates the visions, it cannot be destructive to the area itself. Speaking not as a prognosticator or moralist, but only as a writer, my personal feelings are that a cycle such as this is good for the field, that if nothing else it promotes a reexamination of our attitudes, whatever they may be, toward the basic man-machine-society relationships. End of digression.

Science fiction's special quality, the means by which it achieves its best effects, is of course the imagination, pitched here several octaves above the notes it sounds elsewhere in literature. To score it properly is one of the major difficulties faced in the writing of science fiction; namely, in addition to the standard requirements encountered in composing a mundane story, one has the added task of explaining the extra plot premises and peculiarities of setting—without visibly slowing the action or lessening the tensions that must be built as the narrative progresses. This has led, over the years, to the development of clichés (I would like to have said "conventions," but the word has a way of not working properly when applied to science fiction), clichés involving the acceptance at mere mention of such phenomena as faster-than-light travel, telepathy, matter transmission, immortality drugs and instant language-translation devices, to name a few. Their use represents an artificiality of an order not found elsewhere in contemporary letters—excepting individual poets with private mythologies, which is not really the same thing as an entire field holding stock in common. Yet the artificiality does not really detract and the illusion does work because of the compensatory effect of a higher level of curiosity aroused as to the nature of the beast. Literally anything may be the subject of a science fiction story. In accepting the clichés of science fiction, one is also abandoning the everyday assumptions that hold for the run of mundane fiction. This in some ways requires a higher degree of sophistication, but the rewards are commensurate.

These are some of the more obvious things that set science fiction apart from the modern realistic story. But, if there must be some grand, overall scheme to literature, where does science fiction fit? I am leery of that great classifier Aristotle in one respect that bears on the issue. The Hellenic world did not view the passage of time as we do. History was considered in an episodic sense, as the struggles of an unchanging mankind against a relentless and unchanging fate. The slow process of organic evolution had not yet been detected, and the grandest model for a world view was the seeming changeless patternings of the stars. It took the same processes that set the stage for science fiction—eighteenth-century rationalism and nineteenth-century science—to provide for the first time in the history of the world a sense of historical direction, of time as a developmental, nonrepetitive sequence.

This particular world view became a part of science fiction in a far more explicit fashion than in any other body of storytelling, as it provided the basis for its favorite exercise: extrapolation. I feel that because of this, science fiction is the form of literature least affected by Aristotle's dicta with respect to the nature of the human condition, which he saw as immutable, and the nature of man's fate, which he saw as inevitable.

Yet science fiction is concerned with the human condition and with man's fate. It is the speculative nature of its concern that required the abandonment of the Aristotelian strictures involving the given imponderables. Its methods have included a retention of the higher modes of character, a historical, developmental time sense, assimilation of the tensions of a technological society and the production of a "sense of wonder" by exercises of imagination extending awareness into new realms—a sensation capable, at its best, of matching the power of that experience of recognition which Aristotle held to be the strongest effect of tragedy. It might even be argued that the sense of wonder represents a different order of recognition, but I see no reason to ply the possible metaphysics of it at this point.

Since respectability tends to promote a concern for one's ancestors, we are fortunate to be in on things at the beginning today when one can still aim high and compose one's features into an attitude of certainty while hoping for agreement. It occurs to me then that there is a relationship between the entire body of science fiction and that high literary form, the epic. Traditionally, the epic was regarded as representing the spirit of an entire people—the *Iliad*, the *Mahābhārata*, the *Aeneid* showing us the values, the concerns, the hoped-for destinies of the Greeks, the ancient Indians, the Romans. Science fiction is less provincial, for it really deals with humanity as such. I am not so temerarious as to suggest that any single work of science fiction has ever come near the epic level (though Olaf Stapledon probably came closest), but wish rather to observe that the impulse behind it is akin to that of the epic chronicler, and is reflected in the desire to deal with the future of humanity, describing in every way possible the spirit and destiny not of a single nation but of Man.

High literature, unfortunately, requires more than good intentions, and so I feel obliged to repeat my caveat to prevent my being misunderstood any more than is usually the case. In speaking of the epic, I am attempting to indicate a similarity in spirit and substance between science fiction as a whole and some of the classical features of the epic form. I am not maintaining that it has been achieved in any particular case or even by the entire field viewed as a single entity. It may have; it may not. I stand too near to see that clearly. I suggest only that science fiction is animated in a similar fashion, occasionally possesses something like a Homeric afflatus and that its general aims are of the same order, producing a greater kinship here than with the realistic novel beside which it was born and bred. The source of this particular vitality may well be the fact that, like its subject, it keeps growing but remains unfinished.

❖ ❖ ❖

These were some of the thoughts that occurred to me when I was asked to do a piece on the parameters of science fiction. I reviewed my association with the area, first as a reader and fan, recalling that science fiction is unique in possessing a fandom and a convention system that make for personal contacts between authors and readers, a situation that may be of peculiar significance. When an author is in a position to meet and speak with large numbers of his readers, he cannot help, at least for a little while, feeling somewhat as the old-time storytellers must have felt in facing the questions and the comments of a live audience. The psychological process involved in this should be given some consideration as an influence on the field. I thought of my connection as a writer, self-knowledge suggesting that the remedy for the biggest headache in its composition—furnishing the extra explanations as painlessly as possible—may be the mechanism by which the imagination is roused to climb those several extra steps to the point where the unusual becomes plausible—and thus the freshness; thus, when it is well done, the wonder. And then I thought of all the extracurricular things that many of us either care about because we are science fiction writers or are science fiction writers because we care about.

Which takes me back to the stands at the Cape, to the vibrations, to the shouting, to my "I've waited for this." My enthusiasm at the successful launching of a manned flight to the moon perhaps tells you more about me than it does about science fiction and its parameters, for space flight is only a part—a colorful part, to be sure—of the story we have been engaged in telling of Man and his growing awareness. For on reflection, having watched the fire, felt the force and seen the vessel lifted above the Earth, it seemed a triumph for Pygmalion; and that, I realized, had more to do with my view that day than the fire, the force or the vessel.

A Word from Zelazny

"I wrote this piece in response to a request from Jim Baen that I do a guest column for *Galaxy*, which he was then editing."[1]

Notes

Belles letters is literature of the finest sort, appreciated for its sheer beauty. A **chimera** is a natural or artifical organism composed of two or more distinct species; the mythological chimera had a lion's head, a goat's body, and a serpent's tail. **Antoine de Saint-Exupéry** was a writer and aviator who published several novels about flight; he is best known for *The Little Prince.* **Jacques Cousteau** developed the Aqua-Lung. **Northrop Frye** was a Canadian author whose interest in mythology influenced Zelazny. **Pygmalion** carved a statue of a woman and then fell in love with it; the goddess Venus pitied him and brought it to life. Plato's pupil The ***Mahābhārata*** is an Indian epic poem that describes the conflict between the Pandavas and the Kauravas in ninth century BC. The ***Aeneid*** is Virgil's epic which recounts Aeneas's adventures after the fall of Troy. **Temerarious** is reckless.

1 *Unicorn Variations*, 1983.

Black Is the Color and None Is the Number

Written 1976; previously unpublished.

What is black, infinitely dense, occupies zero volume and eats anything?

Answer: A thing concerning which we possess certain theoretical knowledge and a large collection of guesses, ranging from likely to wild: A black hole.

Let's take a walk on the wild side first.

The things referred to as black holes have been guessed to possess "wormhole" gateways to other universes. They have also been nominated as counterparts of "white holes" out of which matter erupts at some undetermined points in our own universe. Because of this, they have been suggested as "space warp" travel devices, or inter-universe rapid transits.

Black holes have been offered as potential destroyers of the universe, destined eventually to suck away all matter. It has even half-seriously been submitted that this has already occurred—with a calculation of the average density of the universe at 10^{-29} grams per cubic centimeter and a radius of 10^{10} lightyears we may already be within our Schwarzchild radius and collapsing toward our own singularity. (More about these terms shortly.)

A number of plans for extracting energy from the ergospheres of black holes have been suggested. All of them contain major snags, not the least of which resembles the old recipe for tiger soup: "First you obtain a black hole."

Black holes have been suggested as the power sources for quasars, those mysterious distant objects fleeing from us at relativistic velocities, emitting energies equivalent to the output of an entire galaxy. Our galaxy itself has been nominated for the honor of possessing an immense black hole at its center.

Which of these are worth worrying or rejoicing over? Which are the likeliest to represent a true state of affairs? To answer properly we must first understand what a black hole is and how it relates to the known varieties of collapsed objects. We must begin with the birth of a star.

Cosmic compaction produces various spectacular results, all of them, paradoxically, governed by the weakest of the fundamental forces that hold the universe together. The most powerful force [the strong nuclear force] is that which binds protons and neutrons together in the nucleus of the atom.[1] Then there is the electromagnetic force, a hundred times weaker than this, which holds the electrons in place about the nucleus, which ties atoms together to form matter. And then comes gravity, 10^{38} times weaker than the nuclear force, 10^{36} times weaker than the electrical. Gravity is simple as well—it just attracts, pulls things together—unlike the fickle electrical, coming in positive and negative varieties, repelling as well as attracting.

Weak though it is, relative to the other forces, it is gravity which draws together the hydrogen nuclei which move in eddies and swirls throughout the universe, giving us the recipe for a star. The random motions of hydrogen nuclei eventually result in a large enough accumulation to hold a small pocket of them together, to attract more, to create a cloud, to draw all the atoms closer together, contracting the cloud, speeding up the atoms and increasing their energy to the point where the gas rises in temperature. Shrinking, heating, under the pressure of its own weight, the cloud undergoes a change. At around 55,000 K the atoms collide with such force that electrons are stripped from their orbits about the protons[2]. Continue to stir, and wait another 10 million years, while the cloud contracts further and heats to a temperature of around 11 million K. At this point, something new occurs. Up until then, the positively charged protons had repelled one another electrically. Now, however, they are forced so close together that the electrical repulsion yields to the even stronger force of nuclear attraction. They pick up speed and rush together. They fuse to form a new nucleus and give off heat and light. A star is born.

---

1 There is also a weak nuclear force, worth nothing more than a footnote here, to show it is there. —RZ

2 Ionization begins at 10,000 K and rises with temperature. There is no sharp boundary at 55,000 K. —eds.

If it is an average star, like our own sun, the progress has been from a relatively cool gas cloud of about 10 trillion miles in diameter to a blazing globe perhaps a million miles in diameter—ours is actually around 864,000—with a variety of possible surface temperatures, ours being around 6000 K.

It is the weakest force, gravity, operating over a great span of time and space, which brought it all together, introducing the protons to one another at a proximity which would permit the strongest force to begin the reaction. Two additional protons, to give the final step, join the initial pair, lose their positive charges[3] and become neutrons, producing a helium atom. Hydrogen fuses to form helium, and this goes on, and on and on, a slow-burning hydrogen bomb, for most of the lifetime of the star.

Standing on my hilltop regarding the heavens, the stars all look pretty much alike—some brighter, some dimmer, to be sure, but basically a lovely collection of light-points. However, they represent a great variety of sizes, luminosities, surface temperatures, permitting them to be grouped along the diagonal highway of the Hertzsprung-Russell diagram, a chart describing their positions in a progression known as the main sequence, by indicating just how energetic they are. A hot, white star (called type B) would be located up at the top, a cooler red dwarf (type M) down at the bottom. It was originally felt by the chart's designers that the sequence represented an evolutionary progression, that a star would begin its life at the top and over a great period of time burn its way down to the bottom, exhausting its mass and energy on the way. R.I.P. However, Hans Bethe and Carl von Weizäcker determined otherwise, back in 1939, showing that a star dies not by a breaking down but by a building up of its elements, not by a gradual, straightforward loss of heat, but by an enormous expenditure of it.

There comes a time when the hydrogen fuel at a star's center is exhausted. What then? Like a moribund patient able to draw for a time on nervous resources it turns to its own center of existence. It draws additional energy from gravitational contraction of its core. Just as the initial dust cloud was heated by this effect of that weakest of forces, gravity, the helium core contracts, heats up. At this point, the outer envelope of the star expands and cools. It grows to many times its main sequence size and becomes a red giant. As the core

---

3 By emitting positrons. The third proton joins to form He^3, then pairs of He^3 combine to form He^4, emitting two protons into the continuing reaction. —eds.

continues to shrink and heat, another nuclear reaction begins. The helium nuclei now fuse to become carbon nuclei, and oxygen. As it grows hotter other reactions occur: the carbon fuses to neon and magnesium, the oxygen to silicon and sulfur. These, in turn, eventually form iron, and that is the dead end. More energy would be required to do something further with iron, and that energy is not available.

But a star which has become a geriatric case is a thing of great interest. Like people, they do not all go out in the same way. Just as a person's excessive body weight may make him a candidate for cardiac arrest rather than another condition, so does the mass of a star affect the manner of its passing.

One possibility is the way of the white dwarf. Gravity continues to tug at the exhausted core, but a form of resistance to further shrinkage arises. This is known as degeneracy pressure. It is a function of density[4], deriving from the degenerate condition of the electrons in the high-density state and has nothing to do with the temperature. This resistance to compaction halts the collapse. The star Sirius has a small companion star, which is sometimes called the Pup. The Pup is a white dwarf, a compacted mass of degenerate matter, smaller than the Earth itself yet containing as much mass as our own sun. A piece of it the size of a package of cigarettes would weight around 20 tons. According to the generally accepted theory put forward by the astronomers B. Paczynski and William Rose, the Pup reached the red giant stage possessing 2.5 to 3 times the mass of our own sun. The core contracted to a white dwarf state while the envelope around it still resembled a red giant. The core at this point contained about one solar mass. Eventually, the pressure of its radiation overbalanced the pull of its gravity on the envelope which then drifted off to become the gas cloud seen to surround the small, white star, a star which tens of billions of years from now will become a dead, cold black dwarf.

But let us think again of that weakest force, gravity, pitted against degeneracy pressure. One solar mass can be compacted to a high-density state which will cause the body to resist further collapse. But supposing we began with a larger star, having a core of more than one solar mass? Roughly, 1.4 solar masses, to be specific? This figure to known as Chandresekhar's limit—and, yes, something different would occur.

---

4 This is not mass density, but a kind of quantum density where particles (Fermions) resist being in the same quantum state. —eds.

Let us be brief, and take the giant star Betelgeuse in the constellation Orion as an example of what else could occur. If a star is roughly over one-and-a-half (and under approximately 3) times as massive as our sun it will not simply evolve into a red giant and then a white dwarf. It will grow large, as Betelgeuse now is, and when it collapses there will be a catastrophic explosion known as a supernova. In this case, degeneracy pressure will not be sufficient to halt the collapse of the shrinking remnant. Betelgeuse's protons and electrons will one day run together, forming neutrons. The result will be a small superdense body known an a neutron star. It will be about 12 miles in diameter and a thimbleful of its material would weigh in the neighborhood of a billion tons.

Fritz Zwicky and Walter Baade had speculated as far back as 1934 that the supernovae represented the transitions from ordinary stars into neutron stars. In 1939, while Bethe and Weizäcker were considering the internal evolution of a dying star, J. Robert Oppenheimer and George M. Volkoff showed mathematically that neutron stars could indeed exist. It was not until 1967, however, that Jocelyn Bell and Anthony Hewish at Cambridge University, England, discovered pulsars, or pulsating radio sources. In October of 1968, David Staelin and Edward Reifenstein of the National Radio Observatory in Green Bank, West Virginia, located a pulsar in the Crab Nebula, the known remnant of a supernova which occurred in the year 1054 AD. This coincidence was pursued, and Thomas Gold of Cornell offered the explanation that pulsars were spinning neutron stars, a pulse emitted each time they rotate. This is the generally accepted explanation today, although the exact nature of the pulse itself has not yet really been worked out.

These things are known and have been verified to a point of reasonable reliability. That there is a third and particularly bizarre way for a star to die is a new notion on the one hand, because a few likely candidates have but recently been found, and an older idea on the other, going back to 1916, when the German physicist Karl Schwarzchild was considering an aspect of relativity theory. When the radius of an object shrinks to a certain critical point, he suggested, the object would distort spacetime to such an extent that not even light could escape from it. This point is now known as the "Schwarzchild radius," and the boundary around the body having this radius is the "event horizon." No one outside the event horizon could become aware of happenings within it. It would have become a "black hole."

This remained a theoretical concept for years. After all, the Earth itself would have to be compacted to the size of a grape to reach its Schwarzchild radius, and our sun to something under two miles in diameter. What force or forces could possibly effect such shrinkage in real life?

Unfair question. With respect to our sun and the Earth, the answer is: nothing that we know of. As we understand it, they are too small to ever suffer this fate. But let us consider a much larger object. Say, a star of ten or twenty solar masses, or more. If such an object were to begin to collapse, it would not stop at the white dwarf stage, being well beyond Chandresekhar's limit. Degeneracy pressure could not halt it, and neither—according to the theory—could neutron compacting. It would simply collapse and collapse and never stop, retreating into its own small pocket of Somewhere, beyond the spacetime continuum we tend to regard as our own, taking pieces of our universe with it, now and forever[5], and compacting, compacting, compacting, amen.

The concept is reminiscent of trying to grasp a Zen *koan*. It does not proceed from the world of the senses, it boggles the mind. A black hole would be created by this collapse. A hole, not a solid body, a region of space into which matter has fallen and from which it can never return. The matter inside the hole may not occupy any volume at all. The weakest of forces, gravity, would suddenly become infinite, and Einstein's theory of gravity would break down—for the center of the black hole would represent a "singularity," which may be regarded as the heart of the *koan*. It would be a point containing all the mass of the hole at infinite density and occupying zero volume.[6]

Rather than attempting to push definition beyond this near-metaphysical point, let us look away and regard the black hole from the outside. There would be nothing to see but black for, as noted earlier, not even light would escape from it. Hence, the thorn in the side of physical theory, the singularity, would decently perform its violations of field theory within the event horizon and so remain out of sight. There would be tidal gravitational forces to betray its presence, however, which is how the best candidate for the title has been detected.

To simplify a longer story, Cygnus X-1 is a source of X-rays. It was located by the astronomical satellite *Uhuru*. It coincides with the

---

5 No longer forever. See the end note about Hawking radiation. —eds.

6 Zelazny treats "black hole" and "singularity" as interchangeable. They are not. The singularity has infinities associated with it whereas the black hole can be measured. —eds.

star known by the catalog number HDE 226868 in the constellation Cygnus, the Swan. HDE 226868 is a hot supergiant star of the spectral type known as B0, around 30 times the size of our own sun with a surface temperature five times as great. It has an invisible companion, the apparent source of the X-ray emissions, the two of them rotating around the center of mass of the system in 5.6 days. From this, C. T. Bolton of the David Dunlap Observatory in Canada has estimated the mass of the invisible companion at around 14 times that of the sun. This is too great for a white dwarf or even a neutron star. The X-ray radiation, it has been theorized, could be caused by the compression and consequent heating of gas being drawn into a black hole. The strongest case for black holehood to date has been made for Cygnus X-1.

What would a black hole be like, close up?

The area immediately above the event horizon is referred to as the "ergosphere." It would be theoretically possible to orbit the black hole within the ergosphere, staying clear of the event horizon, and experience a time-dilation effect. One would not, however, gain additional length of days by so risking one's life. Time would continue to seem to pass in its petty pace fashion, but when one came away into a more normal area of spacetime a far greater period of time would be found to have elapsed, just how much depending upon one's length of stay in the ergosphere and one's proximity to the event horizon while inside. As a time-travel device, it would be strictly one-way, reminding me again that the ideal means of journeying into the future involves an armchair, a pipe and patience.

But let us consider the zealous astronaut who would venture into the ergosphere and down, down toward the event horizon. He would be killed by tidal gravitational forces—that is to say, the effect of gravity on his extremities nearer the hole would be so much stronger than on those portions of his anatomy farther away that he would literally be pulled apart, so great is the increase over a short distance as one nears the event horizon. But forget that if you can for a moment and consider the fact that while his personal sense of the passage of time remains unchanged, a more distant observer would see him as slowing, slowing. He would pass the event horizon, heading for whatever fate awaits at the singularity—but the observer would never witness this passage. At the event horizon time would be seen as frozen, from the point of view of the distant observer. The astronaut would seem to stop falling, would never be seen to penetrate the event horizon.

When I first heard of this effect, I conjured up a mental image of the event horizon as looking like an enormous Christmas tree, strewn for eternity with whatever cosmic debris had come its way—comets, wrecked spaceships, filaments of dust, broken asteroids…

Which brings us to the end of the story, so far as legitimate pictures based on knowledge and theory. Some of the speculation was aired at the beginning of this piece. Let us return to the wild side and consider some more.

The one force possibly capable of compressing smaller masses than those we have mentioned within their Schwarzchild radii—the "Big Bang" version of the creation of the universe—has been offered as a producer of mini-black holes, cute little ones perhaps smaller than a trash compactor but capable of a more efficient job in that they would never have to be emptied.

In an article in the September 1973 issue of *Nature*, Jackson and Ryan of the University of Texas suggested a mini-black hole as the cause of the "Tungus Event" of 1908—that tremendous explosion in Tunguska, Siberia, which destroyed trees for hundreds of miles around and has been judged equal to the explosion of a 20-megaton H-bomb. They proposed that it could have been a black hole less than a millionth of a centimeter in radius and possessing the mass of a small planet or large asteroid, moving at a velocity greater than the Earth's escape velocity, so that it passed right through our planet and kept going. This idea has been met with considerable skepticism, as there is no real evidence for the existence of mini-black holes. However… If the Jackson and Ryan notion is correct and if the black hole had not possessed escape velocity it would have settled to the center of the Earth. There, its tidal forces would have torn apart all adjacent matter and it would have digested it. As it grew larger the process would have accelerated. In which case, the Earth and everything on it would have disappeared into that microscopic black speck, so that we would have gone out with neither a bang nor a whimper but rather the inexorable pressures of a cosmic trash compactor.

It has been said that the singularity within a black hole can never be seen, as it will always be hidden by its event horizon. However, this is based upon current knowledge and theory as to the natural formation of collapsed objects, which involves the collapsar's being symmetrical. It has been suggested, though, that the collapse of a rapidly rotating asymmetrical object might produce a donut-shaped singularity rather than a point, possessed of no event horizon in its plane. This "naked singularity" would then be visible, thumbing its singular nose, so to speak, at physical theory by granting a view of a region in which its laws do not hold. But there is no evidence that such a bizarrely distorted, unsymmetrical collapse has ever actually occurred.

There is more evidence these days in favor of the Big Bang theory of the origin of the universe than there is for the "steady state"[7] idea. There has even been some recent thinking to the effect that the creation of the universe may have involved a spacetime singularity with the matter erupting outward—that is, a notion of the Big Bang as a cosmic outpouring through a gigantic white hole.[8]

As for the white hole and wormhole notions themselves, there is nothing in the general theory of relativity to indicate that they could not occur, but then there is no real evidence for their existence either.

The growth of radio astronomy in the past ten years has brought about an explosion in astronomical knowledge and wrought many new turns of thought within the area, with much more promised in the very near future. But even Cygnus X-1 has not actually been confirmed as a black hole. Consensus of opinion among experts could probably have it so, but a bit more data is needed to have it really certain. However, none is the number—at this point—to be perfectly honest.

It is interesting, fascinating, stunning even, to contemplate these possibilities: the nightmare aspect of that statistical unlikelihood of the Earth's being devoured by one, the fantastic notion of traveling through a singularity to emerge at another point in spacetime. This of course is guesswork—fun guesswork, surely—but no more than that just now. Yet, I wonder whether the strange deaths of stars are in any way a greater marvel than their births, with the possibility of the formation of planets and the development of life upon them—a far frailer phenomenon, to be sure, than any star, collapsed or otherwise, yet perhaps capable of a sentience able in its small way to regard these larger processes and to know wonder at their contemplation, a thing of which even the spectacularly inanimate is incapable, sealed in mysterious pockets of Somewhere, retreating down alleyways of darkness forever.

---

7 The "steady state" theory is no longer considered viable. No proposed evidence for it ever survived scrutiny. —eds.

8 Current discussions of the Big Bang do not talk of explosions or eruptions, but of expansions or inflations of space itself. —eds.

A Word from Zelazny

Zelazny wrote this 1976 essay—which takes its title from the lyrics of the 1963 Bob Dylan tune "A Hard Rain's a-Gonna Fall"—for the men's magazine *Oui*. His son had asked him how a trash compactor worked, and from there Zelazny made the leap to black holes, sending it in on June 9.

On June 22, Terry Catchpole returned it for revisions. "What we would like in this, preferably at the beginning, would be more discussion of the cosmic implications of black holes, to go along with the astrophysical material you so ably provide; more material, that is, along the lines of: Are black holes yet another reason for us not to get out of bed in the morning? ...use your considerable powers of imagination and narrative to tell us *what it all means*."[9] Zelazny promised a "longer, flashier opening dealing with the speculative aspects"[10] and submitted the revised version on July 13, 1976. *Oui* never published the article and no further correspondence is available concerning its fate.

The revision appears here with a few footnotes which reflect today's perspective. Zelazny used his updated knowledge of black holes and cosmic string theory for his 1995 story "The Three Descents of Jeremy Baker."

Notes

Hawking radiation (aka Bekenstein-Hawking radiation) is a generally accepted mechanism whereby matter or energy can escape from black holes, with escape more probable from smaller ones. The imminent operation of the Large Hadron Collider (near Geneva) has caused controversy over whether it could produce microscopic black holes—and whether this possibility poses a threat. The scientific consensus is that there is no real threat. Any microscopic black holes the collider created would evaporate via Hawking radiation, rather than grow.

A **koan** is a paradoxical question posed by a Zen master, such as "What is the sound of one hand clapping?"

Astrophysicists generally believe that there are black holes at the core of most large galaxies, and the evidence for other black holes (e.g. **Cygnus X-1**) is overwhelming.

---

9 Letter from Terry Catchpole, *Oui Magazine*, to Roger Zelazny, dated June 22, 1976.
10 Letters from Roger Zelazny to Terry Catchpole dated June 26 and July 13, 1976.

The Parts That Are Only Glimpsed: Three Reflexes

SFWA Bulletin #67, Summer 1978.

Jacques Barzun once said that the ideal writer would recast his own death sentence as he was reading it, if it were a bad sentence. While I have never had the pleasure, I feel that this might well be true, because writing at an acceptable level comes to be a reflex after a time, gets imposed critically on one's reading and produces a twitch if frustrated. But there are death sentence reflexes and there are other, less immediately essential but ultimately valuable reflexes upon which one comes to rely.

One way or another, writers acquire a set of mental habits that advise us as to when we should describe a character and to what extent, how much physical description is warranted, or tolerable, at a given point in narration, where to drop plot clues, when to begin a new paragraph, when a simple sentence is preferable to a lengthier, more complex one, *et cetera*. These are the death sentence reflexes. I have a few others that may be nonstandard, so I thought I'd run some of them out for your inspection, in case you're in the market for them. Who knows?

Hemingway said, in *A Moveable Feast:*

> It was a very simple story called "Out of Season" and I had omitted the real end of it which was that the old man hanged himself. This was omitted on my new theory that you could omit anything if you knew that

> you omitted and the omitted part would strengthen the story and make people feel something more than they understood.

This observation bothered me for a long while, because it struck a certain chord in echoing amid my own feelings and practices in writing. I was not at all sure that I believed it as he stated it, but I decided that the observation warranted a little meditation because it suggested a great number of effects, some of which I had attempted in my own ways.

First of all, any story we tell is as much an exercise in omission as inclusion. Our death sentence reflexes normally take care of this, so that we hardly think of the bits of scenery, stray thoughts, passing faces, unimportant physical details we are leaving out.

Somewhere, sometime early I came to believe in tossing in a bit of gratuitous characterization as I went along. It seemed to add something to a story as a whole if—by means of a few extra sentences—a stock character could be shown to have an existence beyond his walk-on role. I remember doing this with the civil servant Briggs—and showing something of the bureaucracy behind him—in *Isle of the Dead.* This I suppose to be a corollary of the Hemingway principle—an indication of the presence of things perhaps important in their own right but not essential to the story itself—actually the reverse of cutting an essential item and hoping that its light shines through. But I believe the effect is similar—in making people feel something more than they understand. It works to expand the setting of the entire piece and to provide evidence of the larger reality surrounding the action by giving the reader a momentary, possibly even subliminal, feeling that there is something more there.

Then, I guess we have Freud to thank for the introduction of childhood trauma into the modern novel, as a key to adult character and actions. I am against the notion on principle, but I do like the technically nonessential flashback. I like it because over the years I have read too many novels where the main characters seemed to come into existence on the first page and plunge immediately into whatever conflict was brewing. In general, I do not like pastless characters. So, I decided early that when more complicated techniques are not required, a quick, brief flashback or even just a reference or two to something in the protagonist's past not connected with anything that is going on in the story's present could efficiently remedy the situation. In *This Immortal*, Conrad explains being late for an engagement because of having attended a birthday party for the seven-year-old daughter of a friend. Nothing more is ever mentioned about it. It is of no consequence to the plot, but I wanted to show that he still had other friends in town and that he was the kind of person who would go to a kid's birthday party. Three birds with one sentence.

Obviously, I am not of the school which holds that everything in a story should advance the action. The shorter the story the more I will concede on this point, for purely practical reasons involving the economy of the briefer form, but there is elbow room in a novel, novella or novelette and I believe in using it to strengthen characterization and to suggest something of the broader world beyond the story's scope.

And finally, there is a small exercise I do in writing longer fiction. I do not know how it would work for anyone else, or even whether it actually works for me—that is, whether my books would be any different if I did not do it. It is the closest I come to the original Hemingway dictum, however, and it is the main reason I was so intrigued by his notion when I first came across it. I do leave something out; or rather, there is something which I do not include.

In writing anything of length, I always compose—either on paper and then destroy it, or in my head and let it be—a scene or scenes involving my protagonist (and possibly separate ones for other important characters) having nothing to do with the story itself—just something that happened to him/her/it once upon a time. I accept it as a real experience, a part of the character's life history, and I may even refer to it in the story itself. But I never include it. I do this under the belief that the character should be larger than his present circumstances indicate, should be defined for me in terms of a bigger picture of his life than the reader ever sees.

The only time I broke my rule and saw one such incident published was when Fred Pohl asked me for a story while I was tied up tight doing *Isle of the Dead*, and I gave him such a sequence ("Dismal Light") rather than take the time to write something new. If you are familiar with both the short story and the novel, I suppose that—viewed from the outside—it is a shoulder-shrugging matter as to what effect that story might have had on the book. I feel it helped me, however, because that offstage piece of Sandow's past showed me how he would behave immediately after he left Homefree.

So, I propose that minor characters, then, by quick reference to their occupations and/or off-scene problems, can be used to expand the general setting of the story, while adding to its verisimilitude with their own improved status as individuals—a double gain; I suggest, also, that even a brief reference to his/her/its past can strengthen a character by adding another point to that character's lifeline; and I feel that a fully realized but not included incident in your character's past can help you to deal with that character in the present—and that all of these devices serve to "make people feel something more than they understand" in your story. Life being full of things felt but not understood, I look upon this as enriching the tale by imitating the actual experience of existence.

I do these sorts of things now without spending much thought over them because I have reduced them to reflexes. In fact, this is the first I have thought about them in years. While they are not of the variety of reflex normally used for recasting death sentences, I do feel they serve to add life to a narrative.

A Word from Zelazny

Zelazny's self-directed reading program used Leonardo da Vinci and historian Jacques Barzun as role models. "When I considered da Vinci, I was taken by the notion of building up a complete working model of the universe in one's mind, which seemed an overwhelming task—as well as a disastrous one for [da Vinci] himself, tending to give too many irons in the fire. A concept from Jacques Barzun's writings came to my aid about then, however; *viz.*, a sufficient accumulation of knowledge will grow. I don't mean by one's studiously, conscientiously adding to it either. I believe that there is something like a 'critical mass' in every area of learning, & that if one considers the information in that area till one achieves that point it becomes a part of the architecture of the mind rather than a mere assemblage of facts."[1] The self-directed reading program is described in more detail in volume 3's "...And Call Me Roger," page 520.

1 *Roger Zelazny*. Jane M. Lindskold, 1993.

FUTURE CRIME

Future Life #10, May 1979.

Does anyone recall that back in the 1930s F. D. R. set up a blue ribbon panel of science advisors and asked them to report on the most likely major scientific developments to come in the next 25 years? Their finished report made no mention of rocketry, computers or atomic energy—enough to make any prophet leery.

Now, all three items were capable of benefitting the world greatly during those next 25 years. All three items were also, of course, subject to abuse. And all three items were, indeed, abused. Yet, in the longer run, they have benefitted mankind.

I have reviewed the preceding essays in this series, and I've seen an impressive list of bright possibilities, baring major catastrophes and blunders. A stable population, sexual equality, longer life and increased leisure seem desirable, especially when accompanied by clean alternative energy sources (say, fusion plants and power satellites), with an increased shifting of tedious chores to computerized servants.

Many beneficial things could come of this projected leisure. Handcrafted items, for instance, would be increasingly desirable in a world of mass production, thus providing a fine outlet for the manually creative. With less pressure to get places in a hurry (so much business being transactable from the home with increased communications potential), we might see a revolution in travel, such as a return of the clean, leisurely dirigible. We might also witness an upswing in continuing education—people picking up the liberal arts courses they hadn't had time for when learning more technical skills.

I could go on and turn this entire column into such a list. But, as a student of history, something else occurs to me. Anything exploitable will be exploited.

I am thinking of the future of crime.

If I were, at present, a successful criminal and my son expressed a desire to follow in my footsteps, I would send him off to get an education in engineering and computer science. Almost everyone I know with such a background has stories of people figuring ways to beat the system using those skills; of crediting accounts improperly, stealing time, crashing programs, altering grades by piercing the school's records system, or placing free phone calls with "black box"-type gimmicks. I've heard amazing electronic crime stories from bankers which I will not detail here.

And, of course, programs themselves can be stolen, systems penetrated and data stolen, et cet, et cet. The potential for the criminal exploitation of a highly computerized world is immense—and to quote John Gall, "When a fail-safe system fails, it fails by failing to fail-safe." This does not seem so far-fetched as it might when someone is actively seeking to circumvent the system's safeguards.

I've a feeling that with increased security, crimes against the individual may well fall off—and this, of course, would be a very good thing. But when any system or organization gets big and depersonalized, people tend to feel a lot less guilty about ripping it off. It is the "white collar crime" syndrome, even if we won't be wearing white collars then. There is a natural human tendency—which I find laudable, a mark of the primate ingenuity which has brought us as far as we have come—to attempt, often successfully, to find ways to beat any system, whether or not one actually intends to do it. And then…

I (who have had a book go out of print prematurely because of an incorrect computer instruction) can see nonviolent hijackings managed by the intentional misrouting of goods, the instructions later doctored. I can see phony orders, phony receipts, phony accounts. I can see entire corporations existing only on printouts. Several books have already been written on these subjects.

Enough. In a number of instances today, people who have done such things, rather than being prosecuted, have been hired as troubleshooters by their victims. Hopefully, they make it more difficult for the next guy.

In this column, Ben Bova pointed out the dangers of a hostage power satellite. Consider fusion plants down here on the surface of Earth. According to my Los Alamos informant, these plants would likely be the size of a small city and there would not have to be an enormous number of them. What does that suggest? Strategically, if we were relying on them exclusively for power and if even one of them were put out of commission, it would make the New York Blackout look like very small beer. Who would do such a thing?

The point I am aiming at is that for every addition to the complexity of society some new means of criminal exploitation will suggest itself to someone. I do not see any way around this, because it is in the nature of the human animal to try to solve problems. Any new situation causes someone to look for an angle. Science fiction writers do it all the time—in pleasant, socially acceptable ways, I hasten to add.

Will the future see people living longer? I think so. Will we wipe out V.D. as we have smallpox—once the hangups surrounding such a public health project have been outgrown—thus, finally taking all the danger out of being close? I think so. Will our current lifestyle be the subject of a nostalgia kick one day? Probably. Will we mine the asteroids, have labs in space, a base on the Moon and well-populated O'Neill colonies? It seems likely. Will we wipe out crime? I doubt it. Is this a bad thing? Again, I doubt it. Society has always absorbed its losses from theft and continued on.

If there is a decline in violent crimes against people I think we will be coming out ahead of the game. The others, the sophisticated crimes coming from more sophisticated criminals in a more sophisticated society, should, when detected, serve to strengthen the systems they offend against—and this, too, is a kind of growth.

If the human race ever loses the tendency to scheme against the system, we will be in bad shape. It is another aspect of this same quality that helps us to keep the system itself in line and, if it becomes unbearable, to find ways of destroying it. It is a part of the human survival mechanism, and we know of no way to selectively stifle it.

And when most of the bugs in new systems have been stepped on, of course the very next development to come along will provide new opportunities for exploitation. It will be a fascinating time in which to be a cop. Security systems of all sorts will be good investments.

Can you imagine the following *Adam-12* episode?

A sinister-appearing individual sits before a computer terminal. He checks some papers and encodes instructions.

CUT TO: Two cops sitting in a similar room elsewhere, drinking coffee and talking about the girls/guys on *O'Neill II.* A buzzer sounds, a telltale light appears on their console. They encode a "tail" for the illegal program, following, recording and canceling it, while tracing its origin.

A number flashes on the CRT. They dial it and turn it over to the arrest program.

CUT TO: Sinister-looking person answering his/her phone.

"You are under arrest. These are your rights…" says the recording. "If you attempt to flee custody, your credit account will be canceled. We are now shutting down your terminal. Will you report to your local Precinct at 9:30 tomorrow morning?"

"Could you make it 10:30? I have a dental implant appointment then."

"Surely."

"Thank you."

Click.

CUT TO: The cops, who log it and discuss the latest weather-control foul-up. Wouldn't it be something if some vandal had gotten to the Weather Exchange Teleoperator (WET) and was about to threaten the city with a storm during the tickertape parade for the astronauts returning from Titan? Nonsense. Nonsense? Better run it through and see if it could be done…

Click.

The future, as I see it, holds many such "clicks."

As with Roosevelt's think tank, though, there must be a lot that we are missing/have missed, both in science fiction and among professional futurologists. There is the wondrous, serendipitous shaping of the future by the billions of little decisions Fred Pohl referred to in this column. Who knows what inspired future criminal is being shaped by them at this very moment? And in what strange fashion?

And then there are always the big unguessable imponderables, such as the possibility of our encountering or communicating with an alien race. Now, there may be criminally exploitable possibilities there that would make our most satisfying conglomerate-shuffling look like petty shoplifting. We may have a lot to learn from them, but then we may have a lot to teach them, too.

In the abstract—in the future, in the past—notions such as these can always be treated humorously. But when the future comes it will of course be the present, and it will be prudent if you recall that every new thing under the Sun provides an opening for an abuse as old as society, at least for a little while...and there will always be another.

Keep your hands on your credit cards, or whatever they're using. And never play cards with a computer named DOC.

Notes

Preceding essays in this series refers to the monthly column "Tomorrow" in *Future Life*, of which this essay was a part; Zelazny mentions prior columns by Frederik Pohl and Ben Bova. Author **John Gall** analyzed systems theory in *Systemantics*, also known as *The Systems Bible*. Physicist Gerard K. **O'Neill** designed a mass driver and a human space habitat called the O'Neill Cylinder. The television police drama ***Adam-12*** ran from 1968 to 1975. **And never play cards with a computer named DOC** alludes to "three rules of life" from Nelson Algren's 1956 *A Walk on the Wild Side*: "Never play cards with a man called Doc. Never eat at a place called Mom's. Never sleep with a woman whose troubles are worse than your own."

A Number of Princes in Amber

Kolvir: Heroic Fiction Issue, 1980, as "The Road to Amber."

I have been asked on numerous occasions whether the Amber books were influenced by Jessie L. Weston's *From Ritual to Romance*, by Philip José Farmer's World of Tiers novels, by Celtic mythology and Arthurian legend. The answer to all of these, in varying degrees, is yes.

I had been reading the World of Tiers novels before beginning work on *Nine Princes in Amber*, and I decided at that time that I would one day write something involving a large family of peculiarly endowed near-immortals who did not get along very well with each other.

As for the Weston book and the legendary and mythological materials—their substance was already present in my mind and had been for a long while. I had no conscious intention of combining these themes, motifs, ideas, with the family situation suggested to me by the Farmer books.

Then I began to write a book. I had no plot, no story, only an opening situation. I sometimes work that way, because I enjoy seeing what will turn up. What I wanted to try was the more or less classical amnesia beginning. I had, at the time, no notion that this was to be the book which would involve all those elements I just mentioned. I did not even know who Corwin was, or what he would do once he had delivered himself from Greenwood.

Somewhere along the way, in writing that first chapter, I recalled once having played with a title in the abstract—something involving the words "Amber" and "Princes". I did not, during the title games, know what they represented. But the words "Princes in Amber" came back to me while writing that sequence. When they did, it felt that they belonged, and I decided to retain them for that story. It was not until Corwin, whose name I discovered at the same time he did, had gotten to Flora's place and located a set of the Trumps that I learned exactly how many "Princes in Amber" there would be. The idea of a particular number in the title did not occur to me until Corwin began going through the deck of cards. "Seven Princes in Amber"? I asked myself. "Ten?" "Five?" Naw. I just went along, creating the portraits of the people on the cards—which seemed a good device for getting everyone described in a story I felt was going to involve a lot of characters—and when I was finished, I counted them. Nine? Okay. It would be *Nine Princes in Amber*. And it struck me at this time that this was going to be the piece that the Farmer books had suggested to me.

Then it occurred to me that it was rather odd for anyone to have a deck of cards such as that hidden carefully away. They must have some special function.

Suddenly, I knew what the Trumps were and how they worked.

And now that the characters had been described, it was time to bring another of them onto the scene. A random choice followed.

By the time Corwin and Random got together, the plot had unfolded considerably for me. I could see the journey to Amber, Corwin's walking the Pattern and recovering his memory, the attack on Amber, Corwin's capture…

I had better pause here to explain that I do not write all of my books in this fashion. There are some that I actually outline, to various extents, before I begin writing. For this reason, they invariably get written quickly. On the other hand, I know that I possess a subconscious plotting mechanism and that it always delivers. Sometimes it is a lot slower, though. It is more fun, however, because it combines the best features of writing and reading—in that I do not really know in advance how everything is going to turn out, but I do get to be right on the scene, even participating in its happening. And, as the various incidents emerge, I do see where some of them are coming from; hence, my awareness of Weston and the mythological and legendary sources.

As it happened, *Nine Princes in Amber* moved right along, and the book was written in less than a month. And by the time Corwin was blinded and imprisoned, I knew that there would have to be at least one more book to wind things up. Until then, I had had no intention of making the story into a series.

I considered doing the next book from a different character's point of view. I could foresee technical difficulties in that approach, though; and besides, I had grown fond enough of Corwin to be willing to follow through more than one book.

So I did. I began *The Guns of Avalon* and wrote the first quarter of it during the next couple of weeks. Then I put it in a drawer and didn't look at it again for two years. Why? I had begun the Amber books on spec—i.e., without a contract, and at that point I realized that I had to get back to work on some pending pay copy. One thing after another occupied me during the next two years.

In the meantime, I had let a typist do up the final copy of *Nine Princes in Amber*, as the draft was kind of messy. I sold the book to Doubleday, made a lip-service resolution to get back to *Guns...* one day and went on with the other business. At some later date, though, I had a *carte blanche* contract to fulfill for Doubleday and the deadline was drawing nearer. It was obvious that less work would be involved in completing a quarter-written novel than in starting a new one from scratch. So I dusted off the MS of *Guns...* and completed it. Several people have claimed to have noticed some sort of change in the writing of this book—and since, without prompting, they put their fingers on the spot where I resumed writing (page 51 of the hardcover copy), it is likely that my writing changed or the material suspended in limbo had rearranged itself a bit—or both in the interim. Whatever, as I wrote I knew that there would have to be at least another book. But I still did not know how many. Maybe I could wind it up as a trilogy.

Later, somewhere in the midst of *Sign of the Unicorn*, I began to see how the entire story was going to work out—in general terms—and I was not certain that even a fourth book would do it. *Sign of the Unicorn*, *The Hand of Oberon*, and *The Courts of Chaos* were each written straight through, without recourse to the drawer, but I wrote other books between them, partly to vacation from Amber, and partly because I like to vary my output between first and third person narratives.

As I've said in other places, I do not like the idea of an interminable series, of leaving the reader and the main issues suspended forever. This seems unfair to both. At some point, therefore, I had to conclude the story I had begun in *Nine Princes in Amber*. I did so in *The Courts of Chaos*. That story is now told, and any inconsistencies can clearly be laid to some residual shakiness in Corwin's crowded memory. I do not feel that the conclusion of the story I was telling precludes my ever returning to Amber or the surviving Amberites to tell another, different story, or stories.

At this time, though, I am not about to. I am doing other things and I want to give the Amberites a rest. Also, all five Amber books are currently under film option, with a clause in the option agreement saying that if they were to go ahead and make several Amber movies, exhausting the entire existing plot-line, and if such films were sufficiently popular to warrant an additional movie, I would then be willing to write another book to provide such material. It is highly unlikely that this will ever come to pass (though one can always dream), but it further justifies some of the scandalous things Flora has been doing by way of recreation, Gerard's almost pure sword and sorcery activities of late and some of the strange trips Julian has been taking now that the pressure is off. We are all enjoying the respite.

Whatever course the film situation takes—say, even the worst—I have not barred myself from writing more Amber stories by the nature of the option agreement, though prudence counsels waiting for a time to see what sort of Amber tale might be next in order. It is a similar situation to that which I knew partway through the writing of the series—"Seven Princes in Amber?" "Ten?"—"Five books?" "Six?"

Life is uncertain.

Notes

In 1980, during a 7-year hiatus between finishing ***The Courts of Chaos*** and starting *Trumps of Doom* (the first book in the second Amber series), Zelazny looked back at how ***Nine Princes in Amber*** began in January 1967. He recalled some details incorrectly (rf. the details on writing *Nine Princes in Amber* and his contemporary correspondence in volume 2's monograph "...And Call Me Roger" beginning on page 544). He had already planned a trilogy—*Nine Princes in Amber*, *The Guns of Avalon*, and *The Courts of Chaos*—before finishing the first novel in January 1967.[1] This essay originally appeared as "The Road to Amber"; to avoid confusion with a 1995 essay also entitled "The Road to Amber," it has Zelazny's original title here.

1 Letter from Roger Zelazny to Doubleday Editor Lawrence P. Ashmead, dated February 13, 1967.

The Balance between Art and Commerce

Bulletin of the Science Fiction Writers of America #90, Volume 19, Number 4, Winter 1985.

There comes a point—and I don't know precisely where it occurs —when you've been around long enough and are sufficiently well-known that you sell everything you write. If I want to try something experimental I do it in confidence that it will appear somewhere. I no longer even think of something not selling. So, to this extent, the question concerns something which no longer seems to apply to me. I will have to return to an earlier period in my career to consider market influences.

When I was just beginning to submit stories to magazines and found them being returned to me with rejection slips, I did make it a point to read every issue of every magazine I was trying to hit (including lots of back issues), cover to cover, in hope of learning the sorts of ideas and narrative techniques which were selling. So I was influenced to the extent of using the contemporary market as something of a model for my own efforts. This worked for me in a short time, with my first sale and with a horde of others which followed. These were mostly short, forgettable gimmick-stories, but that was fine with me. I couldn't write anything else at the time, and I considered the period an apprenticeship. Selling gave me an incentive to keep writing, and writing those sorts of things was practice which I knew I needed while I figured out what it was that I really did want to say when I found my voice and moved on to greater lengths. And when this finally occurred I could not but be grateful for the support of a sympathetic editor and an earn-while-you-learn situation.

Several years later when I began to write full-time I shifted the bulk of my writing activity to novels, for which I would first sign contracts and then do the books. I was only happy that that sort of market situation existed, and following the personal *angst* of a psychological shifting of gears I felt nothing else in the way of pressure or influence. I encountered very little in the way of editorial suggestions concerning the material I was turning out.

So, in my case, I found that the marketplace of those days helped me to develop as a writer. And I'm now past that point I mentioned in my first sentence, so that I do not really know what the marketplace of today is like for a person just starting.

In general, what kind of balance do I feel should exist between art and commerce, craft and commerce? I feel that a sufficiently good story will sell. I do not feel that publishers exist to provide writing lessons or vocational therapy. Will I change a story if I am asked to? Yes. Up to a point. If I feel the change is a good idea, great. If I feel it doesn't make much difference one way or another, okay; I'm a reasonable guy, and if it makes the buyer happy without hurting things, I'll go along with it. If it's something I feel very strongly should not be changed? Then I'll tell them so, and if we can't work it out I'll take the story someplace else. But I've always felt that we both want the same thing—a good story that will make us money. And I've had a very frictionless life in this regard.

So, I am happy with the situation as it is right now, for me. I am more than a little curious how newer writers view it, however, as their general apprehension of these matters today is doubtless clearer than my own.

Notes

The *SFWA Bulletin* editors asked: "In what way has the marketplace, in your opinion, deformed, enhanced, or helped your work? What kind of balance do you think should exist between art and commerce, or craft and commerce?" Zelazny and thirteen other authors responded with essays, including Brian Aldiss, Isaac Asimov, Jack Williamson, Anne McCaffrey, and Arthur C. Clarke.

AMBER AND THE AMBERITES

Combat Command in the World of Roger Zelazny's Nine Princes in Amber: The Black Road War, Neil Randall, Ace 1988, as "Introduction."

This seems a good place to talk about the characters in the Amber series and their evolving relationships, since a number of them put in appearances in this book. I am often asked about the order of their birth and their parentage—matters capable of causing considerable confusion.

There are all manner of apocryphal stories with respect to the founding of Amber as an offshoot of the Courts of Chaos, and the descent of its ruling family from Dworkin of Chaos and the sacred Unicorn. The extent to which this genealogical statement describes an authentic event is unclear, in that Dworkin was insane for many years and the Unicorn isn't talking. Whatever the situation, Oberon, the immortal King of Amber, was referred to as "son of Dworkin" and also as "son of the Unicorn."

Over the centuries Oberon married many times and also had many mistresses as well as numerous passing liaisons, leading to a large number of offspring as long-lived as himself. It has been speculated by Court philosophers that Henry of Navarre was an Earth-shadow of Oberon, and that the Court itself may well have cast particularly strong shadows into Merovingian times. (Consider Gregory of Tours' *History of the Franks.*)

At any rate, there is a section in the third Amber novel, *Sign of the Unicorn*, where Oberon in his disguise as Ganelon asks Corwin to explain the succession, hoping better to understand his children's obviously conflicting feelings on the matter. Corwin says:

"...Benedict is the eldest. His mother was Cymnea. She bore Dad two other sons, also—Osric and Finndo. Then—how does one put these things?—Faiella bore Eric. After that, Dad found some defect in his marriage with Cymnea and had it dissolved—*ab initio*, as they would say in my old shadow—from the beginning. Neat trick, that. But he was the king."

"Didn't that make all of them illegitimate?"

"Well, it left their status less certain. Osric and Finndo were more than a little irritated, as I understand it, but they died shortly thereafter. Benedict was either less irritated or more politic about the entire affair. He never raised a fuss. Dad then married Faiella."

"And that made Eric legitimate?"

"It would have, if he had acknowledged Eric as his son. He treated him as if he were, but he never did anything formal in that regard. It involved the smoothing-over process with Cymnea's family, which had become a bit stronger around that time."

"Still, if he treated him as his own..."

"Ah! But he later *did* acknowledge Llewella formally. She was born out of wedlock, but he decided to recognize her, poor girl. All of Eric's supporters hated her for its effect on his status. Anyway, Faiella was later to become my mother. I was born safely in wedlock, making me the first with a clean claim on the throne. Talk to one of the others and you may get a different line of reasoning, but those are the facts it will have to be based on..."

...

"Who is next? That is to say, if anything were to happen to you?"

I shook my head.

"It gets even more complicated there, now. Caine would have been next. With him dead, I see it as swinging over to Clarissa's brood—the redheads. Bleys would have followed, then Brand."

"Clarissa? What became of your mother?"

"She died in childbirth. Deirdre was the child. Dad did not remarry for many years after mother's death. When

> he did, it was a redheaded wench from a far southern shadow. I never liked her. He began feeling the same way after a time and started fooling around again. They had one reconciliation after Llewella's birth in Rebma, and Brand was the result. When they were finally divorced, he recognized Llewella to spite Clarissa. At least, that is what I think happened."
>
> "So you are not counting the ladies in the succession?"

There follows a somewhat sexist negative remark, as he was not getting along well with all of his sisters at that point, then he works it out the rest of the way:

> "...Fiona would precede Bleys and Llewella would follow him. After Clarissa's crowd, it would swing over to Julian, Gèrard, and Random, in that order. Excuse me—count Flora before Julian. The marriage data is even more involved, but no one will dispute the final order. Let it go at that."

This has caused some confusion because in the fourth chapter of the first book—*Nine Princes in Amber*—Corwin had said of Random, as they were driving back to Amber, "...I realized, with that, that we shared common parents, which I suddenly knew was not the case with me and Eric..." Well, it was too the case with him and Eric, and it wasn't the case with him and Random. Merlin had every right to wonder as he did (in *Sign of Chaos*) just how edited—either intentionally or unconsciously—his father's tale might have been. I personally feel that because Corwin was still suffering from considerable amnesia and trauma at that point he indulged in some wishful thinking and actually believed it to be the case; i.e., he felt closer then to Random, who was helping him, and would rather be a half-brother than a full brother to Eric, whom he disliked.

Here is the proper listing of parents for various of the Amberites, and a few observations concerning the relationships. As I will explain shortly, however, it cannot be regarded as representing a proper chronological order:

[chart on following page]

MOTHER	OFFSPRING
Moins	Llewella
Rilga (aged more rapidly than many; retired to a Shrine of the Unicorn and spent her final years as something of a recluse)	Caine, Julian, Gérard
Paulette (high-strung; a suicide; possibly from our shadow Earth)	Random, Mirelle
Dybele (died in childbirth)	Flora
Lora (Oberon married her in another shadow while Rilga was still living at her shrine; different timestream, though; tricky to date)	Sand, Delwin
Kinta	Coral
Deela the Desacratrix (died leading her troops in battle)	Dalt
Harla (didn't work out, and they separated by mutual consent; no record of divorce or annulment; no record of marriage either; peculiar, as Oberon did for a time refer to her as his wife)	*None Known*

Questions of sequence do arise with respect to various Shadow-paradoxes to which Merlin refers later in the series when thinking upon the ease with which interpretations of birth precedence could be challenged. This has mainly to do with the fact that some of the Amberites were born in shadows possessed of radically different time-streams.

For the Amber board game, due out in mid-1988, I was asked to provide a list of colors, and of the several devices so far referred to as associated with many of the Amberites. These follow:

Random	Orange, red, brown
Julian	White and black (Tree)
Caine	Black and green
Eric	Black and red
Benedict	Orange, yellow, brown
Corwin	Black and silver (Silver rose)

Gérard	Blue and gray (Bronze three-masted ship)
Bleys	Red and orange
Brand	Green
Rinaldo	Green (Phoenix)
Merlin	Gray and purple
Flora	Green and gray
Deirdre	Black and silver
Llewella	Gray, green, lavender
Fiona	Green, lavender, purple
Sand	Pale tan and dark brown
Delwin	Brown and black
Mirelle	Red and yellow
Dalt	Black and green (Lion rending Unicorn)
Osric	Silver and red
Finndo	Green and gold

That provides something of a glimpse into the Family Album of Amber. Try now this variation where you get to flip through pages in your own order, letting the shadows fall where they may.

A Word from Zelazny

Zelazny likely didn't keep a consistent record of every detail about his characters. When he dictated notes to Neil Randall for the *Visual Guide to Castle Amber,* he listed Delwin and Sand as Lora's offspring as in the chart above. However, in the 1987 book *Blood of Amber,* the character Merlin says that Oberon's bigamous marriage to Harla produced Delwin and Sand. Zelazny later verified Merlin's account and suggested that the *Visual Guide* had it wrong.[1] Some other details in this 1988 chart also differ from a 1978 essay "The Great Amber Questionnaire," where Zelazny declared Julian's colors to be white and red, Fiona's colors to be green and brown, and Llewella to be the daughter of "Moire's younger sister, the late Lady Fraye."[2]

1 *Amberzine #3,* April 1993.
2 *Hellride #3,* 1978.

Notes

This essay appears here under Zelazny's manuscript title.

Henry of Navarre was King Henry IV of France, the inspiration for the character Oberon. Henry had six legitimate children with Marie de Médicis and at least eleven illegitimate children by four other women. **Merovingian times** refers to AD 500 to 750, when a Frankish dynasty founded by Clovis I reigned in Gaul and Germany. **Gregory**, bishop **of Tours**, born Georgius Florentius Gregorius, now Saint Gregory, wrote the *Historia Francorum* or ***History of the Franks*** during the sixth century AD. **The Amber board game, due out in mid-1988** was developed by Eon Games but never released. The *Amber Diceless Role-Playing Game*, designed by Erick Wujcik, using similar information from Zelazny, came out in 1991.

"...And Call Me Roger"
The Literary Life of Roger Zelazny, Part 4

by Christopher S. Kovacs, MD

——————1975——————

Move to Santa Fe

In January 1975 Zelazny moved his family to an acre lot on Stagecoach Road that bordered the Pecos Wilderness in Santa Fe, New Mexico.[1] Successful at full-time writing, he could live anywhere. He wanted water or mountains nearby—and Santa Fe certainly had mountains.

"My living in Santa Fe, New Mexico, is a result of a search I'd begun in the early 1970s for a congenial place to live and work. I was living in Baltimore at the time, had become established as a full-time, self-supporting writer and had begun to feel that it was silly to remain where the fates had cast me when I could reside just about anyplace. My New York agent [Henry Morrison] took care of the business end of things and all I had to do was write. So I started looking... We moved here in January of 1975 and still live in the same, though much-augmented, home. The reason for this instance of love at first sight was that the town met almost all our needs. We were tired of large urban centers, but we wanted the amenities—such as good restaurants, bookstores, theater. The climate, the picturesque quality and the proximity of wilderness and skiing helped. The tricultural mixture made the place very interesting. The absence of industry was pleasing. It *felt* like a good place to raise kids… After a while, bits of New Mexico began finding their way into my stories."[2] *Bridge of Ashes* was first to echo Santa Fe, followed by *Eye of Cat* and the last five Amber novels.

Deus Irae completed

Following the move, Zelazny exhumed *Deus Irae* and finished it quickly. In his 1978 Guest of Honor speech at Unicon, he recalled how the project began. "I read [the 50 page draft] over, and wrote to Phil [Dick], saying that I would like to try finishing the book. He said 'Fine. I like your stuff. You like my stuff. Let's do it.' So I wrote a few sections and sent them off to him. He waited awhile. We didn't look upon this project as anything to be completed in a hurry. I'd put it in a drawer and, a year or two later, Phil would remind me that we were doing a book, and I would write another section and send it back to him."[3]

The writing was episodic. Zelazny said, "I just finished the sentence where it stopped partway through and kept writing from there. I sent him what I had done, and when he read my section he became unblocked and continued a bit from the point where I had stopped, and sent me his pages. I read them over, and wrote some more, continuing it from that point. We didn't really…we'd speak on the telephone periodically, but we gave each other all sorts of elbow room. We each picked up from where the other left off. It worked out fine."[4]

Both authors neglected the project. "We moved from Baltimore to Santa Fe, New Mexico. About three years went by [since the last work on it], and I had sort of forgotten about this book in a drawer. A cat had gotten in and done something on the manuscript. Phil finally sent me a frantic letter a week before I was due to leave town, saying that twelve years had gone by and Doubleday was threatening to withhold royalties due him in order to recover the advance on that book if it was not in in six weeks. So I sat down and finished it that day… Anyway, that's how the book was done, and it was very enjoyable."[3]

In his 1993 Guest of Honor speech at Kaleidoscope, Zelazny admitted that the cat had peed on the manuscript. This feline editorial comment amused and horrified him. He copied the affected pages, but Doubleday demanded the originals. He reluctantly sent them off. He never saw the manuscript again, and he advised the wary collector to look for these "tell-tail" signs of authenticity.[5] A carbon copy compiled from several different typescripts (one from Dick, two from Zelazny) eventually surfaced and sold to a collector, but whether it sports the soiling certification is unknown.[6]

He adapted his technique. "I changed my style—I didn't want it to seem too discontinuous, so I aimed for something sort of like Phil but not quite. I sent him a chunk, and he liked them, and said he thought he might be able to continue writing himself from that point. He took it from where I'd stopped, and he wrote the next section. It just went back and forth that way, until we finished the thing. This went on for several years. There was no rush, until Doubleday finally did notice this old contract outstanding... I finished the book in something like three days [he said *one* day in the earlier quote]. He wanted a few changes. The last four [of the 240 manuscript] pages were his, as a sort of wrap. Then we sent the whole thing off to Doubleday. There wasn't a complete overall rewrite."[7]

Zelazny was familiar with Dick's writing but "read or re-read sufficient of his material to teach myself how to mimic his style. I didn't do it, though, but chose a style partway between his & mine, a kind of meta-Phil style which blended well [with] his own & made the thing come out sounding like something reminiscent of both of us but not exactly like us either."[8]

The book pleased him. "I considered [*Deus Irae*] a successful collaboration, defining such as being an effective work that neither of the collaborators could have produced solo, and not sounding exactly like either."[9]

Dick's 1976 recollection partly contradicts statements he made in 1968 (cited earlier in this monograph) and differs from Zelazny's. "A novel that Roger Zelazny and I wrote, *Deus Irae* took twelve years to write. I signed a contract with Doubleday in 1964, and this is 1976, right? Well, that's how long it took the two of us to write it. I got maybe a third of it done and discovered that I didn't know anything about the subject matter, which is Christianity. I could sing a few hymns, you know, and I could cross myself, but that was about all. Anyway, I had embarked on a theological novel without knowing anything about theology. So when I ran across Zelazny in 1968, I'd been working for four years on the novel, and I said, 'Zelazny, do you know anything about theology?' He said, 'You better believe it, Jack,' and I said, 'How would you like to collaborate with me? I got one-third of this thing done, and it's all about Christianity.' So he took it. [Zelazny took the manuscript from Ted White in early 1968, and he didn't meet Dick until the fall.] And then eight years went by, and I didn't hear from Roger until I got a postcard one time from him from the East Coast. [They had actually corresponded more frequently.] Roger's in over his head just like me, but he's doing research. We each got four hundred dollars apiece or something like that. We'll never be able to earn back what we put into that book in the way of research and work."[10]

Doubleday Editor Sharon Jarvis wanted them to remove the obscenities or coin futuristic profanity. "I've got to take some of the four-letter words (at least the 'fucks') out of *Deus Irae* or the book will lose several thousand sales."[11] Dick "irreverently suggested that 'fuck' be changed to 'gee, whiz'—but that's obviously silly."[12] The editor then appealed to Zelazny, adding "what substitute do you prefer? I'm sure you could invent an obscenity of the future."[12] Four years earlier, Zelazny had deleted the sex scene in *The Guns of Avalon*. But now, more established and having Dick as co-author, he objected. "With respect to the language in *Deus Irae*, it has been my experience that attempts to manufacture future obscenities come off sounding either artificial or just plain cute. Either way, they tend to broadcast the fact that a change has been made. Also, the language should not really have changed that much in the few generations between now and the time of the story. So, I cannot conscionably provide new words.

"With this in mind, I would suggest that, if they must go, they either be omitted entirely or, since your editorial policy does seem to allow lesser profanities, that a simple "damn!" or "hell!" be substituted—two words which are close to being technical terms in a book possessed of a theological theme.

"I would rather see it go this way than risk the artificiality of neologisms."[13]

Zelazny mostly won the argument, but he lost out on *fuck*. Jarvis said, "OK, I substituted some lesser profanities for some words, but let the rest stand untouched. As a matter of fact, I didn't lay a finger on the text, it didn't need a thing done to it."[14]

The Hand of Oberon

In April 1975 Zelazny wrote to Jarvis, "Regarding the fourth Amber book, I am doing it right now and am well along into it. You will definitely have it before the end of the year. Probably much sooner. In fact, it would have been ready by now, except that my move out here, with the work involved on both ends, had kept me from writing for close to two months. At any rate, I am settled now and back at the typewriter. It shouldn't be too much longer."[15] And he did, as usual, turn it in before deadline—a copyedited version arrived at Doubleday on December 12. Corrected galleys went back by February 19, 1976.

The Hand of Oberon contains a scene in which the author himself appears.

> "Good evening, Lord Corwin," said the lean, cadaverous figure who rested against a storage rack, smoking his pipe, grinning around it.
>
> "Good evening, Roger. How are things in the nether world?"
>
> "A rat, a bat, a spider. Nothing much else astir. Peaceful."
>
> "You enjoy this duty?"
>
> He nodded.
>
> "I am writing a philosophical romance shot through with elements of horror and morbidity. I work on those parts down here."
>
> "Fitting, fitting," I said. "I'll be needing a lantern."
>
> He took one from the rack, brought it to flame from his candle.
>
> "Will it have a happy ending?" I inquired.
>
> He shrugged.
>
> "I'll be happy."
>
> "I mean, does good triumph and hero bed heroine? Or do you kill everybody off?"
>
> "That's hardly fair," he said.
>
> "Never mind. Maybe I'll read it one day."
>
> "Maybe," he said.[16]

This is Zelazny's only cameo in one of his novels. "I was in a quirky mood when I was writing that. Kind of an Alfred Hitchcock."[17] He later gave himself two cameos in his short fiction: he and his sentient home computer appeared in the short story "LOKI 7281," and he referred to himself as "Roger Z." in the experimental piece "Recital". He showed up again in the *Visual Guide to Castle Amber* as a madman in the dungeon, but that cameo was written by Neil Randall:

> One of the insane is fascinating. He claims to be an author, and he insists that Amber is his subject. So mad is he that he says he—and not Corwin—composed the tale of Corwin's fight against the black road and the Courts of Chaos. But the best part is his demand to see Prince Corwin. The prince, he says, knows him by name.[18]

Theodore Krulik included a page-long entry for "Roger" in *The Complete Amber Sourcebook*, a "Guard of the royal dungeons in the palace of Amber. His last name is known, but is of foreign origin, difficult to pronounce, and nearly impossible to spell… He prefers to spend his spare time writing fictional works of horror and melodramatic romances, partly for personal pleasure and partly for publication in his shadow of origin."[19]

"Home Is the Hangman" and *My Name Is Legion*

Zelazny's short stories became infrequent, but their careful craft was often reminiscent of his best, earlier works. "The Engine at Heartspring's Center" became a finalist for the Nebula and Jupiter Awards in 1976 and placed #5 on the Locus Poll for best short story.

"Home Is the Hangman" appeared in *Analog* and won the 1976 Hugo and Nebula Awards for best novella. This hard science fiction tale sprang from his reading about artificial intelligence, psychology, and self-awareness.

"Hangman" was the last of a trilogy of novellas—published in one volume as *My Name Is Legion*—about a nameless protagonist who lives apart from a society rigidly controlled and surveilled by government computers. The trilogy reflects Zelazny's years in the

Social Security Administration, an experience which made him cynical about government and authority, a sentiment the protagonist shared. "I tend to go along with the idea that any organization is going to get more and more layers of fat on it the longer it is in existence, so that things get done more and more slowly."[20] He and an SSA colleague, Bill Spangler, had discussed progressive computerization and government invasion of privacy, which would create the future that his protagonist was trying to escape.[8] Zelazny dedicated *My Name Is Legion* to Spangler and to Fred Lerner, sf historian and IT expert.

Zelazny was quite fond of the anonymous character and the stories. "He's a special character of mine...I like him. I don't think I've finished with him yet."[21] "He is a character I enjoy writing about, so I save him until I have an idea I would like to use. Generally, he's the character I save for the 'harder' science type."[22] "I employed the tighter plotting of a mystery format with ideas I liked."[9] Sadly, Zelazny did not write any more stories involving this character.

The publisher requested an introduction for *My Name Is Legion*, and initially Zelazny resisted.[23] Ultimately, the introduction did not appear in the book but is included on page 21 of this volume.

"Checkup"

In 1975 the quarterly *UNICEF News* planned a special issue, extrapolating children's health in 100 years, and they commissioned short stories from several science fiction writers. Zelazny's 1,500 word contribution was "Checkup."[24] UNICEF paid for the story, but that special issue never appeared. The manuscript itself is missing; Zelazny retained no copy, nor did his Estate or his Agent Henry Morrison.[25] *UNICEF News* ceased publication in the 1980s. This writer contacted the publications office of UNICEF and learned that while the manuscript may be filed away somewhere, "We simply do not have the capacity to access documents that were never officially published with UNICEF. Furthermore, it appears that the specific document you requested, cannot be accessed via UNICEF channels."[26]

"Checkup" is the single sold Zelazny story which eluded recovery in preparing this collection.

Distinctions:

Nebula nomination for short story
"The Engine at Heartspring's Center"
Locus Poll short story #5: "The Engine at Heartspring's Center"
Jupiter nomination for short story
"The Engine at Heartspring's Center"
Locus Poll all-time best novel #10: *Lord of Light*

Book Published:

Sign of the Unicorn

————1976————

Bridge of Ashes

Bridge of Ashes, written under contract to NAL/Signet, was experimental. The editor was quite enthusiastic about it. "As I told Henry Morrison, I have just finished reading *Bridge of Ashes* and think it's simply wonderful."[27]

Zelazny had mixed feelings. "*Bridge of Ashes* was a very difficult book for me to write…and of all my works it is the one on which I have had the least feedback. About the only comment of any cogency came from fellow writer Steven Brust, who told me that it was when he read the final line of Part I, 'I begin to understand,' that it was precisely at that point that he realized what it was that had gone before. I appreciated this, because it had been my intention that it work that way and because I did have some misgivings after the book had grown cool for me, wondering at the appropriateness of puzzling the reader for 18 pages before beginning to show what was actually happening. It had seemed a good idea while I was about it, but I feared its possible failure as a perfect example of something the writer would be the last person to know.

"On the other hand, I felt that if I could pull it off I could achieve some powerful effects… What I learned from this book is something of the limits of puzzlement in that no man's land between suspense and the weakening of communication. I feel I came down on the side of angels, and the final quarter of *Eye of Cat* would not have been what it was without the realizations I achieved here [in *Bridge of Ashes*].

"So, this is one of the five key books from which I learned things that have borne me through 30 or so others. For this reason it would be special to me. But I feel it has a soul of its own as well."[28]

Elsewhere, he admitted that "the ideas may have run away with the story a bit, here and there."[9] Because of its experimental nature, *Bridge of Ashes* is one of the least successful or popular of Zelazny's solo novels. Only *To Die in Italbar* was less well-received.

The Courts of Chaos and *Roadmarks*

Fans impatiently awaited the next Amber novel, but Zelazny's other obligations took precedence over the fifth installment. In June 1976 he wrote, "At present, I am writing a novel for Ballantine, and I am bit behind on it. After this, I have contracted to do a second book for them, due next summer. As things stand, I am not yet certain how long the current one is going to take me. If I were to wrap it up quickly, I had had hopes of writing the fifth Amber book before doing the next Ballantine novel. Now, I am not sure that I would be able to get it in between the two, in which case I would have to do it after the next one, next summer. It is this uncertainty factor which would make it difficult at this time to specify a due date, which is what is holding me up on making the commitment. I should know better in a couple more months and be able to tell Henry [Morrison, his agent] then and have him get in touch on the last one."[29]

The Ballantine novel was *Roadmarks*. It took longer to write than anticipated, and pressure from Doubleday and fans led him to complete *The Courts of Chaos* first.

Zelazny Household Expands

Zelazny's second son, Jonathan Trent, was born November 28, 1976.

Over the years the Zelazny household expanded to include a number of stray cats, of whom the longest lived and best was named Amber (for her eyes, not the books). Zelazny's aborted drafts became cat toys. "...the first five [drafts], wisely, are paper snowballs which my cat at least is enjoying. By and large, though, her tastes differ from yours and mine. Good thing, too...the cat ate the rest and is grinning."[30] There were no dogs among these cats. As a child Zelazny kept a beloved dog Terry for 16 years, but he never owned a dog as an adult.

The Illustrated Roger Zelazny

In 1976 Publisher Byron Preiss and Zelazny discussed what became *The Illustrated Roger Zelazny.* It featured several classic Zelazny stories adapted into graphic-novel style and a new story, "Shadowjack." Artist Gray Morrow conceived this prequel to *Jack of Shadows* so he could illustrate a Jack tale. More details on the genesis of that story figure in its afterword. Most of *The Illustrated Roger Zelazny* was completed in 1977; Zelazny wrote additional captions in 1978 for the mass market paperback.[31–33]

The collection appeared in 1978 as a signed, limited edition hardcover and a trade paperback. The 1979 paperback contained revised material. It ranked #5 on the Locus Poll for Art or Illustrated books.

More Awards

For the rest of his career Zelazny endured criticism that his recent work was inferior to what he'd written in the 1960s. Yet additional award nominations, strong sales, and increasing popularity vindicated him. His productivity improved with five books published in 1976.

Distinctions:

Nebula nomination for novel *Doorways in the Sand*
Nebula for novella "Home Is the Hangman"
Hugo nomination for novel *Doorways in the Sand*
Hugo for novella "Home Is the Hangman"
Best Books for Young Adults by American Library Association *Doorways in the Sand*
Seiun for novel *This Immortal*

Locus Poll novel #8: *Doorways in the Sand*
Locus Poll novel #11: *Sign of the Unicorn*
Locus Poll novella #2: "Home Is the Hangman"

Books Published:

Doorways in the Sand
My Name Is Legion
The Hand of Oberon
Bridge of Ashes
Deus Irae

——————1977——————

Damnation Alley: The Movie

Damnation Alley premiered on October 21, 1977. "My crusty Hell's Angels protagonist was taken into the back room and worked over more than a bit for the Hollywood version of the story, which basically preserves the title and the special effects. Interested parties can always read the book."[34] Hell Tanner morphed from the novel's bearded ex-con biker rebel into the movie's clean-cut Air Force Captain Tanner, a nice guy who only briefly rides a motorcycle. Jan-Michael Vincent played Tanner, and George Peppard starred as Major Eugene Denton, a major character not found in the novel. They shared laughable dialogue such as: "Tanner, this is Denton! This whole town is infested with killer cockroaches. I repeat: KILLER COCKROACHES!"[35] In Zelazny's story, the authorities *forced* ruthless Hell Tanner to battle post-apocalyptic elements and transport desperately needed plague serum from Los Angeles to Boston. In the movie version, this journey turned into...a cross-country drive to Albany by Captain Tanner and his Air Force companions in "their futuristic Landmaster [to] encounter giant cockroaches, savage sandstorms and killer outlaws...a beautiful woman...a wily boy...an incredible journey through a nightmare world...one you'll never forget."[35] And why Albany instead of Boston? Let the following un-Zelazny-esque, cringe-inducing dialogue explain:

Tanner: So where are we heading for?
Denton: Albany.
Tanner: *Albany*? You have relatives there?
Denton: It's the only place we ever got a signal from. Albany is the place to aim for.
Tanner: Sort of the *objective* of the operation, right?
Denton: You could call it that.[35]

The afterword to "Damnation Alley" in volume 3 of this collection provides Zelazny's thoughts about the movie. He later joked that Hollywood became interested in the novella after a reviewer mentioned it had bikers, volcanoes and gratuitous violence.[5] He'd seen the "Final Script" by Lukas Heller, which he considered very good and quite true to the story line. "I only learned later that they weren't completely happy with it and brought in another writer who totally revised Heller's script. So I walked into the theater expecting Heller's script because it was marked 'final.' "[36]

In retrospect *Damnation Alley* looks like a "B" movie, but it had an "A" movie budget of $17 million in 1977 [about $58 million in 2009 dollars].[37] Yet he did benefit. It "made a lucrative but unimpressive tour of American theaters in 1977."[34] "On the other hand you've got to look at these things a little philosophically. The money I made from the film rights [a $50,000 advance in 1973, or over $230,000 in 2009 dollars[38]] built this office and the courtyard and now I don't think anything people saw in the movie will interfere with anyone's enjoyment of the book if they want to read it, not that it's the greatest book. If something is not really good it has the tendency to fade and disappear from the scene while the original lives on."[39]

He grew more pragmatic later, noting that *any* author who dealt with Hollywood had his or her work altered. "Hemingway once said that the best way to deal with Hollywood is to stay on the other side of the California state line and have them toss you the money so you can catch it and run. Because they are going to do what they want with your book."[36] Perhaps his best response was this: "When some told Roger Zelazny how sorry they were for what Hollywood had done to his book *Damnation Alley*, Zelazny reached up to his shelf, took down the book, and said, 'My book's right here.' "[40]

The book was reissued in paperback with cover art based on the movie. "The editor went through a couple of thousand shots to find something that looked like it remotely represented something in the book."[41] Sales were brisk, and that version saw several reprints. The movie sometimes reappeared under the alternate title *Survival Run*. It is the only motion picture to date that credits Roger Zelazny.

Life in Santa Fe and *The Courts of Chaos*

The Zelaznys adapted nicely to life in Santa Fe. Being a bestselling author in that small town led to relative celebrity status. Everyone recognized him. The local paper's gossip column reported the family's travels. This attention was not necessarily welcome.

Acquaintances often remarked that Zelazny was quiet and shy. While he frequently spoke elsewhere at conventions and did public readings, to maintain privacy he tended to avoid engagements in Santa Fe. This prompted a New Mexico newspaper columnist to call him a hermit. However, he occasionally did appear in Santa Fe for talks and book signings. He spoke about writing to students at his children's school, and he donated signed copies of his books for auction. Life in Santa Fe affected him positively. The concept that became *Eye of Cat* germinated.

In 1977 he wrote, "We are at an elevation of over 7,000 feet, with the Sangre de Cristo Mountains to the east, the Ortiz Mountains to the south, the Sandias to the southwest and the Jemez to the west. It is generally sunny and clement, there are lots of piñon and juniper trees and no lawns to mow. I can easily see for 60 miles and sunsets are spectacular... New Mexico is the only state in the Union with two official languages spoken in the legislature, though you hear three spoken on the streets (Tewa's the other), and the cultural mix makes life richer. And Santa Fe is filled with people in the arts. I've been here a little over two years now and I like it even better now than when I came."[42]

"Things are pleasant here, save for a bit of wind. The arrival & aftermath of the baby (Trent; 11-28-76) threw me off my writing schedule, but I am almost back in the groove now, with a short story entitled "No Award" in the current (Feb) issue of *The Saturday*

Evening Post & the fifth Amber book (*The Courts of Chaos*) about a third completed. I hope to finish it this spring & see it in print about a year from then; and while hoping, I might as well hope for its serialization before that time. That's about it for the moment. I now have a heavy, swiveling, reclinable chair in a new office, so that I can sprawl with even greater hedonistic abandon with my favorite typewriter."[43] He dedicated *The Courts of Chaos* to his long-time friend Carl Yoke.

Critics

Critics of all kinds continued to compare Zelazny's newer novels to his mid to late 1960s shorter works. Assuming that Zelazny's success meant he could sell material that was "just good enough" instead of "the best you could" an interviewer asked, "Do you then have a sense of cheating your readers, by publishing a lesser work under your quality name? Or does *Jack of Shadows* have the same amount of work in it that *This Immortal* did?"[44] Editor David Hartwell recalled, "But to some of his early fans and to some sf critics he was a fallen idol after 1970. Some of them were mean to him in print, some of them even in person."[45] Some even asked, "why do your recent novels suck?" Zelazny disagreed. "Why is my recent work a let-down you ask? *De gustibus*… You speak of a matter of taste and definition. I personally do not consider my recent books a let-down, but rather a series of different endeavors. I never had the intention of writing the same sort of material *ad nauseam*… I have been doing a variety of things during the past four years, just as I intend to do other sorts of things in the future."[42]

"I began writing as a very naïve person. I trusted everyone—editors, critics… I became wary about critics and reviewers after a time, though, when I noticed that when I began writing, they did not like my stuff a great deal; when I stopped writing the mythological sort of thing and shifted into other things, they said 'It's a shame Zelazny's abandoning all this fine mythological material he used to work with;' and when I did something else, they would harken back and say, 'Zelazny's retrogressing back again into his old ways'… So I stopped reading reviews and criticism."[3]

In a 1982 article, Roger Schlobin observed, "Somehow an author is always supposed to produce uniform, predictable prose that doesn't violate readers' expectations. For those who think of favorite writers as psychological nests, this is great. There are certainly many authors out there who produce identical eggs that hatch predictably, page by repetitious page, beneath readers' warm behinds... What should be acknowledged is that when dealing with an author of Zelazny's obvious intelligence and skill, the wisest course is to watch where he's going, not where he's been. Along that future path lies imagination, energy, and innovation."[46] That was precisely Zelazny's mindset: change, experimentation, instinctive plotting.

Zelazny acknowledged the critics: "I do feel that a critic's role in the literary world is to perform a service for the reader rather than the writer. In this sense, it does not matter whether the critic is right or wrong if the critic is able to provide some new and interesting ways of looking at a piece of writing. This in itself may enhance the understanding and give the reader tools which may be useful in different ways, including the consideration of other writings. And yes, I believe they're sometimes right. For statistical reasons, when I'm feeling cynical; for intellectual ones, when I'm not. Even if the critic is dead on, though, I'm not certain of the value of criticism to the writer. I've read some great Shakespearean criticism over the years, but I still admire Shakespeare more than I do any of his critics. Van Doren and Bradley and Fergusson have said things which I feel have made me appreciate Shakespeare more than I did before I read them, but I don't believe that anything they said would have been of any use to Shakespeare himself could we ship their books through a time-warp back to him."[47]

Amber Popularity

Amber's popularity grew with each novel's release, and by 1977 fans impatiently awaited the final installment, *The Courts of Chaos.* Organizations devoted to the series sprang up worldwide in the early 1970s, and many still exist today. The Amber Society at The Johns Hopkins University was one such group, and in 1975 they created *Kolvir,* the first fanzine inspired by the Amber series.

People came to science fiction conventions dressed as Corwin and other Amberites. Amber conventions sprang up. Fans designed Tarot cards, and many shared their artwork with Zelazny. The film industry repeatedly optioned the novels.

With Zelazny's approval, Ken St. Andre designed the first diceless role-playing system. He operated it through the mail via the newsletter *Amber Herald* and the fanzine *Hellride*. Fan artwork and fiction appeared in *Hellride*, and Zelazny contributed a map and responses to an extensive Amber questionnaire. Eventually, this role-playing system died out when St. Andre became too busy with other things. A decade later Erick Wujcik independently developed the better known *Amber Diceless Role-Playing Game*.

Distinctions:

Locus Poll novel #9: *The Hand of Oberon*
Ditmar nomination for best contemporary novel
The Hand of Oberon
Locus Poll #8 all-time favorite author

——————1978——————

Guest(s) of Honor in Australia

The Zelaznys flew to Auckland, New Zealand, on March 22, and arrived in Melbourne, Australia, on March 23, 1978. Zelazny was Guest of Honor at the Australian National Science Fiction Convention in Melbourne, and an interview done at this time appeared in the Australian magazine *Science Fiction*. His Guest of Honor speech, entitled "A Burnt Out Case?" (included in volume 3 of this collection), featured anecdotes about Philip K. Dick and other tales of life as a writer. Triffid Press approached him there about doing a proper poetry collection. It later became *When Pussywillows Last in the Catyard Bloomed* after Norstrilia Press took over the project.[48] The Zelaznys stayed in Australia and traveled the country for more than a month.

Zelazny accidentally shared Guest of Honor duty with Brian Aldiss. One of the organizers, Roger Weddall, enthusiastically invited both authors, not expecting either to accept. "Within twenty-four hours, both Roger Zelazny and Brian Aldiss accepted Roger's invitation to be *the* Guest of Honour at the convention."[49] The fiasco worried the organizing committee, who even held a Tarot reading and then tried to downplay impending disaster it confirmed. But the convention was a great success. Bruce Gillespie recalled, "The 1978 Convention had two Guests of Honour stalking the corridors glaring at each other. Roger Zelazny and Brian Aldiss each put on good shows for the crowd."[49]

The lengthy trip caused Zelazny to fall behind; he had to back out of some commitments. Increasingly popular, he'd begun to turn down many opportunities, some more significant than others. On June 6 he wrote to Robert Asprin, "I am suddenly crushed by the press of work and apprehensive over the prospect of an unexpected load of work to come. A lot of stuff got backed up during the trip, and a whole mess of things I hadn't anticipated has arisen. I didn't know it would get to this point this soon, but I feel that in good conscience I'd better withdraw from *Thieves' World Anthology* now, rather than juggle things around and gamble on being able to do it later and then mess up. Thanks again for thinking of me in the first place. Sorry it didn't work out for me. Best of luck with the book." The popular *Thieves' World* series grew to include twelve anthologies and seven novels, featuring such authors as John Brunner, C. J. Cherryh, Poul Anderson, and Marion Zimmer Bradley. When he had the opportunity to participate in George R. R. Martin's *Wild Cards* some years later, Zelazny did his best to stay involved in that series.

An interviewer in Australia asked him what he thought about science fiction's being studied as literature in universities. "The only thing that would bother me is if anyone were forced to read something I had written. That would go against my grain. If you're taking a course and you've got to read Zelazny by Thursday! I sold stories to people who were putting together textbooks involved in science fiction, and I've looked through them to see my stories, and I get to the end and they have a series of questions about what the author is trying to do, and what symbolism it involves, and some of the questions I couldn't answer myself, and I wrote the stories!"[50]

Adaptations of Zelazny Works

As of 2009, *Damnation Alley* remains the only film that credits a Zelazny novel. 1984's *Dreamscape* was based on *He Who Shapes* but did not acknowledge the novel, as explained later in the 1981 section of this monograph. Adaptations of his other works frequently appeared as radio or stage plays. Some were local productions while many radio adaptations were broadcast nationally. Sometimes producers neither sought Zelazny's permission nor paid him royalties. For example, the Den of Entropy Company presented *Lord of Light*, a science fiction play written and directed by Jeff Unger, at the Savoy-Tivoli in San Francisco in spring 1978. A newspaper clipping in Zelazny's files bears his handwritten note "son of a bitch"—indicating that he was not aware of this in advance.

On August 26, 1978, Robert Silverberg wrote to advise that *Star Trek*'s William Shatner was planning to do a "non-verbal dramatization" of the Dance of Locar from "A Rose for Ecclesiastes," part of a one-night program, "William Shatner as the Star Traveler." Shatner was acquainted with Silverberg, had read a number of science fiction works, and liked Zelazny's fiction. Silverberg whimsically suggested ways for Zelazny to estimate royalties for use of his name—after all, the Dance of Locar only existed by name in the story, and Shatner would entirely improvise it. To further complicate matters, Shatner planned to release an audio recording of the event—but a recording of the Dance of Locar would consist of an interval of silence (punctuated by Shatner's grunting and gasping), and how should Zelazny calculate royalties for use of his name in connection with an interval of audio silence?[51]

In 2007 Silverberg recalled, "the Shatner theatrical evening never happened. He called me out of the blue (I had been briefly involved in the screenplay for the first *Star Trek* movie) and we met a few times and worked out a plan for the program, and then, as Hollywood projects so often do, it went away."[52]

Love of Science Fiction

Zelazny loved to read and write science fiction. "Each science fiction story is a universe of its own. The author establishes his own ground rules governing the behavior of people and things, as close to or as far removed from current consensus reality as he chooses, and plays out his game within these terms. For me, a large part of the enjoyment of the story is a result of the contemplation of the background premise."[53]

In "Tomorrow Stuff" (included in volume 3 of this collection) he explained, "There is also intellectual gratification in the exercising of these extra freedoms [in writing science fiction or fantasy]. The author may plan whatever future society he chooses to show precisely how he thinks it would function, given the factors upon which he bases it. In this fashion, he is free to explore whatever sociological or philosophical notions he wishes. Or, he may write an 'If this goes on...' story, by projecting some facet of present society into the future and exploring its consequences carried to an extreme...

"Also, there is somewhat of an emotional satisfaction involved in exercising one's god-complex in creating a world all by oneself, in fashioning it and populating it as one would, in working out its destinies, and even, perhaps, destroying it...

"There are certain similarities between science fiction, poetry and the visual arts, which—while so with all of literature—are especially striking here, and which exercise a particular appeal to some people such as me. The poet's striving to produce fresh metaphors, and new and uniquely apt combinations of words is a thing akin to the sf writer's efforts in creating new worlds. It presents a more intensely skewed single vision than is necessary in the bulk of modern writing: i.e., realism-naturalism. Likewise, and especially so in expressionism, impressionism and surrealism, there are some affinities with the visual arts. The representation of several ordinarily incongruous objects on the same plane of existence is a thing which happens constantly in sf, as are extraordinary transformations of the commonplace."[54]

Concerning science fiction versus fantasy, he said, "I find fantasy easier to write. If I'm going to do science fiction, I have to spend a lot more time thinking up justifications. I can write fantasy without thinking as much. I like to balance things out: a certain amount of fantasy and a certain amount of science fiction. Just as I like to switch between third person and first person."[21]

"As to my goals as a writer, they are primarily to expand my writing skills and general knowledge so as to be ready to deal with any subject in my stories, no matter how quickly it may arise and strike me as worth writing about."[55]

A fledgling writer asked him to name a neophyte's most classic mistake. "From a practical standpoint, the Most Common Failing is often trying to begin by writing a novel rather than working in the short story area, where you have to make everything count. The novel, generally, provides too much elbow room and the thing tends to sprawl. You can learn something from this, true. But the price is high in terms of time and effort spent. Often too high... Better to try a great number of short stories... From a technical standpoint, the Most Common Failing in the beginner's short story or novel is the attempt to inject too much background and philosophical matter too soon. The main thing is to begin telling the story itself. Feed in the other material in small doses."[56]

Distinction:

Gandalf nomination for Grand Master of Fantasy

Books Published:

The Courts of Chaos
The Illustrated Roger Zelazny

——————1979——————

Third Child

On September 1, 1979, daughter Shannon Alene was born, completing the Zelazny family.

"The Last Defender of Camelot"

Zelazny finished this story on February 26, 1978.[57] *The Saturday Evening Post* and *Ariel: The Book of Fantasy* rejected it as being too long for their use,[58,59] but George Scithers ran it in the fledging *Asimov's SF Adventure Magazine.* It won the Balrog Award for best short fiction in 1980, and George R. R. Martin adapted it for *The Twilight Zone.* The story saw numerous reprints, including a limited edition chapbook for the 1980 V-Con. This story's title graced three distinct short story collections and two chapbooks, confusing collectors and bibliographers.

Changeling

In the late 1970s Nelvana films in Toronto commissioned Zelazny to write an original script for an animated film. "They flew me up and asked me if I'd be interested in working for them. So they hired me to do an outline of a story, and I did outline *Changeling*. They said they liked the story, but it wasn't particularly suited to animation... Later, when the editor of Ace Books asked for a book, I had the outline of *Changeling* sitting right there, so I wrote the story."[60]

He began this light tale where most heroic or fantasy novels conclude, when the battle between good and evil has ended. He conceived a clash between science and magic. "I'd never really shown a confrontation between two worlds in the way that I did in *Changeling*. There's one brief bit of conversation in the novel where Mark and Pol are talking, and Pol, who is more sophisticated since he's lived in both worlds, says something to the effect that he feels that science and magic might both be special instances of some more general law. I wanted to show that they weren't necessarily two things that were completely opposed; that they were not destined to be in terrible conflict with one another. Possibly they were both aspects of the same thing. If they were both special cases of some more general law, there might be a way for Pol and Mark to work together and find out what the unifying principles are and benefit the worlds. I've never seen that said in any fantasy novel before."[21]

Mark Marakson's character was "drawn intentionally as a figure representing the Engineer [or Science]. He's almost a parody; he's so versatile, he picked up his skills so quickly in learning to deal with electronic circuits and gadgets. In building him up as this figure, I was associating him with technology, with science, which was going to oppose magic in this world. Ultimately in *Changeling*, I wanted to show that science was defeated. It was magic that had won the day."[21]

Esteban Moroto illustrated the book. The original film outline of *Changeling* appears in volume 5 of this collection.

A Night in the Lonesome October

Zelazny wanted Gahan Wilson to illustrate *A Night in the Lonesome October*. "Gahan Wilson's wonderfully twisted caricatures of so many of the area's types made me want to work with him. I wrote him a letter in 1979, asking whether he might be interested in a hazy project involving Jack the Ripper's dog."[61] "I didn't know what it was going to be; I just thought it would be neat to write something about Jack the Ripper's dog, and ask Gahan Wilson to illustrate it, partly because of the fact that a dog is such an unusual person. No matter who owns a dog, if that person is nice to the animal, the dog is going to love him. I thought at the time, if you take a really despicable person, a serial killer or someone like that, and tell a story from his dog's point of view it would make him look pretty good. I just suggested that much to Gahan Wilson. I said I'd like to do something involving Jack the Ripper's dog. He wrote back to me, I still have the letter—that's how I know when I came up with the idea—it's dated May 11, 1979, saying 'I like the idea, but I'm just too busy.' I kept the letter because underneath his signature he drew a picture of the dog. It looked just the way I thought the dog would."[62]

Zelazny wrote the novel much later and published it in 1993. Critics remarked that he had finally returned to his old form. They didn't realize he'd conceived it 14 years earlier.[62]

Roadmarks

Roadmarks was difficult to write. "One of my main reasons for writing [*Roadmarks*] was to set up this futuristic writer's conference by a fellow who's a fan of the Marquis de Sade so that when the Marquis left under duress, he could take some of the manuscripts from the writer's workshop. Think how it would feel if you were really working hard on a story and you turned it in and you get a rejection slip from the Marquis de Sade. There was something about that concept I found real funny. Says a lot about me I guess."[63] Adolph Hitler, Jack the Ripper, Antoine de St. Exupéry, Doc Savage and his arch-enemy John Sunlight, and a lost crusader have cameos in the novel.

"I got the idea for that book during an automobile drive. I was coming up I-25, which is a nice modern highway in New Mexico, and just on a whim, I turned off at random on a turn off I'd never taken before. I drove along it for a while, and I saw a road which was much less kept up. I turned onto that one, and later on I hit a dirt road and I tried it, and pretty soon I came to a place that wasn't on the map. It was just a little settlement. There were log cabins there, and horses pulling carts, and it looked physically as if I'd driven back into the 19th century. I started to think about the way the road kept changing, and I said, 'Gee, that would be neat, to consider time as a superhighway with different turnoffs.' I went back and started writing *Roadmarks* that same afternoon."[7] This parallels his 1966 experience, strolling in a city and observing changes around each corner, inspiring him to create shadow-walking for the Amber series.

Zelazny cited Philip José Farmer's Riverworld as inspiration. "Suppose that instead of all of mankind assembled along the banks of a great river [as in Riverworld], it had been a trans-temporal superhighway?...What I am trying to say, I guess, is that sooner or later everyone, I believe, steals from Phil, and it is nice to have a chance to confess."[64] He admired Farmer's writing—"both for his great astonishing imagination and his great stylistic versatility"—and also borrowed aspects of World of Tiers for the Amber series.[64]

"I did not decide until I was well into the book that since there were really two time-situations being dealt with (on-Road and off-Road—with off-Road being anywhen in history), I needed only two chapter headings, One and Two, to let the reader know where we are. And since the Twos were non-linear, anyway, I clipped each Two chapter into a discrete packet, stacked them and then shuffled them before reinserting them between the Ones. It shouldn't have made any difference, though I wouldn't have had the guts to try doing that without my experience with my other experimental books and the faith it had given me in the feelings I'd developed toward narrative."[28] He bemoaned that "[*Roadmarks*] was harder to write than to read."[9]

Confused by the non-linear "Two" chapters, the editor at Ballantine requested some adjustments. The shuffling also changed the novel's expected opening. Zelazny had promised his readers that his next novel "will be the one that begins with 'Red Dorakeen was on a quiet section of the Road, straight and still as death and faintly sparkling.'"[34] It began instead with: "'Pull over!' cried Leila." The original "One" chapter followed.[65]

The novel's working title was *Last Exit to Babylon* when Darrell K. Sweet began the cover art. The title changed to *Roadmarks* shortly before publication, but the road sign on Sweet's painting says "Last Exit to Babylon."[65] A biographical note in the first edition said that Zelazny was working on a full-length animated film treatment, incorporating American Indian mythology. He finished the outline but the company involved shelved the project.[9] However, he incorporated that mythology soon after in *Eye of Cat.*

Lord of Light: The Motion Picture

Barry Ira Geller optioned *Lord of Light.* Development began in 1979 for a $50 million dollar motion picture (approximately $140 million in 2009 dollars) in conjunction with the development of a theme park, Science Fiction Land. Slated to open in 1984, it would incorporate the movie sets. Geller's vision included computer-controlled rides, magnetically levitating cars operated by voice command, billboard-sized holography, a bullet-train from Japan, and many other features. One thousand acres of land stood leased and ready in Aurora, Colorado.[66] Geller wrote the script, comic book artist Jack Kirby agreed to design the park, and Oscar winning makeup artist John Chambers signed on. A press kit incorporated Kirby's artwork. Major investors backed the project for over $270 million ($680 million in 2009 dollars). However, the FBI shut the project down in a December 1979 raid on the offices. The Bureau had discovered fraud and security violations by the project's supervising producer (whom Geller had hired) and members of the city council.[67] Exonerated of any wrongdoing, Geller retains the film rights to the novel and the internet domain lordoflight.com. He has not developed it further.

Lord of Light's script resurfaced in 1980, in a CIA operation to rescue Americans from Iran, as described later in "*Lord of Light* Meets the CIA."

Support for His Colleagues

Zelazny unassumingly supported several colleagues through crisis. In late 1979, when he moved to Santa Fe, "fresh from a divorce, near broke, and utterly alone," George R. R. Martin did not know

Zelazny well. Zelazny took him under his wing, shared meals, discussed manuscripts, and took him to writers' workshops, parties, and family gatherings. He invited Martin to book signings. "And when my money was running low at the end of my first year in Santa Fe, he offered me a loan to tide me over until I could finish *Fevre Dream.* It wasn't just me. He did as much, and more, for others. Roger was as kind and generous a man as I have ever known."[68]

Gerald Hausman benefited from Zelazny's quiet generosity. "He was a surprising person in all ways. Methodical, but full of surprises. Once, when I was broke and we were writing *Wilderness*, I went to my mailbox and there was a check from Roger covering my mortgage. The note with the check said that it wasn't a loan, but part of that great fraternity of fellow writers helping one another. 'If we don't, who will?' he said."[69]

After Zelazny's death in 1995 from bowel cancer, commemorative donations went to the Emergency Medical Fund of the Science Fiction and Fantasy Writers of America. He hadn't needed it himself—he could afford private medical insurance—but many of his colleagues relied on the SFWA fund.[70]

Other Developments

Frederik Pohl invited Zelazny to be Secretary of SFWA again, but Zelazny turned him down. "I fear that I must decline. I did have that job once before, and I still recall my relief on the last day. I'm just not ready to try again."[71] The good-natured dedication to Robert Silverberg in *Nebula Award Stories Three* commemorated that unexpectedly hellish year: "Thanks for the love, sweat and miserable hours, Bob. We'll remember you for each."[72] Some interviews inaccurately described Zelazny as "Past-President" of SFWA.

Carl Yoke published two critical analyses of Zelazny's work in 1979: *Roger Zelazny: Starmont Reader's Guide 2* and *Roger Zelazny and Andre Norton: Proponents of Individualism*. The former also contained a short biography and bibliography. Joseph Sanders's *Roger Zelazny, A Primary and Secondary Bibliography* part biography, bibliography, and literary critique appeared the following year. It contains material not reprinted in the later bibliographies.

Loss of Agent

In 1979 Zelazny severed his relationship with Henry Morrison over some undisclosed and now forgotten issue and remained without an agent for months.[73,74] He felt that he had "enough work lined up right now—with the paperwork out of the way—to keep me occupied for well over a year, so I'm not going to tie up with a new agent for awhile yet."[74] In 1980 he signed on with Kirby McCauley of the Pimlico Agency.[75]

Distinctions:

Locus Poll novel #9: *The Courts of Chaos*
Locus Poll best art or illustrated book #5:
The Illustrated Roger Zelazny
Gandalf nomination for best novel *The Courts of Chaos*
Gandalf nomination for Grand Master of Fantasy

Books Published:

Roadmarks
The Chronicles of Amber
[2-volume SFBC omnibus of the first five Amber novels]
The Bells of Shoredan [chapbook]

1980

"Unicorn Variation"

Zelazny wrote "Unicorn Variation" during an Alaskan cruise in May 1980. As explained in the afterword to the story, the popular novelette included three elements required to satisfy the needs of three different anthology editors: setting in a bar, chess, and a unicorn. The story reaffirmed Zelazny's facility with the shorter form, winning the Hugo Award in 1982 and the Seuin Award in 1984. It also ranked #2 on the 1982 Locus Poll for best novelette.

More on the Craft of Writing

"There are two ways I proceed when I'm doing a book: one is to start with about ten or fifteen percent of the plot and work it out as I go along; and the other, when I'm in a hurry, is to outline. I've done more books the first way than I have by following outlines."[76] Zelazny elaborated in an introduction to a Fred Saberhagen omnibus, "Raymond Chandler once observed that there are plot writers, such as, say, Agatha Christie, who work everything out in advance, and then there are others, such as himself, who do not know everything that is going to occur in a story beforehand, who enjoy having leeway for improvisation and discovery as they go along. I've written things both ways myself, but I prefer Chandler's route because there is a certain joy in encountering the unexpected as you work... There are days when such a writer curses the free-form muse but the reconciliations are wonderful, and the work seldom seems a mere chore."[77]

Zelazny was an intuitive plotter and worked best without an outline. Even with *Lord of Light* he preconceived only three things: to write it in seven or nine self-contained sections, to incorporate the concept of body-changing, and to have a starship's crew masquerade as Hindu gods to rule the descendants of the colonists. *Nine Princes in Amber* began with an amnesiac's awakening in the hospital. Zelazny did not know who he was or what would happen next. Other stories simply began with an interesting character, and that character helped him find the story.

Interactions with Berkley/Putnam on *The Dead Man's Brother* and *Doorways in the Sand* reinforced his disdain for outlines. "The only trouble I ever ran into with a book was when I tried to follow an outline. I learned later that the publisher did not really care about the outline. He told me after I stopped writing for them that they always got an outline as a matter of form, so that they had a gentlemanly way of rejecting a book if they didn't like it. Rather than just saying that this was a dog of a book, they would pull out the outline, find some point at which an author departs from the outline, and say, 'Well, old man, you really didn't follow your outline, so I'll have to return the book.'

"I found a way of faking outlines, of course. I had it down to a real system. Then I stopped writing for that publisher, and no one ever asked me for an outline again. In case you're curious, the system involved selecting one scene, and writing about ninety per cent of the outline as a detailed synopsis of that scene, and the other ten per cent just generalizing the rest of the book. Then I could sit down and write whatever I wanted, as long as I inserted that one scene in the book. It saved a lot of trouble."[3] He later learned how to write proper outlines when he collaborated with Fred Saberhagen on *Coils.*

Madwand

Zelazny wrote *Changeling* as a solo novel, drawing from his unused film treatment. It sold very well, and his agent requested a sequel, offering to increase Zelazny's royalties if he wrote the second book. *Madwand* is a darker novel than *Changeling* and though written quickly, it is better crafted. "I was taken up by the story, and I thought the second book was stronger than the first, even though the conflict was different. Unlike in *Changeling,* the problems within the world of magic occupy Pol [Detson]."[21] It appeared as a slipcased, signed limited edition by Phantasia Press and as a trade paperback from Ace. Both *Changeling* and *Madwand* were sword & sorcery adventure novels, far lighter than *Lord of Light* or *Bridge of Ashes.* Neither received critical acclaim, but both were popular. Readers requested a trilogy. Zelazny had dedicated *Changeling* to his son Devin (age 8 at the time), and *Madwand* to Trent (age 5 at the time), and so it seemed to him preordained that the *Wizard World* trilogy should conclude with *Deathmask*, dedicated to daughter Shannon.

Lord of Light Meets the CIA

This is how a "stolen" copy of Barry Ira Geller's aborted *Lord of Light* script and Jack Kirby's artwork became tools of the Central Intelligence Agency (CIA) during the 1980 Iran Hostage Crisis. Undercover CIA agents posed as location scouts for a Hollywood movie in Iran. Once rescued, the American hostages would pose as the movie's crew and escape the country. The CIA chose *Lord of Light* because it was science fiction, it used mythology, and it contained Hindu and Buddhist references, "close enough" to Islam to make a shoot in Iran plausible.[78,79]

CIA operative Antonio J. Mendez later explained, "This script fit our purpose beautifully, particularly because no uninitiated person could decipher its complicated story line. The script was based on an award-winning sci-fi novel. The producers had also envisioned building a huge set that would later become a major theme park. They had hired a famous comic strip artist to prepare concepts for the sets. This gave us some good 'eyewash' to add to a production portfolio."[79]

How did the CIA obtain the script? Unbeknownst to *Lord of Light* producer Barry Ira Geller, the film's Chief of Makeup Special Effects—Oscar winner (*Planet of the Apes*) John Chambers—was also the CIA's master disguise creator. When the CIA sought a suitable script in January 1980, Chambers proffered his copy of *Lord of Light*, the project that had shut down just weeks before. He gave the script and copies of Jack Kirby's artwork to CIA operative Mendez, who in turn put the covert operation into action.

The Agency retitled the script *Argo*, changed the author's name to Teresa Harris, and set up a fake company (Studio Six Productions) in Hollywood. They occupied the offices Michael Douglas had just vacated after *The China Syndrome*. Chambers added authenticity by joining this company. The Hollywood press became curious about an upstart outfit's hiring an Oscar-winning makeup artist. The Agency ran full-page ads in *The Hollywood Reporter* and *Variety*, held a press conference, conducted interviews, and contacted actors' agents. This activity fostered authenticity should the Iranians check the bona fides of the crew in Iran. Someone answered the phone for Studio Six Productions. No one in Hollywood or Iran ever realized that the project was a ruse.

The caper succeeded, rescuing six Americans who hid in the Embassy after capture of the main hostage group. In 1997 CBS News, a CIA report, and a book by CIA operative Mendez detailed this operation.[79,80] Mendez later appeared in the episode "The Little Gray Man" on Bravo Television's *First Person*, and he revealed that he had never read the script to find out how the story ended. He'd found *Lord of Light* too complicated to follow.[81]

Zelazny never knew that his novel figured in this rescue. He likely would have been very amused. (See update on page 570.)

Nine Black Doves Resurrected as *The Changing Land*

In 1966 Zelazny abandoned Dilvish, the Damned, following a bitter dispute with the new publisher of *Fantastic*. In 1972 Zelazny hadn't wanted Dilvish to compete with Amber, so he refused renewed requests to write more Dilvish tales.[82] But the Amber series ended with *The Courts of Chaos*. Nagged by several editors and many fans, in 1978 Zelazny resurrected Dilvish for "A City Divided" and submitted it to Stephen Gregg's *Eternity SF*. The magazine folded before the story appeared, but Dilvish and Black now refused to vacate the premises. Zelazny was supposed to be writing *Roadmarks* and then *Eye of Cat*, but tales of Dilvish the Deliverer kept interrupting his thoughts. He wrote five more short Dilvish tales over the next year but still couldn't get the character out of his mind. He knew it was time to write the long-awaited novel *Nine Black Doves*. He wrote it in about a month, renamed it *The Changing Land*, and submitted it to Judy-Lynn Del Rey in early March 1980.[83]

The saga of Dilvish now encompassed 11 short stories and a novel. The short tales began with 1962's "Passage to Dilfar," spanned three other tales from the 1960s, and ended with "Dilvish, the Damned." They were collected together as 1982's *Dilvish, the Damned*.

Curiously, *The Changing Land* appeared as a paperback original in 1981, a year before *Dilvish, the Damned*. Reprint rights on the newly published stories were not available any earlier than 1982, but Ballantine wanted to go ahead with *The Changing Land*. Ballantine wasn't even interested in the Dilvish short stories at first. Separate discussions between Zelazny and Underwood-Miller about a limited edition hardcover of *The Changing Land* initiated plans for *Dilvish, the Damned*. That collection appeared in 1982 as a limited edition hardcover from Underwood-Miller, followed by a paperback from Ballantine.[84]

The eleven short pieces told an episodic tale that preceded the events in *The Changing Land*, developed the Dilvish and Black characters, and provided backstory for the novel. However, readers had not seen many of these tales. Over two decades they had appeared in diverse and obscure magazines and fanzines; none had been collected, and several were still unpublished because magazines had folded before printing them. Ballantine confused many readers who had never heard of Dilvish by releasing *The Changing Land* first.

Zelazny's 1964 outline of the Dilvish stories culminated in *Nine Black Doves*. Its title referred to passages from "The Bells of Shoredan":

> In the sky then he saw the shapes of the nine black doves that must circle the world forever, never to land, seeing all things on the earth and on the sea, and passing all things by.[85]

and

> "There!" he said, gesturing. "There is your sign of his goodness and light!"
>
> Nine black doves circled in the heavens.[85]

It's unclear whether Zelazny followed his 1964 outline when he wrote the later stories and *The Changing Land*. He didn't forget about the doves; they appeared in the final sentence of *The Changing Land*:

> Somewhere in the world the black doves were singing as they headed for their landing and their rest.[86]

The Changing Land mirrors William Hope Hodgson's 1908 novel, *The House on the Borderland*. Zelazny cited the earlier work on the dedication page and named a character Hodgson. Moreover, Zelazny's Castle Timeless echoes the House in Hodgson's novel; it co-exists in two worlds and enables a man to see through time and space.

Time's passage probably caused a later Zelazny creation to influence Dilvish's character. "There is something of [Jack of Shadow's] sardonic attitude as well as his caution in the later tales of *Dilvish the Damned*—another wrongfully punished man whose character was twisted by the act."[87]

Zelazny wasn't finished with Dilvish. "What would be really interesting would be to explore what happens to a guy with a monomania like that after you take it away. What's he got left? I mean, if he's devoted his whole life to this revenge thing and he no longer has to get it, what will he become? So I decided to write a book where we disposed of the sorcerer he'd been chasing for so long… Then after I had gone to all this trouble to denature Dilvish's enemy and get rid of him—the gods finally whisked him away at the end, like a strange insect they wanted to study—I could do whatever I wanted. I had a number of stories in mind."[17] However, other projects occupied him, and he wrote no more of Dilvish.

Eye of Cat

In an interview during his 1978 Guest of Honor appearance in Australia, Zelazny pondered a possible story that would involve either the Hopi-Kachinas or the Navajo. "It's still at that very nebulous stage, though. I'm just absorbing material. Something may come of it one day. I don't like to rush things."[50]

Life in the Southwest fostered impressions that he used in *Eye of Cat.* "At some point I became interested in Indians. I began attending lectures, visiting museums. I became acquainted with Indians. At first, my interest was governed only by my desire to know more than I did. Later, though, I began to feel that a story was taking shape at some lower level of my consciousness. I waited. I continued to acquire information and experience in the area."[88] This was how he germinated most of his novels. "I compose my books using free association, where material can influence what you write without your intending it to. The pattern can creep in, and it would be a long time before you can spot it. It's not necessarily by design that you did that thing."[21]

On December 7, 1980, Zelazny noted that he was working on *Eye of Cat* "right now. It is set in the early twenty-second century. The opening sequences take place a couple hundred miles from here on a Navajo reservation. It has some interesting pursuit sequences in it… It's a possibility that there might be some fantasy touches to it. I'm not sure… I don't really know yet how this one is going to be. To a certain extent the story is going to dictate the form; and I could see it getting a bit involved later on—I haven't written anything of that character yet, but it could come to pass that the book would be something more than straightforward, linear narrative. Hopefully, this will be deeper than *Changeling.* There are the books that I write as stories, purely to entertain, and there are others where I try to use a little more psychological motivation rather than external characterization, and where I play a little more with ideas along with the telling of the story. This book should be one of the latter."[76]

Completed in early 1982, *Eye of Cat* involved research as extensive as that for *Lord of Light.*[20] "I took over a year and did a lot of research, and actually visited the places where the action takes place. I took photographs so that I could describe them better in the book. It's partially set on a Navajo reservation in Arizona, and a Navajo guide took me through some of the area."[20] Later, "as I wrote the portions of the book set in the Canyon [de Chelly], I had before me, along with my memories, a map, my photographs, and archaeological descriptions of the route Billy followed. This use of realism, I hoped, would help to achieve some balance against the impressions and radical storytelling techniques I had employed elsewhere."[88] "But anyone who writes like that full time can't do [extensive location research] on every book, because you have to pay the utility companies, and buy the kids shoes, so in between I write straight adventure books."[20] This exemplifies Zelazny's third compromise: writing the experimental, complex novel that he wanted to write (*Eye of Cat*), sandwiched between two straightforward adventure books (*Changeling* and *Madwand*) that paid the bills in the meantime.

"With *Eye of Cat*, I was trying to use all of the tricks I'd learned plus a few new ones to tell the tale to maximum effect. I combined Joycean language techniques I'd learned from Anthony Burgess' *Joysprick* with Indian folk tales and mythology and Dos Passos-type intercuts from news media with stream-of-consciousness and poetry. I could never have written it without *Creatures of Light and Darkness, Doorways in the Sand*, and *Roadmarks* having shown me how to do what I did, no longer as experiment but as learned technique."[28]

He devoted the essay "Constructing a Science Fiction Novel" to the origins of *Eye of Cat*; it appears in volume 5 of this collection.[88] That essay doesn't mention that a 1981 summer in Ireland provided background as well. When protagonist Billy Singer flees from Cat, he teleports to Ireland and traverses locations that Zelazny had visited—Dublin, Bantry, West Cork, Glengariff, and Kenmare.

The original hardcover edition displayed unjustified right margins, more typical with poetry, because he felt that "the rough-hewn, shaggy look of such pages was [particularly] appropriate for mythic materials."[8] This format disappeared with the paperback editions. He deliberately wrote descriptive passages for each telepath in a stream-of-consciousness style suggestive of Walt Whitman. The dedication reads, "To Joe Leaphorn, Jimmy Chee and Tony Hillerman;" the first two names are Navajo police officers from the novels of Zelazny's friend and colleague, Tony Hillerman.

In 1990 he recalled that *Eye of Cat* "was very influenced by [living in New Mexico]. I lived there for a time and became interested in the Indians, I was interested in the traditions in that area. Actually, my interest was not predicated on the notion that I was going to use this material to write a book. I became interested because I lived there, and it was only later that I thought to employ this sort of thing in a novel."[4]

The Last Defender of Camelot

Zelazny's third short story collection integrated tales from the 1960s with more recent work. It included the title story and the novellas "He Who Shapes" and "Damnation Alley." For the first time he wrote an introduction to the collection and a foreword for each story. Readers liked these preambles, so he continued this practice in future collections.

A signed, limited, hardcover edition of this book from Underwood-Miller contained 4 stories not in the paperback or Science Fiction Book Club edition. Three of them later made it into *Unicorn Variations*, but the fourth tale, "Shadowjack," was not reprinted. It appears in volume 4 of this collection.

Amber and Zelazny Popularity

With the Amber series apparently finished at five novels, its popularity only increased. Fans demanded more tales about Corwin. Beginning in 1979, the Science Fiction Book Club printed a two-volume omnibus of the five novels entitled *The Chronicles of Amber*, with cover art by Boris Vallejo. The SFBC in the US and Canada offered the set free or for one cent to new subscribers, so many more people enjoyed Amber. Amber-themed fanzines appeared and flourished, such as *Shadow Shiftin'*.

Conventions hosted Amber costume contests and Amber-themed weddings in full regalia. Fan letters multiplied; many contained photos of women clad in characters' costumes. At conventions Zelazny—a thin, wiry man—encountered female fans who mistook him for the prototype of the athletic, sexy Corwin. Author Mary Turzillo described him as "slender and wiry, an elegant Keanu Reeves, cyberpunk thin whip of a guy with a long aristocratic nose. After he published the Amber novels, teen girls hung on him as if he were some sort of *noir* rock star… [at a convention] he had agreed to come only if the management whisked him from appearance to appearance through secret passageways in the hotel to protect him from throngs of fans. He wasn't drop-dead handsome, though; don't get that idea. It was his heroes they were after."[89]

The first paperback editions of *Nine Princes in Amber* and *The Guns of Avalon* bore cover art by Jeff Jones and Ken Barr, respectively. Avon Books eventually released all five Amber paperbacks with black covers and Ron Walotsky artwork. This distinctive set caught readers' attention. Zelazny understood this. He remarked in Walotsky's 1981 *Amber Portfolio*, "Though writers generally like to take all of the credit for high sales, striking covers do help to sell books and I feel that Ron Walotsky's artwork has helped mine. Those intricately wrought little medallion-like pieces seemed to me very appropriate and true to the spirit of the material. Though we share a Cleveland connection, I have never met Ron Walotsky. But I have long felt that particular author-artist sensation of knowing him by virtue of the work that he has done in complement to my own."[90] Walotsky also did the artwork for the magazine appearance of *Jack of Shadows*; Avon paperback editions of *Lord of Light*, *Creatures of Light and Darkness*, *Doorways in the Sand*, and *Isle of the Dead;* the frontispiece to the Easton Press editions of *Nine Princes in Amber* and *Donnerjack*; and the last nine Amber novels in G. K. Hall large print hardcovers.

The Amber Corporation

On July 31, 1980, Zelazny incorporated himself as The Amber Corporation.[91] His publications after that date bore the notice © The Amber Corporation.

Distinctions:

Locus Poll novel #13: *Roadmarks*
Gandalf nomination for Grand Master of Fantasy
Balrog for short fiction "The Last Defender of Camelot"

Books Published:

Changeling
The Last Defender of Camelot [collection]
The Last Defender of Camelot [chapbook]
When Pussywillows Last in the Catyard Bloomed

——————1981——————

Ireland

For two months in summer 1981, the Zelaznys swapped houses with an Irish family. The Irish home was in Carrigeen House on Roaring Water Bay, a couple of miles out of Ballydehob, in County Cork. The Zelaznys explored ruined castles, abbeys, pubs, and the landscape itself. They visited Killarney, Blarney, Mizen Head, and additional locations. Zelazny read *Finnegan's Wake* and other classic Irish works. Deliberately not writing, he assimilated impressions for later use. Some of these Irish locations appeared in *Eye of Cat.* Overall, the vacation was a very pleasant diversion.

But then one day the mailman delivered an ominous looking envelope from Twentieth Century-Fox. Before leaving for Ireland, he had spent a day in Hollywood, discussing a project. He wrote an outline and submitted it. Now the studio urgently tracked him down, seeking clarifications via teleconference. The quaint old telephone system—described by locals as "the bane of our existence"—involved a telephone with a hand-crank that would reach the village operator, whom one could ask for a connection. It took Zelazny twenty minutes to place a collect call, only to have the Fox switchboard refuse it. He sent a telegram, asking them to call him, only to receive a telegram the next day, replying that Fox could not get through to him either. Finally he managed to reach them. The two parties negotiated changes to the film outline, and then he had to write them. However, the only typewriter he could find had a badly faded ribbon, and no local merchants carried office supplies. He had to make a day's journey to Killarney just to get the ribbon. This near tragedy prompted him forever after to tote an "emergency writing kit" in his luggage. He also learned that "too picturesque and interesting a place can distract as well as stimulate a writer."[92]

The film project in question was *Dreamscape*, based on "He Who Shapes"/*The Dream Master.*

Dreamscape

In 1981, Twentieth Century-Fox approached Zelazny to develop a story that involved dreams for a high-tech, big-budget fantasy film.

"[They] had wanted to do a highly experimental fantasy film, to be called *Dreamscape*, wherein they'd use a bunch of tricks just out of research & development—including a wraparound triple-screen setup on black screens, with the gimmick of firing laser beams above the audience's heads from one screen to the other."[93]

Zelazny excitedly wrote three film outlines. One proposal, a mystical tale, involved the Knights Templar. The studio rejected it. Zelazny later revised that outline (entitled "The Ahriman Factor"), and Thomas T. Thomas used it in the collaborative novel *The Mask of Loki*. The studio also rejected the second outline, *Dreamscape*. Little information is available about it, except Zelazny's passing remarks that it involved "garment changes near the end at their request...because they were talking about merchandising Action Figures, and that bit about the last two decades of the century holding a possible rematch because they were also talking sequels in case this one did well."[93]

Zelazny based a third, "totally different," outline on his novel *The Dream Master*. Fox bought it but then informed him "that it was too big a financial gamble to equip a mess of theaters with the fancy screens and lasers."[93] Zelazny was out of the picture; the studio developed his outline into the movie *Dreamscape*.

Zelazny was cynical but realistic. "There is a movie with the title *Dreamscape* coming out shortly. I did the outline for it, but not the treatment or script; hence, I have no credit on it, only money... So, the outline that I sold them was given to a Hollywood writer [David Loughery] to turn into a treatment and I believe to another one [Chuck Russell and director Joseph Ruben] for final scripting—and I will doubtless not even recognize the thing when I see it. Frankly, in cold contemplation, I think that they may have just wanted to use the gimmick of entering a person's dreams and wanted to avoid a lawsuit from me, because it could be construable as a ripoff of my novel *The Dream Master.* At least, that's what they were advised, I gather, after their researchers told them that the dream-entering gimmick was unique to my book. I think they may have hired me so as to have something in file with my name on it, to defuse the lawsuit possibility."[93] Hollywood's fascination with *The Dream Master* may not have ended there. In the 2000 film *The Cell*, Jennifer Lopez played a psychotherapist who went into the mind of a serial killer. Several film critics noted the resemblance to Zelazny's "He Who Shapes"/*The Dream Master*, but Zelazny received no credit.

Zelazny renamed the unsold *Dreamscape* outline *The Killer at the Heart of the Dream* and later considered it for development as a graphic novel.[93] Archival correspondence about it is available, but the outline itself is not. It remained unproduced and may no longer exist. Zelazny later used *The Killer at the Heart of the Dream* as a subtitle in "The Sleeper," which introduced Croyd Crenson from *Wild Cards.*

From Shyness to the *Chicken Effect*

Zelazny enjoyed a reputation for witty speeches as Guest of Honor at sf conventions, a contrast to his unassuming demeanor. Joe Haldeman said, "it's funny for a guy who wound up with such captivating stage presence, but when I first met Roger, in the mid-sixties, he was very shy, and didn't like listening to people tell him how great he was."[94] Karen Haber recalled that Zelazny typically stood "at the back of a room at a convention party, unobtrusive, with a shyness that might have been taken for aloofness."[95] George R. R. Martin called him "a shy man, always kind, often funny, but quiet."[68] But once engaged in conversation or on stage to give a speech, the veil would drop and the lively, humorous Zelazny emerged.

Sadly, most of his Guest of Honor speeches were delivered off-the-cuff and not recorded. This included the two funniest speeches, the "I am NOT Roger Zelazny" address and the "Chicken Effect" discourse. In his eulogy for Zelazny, George R. R. Martin declared that "no one who heard the 'Chicken Effect' speech at Bubonicon will ever forget it."[68] One fan said it was a "long, convoluted [tale] about weightless chickens, eggs defying gravity, and a whole new meaning to the words 'sunnyside up.' "[96] Joe Haldeman recalled the gist of this 1981 speech. "It really brought down the house. I think one reason it was so funny was Roger's jerky body language—I mean, here was this really serious New Wave writer, pantomiming a guy dropping a crate of chicken eggs!

"I think he called it the 'lucky chicken' story, or the luckiest chicken. The idea was to take a crate of fertilized eggs and keep dropping it until only one egg was intact. Hatch that chicken and breed it, and when you had a bunch of her eggs, drop them as well, and save the survivor. You keep doing that a sufficient number of times, and you wind up with the luckiest chicken in the world.

In one elaboration of the story, it was the Secret Service who did this, and the lucky chicken was always in the entourage when the President traveled."[97]

More on Creative Writing

"Thomas Wolfe said anything a person writes is to some degree autobiographical... I suppose there's a little bit of me in each of my characters, but there's no particular one that I identify with. I do try to keep myself out of the things I write, at least to the extent of not using any character as a personal spokesman."[41] Zelazny said that Michael Gallinger from "A Rose for Ecclesiastes" and Fred Cassidy from *Doorways in the Sand* resembled him the most.

Why did science fiction and fantasy continue to appeal to him? "SF is built on the premise that everything is explainable, not that everything has been explained. The fact that everything isn't known leaves an area of darkness for my stories. I do prefer a world which has some dark corners and dark places. I'm on the side of darkness and I want to defend it for sf."[98]

His large office was the family den, a comfortable, wood-paneled room with lots of windows and little empty space. It was originally the house's two-car garage. A fireplace dominated one wall. Overflowing bookshelves covered the walls, and filing cabinets congested the floor. Most books were references on diverse subjects that he'd read during his self-learning program. Table and desk were cluttered with manuscripts, hand-carved pipes, empty tobacco cans, notes, pencils, and coffee cups. Maintaining his habitual schedule, he wrote after everyone else had gone to bed. "That's when I do my best stuff, after midnight when it's quiet."[99] The office and master bedroom displayed a kaleidoscope of art. Works included Hannes Bok's cover art for "A Rose for Ecclesiastes," the Polly Jackson painting of a red '57 Chevy that the character Merlin also owned, a Yoshitoshi Mori woodcut similar to the one that Corwin had in his house on the Shadow Earth, and various examples of Trump art.[100] Ron Walotsky's cover painting for the Avon Books' edition of *Lord of Light* held a place of honor in Zelazny's study. "The original of that last one is in my office and is the only piece of artwork I have hung so as to face my favorite chair."[90] Zelazny did most of his writing in that chair, a portable typewriter in his lap.

Zelazny developed a ritual. "I hit the typewriter about four times a day for brief periods. If I don't feel like writing more than three sentences I stop. I'll write those three sentences though. If I do feel like writing I'll keep going as long as the mood holds. I have a soundproof office out of the traffic stream at the house. I've found that I tend to do my best writing at night."[41] He preferred those hours even though he had the day to himself. "One of the virtues of the sort of life I lead is that I have a lot of freedom. I don't have to get up at a particular time and be at a particular place of work. I can write anywhere. I don't have to dress in any particular way. If I don't like it here I can go away. This is a consequence of the accommodation-type aspect of life that I enjoy."[21]

Although they noticed his name on the books in his office, the Zelazny children had a casual attitude toward his routine. A fan might not have dared to disturb him when he wrote, but the door was always open for his kids. His son Trent said, "Embarrassed to say now, but the three of us never seemed to have a problem with interrupting him while he was in his office."[91]

Had his degree in dramatic literature influenced his writing? "I sometimes find myself looking at the story—I visualize it. I look at the story, the characters in it, almost as though I'm setting a stage, manipulating the scenery, the props, everything. I can't trace anything to the theatrical experience directly, but I think there's been some sort of influence on the periphery of things." He acknowledged "my fascination with the Faust theme, with bits of grotesque humor, with low counterpoint to high action, with an occasional pun—all owe much to this period. I would be a very different sort of writer had it not been for early exposure to 'Bloody Elizabethans.'"[8] He did return to dramatic literature in his final year, when he wrote the musical "Godson: A Play in Three Acts."

Space Program

Having followed the US space program with great interest, Zelazny was disappointed when it stalled. He recognized that the economy in 1981 was a factor, but lack of national pride was another. "The Administration and Congress [are] more cost-conscious. This has made it more difficult for NASA, with a shrinking budget, to set up long-term goals and hence make predictions about achievements in space. A reliable space time-table would help in focusing public attention on the space program. We simply do not have one which arouses any great interest. For example, no date has yet been predicted for a permanent manned space station.

"The second thing seems to be that we do not seem to look upon the space program as representing national strength in the same way that the Soviets do. They have sent twenty-six cosmonauts into space in the past four years, to break all of our Skylab records and to log half again as many man-hours as we have overall. And they talk about it with obvious pride, as demonstration of their technical achievements, as a matter of international prestige."[101]

He predicted that within three years the Soviets would have a space shuttle and a crude but permanently manned space station. He hoped their achievement would spark the American space program as Sputnik had in 1957, and we would soon after assemble interplanetary vehicles in orbit. Nearly thirty years later we remain far from that milestone.

Coils

Coils apparently originated as an animated film treatment. When it didn't go ahead, he discussed the idea with Fred Saberhagen. "Fred Saberhagen is an old friend of mine...some years back we were walking through the Zoo. We stopped outside the giraffe house and Fred looked at me and said 'Do you want to do a collaboration?' So we did *Coils*."[63] Saberhagen's recollection about this was somewhat different. "As I recall, it was during one of these family visits to our house [in Albuquerque] that Roger began to tell me about a story idea that had been growing in his mind. Somehow it was decided that the idea was to be a subject of collaboration between us—but *how* that decision was reached I do not remember now, nor, I suspect, did I remember a day after it happened."[102]

However it came about, both authors acknowledged that the concept was Zelazny's. "*Coils* was my idea. I did a general outline of the story, and Fred took my outline and elaborated on it, producing a big, chapter-by-chapter breakdown. He does wonderful outlines. He can knock out an outline that runs like 60 or 70 pages—which I won't do."[7] An early outline of *Coils*, taken from Zelazny's handwritten draft on hotel stationery, appears in volume 5 of this collection.

Zelazny gained something from each collaboration. With *Coils* he learned to outline from Fred Saberhagen, and this later served him well. "Fred is very good at outlining things. I had this general idea which I put into writing, about 14 or 16 pages. Fred broke that down into a very detailed chapter-by-chapter outline of the action. When he fed those back to me, I was able to follow it very closely. I could run those through the typewriter very quickly. As a result, it was much faster working with Fred than with Phil [Dick, on *Deus Irae*]. That stretched over a year, while working with Fred lasted a couple of months."[103]

Coils appeared as an illustrated, large format trade paperback; the Science Fiction Book Club released a hardcover edition. Many readers consider it the best of Zelazny's collaborative works.

Music, Dance, and Theater

Many authors listen to music while writing; some list what accompanied various scenes during the writing. While Zelazny loved music and sometimes incorporated it into his work, he generally didn't listen as he wrote. "I listen to a great variety of music. But I don't listen while writing. If I run into a particularly difficult problem, I'll play a piece of folk music. I like jazz and classical music, too, but folk music offers just enough distraction. Often a writer needs a certain level of distraction to let the subconscious push up the images and information he needs."[41]

Zelazny occasionally mentioned a favorite piece in his fiction, such as a jazz piece from Bruce Dunlap's *Los Animales* in *Prince of Chaos* or Death's favorite music—Schubert's *Quartet in D Minor*, also called *Death and the Maiden Quartet*—in "Godson."

He enjoyed dance, having taken lessons in school and later with Judy. The way dance created form out of chaos attracted him.[104] He frequently depicted dance in his poetry but infrequently in his fiction—one example is Braxa's Dance of Locar in "A Rose for Ecclesiastes." In that story Zelazny alluded to psychologist Havelock Ellis who (in *The Dance of Life*, a book that influenced Zelazny) considered dance to be the most moving of arts, not a mere metaphor for life but the controlling influence of form. Elsewhere in that story Zelazny alluded to poet Ranier Maria Rilke who, especially in his "Sonnets to Orpheus," wrote about dance ("I see first the dancer, checked by lingering fate") and roses ("behold the rose in bloom; || resurrected in one thing and another beyond our || power to name"). Rilke proposed that the rose and dance had a common source, with dance symbolizing transformation and the rhythm of the universe.[105]

Fond of musicals and theater, Zelazny frequented the Santa Fe arts scene. The Syracuse University archives have his collection of theater programs from every performance he attended while he lived in Santa Fe. During the 1960s, he had haunted the Greenwich Village music scene, where he met his first fiancée, folk singer Hedy West.

Distinctions:

Locus Poll fantasy novel #4: *Changeling*
Locus Poll collection #3: *The Last Defender of Camelot*

Books Published:

Madwand
The Changing Land
A Rhapsody in Amber
To Spin Is Miracle Cat
The Last Defender of Camelot [Underwood-Miller limited edition]
Alternities #6 issue devoted to Zelazny

References

A note about the format of references:

JOURNALS/MAGAZINES/FANZINES

Author. Title of article. *Journal Name*. Year; Volume (Issue Number [#Whole Number and/or Month]): pages.

BOOK SECTIONS

Author. Title of article. In: Editor. *Book Title*. City, State: Publisher, Year: pages.

WHOLE BOOKS

Author. *Book Title*. City, State: Publisher, Year.

CORRESPONDENCE

Author. Letter/Email to recipient, date.

INTERNET RESOURCES

Author. Title. Year created. URL. Date accessed.

1. Zelazny, Roger. Letter to Doubleday Editor Sharon Jarvis dated January 21, 1975.
2. Zelazny, Roger. Introduction to "For a Breath I Tarry". In: Snodgrass, Melinda M., ed. *A Very Large Array*. Albuquerque, NM: University of New Mexico Press, 1987: p 3–4.
3. Zelazny, Roger. A Burnt-Out Case? *SF Commentary* 1978; (54 [November]): p 22–28.
4. Elliott, Elton. Interview with Roger Zelazny. *Science Fiction Review* 1990; 1 (2 [Summer]): p 35–38.
5. Dellinger, Paul. Afterword. In: Greenberg, Martin H., ed. *Lord of the Fantastic*. New York, NY: Avon Eos, 1998: p 286–287.
6. Lopez, Ken. *Philip K. Dick: A Collection*, 1994. http://lopezbooks.com/catalog/pkd/pkd-03.html Accessed: December 21, 2008
7. Brown, Charles N. Forever Amber: Roger Zelazny Interview. *Locus* 1991; 27 (4 [#369 October]): p 5, 68.
8. Lindskold, Jane M. *Roger Zelazny*. New York, NY: Twayne Publishers, 1993.
9. Wilgus, Neal. Roger Zelazny. *Science Fiction Review* 1980; 9 (3 [#36, August]): p 14–16.
10. Hodel, Mike. The Mainstream That Through the Ghetto Flows: An Interview With Philip K. Dick. *Missouri Review* 1984; 7 (2): p 164–185.
11. Jarvis, Sharon. Letter to Philip K. Dick cc'd to Roger Zelazny dated September 18, 1975.
12. Jarvis, Sharon. Letter to Roger Zelazny dated November 6, 1975.
13. Zelazny, Roger. Letter to Doubleday Editor Sharon Jarvis dated November 14, 1975.
14. Jarvis, Sharon. Letter to Roger Zelazny dated November 19, 1975.
15. Zelazny, Roger. Letter to Doubleday Editor Sharon Jarvis dated April 19, 1975.
16. Zelazny, Roger. *The Hand of Oberon*. Garden City, NY: Doubleday, 1965.
17. Shannon, J.C. Staying Power: An Interview with Roger Zelazny. *Leading Edge* 1994; (29 [August]): p 33–47.

18. Zelazny, Roger; Randall, Neil. *Roger Zelazny's Visual Guide to Castle Amber*. New York, NY: Avon Books, 1988.
19. Krulik, Theodore. *The Complete Amber Sourcebook*. New York, NY: Avon Books, 1996.
20. Vance, Michael; Eads, Bill. An Interview with Roger Zelazny. *Fantasy Newsletter* 1983; (55 [January]): p 8–10.
21. Krulik, Theodore. *Roger Zelazny*. New York, NY: Ungar Publishing, 1986.
22. McGuire, Paul; Truesdale, David A. Tangent Interviews: Roger Zelazny. *Tangent* 1976; (4 [February]): p 5–10.
23. Zelazny, Roger. Letter to Henry Morrison dated October 29, 1974.
24. Zelazny, Roger. Letter to Henry Morrison dated August 11, 1975.
25. Morrison, Henry. Email to Dr. Christopher Kovacs dated December 17, 2007.
26. Broughel, Tara. Email to Dr. Christopher Kovacs dated April 11, 2008.
27. Vezeris, Olga. Letter to Roger Zelazny dated February 9, 1976.
28. Zelazny, Roger. Introduction. In: Zelazny, Roger, ed. *Bridge of Ashes*. New York, NY: Signet, 1989: unpaginated.
29. Zelazny, Roger. Letter to Doubleday Editor Sharon Jarvis dated June 15, 1976.
30. Zelazny, Roger. The Search for the Historical L. Sprague de Camp, or, The Compleat Dragon-Catcher. *Tricon (24th World Science Fiction Convention) Progress Report No. 1* 1966; p 3–4.
31. Preiss, Byron. Letter to Roger Zelazny dated October 17, 1977.
32. Zelazny, Roger. Letter to Byron Preiss dated October 26, 1977.
33. Zelazny, Roger. Letter to Byron Preiss dated September 22, 1978.
34. Zelazny, Roger. *The Illustrated Roger Zelazny*. New York, NY: Baronet, 1978.
35. Smight, Jack [director]. *Damnation Alley*, starring Jan-Michael Vincent, George Peppard and Paul Winfield, Twentieth Century-Fox: Color, 91 minutes; original theatrical release October 21, 1977; Key Video [CBS/Fox] VHS release 1985.
36. Nizalowski, John. An Interview with Roger Zelazny. *The New York Review of Science Fiction* 2006; 18 (7 [#211 March]): p 1, 6–7.
37. IMDb. Damnation Alley (1977) - Box office / business, 1990. http://www.imdb.com/title/tt0075909/business Accessed: April 20, 2007
38. Morrison, Henry. Letter to Roger Zelazny dated January, 1973.
39. Murphy, Ian. Roger Zelazny Interview. *Imagination* 1991; (9 [August/September]): p 4–8.
40. Leeper, Evelyn C. Torcon 3: A convention report: Conversations with George and Howard, 2003. http://www.fanac.org/worldcon/Torcon/x03-rpt.html Accessed: July 4, 2008
41. Thompson, W.B. Interview: Roger Zelazny. *Future Life* 1981; (25 [March]): p 40–42.
42. Zelazny, Roger. An Interview with Roger Zelazny [self-interview]. In: Walker, Paul, ed. *Speaking of Science Fiction*. Ordell, NJ: Luna Publications, 1978: p 78–84.
43. Zelazny, Roger. Letter to the Editor dated February 6, 1977. *Science Fiction Review* 1977; (21): p 34.
44. Smith, Jeffrey D. Up Against The Wall: Roger Zelazny. *Phantasmicom* 1972; (10 [November]): p 14–18.
45. Hartwell, David G. Home is the Hunter: Roger Zelazny and "Home Is the Hangman". *The New York Review of Science Fiction* 1996; 9 (1 [#97, September]): p 21–22.

46. Schlobin, Roger C. The Dragon's Well. *Fantasy Newsletter* 1983; 6 (2 [#56, February]): p 30–31.
47. Zelazny, Roger. Manuscript of typewritten answers to additional questions posed by interviewer Neal Wilgus but unused in the published interview that appeared in *Science Fiction Review* #36, 1980.
48. Handfield, Carey. Letter from Norstrilia Press to Roger Zelazny, dated March 17, 1980.
49. Gillespie, Bruce. The Lark Ascended: Roger Weddall 1956–1992. *Scratch Pad* 1993; (5): p 4–10.
50. Dowling, Terry; Curtis, Keith. A Conversation with Roger Zelazny. *Science Fiction (Australia)* 1978; 1 (2 [June]): p 11–23.
51. Silverberg, Robert. Letter to Henry Morrison and Roger Zelazny dated August 26, 1978.
52. Silverberg, Robert. Reply to Question about Silverberg / Zelazny / Shatner connection dated August 22, 2007. http://groups.yahoo.com/group/theworldsofrobertsilverberg/message/3604 Accessed: October 19, 2007
53. Zelazny, Roger. Foreword. In: Harding, Lee, ed. *Rooms of Paradise*. Melbourne, Australia: Quartet, 1978: p v-viii.
54. Zelazny, Roger. Tomorrow Stuff. *Unpublished* 1968; p 1–6.
55. Zelazny, Roger. Letter to Mr. Eglitis dated October 28, 1975.
56. Zelazny, Roger. Letter to James Moses dated April 29, 1975.
57. Zelazny, Roger. Original manuscript of "The Last Defender of Camelot," signed and dated February 26, 1978.
58. Zelazny, Roger. *The Last Defender of Camelot*. New York, NY: Pocket Books, 1980.
59. Durwood, Tom. Letter to Roger Zelazny dated April 18, 1978.
60. Vance, Michael; Eads, Bill. Roger Zelazny: The New Wave King of Science Fiction. *Media Sight* 1984; 3 (1): p 39–42.
61. Zelazny, Roger. The Art of Fantasy. *Science Fiction Age* 1994; 2 (2 [January]): p 70–75.
62. Lapine, Warren. An Interview with Roger Zelazny. *Absolute Magnitude* 1994; 1 (1 [Fall/Winter]): p 58–61.
63. Heatley, Alex J. An Interview with Roger Zelazny. *Phlogiston* 1995; (44): p 3–6.
64. Zelazny, Roger. The Guest of Honor: Philip José Farmer. *Norwescon 2 Program Booklet* 1979; p 7–8.
65. Zelazny, Roger. *Roadmarks*. New York, NY: Del Rey / Ballantine, 1980.
66. Mitchell, Blake; Ferguson, James. Lord of Light: More Than Just a New SF Movie. *Fantastic Films* 1980; 3 (1 [May]): p 48–49, 56.
67. Morrow, John. Seeking the Lord of Light: Producer Barry Ira Geller. *The Jack Kirby Collector* 1996; 3 (11 [July]): p 22–27.
68. Martin, George R. R. The Lord of Light. *Locus* 1995; 35 (2 [#415 August]): p 39–40.
69. Hausman, Gerald. Email to Dr. Christopher Kovacs dated May 7, 2008.
70. Lindskold, Jane. Email to Dr. Christopher Kovacs dated November 1, 2007.
71. Zelazny, Roger. Letter to Frederik Pohl dated January 30, 1979.
72. Zelazny, Roger. *Nebula Award Stories Three*. New York, NY: Doubleday, 1968.
73. Morrison, Henry. Email to Dr. Christopher Kovacs dated December 27, 2007.
74. Zelazny, Roger. Letter to Pat at Doubleday dated June 22, 1979.

75. Zelazny, Roger. Letter to Michael Lobell dated December 23, 1980.

76. Becker, Matthew. Interview. *Alternities* 1981; (6 [Summer]): p 24–31.

77. Zelazny, Roger. Prologue. In: Saberhagen, Fred, ed. *Empire of the East*. New York, NY: Ace Books, 1979: p vii-ix.

78. Bearman, Joshua. How the CIA Used a Fake Sci-Fi Flick to Rescue Americans from Tehran. *Wired Magazine* 2007; 15 (5): p http://www.wired.com/wired/archive/15.05/feat_cia.html.

79. Mendez, Antonio J. CIA Goes Hollywood: A Classic Case of Deception, 1999. https://www.cia.gov/library/center-for-the-study-of-intelligence/csi-publications/csi-studies/studies/winter99-00/art1.html Accessed: February 2, 2007.

80. Mendez, Antonio J. *Master of Disguise: My Secret Life in the CIA*. Niagara Falls, NY: William Morrow, 1999.

81. Morris, Errol. *The Little Gray Man*. In: *First Person*. Bravo Television. 2001: Online clip: http://www.youtube.com/watch?v=AQJa4xk5rss Accessed: April 3, 2009.

82. Zelazny, Roger. Letter to Henry Morrison dated July 31, 1972.

83. Zelazny, Roger. Letter to Ballantine Books Editor Judy Lynn Del Rey dated March 12, 1980.

84. Zelazny, Roger. Letter to Chuck Miller dated August 1, 1979.

85. Zelazny, Roger. The Bells of Shoredan. *Fantastic Stories of the Imagination* 1966; 15 (4 [March]): p 6–21.

86. Zelazny, Roger. *The Changing Land*. New York, NY: Del Rey / Ballantine, 1981.

87. Zelazny, Roger. Foreword. *Jack of Shadows*. New York, NY: Signet Press, 1989: p 5–8.

88. Zelazny, Roger. Constructing a Science Fiction Novel. *The Writer* 1984; 97 (October): p 9–12, 46.

89. Turzillo, Mary A. Roger Zelazny, Hero Maker. *Ohioana Quarterly* 2003; 46 (4 [Winter]): p 414–420.

90. Zelazny, Roger. Introduction. In: Walotsky, Ron, ed. *Amber Portfolio*. Farmington, CT: Chimera Press, 1981: single sheet, unpaginated.

91. Zelazny, Trent. Email to Dr. Christopher Kovacs dated January 11, 2008.

92. Zelazny, Roger. "I remember tea rooms, small shops, ruined Muckross Abbey": A Writer's Guide to Getting Away from it all in Ireland. *Writer's Yearbook* 1984; p 90–92.

93. Zelazny, Roger. Letter to Bill Willingham at Texas Comics, 1983.

94. Haldeman, Joe. Email to Dr. Christopher Kovacs dated May 7, 2008.

95. Haber, Karen. Memories of Roger. *Locus* 1995; 35 (2 [#415 August]): p 42.

96. Kimbriel, Katharine Eliska. Roger Zelazny. *Dallas Fantasy Fair July 1984 Program Book*. Dallas, TX: Bulldog Productions, 1984: p 31.

97. Haldeman, Joe. Email to Dr. Christopher Kovacs dated May 8, 2008.

98. Conner, Bill. Zelazny at Marcon '72. *Cozine* 1972; (3 [March 30]): p 17–18.

99. Mays, Buddy. Roger Zelazny—Dreamer in the World of Real. *New Mexico Magazine* 1981; (February): p 30–31.

100. Lindskold, Jane M. Zelazny's Santa Fe. *Amberzine* 1992; (1 [March]): p 19–23.

101. Zelazny, Roger. The Future of the Space Program. In: Elliott, Jeffrey M., ed. *The Future of the Space Program / Large Corporations and Society*. San Bernardino, CA: Borgo Press, 1981: p.

102. Saberhagen, Fred. Introduction. In: Greenberg, Martin H., ed. *Lord of the Fantastic: Stories in Honor of Roger Zelazny*. New York, NY: Avon Eos, 1998: p 1–3.

103. Cawley, Rusty. Sky's the Limit for Roger Zelazny. *Bryan-College Station Eagle* 1982; Sec C (April 10): p 14.

104. Yoke, Carl B. Email to Dr. Christopher Kovacs dated January 30, 2008.

105. Yoke, Carl B. Zelazny's Form and Chaos Philosophy. *Amberzine* 1993; (3 [April]): p 27–47.

Addendum 2020[1]

As noted on pages 546 and 550–551, in 1979 *Lord of Light* almost became a motion picture and major theme park in Colorado until an FBI raid abruptly shut everything down. In 1980, the film's script (retitled *Argo*), artwork, and makeup artist became key elements in a CIA caper that enabled fugitive US Embassy employees to be extracted from Iran. The 1980 rescue provided the framework for the 2012 Academy Award-winning motion picture *Argo*, starring, produced, and directed by Ben Affleck. However, the movie made no mention of Zelazny, *Lord of Light*, the artwork and set design by Jack Kirby, the *Lord of Light* script written by Barry Geller, or how makeup artist John Chambers suggested the movie ruse and proffered his copy of the script to the CIA. Instead, the film suggests that CIA agent Tony Mendez alone conceived the plan and legitimately purchased the rights to a Star Wars-like script named *Argo*. It also minimized Canadian involvement in the rescue, prompting former President Jimmy Carter to declare on CNN that "90 per cent of the contributions to the ideas and the consummation of the plan was Canadian."

A documentary, *Science Fiction Land*, directed by Judd Ehrlich and produced by Flatbush Pictures, began production long before *Argo* and was set for release in 2014. It explored the complex back story that *Argo* leaves out, beginning with the development of the *Lord of Light* theme park and motion picture; the involvement of Jack Kirby, Ray Bradbury, John Chambers, architect Paolo Soleri, and futurist Buckminster Fuller; how and why that dream collapsed in the 1979 FBI raid; and how the script and Kirby's artwork later came to be used by the CIA in their rescue operation. However, a lawsuit shut down the documentary with no details provided. Whether Geller's infamous *Lord of Light* screenplay will ever be published or filmed remains to be seen.

---

1 For more details, see "The reality and mythology enveloping Zelazny's *Lord of Light*, the FBI, the CIA, and Ben Affleck's *Argo*" by Christopher S. Kovacs in *The New York Review of Science Fiction* #297, May 2013, p 1, 8–15.

Publication History

Frontispiece portrait by Jack Gaughan first appeared on the cover of "Marcon VII Program and Schedule Book, 1972" where Roger Zelazny was Guest of Honor.

"The Prince of Amber" *by Joe Haldeman* first appears in this volume.

"What I Didn't Learn from Reading Roger Zelazny" *by Steven Brust* first appears in this volume.

"My Name Is Legion: Précis" first appears in this volume. (written in 1974)

"The Eve of RUMOKO" first appeared in *Three for Tomorrow*, ed. Robert Silverberg, Meredith Press 1969.

"'Kjwalll'kje'k'koothaïlll'kje'k" first appeared in *An Exaltation of Stars*, ed. Terry Carr, Simon & Schuster 1973.

"Home Is the Hangman" first appeared in *Analog*, November 1975.

"Stand Pat, Ruby Stone" first appeared in *Destinies* Vol 1 No 1, ed. James Baen, Ace, Nov-Dec 1978.

"Go Starless in the Night" first appeared in *Destinies* Vol 1 No 5, ed. James Baen, Ace, Oct-Dec 1979.

"Halfjack" first appeared in *Omni,* June 1979.

"The Last Defender of Camelot" first appeared in *Asimov's SF Adventure Magazine #3*, Summer 1979.

"Fire and/or Ice" first appeared in *After The Fall*, ed. Robert Sheckley, Ace Books 1980.

"Exeunt Omnes" first appeared in *After The Fall*, ed. Robert Sheckley, Ace Books 1980.

"A Very Good Year..." first appeared in *Harvey*, December 1979.

"The Places of Aache" first appeared in *Other Worlds 2*, ed. Roy Torgeson, Zebra 1979.

"A City Divided" first appeared in *Dilvish, the Damned,* Del Rey/Ballantine 1982.

"The White Beast" first appeared in *Whispers #13-14*, ed. Stuart David Schiff, Whispers Press, October 1979.

"Tower of Ice" first appeared in *Flashing Swords #5: Demons and Daggers*, ed. Lin Carter, Nelson Doubleday 1981.

"The George Business" first appeared in *Dragons of Light*, ed. Orson Scott Card, Ace 1980.

"The Naked Matador" first appeared in *Amazing*, July 1981.

"Walpurgisnacht" first appeared in *A Rhapsody in Amber*, Cheap Street 1981.

"The Last of the Wild Ones" first appeared in *Omni*, March 1981.

"The Horses of Lir" first appeared in *Whispers III*, ed. Stuart David Schiff, Doubleday 1981.

"Recital" first appeared in *A Rhapsody in Amber*, Cheap Street 1981.

"And I Only Am Escaped to Tell Thee" first appeared in *Twilight Zone* #2, May 1981.

"Shadowjack" first appeared in its current form in the collection, *The Last Defender of Camelot*, Underwood-Miller edition only, 1981. An earlier, shorter version, with added graphics, appeared in *The Illustrated Roger Zelazny*, Baronet 1978.

"Shadowjack: Character Biography" first appeared in *Wizards*, ed Bill Fawcett, Mayfair Games 1983. Previously uncollected.

"Unicorn Variation" first appeared in *Isaac Asimov's Science Fiction Magazine,* April 1981.

"Some Science Fiction Parameters: A Biased View" first appeared in *Galaxy*, July 1975.

"Black Is the Color and None Is the Number" first appears in this volume. Written 1976.

"The Parts That Are Only Glimpsed: Three Reflexes" first appeared in *SFWA Bulletin #67*, Summer 1978.

"Future Crime" first appeared in *Future Life #10*, May 1979. Previously uncollected.

"A Number of Princes in Amber" first appeared in *Kolvir: Heroic Fiction Issue,* 1980, as "The Road to Amber". Previously uncollected.

"The Balance between Art and Commerce" first appeared in the *Bulletin of the Science Fiction Writers of America #90*, Volume 19, Number 4, Winter 1985. Previously uncollected.

"Amber and the Amberites" first appeared in *Combat Command in the World of Roger Zelazny's Nine Princes in Amber: The Black Road War*, Neil Randall, Ace 1988, as "Introduction". Previously uncollected.

"'...And Call Me Roger': The Literary Life of Roger Zelazny, Part 4" by Christopher S. Kovacs, MD first appears in this volume.

Poems

"Diadoumenos of Polycletus" first appeared in *Haunted #3*, June 1968. Previously uncollected. Written 1955–60 for *Chisel in the Sky*.

"Come, Let Us Pace the Sky-Aspiring Wave" first appeared in *Polemic* v5 Spring 1960. Written 1955–60 for *Chisel in the Sky.* Previously uncollected.

"On the Death of a Manned Stellar Observation Satellite" first appears in this volume. Written in 1964.

"I, a Stranger and Revisited" first appeared in *First Mercenary*, Spring 1965, as by Harrison Denmark. Previously uncollected.

"On the Return of the Mercurian Flamebird After Nesting" first appeared in *Second Mercenary*, Summer 1965. Previously uncollected.

"There Is Always a Poem" first appeared in *Double:Bill #18* March-April 1968. Previously uncollected.

"The Doctrine of the Perfect Lie" first appeared in *Science Fiction* (Australian) Vol 1 No 3 Dec 1978.

"Pelias Waking, within the S. C." first appears in this volume. Written 1965–68.

"Torlin Dragonson" and "Wriggle Under George Washington Bridge" first appeared in *To Spin Is Miracle Cat*, Underwood-Miller 1981.

"Lamentations of the Prematurely Old Satyr" first appeared in *Yandro #149*, July 1965. Previously uncollected.

"Moonsong" first appeared in *Sirruish #7* July 1968. Previously uncollected.

"Nuages" first appeared in *The Dipple Chronicle #1*, Jan-March 1971. Written 1955–60 for *Chisel in the Sky*.

"Friend" and "Shadows" first appeared in *To Spin Is Miracle Cat*, Underwood-Miller 1981. Written 1955–60 for *Chisel in the Sky*.

"The Burning" first appeared in *When Pussywillows Last in the Catyard Bloomed*, Norstrilia Press 1980.

"Dance" first appeared in *Amazing*, July 1981.

"Ye Who Would Wish to Live" appears as part of "Shadowjack".

"great cummings" first appears in this volume. Written 1955–60 for *Chisel in the Sky.*

"The Man Without a Shadow" first appeared in *Skyline*, April 1958. Written 1955–58 for *Chisel in the Sky.*

"When Pussywillows Last in the Catyard Bloomed" first appeared in *When Pussywillows Last in the Catyard Bloomed*, Norstrilia Press 1980.

ACKNOWLEDGMENTS

Thanks go in many directions: to Roger Zelazny for his life's work, a body of writing that made this project a joy to work on; to my wife, Leah Anderson, without whose support this project would never have started; to Chris Kovacs, whose research efforts not only produced a comprehensive collection of material, but whose insights added depth to the whole project; to Ann Crimmins for her dedication to all things grammatical; to Kirby McCauley, who promoted the project and arranged for us the right to print Zelazny's writing; to Joe Haldeman and Steven Brust for their engaging introductions; to Michael Whelan for his spectacular dust jacket painting; and to Alice Lewis for her polished dust jacket design and her invaluable advice in design issues. Thanks also go to: Mark Olson for his help in book production, Geri Sullivan for design advice and our stalwart band of proofreaders:

Rick Katze, Tim Szczesuil, Ann Broomhead, Larry Pfeffer,
Peter Olson, Jim Burton, Sharon Sbarsky,
Ann Crimmins, Chris Kovacs, and Mark Olson.

David G. Grubbs
May, 2009

In order to write the "A Word from Zelazny" sections, the annotations, and the literary biography, I relied on many individuals. Some aided in the extensive search to locate original manuscripts, correspondence, rare fanzines, and obscure interviews. Colleagues, family, and friends of Roger Zelazny helped to clarify details and quash rumors about his life and work. My own colleagues helped with translations of Greek, German, Japanese and other foreign language phrases. Apologies to anyone who might have been overlooked in compiling the following list:

Charles Ardai, John Ayotte, George Beahm, Greg Bear, John Betancourt, Paul Bradford, Rick Bradford, Ned Brooks, Lois McMaster Bujold, John Callender, George Carayanniotis, Ung-il Chung, Michael Citrak, Giovanna Clairval, Bob Collins, Lloyd Currey, Jack Dann, Chris DeVito, Jane Frank, c Shell Franklin, Paul Gilster, Dave Goldman, Simon Gosden, Ed Greenwood, Joe Haldeman, David Hartwell, Gerald Hausman, Graham Holroyd, Patrick Hulman, Tom Jackson, Beate Lanske, Elizabeth LaVelle, Jane Lindskold, George R. R. Martin, Bryan McKinney, Henry Morrison, Kari Mozena, Rias Nuninga, Richard Patt, Greg Pickersgill, Bob Pylant, Mike Resnick, Andy Richards, Fred Saberhagen, Roger Schlobin, Dean Schramm, Darrell Schweitzer, Robert Silverberg, Dan Simmons, Dean Wesley Smith, Ken St. Andre, Richard Stegall, Thomas T. Thomas, Norris Thomlinson, Josh Wanisko, Erick Wujcik, Carl Yoke, Trent Zelazny, Cindy Ziesing, and Scott Zrubek.

Diane Cooter, Nicolette Schneider, Lara Chmela
Roger Zelazny Papers, Special Collections Research Center, Syracuse University Library

Thomas Beck, Susan Graham, Marcia Peri, Shaun Lusby
Azriel Rosenfeld Science Fiction Research Collection, University of Maryland, Baltimore County.

Sara Stille, Eric Milenkiewicz, Audrey Pearson
Bruce Pelz and Terry Carr Fanzine Collections, Special Collections Library, University of California, Riverside

Greg Prickman, Jacque Roethler, Kathryn Hodson, Jeremy Brett
M. Horvat Collection, Special Collections, University of Iowa Libraries

Jill Tatem
University Archives, Case Western Reserve University

Thomas M. Whitehead
Whitehead Collection, Special Collections Department, Temple University Libraries

Patti Thistle, Dion Fowlow, George Beckett
Document Delivery Office, Health Sciences Library, Memorial University of Newfoundland.

And then there are the personal thanks that I need to make. Of course none of this would have been possible without Roger Zelazny creating the very stories and characters that I find myself returning to again and again. When I finally met him at Ad Astra in 1986, I interrupted his rapid departure from the convention and asked "Mr. Zelazny" to sign the books I'd carried with me. He kindly took care of that and the requests of my companions. "Everybody OK, then? Right, gotta get to the airport"—and then his parting comment to me was "…and call me Roger." From that memory came the fitting title for the monograph in these volumes.

My mother handed me that paperback *Nine Princes in Amber* one dull day so long ago when I complained that I had nothing to read, and my parents drove me to countless new and used bookstores on the very first Zelazny quest to find copies of all of his books. The Internet makes searches so much easier now, and I couldn't have gathered much of this material if I'd had to rely on physical searches and postal mail. My buddy Ed Hew and his cousins drove me to Ad Astra for that fateful meeting. Dave Grubbs believed in and fought to see this project succeed when my involvement made it expand well beyond what he'd anticipated, and Ann Crimmins pruned, weeded, and used a flamethrower where necessary to turn my sometimes passive prose into something more readable. And none of this would have been possible without the support of my wife, Susan, and our children Caileigh and Jamieson, who put up with my additional absences from home and the other blocks of time consumed in creating this project. If their eyes should roll at mention of the name Zelazny, you may now understand why. And the fact that Susan's birthday is also May 13, or that my last name also refers to what happens in a smithy, are just examples of those Strange and Odd Coincidences in Life realized while researching this project. That one of our beloved Golden Retrievers was named Amber is *not* one of those coincidences.

Christopher S. Kovacs, MD
May, 2009 (updated May 2013)

I wish to thank my daughters Fiona and Deirdre, whom I dragged to cons as children and who have grown to love sf and fantasy as much as I do. Particular thanks to my husband Peter Havriluk for patience, encouragement, and easing the log jam at the p.c. by buying himself a laptop. Thanks to Elizabeth Zaborskis Fernandez, for help with the Spanish. Dave and Chris, I'm delighted to have worked with you. Thanks also to the various Crimmins/Havriluk cats who warmed my lap as I edited.

Ann Crimmins
May, 2009

TECHNICAL NOTES

This book is set in Adobe Garamond Pro, except for the titles (which are set in Trajan Pro), using Adobe InDesign 2. The book was printed and bound by Sheridan Books of Ann Arbor, Michigan, on acid-free paper.